The Best Mysteries of

MARY
ROBERTS
RINEHART

The Best Mysteries of

MARY ROBERTS RINEHART

Reader's Digest

THE BEST MYSTERIES OF MARY ROBERTS RINEHART

Copyright © 2002 by The Reader's Digest Association, Inc.

This book contains the complete texts of the original works first published in the years indicated: *The Circular Staircase,* 1908; *The Man in Lower Ten,* 1909; *The Window at the White Cat,* 1910; and *The Buckled Bag,* 1914.

Book design by Robin Arzt

Library of Congress Cataloging-in-Publication Data

Rinehart, Mary Roberts, 1876-1958.
  [Novels. Selections]
  The best mysteries of Mary Roberts Rinehart / by Mary Roberts
Rinehart.
     p. cm.
  ISBN 0-7621-8877-4
  1. Detective and mystery stories, American. I. Title.
  PS3535.I73 A6 2002
  813'.52--dc21

                                     2002004199

PRINTED IN THE UNITED STATES OF AMERICA

2 4 6 8 10 9 7 5 3 1

CONTENTS

Introduction

ALMOST a hundred years have gone by since Mary Roberts Rinehart wrote her first full-length novel, in 1905. It is a century that has seen all manner of suspense writing—mysteries, detective stories, and thrillers—take a prominent place on fiction bestseller lists, and today it is not unusual to see that spot occupied by women authors. Indeed, the American crime-writing sisterhood that stars Patricia Cornwell, Mary Higgins Clark, and Sue Grafton takes up at least half the shelf space in the mystery aisle of any respectable bookstore.

Things were different in 1905.

When America's "Mistress of Mystery" launched her career, detective writing was relatively new. Edgar Allan Poe is credited with inventing it in the 1840s and Arthur Conan Doyle with perfecting it in the 1890s. Aside from these groundbreaking classic authors, mystery readers had only the "penny dreadfuls"—paperback novellas with lurid plots and rococo prose that catered to the lowest common denominator of Victorian taste—and the novels of Rinehart's sole female predecessor, Brooklyn-born Anna Katharine Green. Green's debut legal thriller, *The Leavenworth Case,* was published in 1878.

However, it was Mary Roberts Rinehart who really captured the popular imagination of twentieth-century America and made the mystery novel into the preeminent genre that it is today.

MARY ELLA ROBERTS WAS BORN IN 1876 in Allegheny, Pennsylvania, which today is inside the Pittsburgh city limits. Her parents, Cornelia and Tom Roberts, began married life in the second-story front bedroom of Tom's mother's house, which was also home to his brother and sister-in-law, three younger sisters, and the workshop of Grandmother Roberts's seamstress business. Money was tight, but Mary remembers the house as "busy enough and gay enough." It must have been crowded enough as well, and Cornelia was no doubt delighted when Tom, an inventor and visionary who sold sewing machines for a modest living, was at last able to rent a little brick house for his growing family. (A second daughter, Olive, was born four years after Mary.)

When it came to formal schooling, Mary Roberts did not excel. A lefty, she found the enforced torture of right-handed penmanship particularly onerous. It is painful to imagine the woman who later covered page after page of lined tablets with breakneck flights of elegant prose hunkered over a small desk, struggling to keep her wrist flat, her forefinger slightly curved, and three fingers resting on the page in the approved fashion of the day. In high school she joined the debating society, wrote for the school newspaper, and graduated with an undistinguished C average.

The family's precarious finances suffered a serious downturn in Mary's adolescent years. Tom Roberts had risked investing in a new house that the family could ill afford, and in less than a year the money ran out. The maid was let go, Mary's piano lessons ceased, and—most humiliating of all—the family took in boarders.

By now Mary was eager to make her own way in the world. She conceived a notion to attend medical school. It was a sign of high personal aspirations that was not in line with her family's budget or with Mary's undistinguished academic record, so she lowered her sights. She would train as a nurse.

Her mother was horrified. A hospital ward was no place for a young lady. Undaunted, Mary paid a visit to the Roberts's physician. "I put up my hair for the first time, let a tuck out of a pink and white dimity dress, put on my best hat, white with pink roses, and with a rose parasol to complete my maturity, went to see the family doctor." He was on vacation, however, and Mary was confronted with his summer replacement—"A very dark young man, black hair, small black mustache, black eyes behind *pince-nez.* A rather severe young man, too, when I told him my errand."

He did his best to discourage her. "You have an idea that nursing is a romantic business," he said. "You think it is nothing but smoothing pillows and stroking foreheads." But Mary persisted, and the young doctor relented. He took her on a tour of the wards, and in August of that year, 1893, she enrolled in the Pittsburgh Training School for Nurses.

In her autobiography she is honest about her motives. She was more eager to leave home than she was moved to relieve suffering. "The hospital lured me . . . as an adventure, an experience, and as the solution of a practical difficulty." Eventually she got her adventure, and a sizable dose of drudgery as well, for nurses' schooling in those days was 90 percent on-the-job training. At age seventeen, well-bred middle-class Mary Roberts endured twelve-hour shifts looking after prostitutes, alcoholics, drug addicts, laborers horribly injured in Pittsburgh's steel mills, and victims of typhoid, smallpox, and venereal diseases.

In the wards of that inner-city hospital Mary lost her young girl's illusions and gained a fount of understanding and compassion for human suffering. A new world opened to her, dark and untidy; and largely unawares, she began to collect stories and experiences that would serve her well as a crime writer. One of the two series characters Rinehart invented was, not surprisingly, a nurse-detective named Hilda Adams. (The fourth selection in this volume, *The Buckled Bag,* is Hilda's first adventure.)

Even as she lived through these sobering experiences, Mary felt an urge to record them: "I wanted to put on paper the faces of the men as they waited for their turns; their hands, with the callouses peeling off and strangely white, gripping the tops of the beds while the probe went in; I wanted to put down the whirr of the bandage machines as I rolled bandages. . . . But I could not write it. I would go to my little room on my off duty with a pencil and pad, and bravely go to work: 'The ambulance is ringing furiously in the courtyard below.' Then I would stop. I was too tired."

What little energy she did have left at the end of each long day was directed elsewhere. For Mary Roberts had discovered a softer side of Dr. Stanley Marshall Rinehart, the severe young doctor with the black eyes and mustache who had escorted her on her first visit to the hospital. Dr. Rinehart was, it seemed, wonderful with children. When he walked into the ward, they flocked to him, and he played gentle games with them. Mary was charmed, and she began to see more of the good doctor. Before a year went by, they were engaged.

Doctors and nurses working together were under strict orders not to socialize, so the engagement was kept secret. For two years Mary wore her ring on a ribbon around her neck and went on with her training. They were years of quiet joy marred by one great sorrow.

She was out of town tending a private patient when she received word that her father had died. "It stunned me. Early the next morning I took a train home, and I bought a paper to see if there was any explanation. There was indeed. It was blazoned on the front page. He had gone to a hotel in Buffalo and killed himself. Shot himself. I had not even known he owned a revolver."

Depressed over escalating financial troubles, Tom Roberts had taken his own life. Mary arrived home to find reporters parked on the lawn, ravenous for all the unpleasant details. She never forgot or forgave, and packs of parasitic newsmen feeding on tragedy are regular villains in her novels. Cornelia grieved and busied herself with preparations for her elder daughter's wedding, which was, understandably, a quiet affair.

Nineteen-year-old Mrs. Stanley Rinehart delighted in her status as the wife of a handsome doctor, and motherhood came quickly. Stanley Marshall Rinehart, Jr., was born in 1897, Alan Gillespie in 1900, and her youngest, Frederick, in 1902. The Rineharts employed two maids and a houseboy, but Mary took full charge of the children, sewing their clothes, serving them their early supper "on a tiny table with three diminutive bentwood chairs," and nursing them through life-threatening childhood illnesses. When her eldest came down with diphtheria, Mary caught it as well.

In later years she could not recall the name of the nurse who stayed with her through that illness, but Rinehart's fans are forever in the woman's debt. It was she who showed Mary a magazine ad advertising for verse and suggested that Mary, who was bored with bed rest, might give it try.

Rinehart wrote two poems and sent them off. They were accepted, and she received twenty-two dollars in payment. "The incredible had happened. I was writing. Not stories, of course. Only verse. I wrote reams of it." In her autobiography she admits it was rather poor stuff, but now and then the mail would bring a check for ten or twelve dollars. Encouraged, Rinehart churned out an entire book of verse and traveled to New York in pursuit of a publisher. She was unsuccessful, and her literary career went to the back burner. "I gave it up, this strange itch to put words on paper. I was twenty-seven, and what did I know to write?"

When she made her next literary venture, Mary was no longer fighting boredom or responding to "an itch." Instead, her motive was distressingly practical. Dr. Rinehart had suffered losses in a stock market crash, the family was seriously in debt, and Mary hoped to earn a few dollars to help make ends meet.

Verse would no longer do. She must write longer pieces that could earn real money.

Starting out was difficult. To economize, the Rineharts had dismissed their servants—all but one. Mary was left to run the big house, help her husband with his practice, and care for three small boys, including a sickly baby who required warm milk every two hours. She knew she had it in her to write, but again she could not summon the energy.

And then one day Dr. Rinehart brought home a ready-made plot. A patient had received a knock on the head that sent him back to an earlier stage in his life. He did not recognize his wife or children and claimed never to have seen a "modern" trolley car. Mary was intrigued. In one evening she wrote a story based on the incident and sent it off to *Munsey's Magazine*. In response, she received a check for thirty-four dollars (two cents a word) and a request for more stories. She was off and running.

"I devised weird and often horrible plots. I could think faster than I could write, devise plots and put them on paper with amazing speed. That first year I sold a total of forty-five stories and novelettes . . . and at the end I found that I had earned a total of eighteen hundred and forty-two dollars, and fifty cents!"

Forty-five stories in a year is a great deal of writing by any standard. But it was only the beginning, for in the years to come, Mary Roberts Rinehart would write more than thirty full-length novels, a dozen nonfiction works, an autobiography, and countless short stories and articles.

In 1905 Bob Davis, her editor at *Munsey's Magazine,* asked her for a long story that could be serialized over several issues. Rinehart was reluctant. "I had no confidence in my ability to sustain interest for any length of time, and no desire whatever to write a book. A book was for real writers." But she obliged. The Rineharts had taken a summerhouse in the suburbs; Mary planted herself on the porch and went to work. *The Man in Lower Ten* was the result: a fully formed, stylish novel with a satisfying, multilayered plot, fully developed characters, and pleasing touches of romance and humor. Mary Roberts Rinehart had hit her stride. She had discovered the irresistible recipe that would become her trademark and inspire countless imitators.

The Circular Staircase and *The Window at the White Cat* (originally titled *The Mystery of 1122*) quickly followed, also printed as magazine serials. And in magazines they might have remained were it not for Mary's favorite uncle, John.

Uncle John read *The Circular Staircase* and proclaimed, "That's a book, Mary. You ought to have it published."

"It isn't good enough for a book," she insisted.

"Certainly it is," he said stubbornly. "I've read a lot of worse books."

Having had no success in finding a publisher for her poetry collection by contacting companies at random, the ever practical Rinehart found a more efficient way. "I picked a publisher," she explains, "by the simple method of taking a story by Anna Katharine Green from the book case, noted the name Bobbs-Merrill of Indianapolis, and sent it off."

She was at the butcher's when the editor's reply arrived. Stanley phoned and read it to her. " 'My dear Mrs. Rinehart: I have read *The Circular Staircase,* not only with pleasure but with thrills and shivers.' " He would publish the book! What's more, he wanted to visit her to discuss other books.

Mary was ecstatic. "Other books, and I had two ready for him; two books and a million ideas! I wired him to come on . . . and I baked a cake that afternoon. I beat eggs and whipped icing and sang, and we had ice cream and cake for dinner that night."

Bobbs-Merrill published *The Circular Staircase* in 1908. Mary braced herself. On the day of publication she took her children to the country to get away from bad reviews. To her surprise they were excellent. "I read that I had developed a new technique of the detective novel; that I had made the first advance in the technique of the crime story since Edgar Allan Poe! I was stunned."

The Man in Lower Ten was published in hardcover at the end of 1909 and zoomed up 1910's sales charts to become the first detective novel by an American author to become a bestseller. *The Window at the White Cat* followed a year later.

These three mysteries, written during a short period of intense activity, established Rinehart's reputation. Critics agree that they are vastly superior to the vigorous but somewhat undisciplined short story experiments that went before and that they are more carefully crafted than the majority of her later books. They have stood the test of time and stand today as her finest achievements. This anthology brings together *The Circular Staircase, The Man in Lower Ten,* and *The Window at the White Cat* for the first time, along with *The Buckled Bag* (1914), an exquisite novella that many consider Rinehart's most perfect mystery.

Public reaction to the books was little short of phenomenal. Mary's annual earnings soon topped $100,000, ten times the Rineharts' stock market loss. Mary and Stan bought a grand Premier touring car, the maids were rehired, and the boys were transferred to private schools. The family went to Europe for six months—Stanley studied thoracic medicine in Vienna, while Mary and the boys took in the arts and the pastries—and upon their return to the United States they moved into a twenty-room mansion on a bluff overlooking the Ohio River.

The mediocre schoolgirl was now a full-fledged American icon. By dint of hard work and a seemingly bottomless well of ideas, Mary Roberts Rinehart would hold on to that status for many years to come.

After the First World War the family moved to Washington, D.C. Dr. Rinehart was appointed to the Veterans' Bureau and later commissioned to the medical section of the army's Officer Reserve Corps. The war turned Mary's mind to weighty matters, beginning what would be a lifelong crusade for recognition as a serious writer. She convinced *The Saturday Evening Post* to send her to Europe, where she visited the troops in the trenches and interviewed Winston Churchill, as well as Britain's Queen Mary and the King and Queen of Belgium. The series of articles she wrote for *The Post* were later collected and reprinted as *Kings, Queens, and Pawns.*

In the 1920s and '30s Rinehart returned to her mystery writing, for which there was nonstop demand. Woodrow Wilson and Herbert Hoover were among her fans, as was Gertrude Stein. Rinehart also wrote travel pieces—descriptions of holidays roughing it in the western states and an account of a journey to the Middle East. She authored several successful Broadway plays, including *The Bat,* a 1920's adaptation of *The Circular Staircase.* America's premier magazines—*McCall's, Ladies' Home Journal, The Saturday Evening Post,* and *Good Housekeeping*—published her short stories and essays on topics ranging from political philosophy to fashion. She held the American public in the palm of her hand, but try as she might, it was always the whodunits that defined Mary Roberts Rinehart's image and paid the bills. In 1929 her sons Stan junior and Frederick helped found the publishing house of Farrar and Rinehart and built its success largely on the strength of their mother's mysteries.

Mary was disillusioned with the changing face of postwar America. It was, she said, "a jazzed America, drinking, dancing, spending; developing a cult of ugliness and calling it modernity." She would buck the trend. Politically and socially conservative, she insisted on the highest standards of language and decorum in her novels. Murder and mayhem were all very well, but they must not offend the sensibilities of ladies and children. She also steered clear of feminism, insisting that she herself was a wife and mother first, a career woman only by force of circumstances.

Dr. Rinehart died in 1932, and a year later Mary suffered the first of a series of heart attacks. She left Washington, D.C., and moved to a lavish apartment on Park Avenue in New York City, where she could be near her sons, her grandchildren, and her great-grandchildren. Her public persona receded, and doctors forbade a trip to Europe to report firsthand on World War II, but the pace of her writing did not slow. She published twenty books in the 1930s and '40s, along with dozens of articles.

In her sixtieth year Rinehart was diagnosed with breast cancer and underwent a successful radical mastectomy. She talked about the illness openly and frankly in a 1947 interview with *Ladies' Home Journal.* It was the first time this previously taboo subject was discussed in a public forum, and the article did a great deal to increase awareness of the disease. The compassionate young nurse was still alive and well, it would seem, in the heart of America's grande dame of mystery.

Mary Roberts Rinehart's last novel, *The Frightened Wife,* was written in 1953. She died of a severe heart attack on September 22, 1958, at the age of eighty-three, and was buried next to her husband in Arlington National Cemetery.

I HAVE a personal childhood memory of my mother absorbed in one of Mary Roberts Rinehart's mysteries. She's reading in our 1950s living room, in a monstrous armchair upholstered with large pink and yellow flowers. Mother was a refugee from Latvia, and Rinehart's elegant prose must have challenged her imperfect English, but the stories were too good to put down. I did not learn to love them until very nearly fifty years later, when I first met the unstoppable Miss Rachel Innes and fell under the spell of the circular staircase at Sunnyside.

Today it is my pleasure to share *The Best Mysteries of Mary Roberts Rinehart* with a new generation of mystery lovers.

—*Eva Jaunzems*
Editor

Sources

Jan Cohn, *Improbable Fiction: The Life of Mary Roberts Rinehart,* 1980.

Martha Hailey Dubose, "Mary Roberts Rinehart: The Buried Story," in *Women of Mystery: The Lives and Works of Notable Women Crime Novelists,* 2000.

Mary Roberts Rinehart's autobiography, *My Story,* 1931.

The Best Mysteries of

MARY
ROBERTS
RINEHART

The Circular Staircase

Chapter I

I Take a Country House

⌐≫⌐

THIS is the story of how a middle-aged spinster lost her mind, deserted her domestic gods in the city, took a furnished house for the summer out of town, and found herself involved in one of those mysterious crimes that keep our newspapers and detective agencies happy and prosperous. For twenty years I had been perfectly comfortable; for twenty years I had had the window boxes filled in the spring, the carpets lifted, the awnings put up and the furniture covered with brown linen; for as many summers I had said good-bye to my friends, and, after watching their perspiring hegira, had settled down to a delicious quiet in town, where the mail comes three times a day, and the water supply does not depend on a tank on the roof.

And then—the madness seized me. When I look back over the months I spent at Sunnyside, I wonder that I survived at all. As it is, I show the wear and tear of my harrowing experiences. I have turned very gray—Liddy reminded me of it, only yesterday, by saying that a little bluing in the rinse water would make my hair silvery, instead of a yellowish white. I hate to be reminded of unpleasant things and I snapped her off.

"No," I said sharply, "I'm not going to use bluing at my time of life, or starch, either."

Liddy's nerves are gone, she says, since that awful summer, but she has enough left, goodness knows! And when she begins to go around with a lump in her throat, all I have to do is to threaten to return to Sunnyside, and she is frightened into a semblance of cheerfulness—from which you may judge that the summer there was anything but a success.

The newspaper accounts have been so garbled and incomplete—one of them mentioned me but once, and then only as the tenant at the time the thing happened—that I feel it my due to tell what I know. Mr. Jamieson, the detective, said himself he could never have done without me, although he gave me little enough credit, in print.

I shall have to go back several years—thirteen, to be exact—to start my story. At that time my brother died, leaving me his two children. Halsey was eleven then, and Gertrude was seven. All the responsibilities of maternity were thrust upon me suddenly; to perfect the profession of motherhood requires precisely as many years as the child has lived, like the man who started to carry the calf and ended by walking along with the bull on his shoulders. However, I did the best I could. When Gertrude got past the hair-ribbon age, and Halsey asked for a scarf pin and put on long trousers—and a wonderful help that was to the darning—I sent them away to good schools. After that, my responsibility was chiefly postal, with three months every summer in which to replenish their wardrobes, look over their lists of acquaintances, and generally to take my foster-motherhood out of its nine months' retirement in camphor.

I missed the summers with them when, somewhat later, at boarding school and college, the children spent much of their vacations with friends. Gradually I found that my name signed to a check was even more welcome than when signed to a letter, though I wrote them at stated intervals. But when Halsey had finished his electrical course and Gertrude her boarding school, and both came home to stay, things were suddenly changed. The winter Gertrude came out was nothing but a succession of sitting up late at night to bring her home from things, taking her to the dressmakers between naps the next day, and discouraging ineligible youths with either more money than brains, or more brains than money. Also, I acquired a great many things: to say "lingerie" for undergarments, "frocks" and "gowns" instead of dresses, and that beardless sophomores are not college boys, but college men. Halsey required less personal supervision, and as they both got their mother's fortune that winter, my responsibility became purely moral. Halsey bought a car, of course, and I learned how to tie over my bonnet a gray baize veil, and, after a time, never to stop to look at the dogs one has run down. People are apt to be so unpleasant about their dogs.

The additions to my education made me a properly equipped maiden aunt, and by spring I was quite tractable. So when Halsey suggested camping in the Adirondacks and Gertrude wanted Bar Harbor, we compromised on a good country house with links near, within motor distance of town and telephone distance of the doctor. That was how we went to Sunnyside.

We went out to inspect the property, and it seemed to deserve its name. Its cheerful appearance gave no indication whatever of anything out of the ordinary. Only one thing seemed unusual to me: the housekeeper, who had been left in charge, had moved from the house to the gardener's lodge, a few days before. As the lodge was far enough away from the house, it seemed to me that either fire or thieves could complete their work of destruction undisturbed. The property was an extensive one: the house on the top of a hill, which sloped away in great stretches of green lawn and clipped hedges, to the road; and across the valley, perhaps a couple of miles away, was the Greenwood Club. Gertrude and Halsey were infatuated.

"Why, it's everything you want," Halsey said "View, air, good water and good roads. As for the house, it's big enough for a hospital, if it has a Queen Anne front and a Mary Anne back," which was ridiculous: it was pure Elizabethan.

Of course we took the place; it was not my idea of comfort, being much too large and sufficiently isolated to make the servant question serious. But I give my self credit for this: whatever has happened since, I never blamed Halsey and Gertrude for taking me there. And another thing: if the series of catastrophes there did nothing else, it taught me one thing—that somehow, somewhere, from perhaps a half-civilized ancestor who wore a sheepskin garment and trailed his food or his prey, I have in me the instinct of the chase. Were I a man I should be a trapper of criminals, trailing them as relentlessly as no doubt my sheepskin ancestor did his wild boar. But being an unmarried woman, with the handicap of my sex, my first acquaintance with crime will probably be my last. Indeed, it came near enough to being my last acquaintance with anything.

The property was owned by Paul Armstrong, the president of the Traders' Bank, who at the time we took the house was in the West with his wife and daughter, and a Dr. Walker, the Armstrong family physician. Halsey knew Louise Armstrong—had been rather attentive to her the winter before, but as Halsey was always attentive to somebody, I had not thought of it seriously, although she was a charming girl. I knew of Mr. Armstrong only through his connection with the bank, where the children's money was largely invested, and through an ugly story about the son, Arnold Armstrong, who was reported to have forged his father's name, for a considerable amount, to some bank paper. However, the story had had no interest for me.

I cleared Halsey and Gertrude away to a house party and moved out to Sunnyside the first of May. The roads were bad, but the trees were in leaf, and there were still tulips in the borders around the house. The arbutus was fragrant in the woods under the dead leaves, and on the way from the station, a short mile, while the car stuck in the mud, I found a bank showered with tiny forget-me-nots. The birds—don't ask me what kind; they all look alike to me, unless they have a hallmark of some bright color—the birds were chirping in the hedges, and everything breathed of peace. Liddy, who was born and bred on a brick pavement, got a little bit down-spirited when the crickets began to chirp, or scrape their legs together, or whatever it is they do, at twilight.

The first night passed quietly enough. I have always been grateful for that one night's peace; it shows what the country might be, under favorable circumstances. Never after that night did I put my head on my pillow with any assurance how long it would be there; or on my shoulders, for that matter.

On the following morning Liddy and Mrs. Ralston, my own housekeeper, had a difference of opinion, and Mrs. Ralston left on the eleven train. Just after luncheon, Burke, the butler, was taken unexpectedly with a pain in his right side, much worse when I was within hearing distance, and by afternoon he was started cityward. That night the cook's sister had a baby—the cook, seeing indecision in my face, made it twins on second thought—and, to be short, by noon the next day the household staff was down to Liddy and myself. And this in a house with twenty-two rooms and five baths!

Liddy wanted to go back to the city at once, but the milk boy said that Thomas Johnson, the Armstrongs' colored butler, was working as a waiter at the Greenwood Club, and might come back. I have the usual scruples about coercing people's servants away, but few of us have any conscience regarding institutions or corporations—witness the way we beat railroads and streetcar companies when we can—so I called up the club, and about eight o'clock Thomas Johnson came to see me. Poor Thomas!

Well, it ended by my engaging Thomas on the spot, at outrageous wages, and with permission to sleep in the gardener's lodge, empty since the house was rented. The old man—he was white-haired and a little stooped, but with an immense idea of his personal dignity—gave me his reasons hesitatingly.

"I ain't sayin' nothin', Mis' Innes," he said, with his hand on the door-knob, "but there's been goin's-on here this las' few months as ain't natchal. 'Tain't one thing an' 'tain't another—it's jest a door squealin' here, an' a winder closin' there, but when doors an' winders gets to cuttin' up capers and there's nobody nigh 'em, it's time Thomas Johnson sleeps somewhar's else."

Liddy, who seemed to be never more than ten feet away from me that night, and was afraid of her shadow in that great barn of a place, screamed a little, and turned a yellow green. But I am not easily alarmed.

It was entirely in vain; I represented to Thomas that we were alone, and that he would have to stay in the house that night. He was politely firm, but he would come over early the next morning, and if I gave him a key, he would come in time to get some sort of breakfast. I stood on the huge veranda and watched him shuffle along down the shadowy drive, with mingled feelings—irritation at his cowardice and thankfulness at getting him at all. I am not ashamed to say that I double-locked the hall door when I went in.

"You can lock up the rest of the house and go to bed, Liddy," I said severely. "You give me the creeps standing there. A woman of your age ought to have better sense." It usually braces Liddy to mention her age: she owns to forty—which is absurd. Her mother cooked for my grandfather, and Liddy must be at least as old as I. But that night she refused to brace.

"You're not going to ask me to lock up, Miss Rachel!" she quavered. "Why, there's a dozen French windows in the drawing room and the billiard-room wing, and every one opens on a porch. And Mary Anne said that last night there was a man standing by the stable when she locked the kitchen door."

"Mary Anne was a fool," I said sternly. "If there had been a man there, she would have had him in the kitchen and been feeding him what was left from dinner, inside of an hour, from force of habit. Now don't be ridiculous. Lock up the house and go to bed. I am going to read."

But Liddy set her lips tight and stood still.

"I'm not going to bed," she said. "I am going to pack up, and tomorrow I am going to leave."

"You'll do nothing of the sort," I snapped. Liddy and I often desire to part company, but never at the same time. "If you are afraid, I will go with you, but for goodness' sake don't try to hide behind me."

The house was a typical summer residence on an extensive scale. Wherever possible, on the first floor, the architect had done away with partitions, using arches and columns instead. The effect was cool and spacious, but scarcely cozy. As Liddy and I went from one window to another, our voices echoed back at us uncomfortably. There was plenty of light—the electric plant down in the village supplied us—but there were long vistas of polished floor, and mirrors which reflected us from unexpected corners, until I felt some of Liddy's foolishness communicate itself to me.

The house was very long, a rectangle in general form, with the main entrance in the center of the long side. The brick-paved entry opened into a short hall to the right of which, separated only by a row of pillars, was a huge living room. Beyond that was the drawing room and, in the end, the billiard room. Off the billiard room, in the extreme right wing, was a den, or cardroom, with a small hall opening on the east veranda, and from there went up a narrow circular staircase. Halsey had pointed it out with delight.

"Just look, Aunt Rachel," he said with a flourish. "The architect that put up this joint was wise to a few things. Arnold Armstrong and his friends could sit here and play cards all night and stumble up to bed in the early morning, without having the family send in a police call."

Liddy and I got as far as the cardroom and turned on all the lights. I tried the small entry door there, which opened on the veranda, and examined the windows. Everything was secure, and Liddy, a little less nervous now, had just pointed out to me the disgracefully dusty condition of the hardwood floor, when suddenly the lights went out. We waited a moment; I think Liddy was stunned with fright, or she would have screamed. And then I clutched her by the arm and pointed to one of the windows opening on the porch. The sudden change threw the window into relief, an oblong of grayish light, and showed us a figure standing close, peering in. As I looked it darted across the veranda and out of sight in the darkness.

Chapter II

A Link Cuff-Button

∽∽

LIDDY'S knees seemed to give away under her. Without a sound she sank down, leaving me staring at the window in petrified amazement. Liddy began to moan under her breath, and in my excitement I reached down and shook her.

"Stop it," I whispered. "It's only a woman—maybe a maid of the Armstrongs'. Get up and help me find the door." She groaned again. "Very well," I said, "then I'll have to leave you here. I'm going."

She moved at that, and holding to my sleeve, we felt our way, with numerous collisions, to the billiard room, and from there to the drawing room. The lights came on then, and with the long French windows unshuttered, I had a creepy feeling that each one sheltered a peering face. In fact, in the light of what happened afterward, I am pretty certain we were under surveillance during the entire ghostly evening. We hurried over the rest of the locking-up and got upstairs as quickly as we could. I left the lights all on, and our footsteps echoed cavernously. Liddy had a stiff neck the next morning, from looking back over her shoulder, and she refused to go to bed.

"Let me stay in your dressing room, Miss Rachel," she begged. "If you don't, I'll sit in the hall outside the door. I'm not going to be murdered with my eyes shut."

"If you're going to be murdered," I retorted, "it won't make any difference whether they are shut or open. But you may stay in the dressing room, if you will lie on the couch: when you sleep in a chair, you snore."

She was too far gone to be indignant, but after a while she came to the door and looked in to where I was composing myself for sleep with Drummond's *Spiritual Life*.

"That wasn't a woman, Miss Rachel," she said, with her shoes in her hand. "It was a man in a long coat."

"What woman was a man?" I discouraged her without looking up, and she went back to the couch.

It was eleven o'clock when I finally prepared for bed. In spite of my assumption of indifference, I locked the door into the hall, and finding the transom did not catch, I put a chair cautiously before the door—it was not necessary to rouse Liddy—and climbing up put on the ledge of the transom a small dressing mirror, so that any movement of the frame would send it crashing down. Then, secure in my precautions, I went to bed.

I did not go to sleep at once. Liddy disturbed me just as I was growing drowsy, by coming in and peering under the bed. She was afraid to speak, however, because of her previous snubbing, and went back, stopping in the doorway to sigh dismally.

Somewhere downstairs a clock with a chime sang away the hours—eleven thirty, forty-five, twelve. And then the lights went out to stay. The Casanova Electric Company shuts up shop and goes home to bed at midnight: when one has a party, I believe it is customary to fee the company, which will drink hot coffee and keep awake a couple of hours longer. But the lights were gone for good that night. Liddy had gone to sleep, as I knew she would. She was a very unreliable person: always awake and ready to talk when she wasn't wanted and dozing off to sleep when she was. I called her once or twice, the only result being an explosive snore that threatened her very windpipe—then I got up and lighted a bedroom candle.

My bedroom and dressing room were above the big living room on the first floor. On the second floor a long corridor ran the length of the house, with rooms opening from both sides. In the wings were small corridors crossing the main one—the plan was simplicity itself. And just as I got back into bed, I heard a sound from the east wing, apparently, that made me stop, frozen, with one bedroom slipper half off, and listen. It was a rattling metallic sound, and it reverberated along the empty halls like the crash of doom. It was for all the world as if something heavy, perhaps a piece of steel, had rolled clattering and jangling down the hardwood stairs leading to the cardroom.

In the silence that followed, Liddy stirred and snored again. I was exasperated: first she kept me awake by silly alarms; then when she was needed, she slept like Joe Jefferson, or Rip—they are always the same to me. I went in and aroused her, and I give her credit for being wide awake the minute I spoke.

"Get up," I said, "if you don't want to be murdered in your bed."

"Where? How?" she yelled vociferously, and jumped up.

"There's somebody in the house," I said. "Get up. We'll have to get to the telephone."

"Not out in the hall!" she gasped. "Oh, Miss Rachel, not out in the hall!" trying to hold me back. But I am a large woman and Liddy is small. We got to the door, somehow, and Liddy held a brass andiron, which it was all she could do to lift, let alone brain anybody with. I listened and, hearing nothing, opened the door a little and peered into the hall. It was a black void, full of terrible suggestion, and my candle only emphasized the gloom. Liddy squealed and drew me back again, and as the door slammed, the mirror I had put on the transom came down and hit her on the head. That completed our demoralization. It was some time before I could persuade her she had not been attacked from behind by a burglar, and when she found the mirror smashed on the floor she wasn't much better.

"There's going to be a death!" she wailed. "Oh, Miss Rachel, there's going to be a death!"

"There will be," I said grimly, "if you don't keep quiet, Liddy Allen."

And so we sat there until morning, wondering if the candle would last until dawn, and arranging what trains we could take back to town. If we had only stuck to that decision and gone back before it was too late!

The sun came finally, and from my window I watched the trees along the drive take shadowy form, gradually lose their ghostlike appearance, become gray and then green. The Greenwood Club showed itself a dab of white against the hill across the valley, and an early robin or two hopped around in the dew. Not until the milk boy and the sun came, about the same time, did I dare to open the door into the hall and look around. Everything was as we had left it. Trunks were heaped here and there, ready for the trunk room, and through an end window of stained glass came a streak of red and yellow daylight that was eminently cheerful. The milk boy was pounding somewhere below, and the day had begun.

Thomas Johnson came ambling up the drive about half-past six, and we could hear him clattering around on the lower floor, opening shutters. I had to take Liddy to her room upstairs, however—she was quite sure she would find something uncanny. In fact, when she did not, having now the courage of daylight, she was actually disappointed.

Well, we did not go back to town that day.

The discovery of a small picture fallen from the wall of the drawing room was quite sufficient to satisfy Liddy that the alarm had been a false one, but I was anything but convinced. Allowing for my nerves and the fact that small noises magnify themselves at night, there was still no possibility that the picture had made the series of sounds I heard. To prove it, however, I dropped it again. It fell with a single muffled crash of its wooden frame, and incidentally ruined itself beyond repair. I justified myself by reflecting that if the Armstrongs chose to leave pictures in unsafe positions, and to rent a house with a family ghost, the destruction of property was their responsibility, not mine.

I warned Liddy not to mention what had happened to anybody, and telephoned to town for servants. Then after a breakfast which did more credit to Thomas' heart than his head, I went on a short tour of investigation. The sounds had come from the east wing, and not without some qualms I began there. At first I found nothing. Since then I have developed my powers of observation, but at that time I was a novice. The small cardroom seemed undisturbed. I looked for footprints, which is, I believe, the conventional thing to do, although my experience has been that as clues both footprints and thumbmarks are more useful in fiction than in fact. But the stairs in that wing offered something.

At the top of the flight had been placed a tall wicker hamper, packed with linen that had come from town. It stood at the edge of the top step, almost barring passage, and on the step below it was a long fresh scratch. For three steps the scratch was repeated, gradually diminishing, as if some object had fallen, striking each one. Then for four steps nothing. On the fifth step below was a round dent in the hard wood. That was all, and it seemed little enough, except that I was positive the marks had not been there the day before.

It bore out my theory of the sound, which had been for all the world like the bumping of a metallic object down a flight of steps. The four steps had been skipped. I reasoned that an iron bar, for instance, would do something of the sort—strike two or three steps, end down, then turn over, jumping a few stairs, and landing with a thud.

Iron bars, however, do not fall downstairs in the middle of the night alone. Coupled with the figure on the veranda the agency by which it climbed might be assumed. But—and here was the thing that puzzled me most—the doors were all fastened that morning, the windows unmolested, and the particular door from the cardroom to the veranda had a combination lock of which I held the key, and which had not been tampered with.

I fixed on an attempt at burglary, as the most natural explanation—an attempt frustrated by the falling of the object, whatever it was, that had roused me. Two things I could not understand: how the intruder had escaped with everything locked, and why he had left the small silver, which, in the absence of a butler, had remained downstairs overnight.

Under pretext of learning more about the place, Thomas Johnson led me through the house and the cellars, without result. Everything was in good order and repair; money had been spent lavishly on construction and plumbing. The house was full of conveniences, and I had no reason to repent my bargain, save the fact that, in the nature of things, night must come again. And other nights must follow—and we were a long way from a police station.

In the afternoon a hack came up from Casanova, with a fresh relay of servants. The driver took them with a flourish to the servants' entrance, and drove around to the front of the house, where I was awaiting him.

"Two dollars," he said in reply to my question. "I don't charge full rates, because, bringin' 'em up all summer as I do, it pays to make a special price. When they got off the train, I sez, sez I, 'There's another bunch for Sunnyside, cook, parlormaid and all.' Yes'm—six summers, and a new lot never less than once a month. They won't stand for the country and the lonesomeness, I reckon."

But with the presence of the "bunch" of servants my courage revived, and late in the afternoon came a message from Gertrude that she and Halsey would arrive that night at about eleven o'clock, coming in the car from Richfield. Things were looking up; and when Beulah, my cat, a most intelligent animal, found some early catnip on a bank near the house and rolled in it in a feline ecstasy, I decided that getting back to nature was the thing to do.

While I was dressing for dinner, Liddy rapped at the door. She was hardly herself yet, but privately I think she was worrying about the broken mirror and its augury, more than anything else. When she came in, she was holding something in her hand, and she laid it on the dressing table carefully.

"I found it in the linen hamper," she said. "It must be Mr. Halsey's, but it seems queer how it got there."

It was the half of a link cuff-button of unique design, and I looked at it carefully.

"Where was it? In the bottom of the hamper?" I asked.

"On the very top," she replied. "It's a mercy it didn't fall out on the way."

When Liddy had gone, I examined the fragment attentively. I had never seen it before, and I was certain it was not Halsey's. It was of Italian workmanship, and consisted of a mother-of-pearl foundation, encrusted with tiny seed pearls, strung on horsehair to hold them. In the center was a small ruby. The trinket was odd enough, but not intrinsically of great value. Its interest for me lay in this: Liddy had found it lying in the top of the hamper which had blocked the east-wing stairs.

That afternoon the Armstrongs' housekeeper, a youngish good-looking woman, applied for Mrs. Ralston's place, and I was glad enough to take her. She looked as though she might be equal to a dozen of Liddy, with her snapping black eyes and heavy jaw. Her name was Anne Watson, and I dined that evening for the first time in three days.

Chapter III
Mr. John Bailey Appears

⌒◈◇◈⌒

I HAD dinner served in the breakfast room. Somehow the huge dining room depressed me, and Thomas, cheerful enough all day, allowed his spirits to go down with the sun. He had a habit of watching the corners of the room, left shadowy by the candles on the table, and altogether it was not a festive meal.

Dinner over I went into the living room. I had three hours before the children could possibly arrive, and I got out my knitting. I had brought along two dozen pairs of slipper soles in assorted sizes—I always send knitted slippers to the Old Ladies' Home at Christmas—and now I sorted over the wools with a grim determination not to think about the night before. But my mind was not on my work: at the end of a half hour I found I had put a row of blue scallops on Eliza Klinefelter's lavender slippers, and I put them away.

I got out the cuff link and went with it to the pantry. Thomas was wiping silver and the air was heavy with tobacco smoke. I sniffed and looked around, but there was no pipe to be seen.

"Thomas," I said, "you have been smoking."

"No, ma'am." He was injured innocence itself. "It's on my coat, ma'am. Over at the club the gentlemen—"

But Thomas did not finish. The pantry was suddenly filled with the odor of singeing cloth. Thomas gave a clutch at his coat, whirled to the sink, filled a tumbler with water and poured it into his right pocket with the celerity of practice.

"Thomas," I said, when he was sheepishly mopping the floor, "smoking is a filthy and injurious habit. If you must smoke, you must; but don't stick a lighted pipe in your pocket again. Your skin's your own: you can blister it if you like. But this house is not mine, and I don't want a conflagration. Did you ever see this cuff link before?"

No, he never had, he said, but he looked at it oddly.

"I picked it up in the hall," I added indifferently. The old man's eyes were shrewd under his bushy eyebrows.

"There's strange goin's-on here, Mis' Innes," he said, shaking his head. "Somethin's goin' to happen, sure. You ain't took notice that the big clock in the hall is stopped, I reckon?"

"Nonsense," I said. "Clocks have to stop, don't they, if they're not wound?"

"It's wound up, all right, and it stopped at three o'clock last night," he answered solemnly. "More'n that, that there clock ain't stopped for fifteen years, not since Mr. Armstrong's first wife died. And that ain't all— no, ma'am. Last three nights I slep' in this place, after the electrics went out I had a token. My oil lamp was full of oil, but it kep' goin' out, do what I would. Minute I shet my eyes, out that lamp'd go. There ain't no surer token of death. The Bible sez, Let yer light shine! When a hand you can't see puts yer light out, it means death, sure."

The old man's voice was full of conviction. In spite of myself I had a chilly sensation in the small of my back, and I left him mumbling over his dishes. Later on I heard a crash from the pantry, and Liddy reported that Beulah, who is coal black, had darted in front of Thomas just as he picked up a tray of dishes; that the bad omen had been too much for him, and he had dropped the tray.

The chug of the automobile as it climbed the hill was the most welcome sound I had heard for a long time, and with Gertrude and Halsey actually before me, my troubles seemed over for good. Gertrude stood smiling in the hall, with her hat quite over one ear, and her hair in every direction under her pink veil. Gertrude is a very pretty girl, no matter how her hat is, and I was not surprised when Halsey presented a good-looking young man, who bowed at me and looked at Trude—that is the ridiculous nickname Gertrude brought from school.

"I have brought a guest, Aunt Ray," Halsey said. "I want you to adopt him into your affections and your Saturday-to-Monday list. Let me present John Bailey, only you must call him Jack. In twelve hours he'll be calling you 'Aunt': I know him."

We shook hands, and I got a chance to look at Mr. Bailey; he was a tall fellow, perhaps thirty, and he wore a small mustache. I remember wondering why: he seemed to have a good mouth, and when he smiled, his teeth were above the average. One never knows why certain men cling to a messy upper lip that must get into things, any more than one understands some women building up their hair on wire atrocities. Otherwise, he was very good to look at, stalwart and tanned, with the direct gaze that I like. I am particular about Mr. Bailey, because he was a prominent figure in what happened later.

Gertrude was tired with the trip and went up to bed very soon. I made up my mind to tell them nothing until the next day, and then to make as light of our excitement as possible. After all, what had I to tell? An inquisitive face peering in at a window, a crash in the night, a scratch or two on the stairs, and half a cuff-button! As for Thomas and his forebodings, it was always my belief that a negro is one part thief, one part pigment, and the rest superstition.

It was Saturday night. The two men went to the billiard room, and I could hear them talking as I went upstairs. It seemed that Halsey had stopped at the Greenwood Club for gasoline and found Jack Bailey there, with the Sunday golf crowd. Mr. Bailey had not been hard to persuade—probably Gertrude knew why—and they had carried him off triumphantly. I roused Liddy to get them something to eat— Thomas was beyond reach in the lodge—and paid no attention to her evident terror of the kitchen regions. Then I went to bed. The men were still in the billiard room when I finally dozed off, and the last thing I remember was the howl of a dog in front of the house. It wailed a crescendo of woe that trailed off hopefully, only to break out afresh from a new point of the compass.

At three o'clock in the morning I was roused by a revolver shot. The sound seemed to come from just outside my door. For a moment I could not move. Then I heard Gertrude stirring in her room, and the next moment she had thrown open the connecting door.

"O Aunt Ray! Aunt Ray!" she cried hysterically. "Someone has been killed, killed!"

"Thieves," I said shortly. "Thank goodness, there are some men in the house tonight." I was getting into my slippers and a bathrobe, and Gertrude with shaking hands was lighting a lamp. Then we opened the door into the hall, where, crowded on the upper landing of the stairs, the maids, white-faced and trembling, were peering down, headed by

Liddy. I was greeted by a series of low screams and questions, and I tried to quiet them. Gertrude had dropped on a chair and sat there limp and shivering.

I went at once across the hall to Halsey's room and knocked; then I pushed the door open. It was empty; the bed had not been occupied!

"He must be in Mr. Bailey's room," I said excitedly, and followed by Liddy, we went there. Like Halsey's, it had not been occupied! Gertrude was on her feet now, but she leaned against the door for support.

"They have been killed!" she gasped. Then she caught me by the arm and dragged me toward the stairs. "They may only be hurt, and we must find them," she said, her eyes dilated with excitement.

I don't remember how we got down the stairs: I do remember expecting every moment to be killed. The cook was at the telephone upstairs, calling the Greenwood Club, and Liddy was behind me, afraid to come and not daring to stay behind. We found the living room and the drawing room undisturbed. Somehow I felt that whatever we found would be in the cardroom or on the staircase, and nothing but the fear that Halsey was in danger drove me on; with every step my knees seemed to give way under me. Gertrude was ahead and in the cardroom she stopped, holding her candle high. Then she pointed silently to the doorway into the hall beyond. Huddled there on the floor, facedown, with his arms extended, was a man.

Gertrude ran forward with a gasping sob. "Jack," she cried, "oh, Jack!"

Liddy had run, screaming, and the two of us were there alone. It was Gertrude who turned him over, finally, until we could see his white face, and then she drew a deep breath and dropped limply to her knees. It was the body of a man, a gentleman, in a dinner coat and white waist-coat, stained now with blood—the body of a man I had never seen before.

Chapter IV

Where Is Halsey?

GERTRUDE gazed at the face in a kind of fascination. Then she put out her hands blindly, and I thought she was going to faint.

"He has killed him!" she muttered almost inarticulately; and at that, because my nerves were going, I gave her a good shake.

"What do you mean?" I said frantically. There was a depth of grief and conviction in her tone that was worse than anything she could have said. The shake braced her, anyhow, and she seemed to pull herself together. But not another word would she say: she stood gazing down at that gruesome figure on the floor, while Liddy, ashamed of her flight and afraid to come back alone, drove before her three terrified women servants into the drawing room, which was as near as any of them would venture.

Once in the drawing room, Gertrude collapsed and went from one fainting spell into another. I had all I could do to keep Liddy from drowning her with cold water, and the maids huddled in a corner, as much use as so many sheep. In a short time, although it seemed hours, a car came rushing up, and Anne Watson, who had waited to dress, opened the door. Three men from the Greenwood Club, in all kinds of costumes, hurried in. I recognized a Mr. Jarvis, but the others were strangers.

"What's wrong?" the Jarvis man asked—and we made a strange picture, no doubt. "Nobody hurt, is there?" He was looking at Gertrude.

"Worse than that, Mr. Jarvis," I said. "I think it is murder."

At the word there was a commotion. The cook began to cry, and Mrs. Watson knocked over a chair. The men were visibly impressed.

"Not any member of the family?" Mr. Jarvis asked, when he had got his breath.

"No," I said; and motioning Liddy to look after Gertrude, I led the way with a lamp to the cardroom door. One of the men gave an exclamation, and they all hurried across the room. Mr. Jarvis took the lamp from me—I remember that—and then, feeling myself getting dizzy and light-headed, I closed my eyes. When I opened them their brief examination was over, and Mr. Jarvis was trying to put me in a chair.

"You must get upstairs," he said firmly, "you and Miss Gertrude, too. This has been a terrible shock. In his own home, too."

I stared at him without comprehension. "Who is it?" I asked with difficulty. There was a band drawn tight around my throat.

"It is Arnold Armstrong," he said, looking at me oddly, "and he has been murdered in his father's house."

After a minute I gathered myself together and Mr. Jarvis helped me into the living room. Liddy had got Gertrude upstairs, and the two strange men from the club stayed with the body. The reaction from the shock and strain was tremendous: I was collapsed—and then Mr. Jarvis asked me a question that brought back my wandering faculties.

"Where is Halsey?" he asked.

"Halsey!" Suddenly Gertrude's stricken face rose before me—the empty rooms upstairs. Where was Halsey?

"He was here, wasn't he?" Mr. Jarvis persisted. "He stopped at the club on his way over."

"I—don't know where he is," I said feebly.

One of the men from the club came in, asked for the telephone, and I could hear him excitedly talking, saying something about coroners and detectives. Mr. Jarvis leaned over to me.

"Why don't you trust me, Miss Innes?" he said. "If I can do anything I will. But tell me the whole thing."

I did, finally, from the beginning, and when I told of Jack Bailey's being in the house that night, he gave a long whistle.

"I wish they were both here," he said when I finished. "Whatever mad prank took them away, it would look better if they were here. Especially—"

"Especially what?"

"Especially since Jack Bailey and Arnold Armstrong were notoriously bad friends. It was Bailey who got Arnold into trouble last spring—something about the bank. And then, too—"

"Go on," I said. "If there is anything more, I ought to know."

"There's nothing more," he said evasively. "There's just one thing we may bank on, Miss Innes. Any court in the country will acquit a man who kills an intruder in his house, at night. If Halsey—"

"Why, you don't think Halsey did it!" I exclaimed. There was a queer feeling of physical nausea coming over me.

"No, no, not at all," he said with forced cheerfulness. "Come, Miss Innes, you're a ghost of yourself and I am going to help you upstairs and call your maid. This has been too much for you."

Liddy helped me back to bed, and under the impression that I was in danger of freezing to death, put a hot-water bottle over my heart and another at my feet. Then she left me. It was early dawn now, and from voices under my window I surmised that Mr. Jarvis and his companions were searching the grounds. As for me, I lay in bed, with every faculty awake. Where had Halsey gone? How had he gone, and when? Before the murder, no doubt, but who would believe that? If either he or Jack Bailey had heard an intruder in the house and shot him—as they might have been justified in doing—why had they run away? The whole thing was unheard of, outrageous, and—impossible to ignore.

About six o'clock Gertrude came in. She was fully dressed, and I sat up nervously.

"Poor Aunty!" she said. "What a shocking night you have had!" She came over and sat down on the bed, and I saw she looked very tired and worn.

"Is there anything new?" I asked anxiously.

"Nothing. The car is gone, but Warner"—he is the chauffeur—"Warner is at the lodge and knows nothing about it."

"Well," I said, "if I ever get my hands on Halsey Innes, I shall not let go until I have told him a few things. When we get this cleared up, I am going back to the city to be quiet. One more night like the last two will end me. The peace of the country—fiddlesticks!"

Whereupon I told Gertrude of the noises the night before, and the figure on the veranda in the east wing. As an afterthought I brought out the pearl cuff link.

"I have no doubt now," I said, "that it was Arnold Armstrong the night before last, too. He had a key, no doubt, but why he should steal into his father's house I cannot imagine. He could have come with my permission, easily enough. Anyhow, whoever it was that night, left this little souvenir."

Gertrude took one look at the cuff link and went as white as the pearls in it; she clutched at the foot of the bed and stood staring. As for me, I was quite as astonished as she was.

"Where did—you—find it?" she asked finally, with a desperate effort at calm. And while I told her she stood looking out of the window with a look I could not fathom on her face. It was a relief when Mrs. Watson tapped at the door and brought me some tea and toast. The cook was in bed, completely demoralized, she reported, and Liddy, brave with the daylight, was looking for footprints around the house. Mrs. Watson herself was a wreck; she was blue-white around the lips, and she had one hand tied up. She said she had fallen downstairs in her excitement. It was natural, of course, that the thing would shock her, having been the Armstrongs' housekeeper for several years, and knowing Mr. Arnold well.

Gertrude had slipped out during my talk with Mrs. Watson, and I dressed and went downstairs. The billiard and cardrooms were locked until the coroner and the detectives got there, and the men from the club had gone back for more conventional clothing.

I could hear Thomas in the pantry, alternately wailing for Mr. Arnold, as he called him, and citing the tokens that had precursed the murder. The house seemed to choke me, and slipping a shawl around me, I went out on the drive. At the corner by the east wing I met Liddy. Her skirts were draggled with dew to her knees, and her hair was still in crimps.

"Go right in and change your clothes," I said sharply. "You're a sight, and at your age!"

She had a golf stick in her hand, and she said she had found it on the lawn. There was nothing unusual about it, but it occurred to me that a golf-stick with a metal end might have been the object that had scratched the stairs near the cardroom. I took it from her and sent her up for dry garments. Her daylight courage and self-importance, and her shuddering delight in the mystery, irritated me beyond words. After I left her I made a circuit of the building. Nothing seemed to be disturbed: the house looked as calm and peaceful in the morning sun as it had the day I had been coerced into taking it. There was nothing to show that inside had been mystery and violence and sudden death.

In one of the tulip beds back of the house an early blackbird was pecking viciously at something that glittered in the light. I picked my way gingerly over through the dew and stooped down: almost buried in the soft ground was a revolver! I scraped the earth off it with the tip of my shoe, and, picking it up, slipped it into my pocket. Not until I had got into my bedroom and double-locked the door did I venture to take it out and examine it. One look was all I needed. It was Halsey's revolver. I had unpacked it the day before and put it on his shaving stand, and there could be no mistake. His name was on a small silver plate on the handle.

I seemed to see a network closing around my boy, innocent as I knew he was. The revolver—I am afraid of them, but anxiety gave me courage to look through the barrel—the revolver had still two bullets in it. I could only breathe a prayer of thankfulness that I had found the revolver before any sharp-eyed detective had come around.

I decided to keep what clues I had, the cuff link, the golf stick and the revolver, in a secure place until I could see some reason for displaying them. The cuff link had been dropped into a little filigree box on my toilet table. I opened the box and felt around for it. The box was empty—the cuff link had disappeared!

Chapter V

Gertrude's Engagement

∞

AT TEN o'clock the Casanova hack brought up three men. They introduced themselves as the coroner of the county and two detectives from the city. The coroner led the way at once to the locked wing, and with the aid of one of the detectives examined the rooms and the body. The other detective, after a short scrutiny of the dead man, busied himself with the outside of the house. It was only after they had got a fair idea of things as they were that they sent for me.

I received them in the living room, and I had made up my mind exactly what to tell. I had taken the house for the summer, I said, while the Armstrongs were in California. In spite of a rumor among the servants about strange noises—I cited Thomas—nothing had occurred the first two nights. On the third night I believed that someone had been in the house: I had heard a crashing sound, but being alone with one maid had not investigated. The house had been locked in the morning and apparently undisturbed.

Then, as clearly as I could, I related how, the night before, a shot had roused us; that my niece and I had investigated and found a body; that I did not know who the murdered man was until Mr. Jarvis from the club informed me, and that I knew of no reason why Mr. Arnold Armstrong should steal into his father's house at night. I should have been glad to allow him entree there at any time.

"Have you reason to believe, Miss Innes," the coroner asked, "that any member of your household, imagining Mr. Armstrong was a burglar, shot him in self-defense?"

"I have no reason for thinking so," I said quietly.

"Your theory is that Mr. Armstrong was followed here by some enemy, and shot as he entered the house?"

"I don't think I have a theory," I said. "The thing that has puzzled me is why Mr. Armstrong should enter his father's house two nights in succession, stealing in like a thief, when he needed only to ask entrance to be admitted."

The coroner was a very silent man: he took some notes after this, but he seemed anxious to make the next train back to town. He set the inquest for the following Saturday, gave Mr. Jamieson, the younger of the two detectives, and the more intelligent looking, a few instructions, and, after gravely shaking hands with me and regretting the unfortunate affair, took his departure, accompanied by the other detective.

I was just beginning to breathe freely when Mr. Jamieson, who had been standing by the window, came over to me.

"The family consists of yourself alone, Miss Innes?"

"My niece is here," I said.

"There is no one but yourself and your niece?"

"My nephew." I had to moisten my lips.

"Oh, a nephew. I should like to see him, if he is here."

"He is not here just now," I said as quietly as I could. "I expect him—at any time."

"He was here yesterday evening, I believe?"

"No—yes."

"Didn't he have a guest with him? Another man?"

"He brought a friend with him to stay over Sunday, Mr. Bailey."

"Mr. John Bailey, the cashier of the Traders' Bank I believe." And I knew that someone at the Greenwood Club had told. "When did they leave?"

"Very early—I don't know at just what time."

Mr. Jamieson turned suddenly and looked at me.

"Please try to be more explicit," he said. "You say your nephew and Mr. Bailey were in the house last night, and yet you and your niece, with some women servants, found the body. Where was your nephew?"

I was entirely desperate by that time.

"I do not know," I cried, "but be sure of this: Halsey knows nothing of this thing, and no amount of circumstantial evidence can make an innocent man guilty."

"Sit down," he said, pushing forward a chair. "There are some things I have to tell you, and, in return, please tell me all you know. Believe me, things always come out. In the first place, Mr. Armstrong was shot from above. The bullet was fired at close range, entered below the shoulder and came out, after passing through the heart, well down the back. In other words, I believe the murderer stood on the stairs and fired down. In the second place, I found on the edge of the billiard table a charred cigar which had burned itself partly out, and a cigarette which had consumed itself to the cork tip. Neither one had been more than lighted, then put down and forgotten. Have you any idea what it was that made your nephew and Mr. Bailey leave their cigars and their game, take out the automobile without calling the chauffeur, and all this at— let me see certainly before three o'clock in the morning?"

"I don't know," I said; "but depend on it, Mr. Jamieson, Halsey will be back himself to explain everything."

"I sincerely hope so," he said. "Miss Innes, has it occurred to you that Mr. Bailey might know something of this?"

Gertrude had come downstairs, and just as he spoke, she came in. I saw her stop suddenly, as if she had been struck.

"He does not," she said in a tone that was not her own. "Mr. Bailey and my brother know nothing of this. The murder was committed at three. They left the house at a quarter before three."

"How do you know that?" Mr. Jamieson asked oddly. "Do you know at what time they left?"

"I do," Gertrude answered firmly. "At a quarter before three my brother and Mr. Bailey left the house, by the main entrance. I—was—there."

"Gertrude," I said excitedly, "you are dreaming! Why, at a quarter to three—"

"Listen," she said. "At half-past two the downstairs telephone rang. I had not gone to sleep, and I heard it. Then I heard Halsey answer it, and in a few minutes he came upstairs and knocked at my door. We—we talked for a minute, then I put on my dressing gown and slippers, and went downstairs with him. Mr. Bailey was in the billiard room. We—we all talked together for perhaps ten minutes. Then it was decided that—that they should both go away—"

"Can't you be more explicit?" Mr. Jamieson asked. "Why did they go away?"

"I am only telling you what happened, not why it happened," she said evenly. "Halsey went for the car, and instead of bringing it to the house and rousing people, he went by the lower road from the stable. Mr. Bailey was to meet him at the foot of the lawn. Mr. Bailey left—"

"Which way?" Mr. Jamieson asked sharply.

"By the main entrance. He left—it was a quarter to three. I know exactly."

"The clock in the hall is stopped, Miss Innes," said Jamieson. Nothing seemed to escape him.

"He looked at his watch," she replied, and I could see Mr. Jamieson's eyes snap, as if he had made a discovery. As for myself, during the whole recital I had been plunged into the deepest amazement.

"Will you pardon me for a personal question?" The detective was a youngish man, and I thought he was somewhat embarrassed. "What are your—your relations with Mr. Bailey?"

Gertrude hesitated. Then she came over and put her hand lovingly in mine.

"I am engaged to marry him," she said simply.

I had grown so accustomed to surprises that I could only gasp again, and as for Gertrude, the hand that lay in mine was burning with fever.

"And—after that," Mr. Jamieson went on, "you went directly to bed?"

Gertrude hesitated.

"No," she said finally. "I—I am not nervous; and after I had extinguished the light, I remembered something I had left in the billiard room, and I felt my way back there through the darkness."

"Will you tell me what it was you had forgotten?"

"I cannot tell you," she said slowly. "I—I did not leave the billiard room at once—"

"Why?" The detective's tone was imperative. "This is very important, Miss Innes."

"I was crying," Gertrude said in a low tone. "When the French clock in the drawing room struck three, I got up, and then—I heard a step on the east porch, just outside the cardroom. Someone with a key was working with the latch, and I thought, of course, of Halsey. When we took the house he called that his entrance, and he had carried a key for it ever since. The door opened and I was about to ask what he had forgotten, when there was a flash and a report. Some heavy body dropped, and half crazed with terror and shock, I ran through the drawing room and got upstairs—I scarcely remember how."

She dropped into a chair, and I thought Mr. Jamieson must have finished. But he was not through.

"You certainly clear your brother and Mr. Bailey admirably," he said. "The testimony is invaluable, especially in view of the fact that your brother and Mr. Armstrong had, I believe, quarreled rather seriously some time ago."

"Nonsense," I broke in. "Things are bad enough, Mr. Jamieson, without inventing bad feeling where it doesn't exist. Gertrude, I don't think Halsey knew the—the murdered man, did he?"

But Mr. Jamieson was sure of his ground.

"The quarrel, I believe," he persisted, "was about Mr. Armstrong's conduct to you, Miss Gertrude. He had been paying you unwelcome attentions."

And I had never seen the man!

When she nodded a "yes" I saw the tremendous possibilities involved. If this detective could prove that Gertrude feared and disliked the murdered man, and that Mr. Armstrong had been annoying and possibly pursuing her with hateful attentions, all that, added to Gertrude's confession of her presence in the billiard room at the time of the crime, looked strange, to say the least. The prominence of the family assured a strenuous effort to find the murderer, and if we had nothing worse to look forward to, we were sure of a distasteful publicity.

Mr. Jamieson shut his notebook with a snap and thanked us.

"I have an idea," he said, apropos of nothing at all, "that at any rate the ghost is laid here. Whatever the rappings have been—and the colored man says they began when the family went west three months ago—they are likely to stop now."

Which shows how much he knew about it. The ghost was not laid: with the murder of Arnold Armstrong he, or it, only seemed to take on fresh vigor.

Mr. Jamieson left then, and when Gertrude had gone upstairs, as she did at once, I sat and thought over what I had just heard. Her engagement, once so engrossing a matter, paled now beside the significance of her story. If Halsey and Jack Bailey had left before the crime, how came Halsey's revolver in the tulip bed? What was the mysterious cause of their sudden flight? What had Gertrude left in the billiard room? What was the significance of the cuff link, and where was it?

Chapter VI

In the East Corridor

WHEN the detective left, he enjoined absolute secrecy on everybody in the household. The Greenwood Club promised the same thing, and as there are no Sunday afternoon papers, the murder was not publicly known until Monday. The coroner himself notified the Armstrong family lawyer, and early in the afternoon he came out. I had not seen Mr. Jamieson since morning, but I knew he had been interrogating the servants. Gertrude was locked in her room with a headache, and I had luncheon alone.

Mr. Harton, the lawyer, was a little, thin man, and he looked as if he did not relish his business that day.

"This is very unfortunate, Miss Innes," he said, after we had shaken hands. "Most unfortunate—and mysterious. With the father and mother

in the West, I find everything devolves on me; and as you can understand, it is an unpleasant duty."

"No doubt," I said absently. "Mr. Harton, I am going to ask you some
questions, and I hope you will answer them. I feel that I am entitled to
some knowledge, because I and my family are just now in a most
ambiguous position."

I don't know whether he understood me or not: he took off his glasses
and wiped them.

"I shall be very happy," he said with old-fashioned courtesy.

"Thank you. Mr. Harton, did Mr. Arnold Armstrong know that Sunnyside had been rented?"

"I think—yes, he did. In fact, I myself told him about it."

"And he knew who the tenants were?"

"Yes."

"He had not been living with the family for some years, I believe?"

"No. Unfortunately, there had been trouble between Arnold and his
father. For two years he had lived in town."

"Then it would be unlikely that he came here last night to get possession of anything belonging to him?"

"I should think it hardly possible," he admitted.

"To be perfectly frank, Miss Innes, I cannot think of any reason whatever for his coming here as he did. He had been staying at the clubhouse across the valley for the last week, Jarvis tells me, but that only
explains how he came here, not why. It is a most unfortunate family."

He shook his head despondently, and I felt that this dried-up little
man was the repository of much that he had not told me. I gave up trying to elicit any information from him, and we went together to view
the body before it was taken to the city. It had been lifted on to the billiard table and a sheet thrown over it; otherwise nothing had been
touched. A soft hat lay beside it, and the collar of the dinner coat was
still turned up. The handsome, dissipated face of Arnold Armstrong,
purged of its ugly lines, was now only pathetic. As we went in Mrs. Watson appeared at the cardroom door.

"Come in, Mrs. Watson," the lawyer said. But she shook her head and
withdrew: she was the only one in the house who seemed to regret the
dead man, and even she seemed rather shocked than sorry.

I went to the door at the foot of the circular staircase and opened it.

If I could only have seen Halsey coming at his usual harebrained clip up the drive, if I could have heard the throb of the motor, I would have felt that my troubles were over. But there was nothing to be seen. The countryside lay sunny and quiet in its peaceful Sunday afternoon calm, and far down the drive Mr. Jamieson was walking slowly, stooping now and then, as if to examine the road. When I went back, Mr. Harton was furtively wiping his eyes.

"The prodigal has come home, Miss Innes," he said. "How often the sins of the fathers are visited on the children!" Which left me pondering.

Before Mr. Harton left, he told me something of the Armstrong family. Paul Armstrong, the father, had been married twice. Arnold was a son by the first marriage. The second Mrs. Armstrong had been a widow, with a child, a little girl. This child, now perhaps twenty, was Louise Armstrong, having taken her stepfather's name, and was at present in California with the family.

"They will probably return at once," he concluded, "and part of my errand here today is to see if you will relinquish your lease here in their favor."

"We would better wait and see if they wish to come," I said. "It seems unlikely, and my town house is being remodeled." At that he let the matter drop, but it came up unpleasantly enough, later.

At six o'clock the body was taken away, and at seven thirty, after an early dinner, Mr. Harton went. Gertrude had not come down, and there was no news of Halsey. Mr. Jamieson had taken a lodging in the village, and I had not seen him since midafternoon. It was about nine o'clock, I think, when the bell rang and he was ushered into the living room.

"Sit down," I said grimly. "Have you found a clue that will incriminate me, Mr. Jamieson?"

He had the grace to look uncomfortable. "No," he said. "If you had killed Mr. Armstrong, you would have left no clues. You would have had too much intelligence."

After that we got along better. He was fishing in his pocket, and after a minute he brought out two scraps of paper. "I have been to the clubhouse," he said, "and among Mr. Armstrong's effects, I found these. One is curious; the other is puzzling."

The first was a sheet of club notepaper, on which was written, over and over, the name "Halsey B. Innes." It was Halsey's flowing signature to a dot, but it lacked Halsey's ease. The ones toward the bottom of the sheet were much better than the top ones. Mr. Jamieson smiled at my face.

"His old tricks," he said. "That one is merely curious; this one, as I said before, is puzzling."

The second scrap, folded and refolded into a compass so tiny that the writing had been partly obliterated, was part of a letter—the lower half of a sheet, not typed, but written in a cramped hand.

"—by altering the plans for—rooms, may be possible. The best way, in my opinion, would be to—the plan for—in one of the—rooms—chimney."

That was all.

"Well?" I said, looking up. "There is nothing in that, is there? A man ought to be able to change the plan of his house without becoming an object of suspicion."

"There is little in the paper itself," he admitted; "but why should Arnold Armstrong carry that around, unless it meant something? He never built a house, you may be sure of that. If it is this house, it may mean anything, from a secret room—"

"To an extra bathroom," I said scornfully. "Haven't you a thumbprint, too?"

"I have," he said with a smile, "and the print of a foot in a tulip bed, and a number of other things. The oddest part is, Miss Innes, that the thumbmark is probably yours and the footprint certainly."

His audacity was the only thing that saved me: his amused smile put me on my mettle, and I ripped out a perfectly good scallop before I answered.

"Why did I step into the tulip bed?" I asked with interest.

"You picked up something," he said good-humoredly, "which you are going to tell me about later."

"Am I, indeed?" I was politely curious. "With this remarkable insight of yours, I wish you would tell me where I shall find my four-thousand-dollar motor car."

"I was just coming to that," he said. "You will find it about thirty miles away, at Andrews Station, in a blacksmith shop, where it is being repaired."

I laid down my knitting then and looked at him.

"And Halsey?" I managed to say.

"We are going to exchange information," he said "I am going to tell you that, when you tell me what you picked up in the tulip bed."

We looked steadily at each other: it was not an unfriendly stare; we were only measuring weapons. Then he smiled a little and got up.

"With your permission," he said, "I am going to examine the card-room and the staircase again. You might think over my offer in the meantime."

He went on through the drawing room, and I listened to his footsteps growing gradually fainter. I dropped my pretense at knitting, and leaning back, I thought over the last forty-eight hours. Here was I, Rachel Innes, spinster, a granddaughter of old John Innes of Revolutionary days, a D.A.R., a Colonial Dame, mixed up with a vulgar and revolting crime, and even attempting to hoodwink the law! Certainly I had left the straight and narrow way.

I was roused by hearing Mr. Jamieson coming rapidly back through the drawing room. He stopped at the door.

"Miss Innes," he said quickly, "will you come with me and light the east corridor? I have fastened somebody in the small room at the head of the cardroom stairs."

I jumped up at once.

"You mean—the murderer?" I gasped.

"Possibly," he said quietly, as we hurried together up the stairs. "Someone was lurking on the staircase when I went back. I spoke; instead of an answer, whoever it was turned and ran up. I followed—it was dark—but as I turned the corner at the top a figure darted through this door and closed it. The bolt was on my side, and I pushed it forward. It is a closet, I think." We were in the upper hall now. "If you will show me the electric switch, Miss Innes, you would better wait in your own room."

Trembling as I was, I was determined to see that door opened. I hardly knew what I feared, but so many terrible and inexplicable things had happened that suspense was worse than certainty.

"I am perfectly cool," I said, "and I am going to remain here."

The lights flashed up along that end of the corridor, throwing the doors into relief. At the intersection of the small hallway with the larger, the circular staircase wound its way up, as if it had been an afterthought of the architect. And just around the corner, in the small corridor, was the door Mr. Jamieson had indicated. I was still unfamiliar with the house, and I did not remember the door. My heart was thumping wildly in my ears, but I nodded to him to go ahead. I was perhaps eight or ten feet away—and then he threw the bolt back.

"Come out," he said quietly. There was no response. "Come—out," he repeated. Then—I think he had a revolver, but I am not sure—he stepped aside and threw the door open.

From where I stood I could not see beyond the door, but I saw Mr. Jamieson's face change and heard him mutter something, then he bolted down the stairs, three at a time. When my knees had stopped shaking, I moved forward, slowly, nervously, until I had a partial view of what was beyond the door. It seemed at first to be a closet, empty. Then I went close and examined it, to stop with a shudder. Where the floor should have been was black void and darkness, from which came the indescribable, damp smell of the cellars.

Mr. Jamieson had locked somebody in the clothes chute. As I leaned over I fancied I heard a groan—or was it the wind?

Chapter VII

A Sprained Ankle

I WAS panic-stricken. As I ran along the corridor I was confident that the mysterious intruder and probable murderer had been found, and that he lay dead or dying at the foot of the chute. I got down the staircase somehow, and through the kitchen to the basement stairs. Mr. Jamieson had been before me, and the door stood open. Liddy was standing in the middle of the kitchen, holding a frying pan by the handle as a weapon.

"Don't go down there," she yelled when she saw me moving toward the basement stairs. "Don't you do it, Miss Rachel. That Jamieson's down there now. There's only trouble comes of hunting ghosts; they lead you into bottomless pits and things like that. Oh, Miss Rachel, don't—" as I tried to get past her.

She was interrupted by Mr. Jamieson's reappearance. He ran up the stairs two at a time, and his face was flushed and furious.

"The whole place is locked," he said angrily. "Where's the laundry key kept?"

"It's kept in the door," Liddy snapped. "That whole end of the cellar is kept locked, so nobody can get at the clothes, and then the key's left in the door, so that unless a thief was as blind as—as some detectives, he could walk right in."

"Liddy," I said sharply, "come down with us and turn on all the lights."

She offered her resignation, as usual, on the spot, but I took her by the arm, and she came along finally. She switched on all the lights and pointed to a door just ahead.

"That's the door," she said sulkily. "The key's in it."

But the key was not in it. Mr. Jamieson shook it, but it was a heavy door, well locked. And then he stooped and began punching around the keyhole with the end of a lead pencil. When he stood up his face was exultant.

"It's locked on the inside," he said in a low tone. "There is somebody in there."

"Lord have mercy!" gasped Liddy, and turned to run.

"Liddy," I called, "go through the house at once and see who is missing, or if anyone is. We'll have to clear this thing at once. Mr. Jamieson, if you will watch here I will go to the lodge and find Warner. Thomas would be of no use. Together you may be able to force the door."

"A good idea," he assented. "But—there are windows, of course, and there is nothing to prevent whoever is in there from getting out that way."

"Then lock the door at the top of the basement stairs," I suggested, "and patrol the house from the outside."

We agreed to this, and I had a feeling that the mystery of Sunnyside was about to be solved. I ran down the steps and along the drive. Just at the corner I ran full tilt into somebody who seemed to be as much alarmed as I was. It was not until I had recoiled a step or two that I recognized Gertrude, and she me.

"Good gracious, Aunt Ray," she exclaimed, "what is the matter?"

Mary Roberts Rinehart

"There's somebody locked in the laundry," I panted. "That is—unless—you didn't see anyone crossing the lawn or skulking around the house, did you?"

"I think we have mystery on the brain," Gertrude said wearily. "No, I haven't seen anyone, except old Thomas, who looked for all the world as if he had been ransacking the pantry. What have you locked in the laundry?"

"I can't wait to explain," I replied. "I must get Warner from the lodge. If you came out for air, you'd better put on your overshoes." And then I noticed that Gertrude was limping—not much, but sufficiently to make her progress very slow, and seemingly painful.

"You have hurt yourself," I said sharply.

"I fell over the carriage block," she explained. "I thought perhaps I might see Halsey coming home. He—he ought to be here."

I hurried on down the drive. The lodge was some distance from the house, in a grove of trees where the drive met the county road. There were two white stone pillars to mark the entrance, but the iron gates, once closed and tended by the lodge-keeper, now stood permanently open. The day of the motorcar had come; no one had time for closed gates and lodge-keepers. The lodge at Sunnyside was merely a sort of supplementary servants' quarters: it was as convenient in its appointments as the big house and infinitely more cozy.

As I went down the drive, my thoughts were busy. Who would it be that Mr. Jamieson had trapped in the cellar? Would we find a body or someone badly injured? Scarcely either. Whoever had fallen had been able to lock the laundry door on the inside. If the fugitive had come from outside the house, how did he get in? If it was some member of the household, who could it have been? And then—a feeling of horror almost overwhelmed me. Gertrude! Gertrude and her injured ankle! Gertrude found limping slowly up the drive when I had thought she was in bed!

I tried to put the thought away, but it would not go. If Gertrude had been on the circular staircase that night, why had she fled from Mr. Jamieson? The idea, puzzling as it was, seemed borne out by this circumstance. Whoever had taken refuge at the head of the stairs could scarcely have been familiar with the house, or with the location of the chute. The mystery seemed to deepen constantly. What possible connection could there be between Halsey and Gertrude, and the murder of Arnold Armstrong? And yet, every way I turned I seemed to find something that pointed to such a connection.

At the foot of the drive the road described a long, sloping, horseshoe-shaped curve around the lodge. There were lights there, streaming cheerfully out onto the trees, and from an upper room came wavering shadows, as if someone with a lamp was moving around. I had come almost silently in my evening slippers, and I had my second collision of the evening on the road just above the house. I ran full into a man in a long coat, who was standing in the shadow beside the drive, with his back to me, watching the lighted windows.

"What the hell!" he ejaculated furiously, and turned around. When he saw me, however, he did not wait for any retort on my part. He faded away—this is not slang; he did—he absolutely disappeared in the dusk without my getting more than a glimpse of his face. I had a vague impression of unfamiliar features and of a sort of cap with a visor. Then he was gone.

I went to the lodge and rapped. It required two or three poundings to bring Thomas to the door, and he opened it only an inch or so.

"Where is Warner?" I asked.

"I—I think he's in bed, ma'am."

"Get him up," I said, "and for goodness' sake open the door, Thomas. I'll wait for Warner."

"It's kind o' close in here, ma'am," he said, obeying gingerly, and disclosing a cool and comfortable-looking interior. "Perhaps you'd keer to set on the porch an' rest yo'self."

It was so evident that Thomas did not want me inside that I went in.

"Tell Warner he is needed in a hurry," I repeated, and turned into the little sitting room. I could hear Thomas going up the stairs, could hear him rouse Warner, and the steps of the chauffeur as he hurriedly dressed. But my attention was busy with the room below.

On the center table, open, was a sealskin traveling bag. It was filled with gold-topped bottles and brushes, and it breathed opulence, luxury, femininity from every inch of surface. How did it get there? I was still asking myself the question when Warner came running down the stairs and into the room. He was completely but somewhat incongruously dressed, and his open, boyish face looked abashed. He was a country boy, absolutely frank and reliable, of fair education and intelligence—one of the small army of American youths who turn a natural aptitude for mechanics into the special field of the automobile and earn good salaries in a congenial occupation.

"What is it, Miss Innes?" he asked anxiously.

"There is someone locked in the laundry," I replied. "Mr. Jamieson wants you to help him break the lock. Warner, whose bag is this?"

He was in the doorway by this time, and he pretended not to hear.

"Warner," I called, "come back here. Whose bag is this?"

He stopped then, but he did not turn around.

"It's—it belongs to Thomas," he said, and fled up the drive.

To Thomas! A London bag with mirrors and cosmetic jars of which Thomas could not even have guessed the use! However, I put the bag in the back of my mind, which was fast becoming stored with anomalous and apparently irreconcilable facts, and followed Warner to the house.

Liddy had come back to the kitchen: the door to the basement stairs was double-barred and had a table pushed against it; and beside her on the table was most of the kitchen paraphernalia.

"Did you see if there was anyone missing in the house?" I asked, ignoring the array of saucepans rolling pins, and the poker of the range.

"Rosie is missing," Liddy said with unction. She had objected to Rosie, the parlormaid, from the start. "Mrs. Watson went into her room, and found she had gone without her hat. People that trust themselves a dozen miles from the city, in strange houses, with servants they don't know, needn't be surprised if they wake up some morning and find their throats cut."

After which carefully veiled sarcasm Liddy relapsed into gloom. Warner came in then with a handful of small tools, and Mr. Jamieson went with him to the basement. Oddly enough, I was not alarmed. With all my heart I wished for Halsey, but I was not frightened. At the door he was to force, Warner put down his tools and looked at it. Then he turned the handle. Without the slightest difficulty the door opened, revealing the blackness of the drying room beyond!

Mr. Jamieson gave an exclamation of disgust.

"Gone!" he said. "Confound such careless work! I might have known."

It was true enough. We got the lights on finally and looked all through the three rooms that constituted this wing of the basement. Everything was quiet and empty. An explanation of how the fugitive had escaped injury was found in a heaped-up basket of clothes under the chute. The basket had been overturned, but that was all. Mr. Jamieson examined the windows: one was unlocked and offered an easy escape. The window or the door? Which way had the fugitive escaped? The door seemed most probable, and I hoped it had been so. I could not have borne, just then, to think that it was my poor Gertrude we had been hounding through the darkness, and yet—I had met Gertrude not far from that very window.

I went upstairs at last, tired and depressed. Mrs. Watson and Liddy were making tea in the kitchen. In certain walks of life the teapot is the refuge in times of stress, trouble or sickness: they give tea to the dying and they put it in the baby's nursing bottle. Mrs. Watson was fixing a tray to be sent in to me, and when I asked her about Rosie, she confirmed her absence.

"She's not here," she said; "but I would not think much of that, Miss Innes. Rosie is a pretty young girl, and perhaps she has a sweetheart. It will be a good thing if she has. The maids stay much better when they have something like that to hold them here."

Gertrude had gone back to her room, and while I was drinking my cup of hot tea, Mr. Jamieson came in.

"We might take up the conversation where we left off an hour and a half ago," he said. "But before we go on, I want to say this: the person who escaped from the laundry was a woman with a foot of moderate size and well arched. She wore nothing but a stocking on her right foot, and in spite of the unlocked door, she escaped by the window."

And again I thought of Gertrude's sprained ankle. Was it the right or the left?

Chapter VIII
The Other Half of the Line

⁂

"Miss Innes," the detective began, "what is your opinion of the figure you saw on the east veranda the night you and your maid were in the house alone?"

"It was a woman," I said positively.

"And yet your maid affirms with equal positiveness that it was a man."

"Nonsense," I broke in. "Liddy had her eyes shut—she always shuts them when she's frightened."

"And you never thought then that the intruder who came later that night might be a woman—the woman, in fact, whom you saw on the veranda?"

"I had reasons for thinking it was a man," I said, remembering the pearl cuff link.

"Now we are getting down to business. What were your reasons for thinking that?"

I hesitated.

"If you have any reason for believing that your midnight guest was Mr. Armstrong, other than his visit here the next night, you ought to tell me, Miss Innes. We can take nothing for granted. If, for instance, the intruder who dropped the bar and scratched the staircase—you see, I know about that—if this visitor was a woman, why should not the same woman have come back the following night, met Mr. Armstrong on the circular staircase, and in alarm shot him?"

"It was a man," I reiterated. And then, because I could think of no other reason for my statement, I told him about the pearl cuff link. He was intensely interested.

"Will you give me the link," he said when I finished, "or, at least, let me see it? I consider it a most important clue."

"Won't the description do?"

"Not as well as the original."

"Well, I'm very sorry," I said, as calmly as I could, "I—the thing is lost. It—it must have fallen out of a box on my dressing table."

Whatever he thought of my explanation, and I knew he doubted it, he made no sign. He asked me to describe the link accurately, and I did so, while he glanced at a list he took from his pocket.

"One set monogram cuff links," he read, "one set plain pearl links, one set cuff links, woman's head set with diamonds and emeralds. There is no mention of such a link as you describe, and yet, if your theory is right, Mr. Armstrong must have taken back in his cuffs one complete cuff link, and a half, perhaps, of the other."

The idea was new to me. If it had not been the murdered man who had entered the house that night, who had it been?

"There are a number of strange things connected with this case," the detective went on. "Miss Gertrude Innes testified that she heard some-one fumbling with the lock, that the door opened, and that almost immediately the shot was fired. Now, Miss Innes, here is the strange part of that. Mr. Armstrong had no key with him. There was no key in the lock or on the floor. In other words, the evidence points absolutely to this: Mr. Armstrong was admitted to the house from within."

"It is impossible," I broke in. "Mr. Jamieson, do you know what your words imply? Do you know that you are practically accusing Gertrude Innes of admitting that man?"

"Not quite that," he said, with his friendly smile. "In fact, Miss Innes, I am quite certain she did not. But as long as I learn only parts of the truth, from both you and her, what can I do? I know you picked up something in the flower bed: you refuse to tell me what it was. I know Miss Gertrude went back to the billiard room to get something, she refuses to say what. You suspect what happened to the cuff link, but you won't tell me. So far, all I am sure of is this: I do not believe Arnold Armstrong was the midnight visitor who so alarmed you by dropping— shall we say, a golf stick? And I believe that when he did come he was admitted by someone in the house. Who knows—it may have been— Liddy!"

I stirred my tea angrily.

"I have always heard," I said dryly, "that undertakers' assistants are jovial young men. A man's sense of humor seems to be in inverse pro-portion to the gravity of his profession."

"A man's sense of humor is a barbarous and a cruel thing, Miss Innes," he admitted. "It is to the feminine as the hug of a bear is to the scratch of—well—anything with claws. Is that you, Thomas? Come in."

Thomas Johnson stood in the doorway. He looked alarmed and apprehensive, and suddenly I remembered the sealskin dressing bag in the lodge. Thomas came just inside the door and stood with his head drooping, his eyes, under their shaggy gray brows, fixed on Mr. Jamieson.

"Thomas," said the detective, not unkindly, "I sent for you to tell us what you told Sam Bohannon at the club, the day before Mr. Arnold was found here, dead. Let me see. You came here Friday night to see Miss Innes, didn't you? And came to work here Saturday morning?"

For some unexplained reason Thomas looked relieved.

"Yas, sah," he said. "You see it were like this: When Mistah Armstrong and the fam'ly went away, Mis' Watson an' me, we was lef' in charge till the place was rented. Mis' Watson, she've bin here a good while, an' she warn' skeery. So she slep' in the house. I'd bin havin' tokens—I tol' Mis' Innes some of 'em—an' I slep' in the lodge. Then one day Mis' Watson, she came to me an she sez, sez she, 'Thomas, you'll hev to sleep up in the big house. I'm too nervous to do it anymore.' But I jes' reckon to myself that ef it's too skeery fer her, it's too skeery fer me. We had it, then, sho' nuff, and it ended up with Mis' Watson stayin' in the lodge nights an' me lookin' fer work at de club."

"Did Mrs. Watson say that anything had happened to alarm her?"

"No, sah. She was jes' natchally skeered. Well, that was all, far's I know, until the night I come over to see Mis' Innes. I come across the valley, along the path from the clubhouse, and I goes home that way. Down in the creek bottom I almost run into a man. He wuz standin' with his back to me, an' he was workin' with one of these yere electric light things that fit in yer pocket. He was havin' trouble—one minute it'd flash out, an' the nex' it'd be gone. I hed a view of 'is white dress shirt an' tie, as I passed. I didn't see his face. But I know it warn't Mr. Arnold. It was a taller man than Mr. Arnold. Beside that, Mr. Arnold was playin' cards when I got to the clubhouse, same's he'd been doin' all day."

"And the next morning you came back along the path," pursued Mr. Jamieson relentlessly.

"The nex' mornin' I come back along the path an' down where I dun see the man night befoh, I picked up this here." The old man held out a tiny object and Mr. Jamieson took it. Then he held it on his extended palm for me to see. It was the other half of the pearl cuff link!

But Mr. Jamieson was not quite through questioning him.

"And so you showed it to Sam, at the club, and asked him if he knew anyone who owned such a link, and Sam said—what?"

"Wal, Sam, he 'lowed he'd seen such a pair of cuff-buttons in a shirt belongin' to Mr. Bailey—Mr. Jack Bailey, sah."

"I'll keep this link, Thomas, for a while," the detective said. "That's all I wanted to know. Good night."

As Thomas shuffled out, Mr. Jamieson watched me sharply.

"You see, Miss Innes," he said, "Mr. Bailey insists on mixing himself with this thing. If Mr. Bailey came here that Friday night expecting to meet Arnold Armstrong, and missed him—if, as I say, he had done this, might he not, seeing him enter the following night, have struck him down, as he had intended before?"

"But the motive?" I gasped.

"There could be motive proved, I think. Arnold Armstrong and John Bailey have been enemies since the latter, as cashier of the Traders' Bank, brought Arnold almost into the clutches of the law. Also, you forget that both men have been paying attention to Miss Gertrude. Bailey's flight looks bad, too."

"And you think Halsey helped him to escape?"

"Undoubtedly. Why, what could it be but flight? Miss Innes, let me reconstruct that evening, as I see it. Bailey and Armstrong had quarreled at the club. I learned this today. Your nephew brought Bailey over. Prompted by jealous, insane fury, Armstrong followed, coming across by the path. He entered the billiard room wing—perhaps rapping, and being admitted by your nephew. Just inside he was shot by someone on the circular staircase. The shot fired, your nephew and Bailey left the house at once, going toward the automobile house. They left by the lower road, which prevented them being heard, and when you and Miss Gertrude got downstairs, everything was quiet."

"But—Gertrude's story," I stammered.

"Miss Gertrude only brought forward her explanation the following morning. I do not believe it, Miss Innes. It is the story of a loving and ingenious woman."

"And—this thing tonight?"

"May upset my whole view of the case. We must give the benefit of every doubt, after all. We may, for instance, come back to the figure on the porch: if it was a woman you saw that night through the window, we might start with other premises. Or Mr. Innes' explanation may turn us in a new direction. It is possible that he shot Arnold Armstrong as a burglar and then fled, frightened at what he had done. In any case, however, I feel confident that the body was here when he left. Mr. Armstrong left the club ostensibly for a moonlight saunter, about half after eleven o'clock. It was three when the shot was fired."

I leaned back bewildered. It seemed to me that the evening had been full of significant happenings, had I only held the key. Had Gertrude been the fugitive in the clothes chute? Who was the man on the drive near the lodge, and whose gold-mounted dressing-bag had I seen in the lodge sitting room?

It was late when Mr. Jamieson finally got up to go. I went with him to the door, and together we stood looking out over the valley. Below lay the village of Casanova, with its Old World houses, its blossoming trees and its peace. Above on the hill across the valley were the lights of the Greenwood Club. It was even possible to see the curving row of parallel lights that marked the carriage road. Rumors that I had heard about the club came back—of drinking, of high play, and once, a year ago, of a suicide under those very lights.

Mr. Jamieson left, taking a shortcut to the village, and I still stood there. It must have been after eleven, and the monotonous tick of the big clock on the stairs behind me was the only sound. Then I was conscious that someone was running up the drive. In a minute a woman darted into the area of light made by the open door and caught me by the arm. It was Rosie—Rosie in a state of collapse from terror, and not the least important, clutching one of my Coalport plates and a silver spoon.

She stood staring into the darkness behind, still holding the plate. I got her into the house and secured the plate; then I stood and looked down at her where she crouched tremblingly against the doorway.

"Well," I asked, "didn't your young man enjoy his meal?"

She couldn't speak. She looked at the spoon she still held—I wasn't so anxious about it: thank Heaven, it wouldn't chip—and then she stared at me.

"I appreciate your desire to have everything nice for him," I went on, "but the next time, you might take the Limoges china. It's more easily duplicated and less expensive."

"I haven't a young man—not here." She had got her breath now, as I had guessed she would. "I—I have been chased by a thief, Miss Innes."

"Did he chase you out of the house and back again?" I asked.

Then Rosie began to cry—not silently, but noisily, hysterically. I stopped her by giving her a good shake.

"What in the world is the matter with you?" I snapped. "Has the day of good common sense gone by! Sit up and tell me the whole thing." Rosie sat up then and sniffled.

"I was coming up the drive—" she began.

"You must start with when you went *down* the drive, with my dishes and my silver," I interrupted, but seeing more signs of hysteria, I gave in. "Very well. You were coming up the drive—"

"I had a basket of—of silver and dishes on my arm and I was carrying the plate, because—because I was afraid I'd break it. Partway up the road a man stepped out of the bushes and held his arm like this, spread out, so I couldn't get past. He said—he said—'Not so fast, young lady; I want you to let me see what's in that basket.' "

She got up in her excitement and took hold of my arm.

"It was like this, Miss Innes," she said, "and say you was the man. When he said that, I screamed and ducked under his arm like this. He caught at the basket and I dropped it. I ran as fast as I could, and he came after as far as the trees. Then he stopped. Oh, Miss Innes, it must have been the man that killed that Mr. Armstrong!"

"Don't be foolish," I said. "Whoever killed Mr. Armstrong would put as much space between himself and this house as he could. Go up to bed now; and mind, if I hear of this story being repeated to the other maids, I shall deduct from your wages for every broken dish I find in the drive."

I listened to Rosie as she went upstairs, running past the shadowy places and slamming her door. Then I sat down and looked at the Coalport plate and the silver spoon. I had brought my own china and silver, and, from all appearances, I would have little enough to take back. But though I might jeer at Rosie as much as I wished, the fact remained that someone had been on the drive that night who had no business there. Although neither had Rosie, for that matter.

I could fancy Liddy's face when she missed the extra pieces of china— she had opposed Rosie from the start. If Liddy once finds a prophecy fulfilled, especially an unpleasant one, she never allows me to forget it. It seemed to me that it was absurd to leave that china dotted along the road for her to spy the next morning; so with a sudden resolution, I opened the door again and stepped out into the darkness. As the door closed behind me I half regretted my impulse; then I shut my teeth and went on.

I have never been a nervous woman, as I said before. Moreover, a minute or two in the darkness enabled me to see things fairly well. Beulah gave me rather a start by rubbing unexpectedly against my feet; then we two, side by side, went down the drive.

There were no fragments of china, but where the grove began I picked up a silver spoon. So far Rosie's story was borne out: I began to wonder if it were not indiscreet, to say the least, this midnight prowling in a neighborhood with such a deservedly bad reputation. Then I saw something gleaming, which proved to be the handle of a cup, and a step or two farther on I found a V-shaped bit of a plate. But the most surprising thing of all was to find the basket sitting comfortably beside the road, with the rest of the broken crockery piled neatly within, and a handful of small silver, spoons, forks, and the like, on top! I could only stand and stare. Then Rosie's story was true. But where had Rosie carried her basket? And why had the thief, if he were a thief, picked up the broken china out of the road and left it, with his booty?

It was with my nearest approach to a nervous collapse that I heard the familiar throbbing of an automobile engine. As it came closer I recognized the outline of the Dragon Fly and knew that Halsey had come back.

Strange enough it must have seemed to Halsey, too, to come across me in the middle of the night, with the skirt of my gray silk gown over my shoulders to keep off the dew, holding a red-and-green basket under one arm and a black cat under the other. What with relief and joy, I began to cry, right there, and very nearly wiped my eyes on Beulah in the excitement.

Chapter IX
Just Like a Girl

"AUNT RAY!" Halsey said from the gloom behind the lamps. "What in the world are you doing here?"

"Taking a walk," I said, trying to be composed. I don't think the answer struck either of us as being ridiculous at the time. "Oh, Halsey, where have you been?"

"Let me take you up to the house." He was in the road, and had Beulah and the basket out of my arms in a moment. I could see the car plainly now, and Warner was at the wheel—Warner in an ulster and a pair of slippers, over Heaven knows what. Jack Bailey was not there. I got in, and we went slowly and painfully up to the house.

We did not talk. What we had to say was too important to commence there, and, besides, it took all kinds of coaxing from both men to get the Dragon Fly up the last grade. Only when we had closed the front door and stood facing each other in the hall, did Halsey say anything. He slipped his strong young arm around my shoulders and turned me so I faced the light.

"Poor Aunt Ray!" he said gently. And I nearly wept again. "I—I must see Gertrude, too; we will have a three-cornered talk."

And then Gertrude herself came down the stairs. She had not been to bed, evidently: she still wore the white negligee she had worn earlier in the evening, and she limped somewhat. During her slow progress down the stairs I had time to notice one thing: Mr. Jamieson had said the woman who escaped from the cellar had worn no shoe on her right foot. Gertrude's right ankle was the one she had sprained!

The meeting between brother and sister was tense, but without tears. Halsey kissed her tenderly, and I noticed evidences of strain and anxiety in both young faces.

"Is everything—right?" she asked.

"Right as can be," with forced cheerfulness.

I lighted the living room and we went in there. Only a half hour before

I had sat with Mr. Jamieson in that very room, listening while he overtly accused both Gertrude and Halsey of at least a knowledge of the death of Arnold Armstrong. Now Halsey was here to speak for himself: I should learn everything that had puzzled me.

"I saw it in the paper tonight for the first time," he was saying. "It knocked me dumb. When I think of this houseful of women, and a thing like that occurring!"

Gertrude's face was still set and white. "That isn't all, Halsey," she said. "You and—and Jack left almost at the time it happened. The detective here thinks that you—that we—know something about it."

"The devil he does!" Halsey's eyes were fairly starting from his head. "I beg your pardon, Aunt Ray, but—the fellow's a lunatic."

"Tell me everything, won't you, Halsey?" I begged. "Tell me where you went that night, or rather morning, and why you went as you did. This has been a terrible forty-eight hours for all of us."

He stood staring at me, and I could see the horror of the situation dawning in his face.

"I can't tell you where I went, Aunt Ray," he said after a moment. "As to why, you will learn that soon enough. But Gertrude knows that Jack and I left the house before this thing—this horrible murder—occurred."

"Mr. Jamieson does not believe me," Gertrude said drearily. "Halsey, if the worst comes, if they should arrest you, you must—tell."

"I shall tell nothing," he said with a new sternness in his voice. "Aunt Ray, it was necessary for Jack and me to leave that night. I cannot tell you why—just yet. As to where we went, if I have to depend on that as an alibi, I shall not tell. The whole thing is an absurdity, a trumped-up charge that cannot possibly be serious."

"Has Mr. Bailey gone back to the city," I demanded, "or to the club?"

"Neither," defiantly; "at the present moment I do not know where he is."

"Halsey," I asked gravely, leaning forward, "have you the slightest suspicion who killed Arnold Armstrong? The police think he was admitted from within, and that he was shot down from above, by someone on the circular staircase."

"I know nothing of it," he maintained; but I fancied I caught a sudden glance at Gertrude, a flash of something that died as it came.

As quietly, as calmly as I could, I went over the whole story, from the night Liddy and I had been alone up to the strange experience of Rosie and her pursuer. The basket still stood on the table, a mute witness to this last mystifying occurrence.

"There is something else," I said hesitatingly, at the last. "Halsey, I have never told this even to Gertrude, but the morning after the crime, I found, in a tulip bed, a revolver. It—it was yours, Halsey."

For an appreciable moment Halsey stared at me. Then he turned to Gertrude.

"My revolver, Trude!" he exclaimed. "Why, Jack took my revolver with him, didn't he?"

"Oh, for Heaven's sake don't say that," I implored. "The detective thinks possibly Jack Bailey came back, and—and the thing happened then."

"He didn't come back," Halsey said sternly. "Gertrude, when you brought down a revolver that night for Jack to take with him, what one did you bring? Mine?"

Gertrude was defiant now.

"No. Yours was loaded, and I was afraid of what Jack might do. I gave him one I have had for a year or two. It was empty."

Halsey threw up both hands despairingly.

"If that isn't like a girl!" he said. "Why didn't you do what I asked you to, Gertrude? You send Bailey off with an empty gun, and throw mine in a tulip bed, of all places on earth! Mine was a thirty-eight caliber. The inquest will show, of course, that the bullet that killed Armstrong was a thirty-eight. Then where shall I be?"

"You forget," I broke in, "that I have the revolver, and that no one knows about it."

But Gertrude had risen angrily.

"I cannot stand it; it is always with me," she cried. "Halsey, I did not throw your revolver into the tulip bed. I—think—you—did it—yourself!"

They stared at each other across the big library table, with young eyes all at once hard, suspicious. And then Gertrude held out both hands to him appealingly.

"We must not," she said brokenly. "Just now, with so much at stake, it—is shameful. I know you are as ignorant as I am. Make me believe it, Halsey."

Halsey soothed her as best he could, and the breach seemed healed. But long after I went to bed he sat downstairs in the living room alone, and I knew he was going over the case as he had learned it. Some things were clear to him that were dark to me. He knew, and Gertrude, too, why Jack Bailey and he had gone away that night, as they did. He knew where they had been for the last forty-eight hours, and why Jack Bailey had not returned with him. It seemed to me that without fuller confidence from both the children—they are always children to me—I should never be able to learn anything.

As I was finally getting ready for bed, Halsey came upstairs and knocked at my door. When I had got into a negligee—I used to say "wrapper" before Gertrude came back from school—I let him in. He stood in the doorway a moment, and then he went into agonies of silent mirth. I sat down on the side of the bed and waited in severe silence for him to stop, but he only seemed to grow worse. When he had recovered, he took me by the elbow and pulled me in front of the mirror.

" 'How to be beautiful,' " he quoted. " 'Advice to maids and matrons,' by Beatrice Fairfax!" And then I saw myself. I had neglected to remove my wrinkle eradicators, and I presume my appearance was odd. I believe that it is a woman's duty to care for her looks, but it is much like telling a necessary falsehood—one must not be found out. By the time I got them off Halsey was serious again, and I listened to his story.

"Aunt Ray," he began, extinguishing his cigarette on the back of my ivory hairbrush, "I would give a lot to tell you the whole thing. But—I can't, for a day or so, anyhow. But one thing I might have told you a long time ago. If you had known it, you would not have suspected me for a moment of—of having anything to do with the attack on Arnold Armstrong. Goodness knows what I might do to a fellow like that, if there was enough provocation, and I had a gun in my hand—under ordinary circumstances. But—I care a great deal about Louise Armstrong, Aunt Ray. I hope to marry her someday. Is it likely I would kill her brother?"

"Her stepbrother," I corrected. "No, of course, it isn't likely, or possible. Why didn't you tell me, Halsey?"

"Well, there were two reasons," he said slowly.

"One was that you had a girl already picked out for me—"

"Nonsense," I broke in, and felt myself growing red. I had, indeed, one of the—but no matter."

"And the second reason," he pursued, "was that the Armstrongs would have none of me."

I sat bolt upright at that and gasped.

"The Armstrongs!" I repeated. "With old Peter Armstrong driving a stage across the mountains while your grandfather was war governor—"

"Well, of course, the war governor's dead, and out of the matrimonial market," Halsey interrupted. "And the present Innes admits himself he isn't good enough for—for Louise."

"Exactly," I said despairingly, "and, of course, you are taken at your own valuation. The Inneses are not always so self-depreciatory."

"Not always, no," he said, looking at me with his boyish smile. "Fortunately, Louise doesn't agree with her family. She's willing to take me, war governor or no, provided her mother consents. She isn't overly fond of her stepfather, but she adores her mother. And now, can't you see where this thing puts me? Down and out, with all of them."

"But the whole thing is absurd," I argued. "And besides, Gertrude's sworn statement that you left before Arnold Armstrong came would clear you at once."

Halsey got up and began to pace the room, and the air of cheerfulness dropped like a mask.

"She can't swear it," he said finally. "Gertrude's story was true as far as it went, but she didn't tell everything. Arnold Armstrong came here at two thirty—came into the billiard room and left in five minutes. He came to bring—something."

"Halsey," I cried, "you must tell me the whole truth. Every time I see a way for you to escape you block it yourself with this wall of mystery. What did he bring?"

"A telegram—for Bailey," he said. "It came by special messenger from town and was—most important. Bailey had started for here, and the messenger had gone back to the city. The steward gave it to Arnold, who had been drinking all day and couldn't sleep, and was going for a stroll in the direction of Sunnyside."

"And he brought it?"

"Yes."

"What was in the telegram?"

"I can tell you—as soon as certain things are made public. It is only a matter of days now," gloomily.

"And Gertrude's story of a telephone message?"

"Poor Trude!" he half whispered. "Poor loyal little girl! Aunt Ray, there was no such message. No doubt your detective already knows that and discredits all Gertrude told him."

"And when she went back, it was to get—the telegram?"

"Probably," Halsey said slowly. "When you get to thinking about it, Aunt Ray, it looks bad for all three of us, doesn't it? And yet—I will take my oath none of us even inadvertently killed that poor devil."

I looked at the closed door into Gertrude's dressing room and lowered my voice.

"The same horrible thought keeps recurring to me," I whispered. "Halsey, Gertrude probably had your revolver: she must have examined it, anyhow, that night. After you—and Jack had gone, what if that ruffian came back, and she—and she—"

I couldn't finish. Halsey stood looking at me with shut lips.

"She might have heard him fumbling at the door—he had no key, the police say—and thinking it was you, or Jack, she admitted him. When she saw her mistake she ran up the stairs, a step or two, and turning, like an animal at bay, she fired."

Halsey had his hand over my lips before I finished, and in that position we stared each at the other, our stricken glances crossing.

"The revolver—my revolver—thrown into the tulip bed!" he muttered to himself. "Thrown perhaps from an upper window: you say it was buried deep. Her prostration ever since, her—Aunt Ray, you don't think it was Gertrude who fell down the clothes chute?"

I could only nod my head in a hopeless affirmative.

Chapter X

The Traders' Bank

THE morning after Halsey's return was Tuesday. Arnold Armstrong had been found dead at the foot of the circular staircase at three o'clock on Sunday morning. The funeral services were to be held on Tuesday, and the interment of the body was to be deferred until the Armstrongs arrived from California. No one, I think, was very sorry that Arnold Armstrong was dead, but the manner of his death aroused some sympathy and an enormous amount of curiosity. Mrs. Ogden Fitzhugh, a cousin, took charge of the arrangements, and everything, I believe, was as quiet as possible. I gave Thomas Johnson and Mrs. Watson permission to go into town to pay their last respects to the dead man, but for some reason they did not care to go.

Halsey spent part of the day with Mr. Jamieson, but he said nothing of what happened. He looked grave and anxious, and he had a long conversation with Gertrude late in the afternoon.

Tuesday evening found us quiet, with the quiet that precedes an explosion. Gertrude and Halsey were both gloomy and distraught, and as Liddy had already discovered that some of the china was broken—it is impossible to have any secrets from an old servant—I was not in a pleasant humor myself. Warner brought up the afternoon mail and the evening papers at seven—I was curious to know what the papers said of the murder. We had turned away at least a dozen reporters. But I read over the headline that ran halfway across the top of the *Gazette* twice before I comprehended it. Halsey had opened the *Chronicle* and was staring at it fixedly.

THE TRADERS' BANK CLOSES ITS DOORS! was what I read, and then I put down the paper and looked across the table.

"Did you know of this?" I asked Halsey.

"I expected it. But not so soon," he replied.

"And you?" to Gertrude.

"Jack—told us—something," Gertrude said faintly. "Oh, Halsey, what can he do now?"

"Jack!" I said scornfully. "Your Jack's flight is easy enough to explain now. And you helped him, both of you, to get away! You get that from your mother; it isn't an Innes trait. Do you know that every dollar you have, both of you, is in that bank?"

Gertrude tried to speak, but Halsey stopped her.

"That isn't all, Gertrude," he said quietly; "Jack is—under arrest."

"Under arrest!" Gertrude screamed, and tore the paper out of his hand. She glanced at the heading, then she crumpled the newspaper into a ball and flung it to the floor. While Halsey, looking stricken and white, was trying to smooth it out and read it, Gertrude had dropped her head on the table and was sobbing stormily.

I have the clipping somewhere, but just now I can remember only the essentials.

On the afternoon before, Monday, while the Traders' Bank was in the rush of closing hour, between two and three, Mr. Jacob Trautman, President of the Pearl Brewing Company, came into the bank to lift a loan. As security for the loan he had deposited some three hundred International Steamship Company 5's, in total value three hundred thousand dollars. Mr. Trautman went to the loan clerk and, after certain formalities had been gone through, the loan clerk went to the vault. Mr. Trautman, who was a large and genial German, waited for a time, whistling under his breath. The loan clerk did not come back. After an interval, Mr. Trautman saw the loan clerk emerge from the vault and go to the assistant cashier: the two went hurriedly to the vault. A lapse of another ten minutes, and the assistant cashier came out and approached Mr. Trautman. He was noticeably white and trembling. Mr. Trautman was told that through an oversight the bonds had been misplaced, and was asked to return the following morning, when everything would be made all right.

Mr. Trautman, however, was a shrewd business man, and he did not like the appearance of things. He left the bank apparently satisfied, and within thirty minutes he had called up three different members of the Traders' Board of Directors. At three thirty there was a hastily convened board meeting, with some stormy scenes, and late in the afternoon a national bank examiner was in possession of the books. The bank had not opened for business on Tuesday.

At twelve thirty o'clock the Saturday before, as soon as the business of the day was closed, Mr. John Bailey, the cashier of the defunct bank, had taken his hat and departed. During the afternoon he had called up Mr. Aronson, a member of the board, and said he was ill, and might not be at the bank for a day or two. As Bailey was highly thought of, Mr. Aronson merely expressed a regret. From that time until Monday night, when Mr. Bailey had surrendered to the police, little was known of his movements. Sometime after one on Saturday he had entered the Western Union office at Cherry and White Streets and had sent two telegrams. He was at the Greenwood Country Club on Saturday night, and appeared unlike himself. It was reported that he would be released under enormous bond, sometime that day, Tuesday.

The article closed by saying that while the officers of the bank refused to talk until the examiner had finished his work, it was known that securities aggregating a million and a quarter were missing. Then there was a diatribe on the possibility of such an occurrence; on the folly of a one-man bank, and of a Board of Directors that met only to lunch together and to listen to a brief report from the cashier; and on the poor policy of a government that arranges a three- or four-day examination twice a year. The mystery, it insinuated, had not been cleared by the arrest of the cashier. Before now minor officials had been used to cloak the misdeeds of men higher up. Inseparable as the words "speculation" and "peculation" have grown to be, John Bailey was not known to be in the stock market. His only words, after his surrender, had been "Send for Mr. Armstrong at once." The telegraph message which had finally reached the President of the Traders' Bank, in an interior town in California, had been responded to by a telegram from Dr. Walker, the young physician who was traveling with the Armstrong family, saying that Paul Armstrong was very ill and unable to travel.

That was how things stood that Tuesday evening. The Traders' Bank had suspended payment, and John Bailey was under arrest, charged with wrecking it; Paul Armstrong lay very ill in California, and his only son had been murdered two days before. I sat dazed and bewildered. The children's money was gone: that was bad enough, though I had plenty, if they would let me share. But Gertrude's grief was beyond any power of mine to comfort; the man she had chosen stood accused of a colossal embezzlement—and even worse. For in the instant that I sat there I seemed to see the coils closing around John Bailey as the murderer of Arnold Armstrong.

Gertrude lifted her head at last and stared across the table at Halsey.

"Why did he do it?" she wailed. "Couldn't you stop him, Halsey? It was suicidal to go back!"

Halsey was looking steadily through the windows of the breakfast room, but it was evident he saw nothing.

"It was the only thing he could do, Trude," he said at last. "Aunt Ray, when I found Jack at the Greenwood Club last Saturday night, he was frantic. I cannot talk until Jack tells me I may, but—he is absolutely innocent of all this, believe me. I thought, Trude and I thought, we were helping him, but it was the wrong way. He came back. Isn't that the act of an innocent man?"

"Then why did he leave at all?" I asked, unconvinced. "What innocent man would run away from here at three o'clock in the morning? Doesn't it look rather as though he thought it impossible to escape?"

Gertrude rose angrily. "You are not even just!" she flamed. "You don't know anything about it, and you condemn him!"

"I know that we have all lost a great deal of money," I said. "I shall believe Mr. Bailey innocent the moment he is shown to be. You profess to know the truth, but you cannot tell me! What am I to think?"

Halsey leaned over and patted my hand.

"You must take us on faith," he said. "Jack Bailey hasn't a penny that doesn't belong to him; the guilty man will be known in a day or so."

"I shall believe that when it is proved," I said grimly. "In the meantime, I take no one on faith. The Inneses never do."

Gertrude, who had been standing aloof at a window, turned suddenly. "But when the bonds are offered for sale, Halsey, won't the thief be detected at once?"

Halsey turned with a superior smile.

"It wouldn't be done that way," he said. "They would be taken out of the vault by someone who had access to it and used as collateral for a loan in another bank. It would be possible to realize eighty percent of their face value."

"In cash?"

"In cash."

"But the man who did it—he would be known?"

"Yes. I tell you both, as sure as I stand here, I believe that Paul Armstrong looted his own bank. I believe he has a million at least, as the result, and that he will never come back. I'm worse than a pauper now. I can't ask Louise to share nothing a year with me, and when I think of this disgrace for her, I'm crazy."

The most ordinary events of life seemed pregnant with possibilities that day, and when Halsey was called to the telephone, I ceased all pretense at eating. When he came back from the telephone, his face showed that something had occurred. He waited, however, until Thomas left the dining room; then he told us.

"Paul Armstrong is dead," he announced gravely. "He died this morning in California. Whatever he did, he is beyond the law now."

Gertrude turned pale.

"And the only man who could have cleared Jack can never do it!" she said despairingly.

"Also," I replied coldly, "Mr. Armstrong is forever beyond the power of defending himself. When your Jack comes to me, with some two hundred thousand dollars in his hands, which is about what you have lost, I shall believe him innocent."

Halsey threw his cigarette away and turned on me.

"There you go!" he exclaimed. "If he was the thief, he could return the money, of course. If he is innocent, he probably hasn't a tenth of that amount in the world. In his hands! That's like a woman."

Gertrude, who had been pale and despairing during the early part of the conversation, had flushed an indignant red. She got up and drew herself to her slender height, looking down at me with the scorn of the young and positive.

"You are the only mother I ever had," she said tensely. "I have given you all I would have given my mother, had she lived—my love, my trust. And now, when I need you most, you fail me. I tell you, John Bailey is a good man, an honest man. If you say he is not, you—you—"

"Gertrude," Halsey broke in sharply. She dropped beside the table and, burying her face in her arms, broke into a storm of tears.

"I love him—love him," she sobbed, in a surrender that was totally unlike her. "Oh, I never thought it would be like this."

Halsey and I stood helpless before the storm of her emotion. I would have soothed her, but she had put me away, and there was something aloof in her grief, something new and strange. At last, when her sorrow had subsided to the dry shaking sobs of a tired child, without raising her head she put out one groping hand.

"Aunt Ray!" she whispered. In a moment I was on my knees beside her, her arm around my neck, her cheek against my hair.

"Where am I in this?" Halsey said suddenly, and tried to put his arms around us both. It was a welcome distraction, and Gertrude was soon herself again. The little storm had cleared the air. Nevertheless, my opinion remained unchanged. There was much to be cleared up before I would consent to any renewal of my acquaintance with John Bailey. And Halsey and Gertrude knew it, knowing me.

Chapter XI
Halsey Makes a Capture

⤠

IT WAS about half-past eight when we left the dining room and still engrossed with one subject, the failure of the bank and its attendant evils, Halsey and I went out into the grounds for a stroll. Gertrude followed us shortly. "The light was thickening," to appropriate Shakespeare's description of twilight, and once again the tree toads and the crickets were making night throb with their tiny life. It was almost oppressively lonely, in spite of its beauty, and I felt a sickening pang of homesickness for my city at night—for the clatter of horses' feet on cemented paving, for the lights, the voices, the sound of children playing. The country after dark oppresses me. The stars, quite eclipsed in the city by the electric lights, here become insistent, assertive. Whether I want to or not, I find myself looking for the few I know by name, and feeling ridiculously new and small by contrast—always an unpleasant sensation.

After Gertrude joined us, we avoided any further mention of the murder. To Halsey, as to me, there was ever present, I am sure, the thought of our conversation of the night before. As we strolled back and forth along the drive, Mr. Jamieson emerged from the shadow of the trees.

"Good evening," he said, managing to include Gertrude in his bow. Gertrude had never been even ordinarily courteous to him, and she nodded coldly. Halsey, however, was more cordial, although we were all constrained enough. He and Gertrude went on together, leaving the detective to walk with me. As soon as they were out of earshot, he turned to me.

"Do you know, Miss Innes," he said, "the deeper I go into this thing, the more strange it seems to me. I am very sorry for Miss Gertrude. It looks as if Bailey, whom she has tried so hard to save, is worse than a rascal; and after her plucky fight for him, it seems hard."

I looked through the dusk to where Gertrude's light dinner dress gleamed among the trees. She had made a plucky fight, poor child. Whatever she might have been driven to do, I could find nothing but a deep sympathy for her. If she had only come to me with the whole truth then!

"Miss Innes," Mr. Jamieson was saying, "in the last three days, have you seen a—any suspicious figures around the grounds? Any woman?"

"No," I replied. "I have a houseful of maids that will bear watching, one and all. But there has been no strange woman near the house or Liddy would have seen her, you may be sure. She has a telescopic eye."

Mr. Jamieson looked thoughtful.

"It may not amount to anything," he said slowly. "It is difficult to get any perspective on things around here, because everyone down in the village is sure he saw the murderer, either before or since the crime. And half of them will stretch a point or two as to facts, to be obliging. But the man who drives the hack down there tells a story that may possibly prove to be important."

"I have heard it, I think. Was it the one the parlor maid brought up yesterday, about a ghost wringing its hands on the roof? Or perhaps it's the one the milk boy heard: a tramp washing a dirty shirt, presumably bloody, in the creek below the bridge?"

I could see the gleam of Mr. Jamieson's teeth as he smiled.

"Neither," he said. "But Matthew Geist, which is our friend's name, claims that on Saturday night, at nine thirty, a veiled lady—"

"I knew it would be a veiled lady," I broke in.

"A veiled lady," he persisted, "who was apparently young and beautiful, engaged his hack and asked to be driven to Sunnyside. Near the gate, however, she made him stop, in spite of his remonstrances, saying she preferred to walk to the house. She paid him, and he left her there. Now, Miss Innes, you had no such visitor, I believe?"

"None," I said decidedly.

"Geist thought it might be a maid, as you had got a supply that day. But he said her getting out near the gate puzzled him. Anyhow, we have now one veiled lady, who, with the ghostly intruder of Friday night, makes two assets that I hardly know what to do with."

"It is mystifying," I admitted, "although I can think of one possible explanation. The path from the Greenwood Club to the village enters the road near the lodge gate. A woman who wished to reach the Country Club, unperceived, might choose such a method. There are plenty of women there."

I think this gave him something to ponder, for in a short time he said good night and left. But I myself was far from satisfied. I was determined, however, on one thing. If my suspicions—for I had suspicions— were true, I would make my own investigations, and Mr. Jamieson should learn only what was good for him to know.

We went back to the house, and Gertrude, who was more like herself since her talk with Halsey, sat down at the mahogany desk in the living room to write a letter. Halsey prowled up and down the entire east wing, now in the cardroom, now in the billiard room, and now and then blowing his clouds of tobacco smoke among the pink-and-gold hangings of the drawing room. After a little I joined him in the billiard room, and together we went over the details of the discovery of the body.

The cardroom was quite dark. Where we sat, in the billiard room, only one of the side brackets was lighted, and we spoke in subdued tones, as the hour and the subject seemed to demand. When I spoke of the figure Liddy and I had seen on the porch through the cardroom window Friday night, Halsey sauntered into the darkened room, and together we stood there, much as Liddy and I had done that other night.

The window was the same grayish rectangle in the blackness as before. A few feet away in the hall was the spot where the body of

Arnold Armstrong had been found. I was a bit nervous, and I put my hand on Halsey's sleeve. Suddenly, from the top of the staircase above us came the sound of a cautious footstep. At first I was not sure, but Halsey's attitude told me he had heard and was listening. The step, slow, measured, infinitely cautious, was nearer now. Halsey tried to loosen my fingers, but I was in a paralysis of fright.

The swish of a body against the curving rail, as if for guidance, was plain enough, and now whoever it was had reached the foot of the staircase and had caught a glimpse of our rigid silhouettes against the billiard-room doorway. Halsey threw me off then and strode forward.

"Who is it?" he called imperiously, and took a half dozen rapid strides toward the foot of the staircase. Then I heard him mutter something; there was the crash of a falling body, the slam of the outer door, and, for an instant, quiet. I screamed, I think. Then I remember turning on the lights and finding Halsey, white with fury, trying to untangle himself from something warm and fleecy. He had cut his forehead a little on the lowest step of the stairs, and he was rather a ghastly sight. He flung the white object at me, and, jerking open the outer door, raced into the darkness.

Gertrude had come on hearing the noise, and now we stood, staring at each other over—of all things on earth—a white silk-and-wool blanket, exquisitely fine! It was the most unghostly thing in the world, with its lavender border and its faint scent. Gertrude was the first to speak.

"Somebody—had it?" she asked.

"Yes. Halsey tried to stop whoever it was and fell. Gertrude, that blanket is not mine. I have never seen before."

She held it up and looked at it: then she went to the door onto the veranda and threw it open. Perhaps a hundred feet from the house were two figures that moved slowly toward us as we looked. When they came within range of the light, I recognized Halsey, and with him Mrs. Watson, the housekeeper.

Chapter XII

One Mystery for Another

THE most commonplace incident takes on a new appearance if the attendant circumstances are unusual. There was no reason on earth why Mrs. Watson should not have carried a blanket down the east wing staircase, if she so desired. But to take a blanket down at eleven o'clock at night, with every precaution as to noise, and, when discovered, to fling it at Halsey and bolt—Halsey's word, and a good one—into the grounds—this made the incident more than significant.

They moved slowly across the lawn and up the steps. Halsey was talking quietly, and Mrs. Watson was looking down and listening. She was a woman of a certain amount of dignity, most efficient, so far as I could see, although Liddy would have found fault if she dared. But just now Mrs. Watson's face was an enigma. She was defiant, I think, under her mask of submission, and she still showed the effect of nervous shock.

"Mrs. Watson," I said severely, "will you be so good as to explain this rather unusual occurrence?"

"I don't think it so unusual, Miss Innes." Her voice was deep and very clear: just now it was somewhat tremulous. "I was taking a blanket down to Thomas, who is—not well tonight, and I used this staircase, as being nearer the path to the lodge. When—Mr. Innes called and then rushed at me, I—I was alarmed, and flung the blanket at him." Halsey was examining the cut on his forehead in a small mirror on the wall. It was not much of an injury, but it had bled freely, and his appearance was rather terrifying.

"Thomas ill?" he said, over his shoulder. "Why, I thought I saw Thomas out there as you made that cyclonic break out of the door and over the porch."

I could see that under pretense of examining his injury he was watching her through the mirror.

"Is this one of the servants' blankets, Mrs. Watson?" I asked, holding up its luxurious folds to the light.

"Everything else is locked away," she replied. Which was true enough, no doubt. I had rented the house without bed furnishings.

"If Thomas is ill," Halsey said, "some member of the family ought to go down to see him. You needn't bother, Mrs. Watson. I will take the blanket."

She drew herself up quickly, as if in protest, but she found nothing to say. She stood smoothing the folds of her dead black dress, her face as white as chalk above it. Then she seemed to make up her mind.

"Very well, Mr. Innes," she said. "Perhaps you would better go. I have done all I could."

And then she turned and went up the circular staircase, moving slowly and with a certain dignity. Below, the three of us stared at one another across the intervening white blanket.

"Upon my word," Halsey broke out, "this place is a walking nightmare. I have the feeling that we three outsiders who have paid our money for the privilege of staying in this spook factory are living on the very top of things. We're on the lid, so to speak. Now and then we get a sight of the things inside, but we are not a part of them."

"Do you suppose," Gertrude asked doubtfully, "that she really meant that blanket for Thomas?"

"Thomas was standing beside that magnolia tree," Halsey replied, "when I ran after Mrs. Watson. It's down to this, Aunt Ray. Rosie's basket and Mrs. Watson's blanket can only mean one thing: there is somebody hiding or being hidden in the lodge. It wouldn't surprise me if we hold the key to the whole situation now. Anyhow, I'm going to the lodge to investigate."

Gertrude wanted to go, too, but she looked so shaken that I insisted she should not. I sent for Liddy to help her to bed, and then Halsey and I started for the lodge. The grass was heavy with dew, and manlike, Halsey chose the shortest way across the lawn. Halfway, however, he stopped.

"We'd better go by the drive," he said. "This isn't a lawn; it's a field. Where's the gardener these days?"

"There isn't any," I said meekly. "We have been thankful enough, so far, to have our meals prepared and served and the beds aired. The gardener who belongs here is working at the club."

"Remind me tomorrow to send out a man from town," he said. "I know the very fellow."

I record this scrap of conversation, just as I have tried to put down anything and everything that had a bearing on what followed, because the gardener Halsey sent the next day played an important part in the events of the next few weeks—events that culminated, as you know, by stirring the country profoundly. At that time, however, I was busy try-ing to keep my skirts dry, and paid little or no attention to what seemed then a most trivial remark.

Along the drive I showed Halsey where I had found Rosie's basket with the bits of broken china piled inside. He was rather skeptical.

"Warner probably," he said when I had finished. "Began it as a joke on Rosie, and ended by picking up the broken china out of the road, know-ing it would play hob with the tires of the car." Which shows how near one can come to the truth and yet miss it altogether.

At the lodge everything was quiet. There was a light in the sitting room downstairs, and a faint gleam, as if from a shaded lamp, in one of the upper rooms. Halsey stopped and examined the lodge with calcu-lating eyes.

"I don't know, Aunt Ray," he said dubiously; "this is hardly a woman's affair. If there's a scrap of any kind, you hike for the timber." Which was Halsey's solicitous care for me, put into vernacular.

"I shall stay right here," I said, and crossing the small veranda, now shaded and fragrant with honeysuckle, I hammered the knocker on the door.

Thomas opened the door himself—Thomas, fully dressed and in his customary health. I had the blanket over my arm.

"I brought the blanket, Thomas," I said; "I am sorry you are so ill."

The old man stood staring at me and then at the blanket. His confu-sion under other circumstances would have been ludicrous.

"What! Not ill?" Halsey said from the step. "Thomas, I'm afraid you've been malingering."

Thomas seemed to have been debating something with himself. Now he stepped out on the porch and closed the door gently behind him.

"I reckon you bettah come in, Mis' Innes," he said, speaking cau-tiously. "It's got so I dunno what to do, and it's boun' to come out some time er ruther."

He threw the door open then, and I stepped inside, Halsey close behind. In the sitting room the old negro turned with quiet dignity to Halsey.

"You bettah sit down, sah," he said. "It's a place for a woman, sah."

Things were not turning out the way Halsey expected. He sat down on the center table, with his hands thrust in his pockets, and watched me as I followed Thomas up the narrow stairs. At the top a woman was standing, and a second glance showed me it was Rosie. She shrank back a little, but I said nothing. And then Thomas motioned to a partly open door, and I went in.

The lodge boasted three bedrooms upstairs, all comfortably furnished. In this one, the largest and airiest, a night lamp was burning, and by its light I could make out a plain white metal bed. A girl was asleep there— or in a half stupor, for she muttered something now and then. Rosie had taken her courage in her hands and coming in had turned up the light. It was only then that I knew. Fever-flushed, ill as she was, I recognized Louise Armstrong.

I stood gazing down at her in a stupor of amazement. Louise here, hiding at the lodge, ill and alone! Rosie came up to the bed and smoothed the white counterpane.

"I am afraid she is worse tonight," she ventured at last. I put my hand on the sick girl's forehead. It was burning with fever, and I turned to where Thomas lingered in the hallway.

"Will you tell me what you mean, Thomas Johnson, by not telling me this before?" I demanded indignantly.

Thomas quailed.

"Mis' Louise wouldn' let me," he said earnestly. "I wanted to. She ought to 'a' had a doctor the night she came, but she wouldn' hear to it. Is she—is she very bad, Mis' Innes?"

"Bad enough," I said coldly. "Send Mr. Innes up."

Halsey came up the stairs slowly, looking rather interested and inclined to be amused. For a moment he could not see anything distinctly in the darkened room; he stopped, glanced at Rosie and at me, and then his eyes fell on the restless head on the pillow. I think he felt who it was before he really saw her; he crossed the room in a couple of strides and bent over the bed.

"Louise!" he said softly; but she did not reply, and her eyes showed no recognition. Halsey was young, and illness was new to him. He straightened himself slowly, still watching her, and caught my arm.

"She's dying, Aunt Ray!" he said huskily. "Dying! Why, she doesn't know me!"

"Fudge!" I snapped, being apt to grow irritable when my sympathies are aroused. "She's doing nothing of the sort—and don't pinch my arm. If you want something to do, go and choke Thomas."

But at that moment Louise roused from her stupor to cough, and at the end of the paroxysm, as Rosie laid her back, exhausted, she knew us. That was all Halsey wanted; to him consciousness was recovery. He dropped on his knees beside the bed and tried to tell her she was all right, and we would bring her around in a hurry, and how beautiful she looked only to break down utterly and have to stop. And at that I came to my senses and put him out.

"This instant!" I ordered as he hesitated. "And send Rosie here."

He did not go far. He sat on the top step of the stairs, only leaving to telephone for a doctor, and getting in everybody's way in his eagerness to fetch and carry. I got him away finally by sending him to fix up the car as a sort of ambulance, in case the doctor would allow the sick girl to be moved. He sent Gertrude down to the lodge loaded with all manner of impossible things, including an armful of Turkish towels and a box of mustard plasters, and as the two girls had known each other somewhat before, Louise brightened perceptibly when she saw her.

When the doctor from Englewood—the Casanova doctor, Dr. Walker, being away—had started for Sunnyside, and I had got Thomas to stop trying to explain what he did not understand himself, I had a long talk with the old man, and this is what I learned.

On Saturday evening before, about ten o'clock, he had been reading in the sitting room downstairs when someone rapped at the door. The old man was alone, Warner not having arrived, and at first he was uncertain about opening the door. He did so finally and was amazed at being confronted by Louise Armstrong. Thomas was an old family servant, having been with the present Mrs. Armstrong since she was a child, and he was overwhelmed at seeing Louise. He saw that she was excited and tired, and he drew her into the sitting room and made her sit down. After a while he went to the house and brought Mrs. Watson, and they talked until late. The old man said Louise was in trouble and seemed frightened. Mrs. Watson made some tea and took it to the lodge, but Louise made them both promise to keep her presence a secret. She had not known that Sunnyside was rented, and whatever her trouble was, this complicated things. She seemed puzzled. Her stepfather and her mother were still in California—that was all she would say about them. Why she had run away no one could imagine. Mr. Arnold Armstrong was at the Greenwood Club, and at last Thomas, not knowing what else to do, went over there along the path. It was almost midnight. Partway over he met Armstrong himself and brought him to the lodge. Mrs. Watson had gone to the house for some bed linen, it having been arranged that under the circumstances Louise would be better at the lodge until morning. Arnold Armstrong and Louise had a long conference, during which he was heard to storm and become very violent. When he left it was after two. He had gone up to the house—Thomas did not know why—and at three o'clock he was shot at the foot of the circular staircase.

The following morning Louise had been ill. She had asked for Arnold, and was told he had left town. Thomas had not the moral courage to tell her of the crime. She refused a doctor and shrank morbidly from having her presence known. Mrs. Watson and Thomas had had their hands full, and at last Rosie had been enlisted to help them. She carried necessary provisions—little enough—to the lodge and helped to keep the secret.

Thomas told me quite frankly that he had been anxious to keep Louise's presence hidden for this reason: they had all seen Arnold Armstrong that night, and he, himself, for one, was known to have had no very friendly feeling for the dead man. As to the reason for Louise's flight from California, or why she had not gone to the Fitzhughs', or to some of her people in town, he had no more information than I had. With the death of her stepfather and the prospect of the immediate return of the family, things had become more and more impossible. I gathered that Thomas was as relieved as I at the turn events had taken. No, she did not know of either of the deaths in the family.

Taken all around, I had only substituted one mystery for another. If I knew now why Rosie had taken the basket of dishes, I did not know who had spoken to her and followed her along the drive. If I knew that Louise was in the lodge, I did not know why she was there. If I knew that Arnold Armstrong had spent some time in the lodge the night before he was murdered, I was no nearer the solution of the crime. Who was the midnight intruder who had so alarmed Liddy and myself? Who had fallen down the clothes chute? Was Gertrude's lover a villain or a victim? Time was to answer all these things.

Chapter XIII

Louise

⤎⤏

THE doctor from Englewood came very soon, and I went up to see the sick girl with him. Halsey had gone to supervise the fitting of the car with blankets and pillows, and Gertrude was opening and airing Louise's own rooms at the house. Her private sitting room, bedroom and dressing room were as they had been when we came. They occupied the end of the east wing, beyond the circular staircase, and we had not even opened them.

The girl herself was too ill to notice what was being done. When, with the help of the doctor, who was a fatherly man with a family of girls at home, we got her to the house and up the stairs into bed, she dropped into a feverish sleep, which lasted until morning. Dr. Stewart— that was the Englewood doctor—stayed almost all night, giving the medicine himself and watching her closely. Afterward he told me that she had had a narrow escape from pneumonia, and that the cerebral symptoms had been rather alarming. I said I was glad it wasn't an "itis" of some kind, anyhow, and he smiled solemnly.

He left after breakfast, saying that he thought the worst of the danger was over and that she must be kept very quiet.

"The shock of two deaths, I suppose, has done this," he remarked, picking up his case. "It has been very deplorable."

I hastened to set him right.

"She does not know of either, Doctor," I said. "Please do not mention them to her."

He looked as surprised as a medical man ever does.

"I do not know the family," he said, preparing to get into his top buggy. "Young Walker, down in Casanova, has been attending them. I understand he is going to marry this young lady."

"You have been misinformed," I said stiffly. "Miss Armstrong is going to marry my nephew."

The doctor smiled as he picked up the reins.

"Young ladies are changeable these days," he said. "We thought the wedding was to occur soon. Well, I will stop in this afternoon to see how my patient is getting along."

He drove away then, and I stood looking after him. He was a doctor of the old school, of the class of family practitioner that is fast dying out; a loyal and honorable gentleman who was at once physician and confidential adviser to his patients. When I was a girl we called in the doctor alike when we had measles or when mother's sister died in the far West. He cut out redundant tonsils and brought the babies with the same air of inspiring self-confidence. Nowadays it requires a different specialist for each of these occurrences. When the babies cried, old Dr. Wainwright gave them peppermint and dropped warm sweet oil in their ears with sublime faith that if it was not colic it was earache. When, at the end of a year, father met him driving in his high side-bar buggy with the white mare ambling along, and asked for a bill, the doctor used to go home, estimate what his services were worth for that period, divide it in half—I don't think he kept any books—and send father a statement, in a cramped hand, on a sheet of ruled white paper. He was an honored guest at all the weddings, christenings, and funerals—yes, funerals—for everyone knew he had done his best, and there was no gainsaying the ways of Providence.

Ah, well, Dr. Wainwright is gone, and I am an elderly woman with an increasing tendency to live in the past. The contrast between my old doctor at home and the Casanova doctor, Frank Walker, always rouses me to wrath and digression.

Sometime about noon of that day, Wednesday, Mrs. Ogden Fitzhugh telephoned me. I have the barest acquaintance with her—she managed to be put on the governing board of the Old Ladies' Home and ruins their digestions by sending them ice cream and cake on every holiday. Beyond that, and her reputation at bridge, which is insufferably bad—she is the worst player at the bridge club—I know little of her. It was she who had taken charge of Arnold Armstrong's funeral, however, and I went at once to the telephone.

"Yes," I said, "this is Miss Innes."

"Miss Innes," she said volubly, "I have just received a very strange telegram from my cousin, Mrs. Armstrong. Her husband died yesterday, in California and—wait, I will read you the message."

I knew what was coming, and I made up my mind at once. If Louise Armstrong had a good and sufficient reason for leaving her people and coming home, a reason, moreover, that kept her from going at once to Mrs. Ogden Fitzhugh, and that brought her to the lodge at Sunnyside instead, it was not my intention to betray her. Louise herself must notify her people. I do not justify myself now, but remember, I was in a peculiar position toward the Armstrong family. I was connected most unpleasantly with a cold-blooded crime, and my niece and nephew were practically beggared, either directly or indirectly, through the head of the family.

Mrs. Fitzhugh had found the message. " 'Paul died yesterday. Heart disease,' " she read. " 'Wire at once if Louise is with you.' You see, Miss Innes, Louise must have started east, and Fanny is alarmed about her."

"Yes," I said.

"Louise is not here," Mrs. Fitzhugh went on, "and none of her friends—the few who are still in town—has seen her. I called you because Sunnyside was not rented when she went away, and Louise might have gone there."

"I am sorry, Mrs. Fitzhugh, but I cannot help you," I said, and was immediately filled with compunction. Suppose Louise grew worse? Who was I to play Providence in this case? The anxious mother certainly had a right to know that her daughter was in good hands. So I broke in on Mrs. Fitzhugh's voluble excuses for disturbing me.

"Mrs. Fitzhugh," I said. "I was going to let you think I knew nothing about Louise Armstrong, but I have changed my mind. Louise is here, with me." There was a clatter of ejaculations at the other end of the wire. "She is ill and not able to be moved. Moreover, she is unable to see anyone. I wish you would wire her mother that she is with me and tell her not to worry. No, I do not know why she came east."

"But my dear Miss Innes!" Mrs. Fitzhugh began. I cut in ruthlessly.

"I will send for you as soon as she can see you," I said. "No, she is not in a critical state now, but the doctor says she must have absolute quiet."

When I had hung up the receiver, I sat down to think. So Louise had fled from her people in California and had come east alone! It was not a new idea, but why had she done it? It occurred to me that Dr. Walker might be concerned in it, might possibly have bothered her with unwelcome attentions; but it seemed to me that Louise was hardly a girl to take refuge in flight under such circumstances. She had always been high-spirited, with the well-poised head and buoyant step of the outdoors girl. It must have been much more in keeping with Louise's character, as I knew it, to resent vigorously any unwelcome attentions from Dr. Walker. It was the suitor whom I should have expected to see in headlong flight, not the lady in the case.

The puzzle was no clearer at the end of the half hour. I picked up the morning papers, which were still full of the looting of the Traders' Bank, the interest at fever height again, on account of Paul Armstrong's death. The bank examiners were working on the books and said nothing for publication: John Bailey had been released on bond. The body of Paul Armstrong would arrive Sunday and would be buried from the Armstrong town house. There were rumors that the dead man's estate had been a comparatively small one. The last paragraph was the important one.

Walter P. Broadhurst, of the Marine Bank, had produced two hundred American traction bonds, which had been placed as security with the Marine Bank for a loan of one hundred and sixty thousand dollars, made to Paul Armstrong, just before his California trip. The bonds were a part of the missing traction bonds from the Traders' Bank! While this involved the late president of the wrecked bank, to my mind it by no means cleared its cashier.

The gardener mentioned by Halsey came out about two o'clock in the afternoon and walked up from the station. I was favorably impressed by him. His references were good—he had been employed by the Brays until they went to Europe, and he looked young and vigorous. He asked for one assistant, and I was glad enough to get off so easily. He was a pleasant-faced young fellow, with black hair and blue eyes, and his name was Alexander Graham. I have been particular about Alex, because, as I said before, he played an important part later.

That afternoon I had a new insight into the character of the dead banker. I had my first conversation with Louise. She sent for me, and against my better judgment I went. There were so many things she could not be told, in her weakened condition, that I dreaded the interview. It was much easier than I expected, however, because she asked no questions.

Gertrude had gone to bed, having been up almost all night, and Halsey was absent on one of those mysterious absences of his that grew more and more frequent as time went on, until it culminated in the event of the night of June the tenth. Liddy was in attendance in the sickroom. There being little or nothing to do, she seemed to spend her time smoothing the wrinkles from the counterpane. Louise lay under a field of virgin white, folded back at an angle of geometrical exactness and necessitating a readjustment every time the sick girl turned.

Liddy heard my approach and came out to meet me. She seemed to be in a perpetual state of gooseflesh, and she had got in the habit of looking past me when she talked, as if she saw things. It had the effect of making me look over my shoulder to see what she was staring at, and was intensely irritating.

"She's awake," Liddy said, looking uneasily down the circular staircase, which was beside me. "She was talkin' in her sleep something awful—about dead men and coffins."

"Liddy," I said sternly, "did you breathe a word about everything not being right here?"

Liddy's gaze had wandered to the door of the chute, now bolted securely.

"Not a word," she said, "beyond asking her a question or two, which there was no harm in. She says there never was a ghost known here."

I glared at her, speechless, and closing the door into Louise's boudoir, to Liddy's great disappointment, I went on to the bedroom beyond.

Whatever Paul Armstrong had been, he had been lavish with his stepdaughter. Gertrude's rooms at home were always beautiful apartments, but the three rooms in the east wing at Sunnyside, set apart for the daughter of the house, were much more splendid. From the walls to the rugs on the floor, from the furniture to the appointments of the bath, with its pool sunk in the floor instead of the customary unlovely tub, everything was luxurious. In the bedroom Louise was watching for me.

It was easy to see that she was much improved; the flush was going, and the peculiar gasping breathing of the night before was now a comfortable and easy respiration.

She held out her hand and I took it between both of mine.

"What can I say to you, Miss Innes?" she said slowly. "To have come like this—"

I thought she was going to break down, but she did not.

"You are not to think of anything but of getting well," I said, patting her hand. "When you are better, I am going to scold you for not coming here at once. This is your home, my dear, and of all people in the world, Halsey's old aunt ought to make you welcome."

She smiled a little, sadly, I thought.

"I ought not to see Halsey," she said. "Miss Innes, there are a great many things you will never understand, I am afraid. I am an impostor on your sympathy, because I—I stay here and let you lavish care on me, and all the time I know you are going to despise me."

"Nonsense!" I said briskly. "Why, what would Halsey do to me if I even ventured such a thing? He is so big and masterful that if I dared to be anything but rapturous over you, he would throw me out of a window. Indeed, he would be quite capable of it."

She seemed scarcely to hear my facetious tone. She had eloquent brown eyes—the Inneses are fair and are prone to a grayish-green optic that is better for use than appearance—and they seemed now to be clouded with trouble.

"Poor Halsey!" she said softly. "Miss Innes, I cannot marry him, and I am afraid to tell him. I am a coward—a coward!"

I sat beside the bed and stared at her. She was too ill to argue with, and, besides, sick people take queer fancies.

"We will talk about that when you are stronger," I said gently.

"But there are some things I must tell you," she insisted. "You must wonder how I came here, and why I stayed hidden at the lodge. Dear old Thomas has been almost crazy, Miss Innes. I did not know that Sunnyside was rented. I knew my mother wished to rent it, without telling my—stepfather, but the news must have reached her after I left. When I started east, I had only one idea—to be alone with my thoughts for a time, to bury myself here. Then, I—must have taken a cold on the train."

"You came east in clothing suitable for California," I said, "and, like all young girls nowadays, I don't suppose you wear flannels." But she was not listening.

"Miss Innes," she said, "has my stepbrother Arnold gone away?"

"What do you mean?" I asked, startled. But Louise was literal.

"He didn't come back that night," she said, "and it was so important that I should see him."

"I believe he has gone away," I replied uncertainly. "Isn't it something that we could attend to instead?"

But she shook her head. "I must do it myself," she said dully. "My mother must have rented Sunnyside without telling my stepfather, and—Miss Innes, did you ever hear of anyone being wretchedly poor in the midst of luxury?

"Did you ever long, and long, for money—money to use without question, money that no one would take you to task about? My mother and I have been surrounded for years with every indulgence—everything that would make a display. But we have never had any money, Miss Innes; that must have been why mother rented this house. My stepfather pays out bills. It's the most maddening, humiliating existence in the world. I would love honest poverty better."

"Never mind," I said; "when you and Halsey are married, you can be as honest as you like, and you will certainly be poor."

Halsey came to the door at that moment and I could hear him coaxing Liddy for admission to the sickroom.

"Shall I bring him in?" I asked Louise, uncertain what to do. The girl seemed to shrink back among her pillows at the sound of his voice. I was vaguely irritated with her; there are few young fellows like Halsey—straightforward, honest, and willing to sacrifice everything for the one woman. I knew one once, more than thirty years ago, who was like that: he died a long time ago. And sometimes I take out his picture, with its cane and its queer silk hat, and look at it. But of late years it has grown too painful: he is always a boy—and I am an old woman. I would not bring him back if I could.

Perhaps it was some such memory that made me call out sharply.

"Come in, Halsey." And then I took my sewing and went into the boudoir beyond, to play propriety. I did not try to hear what they said, but every word came through the open door with curious distinctness.

Halsey had evidently gone over to the bed and I suppose he kissed her. There was silence for a moment, as if words were superfluous things.

"I have been almost wild, sweetheart,"—Halsey's voice. "Why didn't you trust me, and send for me before?"

"It was because I couldn't trust myself," she said in a low tone. "I am too weak to struggle today; oh, Halsey, how I have wanted to see you!"

There was something I did not hear, then Halsey again.

"We could go away," he was saying. "What does it matter about anyone in the world but just the two of us? To be always together, like this, hand in hand; Louise—don't tell me it isn't going to be. I won't believe you."

"You don't know; you don't know," Louise repeated dully. "Halsey, I care—you know that—but—not enough to marry you."

"That is not true, Louise," he said sternly. "You cannot look at me with your honest eyes and say that."

"I cannot marry you, she repeated miserably. "It's bad enough, isn't it? Don't make it worse. Someday, before long, you will be glad."

"Then it is because you have never loved me." There were depths of hurt pride in his voice. "You saw how much I loved you, and you let me think you cared—for a while. No—that isn't like you, Louise. There is something you haven't told me. Is it—because there is someone else?"

"Yes," almost inaudibly.

"Louise! Oh, I don't believe it."

"It is true," she said sadly. "Halsey, you must not try to see me again. As soon as I can, I am going away from here—where you are all so much kinder than I deserve. And whatever you hear about me, try to think as well of me as you can. I am going to marry—another man. How you must hate me—hate me!"

I could hear Halsey cross the room to the window. Then, after a pause, he went back to her again. I could hardly sit still; I wanted to go in and give her a good shaking.

"Then it's all over," he was saying with a long breath. "The plans we made together, the hopes, the—all of it—over! Well, I'll not be a baby, and I'll give you up the minute you say 'I don't love you and I do love—someone else'!"

"I cannot say that," she breathed, "but, very soon, I shall marry—the other man."

I could hear Halsey's low triumphant laugh.

"I defy him," he said. "Sweetheart, as long as you care for me, I am not afraid."

The wind slammed the door between the two rooms just then, and I could hear nothing more, although I moved my chair quite close. After a discreet interval, I went into the other room and found Louise alone. She was staring with sad eyes at the cherub painted on the ceiling over the bed, and because she looked tired I did not disturb her.

Chapter XIV
An Eggnog and a Telegram

⌒

WE HAD discovered Louise at the lodge Tuesday night. It was Wednesday I had my interview with her. Thursday and Friday were uneventful, save as they marked improvement in our patient. Gertrude spent almost all the time with her, and the two had grown to be great friends. But certain things hung over me constantly; the coroner's inquest on the death of Arnold Armstrong, to be held Saturday, and the arrival of Mrs. Armstrong and young Dr. Walker, bringing the body of the dead president of the Traders' Bank. We had not told Louise of either death.

Then, too, I was anxious about the children. With their mother's inheritance swept away in the wreck of the bank, and with their love affairs in a disastrous condition, things could scarcely be worse. Added to that, the cook and Liddy had a flare-up over the proper way to make beef tea for Louise, and, of course, the cook left.

Mrs. Watson had been glad enough, I think, to turn Louise over to our care, and Thomas went upstairs night and morning to greet his young mistress from the doorway. Poor Thomas! He had the faculty—found still in some old negroes, who cling to the traditions of slavery days—of making his employer's interest his. It was always "we" with Thomas; I miss him sorely; pipe-smoking, obsequious, not over reliable, kindly old man!

On Thursday Mr. Harton, the Armstrongs' legal adviser, called up from town. He had been advised, he said, that Mrs. Armstrong was coming east with her husband's body and would arrive Monday. He came with some hesitation, he went on, to the fact that he had been further instructed to ask me to relinquish my lease on Sunnyside, as it was Mrs. Armstrong's desire to come directly there.

I was aghast.

"Here!" I said. "Surely you are mistaken, Mr. Harton. I should think, after—what happened here only a few days ago, she would never wish to come back."

"Nevertheless," he replied, "she is most anxious to come. This is what she says. 'Use every possible means to have Sunnyside vacated. Must go there at once.'"

"Mr. Harton," I said testily, "I am not going to do anything of the kind. I and mine have suffered enough at the hands of this family. I rented the house at an exorbitant figure and I have moved out here for the summer. My city home is dismantled and in the hands of decorators. I have been here one week, during which I have had not a single night of uninterrupted sleep, and I intend to stay until I have recuperated. Moreover, if Mr. Armstrong died insolvent, as I believe was the case, his widow ought to be glad to be rid of so expensive a piece of property."

The lawyer cleared his throat.

"I am very sorry you have made this decision," he said. "Miss Innes, Mrs. Fitzhugh tells me Louise Armstrong is with you."

"She is."

"Has she been informed of this—double bereavement?"

"Not yet," I said. "She has been very ill; perhaps tonight she can be told."

"It is very sad; very sad," he said. "I have a telegram for her, Mrs. Innes. Shall I send it out?"

"Better open it and read it to me," I suggested. "If it is important, that will save time."

There was a pause while Mr. Harton opened the telegram. Then he read it slowly, judicially. "'Watch for Nina Carrington. Home Monday. Signed F. L. W.'"

"Hum!" I said. "'Watch for Nina Carrington. Home Monday.' Very well, Mr. Harton, I will tell her, but she is not in condition to watch for anyone."

"Well, Miss Innes, if you decide to—er—relinquish the lease, let me know," the lawyer said.

"I shall not relinquish it," I replied, and I imagined his irritation from the way he hung up the receiver.

I wrote the telegram down word for word, afraid to trust my memory, and decided to ask Dr. Stewart how soon Louise might be told the truth. The closing of the Traders' Bank I considered unnecessary for her to know, but the death of her stepfather and stepbrother must be broken to her soon, or she might hear it in some unexpected and shocking manner.

Dr. Stewart came about four o'clock, bringing his leather satchel into the house with a great deal of care, and opening it at the foot of the stairs to show me a dozen big yellow eggs nesting among the bottles.

"Real eggs," he said proudly. "None of your anemic store eggs, but the real thing—some of them still warm. Feel them! Eggnog for Miss Louise."

He was beaming with satisfaction, and before he left, he insisted on going back to the pantry and making an eggnog with his own hands. Somehow, all the time he was doing it, I had a vision of Dr. Willoughby, my nerve specialist in the city, trying to make an eggnog. I wondered if he ever prescribed anything so plebeian—and so delicious. And while Dr. Stewart whisked the eggs he talked.

"I said to Mrs. Stewart," he confided, a little red in the face from the exertion, "after I went home the other day, that you would think me an old gossip, for saying what I did about Walker and Miss Louise."

"Nothing of the sort," I protested.

"The fact is," he went on, evidently justifying himself, "I got that piece of information just as we get a lot of things, through the kitchen end of the house. Young Walker's chauffeur—Walker's more fashionable than I am, and he goes around the country in a Stanhope car—well, his chauffeur comes to see our servant girl, and he told her the whole thing. I thought it was probable, because Walker spent a lot of time up here last summer, when the family was here, and besides, Riggs, that's Walker's man, had a very pat little story about the doctor's building a house on this property, just at the foot of the hill. The sugar, please."

The eggnog was finished. Drop by drop the liquor had cooked the egg, and now, with a final whisk, a last toss in the shaker, it was ready, a symphony in gold and white. The doctor sniffed it.

"Real eggs, real milk, and a touch of real Kentucky whisky," he said.

He insisted on carrying it up himself, but at the foot of the stairs he paused.

"Riggs said the plans were drawn for the house," he said, harking back to the old subject. "Drawn by Huston in town. So I naturally believed him."

When the doctor came down, I was ready with a question.

"Doctor," I asked, "is there anyone in the neighborhood named Carrington? Nina Carrington?"

"Carrington?" He wrinkled his forehead. "Carrington? No, I don't remember any such family. There used to be Covingtons down the creek."

"The name was Carrington," I said, and the subject lapsed.

Gertrude and Halsey went for a long walk that afternoon, and Louise slept. Time hung heavy on my hands, and I did as I had fallen into a habit of doing lately—I sat down and thought things over. One result of my meditations was that I got up suddenly and went to the telephone. I had taken the most intense dislike to this Dr. Walker, whom I had never seen, and who was being talked of in the countryside as the fiancé of Louise Armstrong.

I knew Sam Huston well. There had been a time, when Sam was a good deal younger than he is now, before he had married Anne Endicott, when I knew him even better. So now I felt no hesitation in calling him over the telephone. But when his office boy had given way to his confidential clerk, and that functionary had condescended to connect his employer's desk telephone, I was somewhat at a loss as to how to begin.

"Why, how are you, Rachel?" Sam said sonorously. "Going to build that house at Rock View?" It was a twenty-year-old joke of his.

"Sometime, perhaps," I said. "Just now I want to ask you a question about something which is none of my business."

"I see you haven't changed an iota in a quarter of a century, Rachel." This was intended to be another jest. "Ask ahead: everything but my domestic affairs is at your service."

"Try to be serious," I said. "And tell me this: has your firm made any plans for a house recently, for a Dr. Walker, at Casanova?"

"Yes, we have."

"Where was it to be built? I have a reason for asking."

"It was to be, I believe, on the Armstrong place. Mr. Armstrong himself consulted me, and the inference was—in fact, I am quite certain—the house was to be occupied by Mr. Armstrong's daughter, who was engaged to marry Dr. Walker."

When the architect had inquired for the different members of my family, and had finally rung off, I was certain of one thing. Louise Armstrong was in love with Halsey, and the man she was going to marry was Dr. Walker. Moreover, this decision was not new; marriage had been contemplated for some time. There must certainly be some explanation—but what was it?

That day I repeated to Louise the telegram Mr. Warton had opened. She seemed to understand, but an unhappier face I have never seen. She looked like a criminal whose reprieve is over, and the day of execution approaching.

Chapter XV
Liddy Gives the Alarm

∽

THE next day, Friday, Gertrude broke the news of her stepfather's death to Louise. She did it as gently as she could, telling her first that he was very ill, and finally that he was dead. Louise received the news in the most unexpected manner, and when Gertrude came out to tell me how she had stood it, I think she was almost shocked.

"She just lay and stared at me, Aunt Ray," she said. "Do you know, I believe she is glad, glad! And she is too honest to pretend anything else. What sort of man was Mr. Paul Armstrong, anyhow?"

"He was a bully as well as a rascal, Gertrude," I said. "But I am convinced of one thing; Louise will send for Halsey now, and they will make it all up."

For Louise had steadily refused to see Halsey all that day, and the boy was frantic.

We had a quiet hour, Halsey and I, that evening, and I told him several things; about the request that we give up the lease to Sunnyside, about the telegram to Louise, about the rumors of an approaching marriage between the girl and Dr. Walker, and, last of all, my own interview with her the day before.

He sat back in a big chair, with his face in the shadow, and my heart fairly ached for him. He was so big and so boyish! When I had finished, he drew a long breath.

"Whatever Louise does," he said, "nothing will convince me, Aunt Ray, that she doesn't care for me. And up to two months ago, when she and her mother went west, I was the happiest fellow on earth. Then something made a difference: she wrote me that her people were opposed to the marriage; that her feeling for me was what it had always been, but that something had happened which had changed her ideas as to the future. I was not to write until she wrote me, and whatever occurred, I was to think the best I could of her. It sounded like a puzzle. When I saw her yesterday, it was the same thing, only, perhaps, worse."

"Halsey," I asked, "have you any idea of the nature of the interview between Louise Armstrong and Arnold the night he was murdered?"

"It was stormy. Thomas says once or twice he almost broke into the room, he was so alarmed for Louise."

"Another thing, Halsey," I said, "have you ever heard Louise mention a woman named Carrington, Nina Carrington?"

"Never," he said positively.

For try as we would, our thoughts always came back to that fatal Saturday night, and the murder. Every conversational path led to it, and we all felt that Jamieson was tightening the threads of evidence around John Bailey. The detective's absence was hardly reassuring; he must have had something to work on in town, or he would have returned.

The papers reported that the cashier of the Traders' Bank was ill in his apartments at the Knickerbocker—a condition not surprising, considering everything. The guilt of the defunct president was no longer in doubt; the missing bonds had been advertised and some of them discovered. In every instance they had been used as collateral for large loans, and the belief was current that not less than a million and a half dollars had been realized. Everyone connected with the bank had been placed under arrest and released on heavy bond.

Was he alone in his guilt, or was the cashier his accomplice? Where was the money? The estate of the dead man was comparatively small— a city house on a fashionable street, Sunnyside, a large estate largely mortgaged, an insurance of fifty thousand dollars, and some personal property—this was all. The rest lost in speculation probably, the papers said. There was one thing which looked uncomfortable for Jack Bailey: he and Paul Armstrong together had promoted a railroad company in New Mexico, and it was rumored that together they had sunk large sums of money there. The business alliance between the two men added to the belief that Bailey knew something of the looting. His unexplained absence from the bank on Monday lent color to the suspicion against him. The strange thing seemed to be his surrendering himself on the point of departure. To me, it seemed the shrewd calculation of a clever rascal. I was not actively antagonistic to Gertrude's lover, but I meant to be convinced, one way or the other. I took no one on faith.

That night the Sunnyside ghost began to walk again. Liddy had been sleeping in Louise's dressing room on a couch, and the approach of dusk was a signal for her to barricade the entire suite. Situated as its was, beyond the circular staircase, nothing but an extremity of excitement would have made her pass it after dark. I confess myself that the place seemed to me to have a sinister appearance, but we kept that wing well lighted, and until the lights went out at midnight it was really cheerful, if one did not know its history.

On Friday night, then, I had gone to bed, resolved to go at once to sleep. Thoughts that insisted on obtruding themselves I pushed resolutely to the back of my mind, and I systematically relaxed every muscle. I fell asleep soon, and was dreaming that Doctor Walker was building his new house immediately in front of my windows: I could hear the thump-thump of the hammers, and then I waked to a knowledge that somebody was pounding on my door.

I was up at once, and with the sound of my footstep on the floor the low knocking ceased, to be followed immediately by sibilant whispering through the keyhole.

"Miss Rachel! Miss Rachel!" somebody was saying, over and over.

"Is that you, Liddy?" I asked, my hand on the knob.

"For the love of mercy, let me in!" she said in a low tone.

She was leaning against the door, for when I opened it, she fell in. She was greenish-white, and she had a red-and-black barred flannel petticoat over her shoulders.

"Listen," she said, standing in the middle of the floor and holding on to me. "Oh, Miss Rachel, it's the ghost of that dead man hammering to get in!"

Sure enough, there was a dull thud—thud—thud from someplace near. It was muffled: one rather felt than heard it, and it was impossible to locate. One moment it seemed to come, three taps and a pause, from the floor under us: the next, thud—thud—thud—it came apparently from the wall.

"It's not a ghost," I said decidedly. "If it was a ghost, it wouldn't rap: it would come through the keyhole." Liddy looked at the keyhole. "But it sounds very much as though someone is trying to break into the house."

Liddy was shivering violently. I told her to get me my slippers and she brought me a pair of kid gloves, so I found my things myself and prepared to call Halsey. As before, the night alarm had found the electric lights gone: the hall, save for its night lamp, was in darkness, as I went across to Halsey's room. I hardly know what I feared, but it was a relief to find him there, very sound asleep, and with his door unlocked.

"Wake up, Halsey," I said, shaking him.

He stirred a little. Liddy was half in and half out of the door, afraid as usual to be left alone and not quite daring to enter. Her scruples seemed to fade, however, all at once. She gave a suppressed yell, bolted into the room, and stood tightly clutching the footboard of the bed. Halsey was gradually waking.

"I've seen it," Liddy wailed. "A woman in white down the hall!"

I paid no attention.

"Halsey," I persevered, "someone is breaking into the house. Get up, won't you?"

"It isn't our house," he said sleepily. And then he roused to the exigency of the occasion. "All right, Aunt Ray," he said, still yawning. "If you'll let me get into something—"

It was all I could do to get Liddy out of the room. The demands of the occasion had no influence on her: she had seen the ghost, she persisted, and she wasn't going into the hall. But I got her over to my room at last, more dead than alive, and made her lie down on the bed.

The tappings, which seemed to have ceased for a while, had commenced again, but they were fainter. Halsey came over in a few minutes, and stood listening and trying to locate the sound.

"Give me my revolver, Aunt Ray," he said; and I got it—the one I had found in the tulip bed—and gave it to him. He saw Liddy there and divined at once that Louise was alone.

"You let me attend to this fellow, whoever it is, Aunt Ray, and go to Louise, will you? She may be awake and alarmed."

So in spite of her protests, I left Liddy alone and went back to the east wing. Perhaps I went a little faster past the yawning blackness of the circular staircase; and I could hear Halsey creaking cautiously down the main staircase. The rapping, or pounding, had ceased, and the silence was almost painful. And then suddenly, from apparently under my very feet, there rose a woman's scream, a cry of terror that broke off as suddenly as it came. I stood frozen and still. Every drop of blood in my body seemed to leave the surface and gather around my heart. In the dead silence that followed it throbbed as if it would burst. More dead than alive, I stumbled into Louise's bedroom. She was not there!

Chapter XVI

In the Early Morning

⁂

I STOOD looking at the empty bed. The coverings had been thrown back, and Louise's pink silk dressing gown was gone from the foot, where it had lain. The night lamp burned dimly, revealing the emptiness of the place. I picked it up, but my hand shook so that I put it down again, and got somehow to the door.

There were voices in the hall and Gertrude came running toward me.

"What is it?" she cried. "What was that sound? Where is Louise?"

"She is not in her room," I said stupidly. "I think—it was she—who screamed."

Liddy had joined us now, carrying a light. We stood huddled together at the head of the circular staircase, looking down into its shadows. There was nothing to be seen, and it was absolutely quiet down there. Then we heard Halsey running up the main staircase. He came quickly down the hall to where we were standing.

"There's no one trying to get in. I thought I heard some one shriek. Who was it?"

Our stricken faces told him the truth.

"Someone screamed down there," I said. "And—and Louise is not in her room."

With a jerk Halsey took the light from Liddy and ran down the circular staircase. I followed him, more slowly. My nerves seemed to be in a state of paralysis: I could scarcely step. At the foot of the stairs Halsey gave an exclamation and put down the light.

"Aunt Ray," he called sharply.

At the foot of the staircase, huddled in a heap, her head on the lower stair, was Louise Armstrong. She lay limp and white, her dressing gown dragging loose from one sleeve of her nightdress, and the heavy braid of her dark hair stretching its length a couple of steps above her head, as if she had slipped down. She was not dead: Halsey put her down on the floor and began to rub her cold hands, while Gertrude and Liddy ran for stimulants. As for me, I sat there at the foot of that ghostly staircase—sat, because my knees wouldn't hold me—and wondered where it would all end. Louise was still unconscious, but she was breathing better, and I suggested that we get her back to bed before she came to. There was something grisly and horrible to me, seeing her there in almost the same attitude and in the same place where we had found her brother's body. And to add to the similarity, just then the hall clock, far off, struck faintly three o'clock.

It was four before Louise was able to talk, and the first rays of dawn were coming through her windows, which faced the east, before she could tell us coherently what had occurred. I give it as she told it. She lay propped in bed, and Halsey sat beside her, unrebuffed, and held her hand while she talked.

"I was not sleeping well," she began, "partly, I think, because I had slept during the afternoon. Liddy brought me some hot milk at ten o'clock and I slept until twelve. Then I wakened and—I got to thinking about things, and worrying, so I could not go to sleep.

"I was wondering why I had not heard from Arnold since the—since I saw him that night at the lodge. I was afraid he was ill, because—he was to have done something for me, and he had not come back. It must have been three when I heard someone rapping. I sat up and listened, to be quite sure, and the rapping kept up. It was cautious, and I was about to call Liddy. Then suddenly I thought I knew what it was. The east entrance and the circular staircase were always used by Arnold when he was out late, and sometimes, when he forgot his key, he would rap and I would go down and let him in. I thought he had come back to see me—I didn't think about the time, for his hours were always erratic. But I was afraid I was too weak to get down the stairs. The knocking kept up, and just as I was about to call Liddy, she ran through the room and out into the hall. I got up then, feeling weak and dizzy, and put on my dressing gown. If it was Arnold, I knew I must see him.

"It was very dark everywhere, but, of course, I knew my way. I felt along for the stair rail, and went down as quickly as I could. The knocking had stopped, and I was afraid I was too late. I got to the foot of the staircase and over to the door on to the east veranda. I had never thought of anything but that it was Arnold, until I reached the door. It was unlocked and opened about an inch. Everything was black: it was perfectly dark outside. I felt very queer and shaky. Then I thought perhaps Arnold had used his key; he did—strange things sometimes, and I turned around. Just as I reached the foot of the staircase I thought I heard someone coming. My nerves were going anyhow, there in the dark, and I could scarcely stand. I got up as far as the third or fourth step; then I felt that someone was coming toward me on the staircase. The next instant a hand met mine on the stair rail. Someone brushed past me, and I screamed. Then I must have fainted."

That was Louise's story. There could be no doubt of its truth, and the thing that made it inexpressibly awful to me was that the poor girl had crept down to answer the summons of a brother who would never need her kindly offices again. Twice now, without apparent cause, someone had entered the house by means of the east entrance, had apparently gone his way unhindered through the house, and gone out again as he had entered. Had this unknown visitor been there a third time, the night Arnold Armstrong was murdered? Or a fourth, the time Mr. Jamieson had locked someone in the clothes chute?

Sleep was impossible, I think, for any of us. We dispersed finally to bathe and dress, leaving Louise little the worse for her experience. But I determined that before the day was over she must know the true state of affairs. Another decision I made, and I put it into execution immediately after breakfast. I had one of the unused bedrooms in the east wing, back along the small corridor, prepared for occupancy, and from that time on, Alex, the gardener, slept there. One man in that barn of a house was an absurdity, with things happening all the time, and I must say that Alex was as unobjectionable as anyone could possibly have been.

The next morning, also, Halsey and I made an exhaustive examination of the circular staircase, the small entry at its foot, and the card-room opening from it. There was no evidence of anything unusual the night before, and had we not ourselves heard the rapping noises, I should have felt that Louise's imagination had run away with her. The outer door was closed and locked, and the staircase curved above us, for all the world like any other staircase.

Halsey, who had never taken seriously my account of the night Liddy and I were there alone, was grave enough now. He examined the paneling of the wainscoting above and below the stairs, evidently looking for a secret door, and suddenly there flashed into my mind the recollection of a scrap of paper that Mr. Jamieson had found among Arnold Armstrong's effects. As nearly as possible I repeated its contents to him, while Halsey took them down in a notebook.

"I wish you had told me that before," he said, as he put the memorandum carefully away. We found nothing at all in the house, and I expected little from any examination of the porch and grounds. But as we opened the outer door something fell into the entry with a clatter. It was a cue from the billiard room.

Halsey picked it up with an exclamation.

"That's careless enough," he said. "Some of the servants have been amusing themselves."

I was far from convinced. Not one of the servants would go into that wing at night unless driven by dire necessity. And a billiard cue! As a weapon of either offense or defense it was an absurdity, unless one accepted Liddy's hypothesis of a ghost, and even then, as Halsey pointed out, a billiard-playing ghost would be a very modern evolution of an ancient institution.

That afternoon we, Gertrude, Halsey, and I, attended the coroner's inquest in town. Dr. Stewart had been summoned also, it transpiring that in that early Sunday morning, when Gertrude and I had gone to our rooms, he had been called to view the body. We went, the four of us, in the machine, preferring the execrable roads to the matinee train, with half of Casanova staring at us. And on the way we decided to say nothing of Louise and her interview with her stepbrother the night he died. The girl was in trouble enough as it was.

Chapter XVII

A Hint of Scandal

᭰

IN GIVING the gist of what happened at the inquest, I have only one excuse—to recall to the reader the events of the night of Arnold Armstrong's murder. Many things had occurred which were not brought out at the inquest and some things were told there that were new to me. Altogether, it was a gloomy affair, and the six men in the corner, who constituted the coroner's jury, were evidently the merest puppets in the hands of that all-powerful gentleman, the coroner.

Gertrude and I sat well back, with our veils down. There were a number of people I knew: Barbara Fitzhugh, in extravagant mourning—she always went into black on the slightest provocation, because it was becoming—and Mr. Jarvis, the man who had come over from the Greenwood Club the night of the murder. Mr. Harton was there, too, looking impatient as the inquest dragged, but alive to every particle of evidence. From a corner Mr. Jamieson was watching the proceedings intently.

Dr. Stewart was called first. His evidence was told briefly and amounted to this: on the Sunday morning previous, at a quarter before five, he had been called to the telephone. The message was from a Mr. Jarvis, who asked him to come at once to Sunnyside, as there had been an accident there, and Mr. Arnold Armstrong had been shot. He had dressed hastily, gathered up some instruments, and driven to Sunnyside.

He was met by Mr. Jarvis, who took him at once to the east wing. There, just as he had fallen, was the body of Arnold Armstrong. There was no need of the instruments: the man was dead. In answer to the coroner's question—no, the body had not been moved, save to turn it over. It lay at the foot of the circular staircase. Yes, he believed death had been instantaneous. The body was still somewhat warm and rigor mortis had not set in. It occurred late in cases of sudden death. No, he believed the probability of suicide might be eliminated; the wounds could have been self-inflicted, but with difficulty, and there had been no weapon found.

The doctor's examination was over, but he hesitated and cleared his throat.

"Mr. Coroner," he said, "at the risk of taking up valuable time, I would like to speak of an incident that may or may not throw some light on this matter."

The audience was alert at once.

"Kindly proceed, Doctor," the coroner said.

"My home is in Englewood, two miles from Casanova," the doctor began. "In the absence of Dr. Walker, a number of Casanova people have been consulting me. A month ago—five weeks, to be exact—a woman whom I had never seen came to my office. She was in deep mourning and kept her veil down, and she brought for examination a child, a boy of six. The little fellow was ill; it looked like typhoid, and the mother was frantic. She wanted a permit to admit the youngster to the Children's Hospital in town here, where I am a member of the staff, and I gave her one. The incident would have escaped me, but for a curious thing. Two days before Mr. Armstrong was shot, I was sent for to go to the Country Club: someone had been struck with a golf ball that had gone wild. It was late when I left—I was on foot, and about a mile from the club, on the Claysburg road, I met two people. They were disputing violently, and I had no difficulty in recognizing Mr. Armstrong. The woman, beyond doubt, was the one who had consulted me about the child."

At this hint of scandal, Mrs. Ogden Fitzhugh sat up very straight. Jamieson was looking slightly skeptical, and the coroner made a note.

"The Children's Hospital, you say, Doctor?" he asked.

"Yes. But the child, who was entered as Lucien Wallace, was taken away by his mother two weeks ago. I have tried to trace them and failed."

All at once I remembered the telegram sent to Louise by someone signed F.L.W.—presumably Dr. Walker. Could this veiled woman be the Nina Carrington of the message? But it was only idle speculation. I had no way of finding out, and the inquest was proceeding.

The report of the coroner's physician came next. The postmortem examination showed that the bullet had entered the chest in the fourth left intercostal space and had taken an oblique course downward and backward, piercing both the heart and lungs. The left lung was collapsed, and the exit point of the ball had been found in the muscles of the back to the left of the spinal column. It was improbable that such a wound had been self-inflicted, and its oblique downward course pointed to the fact that the shot had been fired from above. In other words, as the murdered man had been found dead at the foot of a staircase, it was probable that the shot had been fired by someone higher up on the stairs. There were no marks of powder. The bullet, a thirty-eight caliber, had been found in the dead man's clothing, and was shown to the jury.

Mr. Jarvis was called next, but his testimony amounted to little. He had been summoned by telephone to Sunnyside, had come over at once with the steward and Mr. Winthrop, at present out of town. They had been admitted by the housekeeper and had found the body lying at the foot of the staircase. He had made a search for a weapon, but there was none around. The outer entry door in the east wing had been unfastened and was open about an inch.

I had been growing more and more nervous. When the coroner called Mr. John Bailey, the room was filled with suppressed excitement. Mr. Jamieson went forward and spoke a few words to the coroner, who nodded. Then Halsey was called.

"Mr. Innes," the coroner said, "will you tell under what circumstances you saw Mr. Arnold Armstrong the night he died?"

"I saw him first at the Country Club," Halsey said quietly. He was rather pale, but very composed. "I stopped there with my automobile for gasoline. Mr. Armstrong had been playing cards. When I saw him there, he was coming out of the cardroom, talking to Mr. John Bailey."

"The nature of the discussion—was it amicable?"

Halsey hesitated.

"They were having a dispute," he said. "I asked Mr. Bailey to leave the club with me and come to Sunnyside over Sunday."

"Isn't it a fact, Mr. Innes, that you took Mr. Bailey away from the club-house because you were afraid there would be blows?"

"The situation was unpleasant," Halsey said evasively.

"At that time had you any suspicion that the Traders' Bank had been wrecked?"

"No."

"What occurred next?"

"Mr. Bailey and I talked in the billiard room until two thirty."

"And Mr. Arnold Armstrong came there, while you were talking?"

"Yes. He came about half-past two. He rapped at the east door, and I admitted him."

The silence in the room was intense. Mr. Jamieson's eyes never left Halsey's face.

"Will you tell us the nature of his errand?"

"He brought a telegram that had come to the club for Mr. Bailey."

"He was sober?"

"Perfectly, at that time. Not earlier."

"Was not his apparent friendliness a change from his former attitude?"

"Yes. I did not understand it."

"How long did he stay?"

"About five minutes. Then he left, by the east entrance."

"What occurred then?"

"We talked for a few minutes, discussing a plan Mr.Bailey had in mind. Then I went to the stables, where I kept my car, and got it out."

"Leaving Mr. Bailey alone in the billiard room?"

Halsey hesitated.

"My sister was there."

Mrs. Ogden Fitzhugh had the courage to turn and eye Gertrude through her *lorgnon*.

"And then?"

"I took the car along the lower road, not to disturb the household. Mr. Bailey came down across the lawn, through the hedge, and got into the car on the road."

"Then you know nothing of Mr. Armstrong's movements after he left the house?"

"Nothing. I read of his death Monday evening for the first time."

"Mr. Bailey did not see him on his way across the lawn?"

"I think not. If he had seen him he would have spoken of it."

"Thank you. That is all. Miss Gertrude Innes."

Gertrude's replies were fully as concise as Halsey's. Mrs. Fitzhugh subjected her to a close inspection, commencing with her hat and ending with her shoes. I flatter myself she found nothing wrong with either her gown or her manner, but poor Gertrude's testimony was the reverse of comforting. She had been summoned, she said, by her brother, after Mr. Armstrong had gone. She had waited in the billiard room with Mr. Bailey, until the automobile had been ready. Then she had locked the door at the foot of the staircase, and, taking a lamp, had accompanied Mr. Bailey to the main entrance of the house, and had watched him cross the lawn. Instead of going at once to her room, she had gone back to the billiard room for something which had been left there. The card-room and billiard room were in darkness. She had groped around, found the article she was looking for, and was on the point of returning to her room, when she had heard someone fumbling at the lock at the east outer door. She had thought it was probably her brother, and had been about to go to the door, when she heard it open. Almost immediately there was a shot, and she had run panic-stricken through the drawing room and had roused the house.

"You heard no other sound?" the coroner asked. "There was no one with Mr. Armstrong when he entered?"

"It was perfectly dark. There were no voices and I heard nothing. There was just the opening of the door, the shot, and the sound of somebody falling."

"Then, while you went through the drawing room and upstairs to alarm the household, the criminal, whoever it was, could have escaped by the east door?"

"Yes."

"Thank you. That will do."

I flatter myself that the coroner got little enough out of me. I saw Mr. Jamieson smiling to himself, and the coroner gave me up, after a time. I admitted I had found the body, said I had not known who it was until

Mr. Jarvis told me, and ended by looking up at Barbara Fitzhugh and saying that in renting the house I had not expected to be involved in any family scandal. At which she turned purple.

The verdict was that Arnold Armstrong had met his death at the hands of a person or persons unknown, and we all prepared to leave. Barbara Fitzhugh flounced out without waiting to speak to me, but Mr. Harton came up, as I knew he would.

"You have decided to give up the house, I hope, Miss Innes," he said. "Mrs. Armstrong has wired me again."

"I am not going to give it up," I maintained, "until I understand some things that are puzzling me. The day that the murderer is discovered, I will leave."

"Then, judging by what I have heard, you will be back in the city very soon," he said. And I knew that he suspected the discredited cashier of the Traders' Bank.

Mr. Jamieson came up to me as I was about to leave the coroner's office.

"How is your patient?" he asked with his odd little smile.

"I have no patient," I replied, startled.

"I will put it in a different way, then. How is Miss Armstrong?"

"She—she is doing very well," I stammered.

"Good," cheerfully. "And our ghost? Is it laid?"

"Mr. Jamieson," I said suddenly, "I wish you would do one thing: I wish you would come to Sunnyside and spend a few days there. The ghost is not laid. I want you to spend one night at least watching the circular staircase. The murder of Arnold Armstrong was a beginning, not an end."

He looked serious.

"Perhaps I can do it," he said. "I have been doing something else, but—well, I will come out tonight."

We were very silent during the trip back to Sunnyside. I watched Gertrude closely and somewhat sadly. To me there was one glaring flaw in her story, and it seemed to stand out for everyone to see. Arnold Armstrong had had no key, and yet she said she had locked the east door. He must have been admitted from within the house; over and over I repeated it to myself.

That night, as gently as I could, I told Louise the story of her step-brother's death. She sat in her big, pillow-filled chair, and heard me through without interruption. It was clear that she was shocked beyond words: if I had hoped to learn anything from her expression, I had failed. She was as much in the dark as we were.

Chapter XVIII

A Hole in the Wall

∽

MY TAKING the detective out to Sunnyside raised an unexpected storm of protest from Gertrude and Halsey. I was not prepared for it, and I scarcely knew how to account for it. To me Mr. Jamieson was far less formidable under my eyes where I knew what he was doing, than he was off in the city, twisting circumstances and motives to suit himself and learning what he wished to know, about events at Sunnyside, in some occult way. I was glad enough to have him there, when excitements began to come thick and fast.

A new element was about to enter into affairs: Monday, or Tuesday at the latest, would find Dr. Walker back in his green-and-white house in the village, and Louise's attitude to him in the immediate future would signify Halsey's happiness or wretchedness, as it might turn out. Then, too, the return of her mother would mean, of course, that she would have to leave us, and I had become greatly attached to her.

From the day Mr. Jamieson came to Sunnyside there was a subtle change in Gertrude's manner to me. It was elusive, difficult to analyze, but it was there. She was no longer frank with me, although I think her affection never wavered. At the time I laid the change to the fact that I had forbidden all communication with John Bailey and had refused to acknowledge any engagement between the two. Gertrude spent much of her time wandering through the grounds or taking long cross-country walks. Halsey played golf at the Country Club day after day, and after Louise left, as she did the following week, Mr. Jamieson and I were much together. He played a fair game of cribbage, but he cheated at solitaire.

The night the detective arrived, Saturday, I had a talk with him. I told him of the experience Louise Armstrong had had the night before, on the circular staircase, and about the man who had so frightened Rosie on the drive. I saw that he thought the information was important, and to my suggestion that we put an additional lock on the east wing door he opposed a strong negative.

"I think it probable," he said, "that our visitor will be back again, and the thing to do is to leave things exactly as they are, to avoid rousing suspicion. Then I can watch for at least a part of each night and probably Mr. Innes will help us out. I would say as little to Thomas as possible. The old man knows more than he is willing to admit."

I suggested that Alex, the gardener, would probably be willing to help, and Mr. Jamieson undertook to make the arrangement. For one night, however, Mr. Jamieson preferred to watch alone. Apparently nothing occurred. The detective sat in absolute darkness on the lower step of the stairs, dozing, he said afterwards, now and then. Nothing could pass him in either direction, and the door in the morning remained as securely fastened as it had been the night before. And yet one of the most inexplicable occurrences of the whole affair took place that very night.

Liddy came to my room on Sunday morning with a face as long as the moral law. She laid out my things as usual, but I missed her customary garrulousness. I was not regaled with the new cook's extravagance as to eggs, and she even forbore to mention "that Jamieson," on whose arrival she had looked with silent disfavor.

"What's the matter, Liddy?" I asked at last. "Didn't you sleep last night?"

"No, ma'am," she said stiffly.

"Did you have two cups of coffee at your dinner?" I inquired.

"No, ma'am," indignantly.

I sat up and almost upset my hot water—I always take a cup of hot water with a pinch of salt, before I get up. It tones the stomach.

"Liddy Allen," I said, "stop combing that switch and tell me what is wrong with you."

Liddy heaved a sigh.

"Girl and woman," she said, "I've been with you twenty-five years, Miss Rachel, through good temper and bad"—the idea! and what I have taken from her in the way of sulks!—"but I guess I can't stand it any longer. My trunk's packed."

"Who packed it?" I asked, expecting from her tone to be told she had wakened to find it done by some ghostly hand.

"I did; Miss Rachel, you won't believe me when I tell you this house is haunted. Who was it fell down the clothes chute? Who was it scared Miss Louise almost into her grave?"

"I'm doing my best to find out," I said. "What in the world are you driving at?" She drew a long breath.

"There is a hole in the trunk room wall, dug out since last night. It's big enough to put your head in, and the plaster's all over the place."

"Nonsense!" I said. "Plaster is always falling."

But Liddy clenched that.

"Just ask Alex," she said. "When he put the new cook's trunk there last night the wall was as smooth as this. This morning it's dug out, and there's plaster on the cook's trunk. Miss Rachel, you can get a dozen detectives and put one on every stair in the house, and you'll never catch anything. There's some things you can't handcuff."

Liddy was right. As soon as I could, I went up to the trunk room, which was directly over my bedroom. The plan of the upper story of the house was like that of the second floor, in the main. One end, however, over the east wing, had been left only roughly finished, the intention having been to convert it into a ballroom at some future time. The maids' rooms, trunk room, and various storerooms, including a large airy linen room, opened from a long corridor, like that on the second floor. And in the trunk room, as Liddy had said, was a fresh break in the plaster.

Not only in the plaster, but through the lathing, the aperture extended. I reached into the opening, and three feet away, perhaps, I could touch the bricks of the partition wall. For some reason, the architect, in building the house, had left a space there that struck me, even in the surprise of the discovery, as an excellent place for a conflagration to gain headway.

"You are sure the hole was not here yesterday?" I asked Liddy, whose expression was a mixture of satisfaction and alarm. In answer she pointed to the new cook's trunk—that necessary adjunct of the migratory domestic. The top was covered with fine white plaster, as was the floor. But there were no large pieces of mortar lying around—no bits of lathing. When I mentioned this to Liddy she merely raised her eyebrows. Being quite confident that the gap was of unholy origin, she did not concern herself with such trifles as a bit of mortar and lath. No doubt they were even then heaped neatly on a gravestone in the Casanova churchyard!

I brought Mr. Jamieson up to see the hole in the wall, directly after breakfast. His expression was very odd when he looked at it, and the first thing he did was to try to discover what object, if any, such a hole could have. He got a piece of candle, and by enlarging the aperture a little was able to examine what lay beyond. The result was nil. The trunk room, although heated by steam heat, like the rest of the house, boasted of a fireplace and mantel as well. The opening had been made between the flue and the outer wall of the house. There was revealed, however, on inspection, only the brick of the chimney on one side and the outer wall of the house on the other; in depth the space extended only to the flooring. The breach had been made about four feet from the floor, and inside were all the missing bits of plaster. It had been a methodical ghost.

It was very much of a disappointment. I had expected a secret room, at the very least, and I think even Mr. Jamieson had fancied he might at last have a clue to the mystery. There was evidently nothing more to be discovered: Liddy reported that everything was serene among the servants, and that none of them had been disturbed by the noise. The maddening thing, however, was that the nightly visitor had evidently more than one way of gaining access to the house, and we made arrangements to redouble our vigilance as to windows and doors that night.

Halsey was inclined to pooh-pooh the whole affair. He said a break in the plaster might have occurred months ago and gone unnoticed, and that the dust had probably been stirred up the day before. After all, we had to let it go at that, but we put in an uncomfortable Sunday. Gertrude went to church, and Halsey took a long walk in the morning. Louise was able to sit up, and she allowed Halsey and Liddy to assist her downstairs late in the afternoon. The east veranda was shady, green with vines and palms, cheerful with cushions and lounging chairs. We put Louise in a steamer chair, and she sat there passively enough, her hands clasped in her lap.

We were very silent. Halsey sat on the rail with a pipe, openly watching Louise, as she looked broodingly across the valley to the hills. There was something baffling in the girl's eyes; and gradually Halsey's boyish features lost their glow at seeing her about again and settled into grim lines. He was like his father just then.

We sat until late afternoon, Halsey growing more and more moody. Shortly before six, he got up and went into the house, and in a few minutes he came out and called me to the telephone. It was Anna Whitcomb, in town, and she kept me for twenty minutes, telling me the children had had the measles, and how Madame Sweeny had botched her new gown.

When I finished, Liddy was behind me, her mouth a thin line.

"I wish you would try to look cheerful, Liddy," I groaned, "your face would sour milk." But Liddy seldom replied to my gibes. She folded her lips a little tighter.

"He called her up," she said oracularly, "he called her up and asked her to keep you at the telephone, so he could talk to Miss Louise. *A thankless child is sharper than a serpent's tooth.*"

"Nonsense!" I said bruskly. "I might have known enough to leave them. It's a long time since you and I were in love, Liddy, and—we forget."

Liddy sniffed.

"No man ever made a fool of me," she replied virtuously.

"Well, something did," I retorted.

Chapter XIX

Concerning Thomas

∽

"MR. JAMIESON," I said, when we found ourselves alone after dinner that night, "the inquest yesterday seemed to me the merest recapitulation of things that were already known. It developed nothing new beyond the story of Dr. Stewart's, and that was volunteered."

"An inquest is only a necessary formality, Miss Innes," he replied. "Unless a crime is committed in the open, the inquest does nothing beyond getting evidence from witnesses while events are still in their minds. The police step in later. You and I both know how many important things never transpired. For instance: the dead man had no key, and yet Miss Gertrude testified to a fumbling at the lock, and then the opening of the door. The piece of evidence you mention, Dr. Stewart's story, is one of those things we have to take cautiously: the doctor has a patient who wears black and does not raise her veil. Why, it is the typical mysterious lady! Then the good doctor comes across Arnold Armstrong, who was a graceless scamp—*de mortuis*—what's the rest of it?—and he is quarreling with a lady in black. Behold, says the doctor, they are one and the same."

"Why was Mr. Bailey not present at the inquest?"

The detective's expression was peculiar.

"Because his physician testified that he is ill and unable to leave his bed."

"Ill!" I exclaimed. "Why, neither Halsey nor Gertrude has told me that."

"There are more things than that, Miss Innes, that are puzzling. Bailey gives the impression that he knew nothing of the crash at the bank until he read it in the paper Monday night, and that he went back and surrendered himself immediately. I do not believe it. Jonas, the watchman at the Traders' Bank, tells a different story. He says that on the Thursday night before, about eight thirty, Bailey went back to the bank. Jonas admitted him, and he says the cashier was in a state almost of collapse. Bailey worked until midnight, then he closed the vault and went away. The occurrence was so unusual that the watchman pondered over it all the rest of the night. What did Bailey do when he went back to the Knickerbocker apartments that night? He packed a suitcase ready for instant departure. But he held off too long; he waited for something. My personal opinion is that he waited to see Miss Gertrude before flying from the country. Then, when he had shot down Arnold Armstrong that night, he had to choose between two evils. He did the thing that would immediately turn public opinion in his favor, and surrendered himself, as an innocent man. The strongest thing against him is his preparation for flight, and his deciding to come back after the murder of Arnold Armstrong. He was shrewd enough to disarm suspicion as to the graver charge."

The evening dragged along slowly. Mrs. Watson came to my bedroom before I went to bed and asked if I had any arnica. She showed me a badly swollen hand, with reddish streaks running toward the elbow; she said it was the hand she had hurt the night of the murder a week before, and that she had not slept well since. It looked to me as if it might be serious, and I told her to let Dr. Stewart see it.

The next morning Mrs. Watson went up to town on the eleven train, and was admitted to the Charity Hospital. She was suffering from blood poisoning. I fully meant to go up and see her there, but other things drove her entirely from my mind. I telephoned to the hospital that day, however, and ordered a private room for her, and whatever comforts she might be allowed.

Mrs. Armstrong arrived Monday evening with her husband's body, and the services were set for the next day. The house on Chestnut Street, in town, had been opened, and Tuesday morning Louise left us to go home. She sent for me before she went, and I saw she had been crying.

"How can I thank you, Miss Innes?" she said. "You have taken me on faith, and—you have not asked me any questions. Sometime, perhaps, I can tell you; and when that time comes, you will all despise me—Halsey, too."

I tried to tell her how glad I was to have had her, but there was something else she wanted to say. She said it finally, when she had bade a constrained good-bye to Halsey and the car was waiting at the door.

"Miss Innes," she said in a low tone, "if they—if there is any attempt made to—to have you give up the house, do it, if you possibly can. I am afraid—to have you stay."

That was all. Gertrude went into town with her and saw her safely home. She reported a decided coolness in the greeting between Louise and her mother, and that Dr. Walker was there, apparently in charge of the arrangements for the funeral. Halsey disappeared shortly after Louise left and came home about nine that night, muddy and tired. As for Thomas, he went around dejected and sad, and I saw the detective watching him closely at dinner. Even now I wonder—what did Thomas know? What did he suspect?

At ten o'clock the household had settled down for the night. Liddy, who was taking Mrs. Watson's place, had finished examining the tea towels and the corners of the shelves in the cooling room, and had gone to bed. Alex, the gardener, had gone heavily up the circular staircase to his room, and Mr. Jamieson was examining the locks of the windows. Halsey dropped into a chair in the living room and stared moodily ahead. Once he roused.

"What sort of a looking chap is that Walker, Gertrude?" he asked.

"Rather tall, very dark, smooth-shaven. Not bad-looking," Gertrude said, putting down the book she had been pretending to read. Halsey kicked a taboret viciously.

"Lovely place this village must be in the winter," he said irrelevantly. "A girl would be buried alive here."

It was then someone rapped at the knocker on the heavy front door. Halsey got up leisurely and opened it, admitting Warner. He was out of breath from running, and he looked half abashed.

"I am sorry to disturb you," he said. "But I didn't know what else to do. It's about Thomas."

"What about Thomas?" I asked. Mr. Jamieson had come into the hall and we all stared at Warner.

"He's acting queer," Warner explained. "He's sitting down there on the edge of the porch, and he says he has seen a ghost. The old man looks bad, too; he can scarcely speak."

"He's as full of superstition as an egg is of meat," I said. "Halsey, bring some whisky and we will all go down."

No one moved to get the whisky, from which I judged there were three pocket flasks ready for emergency. Gertrude threw a shawl around my shoulders, and we all started down over the hill: I had made so many nocturnal excursions around the place that I knew my way perfectly. But Thomas was not on the veranda, nor was he inside the house. The men exchanged significant glances, and Warner got a lantern.

"He can't have gone far," he said. "He was trembling so that he couldn't stand when I left."

Jamieson and Halsey together made the round of the lodge, occasionally calling the old man by name. But there was no response. No Thomas came, bowing and showing his white teeth through the darkness. I began to be vaguely uneasy, for the first time. Gertrude, who was never nervous in the dark, went alone down the drive to the gate and stood there, looking along the yellowish line of the road, while I waited on the tiny veranda.

Warner was puzzled. He came around to the edge of the veranda and stood looking at it as if it ought to know and explain.

"He might have stumbled into the house," he said, "but he could not have climbed the stairs. Anyhow, he's not inside or outside, that I can see." The other members of the party had come back now, and no one had found any trace of the old man. His pipe, still warm, rested on the edge of the rail, and inside on the table his old gray hat showed that its owner had not gone far.

He was not far, after all. From the table my eyes traveled around the room, and stopped at the door of a closet. I hardly know what impulse moved me, but I went in and turned the knob. It burst open with the impetus of a weight behind it, and something fell partly forward in a heap on the floor. It was Thomas—Thomas without a mark of injury on him, and dead.

Chapter XX

Dr. Walker's Warning

✍

WARNER was on his knees in a moment, fumbling at the old man's collar to loosen it, but Halsey caught his hand.

"Let him alone," he said. "You can't help him; he is dead."

We stood there, each avoiding the other's eyes; we spoke low and reverently in the presence of death, and we tacitly avoided any mention of the suspicion that was in every mind. When Mr. Jamieson had finished his cursory examination, he got up and dusted the knees of his trousers.

"There is no sign of injury," he said, and I know I, for one, drew a long breath of relief. "From what Warner says and from his hiding in the closet, I should say he was scared to death. Fright and a weak heart, together."

"But what could have done it?" Gertrude asked. "He was all right this evening at dinner. Warner, what did he say when you found him on the porch?"

Warner looked shaken: his honest, boyish face was colorless.

"Just what I told you, Miss Innes. He'd been reading the paper down-stairs; I had put up the car, and, feeling sleepy, I came down to the lodge to go to bed. As I went upstairs, Thomas put down the paper and, taking his pipe, went out on the porch. Then I heard an exclamation from him."

"What did he say?" demanded Jamieson.

"I couldn't hear, but his voice was strange; it sounded startled. I waited for him to call out again, but he did not, so I went downstairs. He was sitting on the porch step, looking straight ahead, as if he saw something among the trees across the road. And he kept mumbling about having seen a ghost. He looked queer, and I tried to get him inside, but he wouldn't move. Then I thought I'd better go up to the house."

"Didn't he say anything else you could understand?" I asked.

"He said something about the grave giving up its dead."

Mr. Jamieson was going through the old man's pockets, and Gertrude was composing his arms, folding them across his white shirt-bosom, always so spotless.

Mr. Jamieson looked up at me.

"What was that you said to me, Miss Innes, about the murder at the house being a beginning and not an end? By jove, I believe you were right!"

In the course of his investigations the detective had come to the inner pocket of the dead butler's black coat. Here he found some things that interested him. One was a small flat key, with a red cord tied to it, and the other was a bit of white paper, on which was written some-thing in Thomas' cramped hand. Mr. Jamieson read it: then he gave it to me. It was an address in fresh ink—LUCIEN WALLACE, 14 Elm Street, Richfield.

As the card went around, I think both the detective and I watched for any possible effect it might have, but, beyond perplexity, there seemed to be none.

"Richfield!" Gertrude exclaimed. "Why, Elm Street is the main street; don't you remember, Halsey?"

"Lucien Wallace!" Halsey said. "That is the child Stewart spoke of at the inquest."

Warner, with his mechanic's instinct, had reached for the key. What he said was not a surprise.

"Yale lock," he said. "Probably a key to the east entry."

There was no reason why Thomas, an old and trusted servant, should not have had a key to that particular door, although the servants' entry was in the west wing. But I had not known of this key, and it opened up a new field of conjecture. Just now, however, there were many things to be attended to, and leaving Warner with the body, we all went back to the house. Mr. Jamieson walked with me, while Halsey and Gertrude followed.

"I suppose I shall have to notify the Armstrongs," I said. "They will know if Thomas had any people and how to reach them. Of course, I expect to defray the expenses of the funeral, but his relatives must be found. What do you think frightened him, Mr. Jamieson?"

"It is hard to say," he replied slowly, "but I think we may be certain it was fright, and that he was hiding from something. I am sorry in more than one way: I have always believed that Thomas knew something, or suspected something, that he would not tell. Do you know how much money there was in that worn-out wallet of his? Nearly a hundred dollars! Almost two months' wages—and yet those darkies seldom have a penny. Well—what Thomas knew will be buried with him."

Halsey suggested that the grounds be searched, but Mr. Jamieson vetoed the suggestion.

"You would find nothing," he said. "A person clever enough to get into Sunnyside and tear a hole in the wall, while I watched downstairs, is not to be found by going around the shrubbery with a lantern."

With the death of Thomas, I felt that a climax had come in affairs at Sunnyside. The night that followed was quiet enough. Halsey watched at the foot of the staircase, and a complicated system of bolts on the other doors seemed to be effectual.

Once in the night I wakened and thought I heard the tapping again. But all was quiet, and I had reached the stage where I refused to be disturbed for minor occurrences.

The Armstrongs were notified of Thomas' death, and I had my first interview with Dr. Walker as a result. He came up early the next morning, just as we finished breakfast, in a professional-looking car with a black hood. I found him striding up and down the living room, and in spite of my preconceived dislike, I had to admit that the man was presentable. A big fellow he was, tall and dark, as Gertrude had said, smooth-shaven and erect, with prominent features and a square jaw. He was painfully spruce in his appearance, and his manner was almost obtrusively polite.

"I must make a double excuse for this early visit, Miss Innes," he said as he sat down. The chair was lower than he expected, and his dignity required collecting before he went on. "My professional duties are urgent and long neglected, and"—a fall to the everyday manner—"something must be done about that body."

"Yes," I said, sitting on the edge of my chair. "I merely wished the address of Thomas' people. You might have telephoned, if you were busy."

He smiled.

"I wished to see you about something else," he said. "As for Thomas, it is Mrs. Armstrong's wish that you allow her to attend to the expense. About his relatives, I have already notified his brother, in the village. It was heart disease, I think. Thomas always had a bad heart."

"Heart disease and fright," I said, still on the edge of my chair. But the doctor had no intention of leaving.

"I understand you have a ghost up here, and that you have the house filled with detectives to exorcise it," he said.

For some reason I felt I was being "pumped," as Halsey says. "You have been misinformed," I replied.

"What, no ghost, no detectives!" he said, still with his smile. "What a disappointment to the village!"

I resented his attempt at playfulness. It had been anything but a joke to us.

"Doctor Walker," I said tartly, "I fail to see any humor in the situation. Since I came here, one man has been shot, and another one has died from shock. There have been intruders in the house, and strange noises. If that is funny, there is something wrong with my sense of humor."

"You miss the point," he said, still good-naturedly. "The thing that is funny, to me, is that you insist on remaining here, under the circumstances. I should think nothing would keep you."

"You are mistaken. Everything that occurs only confirms my resolution to stay until the mystery is cleared."

"I have a message for you, Miss Innes," he said, rising at last. "Mrs. Armstrong asked me to thank you for your kindness to Louise, whose whim, occurring at the time it did, put her to great inconvenience. Also—and this is a delicate matter—she asked me to appeal to your natural sympathy for her, at this time, and to ask you if you will not reconsider your decision about the house. Sunnyside is her home; she loves it dearly, and just now she wishes to retire here for quiet and peace."

"She must have had a change of heart," I said, ungraciously enough. "Louise told me her mother despised the place. Besides, this is no place for quiet and peace just now. Anyhow, doctor, while I don't care to force an issue, I shall certainly remain here, for a time at least."

"For how long?" he asked.

"My lease is for six months. I shall stay until some explanation is found for certain things. My own family is implicated now, and I shall do everything to clear the mystery of Arnold Armstrong's murder."

The doctor stood looking down, slapping his gloves thoughtfully against the palm of a well-looked-after hand.

"You say there have been intruders in the house?" he asked. "You are sure of that, Miss Innes?"

"Certain."

"In what part?"

"In the east wing."

"Can you tell me when these intrusions occurred, and what the purpose seemed to be? Was it robbery?"

"No," I said decidedly. "As to time, once on Friday night a week ago, again the following night, when Arnold Armstrong was murdered, and again last Friday night."

The doctor looked serious. He seemed to be debating some question in his mind, and to reach a decision.

"Miss Innes," he said, "I am in a peculiar position; I understand your attitude, of course; but—do you think you are wise? Ever since you have come here there have been hostile demonstrations against you and your family. I'm not a croaker, but—take a warning. Leave before anything occurs that will cause you a lifelong regret."

"I am willing to take the responsibility," I said coldly.

I think he gave me up then as a poor proposition. He asked to be shown where Arnold Armstrong's body had been found, and I took him there. He scrutinized the whole place carefully, examining the stairs and the lock. When he had taken a formal farewell, I was confident of one thing. Dr. Walker would do anything he could to get me away from Sunnyside.

Chapter XXI

'Fourteen 'Elm Street

ᥫᦂ

IT WAS Monday evening when we found the body of poor old Thomas. Monday night had been uneventful; things were quiet at the house and the peculiar circumstances of the old man's death had been carefully kept from the servants. Rosie took charge of the dining room and pantry, in the absence of a butler, and, except for the warning of the Casanova doctor, everything breathed of peace.

Affairs at the Traders' Bank were progressing slowly. The failure had hit small stockholders very hard, the minister of the little Methodist chapel in Casanova among them. He had received as a legacy from an uncle a few shares of stock in the Traders' Bank, and now his joy was turned to bitterness: he had to sacrifice everything he had in the world, and his feeling against Paul Armstrong, dead as he was, must have been bitter in the extreme. He was asked to officiate at the simple services when the dead banker's body was interred in Casanova churchyard, but the good man providentially took cold, and a substitute was called in.

A few days after the services he called to see me, a kind-faced little man, in a very bad frock coat and laundered tie. I think he was uncertain as to my connection with the Armstrong family, and dubious whether I considered Mr. Armstrong's taking away a matter for condolence or congratulation. He was not long in doubt.

I liked the little man. He had known Thomas well and had promised to officiate at the services in the rickety African Zion Church. He told me more of himself than he knew, and before he left, I astonished him—

and myself, I admit—by promising a new carpet for his church. He was much affected, and I gathered that he had yearned over his ragged chapel as a mother over a half-clothed child.

"You are laying up treasure, Miss Innes," he said brokenly, "where neither moth nor rust corrupt, nor thieves break through and steal."

"It is certainly a safer place than Sunnyside," I admitted. And the thought of the carpet permitted him to smile. He stood just inside the doorway, looking from the luxury of the house to the beauty of the view.

"The rich ought to be good," he said wistfully. "They have so much that is beautiful, and beauty is ennobling. And yet—while I ought to say nothing but good of the dead—Mr. Armstrong saw nothing of this fair prospect. To him these trees and lawns were not the work of God. They were property, at so much an acre. He loved money, Miss Innes. He offered up everything to his golden calf. Not power, not ambition, was his fetish: it was money." Then he dropped his pulpit manner, and, turning to me with his engaging smile: "In spite of all this luxury," he said, "the country people here have a saying that Mr. Paul Armstrong could sit on a dollar and see all around it. Unlike the summer people, he gave neither to the poor nor to the church. He loved money for its own sake."

"And there are no pockets in shrouds!" I said cynically.

I sent him home in the car, with a bunch of hothouse roses for his wife, and he was quite overwhelmed. As for me, I had a generous glow that was cheap at the price of a church carpet. I received less gratification—and less gratitude—when I presented the new silver communion set to St. Barnabas.

I had a great many things to think about in those days. I made out a list of questions and possible answers, but I seemed only to be working around in a circle. I always ended where I began. The list was something like this:

Who had entered the house the night before the murder?

Thomas claimed it was Mr. Bailey, whom he had seen on the footpath, and who owned the pearl cuff link.

Why did Arnold Armstrong come back after he had left the house the night he was killed?

No answer. Was it on the mission Louise had mentioned?

Who admitted him?

Gertrude said she had locked the east entry. There was no key on the dead man or in the door. He must have been admitted from within.

Who had been locked in the clothes chute?

Someone unfamiliar with the house, evidently. Only two people missing from the household, Rosie and Gertrude. Rosie had been at the lodge. Therefore—but was it Gertrude? Might it not have been the mysterious intruder again?

Who had accosted Rosie on the drive?

Again—perhaps the nightly visitor. It seemed more likely someone who suspected a secret at the lodge. Was Louise under surveillance?

Who had passed Louise on the circular staircase?

Could it have been Thomas? The key to the east entry made this a possibility. But why was he there, if it were indeed he?

Who had made the hole in the trunk room wall?

It was not vandalism. It had been done quietly, and with deliberate purpose. If I had only known how to read the purpose of that gaping aperture what I might have saved in anxiety and mental strain!

Why had Louise left her people and come home to hide at the lodge?

There was no answer, as yet, to this, or to the next questions.

Why did both she and Dr. Walker warn us away from the house?

Who was Lucien Wallace?

What did Thomas see in the shadows the night he died?

What was the meaning of the subtle change in Gertrude?

Was Jack Bailey an accomplice or a victim in the looting of the Traders' Bank?

What all-powerful reason made Louise determine to marry Dr. Walker?

The examiners were still working on the books of the Traders' Bank, and it was probable that several weeks would elapse before everything was cleared up. The firm of expert accountants who had examined the books some two months before testified that every bond, every piece of valuable paper, was there at that time. It had been shortly after their examination that the president, who had been in bad health, had gone to California. Mr. Bailey was still ill at the Knickerbocker, and in this, as in other ways, Gertrude's conduct puzzled me. She seemed indifferent, refused to discuss matters pertaining to the bank, and never, to my knowledge, either wrote to him or went to see him.

Gradually I came to the conclusion that Gertrude, with the rest of the world, believed her lover guilty, and—although I believed it myself, for that matter—I was irritated by her indifference. Girls in my day did not meekly accept the public's verdict as to the man they loved.

But presently something occurred that made me think that under Gertrude's surface calm there was a seething flood of emotions.

Tuesday morning the detective made a careful search of the grounds, but he found nothing. In the afternoon he disappeared, and it was late that night when he came home. He said he would have to go back to the city the following day, and arranged with Halsey and Alex to guard the house.

Liddy came to me on Wednesday morning with her black silk apron held up like a bag, and her eyes big with virtuous wrath. It was the day of Thomas' funeral in the village, and Alex and I were in the conservatory cutting flowers for the old man's casket. Liddy is never so happy as when she is making herself wretched, and now her mouth drooped while her eyes were triumphant.

"I always said there were plenty of things going on here, right under our noses, that we couldn't see," she said, holding out her apron.

"I don't see with my nose," I remarked. "What have you got there?"

Liddy pushed aside a half-dozen geranium pots, and in the space thus cleared she dumped the contents of her apron—a handful of tiny bits of paper. Alex had stepped back, but I saw him watching her curiously.

"Wait a moment, Liddy," I said. "You have been going through the library paper-basket again!"

Liddy was arranging her bits of paper with the skill of long practice and paid no attention.

"Did it ever occur to you," I went on, putting my hand over the scraps, "that when people tear up their correspondence, it is for the express purpose of keeping it from being read?"

"If they wasn't ashamed of it they wouldn't take so much trouble, Miss Rachel," Liddy said oracularly. "More than that, with things happening every day, I consider it my duty. If you don't read and act on this, I shall give it to that Jamieson, and I'll venture he'll not go back to the city today."

That decided me. If the scraps had anything to do with the mystery ordinary conventions had no value. So Liddy arranged the scraps, like working out one of the puzzle pictures children play with, and she did it with much the same eagerness. When it was finished she stepped aside while I read it.

"Wednesday night, nine o'clock. Bridge," I real aloud. Then, aware of Alex's stare, I turned on Liddy.

"Someone is to play bridge tonight at nine o'clock," I said. "Is that your business, or mine?"

Liddy was aggrieved. She was about to reply when I scooped up the pieces and left the conservatory.

"Now then," I said, when we got outside, "will you tell me why you choose to take Alex into your confidence? He's no fool. Do you suppose he thinks anyone in this house is going to play bridge tonight at nine o'clock, by appointment! I suppose you have shown it in the kitchen, and instead of my being able to slip down to the bridge tonight quietly, and see who is there, the whole household will be going in a procession."

"Nobody knows it," Liddy said humbly. "I found it in the basket in Miss Gertrude's dressing room. Look at the back of the sheet." I turned over some of the scraps, and sure enough, it was a blank deposit slip from the Traders' Bank. So Gertrude was going to meet Jack Bailey that night by the bridge! And I had thought he was ill! It hardly seemed like the action of an innocent man—this avoidance of daylight, and of his fiancée's people. I decided to make certain, however, by going to the bridge that night.

After luncheon Mr. Jamieson suggested that I go with him to Richfield, and I consented.

"I am inclined to place more faith in Dr. Stewart's story," he said, "since I found that scrap in old Thomas' pocket. It bears out the statement that the woman with the child, and the woman who quarreled with Armstrong, are the same. It looks as if Thomas had stumbled onto some affair which was more or less discreditable to the dead man, and, with a certain loyalty to the family, had kept it to himself. Then, you see, your story about the woman at the cardroom window begins to mean something. It is the nearest approach to anything tangible that we have had yet."

Warner took us to Richfield in the car. It was about twenty-five miles by railroad, but by taking a series of atrociously rough shortcuts we got there very quickly. It was a pretty little town, on the river, and back on the hill I could see the Mortons' big country house, where Halsey and Gertrude had been staying until the night of the murder.

Elm Street was almost the only street, and number fourteen was easily found. It was a small white house, dilapidated without having gained anything picturesque, with a low window and a porch only a foot or so above the bit of a lawn. There was a baby carriage in the path, and from a swing at the side came the sound of conflict. Three small children were disputing vociferously, and a faded young woman with a kindly face was trying to hush the clamor. When she saw us she untied her gingham apron and came around to the porch.

"Good afternoon," I said. Jamieson lifted his hat, without speaking. "I came to inquire about a child named Lucien Wallace."

"I am glad you have come," she said. "In spite of the other children, I think the little fellow is lonely. We thought perhaps his mother would be here today."

Mr. Jamieson stepped forward.

"You are Mrs. Tate?" I wondered how the detective knew.

"Yes, sir."

"Mrs. Tate, we want to make some inquiries. Perhaps in the house—"

"Come right in," she said hospitably. And soon we were in the little shabby parlor, exactly like a thousand of its prototypes. Mrs. Tate sat uneasily, her hands folded in her lap.

"How long has Lucien been here?" Mr. Jamieson asked.

"Since a week ago last Friday. His mother paid one week's board in advance; the other has not been paid."

"Was he ill when he came?"

"No, sir, not what you'd call sick. He was getting better of typhoid, she said, and he's picking up fine."

"Will you tell me his mother's name and address?"

"That's the trouble," the young woman said, knitting her brows. "She gave her name as Mrs. Wallace and said she had no address. She was looking for a boardinghouse in town. She said she worked in a department store and couldn't take care of the child properly, and he needed fresh air and milk. I had three children of my own, and one more didn't make much difference in the work, but—I wish she would pay this week's board."

"Did she say what store it was?"

"No, sir, but all the boy's clothes came from King's. He has far too fine clothes for the country."

There was a chorus of shouts and shrill yells from the front door, followed by the loud stamping of children's feet and a throaty "whoa, whoa!" Into the room came a tandem team of two chubby youngsters, a boy and a girl, harnessed with a clothesline and driven by a laughing boy of about seven in tan overalls and brass buttons. The small driver caught my attention at once: he was a beautiful child, and although he showed traces of recent severe illness, his skin had now the clear transparency of health.

"Whoa, Flinders," he shouted. "You're goin' to smash the trap."

Mr. Jamieson coaxed him over by holding out a lead pencil, striped blue and yellow.

"Now, then," he said, when the boy had taken the lead pencil and was testing its usefulness on the detective's cuff, "now then, I'll bet you don't know what your name is!"

"I do," said the boy. "Lucien Wallace."

"Great! And what's your mother's name?"

"Mother, of course. What's your mother's name?" And he pointed to me! I am going to stop wearing black: it doubles a woman's age.

"And where did you live before you came here?" The detective was polite enough not to smile.

"Grossmutter," he said. And I saw Mr. Jamieson's eyebrows go up.

"German," he commented. "Well, young man, you don't seem to know much about yourself."

"I've tried it all week," Mrs. Tate broke in. "The boy knows a word or two of German, but he doesn't know where he lived, or anything about himself."

Mr. Jamieson wrote something on a card and gave it to her.

"Mrs. Tate," he said, "I want you to do something. Here is some money for the telephone call. The instant the boy's mother appears here, call up that number and ask for the person whose name is there. You can run across to the drugstore on an errand and do it quietly. Just say, 'The lady has come.' "

" 'The lady has come,' " repeated Mrs. Tate. "Very well, sir, and I hope it will be soon. The milk bill alone is almost double what it was."

"How much is the child's board?" I asked.

"Three dollars a week, including his washing."

"Very well," I said. "Now, Mrs. Tate, I am going to pay last week's board and a week in advance. If the mother comes, she is to know nothing of this visit—absolutely not a word, and in return for your silence, you may use this money for—something for your own children."

Her tired, faded face lighted up, and I saw her glance at the little Tates' small feet. Shoes, I divined—the feet of the genteel poor being almost as expensive as their stomachs.

As we went back Mr. Jamieson made only one remark: I think he was laboring under the weight of a great disappointment.

"Is King's a children's outfitting place?" he asked.

"Not especially. It is a general department store."

He was silent after that, but he went to the telephone as soon as we got home, and called up King and Company, in the city.

After a time he got the general manager, and they talked for some time. When Mr. Jamieson hung up the receiver he turned to me.

"The plot thickens," he said with his ready smile. "There are four women named Wallace at King's, none of them married, and none over twenty. I think I shall go up to the city tonight. I want to go to the Children's Hospital. But before I go, Miss Innes, I wish you would be more frank with me than you have been yet. I want you to show me the revolver you picked up in the tulip bed."

So he had known all along!

"It was a revolver, Mr. Jamieson," I admitted, cornered at last, "but I cannot show it to you. It is not in my possession."

Chapter XXII

A Ladder Out of Place

AT DINNER Mr. Jamieson suggested sending a man out in his place for a couple of days, but Halsey was certain there would be nothing more, and felt that he and Alex could manage the situation. The detective went back to town early in the evening, and by nine o'clock Halsey, who had been playing golf—as a man does anything to take his mind away from trouble—was sleeping soundly on the big leather davenport in the living room.

I sat and knitted, pretending not to notice when Gertrude got up and wandered out into the starlight. As soon as I was satisfied that she had gone, however, I went out cautiously. I had no intention of eavesdropping, but I wanted to be certain that it was Jack Bailey she was meeting. Too many things had occurred in which Gertrude was, or appeared to be, involved, to allow anything to be left in question.

I went slowly across the lawn, skirted the hedge to a break not far from the lodge, and found myself on the open road. Perhaps a hundred feet to the left the path led across the valley to the Country Club, and only a little way off was the footbridge over Casanova Creek. But just as I was about to turn down the path I heard steps coming toward me, and I shrank into the bushes. It was Gertrude, going back quickly toward the house.

I was surprised. I waited until she had had time to get almost to the house before I started. And then I stepped back again into the shadows. The reason why Gertrude had not kept her tryst was evident. Leaning on the parapet of the bridge in the moonlight, and smoking a pipe, was Alex, the gardener. I could have throttled Liddy for her carelessness in reading the torn note where he could hear. And I could cheerfully have choked Alex to death for his audacity.

But there was no help for it: I turned and followed Gertrude slowly back to the house.

The frequent invasions of the house had effectually prevented any relaxation after dusk. We had redoubled our vigilance as to bolts and window locks but, as Mr. Jamieson had suggested, we allowed the door at the east entry to remain as before, locked by the Yale lock only. To provide only one possible entrance for the invader, and to keep a constant guard in the dark at the foot of the circular staircase, seemed to be the only method.

In the absence of the detective, Alex and Halsey arranged to change off, Halsey to be on duty from ten to two, and Alex from two until six. Each man was armed, and, as an additional precaution, the one off duty slept in a room near the head of the circular staircase and kept his door open, to be ready for emergency.

These arrangements were carefully kept from the servants, who were only commencing to sleep at night, and who retired, one and all, with barred doors and lamps that burned full until morning.

The house was quiet again Wednesday night. It was almost a week since Louise had encountered someone on the stairs, and it was four days since the discovery of the hole in the trunk-room wall. Arnold Armstrong and his father rested side by side in the Casanova churchyard, and at the Zion African Church, on the hill, a new mound marked the last resting-place of poor Thomas.

Louise was with her mother in town, and beyond a polite note of thanks to me, we had heard nothing from her. Dr. Walker had taken up his practice again, and we saw him now and then flying past along the road, always at top speed. The murder of Arnold Armstrong was still unavenged, and I remained firm in the position I had taken—to stay at Sunnyside until the thing was at least partly cleared.

And yet, for all its quiet, it was on Wednesday night that perhaps the boldest attempt was made to enter the house. On Thursday afternoon the laundress sent word she would like to speak to me, and I saw her in my private sitting room, a small room beyond the dressing room.

Mary Anne was embarrassed. She had rolled down her sleeves and tied a white apron around her waist, and she stood making folds in it with fingers that were red and shiny from her soapsuds.

"Well, Mary," I said encouragingly, "what's the matter? Don't dare to tell me the soap is out."

"No, ma'am, Miss Innes." She had a nervous habit of looking first at my one eye and then at the other, her own optics shifting ceaselessly, right eye, left eye, right eye, until I found myself doing the same thing. "No, ma'am. I was askin' did you want the ladder left up the clothes chute?"

"The what?" I screeched, and was sorry the next minute. Seeing her suspicions were verified, Mary Anne had gone white and stood with her eyes shifting more wildly than ever.

"There's a ladder up the clothes chute, Miss Innes," she said. "It's up that tight I can't move it, and I didn't like to ask for help until I spoke to you."

It was useless to dissemble; Mary Anne knew now as well as I did that the ladder had no business to be there. I did the best I could, however. I put her on the defensive at once.

"Then you didn't lock the laundry last night?"

"I locked it tight and put the key in the kitchen on its nail."

"Very well, then you forgot a window."

Mary Anne hesitated.

"Yes'm," she said at last. "I thought I locked them all, but there was one open this morning."

I went out of the room and down the hall, followed by Mary Anne. The door into the clothes chute was securely bolted, and when I opened it I saw the evidence of the woman's story. A pruning ladder had been brought from where it had lain against the stable and now stood upright in the clothes shaft, its end resting against the wall between the first and second floors.

I turned to Mary.

"This is due to your carelessness," I said. "If we had all been murdered in our beds it would have been your fault." She shivered. "Now, not a word of this through the house, and send Alex to me."

The effect on Alex was to make him apoplectic with rage, and with it all I fancied there was an element of satisfaction. As I look back, so many things are plain to me that I wonder I could not see at the time. It is all known now, and yet the whole thing was so remarkable that perhaps my stupidity was excusable.

Alex leaned down the chute and examined the ladder carefully.

"It is caught," he said with a grim smile. "The fools, to have left a warning like that! The only trouble is, Miss Innes, they won't be apt to come back for a while."

"I shouldn't regard that in the light of a calamity," I replied.

Until late that evening Halsey and Alex worked at the chute. They forced down the ladder at last and put a new bolt on the door. As for myself, I sat and wondered if I had a deadly enemy, intent on my destruction.

I was growing more and more nervous. Liddy had given up all pretense at bravery and slept regularly in my dressing room on the couch, with a prayer book and a game knife from the kitchen under her pillow, thus preparing for both the natural and the supernatural. That was the way things stood that Thursday night, when I myself took a hand in the struggle.

Chapter XXIII
While the Stables Burned

⌐⧓⌐

ABOUT nine o'clock that night Liddy came into the living room and reported that one of the housemaids declared she had seen two men slip around the corner of the stable. Gertrude had been sitting staring in front of her, jumping at every sound. Now she turned on Liddy pettishly.

"I declare, Liddy," she said, "you are a bundle of nerves. What if Eliza did see some men around the stable? It may have been Warner and Alex."

"Warner is in the kitchen, miss," Liddy said with dignity. "And if you had come through what I have, you would be a bundle of nerves, too. Miss Rachel, I'd be thankful if you'd give me my month's wages tomorrow. I'll be going to my sister's."

"Very well," I said, to her evident amazement. "I will make out the check. Warner can take you down to the noon train."

Liddy's face was really funny.

"You'll have a nice time at your sister's," I went on. "Five children, hasn't she?"

"That's it," Liddy said, suddenly bursting into tears. "Send me away, after all these years, and your new shawl only half done, and nobody knowin' how to fix the water for your bath."

"It's time I learned to prepare my own bath." I was knitting complacently. But Gertrude got up and put her arms around Liddy's shaking shoulders.

"You are two big babies," she said soothingly. "Neither one of you could get along for an hour without the other. So stop quarreling and be good. Liddy, go right up and lay out Aunty's night things. She is going to bed early."

After Liddy had gone I began to think about the men at the stable, and I grew more and more anxious. Halsey was aimlessly knocking the billiard balls around in the billiard room, and I called to him.

"Halsey," I said when he sauntered in, "is there a policeman in Casanova?"

"Constable," he said laconically. "Veteran of the war, one arm; in office to conciliate the G.A.R. element. Why?"

"Because I am uneasy tonight." And I told him what Liddy had said. "Is there anyone you can think of who could be relied on to watch the outside of the house tonight?"

"We might get Sam Bohannon from the club," he said thoughtfully. "It wouldn't be a bad scheme. He's a smart darky, and with his mouth shut and his shirtfront covered, you couldn't see him a yard off in the dark."

Halsey conferred with Alex, and the result, in an hour, was Sam. His instructions were simple. There had been numerous attempts to break into the house; it was the intention, not to drive intruders away, but to capture them. If Sam saw anything suspicious outside, he was to tap at the east entry, where Alex and Halsey were to alternate in keeping watch through the night.

It was with a comfortable feeling of security that I went to bed that night. The door between Gertrude's rooms and mine had been opened, and with the doors into the hall bolted, we were safe enough. Although Liddy persisted in her belief that doors would prove no obstacles to our disturbers.

As before, Halsey watched the east entry from ten until two. He had an eye to comfort, and he kept vigil in a heavy oak chair, very large and deep. We went upstairs rather early, and through the open door Gertrude and I kept up a running fire of conversation. Liddy was brushing my hair, and Gertrude was doing her own, with a long free sweep of her strong round arms.

"Did you know Mrs. Armstrong and Louise are in the village?" she called.

"No," I replied, startled. "How did you hear it?"

"I met the oldest Stewart girl today, the doctor's daughter, and she told me they had not gone back to town after the funeral. They went directly to that little yellow house next to Dr. Walker's and are apparently settled there. They took the house furnished for the summer."

"Why, it's a bandbox," I said. "I can't imagine Fanny Armstrong in such a place."

"It's true, nevertheless. Ella Stewart says Mrs. Armstrong has aged terribly and looks as if she is hardly able to walk."

I lay and thought over some of these things until midnight. The electric lights went out then, fading slowly until there was only a red-hot loop to be seen in the bulb, and then even that died away and we were embarked on the darkness of another night.

Apparently only a few minutes elapsed, during which my eyes were becoming accustomed to the darkness. Then I noticed that the windows were reflecting a faint pinkish light; Liddy noticed it at the same time, and I heard her jump up. At that moment Sam's deep voice boomed from somewhere just below.

"Fire!" he yelled. "The stable's on fire!"

I could see him in the glare dancing up and down on the drive, and a moment later Halsey joined him. Alex was awake and running down the stairs, and in five minutes from the time the fire was discovered, three of the maids were sitting on their trunks in the drive, although, excepting a few sparks, there was no fire nearer than a hundred yards.

Gertrude seldom loses her presence of mind, and she ran to the telephone. But by the time the Casanova volunteer fire department came toiling up the hill the stable was a furnace, with the Dragon Fly safe but blistered, in the road. Some gasoline exploded just as the volunteer department got to work, which shook their nerves as well as the burning building. The stable, being on a hill, was a torch to attract the population from every direction. Rumor had it that Sunnyside was burning, and it was amazing how many people threw something over their nightclothes and flew to the conflagration. I take it Casanova has few fires, and Sunnyside was furnishing the people, in one way and another, the greatest excitement they had had for years.

The stable was off the west wing. I hardly know how I came to think of the circular staircase and the unguarded door at its foot. Liddy was putting my clothes into sheets, preparatory to tossing them out the window, when I found her, and I could hardly persuade her to stop.

"I want you to come with me, Liddy," I said. "Bring a candle and a couple of blankets."

She lagged behind considerably when she saw me making for the east wing, and at the top of the staircase she balked.

"I am not going down there," she said firmly.

"There is no one guarding the door down there," I explained. "Who knows?—this may be a scheme to draw everybody away from this end of the house, and let someone in here."

The instant I had said it I was convinced I had hit on the explanation, and that perhaps it was already too late. It seemed to me as I listened that I heard stealthy footsteps on the east porch, but there was so much shouting outside that it was impossible to tell. Liddy was on the point of retreat.

"Very well," I said, "then I shall go down alone. Run back to Mr. Halsey's room and get his revolver. Don't shoot down the stairs if you hear a noise: remember—I shall be down there. And hurry."

I put the candle on the floor at the top of the staircase and took off my bedroom slippers. Then I crept down the stairs, going very slowly, and listening with all my ears. I was keyed to such a pitch that I felt no fear: like the condemned who sleep and eat the night before execution, I was no longer able to suffer apprehension. I was past that. Just at the foot of the stairs I stubbed my toe against Halsey's big chair and had to stand on one foot in a soundless agony until the pain subsided to a dull ache. And then—I knew I was right. Someone had put a key into the lock and was turning it. For some reason it refused to work, and the key was withdrawn. There was a muttering of voices outside: I had only a second. Another trial, and the door would open. The candle above made a faint gleam down the well-like staircase, and at that moment, with a second, no more, to spare, I thought of a plan.

The heavy oak chair almost filled the space between the newel post and the door. With a crash I had turned it on its side, wedging it against the door, its legs against the stairs. I could hear a faint scream from Liddy, at the crash, and then she came down the stairs on a run, with the revolver held straight out in front of her.

"Thank God," she said, in a shaking voice. "I thought it was you."

I pointed to the door, and she understood.

"Call out the windows at the other end of the house," I whispered. "Run. Tell them not to wait for anything."

She went up the stairs at that, two at a time. Evidently she collided with the candle, for it went out, and 1 was left in darkness.

I was really astonishingly cool. I remember stepping over the chair and gluing my ear to the door, and I shall never forget feeling it give an

inch or two there in the darkness, under a steady pressure from without. But the chair held, although I could hear an ominous cracking of
one of the legs. And then, without the slightest warning, the cardroom
window broke with a crash. I had my finger on the trigger of the
revolver, and as I jumped it went off, right through the door. Someone
outside swore roundly, and for the first time I could hear what was said.

"Only a scratch . . . Men are at the other end of the house . . . Have
the whole rat's nest on us." And a lot of profanity which I won't write
down. The voices were at the broken window now, and although I was
trembling violently, I was determined that I would hold them until help
came. I moved up the stairs until I could see into the cardroom, or
rather through it, to the window. As I looked a small man put his leg
over the sill and stepped into the room. The curtain confused him for a
moment; then he turned, not toward me, but toward the billiard room
door. I fired again, and something that was glass or china crashed to the
ground. Then I ran up the stairs and along the corridor to the main
staircase. Gertrude was standing there, trying to locate the shots, and I
must have been a peculiar figure, with my hair in crimps, my dressing
gown flying, no slippers, and a revolver clutched in my hands I had no
time to talk. There was the sound of footsteps in the lower hall, and
someone bounded up the stairs.

I had gone berserk, I think. I leaned over the stair rail and fired again.
Halsey, below, yelled at me.

"What are you doing up there?" he yelled. "You missed me by an
inch."

And then I collapsed and fainted. When I came around, Liddy was
rubbing my temples with *eau de quinine,* and the search was in full
blast.

Well, the man was gone. The stable burned to the ground, while the
crowd cheered at every falling rafter, and the volunteer fire department
sprayed it with a garden hose. And in the house Alex and Halsey
searched every corner of the lower floor, finding no one.

The truth of my story was shown by the broken window and the
overturned chair. That the unknown had got upstairs was almost
impossible. He had not used the main staircase, there was no way to
the upper floor in the east wing, and Liddy had been at the window, in
the west wing, where the servants stair went up. But we did not go to

bed at all. Sam Bohannon and Warner helped in the search, and not a closet escaped scrutiny. Even the cellars were given a thorough overhauling, without result. The door in the east entry had a hole through it where my bullet had gone. The hole slanted downward, and the bullet was embedded in the porch. Some reddish stains showed it had done execution.

"Somebody will walk lame," Halsey said, when he had marked the course of the bullet. "It's too low to have hit anything but a leg or foot."

From that time on I watched every person I met for a limp, and to this day the man who halts in his walk is an object of suspicion to me. But Casanova had no lame men: the nearest approach to it was an old fellow who tended the safety gates at the railroad, and he, I learned on inquiry, had two artificial legs. Our man had gone, and the large and expensive stable at Sunnyside was a heap of smoking rafters and charred boards. Warner swore the fire was incendiary, and in view of the attempt to enter the house, there seemed to be no doubt of it.

Chapter XXIV

Flinders

&co;

IF HALSEY had only taken me fully into his confidence, through the whole affair, it would have been much simpler. If he had been altogether frank about Jack Bailey, and if the day after the fire he had told me what he suspected, there would have been no harrowing period for all of us, with the boy in danger. But young people refuse to profit by the experience of their elders, and sometimes the elders are the ones to suffer.

I was much used up the day after the fire, and Gertrude insisted on my going out. The machine was temporarily out of commission, and the carriage horses had been sent to a farm for the summer. Gertrude finally got a trap from the Casanova liveryman, and we went out. Just as we turned from the drive into the road we passed a woman. She had put down a small valise and stood inspecting the house and grounds minutely. I should hardly have noticed her, had it not been for the fact that she had been horribly disfigured by smallpox.

"Ugh!" Gertrude said, when we had passed, "what a face! I shall dream of it tonight. Get up, Flinders."

"Flinders?" I asked. "Is that the horse's name?"

"It is." She flicked the horse's stubby mane with the whip. "He didn't look like a livery horse, and the liveryman said he had bought him from the Armstrongs when they purchased a couple of motors and cut down the stable. Nice Flinders—good old boy!"

Flinders was certainly not a common name for a horse, and yet the youngster at Richfield had named his prancing, curly-haired little horse Flinders! It set me to thinking.

At my request Halsey had already sent word of the fire to the agent from whom we had secured the house. Also, he had called Mr. Jamieson by telephone, and somewhat guardedly had told him of the previous night's events. Mr. Jamieson promised to come out that night, and to bring another man with him. I did not consider it necessary to notify Mrs. Armstrong, in the village. No doubt she knew of the fire, and in view of my refusal to give up the house, an interview would probably have been unpleasant enough. But as we passed Dr. Walker's white-and-green house I thought of something.

"Stop here, Gertrude," I said. "I am going to get out."

"To see Louise?" she asked.

"No, I want to ask this young Walker something."

She was curious, I knew, but I did not wait to explain. I went up the walk to the house, where a brass sign at the side announced the office, and went in. The reception room was empty, but from the consulting room beyond came the sound of two voices, not very amicable.

"It is an outrageous figure," someone was storming. Then the doctor's quiet tone, evidently not arguing, merely stating something. But I had not time to listen to some person probably disputing his bill, so I coughed. The voices ceased at once: a door closed somewhere, and the doctor entered from the hall of the house. He looked sufficiently surprised at seeing me.

"Good afternoon, Doctor," I said formally. "I shall not keep you from your patient. I wish merely to ask you a question."

"Won't you sit down?"

"It will not be necessary. Doctor, has anyone come to you, either early this morning or today, to have you treat a bullet wound?"

"Nothing so startling has happened to me," he said. "A bullet wound! Things must be lively at Sunnyside."

"I didn't say it was at Sunnyside. But as it happens, it was. If any such case comes to you, will it be too much trouble for you to let me know?"

"I shall be only too happy," he said. "I understand you have had a fire up there, too. A fire and shooting in one night is rather lively for a quiet place like that."

"It is as quiet as a boiler shop," I replied as I turned to go.

"And you are still going to stay?"

"Until I am burned out," I responded. And then on my way down the steps, I turned around suddenly.

"Doctor," I asked at a venture, "have you ever heard of a child named Lucien Wallace?"

Clever as he was, his face changed and stiffened. He was on his guard again in a moment.

"Lucien Wallace?" he repeated. "No, I think not. There are plenty of Wallaces around, but I don't know any Lucien."

I was as certain as possible that he did. People do not lie readily to me, and this man lied beyond a doubt. But there was nothing to be gained now; his defenses were up, and I left, half irritated and wholly baffled.

Our reception was entirely different at Dr. Stewart's. Taken into the bosom of the family at once, Flinders tied outside and nibbling the grass at the roadside, Gertrude and I drank some homemade elderberry wine and told briefly of the fire. Of the more serious part of the night's experience, of course, we said nothing. But when at last we had left the family on the porch and the good doctor was untying our steed, I asked him the same question I had put to Dr. Walker.

"Shot!" he said. "Bless my soul, no. Why, what have you been doing up at the big house, Miss Innes?"

"Someone tried to enter the house during the fire, and was shot and slightly injured," I said hastily. "Please don't mention it; we wish to make as little of it as possible."

There was one other possibility, and we tried that. At Casanova station

I saw the stationmaster and asked him if any trains left Casanova between one o'clock and daylight. There was none until six a.m. The next question required more diplomacy.

"Did you notice on the six-o'clock train any person—any man— who limped a little?" I asked. "Please try to remember: we are trying to trace a man who was seen loitering around Sunnyside last night before the fire."

He was all attention in a moment.

"I was up there myself at the fire," he said volubly. "I'm a member of the volunteer company. First big fire we've had since the summer house burned over to the club golf links. My wife was sayin' the other day, 'Dave, you might as well 'a' saved the money in that there helmet and shirt.' And here last night they came in handy. Rang that bell so hard I hadn't time scarcely to get 'em on."

"And—did you see a man who limped?" Gertrude put in, as he stopped for breath.

"Not at the train, ma'am," he said. "No such person got on here today. But I'll tell you where I did see a man that limped. I didn't wait till the fire company left; there's a fast freight goes through at four forty-five, and I had to get down to the station. I seen there wasn't much more to do anyhow at the fire—we'd got the flames under control"— Gertrude looked at me and smiled—"so I started down the hill. There was folks here and there goin' home, and along by the path to the Country Club I seen two men. One was a short fellow. He was sitting on a big rock, his back to me, and he had something white in his hand, as if he was tying up his foot. After I'd gone on a piece I looked back, and he was hobbling on and—excuse me, miss—he was swearing something sickening."

"Did they go toward the club?" Gertrude asked suddenly, leaning forward.

"No, miss. I think they came into the village. I didn't get a look at their faces, but I know every chick and child in the place, and everybody knows me. When they didn't shout at me—in my uniform, you know—I took it they were strangers."

So all we had for our afternoon's work was this: someone had been shot by the bullet that went through the door; he had not left the village, and he had not called in a physician. Also, Dr. Walker knew who

Lucien Wallace was, and his very denial made me confident that, in that one direction at least, we were on the right track.

The thought that the detective would be there that night was the most cheering thing of all, and I think even Gertrude was glad of it. Driving home that afternoon, I saw her in the clear sunlight for the first time in several days, and I was startled to see how ill she looked. She was thin and colorless, and all her bright animation was gone.

"Gertrude," I said, "I have been a very selfish old woman. You are going to leave this miserable house tonight. Annie Morton is going to Scotland next week, and you shall go right with her."

To my surprise, she flushed painfully.

"I don't want to go, Aunt Ray," she said. "Don't make me leave now."

"You are losing your health and your good looks," I said decidedly. "You should have a change."

"I shan't stir a foot." She was equally decided. Then, more lightly: "Why, you and Liddy need me to arbitrate between you every day in the week."

Perhaps I was growing suspicious of everyone, but it seemed to me that Gertrude's gaiety was forced and artificial. I watched her covertly during the rest of the drive, and I did not like the two spots of crimson in her pale cheeks. But I said nothing more about sending her to Scotland: I knew she would not go.

Chapter XXV

A Visit from Lousie

⌒⌒⌒

THAT day was destined to be an eventful one, for when I entered the house and found Eliza ensconced in the upper hall on a chair, with Mary Anne doing her best to stifle her with household ammonia, and Liddy rubbing her wrists—whatever good that is supposed to do—I knew that the ghost had been walking again, and this time in daylight.

Eliza was in a frenzy of fear. She clutched at my sleeve when I went close to her, and refused to let go until she had told her story. Coming just after the fire, the household was demoralized, and it was no surprise to me to find Alex and the under-gardener struggling downstairs with a heavy trunk between them.

"I didn't want to do it, Miss Innes," Alex said. "But she was so excited, I was afraid she would do as she said—drag it down herself, and scratch the staircase."

I was trying to get my bonnet off and to keep the maids quiet at the same time. "Now, Eliza, when you have washed your face and stopped bawling," I said, "come into my sitting room and tell me what has happened."

Liddy put away my things without speaking. The very set of her shoulders expressed disapproval.

"Well," I said, when the silence became uncomfortable, "things seem to be warming up."

Silence from Liddy, and a long sigh.

"If Eliza goes, I don't know where to look for another cook." More silence.

"Rosie is probably a good cook." Sniff.

"Liddy," I said at last, "don't dare to deny that you are having the time of your life. You positively gloat in this excitement. You never looked better. It's my opinion all this running around, and getting jolted out of a rut, has stirred up that torpid liver of yours."

"It's not myself I'm thinking about," she said, goaded into speech. "Maybe my liver was torpid, and maybe it wasn't; but I know this: I've got some feelings left, and to see you standing at the foot of that staircase shootin' through the door—I'll never be the same woman again."

"Well, I'm glad of that—anything for a change," I said. And in came Eliza, flanked by Rosie and Mary Anne.

Her story, broken with sobs and corrections from the other two, was this: At two o'clock (two-fifteen, Rosie insisted) she had gone upstairs to get a picture from her room to show Mary Anne. (A picture of a *lady*, Mary Anne interposed.) She went up the servants' staircase and along the corridor to her room, which lay between the trunk room and the unfinished ballroom. She heard a sound as she went down the corridor, like someone moving furniture, but she was not nervous. She thought it might be men examining the house after the fire the night before, but she looked in the trunk room and saw nobody.

She went into her room quietly. The noise had ceased, and everything was quiet. Then she sat down on the side of her bed, and feeling faint—she was subject to spells—("I told you that when I came, didn't I, Rosie?" "Yes'm, indeed she did!")—she put her head down on her pillow and—

"Took a nap. All right!" I said. "Go on."

"When I came to, Miss Innes, sure as I'm sittin' here, I thought I'd die. Somethin' hit me on the face, and I set up, sudden. And then I seen the plaster drop, droppin' from a little hole in the wall. And the first thing I knew, an iron bar that long" (fully two yards by her measure) "shot through that hole and tumbled on the bed. If I'd been still sleeping" ("Fainting," corrected Rosie) "I'd 'a' been hit on the head and killed!"

"I wisht you'd heard her scream," put in Mary Anne. "And her face as white as a pillow slip when she tumbled down the stairs."

"No doubt there is some natural explanation for it, Eliza," I said. "You may have dreamed it, in your 'fainting' attack. But if it is true, the metal rod and the hole in the wall will show it."

Eliza looked a little bit sheepish.

"The hole's there all right, Miss Innes," she said. "But the bar was gone when Mary Anne and Rosie went up to pack my trunk."

"That wasn't all," Liddy's voice came funereally from a corner. "Eliza said that from the hole in the wall a burning eye looked down at her!"

"The wall must be at least six inches thick," I said with asperity. "Unless the person who drilled the hole carried his eyes on the ends of a stick, Eliza couldn't possibly have seen them."

But the fact remained, and a visit to Eliza's room proved it. I might jeer all I wished: someone had drilled a hole in the unfinished wall of the ballroom, passing between the bricks of the partition, and shooting through the unresisting plaster of Eliza's room with such force as to send the rod flying onto her bed. I had gone upstairs alone, and I confess the thing puzzled me: in two or three places in the wall small apertures had been made, none of them of any depth. Not the least mysterious thing was the disappearance of the iron implement that had been used.

I remembered a story I read once about an impish dwarf that lived in the spaces between the double walls of an ancient castle. I wondered vaguely if my original idea of a secret entrance to a hidden chamber could be right, after all, and if we were housing some erratic guest, who played pranks on us in the dark, and destroyed the walls that he might listen, hidden safely away, to our amazed investigations.

Mary Anne and Eliza left that afternoon, but Rosie decided to stay. It was about five o'clock when the hack came from the station to get them, and to my amazement, it had an occupant. Matthew Geist, the driver, asked for me and explained his errand with pride.

"I've brought you a cook, Miss Innes," he said. "When the message came to come up for two girls and their trunks, I supposed there was something doing, and as this here woman had been looking for work in the village, I thought I'd bring her along."

Already I had acquired the true suburbanite ability to take servants on faith; I no longer demanded written and unimpeachable references. I, Rachel Innes, have learned not to mind if the cook sits down comfortably in my sitting room when she is taking the orders for the day, and I am grateful if the silver is not cleaned with scouring soap. And so that day I merely told Liddy to send the new applicant in. When she came, however, I could hardly restrain a gasp of surprise. It was the woman with the pitted face.

She stood somewhat awkwardly just inside the door, and she had an air of self-confidence that was inspiring. Yes, she could cook; was not a fancy cook, but could make good soups and desserts if there was anyone to take charge of the salads. And so, in the end, I took her. As Halsey said, when we told him, it didn't matter much about the cook's face, if it was clean.

I have spoken of Halsey's restlessness. On that day it seemed to be more than ever a resistless impulse that kept him out until after luncheon. I think he hoped constantly that he might meet Louise driving over the hills in her runabout: possibly he did meet her occasionally, but from his continued gloom I felt sure the situation between them was unchanged.

Part of the afternoon I believe he read—Gertrude and I were out, as I have said, and at dinner we both noticed that something had occurred to distract him. He was disagreeable, which is unlike him, nervous, looking at his watch every few minutes, and he ate almost nothing. He asked twice during the meal on what train Mr. Jamieson and the other detective were coming, and had long periods of abstraction during which he dug his fork into my damask cloth and did not hear when he was spoken to. He refused dessert and left the table early, excusing himself on the ground that he wanted to see Alex.

Alex, however, was not to be found. It was after eight when Halsey ordered the car and started down the hill at a pace that, even for him, was unusually reckless. Shortly after, Alex reported that he was ready to go over the house, preparatory to closing it for the night. Sam Bohannon came at a quarter before nine and began his patrol of the grounds, and with the arrival of the two detectives to look forward to, I was not especially apprehensive.

At half-past nine I heard the sound of a horse driven furiously up the drive. It came to a stop in front of the house, and immediately after there were hurried steps on the veranda. Our nerves were not what they should have been, and Gertrude, always apprehensive lately, was at the door almost instantly. A moment later Louise had burst into the room and stood there bareheaded and breathing hard.

"Where is Halsey?" she demanded. Above her plain black gown her eyes looked big and somber, and the rapid drive had brought no color to her face. I got up and drew forward a chair.

"He has not come back," I said quietly. "Sit down, child; you are not strong enough for this kind of thing."

I don't think she even heard me.

"He has not come back?" she asked, looking from me to Gertrude. "Do you know where he went? Where can I find him?"

"For Heaven's sake, Louise," Gertrude burst out, "tell us what is wrong. Halsey is not here. He has gone to the station for Mr. Jamieson. What has happened?"

"To the station, Gertrude? You are sure?"

"Yes," I said. "Listen. There is the whistle of the train now."

She relaxed a little at our matter-of-fact tone and allowed herself to sink into a chair.

"Perhaps I was wrong," she said heavily. "He—will be here in a few moments if—everything is right."

We sat there, the three of us, without attempt at conversation. Both Gertrude and I recognized the futility of asking Louise any questions: her reticence was a part of a role she had assumed. Our ears were strained for the first throb of the motor as it turned into the drive and commenced the climb to the house. Ten minutes passed, fifteen, twenty. I saw Louise's hands grow rigid as they clutched the arms of her chair. I watched Gertrude's bright color slowly ebbing away, and around my own heart I seemed to feel the grasp of a giant hand.

Twenty-five minutes, and then a sound. But it was not the chug of the motor: it was the unmistakable rumble of the Casanova hack. Gertrude drew aside the curtain and peered into the darkness.

"It's the hack, I am sure," she said, evidently relieved. "Something has gone wrong with the car, and no wonder—the way Halsey went down the hill."

It seemed a long time before the creaking vehicle came to a stop at the door. Louise rose and stood watching, her hand to her throat. And then Gertrude opened the door, admitting Mr. Jamieson and a stocky, middle-aged man. Halsey was not with them. When the door had closed and Louise realized that Halsey had not come, her expression changed. From tense watchfulness to relief, and now again to absolute despair, her face was an open page.

"Halsey?" I asked unceremoniously, ignoring the stranger. "Did he not meet you?"

"No." Mr. Jamieson looked slightly surprised. "I rather expected the car, but we got up all right."

"You didn't see him at all?" Louise demanded breathlessly.

Mr. Jamieson knew her at once, although he had not seen her before. She had kept to her rooms until the morning she left.

"No, Miss Armstrong," he said. "I saw nothing of him. What is wrong?"

"Then we shall have to find him," she asserted. "Every instant is precious. Mr. Jamieson, I have reason for believing that he is in danger, but I don't know what it is. Only—he must be found."

The stocky man had said nothing. Now, however, he went quickly toward the door.

"I'll catch the hack down the road and hold it," he said. "Is the gentleman down in the town?"

"Mr. Jamieson," Louise said impulsively, "I can use the hack. Take my horse and trap outside and drive like mad. Try to find the Dragon Fly—it ought to be easy to trace. I can think of no other way. Only, don't lose a moment."

The new detective had gone, and a moment later Jamieson went rapidly down the drive, the cob's feet striking fire at every step. Louise stood looking after them. When she turned around she faced Gertrude, who stood indignant, almost tragic, in the hall.

"You *know* what threatens Halsey, Louise," she said accusingly. "I believe you know this whole horrible thing, this mystery that we are struggling with. If anything happens to Halsey, I shall never forgive you."

Louise only raised her hands despairingly and dropped them again.

"He is as dear to me as he is to you," she said sadly. "I tried to warn him."

"Nonsense!" I said, as briskly as I could. "We are making a lot of trouble out of something perhaps very small. Halsey was probably late—he is always late. Any moment we may hear the car coming up the road."

But it did not come. After a half hour of suspense, Louise went out quietly and did not come back. I hardly knew she was gone until I heard the station hack moving off. At eleven o'clock the telephone rang. It was Mr. Jamieson.

"I have found the Dragon Fly, Miss Innes," he said. "It has collided with a freight car on the siding above the station. No, Mr. Innes was not there, but we shall probably find him. Send Warner for the car."

But they did not find him. At four o'clock the next morning we were still waiting for news, while Alex watched the house and Sam the grounds. At daylight I dropped into exhausted sleep. Halsey had not come back, and there was no word from the detective.

Chapter XXVI

Halsey's Disappearance

NOTHING that had gone before had been as bad as this. The murder and Thomas' sudden death we had been able to view in a detached sort of way. But with Halsey's disappearance everything was altered. Our little circle, intact until now, was broken. We were no longer onlookers who saw a battle passing around them. We were the center of action. Of course, there was no time then to voice such an idea. My mind seemed able to hold only one thought: that Halsey had been foully dealt with, and that every minute lost might be fatal.

Mr. Jamieson came back about eight o'clock the next morning: he was covered with mud, and his hat was gone. Altogether, we were a sad-looking trio that gathered around a breakfast that no one could eat. Over a cup of black coffee the detective told us what he had learned of Halsey's movements the night before. Up to a certain point the car had made it easy enough to follow him. And I gathered that Mr. Burns, the other detective, had followed a similar car for miles at dawn, only to find it was a touring car on an endurance run.

"He left here about ten minutes after eight," Mr. Jamieson said. "He went alone, and at eight twenty he stopped at Dr. Walker's. I went to the doctor's about midnight, but he had been called out on a case and had not come back at four o'clock. From the doctor's it seems Mr. Innes walked across the lawn to the cottage Mrs. Armstrong and her daughter have taken. Mrs. Armstrong had retired, and he said perhaps a dozen words to Miss Louise. She will not say what they were, but the girl evidently suspects what has occurred. That is, she suspects foul play, but she doesn't know of what nature. Then, apparently, he started directly for the station. He was going very fast—the flagman at the Carol Street crossing says he saw the car pass. He knew the siren. Along somewhere in the dark stretch between Carol Street and the depot he evidently swerved suddenly—perhaps someone in the road—and went full into the side of a freight. We found it there last night."

"He might have been thrown under the train by the force of the shock," I said tremulously.

Gertrude shuddered.

"We examined every inch of track. There was—no sign."

"But surely—he can't be—gone!" I cried. "Aren't there traces in the mud—anything?"

"There is no mud—only dust. There has been no rain. And the foot-path there is of cinders. Miss Innes, I am inclined to think that he has met with bad treatment, in the light of what has gone before. I do not think he has been murdered." I shrank from the word. "Burns is back in the country, on a clue we got from the night clerk at the drugstore.

There will be two more men here by noon, and the city office is on the lookout."

"The creek?" Gertrude asked.

"The creek is shallow now. If it were swollen with rain, it would be different. There is hardly any water in it. Now, Miss Innes," he said, turning to me, "I must ask you some questions. Had Mr. Halsey any possible reason for going away like this, without warning?"

"None whatever."

"He went away once before," he persisted. "And you were as sure then."

"He did not leave the Dragon Fly jammed into the side of a freight car before."

"No, but he left it for repairs in a blacksmith shop, a long distance from here. Do you know if he had any enemies? Anyone who might wish him out of the way?"

"Not that I know of, unless—no, I cannot think of any."

"Was he in the habit of carrying money?"

"He never carried it far. No, he never had more than enough for current expenses."

Mr. Jamieson got up then and began to pace the room. It was an unwonted concession to the occasion.

"Then I think we get at it by elimination. The chances are against flight. If he was hurt, we find no trace of him. It looks almost like an abduction. This young Dr. Walker—have you any idea why Mr. Innes should have gone there last night?"

"I cannot understand it," Gertrude said thoughtfully. "I don't think he knew Dr. Walker at all, and—their relations could hardly have been cordial, under the circumstances."

Jamieson pricked up his ears, and little by little he drew from us the unfortunate story of Halsey's love affair, and the fact that Louise was going to marry Dr. Walker.

Mr. Jamieson listened attentively.

"There are some interesting developments here," he said thoughtfully. "The woman who claims to be the mother of Lucien Wallace has not come back. Your nephew has apparently been spirited away. There is an organized attempt being made to enter this house; in fact, it has been entered. Witness the incident with the cook yesterday. And I have a new piece of information." He looked carefully away from Gertrude. "Mr. John Bailey is not at his Knickerbocker apartments, and I don't know where he is. It's a hash, that's what it is. It's a Chinese puzzle. They won't fit together, unless—unless Mr. Bailey and your nephew have again—"

And once again Gertrude surprised me. "They are not together," she said hotly. "I—know where Mr. Bailey is, and my brother is not with him."

The detective turned and looked at her keenly.

"Miss Gertrude," he said, "if you and Miss Louise would only tell me everything you know and surmise about this business, I should be able to do a great many things. I believe I could find your brother, and I might be able to—well, to do some other things." But Gertrude's glance did not falter.

"Nothing that I know could help you to find Halsey," she said stubbornly. "I know absolutely as little of his disappearance as you do, and I can only say this: I do not trust Dr. Walker. I think he hated Halsey, and he would get rid of him if he could."

"Perhaps you are right. In fact, I had some such theory myself. But Dr. Walker went out late last night to a serious case in Summitville and is still there. Burns traced him there. We have made guarded inquiry at the Greenwood Club, and through the village. There is absolutely nothing to go on but this. On the embankment above the railroad, at the point where we found the machine, is a small house. An old woman and a daughter, who is very lame, live there. They say that they distinctly heard the shock when the Dragon Fly hit the car, and they went to the bottom of their garden and looked over. The automobile was there; they could see the lights, and they thought someone had been injured. It was very dark, but they could make out two figures, standing together. The women were curious, and leaving the fence, they went back and by a roundabout path down to the road. When they got there the car was still standing, the headlight broken and the bonnet crushed, but there was no one to be seen."

The detective went away immediately, and to Gertrude and me was left the woman's part, to watch and wait. By luncheon nothing had been found, and I was frantic. I went upstairs to Halsey's room finally, from sheer inability to sit across from Gertrude any longer, and meet her terror-filled eyes.

Liddy was in my dressing room, suspiciously red-eyed, and trying to put a right sleeve in a left armhole of a new waist for me. I was too much shaken to scold.

"What name did that woman in the kitchen give?" she demanded, viciously ripping out the offending sleeve.

"Bliss. Mattie Bliss," I replied.

"Bliss. M. B. Well, that's not what she has on her suitcase. It is marked N.F.C."

The new cook and her initials troubled me not at all. I put on my bonnet and sent for what the Casanova liveryman called a "stylish turnout." Having once made up my mind to a course of action, I am not one to turn back. Warner drove me; he was plainly disgusted, and he steered the livery horse as he would the Dragon Fly, feeling uneasily with his left foot for the clutch and working his right elbow at an imaginary horn every time a dog got in the way.

Warner had something on his mind, and after we had turned into the road, he voiced it.

"Miss Innes," he said. "I overheard a part of a conversation yesterday that I didn't understand. It wasn't my business to understand it, for that matter. But I've been thinking all day that I'd better tell you. Yesterday afternoon, while you and Miss Gertrude were out driving, I had got the car in some sort of shape again after the fire, and I went to the library to call Mr. Innes to see it. I went into the living room, where Miss Liddy said he was, and halfway across to the library I heard him talking to someone. He seemed to be walking up and down, and he was in a rage, I can tell you."

"What did he say?"

"The first thing I heard was—excuse me, Miss Innes, but it's what he said, 'The damned rascal,' he said, 'I'll see him in'—well, in hell was what he said, 'in hell first.' Then somebody else spoke up; it was a woman. She said, 'I warned them, but they thought I would be afraid.'"

"A woman! Did you wait to see who it was?"

"I wasn't spying, Miss Innes," Warner said with dignity. "But the next thing caught my attention. She said, 'I knew there was something wrong from the start. A man isn't well one day and dead the next, without some reason.' I thought she was speaking of Thomas."

"And you don't know who it was!" I exclaimed. "Warner, you had the key to this whole occurrence in your hands and did not use it!"

However, there was nothing to be done. I resolved to make inquiry when I got home, and in the meantime, my present errand absorbed me. This was nothing less than to see Louise Armstrong, and to attempt to drag from her what she knew, or suspected, of Halsey's disappearance. But here, as in every, direction I turned, I was baffled.

A neat maid answered the bell, but she stood squarely in the doorway, and it was impossible to preserve one's dignity and pass her.

"Miss Armstrong is very ill and unable to see anyone," she said. I did not believe her.

"And Mrs. Armstrong—is she also ill?"

"She is with Miss Louise and cannot be disturbed."

"Tell her it is Miss Innes, and that it is a matter of the greatest importance."

"It would be of no use, Miss Innes. My orders are positive."

At that moment a heavy step sounded on the stairs. Past the maid's white-strapped shoulder I could see a familiar thatch of gray hair, and in a moment I was face to face with Dr. Stewart. He was very grave, and his customary geniality was tinged with restraint.

"You are the very woman I want to see," he said promptly. "Send away your trap, and let me drive you home. What is this about your nephew?"

"He has disappeared, doctor. Not only that, but there is every evidence that he has been either abducted, or—" I could not finish. The doctor helped me into his capacious buggy in silence. Until we had got a little distance he did not speak; then he turned and looked at me.

"Now tell me about it," he said. He heard me through without speaking.

"And you think Louise knows something?" he said when I had finished. "I don't—in fact, I am sure of it. The best evidence of it is this: she asked me if he had been heard from, or if anything had been learned. She won't allow Walker in the room, and she made me promise to see you and tell you this: don't give up the search for him. Find him, and find him soon. He is living."

"Well," I said, "if she knows that, she knows more. She is a very cruel and ungrateful girl."

"She is a very sick girl," he said gravely. "Neither you nor I can judge her until we know everything. Both she and her mother are ghosts of their former selves. Under all this, these two sudden deaths, this bank robbery, the invasions at Sunnyside and Halsey's disappearance, there is some mystery that, mark my words, will come out someday. And when it does, we shall find Louise Armstrong a victim."

I had not noticed where we were going, but now I saw we were beside the railroad, and from a knot of men standing beside the track I divined that it was here the car had been found. The siding, however, was empty. Except a few bits of splintered wood on the ground, there was no sign of the accident.

"Where is the freight car that was rammed?" the doctor asked a bystander.

"It was taken away at daylight, when the train was moved."

There was nothing to be gained. He pointed out the house on the embankment where the old lady and her daughter had heard the crash and seen two figures beside the car. Then we drove slowly home. I had the doctor put me down at the gate, and I walked to the house—past the lodge where we had found Louise, and, later, poor Thomas; up the drive where I had seen a man watching the lodge and where, later, Rosie had been frightened; past the east entrance, where so short a time before the most obstinate effort had been made to enter the house, and where, that night two weeks ago, Liddy and I had seen the strange woman. Not far from the west wing lay the blackened ruins of the stables. I felt like a ruin myself, as I paused on the broad veranda before I entered the house.

Two private detectives had arrived in my absence, and it was a relief to turn over to them the responsibility of the house and grounds. Mr. Jamieson, they said, had arranged for more to assist in the search for the missing man, and at that time the country was being scoured in all directions.

The household staff was again depleted that afternoon. Liddy was waiting to tell me that the new cook had gone, bag and baggage, without waiting to be paid. No one had admitted the visitor whom Warner had heard in the library, unless, possibly, the missing cook. Again I was working in a circle.

Chapter XXVII

Who Is Nina Carrington?

THE four days, from Saturday to the following Tuesday, we lived, or existed, in a state of the most dreadful suspense. We ate only when Liddy brought in a tray, and then very little. The papers, of course, had got hold of the story, and we were besieged by newspaper men. From all over the country false clues came pouring in and raised hopes that crumbled again to nothing. Every morgue within a hundred miles, every hospital, had been visited, without result.

Mr. Jamieson, personally, took charge of the organized search, and every evening, no matter where he happened to be, he called us by long distance telephone. It was the same formula. "Nothing today. A new clue to work on. Better luck tomorrow." And heartsick we would put up the receiver and sit down again to our vigil.

The inaction was deadly. Liddy cried all day, and because she knew I objected to tears, sniffled audibly around the corner.

"For Heaven's sake, smile!" I snapped at her. And her ghastly attempt at a grin, with her swollen nose and red eyes, made me hysterical. I laughed and cried together, and pretty soon, like the two old fools we were, we were sitting together weeping into the same handkerchief.

Things were happening, of course, all the time, but they made little or no impression. The Charity Hospital called up Dr. Stewart and reported that Mrs. Watson was in a critical condition. I understood also that legal steps were being taken to terminate my lease at Sunnyside. Louise was out of danger, but very ill, and a trained nurse guarded her like a gorgon. There was a rumor in the village, brought up by Liddy from the butcher's, that a wedding had already taken place between Louise and Dr. Walker, and this roused me for the first time to action.

On Tuesday, then, I sent for the car and prepared to go out. As I waited at the porte-cochere I saw the under-gardener, an inoffensive, grayish-haired man, trimming borders near the house. The day detective was watching him, sitting on the carriage block. When he saw me, he got up.

"Miss Innes," he said, taking off his hat, "do you know where Alex, the gardener, is?"

"Why, no. Isn't he here?" I asked.

"He has been gone since yesterday afternoon. Have you employed him long?"

"Only a couple of weeks."

"Is he efficient? A capable man?"

"I hardly know," I said vaguely. "The place looks all right, and I know very little about such things. I know much more about boxes of roses than bushes of them."

"This man," pointing to the assistant, "says Alex isn't a gardener. That he doesn't know anything about plants."

"That's very strange," I said, thinking hard. "Why, he came to me from the Brays, who are in Europe."

"Exactly." The detective smiled. "Every man who cuts grass isn't a gardener, Miss Innes, and just now it is our policy to believe every person around here a rascal until he proves to be the other thing."

Warner came up with the car then, and the conversation stopped. As he helped me in, however, the detective said something further.

"Not a word or sign to Alex, if he comes back," he said cautiously.

I went first to Dr. Walker's. I was tired of beating about the bush, and I felt that the key to Halsey's disappearance was here at Casanova, in spite of Mr. Jamieson's theories.

The doctor was in. He came at once to the door of his consulting room, and there was no mask of cordiality in his manner.

"Please come in," he said curtly.

"I shall stay here, I think, Doctor." I did not like his face or his manner; there was a subtle change in both. He had thrown off the air of friendliness, and I thought, too, that he looked anxious and haggard.

"Dr. Walker," I said, "I have come to you to ask some questions. I hope you will answer them. As you know, my nephew has not yet been found."

"So I understand," stiffly.

"I believe, if you would, you could help us, and that leads to one of my questions. Will you tell me what was the nature of the conversation you held with him the night he was attacked and carried off?"

"Attacked! Carried off?" he said, with pretended surprise. "Really,

Miss Innes, don't you think you exaggerate? I understand it is not the first time Mr. Innes has—disappeared."

"You are quibbling, Doctor. This is a matter of life and death. Will you answer my question?"

"Certainly. He said his nerves were bad, and I gave him a prescription for them. I am violating professional ethics when I tell you even as much as that."

I could not tell him he lied. I think I looked it. But I hazarded a random shot.

"I thought perhaps," I said, watching him narrowly, "that it might be about—Nina Carrington."

For a moment I thought he was going to strike me. He grew livid, and a small crooked blood vessel in his temple swelled and throbbed curiously. Then he forced a short laugh.

"Who is Nina Carrington?" he asked.

"I am about to discover that," I replied, and he was quiet at once. It was not difficult to divine that he feared Nina Carrington a good deal more than he did the devil. Our leave-taking was brief; in fact, we merely stared at each other over the waiting room table, with its litter of year-old magazines. Then I turned and went out.

"To Richfield," I told Warner, and on the way I thought, and thought hard.

Nina Carrington, Nina Carrington, the roar and rush of the wheels seemed to sing the words. *Nina Carrington, N.C.* And I then knew, knew as surely as if I had seen the whole thing. There had been an N.C. on the suitcase belonging to the woman with the pitted face. How simple it all seemed. Mattie Bliss had been Nina Carrington. It was she Warner had heard in the library. It was something she had told Halsey that had taken him frantically to Dr. Walker's office, and from there perhaps to his death. If we could find the woman, we might find what had become of Halsey.

We were almost at Richfield now, so I kept on. My mind was not on my errand there now. It was back with Halsey on that memorable night. What was it he had said to Louise, that had sent her up to Sunnyside, half wild with fear for him? I made up my mind, as the car drew up before the Tate cottage, that I would see Louise if I had to break into the house at night.

Almost exactly the same scene as before greeted my eyes at the cottage. Mrs. Tate, the baby carriage in the path, the children at the swing—all were the same.

She came forward to meet me, and I noticed that some of the anxious lines had gone out of her face. She looked young, almost pretty.

"I am glad you have come back," she said. "I think I will have to be honest and give you back your money."

"Why?" I asked. "Has the mother come?"

"No, but someone came and paid the boy's board for a month. She talked to him for a long time, but when I asked him afterward he didn't know her name."

"A young woman?"

"Not very young. About forty, I suppose. She was small and fairhaired, just a little bit gray, and very sad. She was in deep mourning, and, I think, when she came, she expected to go at once. But the child, Lucien, interested her. She talked to him for a long time, and, indeed, she looked much happier when she left."

"You are sure this was not the real mother?"

"O mercy, no! Why, she didn't know which of the three was Lucien. I thought perhaps she was a friend of yours, but, of course, I didn't ask."

"She was not—pockmarked?" I asked at a venture.

"No, indeed. A skin like a baby's. But perhaps you will know the initials. She gave Lucien a handkerchief and forgot it. It was very fine, blackbordered, and it had three handworked letters in the corner—F. B. A."

"No," I said with truth enough, "she is not a friend of mine." F. B. A. was Fanny Armstrong, without a chance of doubt!

With another warning to Mrs. Tate as to silence, we started back to Sunnyside. So Fanny Armstrong knew of Lucien Wallace and was sufficiently interested to visit him and pay for his support. Who was the child's mother and where was she? Who was Nina Carrington? Did either of them know where Halsey was or what had happened to him?

On the way home we passed the little cemetery where Thomas had been laid to rest. I wondered if Thomas could have helped us to find Halsey, had he lived. Farther along was the more imposing burial ground, where Arnold Armstrong and his father lay in the shadow of a tall granite shaft. Of the three, I think Thomas was the only one sincerely mourned.

Chapter XXVIII

A Tramp and the Toothache

⌒✆⌒

THE bitterness toward the dead president of the Traders' Bank seemed to grow with time. Never popular, his memory was execrated by people who had lost nothing, but who were filled with disgust by constantly hearing new stories of the man's grasping avarice. The Traders' had been a favorite bank for small tradespeople, and in its savings department it had solicited the smallest deposits. People who had thought to be self-supporting to the last found themselves confronting the poorhouse, their two- or three-hundred-dollar savings wiped away. All bank failures have this element, however, and the directors were trying to promise twenty percent on deposits.

But, like everything else those days, the bank failure was almost forgotten by Gertrude and myself. We did not mention Jack Bailey: I had found nothing to change my impression of his guilt, and Gertrude knew how I felt. As for the murder of the bank president's son, I was of two minds. One day I thought Gertrude knew or at least suspected that Jack had done it; the next I feared that it had been Gertrude herself, that night alone on the circular staircase. And then the mother of Lucien Wallace would obtrude herself, and an almost equally good case might be made against her. There were times, of course, when I was disposed to throw all those suspicions aside and fix definitely on the unknown, whoever that might be.

I had my greatest disappointment when it came to tracing Nina Carrington. The woman had gone without leaving a trace. Marked as she was, it should have been easy to follow her, but she was not to be found. A description to one of the detectives, on my arrival at home, had started the ball rolling. But by night she had not been found. I told Gertrude, then, about the telegram to Louise when she had been ill before; about my visit to Dr. Walker, and my suspicions that Mattie Bliss and Nina Carrington were the same. She thought, as I did, that there was little doubt of it.

I said nothing to her, however, of the detective's suspicions about Alex. Little things that I had not noticed at the time now came back to me. I had an uncomfortable feeling that perhaps Alex was a spy, and that by taking him into the house I had played into the enemy's hand. But at eight o'clock that night Alex himself appeared, and with him a strange and repulsive individual. They made a queer pair, for Alex was almost as disreputable as the tramp, and he had a badly swollen eye.

Gertrude had been sitting listlessly waiting for the evening message from Mr. Jamieson, but when the singular pair came in, as they did, without ceremony, she jumped up and stood staring. Winters, the detective who watched the house at night, followed them and kept his eyes sharply on Alex's prisoner. For that was the situation as it developed.

He was a tall lanky individual, ragged and dirty, and just now he looked both terrified and embarrassed. Alex was too much engrossed to be either, and to this day I don't think I ever asked him why he went off without permission the day before.

"Miss Innes," Alex began abruptly, "this man can tell us something very important about the disappearance of Mr. Innes. I found him trying to sell this watch."

He took a watch from his pocket and put it on the table. It was Halsey's watch. I had given it to him on his twenty-first birthday: I was dumb with apprehension.

"He says he had a pair of cuff links also, but he sold them—"

"Fer a dollar'n half," put in the disreputable individual hoarsely, with an eye on the detective.

"He is not—dead?" I implored. The tramp cleared his throat.

"No'm," he said huskily. "He was used up pretty bad, but he weren't dead. He was comin' to hisself when I"—he stopped and looked at the detective. "I didn't steal it, Mr. Winters," he whined. "I found it in the road, honest to God, I did."

Mr. Winters paid no attention to him. He was watching Alex.

"I'd better tell what he told me," Alex broke in. "It will be quicker. When Jamieson—when Mr. Jamieson calls up we can start him right. Mr. Winters, I found this man trying to sell that watch on Fifth Street. He offered it to me for three dollars."

"How did you know the watch?" Winters snapped at him.

"I had seen it before, many times. I used it at night when I was watching at the foot of the staircase." The detective was satisfied. "When he offered the watch to me, I knew it, and I pretended I was going to buy it. We went into an alley and I got the watch." The tramp shivered. It was plain how Alex had secured the watch. "Then—I got the story from this fellow. He claims to have seen the whole affair. He says he was in an empty car—in the car the automobile struck."

The tramp broke in here, and told his story, with frequent interpretations by Alex and Mr. Winters. He used a strange medley, in which familiar words took unfamiliar meanings, but it was gradually made clear to us.

On the night in question the tramp had been "pounding his ear"—this stuck to me as being graphic—in an empty boxcar along the siding at Casanova. The train was going west and due to leave at dawn. The tramp and the "brakey" were friendly, and things going well. About ten o'clock, perhaps earlier, a terrific crash against the side of the car roused him. He tried to open the door, but could not move it. He got out of the other side, and just as he did so, he heard someone groan.

The habits of a lifetime made him cautious. He slipped onto the bumper of a car and peered through. An automobile had struck the car, and stood there on two wheels. The taillights were burning, but the headlights were out. Two men were stooping over someone who lay on the ground. Then the taller of the two started on a dogtrot along the train looking for an empty. He found one four cars away and ran back again. The two lifted the unconscious man into the empty boxcar, and, getting in themselves, stayed for three or four minutes. When they came out, after closing the sliding door, they cut up over the railroad embankment toward the town. One, the short one, seemed to limp.

The tramp was wary. He waited for ten minutes or so. Some women came down a path to the road and inspected the automobile. When they had gone, he crawled into the boxcar and closed the door again. Then he lighted a match. The figure of a man, unconscious, gagged, and with his hands tied, lay far at the end. The tramp lost no time; he went through his pockets, found a little money and the cuff links, and took them. Then he loosened the gag—it had been cruelly tight—and went his way, again closing the door of the boxcar. Outside on the road he found the watch. He got on the fast freight east, sometime after, and rode into the city. He had sold the cuff links, but on offering the watch to Alex he had been "copped."

The story, with its cold recital of villainy, was done. I hardly knew if I were more anxious, or less. That it was Halsey, there could be no doubt. How badly he was hurt, how far he had been carried, were the questions that demanded immediate answer. But it was the first real information we had had; my boy had not been murdered outright. But instead of vague terrors there was now the real fear that he might be lying in some strange hospital receiving the casual attention commonly given to the charity cases. Even this, had we known it, would have been paradise to the terrible truth. I wake yet and feel myself cold and trembling with the horror of Halsey's situation for three days after his disappearance.

Mr. Winters and Alex disposed of the tramp with a warning. It was evident he had told us all he knew. We had occasion, within a day or two, to be doubly thankful that we had given him his freedom. When Mr. Jamieson telephoned that night we had news for him; he told me what I had not realized before—that it would not be possible to find Halsey at once, even with this clue. The cars by this time, three days, might be scattered over the Union. But he said to keep on hoping, that it was the best news we had had. And in the meantime, consumed with anxiety as we were, things were happening at the house in rapid succession.

We had one peaceful day—then Liddy took sick in the night. I went in when I heard her groaning, and found her with a hot-water bottle to her face, and her right cheek swollen until it was glassy.

"Toothache?" I asked, not too gently. "You deserve it. A woman of your age, who would rather go around with an exposed nerve in her head than have the tooth pulled! It would be over in a moment."

"So would hanging," Liddy protested, from behind the hot-water bottle.

I was hunting around for cotton and laudanum.

"You have a tooth just like it yourself, Miss Rachel," she whimpered. "And I'm sure Dr. Boyle's been trying to take it out for years."

There was no laudanum, and Liddy made a terrible fuss when I proposed carbolic acid, just because I had put too much on the cotton once and burned her mouth. I'm sure it never did her any permanent harm; indeed, the doctor said afterward that living on liquid diet had been a splendid rest for her stomach. But she would have none of the acid, and she kept me awake groaning, so at last I got up and went to Gertrude's door. To my surprise, it was locked.

I went around by the hall and into her bedroom that way. The bed was turned down, and her dressing gown and nightdress lay ready in the little room next, but Gertrude was not there. She had not undressed.

I don't know what terrible thoughts came to me in the minute I stood there. Through the door I could hear Liddy grumbling, with a squeal now and then when the pain stabbed harder. Then, automatically, I got the laudanum and went back to her.

It was fully a half hour before Liddy's groans subsided. At intervals I went to the door into the hall and looked out, but I saw and heard nothing suspicious. Finally, when Liddy had dropped into a doze, I even ventured as far as the head of the circular staircase, but there floated up to me only the even breathing of Winters, the night detective, sleeping just inside the entry. And then, far off, I heard the rapping noise that had lured Louise down the staircase that other night, two weeks before. It was over my head, and very faint—three or four short muffled taps, a pause, and then again, stealthily repeated.

The sound of Mr. Winters' breathing was comforting; with the thought that there was help within call, something kept me from waking him. I did not move for a moment; ridiculous things Liddy had said about a ghost—I am not at all superstitious, except, perhaps, in the middle of the night, with everything dark—things like that came back to me. Almost beside me was the clothes chute. I could feel it, but I could see nothing. As I stood, listening intently, I heard a sound near me. It was vague, indefinite. Then it ceased; there was an uneasy movement and a grunt from the foot of the circular staircase, and silence again. I stood perfectly still, hardly daring to breathe.

Then I knew I had been right. Someone was stealthily passing the head of the staircase and coming toward me in the dark. I leaned against the wall for support—my knees were giving way. The steps were close now, and suddenly I thought of Gertrude. Of course it was Gertrude. I put out one hand in front of me, but I touched nothing. My voice almost refused me, but I managed to gasp out, "Gertrude!"

"Good Lord!" a man's voice exclaimed, just beside me. And then I collapsed. I felt myself going, felt someone catch me, a horrible nausea—that was all I remembered.

When I came to it was dawn. I was lying on the bed in Louise's room, with the cherub on the ceiling staring down at me, and there was a blanket from my own bed thrown over me. I felt weak and dizzy, but I managed to get up and totter to the door. At the foot of the circular staircase Mr. Winters was still asleep. Hardly able to stand, I crept back to my room. The door into Gertrude's room was no longer locked: she was sleeping like a tired child. And in my dressing room Liddy hugged a cold hot-water bottle and mumbled in her sleep.

"There's some things you can't hold with handcuffs," she was muttering thickly.

Chapter XXIX

A Scrap of Paper

FOR the first time in twenty years, I kept my bed that day. Liddy was alarmed to the point of hysteria and sent for Dr. Stewart just after breakfast. Gertrude spent the morning with me, reading something— I forget what. I was too busy with my thoughts to listen. I had said nothing to the two detectives. If Mr. Jamieson had been there, I should have told him everything, but I could not go to these strange men and tell them my niece had been missing in the middle of the night; that she had not gone to bed at all; that while I was searching for her through the house, I had met a stranger who, when I fainted, had carried me into a room and left me there, to get better or not, as it might happen.

The whole situation was terrible: had the issues been less vital, it would have been absurd. Here we were, guarded day and night by private detectives, with an extra man to watch the grounds, and yet we might as well have lived in a Japanese paper house, for all the protection we had.

And there was something else: the man I had met in the darkness had been even more startled than I, and about his voice, when he muttered his muffled exclamation, there was something vaguely familiar. All that morning, while Gertrude read aloud, and Liddy watched for the doctor, I was puzzling over that voice, without result.

And there were other things, too. I wondered what Gertrude's absence from her room had to do with it all, or if it had any connection. I tried to think that she had heard the rapping noises before I did and gone to investigate, but I'm afraid I was a moral coward that day. I could not ask her.

Perhaps the diversion was good for me. It took my mind from Halsey, and the story we had heard the night before. The day, however, was a long vigil, with every ring of the telephone full of possibilities. Dr. Walker came up, sometime just after luncheon, and asked for me.

"Go down and see him," I instructed Gertrude. "Tell him I am out— for mercy's sake don't say I'm sick. Find out what he wants, and from this time on, instruct the servants that he is not to be admitted. I loathe that man."

Gertrude came back very soon, her face rather flushed.

"He came to ask us to get out," she said, picking up her book with a jerk. "He says Louise Armstrong wants to come here, now that she is recovering."

"And what did you say?"

"I said we were very sorry we could not leave, but we would be delighted to have Louise come up here with us. He looked daggers at me. And he wanted to know if we would recommend Eliza as a cook. He has brought a patient, a man, out from town, and is increasing his establishment—that's the way he put it."

"I wish him joy of Eliza," I said tartly. "Did he ask for Halsey?"

"Yes. I told him that we were on the track last night, and that it was only a question of time. He said he was glad, although he didn't appear to be, but he said not to be too sanguine."

"Do you know what I believe?" I asked. "I believe, as firmly as I believe anything, that Dr. Walker knows something about Halsey, and that he could put his finger on him, if he wanted to."

There were several things that day that bewildered me. About three o'clock Mr. Jamieson telephoned from the Casanova station and Warner went down to meet him. I got up and dressed hastily, and the detective was shown up to my sitting room.

"No news?" I asked, as he entered. He tried to look encouraging, without success. I noticed that he looked tired and dusty, and although he was ordinarily impeccable in his appearance, it was clear that he was at least two days from a razor.

"It won't be long now, Miss Innes," he said. "I have come out here on a peculiar errand, which I will tell you about later. First, I want to ask some questions. Did anyone come out here yesterday to repair the telephone and examine the wires on the roof?"

"Yes," I said promptly; "but it was not the telephone. He said the wiring might have caused the fire at the stable. I went up with him myself, but he only looked around."

Mr. Jamieson smiled.

"Good for you!" he applauded. "Don't allow anyone in the house that you don't trust, and don't trust anybody. All are not electricians who wear rubber gloves."

He refused to explain further, but he got a slip of paper out of his pocketbook and opened it carefully.

"Listen," he said. "You heard this before and scoffed. In the light of recent developments I want you to read it again. You are a clever woman, Miss Innes. Just as surely as I sit here, there is something in this house that is wanted very anxiously by a number of people. The lines are closing up, Miss Innes."

The paper was the one he had found among Arnold Armstrong's effects, and I read it again:

"—by altering the plans for—rooms, may be possible. The best way, in my opinion, would be to—the plan for—in one of the—rooms—chimney."

"I think I understand," I said slowly. "Someone is searching for the secret room, and the invaders—"

"And the holes in the plaster—"

"Have been in the progress of his—"

"Or her—investigations."

"Her?" I asked.

"Miss Innes," the detective said, getting up, "I believe that somewhere in the walls of this house is hidden some of the money, at least, from the Traders' Bank. I believe, just as surely, that young Walker brought home from California the knowledge of something of the sort, and failing in his effort to reinstall Mrs. Armstrong and her daughter here, he, or a confederate, has tried to break into the house. On two occasions I think he succeeded."

"On three, at least," I corrected. And then I told him about the night before. "I have been thinking hard," I concluded, "and I do not believe

the man at the head of the circular staircase was Dr. Walker. I don't
think he could have got in, and the voice was not his."

Mr. Jamieson got up and paced the floor, his hands behind him.

"There is something else that puzzles me," he said, stepping before
me. "Who and what is the woman Nina Carrington? If it was she who
came here as Mattie Bliss, what did she tell Halsey that sent him racing
to Dr. Walker's, and then to Miss Armstrong? If we could find that
woman we would have the whole thing."

"Mr. Jamieson, did you ever think that Paul Armstrong might not
have died a natural death?"

"That is the thing we are going to try to find out," he replied. And
then Gertrude came in, announcing a man below to see Mr. Jamieson.

"I want you present at this interview, Miss Innes," he said. "May
Riggs come up? He has left Dr. Walker and he has something he wants
to tell us."

Riggs came into the room diffidently, but Mr. Jamieson put him at his
ease. He kept a careful eye on me, however, and slid into a chair by the
door when he was asked to sit down.

"Now, Riggs," began Mr. Jamieson kindly. "You are to say what you
have to say before this lady."

"You promised you'd keep it quiet, Mr. Jamieson." Riggs plainly did
not trust me. There was nothing friendly in the glance he turned on me.

"Yes, yes. You will be protected. But, first of all, did you bring what
you promised?"

Riggs produced a roll of papers from under his coat, and handed them
over. Mr. Jamieson examined them with lively satisfaction and passed
them to me. "The blueprints of Sunnyside," he said. "What did I tell
you? Now, Riggs, we are ready."

"I'd never have come to you, Mr. Jamieson," he began, "if it hadn't
been for Miss Armstrong. When Mr. Innes was spirited away, like, and
Miss Louise got sick because of it, I thought things had gone far
enough. I'd done some things for the doctor before that wouldn't just
bear looking into, but I turned a bit squeamish."

"Did you help with that?" I asked, leaning forward.

"No, ma'am. I didn't even know of it until the next day, when it came
out in the Casanova *Weekly Ledger*. But I know who did it, all right. I'd
better start at the beginning.

"When Dr. Walker went away to California with the Armstrong family, there was talk in the town that when he came back he would be married to Miss Armstrong, and we all expected it. First thing I knew, I got a letter from him, in the West. He seemed to be excited, and he said Miss Armstrong had taken a sudden notion to go home and he sent me some money. I was to watch for her, to see if she went to Sunnyside, and wherever she was, not to lose sight of her until he got home. I traced her to the lodge, and I guess I scared you on the drive one night, Miss Innes."

"And Rosie!" I ejaculated.

Riggs grinned sheepishly.

"I only wanted to make sure Miss Louise was there. Rosie started to run, and I tried to stop her and tell her some sort of a story to account for my being there. But she wouldn't wait.

"And the broken china—in the basket?"

"Well, broken china's death to rubber tires," he said. "I hadn't any complaint against you people here, and the Dragon Fly was a good car."

So Rosie's highwayman was explained.

"Well, I telegraphed the doctor where Miss Louise was and I kept an eye on her. Just a day or so before they came home with the body, I got another letter, telling me to watch for a woman who had been pitted with smallpox. Her name was Carrington, and the doctor made things pretty strong. If I found any such woman loafing around, I was not to lose sight of her for a minute until the doctor got back.

"Well, I would have had my hands full, but the other woman didn't show up for a good while, and when she did the doctor was home."

"Riggs," I asked suddenly, "did you get into this house a day or two after I took it, at night?"

"I did not, Miss Innes. I have never been in the house before. Well, the Carrington woman didn't show up until the night Mr. Halsey disappeared. She came to the office late, and the doctor was out. She waited around, walking the floor and working herself into a passion. When the doctor didn't come back, she was in an awful way. She wanted me to hunt him, and when he didn't appear, she called him names; said he couldn't fool her. There was murder being done, and she would see him swing for it.

"She struck me as being an ugly customer, and when she left, about eleven o'clock, and went across to the Armstrong place, I was not far behind her. She walked all around the house first, looking up at the windows. Then she rang the bell, and the minute the door was opened she was through it, and into the hall."

"How long did she stay?"

"That's the queer part of it," Riggs said eagerly. "She didn't come out that night at all. I went to bed at daylight, and that was the last I heard of her until the next day, when I saw her on a truck at the station, covered with a sheet. She'd been struck by the express and you would hardly have known her—dead, of course. I think she stayed all night in the Armstrong house, and the agent said she was crossing the track to take the up-train to town when the express struck her."

"Another circle!" I exclaimed. "Then we are just where we started."

"Not so bad as that, Miss Innes," Riggs said eagerly. "Nina Carrington came from the town in California where Mr. Armstrong died. Why was the doctor so afraid of her? The Carrington woman knew something. I lived with Dr. Walker seven years, and I know him well. There are few things he is afraid of. I think he killed Mr. Armstrong out in the West somewhere, that's what I think. What else he did I don't know—but he dismissed me and pretty nearly throttled me—for telling Mr. Jamieson here about Mr. Innes' having been at his office the night he disappeared, and about my hearing them quarreling."

"What was it Warner overheard the woman say to Mr. Innes, in the library?" the detective asked me.

"She said 'I knew there was something wrong from the start. A man isn't well one day and dead the next without some reason.' "

How perfectly it all seemed to fit!

Chapter XXX
When Churchyards Yawn

⟨❧⟩

IT WAS on Wednesday Riggs told us the story of his connection with some incidents that had been previously unexplained. Halsey had been gone since the Friday night before, and with the passage of each day I felt that his chances were lessening. I knew well enough that he might be carried thousands of miles in the boxcar, locked in, perhaps, without water or food. I had read of cases where bodies had been found locked in cars on isolated sidings in the West, and my spirits went down with every hour.

His recovery was destined to be almost as sudden as his disappearance, and was due directly to the tramp Alex had brought to Sunnyside. It seems the man was grateful for his release, and when he learned something of Halsey's whereabouts from another member of his fraternity—for it is a fraternity—he was prompt in letting us know.

On Wednesday evening Mr. Jamieson, who had been down at the Armstrong house trying to see Louise—and failing—was met near the gate at Sunnyside by an individual precisely as repulsive and unkempt as the one Alex had captured. The man knew the detective, and he gave him a piece of dirty paper, on which was scrawled the words—"He's at City Hospital, Johnsville." The tramp who brought the paper pretended to know nothing, except this: the paper had been passed along from a "hobo" in Johnsville, who seemed to know the information would be valuable to us.

Again the long distance telephone came into requisition. Mr. Jamieson called the hospital, while we crowded around him. And when there was no longer any doubt that it was Halsey, and that he would probably recover, we all laughed and cried together. I am sure I kissed Liddy, and I have had terrible moments since when I seem to remember kissing Mr. Jamieson, too, in the excitement.

Anyhow, by eleven o'clock that night Gertrude was on her way to Johnsville, three hundred and eighty miles away, accompanied by Rosie. The domestic force was now down to Mary Anne and Liddy, with the under-gardener's wife coming every day to help out. Fortunately, Warner and the detectives were keeping bachelor hall in the lodge. Out of deference to Liddy they washed their dishes once a day, and they concocted queer messes, according to their several abilities. They had one triumph that they ate regularly for breakfast, and that clung to their clothes and their hair the rest of the day. It was bacon, hardtack and onions, fried together. They were almost pathetically grateful, however, I noticed, for an occasional broiled tenderloin.

It was not until Gertrude and Rosie had gone and Sunnyside had settled down for the night, with Winters at the foot of the staircase, that Mr. Jamieson broached a subject he had evidently planned before he came.

"Miss Innes," he said, stopping me as I was about to go to my room upstairs, "how are your nerves tonight?"

"I have none," I said happily. "With Halsey found, my troubles have gone."

"I mean," he persisted, "do you feel as though you could go through with something rather unusual?"

"The most unusual thing I can think of would be a peaceful night. But if anything is going to occur, don't dare to let me miss it."

"Something is going to occur," he said. "And you're the only woman I can think of that I can take along." He looked at his watch. "Don't ask me any questions, Miss Innes. Put on heavy shoes, and some old dark clothes, and make up your mind not to be surprised at anything."

Liddy was sleeping the sleep of the just when I went upstairs, and I hunted out my things cautiously. The detective was waiting in the hall, and I was astonished to see Dr. Stewart with him. They were talking confidentially together, but when I came down they ceased. There were a few preparations to be made: the locks to be gone over, Winters to be instructed as to renewed vigilance, and then, after extinguishing the hall light, we crept, in the darkness, through the front door, and into the night.

I asked no questions. I felt that they were doing me honor in making me one of the party, and I would show them I could be as silent as they. We went across the fields, passing through the woods that reached almost to the ruins of the stable, going over stiles now and then, and sometimes stepping over low fences. Once only somebody spoke, and then it was an emphatic bit of profanity from Dr. Stewart when he ran into a wire fence.

We were joined at the end of five minutes by another man, who fell into step with the doctor silently. He carried something over his shoulder which I could not make out. In this way we walked for perhaps twenty minutes. I had lost all sense of direction: I merely stumbled along in silence, allowing Mr. Jamieson to guide me this way or that as the path demanded. I hardly know what I expected. Once, when through a miscalculation I jumped a little short over a ditch and landed above my shoe tops in the water and ooze, I remember wondering if this were really I, and if I had ever tasted life until that summer. I walked along with the water sloshing in my boots, and I was actually cheerful.

I remember whispering to Mr. Jamieson that I had never seen the stars so lovely, and that it was a mistake, when the Lord had made the night so beautiful, to sleep through it!

The doctor was puffing somewhat when we finally came to a halt. I confess that just at that minute even Sunnyside seemed a cheerful spot. We had paused at the edge of a level cleared place, bordered all around with primly trimmed evergreen trees. Between them I caught a glimpse of starlight shining down on rows of white headstones and an occasional more imposing monument, or towering shaft. In spite of myself, I drew my breath in sharply. We were on the edge of the Casanova churchyard.

I saw now both the man who had joined the party and the implements he carried. It was Alex, armed with two long-handled spades. After the first shock of surprise, I flatter myself I was both cool and quiet. We went in single file between the rows of headstones, and although, when I found myself last, I had an instinctive desire to keep looking back over my shoulder, I found that, the first uneasiness past, a cemetery at night is much the same as any other country place, filled with vague shadows and unexpected noises. Once, indeed—but Mr. Jamieson said it was an owl, and I tried to believe him.

In the shadow of the Armstrong granite shaft we stopped. I think the doctor wanted to send me back.

"It's no place for a woman," I heard him protesting angrily. But the detective said something about witnesses, and the doctor only came over and felt my pulse.

"Anyhow, I don't believe you're any worse off here than you would be in that nightmare of a house," he said finally, and put his coat on the steps of the shaft for me to sit on.

There is an air of finality about a grave: one watches the earth thrown in, with the feeling that this is the end. Whatever has gone before, whatever is to come in eternity, that particular temple of the soul has been given back to the elements from which it came. Thus, there is a sense of desecration, of a reversal of the everlasting fitness of things, in resurrecting a body from its mother clay. And yet that night, in the Casanova churchyard, I sat quietly by, and watched Alex and Mr. Jamieson steaming over their work, without a single qualm, except the fear of detection.

The doctor kept a keen lookout, but no one appeared. Once in a while he came over to me and gave me a reassuring pat on the shoulder.

"I never expected to come to this," he said once. "There's one thing sure—I'll not be suspected of complicity. A doctor is generally supposed to be handier at burying folks than at digging them up."

The uncanny moment came when Alex and Jamieson tossed the spades on the grass, and I confess I hid my face. There was a period of stress, I think, while the heavy coffin was being raised. I felt that my composure was going, and, for fear I would shriek, I tried to think of something else—what time Gertrude would reach Halsey—anything but the grisly reality that lay just beyond me on the grass.

And then I heard a low exclamation from the detective and I felt the pressure of the doctor's fingers on my arm.

"Now, Miss Innes," he said gently. "If you will come over—"

I held on to him frantically, and somehow I got there and looked down. The lid of the casket had been raised and a silver plate on it proved we had made no mistake. But the face that showed in the light of the lantern was a face I had never seen before. The man who lay before us was not Paul Armstrong!

Chapter XXXI

Between Two Fireplaces

∽

WHAT with the excitement of the discovery, the walk home under the stars in wet shoes and draggled skirts, and getting upstairs and undressed without rousing Liddy, I was completely used up. What to do with my boots was the greatest puzzle of all, there being no place in the house safe from Liddy, until I decided to slip upstairs the next morning and drop them into the hole the "ghost" had made in the trunk room wall.

I went asleep as soon as I reached this decision, and in my dreams I lived over again the events of the night. Again I saw the group around the silent figure on the grass, and again, as had happened at the grave, I heard Alex's voice, tense and triumphant:

"Then we've got them," he said. Only, in my dreams, he said it over and over until he seemed to shriek it in my ears.

I wakened early, in spite of my fatigue, and lay there thinking. Who was Alex? I no longer believed that he was a gardener. Who was the man whose body we had resurrected? And where was Paul Armstrong? Probably living safely in some extraditionless country on the fortune he had stolen. Did Louise and her mother know of the shameful and wicked deception? What had Thomas known, and Mrs. Watson? Who was Nina Carrington?

This last question, it seemed to me, was answered. In some way the woman had learned of the substitution and had tried to use her knowledge for blackmail. Nina Carrington's own story died with her, but, however it happened, it was clear that she had carried her knowledge to Halsey the afternoon Gertrude and I were looking for clues to the man I had shot on the east veranda. Halsey had been half crazed by what he heard; it was evident that Louise was marrying Dr. Walker to keep the shameful secret, for her mother's sake. Halsey, always reckless, had gone at once to Dr. Walker and denounced him. There had been a scene, and he left on his way to the station to meet and notify Mr. Jamieson of what he had learned. The doctor was active mentally and physically. Accompanied perhaps by Riggs, who had shown himself not overscrupulous until he quarreled with his employer, he had gone across to the railroad embankment, and by jumping in front of the car, had caused Halsey to swerve. The rest of the story we knew.

That was my reconstructed theory of that afternoon and evening: it was almost correct—not quite.

There was a telegram that morning from Gertrude.

HALSEY CONSCIOUS AND IMPROVING. PROBABLY HOME IN DAY OR SO.

—GERTRUDE

With Halsey found and improving in health, and with at last something to work on, I began that day, Thursday, with fresh courage. As Mr. Jamieson had said, the lines were closing up. That I was to be caught and almost finished in the closing was happily unknown to us all.

It was late when I got up. I lay in my bed, looking around the four walls of the room, and trying to imagine behind what one of them a secret chamber might lie. Certainly, in daylight, Sunnyside deserved its name: never was a house more cheery and open, less sinister in general appearance. There was not a corner apparently that was not open and aboveboard, and yet, somewhere behind its handsomely papered walls

I believed firmly that there lay a hidden room, with all the possibilities it would involve.

I made a mental note to have the house measured during the day, to discover any discrepancy between the outer and inner walls, and I tried to recall again the exact wording of the paper Jamieson had found.

The slip had said "chimney." It was the only clue, and a house as large as Sunnyside was full of them. There was an open fireplace in my dressing room, but none in the bedroom, and as I lay there, looking around, I thought of something that made me sit up suddenly. The trunk room, just over my head, had an open fireplace and a brick chimney, and yet, there was nothing of the kind in my room. I got out of bed and examined the opposite wall closely. There was apparently no flue, and I knew there was none in the hall just beneath. The house was heated by steam, as I have said before. In the living room was a huge open fireplace, but it was on the other side.

Why did the trunk room have both a radiator and an open fireplace? Architects were not usually erratic! It was not fifteen minutes before I was upstairs, armed with a tape measure in lieu of a foot rule, eager to justify Mr. Jamieson's opinion of my intelligence, and firmly resolved not to tell him of my suspicion until I had more than theory to go on. The hole in the trunk room wall still yawned there, between the chimney and the outer wall. I examined it again, with no new result. The space between the brick wall and the plaster-and-lath one, however, had a new significance. The hole showed only one side of the chimney, and I determined to investigate what lay in the space on the other side of the mantel.

I worked feverishly. Liddy had gone to the village to market, it being her firm belief that the store people sent short measure unless she watched the scales, and that, since the failure of the Traders' Bank, we must watch the corners; and I knew that what I wanted to do must be done before she came back. I had no tools, but after rummaging around I found a pair of garden scissors and a hatchet, and thus armed, I set to work. The plaster came out easily: the lathing was more obstinate. It gave under the blows, only to spring back into place again, and the necessity for caution made it doubly hard.

I had a blister on my palm when at last the hatchet went through and fell with what sounded like the report of a gun to my overstrained nerves. I sat on a trunk, waiting to hear Liddy fly up the stairs, with the household behind her, like the tail of a comet. But nothing happened, and with a growing feeling of uncanniness I set to work enlarging the opening.

The result was absolutely nil. When I could hold a lighted candle in the opening, I saw precisely what I had seen on the other side of the chimney—a space between the true wall and the false one, possibly seven feet long and about three feet wide. It was in no sense of the word a secret chamber, and it was evident it had not been disturbed since the house was built. It was a supreme disappointment.

It had been Mr. Jamieson's idea that the hidden room, if there was one, would be found somewhere near the circular staircase. In fact, I knew that he had once investigated the entire length of the clothes chute, hanging to a rope, with this in view. I was reluctantly about to concede that he had been right, when my eyes fell on the mantel and fireplace. The latter had evidently never been used: it was closed with a metal fire front, and only when the front refused to move, and investigation showed that it was not intended to be moved, did my spirits revive.

I hurried into the next room. Yes, sure enough, there was a similar mantel and fireplace there, similarly closed. In both rooms the chimney flue extended well out from the wall. I measured with the tape line, my hands trembling so that I could scarcely hold it. They extended two feet and a half into each room, which, with the three feet of space between the two partitions, made eight feet to be accounted for. Eight feet in one direction and almost seven in the other—what a chimney it was!

But I had only located the hidden room. I was not in it, and no amount of pressing on the carving of the wooden mantels, no search of the floors for loose boards, none of the customary methods availed at all. That there was a means of entrance, and probably a simple one, I could be certain. But what? What would I find if I did get in? Was the detective right, and were the bonds and money from the Traders' Bank there? Or was our whole theory wrong? Would not Paul Armstrong have taken his booty with him? If he had not, and if Dr. Walker was in the secret, he would have known how to enter the chimney room. Then—who had dug the other hole in the false partition?

Chapter XXXII

Anne Watson's Story

LIDDY discovered the fresh break in the trunk room wall while we were at luncheon, and ran shrieking down the stairs. She maintained that, as she entered, unseen hands had been digging at the plaster; that they had stopped when she went in, and she had felt a gust of cold damp air. In support of her story she carried in my wet and muddy boots, that I had unluckily forgotten to hide, and held them out to the detective and myself.

"What did I tell you?" she said dramatically. "Look at 'em. They're yours, Miss Rachel—and covered with mud and soaked to the tops. I tell you, you can scoff all you like; something has been wearing your shoes. As sure as you sit there, there's the smell of the graveyard on them. How do we know they weren't tramping through the Casanova churchyard last night, and sitting on the graves!"

Mr. Jamieson almost choked to death. "I wouldn't be at all surprised if they were doing that very thing, Liddy," he said, when he got his breath. "They certainly look like it."

I think the detective had a plan, on which he was working, and which was meant to be a coup. But things went so fast there was no time to carry it into effect. The first thing that occurred was a message from the Charity Hospital that Mrs. Watson was dying, and had asked for me. I did not care much about going. There is a sort of melancholy pleasure to be had out of a funeral, with its pomp and ceremony, but I shrank from a deathbed. However, Liddy got out the black things and the crape veil I keep for such occasions, and I went. I left Mr. Jamieson and the day detective going over every inch of the circular staircase, pounding, probing and measuring. I was inwardly elated to think of the surprise I was going to give them that night; as it turned out, I did surprise them almost into spasms.

I drove from the train to the Charity Hospital, and was at once taken to a ward. There, in a gray-walled room in a high iron bed, lay Mrs.

Watson. She was very weak, and she only opened her eyes and looked at me when I sat down beside her. I was conscience-stricken. We had been so engrossed that I had left this poor creature to die without even a word of sympathy.

The nurse gave her a stimulant, and in a little while she was able to talk. So broken and half coherent, however, was her story that I shall tell it in my own way. In an hour from the time I entered the Charity Hospital, I had heard a sad and pitiful narrative, and had seen a woman slip into the unconsciousness that is only a step from death.

Briefly, then, the housekeeper's story was this:

She was almost forty years old, and had been the sister-mother of a large family of children. One by one they had died and been buried beside their parents in a little town in the Middle West. There was only one sister left, the baby, Lucy. On her the older girl had lavished all the love of an impulsive and emotional nature. When Anne, the elder, was thirty-two and Lucy was nineteen, a young man had come to the town. He was going east, after spending the summer at a celebrated ranch in Wyoming—one of those places where wealthy men send worthless and dissipated sons, for a season of temperance, fresh air and hunting. The sisters, of course, knew nothing of this, and the young man's ardor rather carried them away. In a word, seven years before, Lucy Haswell had married a young man whose name was given as Aubrey Wallace.

Anne Haswell had married a carpenter in her native town, and was a widow. For three months everything went fairly well. Aubrey took his bride to Chicago, where they lived at a hotel. Perhaps the very unsophistication that had charmed him in Valley Mill jarred on him in the city. He had been far from a model husband, even for the three months, and when he disappeared Anne was almost thankful. It was different with the young wife, however. She drooped and fretted, and on the birth of her baby boy, she had died. Anne took the child and named him Lucien.

Anne had had no children of her own, and on Lucien she had lavished all her aborted maternal instinct. On one thing she was determined, however: that was that Aubrey Wallace should educate his boy. It was a part of her devotion to the child that she should be ambitious for him: he must have every opportunity. And so she came east. She drifted around, doing plain sewing and keeping a home somewhere always for the boy. Finally, however, she realized that her only training had been domestic, and she put the boy in an Episcopalian home, and secured the position of housekeeper to the Armstrongs. There she found Lucien's father, this time under his own name. It was Arnold Armstrong.

I gathered that there was no particular enmity at that time in Anne's mind. She told him of the boy, and threatened exposure if he did not provide for him. Indeed, for a time, he did so. Then he realized that Lucien was the ruling passion in this lonely woman's life. He found out where the child was hidden, and threatened to take him away. Anne was frantic. The positions became reversed. Where Arnold had given money for Lucien's support, as the years went on he forced money from Anne Watson instead until she was always penniless. The lower Arnold sank in the scale, the heavier his demands became. With the rupture between him and his family, things were worse. Anne took the child from the home and hid him in a farmhouse near Casanova, on the Claysburg road. There she went sometimes to see the boy, and there he had taken fever. The people were Germans, and he called the farmer's wife Grossmutter. He had grown into a beautiful boy, and he was all Anne had to live for.

The Armstrongs left for California, and Arnold's persecutions began anew. He was furious over the child's disappearance and she was afraid he would do her some hurt. She left the big house and went down to the lodge. When I had rented Sunnyside, however, she had thought the persecutions would stop. She had applied for the position of housekeeper, and secured it.

That had been on Saturday. That night Louise arrived unexpectedly. Thomas sent for Mrs. Watson and then went for Arnold Armstrong at the Greenwood Club. Anne had been fond of Louise—she reminded her of Lucy. She did not know what the trouble was, but Louise had been in a state of terrible excitement. Mrs. Watson tried to hide from Arnold, but he was ugly. He left the lodge and went up to the house about two thirty, was admitted at the east entrance and came out again very soon. Something had occurred, she didn't know what; but very soon Mr. Innes and another gentleman left, using the car.

Thomas and she had got Louise quiet, and a little before three, Mrs.

Watson started up to the house. Thomas had a key to the east entry and gave it to her.

On the way across the lawn she was confronted by Arnold, who for some reason was determined to get into the house. He had a golf stick in his hand, that he had picked up somewhere, and on her refusal he had struck her with it. One hand had been badly cut, and it was that, poisoning having set in, which was killing her. She broke away in a frenzy of rage and fear, and got into the house while Gertrude and Jack Bailey were at the front door. She went upstairs, hardly knowing what she was doing. Gertrude's door was open, and Halsey's revolver lay there on the bed. She picked it up and turning, ran partway down the circular staircase. She could hear Arnold fumbling at the lock outside. She slipped down quietly and opened the door: he was inside before she had got back to the stairs. It was quite dark, but she could see his white shirt bosom. From the fourth step she fired. As he fell, somebody in the billiard room screamed and ran. When the alarm was raised, she had had no time to get upstairs: she hid in the west wing until everyone was down on the lower floor. Then she slipped upstairs and threw the revolver out of an upper window, going down again in time to admit the men from the Greenwood Club.

If Thomas had suspected, he had never told. When she found the hand Arnold had injured was growing worse, she gave the address of Lucien at Richfield to the old man, and almost a hundred dollars. The money was for Lucien's board until she recovered. She had sent for me to ask me if I would try to interest the Armstrongs in the child. When she found herself growing worse, she had written to Mrs. Armstrong, telling her nothing but that Arnold's legitimate child was at Richfield, and imploring her to recognize him. She was dying: the boy was an Armstrong and entitled to his father's share of the estate. The papers were in her trunk at Sunnyside, with letters from the dead man that would prove what she said. She was going; she would not be judged by earthly laws; and somewhere else perhaps Lucy would plead for her. It was she who had crept down the circular staircase, drawn by a magnet, that night Mr. Jamieson had heard someone there. Pursued, she had fled madly, anywhere—through the first door she came to. She had fallen down the clothes chute and been saved by the basket beneath. I could have cried with relief; then it had not been Gertrude, after all!

That was the story. Sad and tragic though it was, the very telling of it seemed to relieve the dying woman. She did not know that Thomas was dead, and I did not tell her. I promised to look after little Lucien, and sat with her until the intervals of consciousness grew shorter and finally ceased altogether. She died that night.

Chapter XXXIII

At the Foot of the Stairs

∽

As I drove rapidly up to the house from Casanova Station in the hack, I saw the detective Burns loitering across the street from the Walker place. So Jamieson was putting the screws on—lightly now, but ready to give them a twist or two, I felt certain, very soon.

The house was quiet. Two steps of the circular staircase had been pried off, without result, and beyond a second message from Gertrude, that Halsey insisted on coming home and they would arrive that night, there was nothing new. Mr. Jamieson, having failed to locate the secret room, had gone to the village. I learned afterwards that he called at Dr. Walker's, under pretense of an attack of acute indigestion, and before he left, had inquired about the evening trains to the city. He said he had wasted a lot of time on the case, and a good bit of the mystery was in my imagination! The doctor was under the impression that the house was guarded day and night. Well, give a place a reputation like that, and you don't need a guard at all—thus Jamieson. And sure enough, late in the afternoon, the two private detectives, accompanied by Mr. Jamieson, walked down the main street of Casanova and took a city-bound train.

That they got off at the next station and walked back again to Sunnyside at dusk was not known at the time. Personally, I knew nothing of either move; I had other things to absorb me at that time.

Liddy brought me some tea while I rested after my trip, and on the tray was a small book from the Casanova library. It was called *The Unseen World* and had a cheerful cover on which a half-dozen sheeted figures linked hands around a headstone.

At this point in my story, Halsey always says, "Trust a woman to add two and two together, and make six." To which I retort that if two and two plus X make six, then to discover the unknown quantity is the simplest thing in the world. That a houseful of detectives missed it entirely was because they were busy trying to prove that two and two make four.

The depression due to my visit to the hospital left me at the prospect of seeing Halsey again that night. It was about five o'clock when Liddy left me for a nap before dinner, having put me into a gray silk dressing gown and a pair of slippers. I listened to her retreating footsteps, and as soon as she was safely below stairs, I went up to the trunk room. The place had not been disturbed, and I proceeded at once to try to discover the entrance to the hidden room. The openings on either side, as I have said, showed nothing but perhaps three feet of brick wall. There was no sign of an entrance—no levers, no hinges, to give a hint. Either the mantel or the roof, I decided, and after a half-hour at the mantel, productive of absolutely no result, I decided to try the roof.

I am not fond of a height. The few occasions on which I have climbed a stepladder have always left me dizzy and weak in the knees. The top of the Washington monument is as impossible to me as the elevation of the presidential chair. And yet—I climbed out onto the Sunnyside roof without a second's hesitation. Like a dog on a scent, like my bearskin progenitor, with his spear and his wild boar, to me now there was the lust of the chase, the frenzy of pursuit, the dust of battle. I got quite a little of the latter on me as I climbed from the unfinished ballroom out through a window to the roof of the east wing of the building, which was only two stories in height.

Once out there, access to the top of the main building was rendered easy—at least it looked easy—by a small vertical iron ladder, fastened to the wall outside of the ball room, and perhaps twelve feet high. The twelve feet looked short from below, but they were difficult to climb. I gathered my silk gown around me and succeeded finally in making the top of the ladder. Once there, however, I was completely out of breath. I sat down, my feet on the top rung, and put my hairpins in more securely, while the wind bellowed my dressing gown out like a sail. I had torn a great strip of the silk loose, and now I ruthlessly finished the destruction of my gown by jerking it free and tying it around my head.

From far below the smallest sounds came up with peculiar distinctness. I could hear the paperboy whistling down the drive, and I heard something else. I heard the thud of a stone, and a spit, followed by a long and startled *meiou* from Beulah. I forgot my fear of a height, and advanced boldly almost to the edge of the roof.

It was half-past six by that time, and growing dusk.

"You boy, down there!" I called.

The paperboy turned and looked around. Then, seeing nobody, he raised his eyes. It was a moment before he located me: when he did, he stood for one moment as if paralyzed, then he gave a horrible yell, and dropping his papers, bolted across the lawn to the road without stopping to look around. Once he fell, and his impetus was so great that he turned an involuntary somersault. He was up and off again without any perceptible pause, and he leaped the hedge—which I am sure under ordinary stress would have been a feat for a man.

I am glad in this way to settle the Gray Lady story, which is still a choice morsel in Casanova. I believe the moral deduced by the village was that it is always unlucky to throw a stone at a black cat.

With Johnny Sweeny a cloud of dust down the road, and the dinner hour approaching, I hurried on with my investigations. Luckily, the roof was flat, and I was able to go over every inch of it. But the result was disappointing; no trap-door revealed itself, no glass window; nothing but a couple of pipes two inches across, and standing perhaps eighteen inches high and three feet apart, with a cap to prevent rain from entering and raised to permit the passage of air. I picked up a pebble from the roof and dropped it down, listening with my ear at one of the pipes. I could hear it strike on something with a sharp, metallic sound, but it was impossible for me to tell how far it had gone.

I gave up finally and went down the ladder again, getting in through the ballroom window without being observed. I went back at once to the trunk room, and sitting down on a box, I gave my mind, as consistently as I could, to the problem before me. If the pipes in the roof were ventilators to the secret room, and there was no trapdoor above, the entrance was probably in one of the two rooms between which it lay—unless, indeed, the room had been built, and the opening then closed with a brick and mortar wall.

The mantel fascinated me. Made of wood and carved, the more I looked the more I wondered that I had not noticed before the absurdity of such a mantel in such a place. It was covered with scrolls and panels, and finally, by the merest accident, I pushed one of the panels to the side. It moved easily, revealing a small brass knob.

It is not necessary to detail the fluctuations of hope and despair, and not a little fear of what lay beyond, with which I twisted and turned the knob. It moved, but nothing seemed to happen, and then I discovered the trouble. I pushed the knob vigorously to one side, and the whole mantel swung loose from the wall almost a foot, revealing a cavernous space beyond.

I took a long breath, closed the door from the trunk room into the hall—thank Heaven, I did not lock it—and pulling the mantel-door wide open, I stepped into the chimney room. I had time to get a hazy view of a small portable safe, a common wooden table and a chair— then the mantel door swung to and clicked behind me. I stood quite still for a moment, in the darkness, unable to comprehend what had happened. Then I turned and beat furiously at the door with my fists. It was closed and locked again, and my fingers in the darkness slid over a smooth wooden surface without a sign of a knob.

I was furiously angry—at myself, at the mantel door, at everything. I did not fear suffocation; before the thought had come to me I had already seen a gleam of light from the two small ventilating pipes in the roof. They supplied air, but nothing else. The room itself was shrouded in blackness.

I sat down in the stiff-backed chair and tried to remember how many days one could live without food and water. When that grew monotonous and rather painful, I got up and, according to the time-honored rule for people shut in unknown and ink-black prisons, I felt my way around—it was small enough, goodness knows. I felt nothing but a splintery surface of boards, and in endeavoring to get back to the chair, something struck me full in the face and fell with the noise of a thousand explosions to the ground. When I had gathered up my nerves again, I found it had been the bulb of a swinging electric light, and that had it not been for the accident, I might have starved to death in an illuminated sepulcher.

I must have dozed off. I am sure I did not faint. I was never more composed in my life. I remember planning, if I were not discovered, who would have my things. I knew Liddy would want my heliotrope poplin, and she's a fright in lavender. Once or twice I heard mice in the partitions, and so I sat on the table, with my feet on the chair. I imagined I could hear the search going on through the house, and once someone came into the trunk room; I could distinctly hear footsteps.

"In the chimney! In the chimney!" I called with all my might, and was rewarded by a piercing shriek from Liddy and the slam of the trunk room door.

I felt easier after that, although the room was oppressively hot and enervating. I had no doubt the search for me would now come in the right direction, and after a little, I dropped into a doze. How long I slept I do not know.

It must have been several hours, for I had been tired from a busy day, and I wakened stiff from my awkward position. I could not remember where I was for a few minutes, and my head felt heavy and congested. Gradually I roused to my surroundings, and to the fact that in spite of the ventilators, the air was bad and growing worse. I was breathing long, gasping respirations, and my face was damp and clammy. I must have been there a long time, and the searchers were probably hunting outside the house, dredging the creek, or beating the woodland. I knew that another hour or two would find me unconscious, and with my inability to cry out would go my only chance of rescue. It was the combination of bad air and heat, probably, for some inadequate ventilation was coming through the pipes. I tried to retain my consciousness by walking the length of the room and back, over and over, but I had not the strength to keep it up, so I sat down on the table again, my back against the wall.

The house was very still. Once my straining ears seemed to catch a footfall beneath me, possibly in my own room. I groped for the chair from the table and pounded with it frantically on the floor. But nothing happened: I realized bitterly that if the sound was heard at all, no doubt it was classed with the other rappings that had so alarmed us recently.

It was impossible to judge the flight of time. I measured five minutes by counting my pulse, allowing seventy-two beats to the minute. But it took eternities, and toward the last I found it hard to count; my head was confused.

And then—I heard sounds from below me, in the house. There was a peculiar throbbing, vibrating noise that I felt rather than heard, much like the pulsing beat of fire engines in the city. For one awful moment I thought the house was on fire, and every drop of blood in my body gathered around my heart; then I knew. It was the engine of the auto-mobile, and Halsey had come back. Hope sprang up afresh. Halsey's clear head and Gertrude's intuition might do what Liddy's hysteria and three detectives had failed in.

After a time I thought I had been right. There was certainly some-thing going on down below; doors were slamming, people were hurry-ing through the halls, and certain high notes of excited voices penetrated to me shrilly. I hoped they were coming closer, but after a time the sounds died away below, and I was left to the silence and heat, to the weight of the darkness, to the oppression of walls that seemed to close in on me and stifle me.

The first warning I had was a stealthy fumbling at the lock of the mantel-door. With my mouth open to scream, I stopped. Perhaps the situation had rendered me acute, perhaps it was instinctive. Whatever it was, I sat without moving, and someone outside, in absolute stillness, ran his fingers over the carving of the mantel and—found the panel.

Now the sounds below redoubled: from the clatter and jarring I knew that several people were running up the stairs, and as the sounds approached, I could even hear what they said.

"Watch the end staircases!" Jamieson was shouting. "Damnation— there's no light here!" And then a second later, "All together now. One— two—three—"

The door into the trunk room had been locked from the inside. At the second that it gave, opening against the wall with a crash and evidently tumbling somebody into the room, the stealthy fingers beyond the man-tel door gave the knob the proper impetus, and—the door swung open, and closed again. Only—and Liddy always screams and puts her fingers in her ears at this point—only now I was not alone in the chimney room. There was someone else in the darkness, someone who breathed hard, and who was so close I could have touched him with my hand.

I was in a paralysis of terror. Outside there were excited voices and incredulous oaths. The trunks were being jerked around in a frantic search, the windows were thrown open, only to show a sheer drop of forty feet. And the man in the room with me leaned against the mantel-door and listened. His pursuers were plainly baffled: I heard him draw a long breath and turn to grope his way through the blackness. Then— he touched my hand, cold, clammy, deathlike.

A hand in an empty room! He drew in his breath, the sharp intaking of horror that fills lungs suddenly collapsed. Beyond jerking his hand away instantly, he made no movement. I think absolute terror had him by the throat. Then he stepped back, without turning, retreating foot by foot from The Dread in the corner, and I do not think he breathed.

Then, with the relief of space between us, I screamed, earsplittingly, madly, and they heard me outside.

"In the chimney!" I shrieked. "Behind the mantel! The mantel!"

With an oath the figure hurled itself across the room at me, and I screamed again. In his blind fury he had missed me; I heard him strike the wall. That one time I eluded him; I was across the room, and I had got the chair. He stood for a second, listening, then—he made another rush, and I struck out with my weapon. I think it stunned him, for I had a second's respite when I could hear him breathing, and someone shouted outside:

"We—can't—get—in. How—does—it—open?"

But the man in the room had changed his tactics. I knew he was creeping on me, inch by inch, and I could not tell from where. And then—he caught me. He held his hand over my mouth, and I bit him. I was helpless, strangling—and someone was trying to break in the mantel from outside. It began to yield somewhere, for a thin wedge of yellowish light was reflected on the opposite wall. When he saw that, my assailant dropped me with a curse; then—the opposite wall swung open noiselessly, closed again without a sound, and I was alone. The intruder was gone.

"In the next room!" I called wildly. "The next room!" But the sound of blows on the mantel drowned my voice. By the time I had made them understand, a couple of minutes had elapsed. The pursuit was taken up then, by all except Alex, who was determined to liberate me. When I stepped out into the trunk room, a free woman again, I could hear the chase far below.

I must say, for all Alex's anxiety to set me free, he paid little enough attention to my plight. He jumped through the opening into the secret room and picked up the portable safe.

"I am going to put this in Mr. Halsey's room, Miss Innes," he said, "and I shall send one of the detectives to guard it."

I hardly heard him. I wanted to laugh and cry in the same breath—to crawl into bed and have a cup of tea, and scold Liddy, and do any of the thousand natural things that I had never expected to do again. And the air! The touch of the cool night air on my face!

As Alex and I reached the second floor, Mr. Jamieson met us. He was grave and quiet, and he nodded comprehendingly when he saw the safe.

"Will you come with me for a moment, Miss Innes?" he asked soberly, and on my assenting, he led the way to the east wing. There were lights moving around below, and some of the maids were standing gaping down. They screamed when they saw me and drew back to let me pass. There was a sort of hush over the scene; Alex, behind me, muttered something I could not hear and brushed past me without ceremony. Then I realized that a man was lying doubled up at the foot of the staircase, and that Alex was stooping over him.

As I came slowly down, Winters stepped back, and Alex straightened himself, looking at me across the body with impenetrable eyes. In his hand he held a shaggy gray wig, and before me on the floor lay the man whose headstone stood in Casanova churchyard—Paul Armstrong.

Winters told the story in a dozen words. In his headlong flight down the circular staircase, with Winters just behind, Paul Armstrong had pitched forward violently, struck his head against the door 'to the east veranda, and probably broken his neck. He had died as Winters reached him.

As the detective finished, I saw Halsey, pale and shaken, in the card-room doorway, and for the first time that night I lost my self-control. I put my arms around my boy, and for a moment he had to support me. A second later, over Halsey's shoulder, I saw something that turned my emotion into other channels, for, behind him, in the shadowy cardroom, were Gertrude and Alex, the gardener, and—there is no use mincing matters—he was kissing her!

I was unable to speak. Twice I opened my mouth: then I turned Halsey around and pointed. They were quite unconscious of us; her head was on his shoulder, his face against her hair. As it happened, it was Mr. Jamieson who broke up the tableau.

He stepped over to Alex and touched him on the arm.

"And now," he said quietly, "how long are you and I to play *our* little comedy, Mr. Bailey?"

Chapter XXXIV
The Odds and Ends

⌒⌘⌒

OF DR. Walker's sensational escape that night to South America, of the recovery of over a million dollars in cash and securities in the safe from the chimney room—the papers have kept the public well informed. Of my share in discovering the secret chamber they have been singularly silent. The inner history has never been told. Mr. Jamieson got all kinds of credit, and some of it he deserved, but if Jack Bailey, as Alex, had not traced Halsey and insisted on the disinterring of Paul Armstrong's casket, if he had not suspected the truth from the start, where would the detective have been?

When Halsey learned the truth, he insisted on going the next morning, weak as he was, to Louise, and by night she was at Sunnyside, under Gertrude's particular care, while her mother had gone to Barbara Fitzhugh's.

What Halsey said to Mrs. Armstrong I never knew, but that he was considerate and chivalrous I feel confident. It was Halsey's way always with women.

He and Louise had no conversation together until that night. Gertrude and Alex—I mean Jack—had gone for a walk, although it was nine o'clock, and anybody but a pair of young geese would have known that dew was falling, and that it is next to impossible to get rid of a summer cold.

At half after nine, growing weary of my own company, I went downstairs to find the young people. At the door of the living room I paused. Gertrude and Jack had returned and were there, sitting together on a divan, with only one lamp lighted. They did not see or hear me, and I beat a hasty retreat to the library. But here again I was driven back. Louise was sitting in a deep chair, looking the happiest I had ever seen her, with Halsey on the arm of the chair, holding her close.

It was no place for an elderly spinster. I retired to my upstairs sitting room and got out Eliza Klinefelter's lavender slippers. Ah, well, the foster motherhood would soon have to be put away in camphor again.

The next day, by degrees, I got the whole story.

Paul Armstrong had a besetting evil—the love of money. Common enough, but he loved money, not for what it would buy, but for its own sake. An examination of the books showed no irregularities in the past year since John had been cashier, but before that, in the time of Anderson, the old cashier, who had died, much strange juggling had been done with the records. The railroad in New Mexico had apparently drained the banker's private fortune, and he determined to retrieve it by one stroke. This was nothing less than the looting of the bank's securities, turning them into money, and making his escape.

But the law has long arms. Paul Armstrong evidently studied the situation carefully. Just as the only good Indian is a dead Indian, so the only safe defaulter is a dead defaulter. He decided to die, to all appearances, and when the hue and cry subsided, he would be able to enjoy his money almost anywhere he wished.

The first necessity was an accomplice. The connivance of Dr. Walker was suggested by his love for Louise. The man was unscrupulous, and with the girl as a bait, Paul Armstrong soon had him fast. The plan was apparently the acme of simplicity: a small town in the west, an attack of heart disease, a body from a medical college dissecting room shipped in a trunk to Dr. Walker by a colleague in San Francisco, and palmed off for the supposed dead banker. What was simpler?

The woman, Nina Carrington, was the cog that slipped. What she only suspected, what she really knew, we never learned. She was a chambermaid in the hotel at C—, and it was evidently her intention to blackmail Dr. Walker. His position at that time was uncomfortable: to pay the woman to keep quiet would be confession. He denied the whole thing, and she went to Halsey.

It was this that had taken Halsey to the doctor the night he disappeared. He accused the doctor of the deception, and, crossing the lawn, had said something cruel to Louise. Then, furious at her apparent connivance, he had started for the station. Dr. Walker and Paul Armstrong—the latter still lame where I had shot him—hurried across to the embankment, certain only of one thing. Halsey must not tell the detective what he suspected until the money had been removed from the chimney room. They stepped into the road in front of the car to stop it, and fate played into their hands. The car struck the train, and they had only to dispose of the unconscious figure in the road. This they did as I have told. For three days Halsey lay in the boxcar, tied hand and foot, suffering tortures of thirst, delirious at times, and discovered by a tramp at Johnsville only in time to save his life.

To go back to Paul Armstrong. At the last moment his plans had been frustrated. Sunnyside, with its hoard in the chimney room, had been rented without his knowledge! Attempts to dislodge me having failed, he was driven to breaking into his own house. The ladder in the chute, the burning of the stable and the entrance through the card-room window—all were in the course of a desperate attempt to get into the chimney room.

Louise and her mother had, from the first, been the great stumbling blocks. The plan had been to send Louise away until it was too late for her to interfere, but she came back to the hotel at C—just at the wrong time. There was a terrible scene. The girl was told that something of the kind was necessary, that the bank was about to close and her stepfather would either avoid arrest and disgrace in this way, or kill himself. Fanny Armstrong was a weakling, but Louise was more difficult to manage. She had no love for her stepfather, but her devotion to her mother was entire, self-sacrificing. Forced into acquiescence by her mother's appeals, overwhelmed by the situation, the girl consented and fled.

From somewhere in Colorado she sent an anonymous telegram to Jack Bailey at the Traders' Bank. Trapped as she was, she did not want to see an innocent man arrested. The telegram, received on Thursday, had sent the cashier to the bank that night in a frenzy.

Louise arrived at Sunnyside and found the house rented. Not knowing what to do, she sent for Arnold at the Greenwood Club and told him a little, not all. She told him that there was something wrong, and that the bank was about to close. That his father was responsible. Of the conspiracy she said nothing. To her surprise, Arnold already knew, through Bailey that night, that things were not right. Moreover, he suspected what Louise did not, that the money was hidden at Sunnyside. He had a scrap of paper that indicated a concealed room somewhere.

His inherited cupidity was aroused. Eager to get Halsey and Jack Bailey out of the house, he went up to the east entry, and in the billiard room gave the cashier what he had refused earlier in the evening—the address of Paul Armstrong in California and a telegram which had been forwarded to the club for Bailey, from Dr. Walker. It was in response to one Bailey had sent, and it said that Paul Armstrong was very ill.

Bailey was almost desperate. He decided to go west and find Paul Armstrong, and to force him to disgorge. But the catastrophe at the bank occurred sooner than he had expected. On the moment of starting west, at Andrews Station, where Mr. Jamieson had located the car, he read that the bank had closed, and, going back, surrendered himself.

John Bailey had known Paul Armstrong intimately. He did not believe that the money was gone; in fact, it was hardly possible in the interval since the securities had been taken. Where was it? And from some chance remark let fall some months earlier by Arnold Armstrong at a dinner, Bailey felt sure there was a hidden room at Sunnyside. He tried to see the architect of the building, but, like the contractor, if he knew of the room, he refused any information. It was Halsey's idea that John Bailey come to the house as a gardener, and pursue his investigations as he could. His smooth upper lip had been sufficient disguise, with his change of clothes, and a haircut by a country barber.

So it was Alex, Jack Bailey, who had been our ghost. Not only had he alarmed Louise—and himself, he admitted—on the circular staircase, but he had dug the hole in the trunk room wall, and later sent Eliza into hysteria. The note Liddy had found in Gertrude's scrap basket was from him, and it was he who had startled me into unconsciousness by the clothes chute, and, with Gertrude's help, had carried me to Louise's room. Gertrude, I learned, had watched all night beside me, in an extremity of anxiety about me.

That old Thomas had seen his master, and thought he had seen the Sunnyside ghost, there could be no doubt. Of that story of Thomas', about seeing Jack Bailey in the footpath between the club and Sunnyside, the night Liddy and I heard the noise on the circular staircase—that, too, was right. On the night before Arnold Armstrong was murdered, Jack Bailey had made an attempt to search for the secret room. He secured Arnold's keys from his room at the club and got into the house, armed with a golf-stick for sounding the walls. He ran against the hamper at the head of the stairs, caught his cuff link in it, and dropped the golf stick with a crash. He was glad enough to get away without an alarm being raised, and he took the "owl" train to town.

The oddest thing to me was that Mr. Jamieson had known for some time that Alex was Jack Bailey. But the face of the pseudo-gardener was very queer indeed, when that night, in the cardroom, the detective turned to him and said: "How long are you and I going to play our little comedy, Mr. Bailey?"

Well, it is all over now. Paul Armstrong rests in Casanova churchyard, and this time there is no mistake. I went to the funeral, because I wanted to be sure he was really buried, and I looked at the step of the shaft where I had sat that night, and wondered if it was all real. Sunnyside is for sale—no, I shall not buy it. Little Lucien Armstrong is living with his step-grandmother, and she is recovering gradually from troubles that had extended over the entire period of her second marriage. Anne Watson lies not far from the man she killed, and who as surely caused her death. Thomas, the fourth victim of the conspiracy, is buried on the hill. With Nina Carrington, five lives were sacrificed in the course of this grim conspiracy.

There will be two weddings before long, and Liddy has asked for my heliotrope poplin to wear to the church. I knew she would. She has wanted it for three years, and she was quite ugly the time I spilled coffee on it. We are very quiet, just the two of us. Liddy still clings to her ghost theory, and points to my wet and muddy boots in the trunk room as proof. I am gray, I admit, but I haven't felt as well in a dozen years. Sometimes, when I am bored, I ring for Liddy, and we talk things over. When Warner married Rosie, Liddy sniffed and said what I took for faithfulness in Rosie had been nothing but mawkishness. I have not yet outlived Liddy's contempt because I gave them silver knives and forks as a wedding gift.

So we sit and talk, and sometimes Liddy threatens to leave, and often I discharge her, but we stay together somehow. I am talking of renting a house next year, and Liddy says to be sure there is no ghost. To be perfectly frank, I never really lived until that summer. Time has passed since I began this story. My neighbors are packing up for another summer. Liddy is having the awnings put up, and the window boxes filled. Liddy or no Liddy, I shall advertise tomorrow for a house in the country, and I don't care if it has a Circular Staircase.

The Man in Lower Ten

Chapter I

I Go To Pittsburgh

⌒∞⌒

MCKNIGHT is gradually taking over the criminal end of the business. I never liked it, and since the strange case of the man in lower ten, I have been a bit squeamish. Given a case like that, where you can build up a network of clues that absolutely incriminate three entirely different people, only one of whom can be guilty, and your faith in circumstantial evidence dies of overcrowding. I never see a shivering, white-faced wretch in the prisoners' dock that I do not hark back with shuddering horror to the strange events on the Pullman car Ontario, between Washington and Pittsburgh, on the night of September ninth, last.

McKnight could tell the story a great deal better than I, although he cannot spell three consecutive words correctly. But while he has imagination and humor, he is lazy.

"It didn't happen to me, anyhow," he protested, when I put it up to him. "And nobody cares for secondhand thrills. Besides, you want the unvarnished and ungarnished truth, and I'm no hand for that. I'm a lawyer."

So am I, although there have been times when my assumption in that particular has been disputed. I am unmarried, and just old enough to dance with the grown-up little sisters of the girls I used to know. I am fond of outdoors, prefer horses to the aforesaid grown-up little sisters, am without sentiment (am crossed out and was substituted.-Ed.) and completely ruled and frequently routed by my housekeeper, an elderly widow.

In fact, of all the men of my acquaintance, I was probably the most prosaic, the least adventurous, the one man in a hundred who would be likely to go without a deviation from the normal through the orderly procession of the seasons, summer suits to winter flannels, golf to bridge.

So it was a queer freak of the demons of chance to perch on my unsusceptible thirty-year-old chest, tie me up with a crime, ticket me with a love affair, and start me on that sensational and not always respectable journey that ended so surprisingly less than three weeks later in the firm's private office. It had been the most remarkable period of my life. I would neither give it up nor live it again under any inducement, and yet all that I lost was some twenty yards off my drive!

It was really McKnight's turn to make the next journey. I had a tournament at Chevy Chase for Saturday, and a short yacht cruise planned for Sunday, and when a man has been grinding at statute law for a week, he needs relaxation. But McKnight begged off. It was not the first time he had shirked that summer in order to run down to Richmond, and I was surly about it. But this time he had a new excuse. "I wouldn't be able to look after the business if I did go," he said. He has a sort of wide-eyed frankness that makes one ashamed to doubt him. "I'm always carsick crossing the mountains. It's a fact, Lollie. Seesawing over the peaks does it. Why, crossing the Allegheny Mountains has the Gulf Stream to Bermuda beaten to a frazzle."

So I gave him up finally and went home to pack. He came later in the evening with his machine, the Cannonball, to take me to the station, and he brought the forged notes in the Bronson case.

"Guard them with your life," he warned me. "They are more precious than honor. Sew them in your chest protector, or wherever people keep valuables. I never keep any. I'll not be happy until I see Gentleman Andy doing the lockstep."

He sat down on my clean collars, found my cigarettes and struck a match on the mahogany bedpost with one movement.

"Where's the Pirate?" he demanded. The Pirate is my housekeeper, Mrs. Klopton, a very worthy woman, so labeled—and libeled—because of a ferocious pair of eyes and what McKnight called a bucaneering nose. I quietly closed the door into the hall.

"Keep your voice down, Richey," I said. "She is looking for the evening paper to see if it is going to rain. She has my raincoat and an umbrella waiting in the hall."

The collars being damaged beyond repair, he left them and went to the window. He stood there for some time, staring at the blackness that represented the wall of the house next door.

"It's raining now," he said over his shoulder, and closed the window and the shutters. Something in his voice made me glance up, but he was watching me, his hands idly in his pockets.

"Who lives next door?" he inquired in a perfunctory tone, after a pause. I was packing my razor.

"House is empty," I returned absently. "If the landlord would put it in some sort of shape—"

"Did you put those notes in your pocket?" he broke in.

"Yes." I was impatient. "Along with my certificates of registration, baptism and vaccination. Whoever wants them will have to steal my coat to get them."

"Well, I would move them if I were you. Somebody in the next house was confoundedly anxious to see where you put them. Somebody right at that window opposite."

I scoffed at the idea, but nevertheless I moved the papers, putting them in my traveling bag, well down at the bottom. McKnight watched me uneasily.

"I have a hunch that you are going to have trouble," he said, as I locked the alligator bag. "Darned if I like starting anything important on Friday."

"You have a congenital dislike to start anything on any old day," I retorted, still sore from my lost Saturday. "And if you knew the owner of that house as I do, you would know that if there was anyone at that window he is paying rent for the privilege."

Mrs. Klopton rapped at the door and spoke discreetly from the hall.

"Did Mr. McKnight bring the evening paper?" she inquired.

"Sorry, but I didn't, Mrs. Klopton," McKnight called. "The Cubs won, three to nothing." He listened, grinning, as she moved away with little irritated rustles of her black silk gown.

I finished my packing, changed my collar and was ready to go. Then very cautiously we put out the light and opened the shutters. The window across was merely a deeper black in the darkness. It was closed and dirty. And yet, probably owing to Richey's suggestion, I had an uneasy sensation of eyes staring across at me. The next moment we were at the door, poised for flight.

"We'll have to run for it," I said in a whisper. "She's down there with a package of some sort, sandwiches probably. And she's threatened me with overshoes for a month. Ready now!"

I had a kaleidoscopic view of Mrs. Klopton in the lower hall, holding out an armful of such traveling impedimenta as she deemed essential, while beside her, Euphemia, the colored housemaid, grinned over a white-wrapped box.

"Awfully sorry—no time—back Sunday," I panted over my shoulder. Then the door closed and the car was moving away.

McKnight bent forward and stared at the façade of the empty house next door as we passed. It was black, staring, mysterious, as empty buildings are apt to be.

"I'd like to hold a postmortem on that corpse of a house," he said thoughtfully. "By George, I've a notion to get out and take a look."

"Somebody after the brass pipes," I scoffed. "House has been empty for a year."

With one hand on the steering wheel McKnight held out the other for my cigarette case. "Perhaps," he said, "but I don't see what she would want with brass pipe."

"A woman!" I laughed outright. "You have been looking too hard at the picture in the back of your watch, that's all. There's an experiment like that: if you stare long enough—"

But McKnight was growing sulky: he sat looking rigidly ahead, and he did not speak again until he brought the Cannonball to a stop at the station. Even then it was only a perfunctory remark. He went through the gate with me, and with five minutes to spare, we lounged and smoked in the train shed. My mind had slid away from my surroundings and had wandered to a polo pony that I couldn't afford and intended to buy anyhow. Then McKnight shook off his taciturnity.

"For Heaven's sake, don't look so martyred," he burst out; "I know you've done all the traveling this summer. I know you're missing a game tomorrow. But don't be a patient mother; confound it, I have to go to Richmond on Sunday. I—I want to see a girl."

"Oh, don't mind me," I observed politely. "Personally, I wouldn't change places with you. What's her name—North? South?"

"West," he snapped. "Don't try to be funny. And all I have to say, Blakeley, is that if you ever fall in love, I hope you make an egregious ass of yourself."

In view of what followed, this came rather close to prophecy.

The trip west was without incident. I played bridge with a furniture dealer from Grand Rapids, a sales agent for a Pittsburgh iron firm and a young professor from an eastern college. I won three rubbers out of four, finished what cigarettes McKnight had left me, and went to bed at one o'clock. It was growing cooler, and the rain had ceased. Once, toward morning, I wakened with a start, for no apparent reason, and sat bolt upright. I had an uneasy feeling that someone had been looking at me, the same sensation I had experienced earlier in the evening at the window. But I could feel the bag with the notes, between me and the window, and with my arm thrown over it for security, I lapsed again into slumber. Later, when I tried to piece together the fragments of that journey, I remembered that my coat, which had been folded and placed beyond my restless tossing, had been rescued in the morning from a heterogeneous jumble of blankets, evening papers and cravat, had been shaken out with profanity and donned with wrath. At the time, nothing occurred to me but the necessity of writing to the Pullman Company and asking them if they ever traveled in their own cars. I even formulated some of the letter.

"If they are built to scale, why not take a man of ordinary stature as your unit?" I wrote mentally. "I cannot fold together like the traveling cup with which I drink your abominable water."

I was more cheerful after I had had a cup of coffee in the Union Station. It was too early to attend to business, and I lounged in the restaurant and hid behind the morning papers. As I had expected, they had got hold of my visit and its object. On the first page was a staring announcement that the forged papers in the Bronson case had been brought to Pittsburgh. Underneath, a telegram from Washington stated that Lawrence Blakeley, of Blakeley and McKnight, had left for Pittsburgh the night before, and that, owing to the approaching trial of the Bronson case and the illness of John Gilmore, the Pittsburgh millionaire, who was the chief witness for the prosecution, it was supposed that the visit was intimately concerned with the trial.

I looked around apprehensively. There were no reporters yet in sight, and thankful to have escaped notice, I paid for my breakfast and left. At the cab stand I chose the least dilapidated hansom I could find, and giving the driver the address of the Gilmore residence, in the East end, I got in.

I was just in time. As the cab turned and rolled off, a slim young man in a straw hat separated himself from a little group of men and hurried toward us.

"Hey! Wait a minute there!" he called, breaking into a trot.

But the cabby did not hear, or perhaps did not care to. We jogged comfortably along, to my relief, leaving the young man far behind. I avoid reporters on principle, having learned long ago that I am an easy mark for a clever interviewer.

It was perhaps nine o'clock when I left the station. Our way was along the boulevard which hugged the side of one of the city's great hills. Far below, to the left, lay the railroad tracks and the seventy times seven looming stacks of the mills. The white mist of the river, the grays and blacks of the smoke blended into a half-revealing haze, dotted here and there with fire. It was unlovely, tremendous. Whistler might have painted it with its pathos, its majesty, but he would have missed what made it infinitely suggestive—the rattle and roar of iron on iron, the rumble of wheels, the throbbing beat, against the ears, of fire and heat and brawn welding prosperity.

Something of this I voiced to the grim old millionaire who was responsible for at least part of it. He was propped up in bed in his East end home, listening to the market reports read by a nurse, and he smiled a little at my enthusiasm.

"I can't see much beauty in it myself," he said. "But it's our badge of prosperity. The full dinner pail here means a nose that looks like a flue. Pittsburgh without smoke wouldn't be Pittsburgh, any more than New York prohibition would be New York. Sit down for a few minutes, Mr. Blakeley. Now, Miss Gardner, Westinghouse Electric."

The nurse resumed her reading in a monotonous voice. She read literally and without understanding, using initials and abbreviations as they came. But the shrewd old man followed her easily. Once, however, he stopped her.

"D-o is ditto," he said gently, "not do."

As the nurse droned along, I found myself looking curiously at a photograph in a silver frame on the bedside table. It was the picture of a girl in white, with her hands clasped loosely before her. Against the dark background her figure stood out slim and young. Perhaps it was the rather grim environment, possibly it was my mood, but although as a general thing photographs of young girls make no appeal to me, this one did. I found my eyes straying back to it. By a little finesse I even made out the name written across the corner, "Alison."

Mr. Gilmore lay back among his pillows and listened to the nurse's listless voice. But he was watching me from under his heavy eyebrows, for when the reading was over, and we were alone, he indicated the picture with a gesture.

"I keep it there to remind myself that I am an old man," he said. "That is my granddaughter, Alison West."

I expressed the customary polite surprise, at which, finding me responsive, he told me his age with a chuckle of pride. More surprise, this time genuine. From that we went to what he ate for breakfast and did not eat for luncheon, and then to his reserve power, which at sixty-five becomes a matter for thought. And so, in a wide circle, back to where we started, the picture.

"Father was a rascal," John Gilmore said, picking up the frame. "The happiest day of my life was when I knew he was safely dead in bed and not hanged. If the child had looked like him, I—well, she doesn't. She's a Gilmore, every inch. Supposed to look like me."

"Very noticeably," I agreed soberly.

I had produced the notes by that time, and replacing the picture, Mr. Gilmore gathered his spectacles from beside it. He went over the four notes methodically, examining each carefully and putting it down before he picked up the next. Then he leaned back and took off his glasses.

"They're not so bad," he said thoughtfully. "Not so bad. But I never saw them before. That's my unofficial signature. I am inclined to think"—he was speaking partly to himself—"to think that he has got hold of a letter of mine, probably to Alison. Bronson was a friend of her rapscallion of a father."

I took Mr. Gilmore's deposition and put it into my traveling bag with
the forged notes. When I saw them again, almost three weeks later, they
were unrecognizable, a mass of charred paper on a copper ashtray. In the
interval other and bigger things had happened: the Bronson forgery case
had shrunk beside the greater and more imminent mystery of the man in
lower ten. And Alison West had come into the story and into my life.

Chapter II

A Torn Telegram

I LUNCHED alone at the Gilmore house, and went back to the city at
once. The sun had lifted the mists, and a fresh summer wind had
cleared away the smoke pall. The boulevard was full of cars flying countryward for the Saturday half-holiday, toward golf and tennis, green
fields and babbling girls. I gritted my teeth and thought of McKnight at
Richmond, visiting the lady with the geographical name. And then, for
the first time, I associated John Gilmore's granddaughter with the
"West" that McKnight had irritably flung at me.

I still carried my traveling bag, for McKnight's vision at the window
of the empty house had not been without effect. I did not transfer the
notes to my pocket, and, if I had, it would not have altered the situation
later. Only the other day McKnight put this very thing up to me.

"I warned you," he reminded me. "I told you there were queer things
coming, and to be on your guard. You ought to have taken your
revolver."

"It would have been of exactly as much use as a bucket of snow in
Africa," I retorted. "If I had never closed my eyes, or if I had kept my
finger on the trigger of a six-shooter (which is novelesque for revolver),
the result would have been the same. And the next time you want a
little excitement with every variety of thrill thrown in, I can put you
by way of it. You begin by getting the wrong berth in a Pullman car,
and end—"

"Oh, I know how it ends," he finished shortly. "Don't you suppose the
whole thing's written on my spinal marrow?"

But I am wandering again. That is the difficulty with the unprofessional storyteller: he yaws back and forth and can't keep in the wind; he drops his characters overboard when he hasn't any further use for them and drowns them; he forgets the coffeepot and the frying pan and all the other small essentials, and, if he carries a love affair, he mutters a fervent "Allah be praised" when he lands them, drenched with adventures, at the matrimonial dock at the end of the final chapter.

I put in a thoroughly unsatisfactory afternoon. Time dragged eternally. I dropped in at a summer vaudeville, and bought some ties at a haberdasher's. I was bored but unexpectant; I had no premonition of what was to come. Nothing unusual had ever happened to me; friends of mine had sometimes sailed the high seas of adventure or skirted the coasts of chance, but all of the shipwrecks had occurred after a woman passenger had been taken on. "Ergo," I had always said, "no women!" I repeated it to myself that evening almost savagely, when I found my thoughts straying back to the picture of John Gilmore's granddaughter. I even argued as I ate my solitary dinner at a downtown restaurant.

"Haven't you troubles enough," I reflected, "without looking for more? Hasn't Bad News gone lame, with a matinee race booked for next week? Otherwise aren't you comfortable? Isn't your house in order? Do you want to sell a pony in order to have the library done over in mission or the drawing room in gold? Do you want somebody to count the empty cigarette boxes lying around every morning?"

Lay it to the long idle afternoon, to the new environment, to anything you like, but I began to think that perhaps I did. I was confoundedly lonely. For the first time in my life its even course began to waver: the needle registered warning marks on the matrimonial seismograph, lines vague enough, but lines.

My alligator bag lay at my feet, still locked. While I waited for my coffee I leaned back and surveyed the people incuriously. There were the usual couples intent on each other: my new state of mind made me regard them with tolerance. But at the next table, where a man and woman dined together, a different atmosphere prevailed. My attention was first caught by the woman's face. She had been speaking earnestly across the table, her profile turned to me. I had noticed casually her earnest manner, her somber clothes, and the great mass of odd, bronze-colored hair on her neck. But suddenly she glanced toward me and the utter hopelessness—almost tragedy of her expression struck me with a shock. She half closed her eyes and drew a long breath, then she turned again to the man across the table.

Neither one was eating. He sat low in his chair, his chin on his chest, ugly folds of thick flesh protruding over his collar. He was probably fifty, bald, grotesque, sullen, and yet not without a suggestion of power. But he had been drinking; as I looked, he raised an unsteady hand and summoned a waiter with a wine list.

The young woman bent across the table and spoke again quickly. She had unconsciously raised her voice. Not beautiful, in her earnestness and stress she rather interested me. I had an idle inclination to advise the waiter to remove the bottled temptation from the table. I wonder what would have happened if I had? Suppose Harrington had not been intoxicated when he entered the Pullman car Ontario that night!

For they were about to make a journey, I gathered, and the young woman wished to go alone. I drank three cups of coffee, which accounted for my wakefulness later, and shamelessly watched the tableau before me. The woman's protest evidently went for nothing: across the table the man grunted monosyllabic replies and grew more and more lowering and sullen. Once, during a brief unexpected pianis-simo in the music, her voice came to me sharply.

"If I could only see him in time!" she was saying. "Oh, it's terrible!"

In spite of my interest I would have forgotten the whole incident at once, erased it from my mind as one does the inessentials and clutter-ings of memory, had I not met them again, later that evening, in the Pennsylvania station. The situation between them had not visibly altered: the same dogged determination showed in the man's face, but the young woman—daughter or wife? I wondered—had drawn down her veil and I could only suspect what white misery lay beneath.

I bought my berth after waiting in a line of some eight or ten people. When, step by step, I had almost reached the window, a tall woman whom I had not noticed before spoke to me from my elbow. She had a ticket and money in her hand.

"Will you try to get me a lower when you buy yours?" she asked. "I have traveled for three nights in uppers."

I consented, of course; beyond that I hardly noticed the woman. I had a vague impression of height and a certain amount of stateliness, but the crowd was pushing behind me, and someone was standing on my foot. I got two lowers easily, and, turning with the change and berths, held out the tickets.

"Which will you have?" I asked. "Lower eleven or lower ten?"

"It makes no difference," she said. "Thank you very much indeed."

At random I gave her lower eleven, and called a porter to help her with her luggage. I followed them leisurely to the train shed, and ten minutes more saw us under way.

I looked into my car, but it presented the peculiarly unattractive appearance common to sleepers. The berths were made up; the center aisle was a path between walls of dingy, breeze-repelling curtains, while the two seats at each end of the car were piled high with suitcases and umbrellas. The perspiring porter was trying to be six places at once: somebody has said that Pullman porters are black so they won't show the dirt, but they certainly show the heat.

Nine-fifteen was an outrageous hour to go to bed, especially since I sleep little or not at all on the train, so I made my way to the smoker and passed the time until nearly eleven with cigarettes and a magazine. The car was very close. It was a warm night, and before turning in I stood a short time in the vestibule. The train had been stopping at frequent intervals, and, finding the brakeman there, I asked the trouble.

It seemed that there was a hotbox on the next car, and that not only were we late, but we were delaying the second section, just behind. I was beginning to feel pleasantly drowsy, and the air was growing cooler as we got into the mountains. I said good night to the brakeman and went back to my berth. To my surprise, lower ten was already occupied—a suitcase projected from beneath, a pair of shoes stood on the floor, and from behind the curtains came the heavy, unmistakable breathing of deep sleep. I hunted out the porter and together we investigated.

"Are you asleep, sir?" asked the porter, leaning over deferentially. No answer forthcoming, he opened the curtains and looked in. Yes, the intruder was asleep—very much asleep—and an overwhelming odor of whisky proclaimed that he would probably remain asleep until morning. I was irritated. The car was full, and I was not disposed to take an upper in order to allow this drunken interloper to sleep comfortably in my berth.

"You'll have to get out of this," I said, shaking him angrily. But he merely grunted and turned over. As he did so, I saw his features for the first time. It was the quarrelsome man of the restaurant.

I was less disposed than ever to relinquish my claim, but the porter, after a little quiet investigation, offered a solution of the difficulty. "There's no one in lower nine," he suggested, pulling open the curtains just across. "It's likely nine's his berth, and he's made a mistake, owing to his condition. You'd better take nine, sir."

I did, with a firm resolution that if nine's rightful owner turned up later, I should be just as unwakable as the man opposite. I undressed leisurely, making sure of the safety of the forged notes, and placing my grip as before between myself and the window.

Being a man of systematic habits, I arranged my clothes carefully, putting my shoes out for the porter to polish, and stowing my collar and scarf in the little hammock swung for the purpose.

At last, with my pillows so arranged that I could see out comfortably, and with the unhygienic-looking blanket turned back—I have always a distrust of those much-used affairs—I prepared to wait gradually for sleep.

But sleep did not visit me. The train came to frequent, grating stops, and I surmised the hotbox again. I am not a nervous man, but there was something chilling in the thought of the second section pounding along behind us. Once, as I was dozing, our locomotive whistled a shrill warning. "You keep back where you belong," it screamed to my drowsy ears, and from somewhere behind came a chastened "All right I will."

I grew more and more wide-awake. At Cresson I got up on my elbow and blinked out at the station lights. Some passengers boarded the train there and I heard a woman's low tones, a southern voice, rich and full. Then quiet again. Every nerve was tense: time passed, perhaps ten minutes, possibly half an hour. Then, without the slightest warning, as the train rounded a curve, a heavy body was thrown into my berth. The incident, trivial as it seemed, was startling in its suddenness, for although my ears were painfully strained and awake, I had heard no step outside. The next instant the curtain hung limp again; still without a sound, my disturber had slipped away into the gloom and darkness. In a frenzy of wakefulness, I sat up, drew on a pair of slippers and fumbled for my bathrobe.

From a berth across, probably lower ten, came that particular aggravating snore which begins lightly, delicately, faintly soprano, goes down the scale a note with every breath, and, after keeping the listener tense with expectation, ends with an explosion that tears the very air. I was more and more irritable: I sat on the edge of the berth and hoped the snorer would choke to death. He had considerable vitality, however; he withstood one shock after another and survived to start again with new vigor. In desperation I found some cigarettes and one match, piled my blankets over my grip, and drawing the curtains together as though the berth were still occupied, I made my way to the vestibule of the car.

I was not clad for dress parade. Is it because the male is so restricted to gloom in his everyday attire that he blossoms into gaudy colors in his pajamas and dressing gowns? It would take a Turk to feel at home before an audience in my red-and-yellow bathrobe, a Christmas remembrance from Mrs. Klopton, with slippers to match.

So, naturally, when I saw a feminine figure on the platform, my first instinct was to dodge. The woman, however, was quicker than I; she gave me a startled glance, wheeled and disappeared, with a flash of two bronze-colored braids, into the next car.

Cigarette box in one hand, match in the other, I leaned against the uncertain frame of the door and gazed after her vanished figure. The mountain air flapped my bathrobe around my bare ankles, my one match burned to the end and went out, and still I stared. For I had seen on her expressive face a haunting look that was horror, nothing less. Heaven knows, I am not psychological. Emotions have to be written large before I can read them. But a woman in trouble always appeals to me, and this woman was more than that. She was in deadly fear.

If I had not been afraid of being ridiculous, I would have followed her. But I fancied that the apparition of a man in a red-and-yellow bathrobe, with an unkempt thatch of hair, walking up to her and assuring her that he would protect her would probably put her into hysterics. I had done that once before, when burglars had tried to break into the house, and had startled the parlor maid into bed for a week. So I tried to assure myself that I had imagined the lady's distress—or caused it, perhaps—and to dismiss her from my mind.

Perhaps she was merely anxious about the unpleasant gentleman of the restaurant. I thought smugly that I could have told her all about him: that he was sleeping the sleep of the just and the intoxicated in a berth that ought, by all that was fair and right, to have been mine, and that if I were tied to a man who snored like that, I should have him anesthetized and his soft palate put where it would never again flap like a loose sail in the wind.

We passed Harrisburg as I stood there. It was starlight, and the great crests of the Alleghenies had given way to low hills. At intervals we passed smudges of gray white, no doubt in daytime comfortable farms, which McKnight says is a good way of putting it, the farms being a lot more comfortable than the people on them.

I was growing drowsy: the woman with the bronze hair and the horrified face was fading in retrospect. It was colder, too, and I turned with a shiver to go in. As I did so a bit of paper fluttered into the air and settled on my sleeve, like a butterfly on a gorgeous red-and-yellow blossom. I picked it up curiously and glanced at it. It was part of a telegram that had been torn into bits.

There were only parts of four words on the scrap, but it left me puzzled and thoughtful. It read, "-ower ten, car seve-."

"Lower ten, car seven," was my berth—the one I had bought and found preempted.

Chapter III

Across the Aisle

NO SOLUTION offering itself, I went back to my berth. The snorer across had apparently strangled, or turned over, and so after a time I dropped asleep, to be awakened by the morning sunlight across my face.

I felt for my watch, yawning prodigiously. I reached under the pillow and failed to find it, but something scratched the back of my hand. I sat up irritably and nursed the wound, which was bleeding a little. Still drowsy, I felt more cautiously for what I supposed had been my scarf pin, but there was nothing there. Wide-awake now, I reached for my traveling bag, on the chance that I had put my watch in there. I had drawn the satchel to me and had my hand on the lock before I realized that it was not my own!

Mine was of alligator hide. I had killed the beast in Florida, after the expenditure of enough money to have bought a house and enough energy to have built one. The bag I held in my hand was a black one, sealskin, I think. The staggering thought of what the loss of my bag meant to me put my finger on the bell and kept it there until the porter came.

"Did you ring, sir?" he asked, poking his head through the curtains obsequiously. McKnight objects that nobody can poke his head through a curtain and be obsequious. But Pullman porters can and do.

"No," I snapped. "It rang itself. What in thunder do you mean by exchanging my valise for this one? You'll have to find it if you waken the entire car to do it. There are important papers in that grip."

"Porter," called a feminine voice from an upper berth nearby. "Porter, am I to dangle here all day?"

"Let her dangle," I said savagely. "You find that bag of mine."

The porter frowned. Then he looked at me with injured dignity. "I brought in your overcoat, sir. You carried your own valise."

The fellow was right! In an excess of caution I had refused to relinquish my alligator bag, and had turned over my other traps to the porter. It was clear enough then. I was simply a victim of the usual sleeping-car robbery. I was in a lather of perspiration by that time: the lady down the car was still dangling and talking about it; still nearer, a feminine voice was giving quick orders in French, presumably to a maid. The porter was on his knees, looking under the berth.

"Not there, sir," he said, dusting his knees. He was visibly more cheerful, having been absolved of responsibility. "Reckon it was taken while you was wanderin' around the car last night."

"I'll give you fifty dollars if you find it," I said. "A hundred. Reach up my shoes and I'll—"

I stopped abruptly. My eyes were fixed in stupefied amazement on a coat that hung from a hook at the foot of my berth. From the coat they traveled, dazed, to the soft-bosomed shirt beside it, and from there to the collar and cravat in the net hammock across the windows.

"A hundred!" the porter repeated, showing his teeth. But I caught him by the arm and pointed to the foot of the berth.

"What—what color's that coat?" I asked unsteadily.

"Gray, sir." His tone was one of gentle reproof.

"And—the trousers?"

He reached over and held up one creased leg. "Gray, too," he grinned.

"Gray!" I could not believe even his corroboration of my own eyes. "But my clothes were blue!" The porter was amused: he dived under the curtains and brought up a pair of shoes. "Your shoes, sir," he said with a flourish. "Reckon you've been dreaming, sir."

Now, there are two things I always avoid in my dress—possibly an idiosyncrasy of my bachelor existence. These tabooed articles are red neckties and tan shoes. And not only were the shoes the porter lifted from the floor of a gorgeous shade of yellow, but the scarf which was run through the turned-over collar was a gaudy red. It took a full minute for the real import of things to penetrate my dazed intelligence. Then I gave a vindictive kick at the offending ensemble.

"They're not mine, any of them," I snarled. "They are some other fellow's. I'll sit here until I take root before I put them on."

"They're nice lookin' clothes," the porter put in, eyeing the red tie with appreciation. "Ain't everybody would have left you anything."

"Call the conductor," I said shortly. Then a possible explanation occurred to me. "Oh, porter—what's the number of this berth?"

"Seven, sir. If you cain't wear those shoes—"

"Seven!" In my relief I almost shouted it. "Why, then, it's simple enough. I'm in the wrong berth, that's all. My berth is nine. Only—where the deuce is the man who belongs here?"

"Likely in nine, sir." The darky was enjoying himself. "You and the other gentleman just got mixed in the night. That's all, sir." It was clear that he thought I had been drinking.

I drew a long breath. Of course, that was the explanation. This was number seven's berth, that was his soft hat, this his umbrella, his coat, his bag. My rage turned to irritation at myself.

The porter went to the next berth and I could hear his softly insinuating voice. "Time to get up, sir. Are you awake? Time to get up."

There was no response from number nine. I guessed that he had opened the curtains and was looking in. Then he came back.

"Number nine's empty," he said.

"Empty! Do you mean my clothes aren't there?" I demanded. "My valise? Why don't you answer me?"

"You doan' give me time," he retorted. "There ain't nothin' there. But it's been slept in."

The disappointment was the greater for my few moments of hope. I sat up in a white fury and put on the clothes that had been left me. Then, still raging, I sat on the edge of the berth and put on the obnoxious tan shoes. The porter, called to his duties, made little excursions back to me, to offer assistance and to chuckle at my discomfiture. He stood by, outwardly decorous, but with little irritating grins of amusement around his mouth, when I finally emerged with the red tie in my hand.

"Bet the owner of those clothes didn't become them any more than you do," he said, as he plied the ubiquitous whisk broom.

"When I get the owner of these clothes," I retorted grimly, "he will need a shroud. Where's the conductor?"

The conductor was coming, he assured me; also that there was no bag answering the description of mine on the car. I slammed my way to the dressing room, washed, choked my fifteen and a half neck into a fifteen collar, and was back again in less than five minutes. The car, as well as its occupants, was gradually taking on a daylight appearance. I hobbled in, for one of the shoes was abominably tight, and found myself facing a young woman in blue with an unforgettable face. ("Three women already." McKnight says: "That's going some, even if you don't count the Gilmore nurse.") She stood, half-turned toward me, one hand idly drooping, the other steadying her as she gazed out at the flying landscape. I had an instant impression that I had met her somewhere, under different circumstances, more cheerful ones, I thought, for the girl's dejection now was evident. Beside her, sitting down, a small dark woman, considerably older, was talking in a rapid undertone. The girl nodded indifferently now and then. I fancied, although I was not sure, that my appearance brought a startled look into the young woman's face. I sat down and, hands thrust deep into the other man's pockets, stared ruefully at the other man's shoes.

The stage was set. In a moment the curtain was going up on the first act of the play. And for a while we would all say our little speeches and sing our little songs, and I, the villain, would hold center stage while the gallery hissed.

The porter was standing beside lower ten. He had reached in and was knocking valiantly. But his efforts met with no response. He winked at me over his shoulder; then he unfastened the curtains and bent forward. Behind him, I saw him stiffen, heard his muttered exclamation, saw the bluish pallor that spread over his face and neck. As he retreated a step the interior of lower ten lay open to the day.

The man in it was on his back, the early morning sun striking full on his upturned face. But the light did not disturb him. A small stain of red dyed the front of his nightclothes and trailed across the sheet; his half-open eyes were fixed, without seeing, on the shining wood above.

I grasped the porter's shaking shoulders and stared down to where the train imparted to the body a grisly suggestion of motion. "Good Lord," I gasped. "The man's been murdered!"

Chapter IV

Numbers Seven and Nine

AFTERWARDS, when I tried to recall our discovery of the body in lower ten, I found that my most vivid impression was not that made by the revelation of the opened curtain. I had an instantaneous picture of a slender blue-gowned girl who seemed to sense my words rather than hear them, of two small hands that clutched desperately at the seat beside them. The girl in the aisle stood, bent toward us, perplexity and alarm fighting in her face.

With twitching hands the porter attempted to draw the curtains together. Then in a paralysis of shock, he collapsed on the edge of my berth and sat there swaying. In my excitement I shook him.

"For Heaven's sake, keep your nerve, man," I said brusquely. "You'll have every woman in the car in hysterics. And if you do, you'll wish you could change places with the man in there." He rolled his eyes.

A man near, who had been reading last night's paper, dropped it quickly and tiptoed toward us. He peered between the partly open curtains, closed them quietly and went back, ostentatiously solemn, to his seat. The very crackle with which he opened his paper added to the bursting curiosity of the car. For the passengers knew that something was amiss: I was conscious of a sudden tension.

With the curtains closed the porter was more himself; he wiped his lips with a handkerchief and stood erect.

"It's my last trip in this car," he remarked heavily. "There's something wrong with that berth. Last trip the woman in it took an overdose of some sleeping stuff, and we found her, jes' like that, dead! And it ain't more'n three months now since there was twins born in that very spot. No, sir, it ain't natural."

At that moment a thin man with prominent eyes and a spare grayish goatee creaked up the aisle and paused beside me.

"Porter sick?" he inquired, taking in with a professional eye the porter's horror-struck face, my own excitement and the slightly gaping curtains of lower ten. He reached for the darky's pulse and pulled out an old-fashioned gold watch.

"Hm! Only fifty! What's the matter? Had a shock?" he asked shrewdly.

"Yes," I answered for the porter. "We've both had one. If you are a doctor, I wish you would look at the man in the berth across, lower ten. I'm afraid it's too late, but I'm not experienced in such matters."

Together we opened the curtains, and the doctor, bending down, gave a comprehensive glance that took in the rolling head, the relaxed jaw, the ugly stain on the sheet. The examination needed only a moment. Death was written in the clear white of the nostrils, the colorless lips, the smoothing away of the sinister lines of the night before. With its new dignity the face was not unhandsome: the gray hair was still plentiful, the features strong and well cut.

The doctor straightened himself and turned to me. "Dead for some time," he said, running a professional finger over the stains. "These are dry and darkened, you see, and rigor mortis is well established. A friend of yours?"

"I don't know him at all," I replied. "Never saw him but once before."

"Then you don't know if he is traveling alone?"

"No, he was not—that is, I don't know anything about him," I corrected myself. It was my first blunder: the doctor glanced up at me quickly and then turned his attention again to the body. Like a flash there had come to me the vision of the woman with the bronze hair and the tragic face, whom I had surprised in the vestibule between the cars, somewhere in the small hours of the morning. I had acted on my first impulse—the masculine one of shielding a woman.

The doctor had unfastened the coat of the striped pajamas and exposed the dead man's chest. On the left side was a small punctured wound of insignificant size.

"Very neatly done," the doctor said with appreciation. "Couldn't have done it better myself. Right through the intercostal space: no time even to grunt."

"Isn't the heart around there somewhere?" I asked. The medical man turned toward me and smiled austerely.

"That's where it belongs, just under that puncture, when it isn't gadding around in a man's throat or his boots."

I had a new respect for the doctor, for anyone indeed who could crack even a feeble joke under such circumstances, or who could run an impersonal finger over that wound and those stains. Odd how a healthy, normal man holds the medical profession in half contemptuous regard until he gets sick, or an emergency like this arises, and then turns meekly to the man who knows the ins and outs of his mortal tenement, takes his pills or his patronage, ties to him like a rudderless ship in a gale.

"Suicide, is it, doctor?" I asked.

He stood erect, after drawing the bed-clothing over the face, and, taking off his glasses, he wiped them slowly.

"No, it is not suicide," he announced decisively. "It is murder."

Of course, I had expected that, but the word itself brought a shiver. I was just a bit dizzy. Curious faces through the car were turned toward us, and I could hear the porter behind me breathing audibly. A stout woman in negligee came down the aisle and querulously confronted the porter. She wore a pink dressing jacket and carried portions of her clothing.

"Porter," she began, in the voice of the lady who had "dangled," "is there a rule of this company that will allow a woman to occupy the dressing room for one hour and curl her hair with an alcohol lamp while respectable people haven't a place where they can hook their—"

She stopped suddenly and stared into lower ten. Her shining pink cheeks grew pasty; her jaw fell. I remember trying to think of something to say, and of saying nothing at all. Then she had buried her eyes in the nondescript garments that hung from her arm and tottered back the way she had come. Slowly a little knot of men gathered around us, silent for the most part. The doctor was making a search of the berth when the conductor elbowed his way through, followed by the inquisitive man, who had evidently summoned him. I had lost sight, for a time, of the girl in blue.

"Do it himself?" the conductor queried, after a businesslike glance at the body.

"No, he didn't," the doctor asserted. "There's no weapon here, and the window is closed. He couldn't have thrown it out, and he didn't swallow it. What on earth are you looking for, man?"

Someone was on the floor at our feet, facedown, head peering under the berth. Now he got up without apology, revealing the man who had summoned the conductor. He was dusty, alert, cheerful, and he dragged up with him the dead man's suitcase. The sight of it brought back to me at once my own predicament.

"I don't know whether there's any connection or not, conductor," I said, "but I am a victim, too, in less degree; I've been robbed of everything I possess, except a red-and-yellow bathrobe. I happened to be wearing the bathrobe, which was probably the reason the thief overlooked it."

There was a fresh murmur in the crowd. Somebody laughed nervously. The conductor was irritated.

"I can't bother with that now," he snarled. "The railroad company is responsible for transportation, not for clothes, jewelry and morals. If people want to be stabbed and robbed in the company's cars, it's their affair. Why didn't you sleep in your clothes? I do."

I took an angry step forward. Then somebody touched my arm, and I unclenched my fist. I could understand the conductor's position, and beside, in the law, I had been guilty myself of contributory negligence.

"I'm not trying to make you responsible," I protested as amiably as I could, "and I believe the clothes the thief left are as good as my own.

They are certainly newer. But my valise contained valuable papers and it is to your interest as well as mine to find the man who stole it."

"Why, of course," the conductor said shrewdly. "Find the man who skipped out with this gentleman's clothes, and you've probably got the murderer."

"I went to bed in lower nine," I said, my mind full again of my lost papers, "and I wakened in number seven. I was up in the night prowling around, as I was unable to sleep, and I must have gone back to the wrong berth. Anyhow, until the porter wakened me this morning I knew nothing of my mistake. In the interval the thief—murderer, too, perhaps—must have come back, discovered my error, and taken advantage of it to further his escape."

The inquisitive man looked at me from between narrowed eyelids, ferretlike.

"Did anyone on the train suspect you of having valuable papers?" he inquired. The crowd was listening intently.

"No one," I answered promptly and positively. The doctor was investigating the murdered man's effects. The pockets of his trousers contained the usual miscellany of keys and small change, while in his hip pocket was found a small pearl-handled revolver of the type women usually keep around. A gold watch with a Masonic charm had slid down between the mattress and the window, while a showy diamond stud was still fastened in the bosom of his shirt. Taken as a whole, the personal belongings were those of a man of some means, but without any particular degree of breeding. The doctor heaped them together.

"Either robbery was not the motive," he reflected, "or the thief overlooked these things in his hurry."

The latter hypothesis seemed the more tenable, when, after a thorough search, we found no pocketbook and less than a dollar in small change.

The suitcase gave no clue. It contained one empty leather-covered flask and a pint bottle, also empty, a change of linen and some collars with the laundry mark S.H. In the leather tag on the handle was a card with the name Simon Harrington, Pittsburgh. The conductor sat down on my unmade berth, across, and made an entry of the name and address. Then, on an old envelope, he wrote a few words and gave it to the porter, who disappeared.

"I guess that's all I can do," he said. "I've had enough trouble this trip to last for a year. They don't need a conductor on these trains anymore; what they ought to have is a sheriff and a posse."

The porter from the next car came in and whispered to him. The conductor rose unhappily.

"Next car's caught the disease," he grumbled. "Doctor, a woman back there has got mumps or bubonic plague, or something. Will you come back?"

The strange porter stood aside.

"Lady about the middle of the car," he said, "in black, sir, with queer-looking hair—sort of copper color, I think, sir."

Chapter V

The Woman in the Next Car

∽

WITH the departure of the conductor and the doctor, the group around lower ten broke up, to re-form in smaller knots through the car. The porter remained on guard. With something of relief I sank into a seat. I wanted to think, to try to remember the details of the previous night. But my inquisitive acquaintance had other intentions. He came up and sat down beside me. Like the conductor, he had taken notes of the dead man's belongings, his name, address, clothing and the general circumstances of the crime. Now with his little notebook open before him, he prepared to enjoy the minor sensation of the robbery.

"And now for the second victim," he began cheerfully. "What is your name and address, please?" I eyed him with suspicion.

"I have lost everything but my name and address," I parried. "What do you want them for? Publication?"

"Oh, no; dear, no!" he said, shocked at my misapprehension. "Merely for my own enlightenment. I like to gather data of this kind and draw my own conclusions. Most interesting and engrossing. Once or twice I have forestalled the results of police investigation—but entirely for my own amusement."

I nodded tolerantly. Most of us have hobbies; I knew a man once who carried his handkerchief up his sleeve and had a mania for old colored prints cut out of *Godey's Lady's Book.*

"I use that inductive method originated by Poe and followed since with such success by Conan Doyle. Have you ever read Gaboriau? Ah, you have missed a treat, indeed. And now, to get down to business, what is the name of our escaped thief and probable murderer?"

"How on earth do I know?" I demanded impatiently. "He didn't write it in blood anywhere, did he?"

The little man looked hurt and disappointed.

"Do you mean to say," he asked, "that the pockets of those clothes are entirely empty?" The pockets! In the excitement I had forgotten entirely the sealskin grip which the porter now sat at my feet, and I had not investigated the pockets at all. With the inquisitive man's pencil taking note of everything that I found, I emptied them on the opposite seat.

Upper left-hand waistcoat, two lead pencils and a fountain pen; lower right waistcoat, matchbox and a small stamp book; right-hand pocket coat, pair of gray suede gloves, new, size seven and a half; left-hand pocket, gun-metal cigarette case studded with pearls, half full of Egyptian cigarettes. The trousers pockets contained a gold penknife, a small amount of money in bills and change, and a handkerchief with the initial "S" on it.

Further search through the coat discovered a card case with cards bearing the name Henry Pinckney Sullivan, and a leather flask with gold mountings, filled with what seemed to be very fair whisky, and mono-grammed H. P. S.

"His name evidently is Henry Pinckney Sullivan," said the cheerful fol-lower of Poe, as he wrote it down. "Address as yet unknown. Blond, probably. Have you noticed that it is almost always the blond men who affect a very light gray, with a touch of red in the scarf? Fact, I assure you. I kept a record once of the summer attire of men, and ninety per-cent followed my rule. Dark men like you affect navy blue, or brown."

In spite of myself I was amused at the man's shrewdness.

"Yes; the suit he took was dark—a blue," I said.

He rubbed his hands and smiled at me delightedly. "Then you wore black shoes, not tan," he said with a glance at the aggressive yellow ones I wore.

"Right again," I acknowledged. "Black low shoes and black embroidered hose. If you keep on, you'll have a motive for the crime, and the murderer's present place of hiding. And if you come back to the smoker with me, I'll give you an opportunity to judge if he knew good whisky from bad."

I put the articles from the pockets back again and got up. "I wonder if there is a diner on?" I said. "I need something sustaining after all this."

I was conscious then of someone at my elbow. I turned to see the young woman whose face was so vaguely familiar. In the very act of speaking she drew back suddenly and colored.

"Oh, I beg your pardon," she said hurriedly. "I thought you were someone else." She was looking in a puzzled fashion at my coat. I felt all the cringing guilt of a man who has accidentally picked up the wrong umbrella: my borrowed collar sat tight on my neck.

"I'm sorry," I said idiotically. "I'm sorry, but I'm not." I have learned since that she has bright brown hair, with a loose wave in it that drops over her ears, and dark blue eyes with black lashes and— But what does it matter? One enjoys a picture as a whole, not as the sum of its parts.

She saw the flask then, and her errand came back to her. "One of the ladies at the end of the car has fainted," she explained. "I thought perhaps a stimulant—"

I picked up the flask at once and followed my guide down the aisle. Two or three women were working over the woman who had fainted. They had opened her collar and taken out her hairpins, whatever good that might do. The stout woman was vigorously rubbing her wrists, with the idea, no doubt, of working up her pulse! The unconscious woman was the one for whom I had secured lower eleven at the station.

I poured a little liquor in a bungling masculine fashion between her lips as she leaned back, with closed eyes. She choked, coughed, and rallied somewhat.

"Poor thing," said the stout lady. "As she lies back that way I could almost think it was my mother; she used to faint so much."

"It would make anybody faint," chimed in another. "Murder and robbery in one night and on one car. I'm thankful I always wear my rings in a bag around my neck—even if they do get under me and keep me awake."

The girl in blue was looking at us with wide, startled eyes. I saw her pale a little, saw the quick, apprehensive glance which she threw at her traveling companion, the small woman I had noticed before. There was an exchange—almost a clash—of glances. The small woman frowned. That was all. I turned my attention again to my patient.

She had revived somewhat, and now she asked to have the window opened. The train had stopped again and the car was oppressively hot. People around were looking at their watches and grumbling over the delay. The doctor bustled in with a remark about its being his busy day. The amateur detective and the porter together mounted guard over lower ten. Outside the heat rose in shimmering waves from the tracks: the very wood of the car was hot to touch. A Camberwell Beauty darted through the open door and made its way, in erratic plunges, great wings waving, down the sunny aisle. All around lay the peace of harvested fields, the quiet of the country.

Chapter VI

The Girl in Blue

⁞∞⁞

I WAS growing more and more irritable. The thought of what the loss of the notes meant was fast crowding the murder to the back of my mind. The forced inaction was intolerable.

The porter had reported no bag answering the description of mine on the train, but I was disposed to make my own investigation. I made a tour of the cars, scrutinizing every variety of hand luggage, ranging from luxurious English bags with gold mountings to the wicker nondescripts of the day coach at the rear. I was not alone in my quest, for the girl in blue was just ahead of me. Car by car she preceded me through the train, unconscious that I was behind her, looking at each passenger as she passed. I fancied the proceeding was distasteful, but that she had determined on a course and was carrying it through. We reached the end of the train almost together—empty-handed, both of us.

The girl went out to the platform. When she saw me, she moved aside, and I stepped out beside her. Behind us the track curved sharply; the early sunshine threw the train, in long black shadow, over the hot earth. Forward somewhere they were hammering. The girl said nothing, but her profile was strained and anxious.

"I—if you have lost anything," I began, "I wish you would let me try to help. Not that my own success is anything to boast of."

She hardly glanced at me. It was not flattering. "I have not been robbed, if that is what you mean," she replied quietly. "I am perplexed. That is all."

There was nothing to say to that. I lifted my hat—the other fellow's hat—and turned to go back to my car. Two or three members of the train crew, including the conductor, were standing in the shadow talking. And at that moment, from a farmhouse near came the swift clang of the breakfast bell, calling in the hands from barn and pasture. I turned back to the girl.

"We may be here for an hour," I said, "and there is no buffet car on. If I remember my youth, that bell means ham and eggs and country butter and coffee. If you care to run the risk—"

"I am not hungry," she said, "but perhaps a cup of coffee— Dear me, I believe I am hungry," she finished. "Only—" She glanced back of her.

"I can bring your companion," I suggested, without enthusiasm. But the young woman shook her head.

"She is not hungry," she objected, "and she is very—well, I know she wouldn't come. Do you suppose we could make it if we run?"

"I haven't any idea," I said cheerfully. "Any old train would be better than this one, if it does leave us behind."

"Yes. Any train would be better than this one," she repeated gravely. I found myself watching her changing expression. I had spoken two dozen words to her and already I felt that I knew the lights and shades in her voice—I, who had always known how a woman rode to hounds, and who never could have told the color of her hair.

I stepped down on the ties and turned to assist her, and together we walked back to where the conductor and the porter from our car were in close conversation. Instinctively my hand went to my cigarette pocket and came out empty. She saw the gesture.

"If you want to smoke, you may," she said. "I have a big cousin who smokes all the time. He says I am 'kippered.' "

I drew out the gun-metal cigarette case and opened it. But this most commonplace action had an extraordinary result: the girl beside me stopped dead still and stood staring at it with fascinated eyes.

"Is—where did you get that?" she demanded, with a catch in her voice; her gaze still fixed on the cigarette case.

"Then you haven't heard the rest of the tragedy?" I asked, holding out the case. "It's frightfully bad luck for me, but it makes a good story. You see—"

At that moment the conductor and porter ceased their colloquy. The conductor came directly toward me, tugging as he came at his bristling gray mustache.

"I would like to talk to you in the car," he said to me, with a curious glance at the young lady.

"Can't it wait?" I objected. "We are on our way to a cup of coffee and a slice of bacon. Be merciful, as you are powerful."

"I'm afraid the breakfast will have to wait," he replied. "I won't keep you long." There was a note of authority in his voice which I resented; but, after all, the circumstances were unusual.

"We'll have to defer that cup of coffee for a while," I said to the girl. "But don't despair; there's breakfast somewhere."

As we entered the car, she stood aside, but I felt rather than saw that she followed us. I was surprised to see a half dozen men gathered around the berth in which I had wakened, number seven. It had not yet been made up.

As we passed along the aisle, I was conscious of a new expression on the faces of the passengers. The tall woman who had fainted was searching my face with narrowed eyes, while the stout woman of the kindly heart avoided my gaze, and pretended to look out the window.

As we pushed our way through the group, I fancied that it closed around me ominously. The conductor said nothing, but led the way without ceremony to the side of the berth.

"What's the matter?" I inquired. I was puzzled, but not apprehensive. "Have you some of my things? I'd be thankful even for my shoes; these are confoundedly tight."

Nobody spoke, and I fell silent, too. For one of the pillows had been turned over, and the underside of the white case was streaked with brownish stains. I think it was a perceptible time before I realized that the stains were blood, and that the faces around were filled with suspicion and distrust.

"Why, it—that looks like blood," I said vacuously. There was an incessant pounding in my ears, and the conductor's voice came from far off.

"It is blood," he asserted grimly.

I looked around with a dizzy attempt at nonchalance. "Even if it is," I remonstrated, "surely you don't suppose for a moment that I know anything about it!"

The amateur detective elbowed his way in. He had a scrap of transparent paper in his hand, and a pencil.

"I would like permission to trace the stains," he began eagerly. "Also"—to me—"if you will kindly jab your finger with a pin—needle—anything—"

"If you don't keep out of this," the conductor said savagely, "I will do some jabbing myself. As for you, sir—" he turned to me. I was absolutely innocent, but I knew that I presented a typical picture of guilt; I was covered with cold sweat, and the pounding in my ears kept up dizzily. "As for you, sir—"

The irrepressible amateur detective made a quick pounce at the pillow and pushed back the cover. Before our incredulous eyes he drew out a narrow steel dirk which had been buried to the small cross that served as a head.

There was a chorus of voices around, a quick surging forward of the crowd. So that was what had scratched my hand! I buried the wound in my coat pocket.

"Well," I said, trying to speak naturally, "doesn't that prove what I have been telling you? The man who committed the murder belonged to this berth, and made an exchange in some way after the crime. How do you know he didn't change the tags so I would come back to this berth?" This was an inspiration; I was pleased with it. "That's what he did, he changed the tags," I reiterated.

There was a murmur of assent around. The doctor, who was standing beside me, put his hand on my arm. "If this gentleman committed this crime, and I for one feel sure he did not, then who is the fellow who got away? And why did he go?"

"We have only one man's word for that," the conductor snarled. "I've traveled some in these cars myself, and no one ever changed berths with me."

Somebody on the edge of the group asserted that hereafter he would travel by daylight. I glanced up and caught the eye of the girl in blue.

"They are all mad," she said. Her tone was low, but I heard her distinctly. "Don't take them seriously enough to defend yourself."

"I am glad you think I didn't do it," I observed meekly, over the crowd. "Nothing else is of any importance."

The conductor had pulled out his notebook again. "Your name, please," he said gruffly.

"Lawrence Blakeley, Washington."

"Your occupation?"

"Attorney. A member of the firm of Blakeley and McKnight."

"Mr. Blakeley, you say you have occupied the wrong berth and have been robbed. Do you know anything of the man who did it?"

"Only from what he left behind," I answered. "These clothes—"

"They fit you," he said with quick suspicion. "Isn't that rather a coincidence? You are a large man."

"Good Heavens," I retorted, stung into fury, "do I look like a man who would wear this kind of a necktie? Do you suppose I carry purple-and-green-barred silk handkerchiefs? Would any man in his senses wear a pair of shoes a full size too small?"

The conductor was inclined to hedge. "You will have to grant that I am in a peculiar position," he said. "I have only your word as to the exchange of berths, and you understand I am merely doing my duty. Are there any clues in the pockets?"

For the second time I emptied them of their contents, which he noted. "Is that all?" he finished. "There was nothing else?"

"Nothing."

"That's not all, sir," broke in the porter, stepping forward. "There was a small black satchel."

"That's so," I exclaimed. "I forgot the bag. I don't even know where it is."

The easily swayed crowd looked suspicious again. I've grown so accustomed to reading the faces of a jury, seeing them swing from doubt to belief, and back again to doubt, that I instinctively watch expressions.

I saw that my forgetfulness had done me harm—that suspicion was roused again.

The bag was found a couple of seats away, under somebody's raincoat another dubious circumstance. Was I hiding it? It was brought to the berth and placed beside the conductor, who opened it at once.

It contained the usual traveling impedimenta—change of linen, collars, handkerchiefs, a bronze-green scarf, and a safety razor. But the attention of the crowd riveted itself on a flat, Russia leather wallet, around which a heavy gum band was wrapped, and which bore in gilt letters the name "Simon Harrington."

Chapter VII

A Fine Gold Chain

⟨∞⟩

THE conductor held it out to me, his face sternly accusing.

"Is this another coincidence?" he asked. "Did the man who left you his clothes and the barred silk handkerchief and the tight shoes leave you the spoil of the murder?"

The men standing around had drawn off a little, and I saw the absolute futility of any remonstrance. Have you ever seen a fly, who, in these hygienic days, finding no cobwebs to entangle him, is caught in a sheet of flypaper, finds himself more and more mired, and is finally quiet with the sticky stillness of despair?

Well, I was the fly. I had seen too much of circumstantial evidence to have any belief that the establishing of my identity would weigh much against the other incriminating details. It meant imprisonment and trial, probably, with all the notoriety and loss of practice they would entail. A man thinks quickly at a time like that. All the probable consequences of the finding of that pocketbook flashed through my mind as I extended my hand to take it. Then I drew my arm back.

"I don't want it," I said. "Look inside. Maybe the other man took the money and left the wallet."

The conductor opened it, and again there was a curious surging forward of the crowd. To my intense disappointment the money was still there.

I stood blankly miserable while it was counted out—five one-hundred-dollar bills, six twenties, and some fives and ones that brought the total to six hundred and fifty dollars.

The little man with the notebook insisted on taking the numbers of the notes, to the conductor's annoyance. It was immaterial to me: small things had lost their power to irritate. I was seeing myself in the prisoner's box, going through all the nerve-racking routine of a trial for murder—the challenging of the jury, the endless cross-examinations, the alternate hope and fear. I believe I said before that I had no nerves, but for a few minutes that morning I was as near as a man ever comes to hysteria.

I folded my arms and gave myself a mental shake. I seemed to be the center of a hundred eyes, expressing every shade of doubt and distrust, but I tried not to flinch. Then someone created a diversion.

The amateur detective was busy again with the sealskin bag, investigating the make of the safety razor and the manufacturer's name on the bronze-green tie. Now, however, he paused and frowned, as though some pet theory had been upset.

Then from a corner of the bag he drew out and held up for our inspection some three inches of fine gold chain, one end of which was blackened and stained with blood!

The conductor held out his hand for it, but the little man was not ready to give it up. He turned to me.

"You say no watch was left you? Was there a piece of chain like that?"

"No chain at all," I said sulkily. "No jewelry of any kind, except plain gold buttons in the shirt I am wearing."

"Where are your glasses?" he threw at me suddenly. Instinctively my hand went to my eyes. My glasses had been gone all morning, and I had not even noticed their absence. The little man smiled cynically and held out the chain.

"I must ask you to examine this," he insisted. "Isn't it a part of the fine gold chain you wear over your ear?"

I didn't want to touch the thing: the stain at the end made me shudder. But with a baker's dozen of suspicious eyes—well, we'll say fourteen: there were no one-eyed men—I took the fragment in the tips of my fingers and looked at it helplessly.

"Very fine chains are much alike," I managed to say. "For all I know, this may be mine, but I don't know how it got into that sealskin bag. I never saw the bag until this morning after daylight."

"He admits that he had the bag," somebody said behind me. "How did you guess that he wore glasses, anyhow?" to the amateur sleuth.

That gentleman cleared his throat. "There were two reasons," he said, "for suspecting it. When you see a man with the lines of his face drooping, a healthy individual with a pensive eye—suspect astigmatism. Besides, this gentleman has a pronounced line across the bridge of his nose and a mark on his ear from the chain."

After this remarkable exhibition of the theoretical as combined with the practical, he sank into a seat nearby, and still holding the chain, sat with closed eyes and pursed lips. It was evident to all the car that the solution of the mystery was a question of moments. Once he bent forward eagerly and putting the chain on the windowsill, proceeded to go over it with a pocket magnifying glass, only to shake his head in disappointment. All the people around shook their heads, too, although they had not the slightest idea what it was about.

The pounding in my ears began again. The group around me seemed to be suddenly motionless in the very act of moving, as if a hypnotist had called "Rigid!" The girl in blue was looking at me, and above the din I thought she said she must speak to me—something vital. The pounding grew louder and merged into a scream. With a grinding and splintering the car rose under my feet. Then it fell away into darkness.

Chapter VIII
The Second Section

HAVE you ever been picked up out of your three-meals-a-day life, whirled around in a tornado of events, and landed in a situation so grotesque and yet so horrible that you laugh even while you are groaning, and straining at its hopelessness? McKnight says that is hysteria, and that no man worthy of the name ever admits to it.

Also, as McKnight says, it sounds like a tank drama. Just as the revolving saw is about to cut the hero into stove lengths, the second villain blows up the sawmill. The hero goes up through the roof and alights on the bank of a stream at the feet of his lady love, who is making daisy chains.

Nevertheless, when I was safely home again, with Mrs. Klopton brewing strange drinks that came in paper packets from the pharmacy, and that smelled to heaven, I remember staggering to the door and closing it, and then going back to bed and howling out the absurdity and the madness of the whole thing. And while I laughed my very soul was sick, for the girl was gone by that time, and I knew by all the loyalty that answers between men for honor that I would have to put her out of my mind.

And yet, all the night that followed, filled as it was with the shrieking demons of pain, I saw her as I had seen her last, in the queer hat with green ribbons. I told the doctor this, guardedly, the next morning, and he said it was the morphia, and that I was lucky not to have seen a row of devils with green tails.

I don't know anything about the wreck of September ninth last. You who swallowed the details with your coffee and digested the horrors with your chop, probably know a great deal more than I do. I remember very distinctly that the jumping and throbbing in my arm brought me back to a world that at first was nothing but sky, a heap of clouds that I thought hazily were the meringue on a blue charlotte russe. As the sense of hearing was slowly added to vision, I heard a woman near me sobbing that she had lost her hat pin, and she couldn't keep her hat on.

I think I dropped back into unconsciousness again, for the next thing I remember was of my blue patch of sky clouded with smoke, of a strange roaring and crackling, of a rain of fiery sparks on my face and of somebody beating at me with feeble hands. I opened my eyes and closed them again: the girl in blue was bending over me. With that imperviousness to big things and keenness to small that is the first effect of shock, I tried to be facetious, when a spark stung my cheek.

"You will have to rouse yourself!" the girl was repeating desperately. "You've been on fire twice already." A piece of striped ticking floated slowly over my head. As the wind caught it its charring edges leaped into flame.

"Looks like a kite, doesn't it?" I remarked cheerfully. And then, as my arm gave an excruciating throb—"Jove, how my arm hurts!"

The girl bent over and spoke slowly, distinctly, as one might speak to a deaf person or a child.

"Listen, Mr. Blakeley," she said earnestly. "You must rouse yourself. There has been a terrible accident. The second section ran into us. The wreck is burning now, and if we don't move, we will catch fire. Do you hear?"

Her voice and my arm were bringing me to my senses. "I hear," I said. "I—I'll sit up in a second. Are you hurt?"

"No, only bruised. Do you think you can walk?"

I drew up one foot after another, gingerly.

"They seem to move all right," I remarked dubiously. "Would you mind telling me where the back of my head has gone? I can't help thinking it isn't there."

She made a quick examination. "It's pretty badly bumped," she said. "You must have fallen on it."

I had got up on my uninjured elbow by that time, but the pain threw me back. "Don't look at the wreck," I entreated her. "It's no sight for a woman. If—if there is any way to tie up this arm, I might be able to do something. There may be people under those cars!"

"Then it is too late to help," she replied solemnly. A little shower of feathers, each carrying its fiery lamp, blew over us from some burning pillow. A part of the wreck collapsed with a crash. In a resolute to play a man's part in the tragedy going on around, I got to my knees. Then I realized what I had not noticed before: the hand and wrist of the broken left arm were jammed through the handle of the sealskin grip. I gasped and sat down suddenly.

"You must not do that," the girl insisted. I noticed now that she kept her back to the wreck, her eyes averted. "The weight of the traveling bag must be agony. Let me support the valise until we get back a few yards. Then you must lie down until we can get it cut off."

"Will it have to be cut off?" I asked as calmly as possible. There were red-hot stabs of agony clear to my neck, but we were moving slowly away from the track.

"Yes," she replied, with dumfounding coolness. "If I had a knife, I could do it myself. You might sit here and lean against this fence."

By that time my returning faculties had realized that she was going to cut off the satchel, not the arm. The dizziness was leaving and I was gradually becoming myself.

"If you pull, it might come," I suggested. "And with that weight gone, I think I will cease to be five feet eleven inches of baby."

She tried gently to loosen the handle, but it would not move, and at last, with great drops of cold perspiration over me, I had to give up.

"I'm afraid I can't stand it," I said. "But there's a knife somewhere around these clothes, and if I can find it, perhaps you can cut the leather."

As I gave her the knife she turned it over, examining it with a peculiar expression, bewilderment rather than surprise. But she said nothing. She set to work deftly, and in a few minutes the bag dropped free.

"That's better," I declared, sitting up. "Now, if you can pin my sleeve to my coat, it will support the arm so we can get away from here."

"The pin might give," she objected, "and the jerk would be terrible." She looked around, puzzled; then she got up, coming back in a minute with a draggled, partly scorched sheet. This she tore into a large square, and after she had folded it, she slipped it under the broken arm and tied it securely at the back of my neck.

The relief was immediate, and, picking up the sealskin bag, I walked slowly beside her, away from the track.

The first act was over: the curtain fallen. The scene was "struck."

Chapter IX

The Halcyon Breakfast

⌒⌒⌒

WE WERE still dazed, I think, for we wandered like two troubled children, our one idea at first to get as far away as we could from the horror behind us. We were both bareheaded, grimy, pallid through the grit. Now and then we met little groups of country folk hurrying to the track: they stared at us curiously, and some wished to question us. But we hurried past them; we had put the wreck behind us. That way lay madness.

Only once the girl turned and looked behind her. The wreck was hidden, but the smoke cloud hung heavy and dense. For the first time I remembered that my companion had not been alone on the train.

"It is quiet here," I suggested. "If you will sit down on the bank, I will go back and make some inquiries. I've been criminally thoughtless. Your traveling companion—"

She interrupted me, and something of her splendid poise was gone. "Please don't go back," she said. "I am afraid it would be of no use. And I don't want to be left alone."

Heaven knows I did not want her to be alone. I was more than content to walk along beside her aimlessly, for any length of time. Gradually, as she lost the exaltation of the moment, I was gaining my normal condition of mind. I was beginning to realize that I had lacked the morning grace of a shave, that I looked like some lost hope of yesterday, and that my left shoe pinched outrageously. A man does not rise triumphant above such handicaps. The girl, for all her disordered hair and the crumpled linen of her waist, in spite of her missing hat and the small gold bag that hung forlornly from a broken chain, looked exceedingly lovely.

"Then I won't leave you alone," I said manfully, and we stumbled on together. Thus far we had seen nobody from the wreck, but well up the lane we came across the tall dark woman who had occupied lower eleven. She was half crouching beside the road, her black hair about her shoulders, and an ugly bruise over her eye. She did not seem to know us, and refused to accompany us. We left her there at last, babbling incoherently and rolling in her hands a dozen pebbles she had gathered in the road.

The girl shuddered as we went on. Once she turned and glanced at my bandage. "Does it hurt very much?" she asked.

"It's growing rather numb. But it might be worse," I answered mendaciously. If anything in this world could be worse, I had never experienced it.

And so we trudged on bareheaded under the summer sun, growing parched and dusty and weary, doggedly leaving behind us the pillar of smoke. I thought I knew of a trolley line somewhere in the direction we were going, or perhaps we could find a horse and trap to take us into Baltimore. The girl smiled when I suggested it.

"We will create a sensation, won't we?" she asked. "Isn't it queer or perhaps it's my state of mind—but I keep wishing for a pair of gloves, when I haven't even a hat!"

When we reached the main road, we sat down for a moment, and her hair, which had been coming loose for some time, fell over her shoulders in little waves that were most alluring. It seemed a pity to twist it up again but when I suggested this, cautiously, she said it was troublesome and got in her eyes when it was loose. So she gathered it up, while I held a row of little shell combs and pins, and when it was done it was vastly becoming, too. Funny about hair: a man never knows he has it until he begins to lose it, but it's different with a girl. Something of the unconventional situation began to dawn on her as she put in the last hairpin and patted some stray locks to place.

"I have not told you my name," she said abruptly. "I forgot that because I know who you are, you know nothing about me. I am Alison West, and my home is in Richmond."

So that was it! This was the girl of the photograph on John Gilmore's bedside table. The girl McKnight expected to see in Richmond the next day, Sunday! She was on her way back to meet him! Well, what difference did it make, anyhow? We had been thrown together by the merest chance. In an hour or two at the most we would be back in civilization and she would recall me, if she remembered me at all, as an unshaven creature in a red cravat and tan shoes, with a soiled Pullman sheet tied around my neck. I drew a deep breath.

"Just a twinge," I said, when she glanced up quickly. "It's very good of you to let me know, Miss West. I have been hearing delightful things about you for three months."

"From Richey McKnight?" She was frankly curious.

"Yes. From Richey McKnight," I assented. Was it any wonder McKnight was crazy about her? I dug my heels into the dust.

"I have been visiting near Cresson, in the mountains," Miss West was saying. "The person you mentioned, Mrs. Curtis, was my hostess. We— we were on our way to Washington together." She spoke slowly, as if she wished to give the minimum of explanation. Across her face had come again the baffling expression of perplexity and trouble I had seen before.

"You were on your way home, I suppose? Richey spoke about seeing you," I floundered, finding it necessary to say something. She looked at me with level, direct eyes.

"No," she returned quietly. "I did not intend to go home. I—well, it doesn't matter; I am going home now."

A woman in a calico dress, with two children, each an exact duplicate of the other, had come quickly down the road. She took in the situation at a glance, and was explosively hospitable.

"You poor things," she said. "If you'll take the first road to the left over there, and turn in at the second pigsty, you will find breakfast on the table and a coffeepot on the stove. And there's plenty of soap and water, too. Don't say one word. There isn't a soul there to see you."

We accepted the invitation and she hurried on toward the excitement and the railroad. I got up carefully and helped Miss West to her feet.

"At the second pigsty to the left," I repeated, "we will find the breakfast I promised you seven eternities ago. Forward to the pigsty!"

We said very little for the remainder of that walk. I had almost reached the limit of endurance: with every step the broken ends of the bone grated together. We found the farmhouse without difficulty, and I remember wondering if I could hold out to the end of the old stone walk that led between hedges to the door.

"Allah be praised," I said with all the voice I could muster. "Behold the coffeepot!" And then I put down the grip and folded up like a jack-knife on the porch floor.

When I came around, something hot was trickling down my neck, and a despairing voice was saying, "Oh, I don't seem to be able to pour it into your mouth. Please open your eyes."

"But I don't want it in my eyes," I replied dreamily. "I haven't any idea what came over me. It was the shoes, I think: the left one is a red-hot torture." I was sitting by that time and looking across into her face.

Never before or since have I fainted, but I would do it joyfully, a dozen times a day, if I could waken again to the blissful touch of soft fingers on my face, the hot ecstasy of coffee spilled by those fingers down my neck. There was a thrill in every tone of her voice that morning. Before long my loyalty to McKnight would step between me and the girl he loved: life would develop new complexities. In those early hours after the wreck, full of pain as they were, there was nothing of the suspicion and distrust that came later. Shorn of our gauds and baubles, we were primitive man and woman, together: our world for the hour was the deserted farmhouse, the slope of wheat field that led to the road, the woodland lot, the pasture.

We breakfasted together across the homely table. Our cheerfulness, at first sheer reaction, became less forced as we ate great slices of bread from the granny oven back of the house, and drank hot fluid that smelled like coffee and tasted like nothing that I have ever swallowed. We found cream in stone jars, sunk deep in the chill water of the spring house. And there were eggs, great yellow-brown ones—a basket of them.

So, like two children awakened from a nightmare, we chattered over our food: we hunted mutual friends, we laughed together at my feeble witticisms, but we put the horror behind us resolutely. After all, it was the hat with the green ribbons that brought back the strangeness of the situation.

All along I had had the impression that Alison West was deliberately putting out of her mind something that obtruded now and then. It brought with it a return of the puzzled expression that I had surprised early in the day, before the wreck. I caught it once, when, breakfast over, she was tightening the sling that held the broken arm. I had prolonged the morning meal as much as I could, but when the wooden clock with the pink roses on the dial pointed to half after ten, and the mother with the duplicate youngsters had not come back, Miss West made the move I had dreaded.

"If we are to get into Baltimore at all, we must start," she said, rising. "You ought to see a doctor as soon as possible."

"Hush," I said warningly. "Don't mention the arm, please; it is asleep now. You may rouse it."

"If I only had a hat," she reflected. "It wouldn't need to be much of one, but—" She gave a little cry and darted to the corner. "Look," she said triumphantly, "the very thing. With the green streamers tied up in a bow, like this—do you suppose the child would mind? I can put five dollars or so here—that would buy a dozen of them."

It was a queer affair of straw, that hat, with a round crown and a rim that flopped dismally. With a single movement she had turned it up at one side and fitted it to her head. Grotesque by itself, when she wore it, it was a thing of joy.

Evidently the lack of head covering had troubled her, for she was elated at her find. She left me, scrawling a note of thanks and pinning it with a bill to the tablecloth, and ran upstairs to the mirror and the promised soap and water.

I did not see her when she came down. I had discovered a bench with a tin basin outside the kitchen door, and was washing, in a helpless, one-sided way. I felt rather than saw that she was standing in the door-way, and I made a final plunge into the basin.

"How is it possible for a man with only a right hand to wash his left ear?" I asked from the roller towel. I was distinctly uncomfortable: men are more rigidly creatures of convention than women, whether they admit it or not. "There is so much soap on me still that if I laugh I will blow bubbles. Washing with rainwater and homemade soap is like motoring on a slippery road. I only struck the high places."

Then, having achieved a brilliant polish with the towel, I looked at the girl.

She was leaning against the frame of the door, her face perfectly col-orless, her breath coming in slow, difficult respirations. The erratic hat was pinned to place, but it had slid rakishly to one side. When I realized that she was staring, not at me, but past me to the road along which we had come, I turned and followed her gaze. There was no one in sight: the lane stretched dust white in the sun—no moving figure on it, no sign of life.

Chapter X

Miss West's Request

⇜

THE surprising change in her held me speechless. All the animation of the breakfast table was gone: there was no hint of the response with which, before, she had met my nonsensical sallies. She stood there, white-lipped, unsmiling, staring down the dusty road. One hand was clenched tight over some small object. Her eyes dropped to it from the distant road, and then closed, with a quick, indrawn breath. Her color came back slowly. Whatever had caused the change, she said nothing.

She was anxious to leave at once, almost impatient over my deliberate masculine way of getting my things together. Afterward I recalled that I had wanted to explore the barn for a horse and some sort of a vehicle to take us to the trolley, and that she had refused to allow me to look. I remembered many things later that might have helped me, and did not. At the time, I was only completely bewildered. Save the wreck, the responsibility for which lay between Providence and the engineer of the second section, all the events of that strange morning were logically connected; they came from one cause, and tended unerringly to one end. But the cause was buried, the end not yet in view.

Not until we had left the house well behind did the girl's face relax its tense lines. I was watching her more closely than I had realized, for when we had gone a little way along the road, she turned to me almost petulantly. "Please don't stare so at me," she said, to my sudden confusion. "I know the hat is dreadful. Green always makes me look ghastly."

"Perhaps it was the green." I was unaccountably relieved. "Do you know, a few minutes ago, you looked almost pallid to me!"

She glanced at me quickly, but I was gazing ahead. We were out of sight of the house, now, and with every step away from it the girl was obviously relieved. Whatever she held in her hand, she never glanced at it. But she was conscious of it every second. She seemed to come to a decision about it while we were still in sight of the gate, for she murmured something and turned back alone, going swiftly, her feet stirring up small puffs of dust at every step. She fastened something to the gatepost—I could see the nervous haste with which she worked. When she joined me again, it was without explanation. But the clenched fingers were free now, and while she looked tired and worn, the strain had visibly relaxed.

We walked along slowly in the general direction of the suburban trolley line. Once a man with an empty wagon offered us a lift, but after a glance at the springless vehicle I declined.

"The ends of the bone think they are castanets as it is," I explained. "But the lady—"

The young lady, however, declined and we went on together. Once, when the trolley line was in sight, she got a pebble in her low shoe, and we sat down under a tree until she found the cause of the trouble.

"I—I don't know what I should have done without you," I blundered. "Moral support and—and all that. Do you know, my first conscious thought after the wreck was of relief that you had not been hurt?"

She was sitting beside me, where a big chestnut tree shaded the road, and I surprised a look of misery on her face that certainly my words had not been meant to produce.

"And my first thought," she said slowly, "was regret that I—that I hadn't been obliterated, blown out like a candle. Please don't look like that! I am only talking."

But her lips were trembling, and because the little shams of society are forgotten at times like this, I leaned over and patted her hand lightly, where it rested on the grass beside me.

"You must not say those things," I expostulated. "Perhaps, after all, your friends—"

"I had no friends on the train." Her voice was hard again, her tone final. She drew her hand from under mine, not quickly, but decisively. A car was in sight, coming toward us. The steel finger of civilization, of propriety, of visiting cards and formal introductions was beckoning us in. Miss West put on her shoe.

We said little on the car. The few passengers stared at us frankly, and discussed the wreck, emphasizing its horrors. The girl did not seem to hear. Once she turned to me with the quick, unexpected movement that was one of her charms.

"I do not wish my mother to know I was in the accident," she said. "Will you please not tell Richey about having met me?"

I gave my promise, of course. Again, when we were almost into Baltimore, she asked to examine the gun-metal cigarette case, and sat silent with it in her hands, while I told of the early morning's events on the Ontario.

"So you see," I finished, "this grip, everything I have on, belongs to a fellow named Sullivan. He probably left the train before the wreck—perhaps just after the murder."

"And so—you think he committed the—the crime?" Her eyes were on the cigarette case.

"Naturally," I said. "A man doesn't jump off a Pullman car in the middle of the night in another man's clothes, unless he is trying to get away from something. Besides the dirk, there were the stains that you saw. Why, I have the murdered man's pocketbook in this valise at my feet. What does that look like?"

I colored when I saw the ghost of a smile hovering around the corners of her mouth. "That is," I finished, "if you care to believe that I am innocent."

The sustaining chain of her small gold bag gave way just then. She did not notice it. I picked it up and slid the trinket into my pocket for safekeeping, where I promptly forgot it. Afterwards I wished I had let it lie unnoticed on the floor of that dirty little suburban car, and even now, when I see a woman carelessly dangling a similar feminine trinket, I shudder involuntarily: there comes back to me the memory of a girl's puzzled eyes under the brim of a flopping hat, the haunting suspicion of the sleepless nights that followed.

Just then I was determined that my companion should not stray back to the wreck, and to that end I was determinedly facetious.

"Do you know that it is Sunday?" she asked suddenly. "And that we are actually ragged?"

"Never mind that," I retorted. "All Baltimore is divided on Sunday into three parts, those who rise up and go to church, those who rise up and read the newspapers, and those who don't rise up. The first are somewhere between the creed and the sermon, and we need not worry about the others."

"You treat me like a child," she said almost pettishly. "Don't try so hard to be cheerful. It—it is almost ghastly."

After that I subsided like a pricked balloon, and the remainder of the ride was made in silence. The information that she would go to friends in the city was a shock: it meant an earlier separation than I had planned for. But my arm was beginning again. In putting her into a cab I struck it and gritted my teeth with the pain. It was probably for that reason that I forgot the gold bag.

She leaned forward and held out her hand. "I may not have another chance to thank you," she said, "and I think I would better not try, anyhow. I cannot tell you how grateful I am." I muttered something about the gratitude being mine. Owing to the knock I was seeing two cabs, and two girls were holding out two hands.

"Remember," they were both saying, "you have never met me, Mr. Blakeley. And if you ever hear anything about me that is not pleasant, I want you to think the best you can of me. Will you?"

The two girls were one now, with little flashes of white light playing all around. "I—I'm afraid that I shall think too well for my own good," I said unsteadily. And the cab drove on.

Chapter XI

The Name Was Sullivan

⌒∞⌒

I HAD my arm done up temporarily in Baltimore and took the next train home. I was pretty far gone when I stumbled out of a cab almost into the scandalized arms of Mrs. Klopton. In fifteen minutes I was in bed, with that good woman piling on blankets and blistering me in unprotected places with hot-water bottles. And in an hour I had a whiff of chloroform and Dr. Williams had set the broken bone.

I dropped asleep then, waking in the late twilight to a realization that I was at home again, without the papers that meant conviction for Andy Bronson, with a charge of murder hanging over my head, and with something more than an impression of the girl my best friend was in love with, a girl, moreover, who was almost as great an enigma as the crime itself.

"And I'm no hand at guessing riddles," I groaned half aloud. Mrs. Klopton came over promptly and put a cold cloth on my forehead.

"Euphemia," she said to someone outside the door, "telephone the doctor that he is still rambling, but that he has switched from green ribbons to riddles."

"There's nothing the matter with me, Mrs. Klopton," I rebelled. "I was only thinking out loud. Confound that cloth: it's trickling all over me!" I gave it a fling, and heard it land with a soggy thud on the floor.

"Thinking out loud is delirium," Mrs. Klopton said imperturbably. "A fresh cloth, Euphemia."

This time she held it on with a firm pressure that I was too weak to resist. I expostulated feebly that I was drowning, which she also laid to my mental exaltation, and then I finally dropped into a damp sleep. It was probably midnight when I roused again. I had been dreaming of the wreck, and it was inexpressibly comforting to feel the stability of my bed, and to realize the equal stability of Mrs. Klopton, who sat, fully attired, by the night light, reading *Science and Health.*

"Does that book say anything about opening the windows on a hot night?" I suggested, when I had got my bearings.

She put it down immediately and came over to me. If there is one time when Mrs. Klopton is chastened—and it is the only time— it is when she reads *Science and Health.* "I don't like to open the shutters, Mr. Lawrence," she explained. "Not since the night you went away."

But, pressed further, she refused to explain. "The doctor said you were not to be excited," she persisted. "Here's your beef tea."

"Not a drop until you tell me," I said firmly. "Besides, you know very well there's nothing the matter with me. This arm of mine is only a false belief." I sat up gingerly. "Now—why don't you open that window?"

Mrs. Klopton succumbed. "Because there are queer goings-on in that house next door," she said. "If you will take the beef tea, Mr. Lawrence, I will tell you."

The queer goings-on, however, proved to be slightly disappointing. It seemed that after I left on Friday night, a light was seen flitting fitfully through the empty house next door. Euphemia had seen it first and called Mrs. Klopton. Together they had watched it breathlessly until it disappeared on the lower floor.

"You should have been a writer of ghost stories," I said, giving my pillows a thump. "And so it was fitting fitfully!"

"That's what it was doing," she reiterated. "Fitting flitfully—I mean flitting fitfully—how you do throw me out, Mr. Lawrence! And what's more, it came again!"

"Oh, come now, Mrs. Klopton," I objected, "ghosts are like lightning; they never strike twice in the same night. That is only worth half a cup of beef tea."

"You may ask Euphemia," she retorted with dignity. "Not more than an hour after, there was a light there again. We saw it through the chinks of the shutters. Only—this time it began at the lower floor and climbed!"

"You oughtn't to tell ghost stories at night," came McKnight's voice from the doorway. "Really, Mrs. Klopton, I'm amazed at you. You old duffer! I've got you to thank for the worst day of my life."

Mrs. Klopton gulped. Then realizing that the "old duffer" was meant for me, she took her empty cup and went out muttering.

"The Pirate's crazy about me, isn't she?" McKnight said to the closing door. Then he swung around and held out his hand.

"By Jove," he said, "I've been laying you out all day, lilies on the doorbell, black gloves, everything. If you had had the sense of a mosquito in a snowstorm, you would have telephoned me."

"I never even thought of it." I was filled with remorse. "Upon my word, Rich, I hadn't an idea beyond getting away from that place. If you had seen what I saw——"

McKnight stopped me. "Seen it! Why, you lunatic, I've been digging for you all day in the ruins! I've lunched and dined on horrors. Give me something to rinse them down, Lollie."

He had fished the key of the cellarette from its hiding place in my shoe bag and was mixing himself what he called a Bernard Shaw—a foundation of brandy and soda, with a little of everything else in sight to give it snap. Now that I saw him clearly, he looked weary and grimy. I hated to tell him what I knew he was waiting to hear, but there was no use wading in by inches. I ducked and got it over.

"The notes are gone, Rich," I said, as quietly as I could. In spite of himself his face fell.

"I—of course I expected it," he said. "But Mrs. Klopton said over the telephone that you had brought home a grip and I hoped—— Well, Lord knows we ought not to complain. You're here, damaged, but here." He lifted his glass. "Happy days, old man!"

"If you will give me that black bottle and a teaspoon, I'll drink that in arnica, or whatever the stuff is; Rich—the notes were gone before the wreck!"

He wheeled and stared at me, the bottle in his hand. "Lost, strayed or stolen?" he queried with forced lightness.

"Stolen, although I believe the theft was incidental to something else."

Mrs. Klopton came in at that moment, with an eggnog in her hand. She glanced at the clock, and, without addressing anyone in particular, she intimated that it was time for self-respecting folks to be at home in bed. McKnight, who could never resist a fling at her back, spoke to me in a stage whisper.

"Is she talking still? Or again?" he asked, just before the door closed. There was a second's indecision with the knob, then, judging discretion the better part, Mrs. Klopton went away.

"Now, then," McKnight said, settling himself in a chair beside the bed, "spit it out. Not the wreck—I know all I want about that. But the theft. I can tell you beforehand that it was a woman.

I had crawled painfully out of bed, and was in the act of pouring the eggnog down the pipe of the washstand. I paused, with the glass in the air.

"A woman!" I repeated, startled. "What makes you think that?"

"You don't know the first principles of a good detective yarn," he said scornfully. "Of course, it was the woman in the empty house next door. You said it was brass pipes, you will remember. Well, on with the dance. Let joy be unconfined."

So I told the story; I had told it so many times that day that I did it automatically. And I told about the girl with the bronze hair, and my suspicions. But I did not mention Alison West. McKnight listened to the end without interruption. When I had finished, he drew a long breath.

"Well!" he said. "That's something of a mess, isn't it? If you can only prove your mild and childlike disposition, they couldn't hold you for the murder—which is a regular ten-twent-thirt crime, anyhow. But the notes—that's different. They are not burned, anyhow. Your man wasn't on the train—therefore, he wasn't in the wreck. If he didn't know what he was taking, as you seem to think, he probably reads the papers, and unless he is a fathead, he's awake by this time to what he's got. He'll try to sell them to Bronson, probably."

"Or to us," I put in.

We said nothing for a few minutes. McKnight smoked a cigarette and stared at a photograph of Candida over the mantel. Candida is the best pony for a heavy mount in seven states.

"I didn't go to Richmond," he observed finally. The remark followed my own thoughts so closely that I started. "Miss West is not home yet from Seal Harbor."

Receiving no response, he lapsed again into thoughtful silence. Mrs. Klopton came in just as the clock struck one, and made preparation for the night by putting a large gaudy comfortable into an armchair in the dressing room, with a smaller, stiff-backed chair for her feet. She was wonderfully attired in a dressing gown that was reminiscent, in parts, of all the ones she had given me for a half dozen Christmases, and she had a purple veil wrapped around her head, to hide Heaven knows what deficiency. She examined the empty eggnog glass, inquired what the evening paper had said about the weather, and then stalked into the dressing room, and prepared, with much ostentatious creaking, to sit up all night.

We fell silent again, while McKnight traced a rough outline of the berths on the white table cover, and puzzled it out slowly. It was something like this:

12	10	8
AISLE		
11	9	7

"You think he changed the tags on seven and nine, so that when you went back to bed, you thought you were crawling into nine, when it was really seven, eh?"

"Probably—yes."

"Then toward morning, when everybody was asleep, your theory is that he changed the numbers again and left the train."

"I can't think of anything else," I replied wearily.

"Jove, what a game of bridge that fellow would play! It was like finessing an eight-spot and winning out. They would scarcely have doubted your story had the tags been reversed in the morning. He certainly left you in a bad way. Not a jury in the country would stand out against the stains, the stiletto, and the murdered man's pocketbook in your possession."

"Then you think Sullivan did it?" I asked.

"Of course," said McKnight confidently. "Unless you did it in your sleep. Look at the stains on his pillow, and the dirk stuck into it. And didn't he have the man Harrington's pocketbook?"

"But why did he go off without the money?" I persisted. "And where does the bronze-haired girl come in?"

"Search me," McKnight retorted flippantly. "Inflammation of the imagination on your part."

"Then there is the piece of telegram. It said lower ten, car seven. It's extremely likely that she had it. That telegram was about me, Richey."

"I'm getting a headache," he said, putting out his cigarette against the sole of his shoe. "All I'm certain of just now is that if there hadn't been a wreck, by this time you'd be sitting in an eight-by-ten cell, and feeling like the rhyme for it."

"But listen to this," I contended, as he picked up his hat, "this fellow Sullivan is a fugitive, and he's a lot more likely to make advances to Bronson than to us. We could have the case continued, release Bronson on bail and set a watch on him."

"Not my watch," McKnight protested. "It's a family heirloom."

"You'd better go home," I said firmly. "Go home and go to bed. You're sleepy. You can have Sullivan's red necktie to dream over if you think it will help any."

Mrs. Klopton's voice came drowsily from the next room, punctuated by a yawn. "Oh, I forgot to tell you," she called, with the suspicious lisp which characterizes her at night, "somebody called up about noon, Mr. Lawrence. It was long distance, and he said he would call again. The name was"—she yawned—"Sullivan."

Chapter XII

The Gold Bag

I HAVE always smiled at those cases of spontaneous combustion which, like fusing the component parts of a seidlitz powder, unite two people in a bubbling and ephemeral ecstasy. But surely there is possible, with but a single meeting, an attraction so great, a community of mind and interest so strong, that between that first meeting and the next the bond may grow into something stronger. This is especially true, I fancy, of people with temperament, the modern substitute for imagination. It is a nice question whether lovers begin to love when they are together, or when they are apart.

Not that I followed any such line of reasoning at the time. I would not even admit my folly to myself. But during the restless hours of that first night after the accident, when my back ached with lying on it, and any other position was torture, I found my thoughts constantly going back to Alison West. I dropped into a doze, to dream of touching her fingers again to comfort her, and awoke to find I had patted a teaspoonful of medicine out of Mrs. Klopton's indignant hand. What was it McKnight had said about making an egregious ass of myself?

And that brought me back to Richey, and I fancy I groaned. There is no use expatiating on the friendship between two men who have gone together through college, have quarreled and made it up, fussed together over politics and debated creeds for years: men don't need to be told, and women cannot understand. Nevertheless, I groaned. If it had been anyone but Rich!

Some things were mine, however, and I would hold them: the halcyon breakfast, the queer hat, the pebble in her small shoe, the gold bag with the broken chain—the bag! Why, it was in my pocket at that moment.

I got up painfully and found my coat. Yes, there was the purse, bulging with an opulent suggestion of wealth inside. I went back to bed again, somewhat dizzy, between effort and the touch of the trinket, so lately hers. I held it up by its broken chain and gloated over it. By careful attention to orders, I ought to be out in a day or so. Then—I could return it to her. I really ought to do that: it was valuable, and I wouldn't care to trust it to the mail. I could run down to Richmond, and see her once—there was no disloyalty to Rich in that.

I had no intention of opening the little bag. I put it under my pillow—which was my reason for refusing to have the linen slips changed, to Mrs. Klopton's dismay. And sometimes during the morning, while I lay under a virgin field of white, ornamented with strange flowers, my cigarettes hidden beyond discovery, and *Science and Health* on a table by my elbow, as if by the merest accident, I slid my hand under my pillow and touched it reverently.

McKnight came in about eleven. I heard his car at the curb, followed almost immediately by his slam at the front door, and his usual clamor on the stairs. He had a bottle under his arm, rightly surmising that I had been forbidden stimulant, and a large box of cigarettes in his pocket, suspecting my deprivation.

"Well," he said cheerfully. "How did you sleep after keeping me up half the night?"

I slid my hand around: the purse was well covered. "Have it now, or wait till I get the cork out?" he rattled on.

"I don't want anything," I protested. "I wish you wouldn't be so darned cheerful, Richey." He stopped whistling to stare at me.

" 'I am saddest when I sing!' " he quoted unctuously. "It's pure reaction, Lollie. Yesterday the sky was low: I was digging for my best friend. Today—he lies before me, his peevish self. Yesterday I thought the notes were burned. Today—I look forward to a good cross-country chase, and with luck we will draw." His voice changed suddenly. "Yesterday—she was in Seal Harbor. Today she is here."

"Here in Washington?" I asked, as naturally as I could.

"Yes. Going to stay a week or two."

"Oh, I had a little hen and she had a wooden leg. And nearly every morning she used to lay an egg—"

"Will you stop that racket, Rich! It's the real thing this time, I suppose?"

"She's the best little chicken that we have on the farm. And another little drink won't do us any harm—" he finished, twisting out the corkscrew. Then he came over and sat down on the bed.

"Well," he said judicially, "since you drag it from me, I think perhaps it is. You—you're such a confirmed woman-hater that I hardly knew how you would take it."

"Nothing of the sort," I denied testily. "Because a man reaches the age of thirty without making maudlin love to every—"

"I've taken to long country rides," he went on reflectively, without listening to me, "and yesterday I ran over a sheep; nearly went into the ditch. But there's a Providence that watches over fools and lovers, and just now I know darned well that I'm one, and I have a sneaking idea I'm both."

"You are both," I said with disgust. "If you can be rational for one moment, I wish you would tell me why that man Sullivan called me over the telephone yesterday morning."

"Probably hadn't yet discovered the Bronson notes—providing you hold to your theory that the theft was incidental to the murder. May have wanted his own clothes again, or to thank you for yours. Search me: I can't think of anything else." The doctor came in just then.

As I said before, I think a lot of my doctor—when I am ill. He is a young man, with an air of breezy self-confidence and good humor. He looked directly past the bottle, which is a very valuable accomplishment, and shook hands with McKnight until I could put the cigarettes under the bedclothes. He had interdicted tobacco. Then he sat down beside the bed and felt around the bandages with hands as gentle as a baby's.

"Pretty good shape," he said. "How did you sleep?"

"Oh, occasionally," I replied. "I would like to sit up, doctor."

"Nonsense. Take a rest while you have an excuse for it. I wish to thunder I could stay in bed for a day or so. I was up all night."

"Have a drink," McKnight said, pushing over the bottle.

"Twins!" The doctor grinned.

"Have two drinks."

But the medical man refused.

"I wouldn't even wear a champagne-colored necktie during business hours," he explained. "By the way, I had another case from your accident, Mr. Blakeley, late yesterday afternoon. Under the tongue, please." He stuck a thermometer in my mouth.

I had a sudden terrible vision of the amateur detective coming to light, notebook, cheerful impertinence and incriminating data. "A small man?" I demanded. "Gray hair—"

"Keep your mouth closed," the doctor said peremptorily. "No. A woman, with a fractured skull. Beautiful case. Van Kirk was up to his eyes and sent for me. Hemorrhage, right-sided paralysis, irregular pupils—all the trimmings. Worked for two hours."

"Did she recover?" McKnight put in. He was examining the doctor with a new awe.

"She lifted her right arm before I left," the doctor finished cheerily, "so the operation was a success, even if she should die."

"Good Heavens," McKnight broke in, "and I thought you were just an ordinary mortal, like the rest of us! Let me touch you for luck. Was she pretty?"

"Yes, and young. Had a wealth of bronze-colored hair. Upon my soul, I hated to cut it."

McKnight and I exchanged glances.

"Do you know her name, doctor?" I asked.

"No. The nurses said her clothes came from a Pittsburgh tailor."

"She is not conscious, I suppose?"

"No; she may be, tomorrow—or in a week."

He looked at the thermometer, murmured something about liquid diet, avoiding my eye—Mrs. Klopton was broiling a chop at the time—and took his departure, humming cheerfully as he went downstairs. McKnight looked after him wistfully.

"Jove, I wish I had his constitution," he exclaimed. "Neither nerves nor heart! What a chauffeur he would make!"

But I was serious.

"I have an idea," I said grimly, "that this small matter of the murder is going to come up again, and that your uncle will be in the deuce of a fix if it does. If that woman is going to die, somebody ought to be around to take her deposition. She knows a lot, if she didn't do it herself. I wish you would go down to the telephone and get the hospital. Find out her name, and if she is conscious."

McKnight went under protest. "I haven't much time," he said, looking at his watch. "I'm to meet Mrs. West and Alison at one. I want you to know them, Lollie. You would like the mother."

"Why not the daughter?" I inquired. I touched the little gold bag under the pillow.

"Well," he said judicially, "you've always declared against the immaturity and romantic nonsense of very young women—"

"I never said anything of the sort," I retorted furiously.

" 'There is more satisfaction to be had out of a good saddle horse!' " he quoted me. " 'More excitement out of a polo pony, and as for the eternal matrimonial chase, give me instead a good stubble, a fox, some decent hounds and a hunter, and I'll show you the real joys of the chase!' "

"For Heaven's sake, go down to the telephone, you make my head ache," I said savagely.

I hardly know what prompted me to take out the gold purse and look at it. It was an imbecile thing to do—call it impulse, sentimentality, what you wish. I brought it out, one eye on the door, for Mrs. Klopton has a ready eye and a noiseless shoe. But the house was quiet. Downstairs

McKnight was flirting with the telephone central and there was an odor of boneset tea in the air. I think Mrs. Klopton was fascinated out of her theories by the "boneset" in connection with the fractured arm.

Anyhow, I held up the bag and looked at it. It must have been unfastened, for the next instant there was an avalanche on the snowfield of the counterpane—some money, a wisp of a handkerchief, a tiny booklet with thin leaves, covered with a powdery substance—and a necklace. I drew myself up slowly and stared at the necklace.

It was one of the semi-barbaric affairs that women are wearing now, a heavy pendant of gold chains and carved cameos, swung from a thin neck chain of the same metal. The necklace was broken: in three places the links were pulled apart and the cameos swung loose and partly detached. But it was the supporting chain that held my eye and fascinated with its sinister suggestion. Three inches of it had been snapped off, and as well as I knew anything on earth, I knew that the bit of chain that the amateur detective had found, bloodstain and all, belonged just there.

And there was no one I could talk to about it, no one to tell me how hideously absurd it was, no one to give me a slap and tell me there are tons of fine gold chains made every year, or to point out the long arm of coincidence!

With my one useful hand I fumbled the things back into the bag and thrust it deep out of sight among the pillows. Then I lay back in a cold perspiration. What connection had Alison West with this crime? Why had she stared so at the gun-metal cigarette case that morning on the train? What had alarmed her so at the farmhouse? What had she taken back to the gate? Why did she wish she had not escaped from the wreck? And last, in Heaven's name, how did a part of her necklace become torn off and covered with blood?

Downstairs McKnight was still at the telephone, and amusing himself with Mrs. Klopton in the interval of waiting.

"Why did he come home in a gray suit, when he went away in a blue?" he repeated. "Well, wrecks are queer things, Mrs. Klopton. The suit may have turned gray with fright. Or perhaps wrecks do as queer stunts as lightning. Friend of mine once was struck by lightning; he and the caddy had taken refuge under a tree. After the flash, when they recovered consciousness, there was my friend in the caddy's clothes, and the caddy in his. And as my friend was a large man and the caddy a very small boy—"

McKnight's story was interrupted by the indignant slam of the dining-room door. He was obliged to wait some time, and even his eternal cheerfulness was ebbing when he finally got the hospital.

"Is Dr. Van Kirk there?" he asked. "Not there? Well, can you tell me how the patient is whom Dr. Williams, from Washington, operated on last night? Well, I'm glad of that. Is she conscious? Do you happen to know her name? Yes, I'll hold the line." There was a long pause, then McKnight's voice.

"Hello—yes. Thank you very much. Good-bye."

He came upstairs, two steps at a time.

"Look here," he said, bursting into the room, "there may be something in your theory, after all. The woman's name—it may be a coincidence, but it's curious—her name is Sullivan."

"What did I tell you?" I said, sitting up suddenly in bed. "She's probably a sister of that scoundrel in lower seven, and she was afraid of what he might do."

"Well, I'll go there some day soon. She's not conscious yet. In the meantime, the only thing I can do is to keep an eye, through a detective, on the people who try to approach Bronson. We'll have the case continued, anyhow, in the hope that the stolen notes will sooner or later turn up."

"Confound this arm," I said, paying for my energy with some excruciating throbs. "There's so much to be looked after, and here I am, bandaged, splinted, and generally useless. It's a beastly shame."

"Don't forget that I am here," said McKnight pompously. "And another thing, when you feel this way, just remember there are two less desirable places where you might be. One is jail, and the other is—" He strummed on an imaginary harp, with devotional eyes.

But McKnight's lightheartedness jarred on me that morning. I lay and frowned under my helplessness. When by chance I touched the little gold bag, it seemed to scorch my fingers. Richey, finding me unresponsive, left to keep his luncheon engagement with Alison West. As he clattered down the stairs, I turned my back to the morning sunshine and abandoned myself to misery. By what strain on her frayed nerves was Alison West keeping up, I wondered? Under the circumstances, would

I dare to return the bag? Knowing that I had it, would she hate me for my knowledge? Or had I exaggerated the importance of the necklace, and in that case had she forgotten me already?

But McKnight had not gone, after all. I heard him coming back, his voice preceding him, and I groaned with irritation.

"Wake up!" he called. "Somebody's sent you a lot of flowers. Please hold the box, Mrs. Klopton; I'm going out to be run down by an automobile."

I roused to feeble interest. My brother's wife is punctilious about such things; all the new babies in the family have silver rattles, and all the sick people flowers.

McKnight pulled up an armful of roses, and held them out to me.

"Wonder who they're from?" he said, fumbling in the box for a card. "There's no name—yes, here's one."

He held it up and read it with exasperating slowness.

> Best wishes for an early recovery.
> —A Companion in Misfortune

"Well, what do you know about that!" he exclaimed. "That's something you didn't tell me, Lollie."

"It was hardly worth mentioning," I said mendaciously, with my heart beating until I could hear it. She had not forgotten, after all.

McKnight took a bud and fastened it in his buttonhole. I'm afraid I was not especially pleasant about it. They were her roses, and anyhow, they were meant for me. Richey left very soon, with an irritating final grin at the box.

"Good-bye, sir woman-hater," he jeered at me from the door.

So he wore one of the roses she had sent me, to luncheon with her, and I lay back among my pillows and tried to remember that it was his game, anyhow, and that I wasn't even drawing cards. To remember that, and to forget the broken necklace under my head!

Chapter XIII

Faded Roses

I WAS in the house for a week. Much of that time I spent in composing and destroying letters of thanks to Miss West, and in growling at the doctor. McKnight dropped in daily, but he was less cheerful than usual. Now and then I caught him eyeing me as if he had something to say, but whatever it was he kept it to himself. Once during the week he went to Baltimore and saw the woman in the hospital there. From the description I had little difficulty in recognizing the young woman who had been with the murdered man in Pittsburgh. But she was still unconscious. An elderly aunt had appeared, a gaunt person in black, who sat around like a buzzard on a fence, according to McKnight, and wept, in a mixed figure, into a damp handkerchief.

On the last day of my imprisonment he stopped in to thrash out a case that was coming up in court the next day, and to play a game of double solitaire with me.

"Who won the ball game?" I asked.

"We were licked. Ask me something pleasant. Oh, by the way, Bronson's out today."

"I'm glad I'm not on his bond," I said pessimistically. "He'll clear out."

"Not he." McKnight pounced on my ace. "He's no fool. Don't you suppose he knows you took those notes to Pittsburgh? The papers were full of it. And he knows you escaped with your life and a broken arm from the wreck. What do we do next? The Commonwealth continues the case. A deaf man on a dark night would know those notes are missing."

"Don't play so fast," I remonstrated. "I have only one arm to your two. Who is trailing Bronson? Did you try to get Johnson?"

"I asked for him, but he had some work on hand."

"The murder's evidently a dead issue," I reflected. "No, I'm not joking. The wreck destroyed all the evidence. But I'm firmly convinced those notes will be offered, either to us or to Bronson very soon. Johnson's a blackguard, but he's a good detective. He could make his fortune as a game dog. What's he doing?"

McKnight put down his cards, and rising, went to the window. As he held the curtain back his customary grin looked a little forced.

"To tell you the truth, Lollie," he said, "for the last two days he has been watching a well-known Washington attorney named Lawrence Blakeley. He's across the street now."

It took a moment for me to grasp what he meant.

"Why, it's ridiculous," I asserted. "What would they trail me for? Go over and tell Johnson to get out of there, or I'll pot at him with my revolver."

"You can tell him that yourself." McKnight paused and bent forward. "Hello, here's a visitor; little man with string halt."

"I won't see him," I said firmly. "I've been bothered enough with reporters."

We listened together to Mrs. Klopton's expostulating tones in the lower hall and the creak of the boards as she came heavily up the stairs. She had a piece of paper in her hand torn from a pocket account book, and on it was the name Mr. Wilson Budd Hotchkiss. "Important business."

"Oh, well, show him up," I said resignedly. "You'd better put those cards away, Richey. I fancy it's the rector of the church around the corner."

But when the door opened to admit a curiously alert little man, adjusting his glasses with nervous fingers, my face must have shown my dismay.

It was the amateur detective of the Ontario!

I shook hands without enthusiasm. Here was the one survivor of the wrecked car who could do me any amount of harm. There was no hope that he had forgotten any of the incriminating details. In fact, he held in his hand the very notebook which contained them.

His manner was restrained, but it was evident he was highly excited. I introduced him to McKnight, who has the imagination I lack, and who placed him at once, mentally.

"I only learned yesterday that you had been—er—saved," he said rapidly. "Terrible accident—unspeakable. Dream about it all night and think about it all day. Broken arm?"

"No. He just wears the splint to be different from other people," McKnight drawled lazily. I glared at him; there was nothing to be gained by antagonizing the little man.

"Yes, a fractured humerus, which isn't as funny as it sounds."

"Humerus—humorous! Pretty good," he cackled. "I must say you keep up your spirits pretty well, considering everything."

"You seem to have escaped injury," I parried. He was fumbling for something in his pockets.

"Yes, I escaped," he replied abstractedly. "Remarkable thing, too. I haven't a doubt I would have broken my neck, but I landed on you'll never guess what! I landed headfirst on the very pillow which was under inspection at the time of the wreck. You remember, don't you? Where did I put that package?"

He found it finally and opened it on a table, displaying with some theatricalism a rectangular piece of muslin and a similar patch of striped ticking.

"You recognize it?" he said. "The stains, you see, and the hole made by the dirk. I tried to bring away the entire pillow, but they thought I was stealing it, and made me give it up."

Richey touched the pieces gingerly. "By George," he said, "and you carry that around in your pocket! What if you should mistake it for your handkerchief?"

But Mr. Hotchkiss was not listening. He stood bent somewhat forward, leaning over the table, and fixed me with his ferretlike eyes.

"Have you see the evening papers, Mr. Blakeley?" he inquired.

I glanced to where they lay unopened, and shook my head.

"Then I have a disagreeable task," he said with evident relish. "Of course, you had considered the matter of the man Harrington's death closed, after the wreck. I did myself. As far as I was concerned, I meant to let it remain so. There were no other survivors, at least none that I knew of, and in spite of circumstances, there were a number of points in your favor."

"Thank you," I put in with a sarcasm that was lost on him.

"I verified your identity, for instance, as soon as I recovered from the shock. Also—I found on inquiring of your tailor that you invariably wore dark clothing."

McKnight came forward threateningly. "Who are you, anyhow?" he demanded. "And how is this any business of yours?" Mr. Hotchkiss was entirely unruffled.

"I have a minor position here," he said, reaching for a visiting card. "I am a very small patch on the seat of government, sir."

McKnight muttered something about certain offensive designs against the said patch and retired grumbling to the window. Our visitor was opening the paper with a tremendous expenditure of energy.

"Here it is. Listen." He read rapidly aloud.

"The Pittsburgh police have sent to Baltimore two detectives who are looking up the survivors of the ill-fated *Washington Flier*. It has transpired that Simon Harrington, the Wood Street merchant of that city, was not killed in the wreck, but was murdered in his berth the night preceding the accident. Shortly before the collision, John Flanders, the conductor of the *Flier*, sent this telegram to the chief of police:

BODY OF SIMON HARRINGTON FOUND STABBED IN HIS BERTH, LOWER TEN, ONTARIO, AT SIX-THIRTY THIS MORNING.

—JOHN FLANDERS, CONDUCTOR

"It is hoped that the survivors of the wrecked car Ontario will be found, to tell what they know of the discovery of the crime.

"Mr. John Gilmore, head of the steel company for which Mr. Harrington was purchasing agent, has signified his intention of sifting the matter to the bottom.

"So you see," Hotchkiss concluded. "there's trouble brewing. You and I are the only survivors of that unfortunate car."

I did not contradict him, but I knew of two others, at least: Alison West, and the woman we had left beside the road that morning, babbling incoherently, her black hair tumbling over her white face.

"Unless we can find the man who occupied lower seven," I suggested.

"I have already tried and failed. To find him would not clear you, of course, unless we could establish some connection between him and the murdered man. It is the only thing I see, however. I have learned this much," Hotchkiss concluded. "Lower seven was reserved from Cresson."

Cresson! Where Alison West and Mrs. Curtis had taken the train!

McKnight came forward and suddenly held out his hand. "Mr. Hotchkiss," he said, "I—I'm sorry if I have been offensive. I thought when you came in, that, like the Irishman and the government, you were 'forninst' us. If you will put those cheerful relics out of sight somewhere, I should be glad to have you dine with me at the Incubator." (His name for his bachelor apartment.) "Compared with Johnson, you are the great original protoplasm."

The strength of this was lost on Hotchkiss, but the invitation was clear. They went out together, and from my window I watched them get into McKnight's car. It was raining, and at the corner the Cannonball skidded. Across the street my detective, Johnson, looked after them with his crooked smile. As he turned up his collar he saw me, and lifted his hat.

I left the window and sat down in the growing dusk. So the occupant of lower seven had got on the car at Cresson, probably with Alison West and her companion. There was someone she cared about enough to shield. I went irritably to the door and summoned Mrs. Klopton.

"You may throw out those roses," I said without looking at her. "They are quite dead."

"They have been quite dead for three days," she retorted spitefully. "Euphemia said you threatened to dismiss her if she touched them."

Chapter XIV

The Trapdoor

By SUNDAY evening, a week after the wreck, my inaction had goaded me to frenzy. The very sight of Johnson across the street or lurking, always within sight of the house, kept me constantly exasperated. It was on that day that things began to come to a focus, a burning-glass of events that seemed to center on me.

I dined alone that evening in no cheerful frame of mind. There had been a polo game the day before and I had lent a pony, which is always a bad thing to do. And she had wrenched her shoulder, besides helping to lose the game. There was no one in town: the temperature was ninety and climbing, and my left hand persistently cramped under its bandage.

Mrs. Klopton herself saw me served, my bread buttered and cut in tidbits, my meat ready for my fork. She hovered around me maternally, obviously trying to cheer me.

"The paper says still warmer," she ventured. "The thermometer is ninety-two now."

"And this coffee is two hundred and fifty," I said, putting down my cup. "Where is Euphemia? I haven't seen her around, or heard a dish smash all day."

"Euphemia is in bed," Mrs. Klopton said gravely. "Is your meat cut small enough, Mr. Lawrence?" Mrs. Klopton can throw more mystery into an ordinary sentence than anyone I know. She can say, "Are your sheets damp, sir?" And I can tell from her tone that the house across the street has been robbed, or that my left-hand neighbor has appendicitis. So now I looked up and asked the question she was waiting for.

"What's the matter with Euphemia?" I inquired idly.

"Frightened into her bed," Mrs. Klopton said in a stage whisper. "She's had three hot-water bottles and she hasn't done a thing all day but moan."

"She oughtn't to take hot-water bottles," I said in my severest tone. "One would make me moan. You need not wait, I'll ring if I need anything."

Mrs. Klopton sailed to the door, where she stopped and wheeled indignantly. "I only hope you won't laugh on the wrong side of your face some morning, Mr. Lawrence," she declared, with Christian fortitude. "But I warn you, I am going to have the police watch that house next door."

I was half inclined to tell her that both it and we were under police surveillance at that moment. But I like Mrs. Klopton, in spite of the fact that I make her life a torment for her, so I refrained.

"Last night, when the paper said it was going to storm, I sent Euphemia to the roof to bring the rugs in. Eliza had slipped out, although it was her evening in. Euphemia went up to the roof—it was eleven o'clock—and soon I heard her running downstairs crying. When she got to my room she just folded up on the floor. She said there was a black figure sitting on the parapet of the house next door—the empty house—and that when she appeared it rose and waved long black arms at her and spit like a cat."

I had finished my dinner and was lighting a cigarette. "If there was anyone up there, which I doubt, they probably sneezed," I suggested. "But if you feel uneasy, I'll take a look around the roof tonight before I turn in. As far as Euphemia goes, I wouldn't be uneasy about her— doesn't she always have an attack of some sort when Eliza rings in an extra evening on her?"

So I made a superficial examination of the window locks that night, visiting parts of the house that I had not seen since I bought it. Then I went to the roof. Evidently it had not been intended for any purpose save to cover the house, for unlike the houses around, there was no staircase. A ladder and a trapdoor led to it, and it required some nice balancing on my part to get up with my useless arm. I made it, however, and found this unexplored part of my domain rather attractive. It was cooler than downstairs, and I sat on the brick parapet and smoked my final cigarette. The roof of the empty house adjoined mine along the back wing, but investigation showed that the trapdoor across the low dividing wall was bolted underneath.

There was nothing out of the ordinary anywhere, and so I assured Mrs. Klopton. Needless to say, I did not tell her that I had left the trap-door open, to see if it would improve the temperature of the house. I went to bed at midnight, merely because there was nothing else to do. I turned on the night lamp at the head of my bed, and picked up a volume of Shaw at random (it was *Arms and the Man,* and I remember thinking grimly that I was a good bit of a chocolate cream soldier myself), and prepared to go to sleep. Shaw always puts me to sleep. I have no apologies to make for what occurred that night, and not even an explanation that I am sure of. I did a foolish thing under impulse, and I have not been sorry.

It was something after two when the doorbell rang. It rang quickly, twice. I got up drowsily, for the maids and Mrs. Klopton always lock themselves beyond reach of the bell at night, and put on a dressing gown. The bell rang again on my way downstairs. I lit the hall light and opened the door. I was wide-awake now, and I saw that it was Johnson. His bald head shone in the light; his crooked mouth was twisted in a smile.

"Good Heavens, man," I said irritably. "Don't you ever go home and go to bed?"

He closed the vestibule door behind him and cavalierly turned out the light. Our dialogue was sharp, staccato.

"Have you a key to the empty house next door?" he demanded. "Somebody's in there, and the latch is caught."

"The houses are alike. The key to this door may fit. Did you see them go in?"

"No. There's a light moving up from room to room. I saw something like it last night, and I have been watching. The patrolman reported queer doings there a week or so ago."

"A light!" I exclaimed. "Do you mean that you—"

"Very likely," he said grimly. "Have you a revolver?"

"All kinds in the gun rack," I replied, and going into the den, I came back with a Smith and Wesson. "I'm not much use," I explained, "with this arm, but I'll do what I can. There may be somebody there. The servants here have been uneasy."

Johnson planned the campaign. He suggested on account of my familiarity with the roof, that I go there and cut off escape in that direction. "I have Robison out there now—the patrolman on the beat," he said. "He'll watch below and you above, while I search the house. Be as quiet as possible."

I was rather amused. I put on some clothes and felt my way carefully up the stairs, the revolver swinging free in my pocket, my hand on the rail. At the foot of the ladder I stopped and looked up. Above me there was a gray rectangle of sky dotted with stars. It occurred to me that with my one serviceable hand holding the ladder, I was hardly in a position to defend myself, that I was about to hoist a body that I am rather careful of into a danger I couldn't see and wasn't particularly keen about anyhow. I don't mind saying that the seconds it took me to scramble up the ladder were among the most unpleasant that I recall.

I got to the top, however, without incident. I could see fairly well after the darkness of the house beneath, but there was nothing suspicious in sight. The roofs, separated by two feet of brick wall, stretched around me, unbroken save by an occasional chimney. I went very softly over to the other trap, the one belonging to the suspected house. It was closed, but I imagined I could hear Johnson's footsteps ascending heavily. Then even that was gone. A nearby clock struck three as I stood waiting. I examined my revolver then, for the first time, and found it was empty!

I had been rather skeptical until now. I had had the usual tolerant attitude of the man who is summoned from his bed to search for burglars, combined with the artificial courage of firearms. With the discovery of my empty gun, I felt like a man on the top of a volcano in lively eruption. Suddenly I found myself staring incredulously at the trapdoor at my feet. I had examined it early in the evening and found it bolted. Did I imagine it, or had it raised about an inch? Wasn't it moving slowly as I looked? No, I am not a hero: I was startled almost into a panic. I had one arm, and whoever was raising that trapdoor had two. My knees had a queer inclination to bend the wrong way.

Johnson's footsteps were distinct enough, but he was evidently far below. The trap, raised perhaps two inches now, remained stationary. There was no sound from beneath it. Once I thought I heard two or three gasping respirations; I am not sure they were not my own. I wanted desperately to stand on one leg at a time and hold the other up out of focus of a possible revolver.

I did not see the hand appear. There was nothing there, and then it was there, clutching the frame of the trap. I did the only thing I could think of; I put my foot on it!

There was not a sound from beneath. The next moment I was kneeling and had clutched the wrist just above the hand. After a second's struggle, the arm was still. With something real to face, I was myself again.

"Don't move, or I'll stand on the trap and break your arm," I panted. What else could I threaten? I couldn't shoot, I couldn't even fight. "Johnson!" I called.

And then I realized the thing that stayed with me for a month, the thing I cannot think of even now without a shudder. The hand lay ice cold, strangely quiescent. Under my fingers, an artery was beating feebly. The wrist was as slender as—I held the hand to the light. Then I let it drop.

"Good Lord," I muttered, and remained on my knees, staring at the spot where the hand had been. It was gone now; there was a faint rustle in the darkness below, and then silence.

I held up my own hand in the starlight and stared at a long scratch in the palm. "A woman!" I said to myself stupidly. "By all that's ridiculous, a woman!"

Johnson was striking matches below and swearing softly to himself. "How the devil do you get to the roof?" he called. "I think I've broken my nose."

He found the ladder after a short search and stood at the bottom, looking up at me. "Well, I suppose you haven't seen him?" he inquired. "There are enough darned cubbyholes in this house to hide a patrol wagon load of thieves." He lighted a fresh match. "Hello, here's another door!"

By the sound of his diminishing footsteps I supposed it was a rear staircase. He came up again in ten minutes or so, this time with the policeman.

"He's gone, all right," he said ruefully. "If you'd been attending to your business, Robison, you'd have watched the back door."

"I'm not twins." Robison was surly.

"Well," I broke in, as cheerfully as I could, "if you are through with this jolly little affair, and can get down my ladder without having my housekeeper ring the burglar alarm, I have some good Monongahela whisky—eh?"

They came without a second invitation across the roof, and with them safely away from the house I breathed more freely. Down in the den I fulfilled my promise, which Johnson drank to the toast, "Coming through the rye." He examined my gun rack with the eye of a connoisseur, and even when he was about to go he cast a loving eye back at the weapons.

"Ever been in the army?" he inquired.

"No," I said with a bitterness that he noticed but failed to comprehend. "I'm a chocolate cream soldier—you don't read Shaw, I suppose, Johnson?"

"Never heard of him," the detective said indifferently. "Well, good night, Mr. Blakeley. Much obliged." At the door he hesitated and coughed.

"I suppose you understand, Mr. Blakeley," he said awkwardly, "that this—er—surveillance is all in the day's work. I don't like it, but it's duty. Every man to his duty, sir."

"Sometime when you are in an open mood, Johnson," I returned, "you can explain why I am being watched at all."

Chapter XV

The Cinematograph

ON MONDAY I went out for the first time. I did not go to the office. I wanted to walk. I thought fresh air and exercise would drive away the blue devils that had me by the throat. McKnight insisted on a long day in his car, but I refused.

"I don't know why not," he said sulkily. "I can't walk. I haven't walked two consecutive blocks in three years. Automobiles have made legs mere ornaments—and some not even that. We could have Johnson out there chasing us over the country at five dollars an hour!"

"He can chase us just as well at five miles an hour," I said. "But what gets me, McKnight, is why I am under surveillance at all. How do the police know I was accused of that thing?"

"The young lady who sent the flowers—she isn't likely to talk, is she?"

"No. That is, I didn't say it was a lady." I groaned as I tried to get my splinted arm into a coat. "Anyhow, she didn't tell," I finished with conviction, and McKnight laughed.

It had rained in the early morning, and Mrs. Klopton predicted more showers. In fact, so firm was her belief and so determined her eye that I took the umbrella she proffered me.

"Never mind," I said. "We can leave it next door; I have a story to tell you, Richey, and it requires proper setting."

McKnight was puzzled, but he followed me obediently round to the kitchen entrance of the empty house. It was unlocked, as I had expected. While we climbed to the upper floor I retailed the events of the previous night.

"It's the finest thing I ever heard of," McKnight said, staring up at the ladder and the trap. "What a vaudeville skit it would make! Only you ought not to have put your foot on her hand. They don't do it in the best circles."

I wheeled on him impatiently.

"You don't understand the situation at all, Richey!" I exclaimed. "What would you say if I tell you it was the hand of a lady? It was covered with rings."

"A lady!" he repeated. "Why, I'd say it was a darned compromising situation, and that the less you say of it the better. Look here, Lawrence, I think you dreamed it. You've been in the house too much. I take it all back: you do need exercise."

"She escaped through this door, I suppose," I said as patiently as I could. "Evidently down the back staircase. We might as well go down that way."

"According to the best precedents in these affairs, we should find a glove about here," he said as we started down. But he was more impressed than he cared to own. He examined the dusty steps carefully, and once, when a bit of loose plaster fell just behind him, he started like a nervous woman.

"What I don't understand is why you let her go," he said, stopping once, puzzled. "You're not usually quixotic."

"When we get out into the country, Richey," I replied gravely, "I am going to tell you another story, and if you don't tell me I'm a fool and a craven, on the strength of it, you are no friend of mine."

We stumbled through the twilight of the staircase into the blackness of the shuttered kitchen. The house had the moldy smell of closed buildings; even on that warm September morning it was damp and chilly. As we stepped into the sunshine McKnight gave a shiver.

"Now that we are out," he said, "I don't mind telling you that I have been there before. Do you remember the night you left, and the face at the window?"

"When you speak of it—yes."

"Well, I was curious about that thing," he went on, as we started up the street, "and I went back. The street door was unlocked, and I examined every room. I was Mrs. Klopton's ghost that carried a light, and clumb."

"Did you find anything?"

"Only a clean place rubbed on the window opposite your dressing room. Splendid view of an untidy interior. If that house is ever occupied, you'd better put stained glass in that window of yours."

As we turned the corner I glanced back. Half a block behind us

Johnson was moving our way slowly. When he saw me, he stopped and proceeded with great deliberation to light a cigar. By hurrying, however, he caught the car that we took, and stood unobtrusively on the rear platform. He looked fagged, and absentmindedly paid our fares, to McKnight's delight.

"We will give him a run for his money," he declared, as the car moved countryward. "Conductor, let us off at the muddiest lane you can find."

At one o'clock, after a six-mile ramble, we entered a small country hotel. We had seen nothing of Johnson for a half hour. At that time he was a quarter of a mile behind us, and losing rapidly. Before we had finished our luncheon he staggered into the inn. One of his boots was under his arm, and his whole appearance was deplorable. He was coated with mud, streaked with perspiration, and he limped as he walked. He chose a table not far from us and ordered Scotch. Beyond touching his hat he paid no attention to us.

"I'm just getting my second wind," McKnight declared. "How do you feel, Mr. Johnson? Six or eight miles more and we'll all enjoy our dinners." Johnson put down the glass he had raised to his lips without replying.

The fact was, however, that I was like Johnson. I was soft from my week's inaction, and I was pretty well done up. McKnight, who was a wellspring of vitality and high spirits, ordered a strange concoction, made of nearly everything in the bar, and sent it over to the detective, but Johnson refused it.

"I hate that kind of person," McKnight said pettishly. "Kind of a fellow that thinks you're going to poison his dog if you offer him a bone."

When we got back to the car line, with Johnson a draggled and drooping tail to the kite, I was in better spirits. I had told McKnight the story of the three hours just after the wreck. I had not named the girl, of course; she had my promise of secrecy. But I told him everything else. It was a relief to have a fresh mind on it. I had puzzled so much over the incident at the farmhouse, and the necklace in the gold bag, that I had lost perspective.

He had been interested, but inclined to be amused, until I came to the broken chain. Then he had whistled softly.

"But there are tons of fine gold chains made every year," he said. "Why in the world do you think that the—er—smeary piece came from that necklace?"

I had looked around. Johnson was far behind, scraping the mud off his feet with a piece of stick.

"I have the short end of the chain in the sealskin bag," I reminded him. "When I couldn't sleep this morning, I thought I would settle it, one way or the other. It was hell to go along the way I had been doing. And there's no doubt about it, Rich. It's the same chain."

We walked along in silence until we caught the car back to town.

"Well," he said finally, "you know the girl, of course, and I don't. But if you like her—and I think myself you're rather hard hit, old man—I wouldn't give a whoop about the chain in the gold purse. It's just one of the little coincidences that hang people now and then. And as for last night—if she's the kind of a girl you say she is, and you think she had anything to do with that, you—you're addled, that's all. You can depend on it, the lady of the empty house last week is the lady of last night. And yet your train acquaintance was in Altoona at that time."

Just before we got off the car, I reverted to the subject again. It was never far back in my mind.

"About the—young lady of the train, Rich," I said, with what I suppose was elaborate carelessness, "I don't want you to get a wrong impression. I am rather unlikely to see her again, but even if I do, I—I believe she is already 'bespoke,' or next thing to it."

He made no reply, but as I opened the door with my latchkey he stood looking up at me from the pavement with his quizzical smile.

"Love is like the measles," he orated. "The older you get it, the worse the attack."

Johnson did not appear again that day. A small man in a raincoat took his place. The next morning I made my initial trip to the office, the raincoat still on hand. I had a short conference with Miller, the district attorney, at eleven. Bronson was under surveillance, he said, and any attempt to sell the notes to him would probably result in their recovery. In the meantime, as I knew, the Commonwealth had continued the case, in hope of such contingency.

At noon I left the office and took a veterinarian to see Candida, the injured pony. By one o'clock my first day's duties were performed, and a long Sahara of hot afternoon stretched ahead. McKnight, always glad to escape from the grind, suggested a vaudeville, and in sheer ennui I consented. I could neither ride, drive nor golf, and my own company bored me to distraction.

"Coolest place in town these days," he declared. "Electric fans, breezy songs, airy costumes. And there's Johnson just behind—the coldest proposition in Washington."

He gravely bought three tickets and presented the detective with one. Then we went in. Having lived a normal, busy life, the theater in the afternoon is to me about on a par with ice cream for breakfast. Up on the stage a very stout woman in short pink skirts, with a smile that McKnight declared looked like a slash in a roll of butter, was singing nasally, with a laborious kick at the end of each verse. Johnson, two rows ahead, went to sleep. McKnight prodded me with his elbow.

"Look at the first box to the right," he said in a stage whisper. "I want you to come over at the end of this act."

It was the first time I had seen her since I put her in the cab at Baltimore. Outwardly I presume I was calm, for no one turned to stare at me, but every atom of me cried out at the sight of her. She was leaning, bent forward, lips slightly parted, gazing raptly at the Japanese conjurer who had replaced what McKnight disrespectfully called the Columns of Hercules. Compared with the draggled lady of the farmhouse, she was radiant.

For that first moment there was nothing but joy at the sight of her. McKnight's touch on my arm brought me back to reality.

"Come over and meet them," he said. "That's the cousin Miss West is visiting, Mrs. Dallas."

But I would not go. After he went I sat there alone, painfully conscious that I was being pointed out and stared at from the box. The abominable Japanese gave way to yet more atrocious performing dogs.

"How many offers of marriage will the young lady in the box have?" The dog stopped sagely at 'none,' and then pulled out a card that said eight. Wild shouts of glee by the audience. "The fools," I muttered.

After a little I glanced over. Mrs. Dallas was talking to McKnight, but she was looking straight at me. She was flushed, but more calm than I, and she did not bow. I fumbled for my hat, but the next moment I saw that they were going, and I sat still. When McKnight came back, he was triumphant.

"I've made an engagement for you," he said. "Mrs. Dallas asked me to bring you to dinner tonight, and I said I knew you would fall all over yourself to go. You are requested to bring along the broken arm, and any other souvenirs of the wreck that you may possess."

"I'll do nothing of the sort," I declared, struggling against my inclination. "I can't even tie my necktie, and I have to have my food cut for me."

"Oh, that's all right," he said easily. "I'll send Stogie over to fix you up, and Mrs. Dal knows all about the arm. I told her."

(Stogie is his Japanese factotum, so-called because he is lean, a yellowish brown in color, and because he claims to have been shipped into this country in a box.)

The cinematograph was finishing the program. The house was dark and the music had stopped, as it does in the circus just before somebody risks his neck at so much a neck in the Dip of Death, or the hundred-foot dive. Then, with a sort of shock, I saw on the white curtain the announcement:

THE NEXT PICTURE IS THE DOOMED *WASHINGTON FLIER*, TAKEN A SHORT DISTANCE FROM THE SCENE OF THE WRECK ON THE FATAL MORNING OF SEPTEMBER TENTH. TWO MILES FURTHER ON IT MET WITH ALMOST COMPLETE ANNIHILATION.

I confess to a return of some of the sickening sensations of the wreck; people around me were leaning forward with tense faces. Then the letters were gone, and I saw a long level stretch of track, even the broken stone between the ties standing out distinctly. Far off under a cloud of smoke a small object was rushing toward us and growing larger as it came.

Now it was on us, a mammoth in size, with huge drivers and a colossal tender. The engine leaped aside, as if just in time to save us from destruction, with a glimpse of a stooping fireman and a grimy engineer. The long train of sleepers followed. From a forward vestibule a porter in a white coat waved his hand. The rest of the cars seemed still wrapped in slumber. With mixed sensations I saw my own car,

Ontario, fly past, and then I rose to my feet and gripped McKnight's shoulder.

On the lowest step at the last car, one foot hanging free, was a man. His black derby hat was pulled well down to keep it from blowing away, and his coat was flying open in the wind. He was swung well out from the car, his free hand gripping a small valise, every muscle tense for a jump.

"Good God, that's my man!" I said hoarsely, as the audience broke into applause. McKnight half rose; in his seat ahead Johnson stifled a yawn and turned to eye me.

I dropped into my chair limply, and tried to control my excitement. "The man on the last platform of the train," I said. "He was just about to leap; I'll swear that was my bag."

"Could you see his face?" McKnight asked in an undertone. "Would you know him again?"

"No. His hat was pulled down and his head was bent. I'm going back to find out where that picture was taken. They say two miles, but it may have been forty."

The audience, busy with its wraps, had not noticed. Mrs. Dallas and Alison West had gone. In front of us Johnson had dropped his hat and was stooping for it.

"This way," I motioned to McKnight, and we wheeled into the narrow passage beside us, back of the boxes. At the end there was a door leading into the wings, and as we went boldly through I turned the key.

The final set was being struck, and no one paid any attention to us. Luckily they were similarly indifferent to a banging at the door I had locked, a banging which, I judged, signified Johnson.

"I guess we've broken up his interference," McKnight chuckled.

Stagehands were hurrying in every direction; pieces of the side wall of the last drawing room menaced us; a switchboard behind us was singing like a tea kettle. Everywhere we stepped we were in somebody's way. At last we were across, confronting a man in his shirt sleeves, who by dots and dashes of profanity seemed to be directing the chaos.

"Well?" he said, wheeling on us. "What can I do for you?"

"I would like to ask," I replied, "if you have any idea just where the last cinematograph picture was taken."

"Broken board—picnickers—lake?"

"No. The *Washington Flier.*"

He glanced at my bandaged arm.

"The announcement says two miles," McKnight put in, "but we should like to know whether it is railroad miles, automobile miles, or policeman miles."

"I am sorry I can't tell you," he replied, more civilly. "We get those pictures by contract. We don't take them ourselves."

"Where are the company's offices?"

"New York." He stepped forward and grasped a super by the shoulder. "What in blazes are you doing with that gold chair in a kitchen set? Take that piece of pink plush there and throw it over a soap box, if you haven't got a kitchen chair."

I had not realized the extent of the shock, but now I dropped into a chair and wiped my forehead. The unexpected glimpse of Alison West, followed almost immediately by the revelation of the picture, had left me limp and unnerved. McKnight was looking at his watch.

"He says the moving picture people have an office downtown. We can make it if we go now."

So he called a cab, and we started at a gallop. There was no sign of the detective. "Upon my word," Richey said, "I feel lonely without him."

The people at the downtown office of the cinematograph company were very obliging. The picture had been taken, they said, at M-, just two miles beyond the scene of the wreck. It was not much, but it was something to work on. I decided not to go home, but to send McKnight's Jap for my clothes, and to dress at the Incubator. I was determined, if possible, to make my next day's investigations without Johnson. In the meantime, even if it was for the last time, I would see her that night. I gave Stogie a note for Mrs. Klopton, and with my dinner clothes there came back the gold bag, wrapped in tissue paper.

Chapter XVI

The Shadow of a Girl

CERTAIN things about the dinner at the Dallas house will always be obscure to me. Dallas was something in the Fish Commission, and I remember his reeling off fish eggs in billions while we ate our caviar. He had some particular stunt he had been urging the government to for years—something about forbidding the establishment of mills and factories on riverbanks—it seems they kill the fish, either the smoke, or the noise, or something they pour into the water.

Mrs. Dallas was there, I think. Of course, I suppose she must have been; and there was a woman in yellow. I took her in to dinner, and I remember she loosened my clams for me so I could get them. But the only real person at the table was a girl across in white, a sublimated young woman who was as brilliant as I was stupid, who never by any chance looked directly at me, and who appeared and disappeared across the candles and orchids in a sort of halo of radiance.

When the dinner had progressed from salmon to roast, and the conversation had done the same thing—from fish to scandal—the yellow gown turned to me. "We have been awfully good, haven't we, Mr. Blakeley?" she asked. "Although I am crazy to hear, I have not said 'wreck' once. I'm sure you must feel like the survivor of Waterloo, or something of the sort."

"If you want me to tell you about the wreck," I said, glancing across the table, "I'm sorry to be disappointing, but I don't remember anything."

"You are fortunate to be able to forget it." It was the first word Miss West had spoken directly to me, and it went to my head.

"There are some things I have not forgotten," I said, over the candles. "I recall coming to myself some time after, and that a girl, a beautiful girl—"

"Ah!" said the lady in yellow, leaning forward breathlessly. Miss West was staring at me coldly, but, once started, I had to stumble on.

"That a girl was trying to rouse me, and that she told me I had been on fire twice already." A shudder went around the table.

"But surely that isn't the end of the story," Mrs. Dallas put in aggrievedly. "Why, that's the most tantalizing thing I ever heard."

"I'm afraid that's all," I said. "She went her way and I went mine. If she recalls me at all, she probably thinks of me as a weak-kneed individual who faints like a woman when everything is over."

"What did I tell you?" Mrs. Dallas asserted triumphantly. "He fainted, did you hear? When everything was over! He hasn't begun to tell it."

I would have given a lot by that time if I had not mentioned the girl. But McKnight took it up there and carried it on.

"Blakeley is a regular geyser," he said. "He never spouts until he reaches the boiling point. And by that same token, although he hasn't said much about the Lady of the Wreck, I think he is crazy about her. In fact, I am sure of it. He thinks he has locked his secret in the caves of his soul, but I call you to witness that he has it nailed to his face. Look at him!"

I squirmed miserably and tried to avoid the startled eyes of the girl across the table. I wanted to choke McKnight and murder the rest of the party.

"It isn't fair," I said as coolly as I could. "I have my fingers crossed; you are five against one."

"And to think that there was a murder on that very train," broke in the lady in yellow. "It was a perfect crescendo of horrors, wasn't it? And what became of the murdered man, Mr. Blakeley?"

McKnight had the sense to jump into the conversation and save my reply.

"They say good Pittsburghers go to Atlantic City when they die," he said. "So—we are reasonably certain the gentleman did not go to the seashore."

The meal was over at last, and once in the drawing room it was clear we hung heavy on the hostess' hands. "It is so hard to get people for bridge in September," she wailed. "There is absolutely nobody in town. Six is a dreadful number."

"It's a good poker number," her husband suggested.

The matter settled itself, however. I was hopeless, save as a dummy; Miss West said it was too hot for cards, and went out on a balcony that overlooked the Mall. With obvious relief Mrs. Dallas had the card table brought, and I was face to face with the minute I had dreaded and hoped for for a week.

Now it had come, it was more difficult than I had anticipated. I do not know if there was a moon, but there was the urban substitute for it—the arc light. It threw the shadow of the balcony railing in long black bars against her white gown, and as it swung sometimes her face was in the light. I drew a chair close so that I could watch her.

"Do you know," I said, when she made no effort at speech, "that you are a much more formidable person tonight, in that gown, than you were the last time I saw you?"

The light swung on her face; she was smiling faintly. "The hat with the green ribbons!" she said. "I must take it back; I had almost forgotten."

"I have not forgotten—anything." I pulled myself up short. This was hardly loyalty to Richey. His voice came through the window just then, and perhaps I was wrong, but I thought she raised her head to listen.

"Look at this hand," he was saying. "Regular pianola: you could play it with your feet."

"He's a dear, isn't he?" Alison said unexpectedly. "No matter how depressed and downhearted I am, I always cheer up when I see Richey."

"He's more than that," I returned warmly. "He is the most honorable fellow I know. If he wasn't so much that way, he would have a career before him. He wanted to put on the doors of our offices, Blakeley and McKnight, P. B. H., which is Poor But Honest."

From my comparative poverty to the wealth of the girl beside me was a single mental leap. From that wealth to the grandfather who was responsible for it was another.

"I wonder if you know that I had been to Pittsburgh to see your grandfather when I met you?" I said.

"You?" She was surprised.

"Yes. And you remember the alligator bag that I told you was exchanged for the one you cut off my arm?" She nodded expectantly. "Well, in that valise were the forged Andy Bronson notes, and Mr. Gilmore's deposition that they were forged."

She was on her feet in an instant. "In that bag!" she cried. "Oh, why didn't you tell me that before? Oh, it's so ridiculous, so—so hopeless. Why, I could—"

She stopped suddenly and sat down again. "I do not know that I am sorry, after all," she said after a pause. "Mr. Bronson was a friend of my father's. I—I suppose it was a bad thing for you, losing the papers?"

"Well, it was not a good thing," I conceded. "While we are on the subject of losing things, do you remember—do you know that I still have your gold purse?"

She did not reply at once. The shadow of a column was over her face, but I guessed that she was staring at me.

"You have it!" She almost whispered.

"I picked it up in the streetcar," I said, with a cheerfulness I did not feel. "It looks like a very opulent little purse."

Why didn't she speak about the necklace? For just a careless word to make me sane again!

"You!" she repeated, horror-stricken.

And then I produced the purse and held it out on my palm. "I should have sent it to you before, I suppose, but, as you know, I have been laid up since the wreck."

We both saw McKnight at the same moment. He had pulled the curtains aside and was standing looking out at us. The tableau of give and take was unmistakable; the gold purse, her outstretched hand, my own attitude. It was over in a second; then he came out and lounged on the balcony railing.

"They're mad at me in there," he said airily, "so I came out. I suppose the reason they call it bridge is because so many people get cross over it."

The heat broke up the card group soon after, and they all came out for the night breeze. I had no more words alone with Alison.

I went back to the Incubator for the night. We said almost nothing on the way home; there was a constraint between us for the first time that I could remember. It was too early for bed, and so we smoked in the living room and tried to talk of trivial things. After a time even those failed, and we sat silent. It was McKnight who finally broached the subject.

"And so she wasn't at Seal Harbor at all."

"No."

"Do you know where she was, Lollie?"

"Somewhere near Cresson."

"And that was the purse—her purse—with the broken necklace in it?"

"Yes, it was. You understand, don't you, Rich, that, having given her my word. I couldn't tell you?"

"I understand a lot of things," he said, without bitterness.

We sat for some time and smoked. Then Richey got up and stretched himself. "I'm off to bed, old man," he said. "Need any help with that game arm of yours?"

"No, thanks," I returned.

I heard him go into his room and lock the door. It was a bad hour for me. The first shadow between us, and the shadow of a girl at that.

Chapter XVII

At the Farmhouse Again

∽

McKNIGHT is always a sympathizer with the early worm. It was late when he appeared. Perhaps, like myself, he had not slept well. But he was apparently cheerful enough, and he made a better breakfast than I did. It was one o'clock before we got to Baltimore. After a half hour's wait we took a local for M-, the station near which the cinematograph picture had been taken.

We passed the scene of the wreck, McKnight with curiosity, I with a sickening sense of horror. Back in the fields was the little farmhouse where Alison West and I had intended getting coffee, and winding away from the track, maple trees shading it on each side, was the lane where we had stopped to rest, and where I had—it seemed presumption beyond belief now—where I had tried to comfort her by patting her hand.

We got out at M-, a small place with two or three houses and a general store. The station was a one-roomed affair, with a railed-off place at the end, where a scale, a telegraph instrument and a chair constituted the entire furnishing.

The station agent was a young man with a shrewd face. He stopped hammering a piece of wood over a hole in the floor to ask where we wanted to go.

"We're not going," said McKnight, "we're coming. Have a cigar?"

The agent took it with an inquiring glance, first at it and then at us.

"We want to ask you a few questions," began McKnight, perching himself on the railing and kicking the chair forward for me. "Or, rather, this gentleman does."

"Wait a minute," said the agent, glancing through the window. "There's a hen in that crate choking herself to death."

He was back in a minute, and took up his position near a sawdust-filled box that did duty as a cuspidor.

"Now fire away," he said.

"In the first place," I began, "do you remember the day the *Washington Flier* was wrecked below here?"

"Do I!" he said. "Did Jonah remember the whale?"

"Were you on the platform here when the first section passed?"

"I was."

"Do you recall seeing a man hanging to the platform of the last car?"

"There was no one hanging there when she passed here," he said with conviction. "I watched her out of sight."

"Did you see anything that morning of a man about my size, carrying a small grip, and wearing dark clothes and a derby hat?" I asked eagerly.

McKnight was trying to look unconcerned, but I was frankly anxious. It was clear that the man had jumped somewhere in the mile of track just beyond.

"Well, yes, I did." The agent cleared his throat. "When the smash came, the operator at MX sent word along the wire, both ways. I got it here, and I was pretty near crazy, though I knew it wasn't any fault of mine.

"I was standing on the track looking down, for I couldn't leave the office, when a young fellow with light hair limped up to me and asked me what that smoke was over there.

"That's what's left of the *Washington Flier*," I said, "and I guess there's souls going up in that smoke."

"Do you mean the first section?" he said, getting kind of greenish yellow.

"That's what I mean," I said. "Split to kindling wood because Rafferty, on the second section, didn't want to be late."

He put his hand out in front of him, and the satchel fell with a bang.

"My God!" he said, and dropped right on the track in a heap.

"I got him into the station and he came around, but he kept on groaning something awful. He'd sprained his ankle, and when he got a little better I drove him over in Carter's milk wagon to the Carter place, and I reckon he stayed there a spell."

"That's all, is it?" I asked.

"That's all—or, no, there's something else. About noon that day one of the Carter twins came down with a note from him asking me to send a long-distance message to someone in Washington."

"To whom?" I asked eagerly.

"I reckon I've forgot the name, but the message was that this fellow—Sullivan was his name—was at M-, and if the man had escaped from the wreck would he come to see him."

"He wouldn't have sent that message to me," I said to McKnight, rather crestfallen. "He'd have every object in keeping out of my way."

"There might be reasons," McKnight observed judicially. "He might not have found the papers then."

"Was the name Blakeley?" I asked.

"It might have been—I can't say. But the man wasn't there, and there was a lot of noise. I couldn't hear well. Then in half an hour down came the other twin to say the gentleman was taking on awful and didn't want the message sent."

"He's gone, of course?"

"Yes. Limped down here in about three days and took the noon train for the city."

It seemed a certainty now that our man, having hurt himself somewhat in his jump, had stayed quietly in the farmhouse until he was able to travel. But, to be positive, we decided to visit the Carter place.

I gave the station agent a five-dollar bill, which he rolled up with a couple of others and stuck in his pocket. I turned as we got to a bend in the road, and he was looking curiously after us.

It was not until we had climbed the hill and turned onto the road to the Carter place that I realized where we were going. Although we approached it from another direction, I knew the farmhouse at once. It was the one where Alison West and I had breakfasted nine days before. With the new restraint between us, I did not tell McKnight. I wondered afterward if he had suspected it. I saw him looking hard at the gatepost which had figured in one of our mysteries, but he asked no questions. Afterward he grew almost taciturn, for him, and let me do most of the talking.

We opened the front gate of the Carter place and went slowly up the walk. Two ragged youngsters, alike even to freckles and squints, were playing in the yard.

"Is your mother around?" I asked.

"In the front room. Walk in," they answered in identical tones.

As we got to the porch we heard voices, and stopped. I knocked, but the people within, engaged in animated, rather one-sided conversation, did not answer.

" 'In the front room. Walk in,' " quoted McKnight, and did so.

In the stuffy farm parlor two people were sitting. One, a pleasant-faced woman with a checked apron, rose, somewhat embarrassed, to meet us. She did not know me, and I was thankful. But our attention was riveted on a little man who was sitting before a table, writing busily. It was Hotchkiss!

He got up when he saw us, and had the grace to look uncomfortable.

"Such an interesting case," he said nervously. "I took the liberty—"

"Look here," said McKnight suddenly, "did you make any inquiries at the station?"

"A few," he confessed. "I went to the theater last night—I felt the need of a little relaxation—and the sight of a picture there, a cinematograph affair, started a new line of thought. Probably the same clue brought you gentlemen. I learned a good bit from the station agent."

"The son of a gun," said McKnight. "And you paid him, I suppose?"

"I gave him five dollars," was the apologetic answer. Mrs. Carter, hearing sounds of strife in the yard, went out, and Hotchkiss folded up his papers.

"I think the identity of the man is established," he said. "What number of hat do you wear, Mr. Blakeley?"

"Seven and a quarter," I replied.

"Well, it's only piling up evidence," he said cheerfully. "On the night of the murder you wore light gray silk underclothing, with the second button of the shirt missing. Your hat had L.B. in gilt letters inside, and there was a very minute hole in the toe of one black sock."

"Hush," McKnight protested. "If word gets to Mrs. Klopton that Mr. Blakeley was wrecked, or robbed, or whatever it was, with a button missing and a hole in one sock, she'll retire to the Old Ladies' Home. I've heard her threaten it."

Mr. Hotchkiss was without a sense of humor. He regarded McKnight gravely and went on.

"I've been up in the room where the man lay while he was unable to get away, and there is nothing there. But I found what may be a possible clue in the dust heap.

"Mrs. Carter tells me that in unpacking his grip the other day she took out of the coat of the pajamas some pieces of a telegram. As I figure it, the pajamas were his own. He probably had them on when he effected the exchange."

I nodded assent. All I had retained of my own clothing was the suit of pajamas I was wearing and my bathrobe.

"Therefore the telegram was his, not yours. I have pieces here, but some are missing. I am not discouraged, however."

He spread out some bits of yellow paper, and we bent over them curiously. It was something like this:

Man with p-Get-

Br-

We spelled it out slowly.

"Now," Hotchkiss announced, "I make it something like this: The 'p-' is one of two things, pistol—you remember the little pearl-handled affair belonging to the murdered man—or it is pocketbook. I am inclined to the latter view, as the pocketbook had been disturbed and the pistol had not."

I took the piece of paper from the table and scrawled four words on it.

"Now," I said, rearranging them, "it happens, Mr. Hotchkiss, that I found one of these pieces of the telegram on the train. I thought it had been dropped by someone else, you see, but that's immaterial.

"Arranged this way it almost makes sense. Fill out that 'p-' with the rest of the word, as I imagine it, and it makes 'papers,' and add this scrap and you have 'Man with papers (in) lower ten, car seven. Get (them).' "

McKnight slapped Hotchkiss on the back. "You're a trump," he said. " 'Br-' is Bronson, of course. It's almost too easy. You see, Mr. Blakeley here engaged lower ten, but found it occupied by the man who was later murdered there. The man who did the thing was a friend of Bronson's, evidently, and in trying to get the papers we have the motive for the crime."

"There are still some things to be explained." Mr. Hotchkiss wiped his glasses and put them on. "For one thing, Mr. Blakeley, I am puzzled by that bit of chain."

I did not glance at McKnight. I felt that the hand with which I was gathering up the bits of torn paper was shaking. It seemed to me that this astute little man was going to drag in the girl in spite of me.

Chapter XVIII

A New World

∽

HOTCHKISS jotted down the bits of telegram and rose.

"Well," he said, "we've done something. We've found where the murderer left the train, we know what day he went to Baltimore, and, most important of all, we have a motive for the crime."

"It seems the irony of fate," said McKnight, getting up, "that a man should kill another man for certain papers he is supposed to be carrying, find he hasn't got them after all, decide to throw suspicion on another man by changing berths and getting out, bag and baggage, and then, by the merest fluke of chance, take with him, in the valise he changed for his own, the very notes he was after. It was a bit of luck for him."

"Then why," put in Hotchkiss doubtfully, "why did he collapse when he heard of the wreck? And what about the telephone message the station agent sent? You remember they tried to countermand it, and with some excitement."

"We will ask him those questions when we get him," McKnight said. We were on the unrailed front porch by that time, and Hotchkiss had put away his notebook. The mother of the twins followed us to the steps.

"Dear me," she exclaimed volubly, "and to think I was forgetting to tell you! I put the young man to bed with a spice poultice on his ankle;

my mother always was a firm believer in spice poultices. It's wonderful what they will do in croup! And then I took the children and went down to see the wreck. It was Sunday, and the mister had gone to church; hasn't missed a day since he took the pledge nine years ago. And on the way I met two people, a man and a woman. They looked half dead, so I sent them right here for breakfast and some soap and water. I always say soap is better than liquor after a shock."

Hotchkiss was listening absently. McKnight was whistling under his breath, staring down across the field to where a break in the woods showed a half dozen telegraph poles, the line of the railroad.

"It must have been twelve o'clock when we got back; I wanted the children to see everything, because it isn't likely they'll ever see another wreck like that. Rows of—"

"About twelve o'clock," I broke in, "and what then?"

"The young man upstairs was awake," she went on, "and hammering at his door like all possessed. And it was locked on the outside!" She paused to enjoy her sensation.

"I would like to see that lock," Hotchkiss said promptly, but for some reason the woman demurred.

"I will bring the key down," she said and disappeared. When she returned she held out an ordinary door key of the cheapest variety.

"We had to break the lock," she volunteered, "and the key didn't turn up for two days. Then one of the twins found the turkey gobbler trying to swallow it. It has been washed since," she hastened to assure Hotchkiss, who showed an inclination to drop it.

"You don't think he locked the door himself and threw the key out of the window?" the little man asked.

"The windows are covered with mosquito netting, nailed on. The mister blamed it on the children, and it might have been Obadiah. He's the quiet kind, and you never know what he's about."

"He's about to strangle, isn't he," McKnight remarked lazily, "or is that Obadiah?"

Mrs. Carter picked the boy up and inverted him, talking amiably all the time. "He's always doing it," she said, giving him a shake. "Whenever we miss anything we look to see if Obadiah's black in the face." She gave him another shake, and the quarter I had given him shot out as if blown from a gun. Then we prepared to go back to the station.

From where I stood I could look into the cheery farm kitchen, where Alison West and I had eaten our al fresco breakfast. I looked at the table with mixed emotions, and then, gradually, the meaning of something on it penetrated my mind. Still in its papers, evidently just opened, was a hat box, and protruding over the edge of the box was a streamer of vivid green ribbon.

On the plea that I wished to ask Mrs. Carter a few more questions, I let the others go on. I watched them down the flagstone walk; saw McKnight stop and examine the gateposts and saw, too, the quick glance he threw back at the house. Then I turned to Mrs. Carter.

"I would like to speak to the young lady upstairs," I said.

She threw up her hands with a quick gesture of surrender. "I've done all I could," she exclaimed. "She won't like it very well, but—she's in the room over the parlor."

I went eagerly up the ladderlike stairs, to the rag-carpeted hall. Two doors were open, showing interiors of four-poster beds and high bureaus. The door of the room over the parlor was almost closed. I hesitated in the hallway; after all, what right had I to intrude on her? But she settled my difficulty by throwing open the door and facing me.

"I—I beg your pardon, Miss West," I stammered. "It has just occurred to me that I am unpardonably rude. I saw the hat downstairs and I—I guessed—"

"The hat!" she said. "I might have known. Does Richey know I am here?"

"I don't think so." I turned to go down the stairs again. Then I halted. "The fact is," I said, in an attempt at justification, "I'm in rather a mess these days, and I'm apt to do irresponsible things. It is not impossible that I shall be arrested, in a day or so, for the murder of Simon Harrington."

She drew her breath in sharply. "Murder!" she echoed. "Then they have found you after all!"

"I don't regard it as anything more than—er—inconvenient," I lied. "They can't convict me, you know. Almost all the witnesses are dead."

She was not deceived for a moment. She came over to me and stood, both hands on the rail of the stair. "I know just how grave it is," she said quietly. "My grandfather will not leave one stone unturned, and he can be terrible—terrible. But"—she looked directly into my eyes as I stood below her on the stairs—"the time may come soon—when I can help you. I'm afraid I shall not want to; I'm a dreadful coward, Mr. Blakeley. But—I will." She tried to smile.

"I wish you would let me help you," I said unsteadily. "Let us make it a bargain: each help the other!"

The girl shook her head with a sad little smile. "I am only as unhappy as I deserve to be," she said. And when I protested and took a step toward her, she retreated, with her hands out before her.

"Why don't you ask me all the questions you are thinking?" she demanded, with a catch in her voice. "Oh, I know them. Or are you afraid to ask?"

I looked at her, at the lines around her eyes, at the drawn look about her mouth. Then I held out my hand. "Afraid!" I said, as she gave me hers. "There is nothing in God's green earth I am afraid of, save of trouble for you. To ask questions would be to imply a lack of faith. I ask you nothing. Someday, perhaps, you will come to me yourself and let me help you."

The next moment I was out in the golden sunshine; the birds were singing carols of joy. I walked dizzily through rainbow-colored clouds, past the twins, cherubs now, swinging on the gate. It was a new world into which I stepped from the Carter farmhouse that morning, for—I had kissed her!

Chapter XIX

At the Table Next

⟨∾⟩

McKnight and Hotchkiss were sauntering slowly down the road as I caught up with them. As usual, the little man was busy with some abstruse mental problem.

"The idea is this," he was saying, his brows knitted in thought. "If a left-handed man, standing in the position of the man in the picture, should jump from a car, would he be likely to sprain his right ankle? When a right-handed man prepares for a leap of that kind, my theory is that he would hold on with his right hand, and alight at the proper time, on his right foot. Of course—"

"I imagine, although I don't know," interrupted McKnight, "that a man either ambidextrous or one-armed, jumping from the *Washington Flier,* would be more likely to land on his head."

"Anyhow," I interposed, "what difference does it make whether Sullivan used one hand or the other? One pair of handcuffs will put both hands out of commission."

As usual when one of his pet theories was attacked, Hotchkiss looked aggrieved.

"My dear sir," he expostulated, "don't you understand what bearing this has on the case? How was the murdered man lying when he was found?"

"On his back," I said promptly, "head toward the engine."

"Very well," he retorted, "and what then? Your heart lies under your fifth intercostal space, and to reach it a right-handed blow would have struck either down or directly in.

"But, gentleman, the point of entrance for the stiletto was below the heart, striking up! As Harrington lay with his head toward the engine, a person in the aisle must have used the left hand."

McKnight's eyes sought mine and he winked at me solemnly as I unostentatiously transferred the hat I was carrying to my right hand. Long training has largely counterbalanced heredity in my case, but I still pitch ball, play tennis and carve with my left hand. But Hotchkiss was too busy with his theories to notice me.

We were only just in time for our train back to Baltimore, but McKnight took advantage of a second's delay to shake the station agent warmly by the hand.

"I want to express my admiration for you," he said beamingly. "Ability of your order is thrown away here. You should have been a city policeman, my friend."

The agent looked a trifle uncertain.

"The young lady was the one who told me to keep still," he said.

McKnight glanced at me, gave the agent's hand a final shake, and climbed on board. But I knew perfectly that he had guessed the reason for my delay.

He was very silent on the way home. Hotchkiss, too, had little to say.

He was reading over his notes intently, stopping now and then to make a penciled addition. Just before we left the train Richey turned to me. "I suppose it was the key to the door that she tied to the gate?"

"Probably. I did not ask her."

"Curious, her locking that fellow in," he reflected.

"You may depend on it, there was a good reason for it all. And I wish you wouldn't be so suspicious of motives, Rich," I said warmly.

"Only yesterday you were the suspicious one," he retorted, and we lapsed into strained silence.

It was late when we got to Washington. One of Mrs. Klopton's small tyrannies was exacting punctuality at meals, and, like several other things, I respected it. There are always some concessions that should be made in return for faithful service.

So, as my dinner hour of seven was long past, McKnight and I went to a little restaurant downtown where they have a very decent way of fixing chicken à la King. Hotchkiss had departed, economically bent, for a small hotel where he lived on the American plan.

"I want to think some things over," he said in response to my invitation to dinner, "and, anyhow, there's no use dining out when I pay the same, dinner or no dinner, where I am stopping."

The day had been hot, and the first floor dining room was sultry in spite of the palms and fans which attempted to simulate the verdure and breezes of the country.

It was crowded, too, with a typical summer night crowd, and, after sitting for a few minutes in a sweltering corner, we got up and went to the smaller dining room upstairs. Here it was not so warm, and we settled ourselves comfortably by a window.

Over in a corner half a dozen boys on their way back to school were ragging a perspiring waiter, a proceeding so exactly to McKnight's taste that he insisted on going over to join them. But their table was full, and somehow that kind of fun had lost its point for me.

Not far from us a very stout, middle-aged man, apoplectic with the heat, was elephantinely jolly for the benefit of a bored-looking girl across the table from him, and at the next table a newspaper woman ate alone, the last edition propped against the water bottle before her, her hat, for coolness, on the corner of the table. It was a motley Bohemian crowd.

I looked over the room casually, while McKnight ordered the meal. Then my attention was attracted to the table next to ours. Two people were sitting there, so deep in conversation that they did not notice us. The woman's face was hidden under her hat, as she traced the pattern of the cloth mechanically with her fork. But the man's features stood out clear in the light of the candles on the table. It was Bronson!

"He shows the strain, doesn't he?" McKnight said, holding up the wine list as if he read from it. "Who's the woman?"

"Search me," I replied, in the same way.

When the chicken came, I still found myself gazing now and then at the abstracted couple near me. Evidently the subject of conversation was unpleasant. Bronson was eating little, the woman not at all. Finally he got up, pushed his chair back noisily, thrust a bill at the waiter and stalked out.

The woman sat still for a moment; then, with an apparent resolution to make the best of it, she began slowly to eat the meal before her.

But the quarrel had taken away her appetite, for the mixture in our chafing dish was hardly ready to serve before she pushed her chair back a little and looked around the room.

I caught my first glimpse of her face then, and I confess it startled me. It was the tall, stately woman of the Ontario, the woman I had last seen cowering beside the road, rolling pebbles in her hand, blood streaming from a cut over her eye. I could see the scar now, a little affair, about an inch long, gleaming red through its layers of powder.

And then, quite unexpectedly, she turned and looked directly at me. After a minute's uncertainty, she bowed, letting her eyes rest on mine with a calmly insolent stare. She glanced at McKnight for a moment, then back to me. When she looked away again, I breathed easier.

"Who is it?" asked McKnight under his breath.

"Ontario." I formed it with my lips rather than said it. McKnight's eyebrows went up and he looked with increased interest at the black-gowned figure.

I ate little after that. The situation was rather bad for me, I began to see. Here was a woman who could, if she wished, and had any motive for so doing, put me in jail under a capital charge. A word from her to the police, and polite surveillance would become active interference.

Then, too, she could say that she had seen me, just after the wreck, with a young woman from the murdered man's car, and thus probably bring Alison West into the case.

It is not surprising, then, that I ate little. The woman across seemed in no hurry to go. She loitered over a demitasse, and that finished, sat with her elbow on the table, her chin in her hand, looking darkly at the changing groups in the room.

The fun at the table where the college boys sat began to grow a little noisy; the fat man, now a purplish shade, ambled away behind his slim companion; the newspaper woman pinned on her businesslike hat and stalked out. Still the woman at the next table waited.

It was a relief when the meal was over. We got our hats and were about to leave the room, when a waiter touched me on the arm.

"I beg your pardon, sir," he said, "but the lady at the table near the window, the lady in black, sir, would like to speak to you."

I looked down between the rows of tables to where the woman sat alone, her chin still resting on her hand, her black eyes still insolently staring, this time at me.

"I'll have to go," I said to McKnight hurriedly. "She knows all about that affair and she'd be a bad enemy."

"I don't like her lamps," McKnight observed, after a glance at her. "Better jolly her a little. Good-bye."

Chapter XX

The Notes and a Bargain

I WENT back slowly to where the woman sat alone.

She smiled rather oddly as I drew near, and pointed to the chair Bronson had vacated.

"Sit down, Mr. Blakeley," she said, "I am going to take a few minutes of your valuable time."

"Certainly." I sat down opposite her and glanced at a cuckoo clock on the wall. "I am sorry, but I have only a few minutes. If you—" She laughed a little, not very pleasantly, and opening a small black fan covered with spangles, waved it slowly.

"The fact is," she said, "I think we are about to make a bargain."

"A bargain?" I asked incredulously. "You have a second advantage of me. You know my name." I paused suggestively and she took the cue.

"I am Mrs. Conway," she said, and flicked a crumb off the table with an over-manicured finger.

The name was scarcely a surprise. I had already surmised that this might be the woman whom rumor credited as being Bronson's common-law wife. Rumor, I remembered, had said other things even less pleasant, things which had been brought out at Bronson's arrest for forgery.

"We met last under less fortunate circumstances," she was saying. "I have been fit for nothing since that terrible day. And you—you had a broken arm, I think."

"I still have it," I said with a lame attempt at jocularity, "but to have escaped at all was a miracle. We have much, indeed, to be thankful for."

"I suppose we have," she said carelessly, "although sometimes I doubt it." She was looking somberly toward the door through which her late companion had made his exit.

"You sent for me—" I said.

"Yes, I sent for you." She roused herself and sat erect. "Now, Mr. Blakeley, have you found those papers?"

"The papers? What papers?" I parried. I needed time to think.

"Mr. Blakeley," she said quietly, "I think we can lay aside all subterfuge. In the first place let me refresh your mind about a few things. The Pittsburgh police are looking for the survivors of the car Ontario; there are three that I know of—yourself, the young woman with whom you left the scene of the wreck, and myself. The wreck, you will admit, was a fortunate one for you."

I nodded without speaking.

"At the time of the collision you were in rather a hole," she went on, looking at me with a disagreeable smile. "You were, if I remember, accused of a rather atrocious crime. There was a lot of corroborative evidence, was there not? I seem to remember a dirk and the murdered man's pocketbook in your possession, and a few other things that were—well, rather unpleasant."

I was thrown a bit off my guard.

"You remember also," I said quickly, "that a man disappeared from the car, taking my clothes, papers and everything."

"I remember that you said so." Her tone was quietly insulting, and I bit my lip at having been caught. It was no time to make a defense.

"You have missed one calculation," I said coldly, "and that is, the discovery of the man who left the train."

"You have found him?" She bent forward, and again I regretted my hasty speech. "I knew it; I said so."

"We are going to find him," I asserted, with a confidence I did not feel. "We can produce at any time proof that a man left the *Flier* a few miles beyond the wreck. And we can find him, I am positive."

"But you have not found him yet?" She was clearly disappointed. "Well, so be it. Now for our bargain. You will admit that I am no fool."

I made no such admission, and she smiled mockingly.

"How flattering you are!" she said. "Very well. Now for the premises. You take to Pittsburgh four notes held by the Mechanics' National Bank, to have Mr. Gilmore, who is ill, declare his endorsement of them forged.

"On the journey back to Pittsburgh two things happen to you: you lose your clothing, your valise and your papers, including the notes, and you are accused of murder. In fact, Mr. Blakeley, the circumstances were most singular, and the evidence—well, almost conclusive."

I was completely at her mercy, but I gnawed my lip with irritation.

"Now for the bargain." She leaned over and lowered her voice. "A fair exchange, you know. The minute you put those four notes in my hand—that minute the blow to my head has caused complete forgetfulness as to the events of that awful morning. I am the only witness, and I will be silent. Do you understand? They will call off their dogs."

My head was buzzing with the strangeness of the idea.

"But," I said, striving to gain time, "I haven't the notes. I can't give you what I haven't got."

"You have had the case continued," she said sharply. "You expect to find them. Another thing," she added slowly, watching my face, "if you don't get them soon, Bronson will have them. They have been offered to him already, but at a prohibitive price."

"But," I said, bewildered, "what is your object in coming to me? If Bronson will get them anyhow—"

She shut her fan with a click and her face was not particularly pleasant to look at.

"You are dense," she said insolently. "I want those papers—for myself, not for Andy Bronson."

"Then the idea is," I said, ignoring her tone, "that you think you have me in a hole, and that if I find those papers and give them to you, you will let me out. As I understand it, our friend Bronson, under those circumstances, will also be in a hole."

She nodded.

"The notes would be of no use to you for a limited length of time," I went on, watching her narrowly. "If they are not turned over to the state's attorney within a reasonable time, there will have to be a nol-pros—that is, the case will simply be dropped for lack of evidence."

"A week would answer, I think," she said slowly. "You will do it, then?"

I laughed, although I was not especially cheerful.

"No, I'll not do it. I expect to come across the notes anytime now, and I expect just as certainly to turn them over to the state's attorney when I get them."

She got up suddenly, pushing her chair back with a noisy grating sound that turned many eyes toward us.

"You're more of a fool than I thought you," she sneered, and left me at the table.

Chapter XXI

McKnight's Theory

᳘

I CONFESS I was staggered. The people at the surrounding tables, after glancing curiously in my direction, looked away again.

I got my hat and went out in a very uncomfortable frame of mind. That she would inform the police at once of what she knew I never doubted, unless possibly she would give a day or two's grace in the hope that I would change my mind.

I reviewed the situation as I waited for a car. Two passed me going in the opposite direction, and on the first one I saw Bronson, his hat over his eyes, his arms folded, looking moodily ahead. Was it imagination? Or was the small man huddled in the corner of the rear seat Hotchkiss?

As the car rolled on I found myself smiling. The alert little man was for all the world like a terrier, ever on the scent, and scouring about in every direction.

I found McKnight at the Incubator, with his coat off, working with enthusiasm and a manicure file over the horn of his auto.

"It's the worst horn I ever ran across," he groaned, without looking up, as I came in. "The blankety-blank thing won't blow."

He punched it savagely, finally eliciting a faint throaty croak.

"Sounds like croup," I suggested. "My sister-in-law uses camphor and goose grease for it. Or how about a spice poultice?"

But McKnight never sees any jokes but his own. He flung the horn clattering into a corner, and collapsed sulkily into a chair.

"Now," I said, "if you're through manicuring that horn, I'll tell you about my talk with the lady in black."

"What's wrong?" asked McKnight languidly. "Police watching her, too?"

"Not exactly. The fact is, Rich, there's the mischief to pay."

Stogie came in, bringing a few additions to our comfort. When he went out, I told my story.

"You must remember," I said, "that I had seen this woman before the morning of the wreck. She was buying her Pullman ticket when I did. Then the next morning, when the murder was discovered, she grew hysterical, and I gave her some whisky. The third and last time I saw her, until tonight, was when she crouched beside the road, after the wreck."

McKnight slid down in his chair until his weight rested on the small of his back, and put his feet on the big reading table.

"It is rather a facer," he said. "It's really too good a situation for a commonplace lawyer. It ought to be dramatized. You can't agree, of course; and by refusing you run the chance of jail, at least, and of having Alison brought into publicity, which is out of the question. You say she was at the Pullman window when you were?"

"Yes. I bought her ticket for her. Gave her lower eleven."

"And you took ten?"

"Lower ten."

McKnight straightened up and looked at me.

"Then she thought you were in lower ten."

"I suppose she did, if she thought at all."

"But listen, man." McKnight was growing excited. "What do you figure out of this? The Conway woman knows you have taken the notes to Pittsburgh. The probabilities are that she follows you there, on the chance of an opportunity to get them, either for Bronson or herself.

"Nothing doing during the trip over or during the day in Pittsburgh; but she learns the number of your berth as you buy it at the Pullman ticket office in Pittsburgh, and she thinks she sees her chance. No one could have foreseen that that drunken fellow would have crawled into your berth.

"Now, I figure it out this way: She wanted those notes desperately—does still—not for Bronson, but to hold over his head for some purpose. In the night, when everything is quiet, she slips behind the curtains of lower ten, where the man's breathing shows he is asleep. Didn't you say he snored?"

"He did!" I affirmed. "But I tell you—"

"Now keep still and listen. She gropes cautiously around in the darkness, finally discovering the wallet under the pillow. Can't you see it yourself?"

He was leaning forward, excitedly, and I could almost see the gruesome tragedy he was depicting.

"She draws out the wallet. Then, perhaps she remembers the alligator bag, and on the possibility that the notes are there, instead of in the pocketbook, she gropes around for it. Suddenly, the man awakes and clutches at the nearest object, perhaps her neck chain, which breaks. She drops the pocketbook and tries to escape, but he has caught her right hand.

"It is all in silence; the man is still stupidly drunk. But he holds her in a tight grip. Then the tragedy. She must get away; in a minute the car will be aroused. Such a woman, on such an errand, does not go without some sort of a weapon, in this case a dagger, which, unlike a revolver, is noiseless.

"With a quick thrust—she's a big woman and a bold one—she strikes. Possibly Hotchkiss is right about the left-hand blow. Harrington may have held her right hand, or perhaps she held the dirk in her left hand as she groped with her right. Then, as the man falls back, and his grasp relaxes, she straightens and attempts to get away. The swaying of the car throws her almost into your berth, and, trembling with terror, she crouches behind the curtains of lower ten until everything is still. Then she goes noiselessly back to her berth."

I nodded.

"It seems to fit partly, at least," I said. "In the morning when she found that the crime had been not only fruitless, but that she had searched the wrong berth and killed the wrong man; when she saw me emerge, unhurt, just as she was bracing herself for the discovery of my dead body, then she went into hysterics. You remember, I gave her some whisky.

"It really seems a tenable theory. But, like the Sullivan theory, there are one or two things that don't agree with the rest. For one thing, how did the remainder of that chain get into Alison West's possession?"

"She may have picked it up on the floor."

"We'll admit that," I said, "and I'm sure I hope so. Then how did the murdered man's pocketbook get into the sealskin bag? And the dirk, how account for that, and the bloodstains?"

"Now what's the use," asked McKnight aggrievedly, "of my building up beautiful theories for you to pull down? We'll take it to Hotchkiss. Maybe he can tell from the bloodstains if the murderer's fingernails were square or pointed."

"Hotchkiss is no fool," I said warmly. "Under all his theories there's a good hard layer of common sense. And we must remember, Rich, that neither of our theories includes the woman at Dr. Van Kirk's hospital, that the charming picture you have just drawn does not account for Alison West's connection with the case, or for the bits of telegram in the Sullivan fellow's pajamas pocket. You are like the man who put the clock together; you've got half of the works left over."

"Oh, go home," said McKnight disgustedly. "I'm no Edgar Allan Poe. What's the use of coming here and asking me things if you're so particular?"

With one of his quick changes of mood, he picked up his guitar.

"Listen to this," he said. "It is a Hawaiian song about a fat lady, oh, ignorant one! And how she fell off her mule."

But for all the lightness of the words, the voice that followed me down the stairs was anything but cheery.

"There was a Kanaka in Balu did dwell,/ Who had for his daughter a monstrous fat girl," he sang in his clear tenor. I paused on the lower floor and listened. He had stopped singing as abruptly as he had begun.

Chapter XXII

At the Boardinghouse

I HAD not been home for thirty-six hours, since the morning of the preceding day. Johnson was not in sight, and I let myself in quietly with my latchkey. It was almost midnight, and I had hardly settled myself in the library when the bell rang and I was surprised to find Hotchkiss, much out of breath, in the vestibule.

"Why, come in, Mr. Hotchkiss," I said. "I thought you were going home to go to bed."

"So I was, so I was." He dropped into a chair beside my reading lamp and mopped his face. "And here it is almost midnight, and I'm wider awake than ever. I've seen Sullivan, Mr. Blakeley."

"You have!"

"I have," he said impressively.

"You were following Bronson at eight o'clock. Was that when it happened?"

"Something of the sort. When I left you at the door of the restaurant, I turned and almost ran into a plainclothesman from the central office. I know him pretty well; once or twice he has taken me with him on interesting bits of work. He knows my hobby."

"You know him, too, probably. It was the man Arnold, the detective whom the state's attorney has had watching Bronson."

Johnson being otherwise occupied, I had asked for Arnold myself.

I nodded.

"Well, he stopped me at once; said he'd been on the fellow's tracks since early morning and had had no time for luncheon. Bronson, it seems, isn't eating much these days. I at once jotted down the fact, because it argued that he was being bothered by the man with the notes."

"It might point to other things," I suggested. "Indigestion, you know."

Hotchkiss ignored me. "Well, Arnold had some reason for thinking that Bronson would try to give him the slip that night, so he asked me to stay around the private entrance there while he ran across the street and got something to eat. It seemed a fair presumption that, as he had gone there with a lady, they would dine leisurely, and Arnold would have plenty of time to get back."

"What about your own dinner?" I asked curiously.

"Sir," he said pompously, "I have given you a wrong estimate of Wilson Budd Hotchkiss if you think that a question of dinner would even obtrude itself on his mind at such a time as this."

He was a frail little man, and tonight he looked pale with heat and overexertion.

"Did you have any luncheon?" I asked.

He was somewhat embarrassed at that.

"I—really, Mr. Blakeley, the events of the day were so engrossing—"

"Well," I said, "I'm not going to see you drop on the floor from exhaustion. Just wait a minute."

I went back to the pantry, only to be confronted with rows of locked doors and empty dishes. Downstairs, in the basement kitchen, however, I found two unattractive-looking cold chops, some dry bread and a piece of cake, wrapped in a napkin, and from its surreptitious and generally hangdog appearance, destined for the coachman in the stable at the rear. Trays there were none—everything but the chairs and tables seemed under lock and key, and there was neither napkin, knife nor fork to be found.

The luncheon was not attractive in appearance, but Hotchkiss ate his cold chops and gnawed at the crusts as though he had been famished, while he told his story.

"I had been there only a few minutes," he said, with a chop in one hand and the cake in the other, "when Bronson rushed out and cut across the street. He's a tall man, Mr. Blakeley, and I had had work keeping close. It was a relief when he jumped on a passing car, although being well behind, it was a hard run for me to catch him. He had left the lady.

"Once on the car, we simply rode from one end of the line to the other and back again. I suppose he was passing the time, for he looked at his watch now and then, and when I did once get a look at his face it made me—er—uncomfortable. He could have crushed me like a fly, sir."

I had brought Mr. Hotchkiss a glass of wine, and he was looking better. He stopped to finish it, declining with a wave of his hand to have it refilled, and continued.

"About nine o'clock or a little later he got off somewhere near Washington Circle. He went along one of the residence streets there, turned to his left a square or two, and rang a bell. He had been admitted when I got there, but I guessed from the appearance of the place that it was a boardinghouse.

"I waited a few minutes and rang the bell. When a maid answered it, I asked for Mr. Sullivan. Of course there was no Mr. Sullivan there.

"I said I was sorry; that the man I was looking for was a new boarder. She was sure there was no such boarder in the house; the only new arrival was a man on the third floor—she thought his name was Stuart.

" 'My friend has a cousin by that name,' I said. 'I'll just go up and see.'

"She wanted to show me up, but I said it was unnecessary. So after telling me it was the bedroom and sitting room on the third floor front, I went up.

"I met a couple of men on the stairs, but neither of them paid any attention to me. A boardinghouse is the easiest place in the world to enter."

"They're not always so easy to leave," I put in, to his evident irritation.

"When I got to the third story, I took out a bunch of keys and posted myself by a door near the ones the girl had indicated. I could hear voices in one of the front rooms, but could not understand what they said.

"There was no violent dispute, but a steady hum. Then Bronson jerked the door open. If he had stepped into the hall, he would have seen me fitting a key into the door before me. But he spoke before he came out.

" 'You're acting like a maniac,' he said. 'You know I can get those things some way; I'm not going to threaten you. It isn't necessary. You know me.'

" 'It would be no use,' the other man said. 'I tell you, I haven't seen the notes for ten days.'

" 'But you will,' Bronson said savagely. 'You're standing in your own way, that's all. If you're holding out expecting me to raise my figure, you're making a mistake. It's my last offer.'

" 'I couldn't take it if it was for a million,' said the man inside the room. 'I'd do it, I expect, if I could. The best of us have our price.'

"Bronson slammed the door then, and flung past me down the hall.

"After a couple of minutes I knocked at the door, and a tall man about your size, Mr. Blakeley, opened it. He was very blond, with a smooth face and blue eyes—what I think you would call a handsome man.

" 'I beg your pardon for disturbing you,' I said. 'Can you tell me which is Mr. Johnson's room? Mr. Francis Johnson?'

" 'I cannot say,' he replied civilly. 'I've only been here a few days.'

"I thanked him and left, but I had had a good look at him, and I think I'd know him readily anyplace."

I sat for a few minutes thinking it over. "But what did he mean by saying he hadn't seen the notes for ten days? And why is Bronson making the overtures?"

"I think he was lying," Hotchkiss reflected. "Bronson hasn't reached his figure."

"It's a big advance, Mr. Hotchkiss, and I appreciate what you have done more than I can tell you," I said. "And now, if you can locate any of my property in this fellow's room, we'll send him up for larceny, and at least have him where we can get at him. I'm going to Cresson tomorrow, to try to trace him a little from there. But I'll be back in a couple of days, and we'll begin to gather in these scattered threads."

Hotchkiss rubbed his hands together delightedly.

"That's it," he said. "That's what we want to do, Mr. Blakeley. We'll gather up the threads ourselves; if we let the police in too soon, they'll tangle it up again. I'm not vindictive by nature; but when a fellow like Sullivan not only commits a murder, but goes to all sorts of trouble to put the burden of guilt on an innocent man, I say hunt him down, sir!"

"You are convinced, of course, that Sullivan did it?"

"Who else?" He looked over his glasses at me with the air of a man whose mental attitude is unassailable.

"Well, listen to this," I said.

Then I told him at length of my encounter with Bronson in the restaurant, of the bargain proposed by Mrs. Conway, and finally of McKnight's new theory. But, although he was impressed, he was far from convinced.

"It's a very vivid piece of imagination," he said dryly; "but while it fits the evidence as far as it goes, it doesn't go far enough. How about the stains in lower seven, the dirk, and the wallet? Haven't we even got motive in that telegram from Bronson?"

"Yes," I admitted, "but that bit of chain—"

"Pooh," he said shortly. "Perhaps, like yourself, Sullivan wore glasses with a chain. Our not finding them does not prove they did not exist."

And there I made an error; half confidences are always mistakes. I could not tell of the broken chain in Alison West's gold purse.

It was one o'clock when Hotchkiss finally left. We had by that time arranged a definite course of action—Hotchkiss to search Sullivan's rooms and if possible find evidence to have him held for larceny, while I went to Cresson.

Strangely enough, however, when I entered the train the following morning, Hotchkiss was already there. He had bought a new notebook, and was sharpening a fresh pencil.

"I changed my plans, you see," he said, bustling his newspaper aside for me. "It is no discredit to your intelligence, Mr. Blakeley, but you lack the professional eye, the analytical mind. You legal gentlemen call a spade a spade, although it may be a shovel."

> "A primrose by the river's brim
> A yellow primrose was to him,
> And nothing more!"

I quoted as the train pulled out.

Chapter XXIII

A Night at the Laurels

I SLEPT most of the way to Cresson, to the disgust of the little detective. Finally he struck up an acquaintance with a kindly-faced old priest on his way home to his convent school, armed with a roll of dance music and surreptitious bundles that looked like boxes of candy. From scraps of conversation I gleaned that there had been mysterious occurrences at the convent—ending in the theft of what the reverend father called vaguely, "a quantity of undermuslins." I dropped asleep at that point, and when I roused a few moments later, the conversation had progressed. Hotchkiss had a diagram on an envelope.

"With this window bolted, and that one inaccessible, and if, as you say, the—er—garments were in a tub here at X, then, as you hold the key to the other door—I think you said the convent dog did not raise any disturbance? Pardon a personal question, but do you ever walk in your sleep?"

The priest looked bewildered.

"I'll tell you what to do," Hotchkiss said cheerfully, leaning forward. "Look around a little yourself before you call in the police. Somnambulism is a queer thing. It's a question whether we are most ourselves sleeping or waking. Ever think of that? Live a saintly life all day, prayers and matins and all that, and the subconscious mind hikes you out of bed at night to steal undermuslins! Subliminal theft, so to speak. Better examine the roof."

I dozed again. When I wakened, Hotchkiss sat alone, and the priest, from a corner, was staring at him dazedly, over his breviary.

It was raining when we reached Cresson, a wind-driven rain that had forced the agent at the newsstand to close himself in, and that beat back from the rails in parallel lines of white spray. As he went up the main street, Hotchkiss was cheerfully oblivious of the weather, of the threatening dusk, of our generally draggled condition. My draggled condition, I should say, for he improved every moment, his eyes brighter, his ruddy face ruddier, his collar newer and glossier. Sometime, when it does not encircle the little man's neck, I shall test that collar with a match.

I was growing steadily more depressed: I loathed my errand and its necessity. I had always held that a man who played the spy on a woman was beneath contempt. Then, I admit I was afraid of what I might learn. For a time, however, this promised to be a negligible quantity. The streets of the straggling little mountain town had been clean-washed of humanity by the downpour. Windows and doors were inhospitably shut, and from around an occasional drawn shade came narrow strips of light that merely emphasized our gloom. When Hotchkiss' umbrella turned inside out, I stopped.

"I don't know where you are going," I snarled. "I don't care. But I'm going to get under cover inside of ten seconds. I'm not amphibious."

I ducked into the next shelter, which happened to be the yawning entrance to a livery stable, and shook myself, dog fashion. Hotchkiss wiped his collar with his handkerchief. It emerged gleaming and unwilted.

"This will do as well as anyplace," he said, raising his voice above the rattle of the rain. "Got to make a beginning."

I sat down on the usual chair without a back, just inside the door, and stared out at the darkening street. The whole affair had an air of unreality. Now that I was there, I doubted the necessity, or the value, of the journey. I was wet and uncomfortable. Around me, with Cresson as a center, stretched an irregular circumference of mountain, with possibly a ten-mile radius, and in it I was to find the residence of a woman whose first name I did not know, and a man who, so far, had been a purely chimerical person.

Hotchkiss had penetrated the steaming interior of the cave, and now his voice, punctuated by the occasional thud of horses' hoofs, came to me.

"Something light will do," he was saying. "A runabout, perhaps." He came forward rubbing his hands, followed by a thin man in overalls. "Mr. Peck says," he began, "—this is Mr. Peck of Peck and Peck—says that the place we are looking for is about seven miles from the town. It's clearing, isn't it?"

"It is not," I returned savagely. "And we don't want a runabout, Mr. Peck. What we require is hermetically sealed diving suits. I suppose there isn't a machine to be had?" Mr. Peck gazed at me in silence; machine to him meant other things than motors. "Automobile," I supplemented. His face cleared.

"None but private affairs. I can give you a good buggy with a rubber apron. Mike, is the doctor's horse in?"

I am still uncertain as to whether the raw-boned roan we took out that night over the mountains was the doctor's horse or not. If it was, the doctor may be a good doctor, but he doesn't know anything about a horse. And furthermore, I hope he didn't need the beast that miserable evening.

While they harnessed the horse, Hotchkiss told me what he had learned.

"Six Curtises in the town and vicinity," he said. "Sort of family name around here. One of them is telegraph operator at the station. Person we are looking for is—was—a wealthy widow with a brother named Sullivan! Both supposed to have been killed on the *Flier*."

"Her brother," I repeated stupidly.

"You see," Hotchkiss went on, "three people, in one party, took the train here that night, Miss West, Mrs. Curtis and Sullivan. The two women had the drawing room, Sullivan had lower seven. What we want to find out is just who these people were, where they came from, if Bronson knew them, and how Miss West became entangled with them. She may have married Sullivan, for one thing."

I fell into gloom after that. The roan was led unwillingly into the weather, Hotchkiss and I in eclipse behind the blanket. The liveryman stood in the doorway and called directions to us. "You can't miss it," he finished. "Got the name over the gate anyhow, 'The Laurels.' The servants are still there; leastways, we didn't bring them down." He even took a step into the rain as Hotchkiss picked up the lines. "If you're going to settle the estate," he bawled, "don't forget us, Peck and Peck. A half-bushel of name and a bushel of service."

Hotchkiss could not drive. Born a clerk, he guided the roan much as he would drive a bad pen. And the roan spattered through puddles and splashed ink—mud, that is—until I was in a frenzy of irritation.

"What are we going to say when we get there?" I asked after I had finally taken the reins in my one useful hand. "Get out there at midnight and tell the servants we have come to ask a few questions about the family? It's an idiotic trip anyhow; I wish I had stayed at home."

The roan fell just then, and we had to crawl out and help him up. By the time we had partly unharnessed him our matches were gone, and the small bicycle lamp on the buggy was wavering only too certainly. We were covered with mud, panting with exertion, and even Hotchkiss showed a disposition to be surly. The rain, which had lessened for a time, came on again, the lightning flashes doing more than anything else to reveal our isolated position.

Another mile saw us, if possible, more despondent. The water in our clothes had had time to penetrate; the roan had sprained his shoulder and drew us along in a series of convulsive jerks. And then through the rain-spattered window of the blanket, I saw a light. It was a small light, rather yellow, and it lasted perhaps thirty seconds. Hotchkiss missed it, and was inclined to doubt me. But in a couple of minutes the roan hobbled to the side of the road and stopped, and I made out a break in the pines and an arched gate.

It was a small gate, too narrow for the buggy. I pulled the horse into as much shelter as possible under the trees, and we got out. Hotchkiss tied the beast and we left him there, head down against the driving rain, drooping and dejected. Then we went toward the house.

It was a long walk. The path bent and twisted, and now and then we lost it. We were climbing as we went. Oddly there were no lights ahead, although it was only ten o'clock—not later. Hotchkiss kept a little ahead of me, knocking into trees now and then, but finding the path in half the time I should have taken. Once, as I felt my way around a tree in the blackness, I put my hand unexpectedly on his shoulder, and felt a shudder go down my back.

"What do you expect me to do?" he protested, when I remonstrated. "Hang out a red lantern? What was that? Listen."

We both stood peering into the gloom. The sharp patter of the rain on leaves had ceased, and from just ahead there came back to us the stealthy padding of feet in wet soil. My hand closed on Hotchkiss' shoulder, and we listened together, warily. The steps were close by, unmistakable. The next flash of lightning showed nothing moving: the house was in full view now, dark and uninviting, looming huge above a terrace, with an Italian garden at the side. Then the blackness again. Somebody's teeth were chattering: I accused Hotchkiss but he denied it.

"Although I'm not very comfortable, I'll admit," he confessed, "there was something breathing right at my elbow here a moment ago.

"Nonsense!" I took his elbow and steered him in what I made out to be the direction of the steps of the Italian garden. "I saw a deer just ahead by the last flash; that's what you heard. By Jove, I hear wheels."

We paused to listen and Hotchkiss put his hand on something close to us. "Here's your deer," he said.

"Bronze."

As we neared the house the sense of surveillance we had had in the park gradually left us. Stumbling over flower beds, running afoul of a sun dial, groping our way savagely along hedges and thorny banks, we reached the steps finally and climbed the terrace.

It was then that Hotchkiss fell over one of the two stone urns which, with tall boxwood trees in them, mounted guard at each side of the door. He didn't make any attempt to get up. He sat in a puddle on the brick floor of the terrace and clutched his leg and swore softly in Government English.

The occasional relief of the lightning was gone. I could not see an outline of the house before me. We had no matches, and an instant's investigation showed that the windows were boarded and the house closed. Hotchkiss, still recumbent, was ascertaining the damage, tenderly peeling down his stocking.

"Upon my soul," be said finally, "I don't know whether this moisture is blood or rain. I think I've broken a bone."

"Blood is thicker than water," I suggested. "Is it sticky? See if you can move your toes."

There was a pause: Hotchkiss moved his toes. By that time I had found a knocker and was making the night hideous. But there was no response save the wind that blew sodden leaves derisively in our faces. Once Hotchkiss declared he heard a window sash lifted, but renewed violence with the knocker produced no effect.

"There's only one thing to do," I said finally. "I'll go back and try to bring the buggy up for you. You can't walk, can you?"

Hotchkiss sat back in his puddle and said he didn't think he could stir, but for me to go back to town and leave him, that he didn't have any family dependent on him, and that if he was going to have pneumonia, he had probably got it already. I left him there, and started back to get the horse.

If possible, it was worse than before. There was no lightning, and only by a miracle did I find the little gate again. I drew a long breath of relief, followed by another, equally long, of dismay. For I had found the hitching strap and there was nothing at the end of it! In a lull of the wind I seemed to hear, far off, the eager thud of stable-bound feet. So for the second time I climbed the slope to the Laurels, and on the way I thought of many things to say.

I struck the house at a new angle, for I found a veranda, destitute of chairs and furnishings, but dry and evidently roofed. It was better than the terrace, and so, by groping along the wall, I tried to make my way to Hotchkiss. That was how I found the open window. I had passed perhaps six, all closed, and to have my hand grope for the next one, and to find instead the soft drapery of an inner curtain, was startling, to say the least.

I found Hotchkiss at last around an angle of the stone wall and told him that the horse was gone. He was disconcerted, but not abased; maintaining that it was a new kind of knot that couldn't slip and that the horse must have chewed the halter through! He was less enthusiastic than I had expected about the window.

"It looks uncommonly like a trap," he said. "I tell you there was someone in the park below when we were coming up. Man has a sixth sense that scientists ignore—a sense of the nearness of things. And all the time you have been gone, someone has been watching me."

"Couldn't see you," I maintained. "I can't see you now. And your sense of contiguity didn't tell you about that flower crock."

In the end, of course, he consented to go with me. He was very lame, and I helped him around to the open window. He was full of moral courage, the little man: it was only the physical in him that quailed. And as we groped along, he insisted on going through the window first.

"If it is a trap," he whispered, "I have two arms to your one, and, besides, as I said before, life holds much for you. As for me, the government would merely lose an indifferent employee."

When he found I was going first, he was rather hurt, but I did not wait for his protests. I swung my feet over the sill and dropped. I made a clutch at the window frame with my good hand when I found no floor under my feet, but I was too late. I dropped probably ten feet and landed with a crash that seemed to split my eardrums. I was thoroughly shaken, but in some miraculous way the bandaged arm had escaped injury.

"For Heaven's sake," Hotchkiss was calling from above, "have you broken your back?"

"No," I returned, as steadily as I could, "merely driven it up through my skull. This is a staircase. I'm coming up to open another window."

It was eerie work, but I accomplished it finally, discovering, not without mishap, a room filled with more tables than I had ever dreamed of, tables that seemed to waylay and strike at me. When I had got a window open, Hotchkiss crawled through, and we were at last under shelter.

Our first thought was for a light. The same laborious investigation that had landed us where we were, revealed that the house was lighted by electricity, and that the plant was not in operation. By accident I stumbled across a tabouret with smoking materials, and found a half dozen matches. The first one showed us the magnitude of the room we stood in, and revealed also a brass candlestick by the open fireplace, a candlestick almost four feet high, supporting a candle of similar colossal proportions. It was Hotchkiss who discovered that it had been recently lighted. He held the match to it and peered at it over his glasses.

"Within ten minutes," he announced impressively, "this candle has been burning. Look at the wax! And the wick! Both soft."

"Perhaps it's the damp weather," I ventured, moving a little nearer to the circle of light. A gust of wind came in just then, and the flame turned over on its side and threatened demise. There was something almost ridiculous in the haste with which we put down the window and nursed the flicker to life.

The peculiarly ghostlike appearance of the room added to the uncanniness of the situation. The furniture was swathed in white covers for the winter; even the pictures wore shrouds. And in a niche between two windows a bust on a pedestal, similarly wrapped, one arm extended under its winding sheet, made a most lifelike ghost, if any ghost can be lifelike.

In the light of the candle we surveyed each other, and we were objects for mirth. Hotchkiss was taking off his sodden shoes and preparing to make himself comfortable, while I hung my muddy raincoat over the ghost in the corner. Thus habited, he presented a rakish but distinctly more comfortable appearance.

"When these people built," Hotchkiss said, surveying the huge dimensions of the room, "they must have bought a mountain and built all over it. What a room!"

It seemed to be a living room, although Hotchkiss remarked that it was much more like a dead one. It was probably fifty feet long and twenty-five feet wide. It was very high, too, with a domed ceiling, and a gallery ran around the entire room, about fifteen feet above the floor. The candlelight did not penetrate beyond the dim outlines of the gallery rail, but I fancied the wall there hung with smaller pictures.

Hotchkiss had discovered a fire laid in the enormous fireplace, and in a few minutes we were steaming before a cheerful blaze. Within the radius of its light and heat, we were comfortable again. But the brightness merely emphasized the gloom of the ghostly corners. We talked in subdued tones, and I smoked a box of Russian cigarettes which I found in a table drawer. We had decided to stay all night, there being nothing else to do. I suggested a game of double-dummy bridge, but did not urge it when my companion asked me if it resembled euchre. Gradually, as the ecclesiastical candle paled in the firelight, we grew drowsy. I drew a divan into the cheerful area and stretched myself out for sleep. Hotchkiss, who said the pain in his leg made him wakeful, sat wide-eyed by the fire, smoking a pipe.

I have no idea how much time had passed when something threw itself violently on my chest. I roused with a start and leaped to my feet, and a large Angora cat fell with a thump to the floor. The fire was still bright, and there was an odor of scorched leather through the room, from Hotchkiss' shoes. The little detective was sound asleep, his dead pipe in his fingers. The cat sat back on its haunches and wailed.

The curtain at the door into the hallway bellied slowly out into the room and fell again. The cat looked toward it and opened its mouth for another howl. I thrust at it with my foot, but it refused to move. Hotchkiss stirred uneasily, and his pipe clattered to the floor.

The cat was standing at my feet, staring behind me. Apparently it was following with its eyes an object unseen to me, that moved behind me. The tip of its tail waved threateningly, but when I wheeled, I saw nothing.

I took the candle and made a circuit of the room. Behind the curtain that had moved the door was securely closed. The windows were shut and locked, and everywhere the silence was absolute. The cat followed me majestically. I stooped and stroked its head, but it persisted in its uncanny watching of the corners of the room.

When I went back to my divan, after putting a fresh log on the fire, I was reassured. I took the precaution, and smiled at myself for doing it, to put the fire tongs within reach of my hand. But the cat would not let me sleep. After a time I decided that it wanted water, and I started out in search of some, carrying the candle without the stand. I wandered through several rooms, all closed and dismantled, before I found a small lavatory opening off a billiard room. The cat lapped steadily, and I filled a glass to take back with me. The candle flickered in a sickly fashion that threatened to leave me there lost in the wanderings of the many hallways, and from somewhere there came an occasional violent puff of wind. The cat stuck by my feet, with the hair on its back raised menacingly. I don't like cats; there is something psychic about them.

Hotchkiss was still asleep when I got back to the big room. I moved his boots back from the fire, and trimmed the candle. Then, with sleep gone from me, I lay back on my divan and reflected on many things: on my idiocy in coming; on Alison West, and the fact that only a week before she had been a guest in this very house; on Richey and the constraint that had come between us. From that I drifted back to Alison, and to the barrier my comparative poverty would be.

The emptiness, the stillness were oppressive. Once I heard footsteps coming, rhythmical steps that neither hurried nor dragged, and seemed to mount endless staircases without coming any closer. I realized finally that I had not quite turned off the tap, and that the lavatory, which I had circled to reach, must be quite close.

The cat lay by the fire, its nose on its folded paws, content in the warmth and companionship. I watched it idly. Now and then the green wood hissed in the fire, but the cat never batted an eye. Through an unshuttered window the lightning flashed. Suddenly the cat looked up. It lifted its head and stared directly at the gallery above. Then it blinked, and stared again. I was amused. Not until it had got up on its feet, eyes still riveted on the balcony, tail waving at the tip, the hair on its back a bristling brush, did I glance casually over my head.

From among the shadows a face gazed down at me, a face that seemed a fitting tenant of the ghostly room below. I saw it as plainly as I might see my own face in a mirror. While I stared at it with horrified eyes, the apparition faded. The rail was there, the Bokhara rug still swung from it, but the gallery was empty.

The cat threw back its head and wailed.

Chapter XXIV

His Wife's Father

$\backsim\!\!\!\infty\!\!\!\backsim$

I JUMPED up and seized the fire tongs. The cat's wail had roused
Hotchkiss, who was wide-awake at once. He took in my offensive attitude, the tongs, the direction of my gaze, and needed nothing more. As
he picked up the candle and darted out into the hall, I followed him. He
made directly for the staircase, and partway up he turned off to the right
through a small door. We were on the gallery itself; below us the fire
gleamed cheerfully, the cat was not in sight. There was no sign of my
ghostly visitant, but as we stood there the Bokhara rug, without warning,
slid over the railing and fell to the floor below.

"Man or woman?" Hotchkiss inquired in his most professional tone.

"Neither—that is, I don't know. I didn't notice anything but the
eyes," I muttered. "They were looking a hole in me. If you'd seen that
cat, you would realize my state of mind. That was a traditional graveyard yowl."

"I don't think you saw anything at all," he lied cheerfully. "You dozed
off, and the rest is the natural result of a meal on a buffet car."

Nevertheless, he examined the Bokhara carefully when we went
down, and when I finally went to sleep, he was reading the only book
in sight—*Elwell on Bridge*. The first rays of daylight were coming mist-
ily into the room when he roused me. He had his finger on his lips, and
he whispered sibilantly while I tried to draw on my distorted boots.

"I think we have him," he said triumphantly. "I've been looking
around some, and I can tell you this much. Just before we came in
through the window last night, another man came. Only—he did not
drop, as you did. He swung over to the stair railing, and then down. The
rail is scratched. He was long enough ahead of us to go into the dining
room and get a decanter out of the sideboard. He poured out the liquor
into a glass, left the decanter there, and took the whisky into the library
across the hall. Then—he broke into a desk, using a paper knife for a
jimmy."

"Good Lord, Hotchkiss!" I exclaimed. "Why, it may have been Sullivan himself! Confound your theories—he's getting farther away every minute."

"It was Sullivan," Hotchkiss returned imperturbably. "And he has not gone. His boots are by the library fire."

"He probably had a dozen pairs where he could get them," I scoffed. "And while you and I sat and slept, the very man we want to get our hands on leered at us over that railing."

"Softly, softly, my friend," Hotchkiss said, as I stamped into my other shoe. "I did not say he was gone. Don't jump at conclusions. It is fatal to reasoning. As a matter of fact, he didn't relish a night on the mountains any more than we did. After he had unintentionally frightened you almost into paralysis, what would my gentleman naturally do? Go out in the storm again? Not if I know the Alice-sit-by-the-fire type. He went upstairs, well up near the roof, locked himself in and went to bed."

"And he is there now?"

"He is there now."

We had no weapons. I am aware that the traditional hero is always armed, and that Hotchkiss as the low comedian should have had a revolver that missed fire. As a fact, we had nothing of the sort. Hotchkiss carried the fire tongs, but my sense of humor was too strong for me; I declined the poker.

"All we want is a little peaceable conversation with him," I demurred. "We can't brain him first and converse with him afterward. And anyhow, while I can't put my finger on the place, I think your theory is weak. If he wouldn't run a hundred miles through fire and water to get away from us, then he is not the man we want."

Hotchkiss, however, was certain. He had found the room and listened outside the door to the sleeper's heavy breathing, and so we climbed past luxurious suites, revealed in the deepening daylight, past long vistas of hall and boudoir. And we were both badly winded when we got there. It was a tower room, reached by narrow stairs, and well above the roof level. Hotchkiss was glowing.

"It is partly good luck, but not all," he panted in a whisper. "If we had persisted in the search last night, he would have taken alarm and fled. Now—we have him. Are you ready?"

He gave a mighty rap at the door with the fire tongs, and stood expectant. Certainly he was right; someone moved within.

"Hello! Hello there!" Hotchkiss bawled. "You might as well come out. We won't hurt you, if you'll come peaceably."

"Tell him we represent the law," I prompted. "That's the customary thing, you know."

But at that moment a bullet came squarely through the door and flattened itself with a sharp pst against the wall of the tower staircase. We ducked unanimously, dropped back out of range, and Hotchkiss retaliated with a spirited bang at the door with the tongs. This brought another bullet. It was a ridiculous situation. Under the circumstances, no doubt, we should have retired, at least until we had armed ourselves, but Hotchkiss had no end of fighting spirit, and as for me, my blood was up.

"Break the lock," I suggested, and Hotchkiss, standing at the side, out of range, retaliated for every bullet by a smashing blow with the tongs. The shots ceased after a half dozen, and the door was giving, slowly. One of us on each side of the door, we were ready for almost any kind of desperate resistance. As it swung open Hotchkiss poised the tongs; I stood, bent forward, my arm drawn back for a blow.

Nothing happened.

There was not a sound. Finally, at the risk of losing an eye which I justly value, I peered around and into the room. There was no desperado there: only a fresh-faced, trembling-lipped servant, sitting on the edge of her bed, with a quilt around her shoulders and the empty revolver at her feet.

We were victorious, but no conquered army ever beat such a retreat as ours down the tower stairs and into the refuge of the living room. There, with the door closed, sprawled on the divan, I went from one spasm of mirth into another, becoming sane at intervals, and suffering relapse again every time I saw Hotchkiss' disgruntled countenance. He was pacing the room, the tongs still in his hand, his mouth pursed with irritation. Finally he stopped in front of me and compelled my attention.

"When you have finished cackling," he said with dignity, "I wish to justify my position. Do you think the—er—young woman upstairs put a pair of number eight boots to dry in the library last night? Do you think she poured the whisky out of that decanter?"

"They have been known to do it," I put in, but his eye silenced me.

"Moreover, if she had been the person who peered at you over the gallery railing last night, don't you suppose, with her—er—belligerent disposition, she could have filled you as full of lead as a window weight?"

"I do," I assented. "It wasn't Alice-sit-by-the-fire. I grant you that. Then who was it?"

Hotchkiss felt certain that it had been Sullivan, but I was not so sure. Why would he have crawled like a thief into his own house? If he had crossed the park, as seemed probable, when we did, he had not made any attempt to use the knocker. I gave it up finally, and made an effort to conciliate the young woman in the tower.

We had heard no sound since our spectacular entrance into her room. I was distinctly uncomfortable as, alone this time, I climbed to the tower staircase. Reasoning from before, she would probably throw a chair at me. I stopped at the foot of the staircase and called.

"Hello up there," I said, in as debonair a manner as I could summon. "Good morning. Wie geht es bei ihen?"

No reply.

"Bon jour, mademoiselle," I tried again. This time there was a movement of some sort from above, but nothing fell on me.

"I—we want to apologize for rousing you so—er—unexpectedly this morning," I went on. "The fact is, we wanted to talk to you, and you—you were hard to waken. We are travelers, lost in your mountains, and we crave a breakfast and an audience."

She came to the door then. I could feel that she was investigating the top of my head from above. "Is Mr. Sullivan with you?" she asked. It was the first word from her, and she was not sure of her voice.

"No. We are alone. If you will come down and look at us, you will find us two perfectly harmless people, whose horse—curses on him—departed without leave last night and left us at your gate."

She relaxed somewhat then and came down a step or two. "I was afraid I had killed somebody," she said. "The housekeeper left yesterday, and the other maids went with her."

When she saw that I was comparatively young and lacked the earmarks of the highwayman, she was greatly relieved. She was inclined to fight shy of Hotchkiss, however, for some reason. She gave us a breakfast of a sort, for there was little in the house, and afterward we telephoned to the town for a vehicle. While Hotchkiss examined scratches and replaced the Bokhara rug, I engaged Jennie in conversation.

"Can you tell me," I asked, "who is managing the estate since Mrs. Curtis was killed?"

"No one," she returned shortly.

"Has—any member of the family been here since the accident?"

"No, sir. There was only the two, and some think Mr. Sullivan was killed as well as his sister."

"You don't?"

"No," with conviction.

"Why?"

She wheeled on me with quick suspicion.

"Are you a detective?" she demanded.

"No."

"You told him to say you represented the law."

"I am a lawyer. Some of them misrepresent the law, but I—"

She broke in impatiently.

"A sheriff's officer?"

"No. Look here, Jennie; I am all that I should be. You'll have to believe that. And I'm in a bad position through no fault of my own. I want you to answer some questions. If you will help me, I will do what I can for you. Do you live near here?"

Her chin quivered. It was the first sign of weakness she had shown.

"My home is in Pittsburgh," she said, "and I haven't enough money to get there. They hadn't paid any wages for two months. They didn't pay anybody."

"Very well," I returned. "I'll send you back to Pittsburgh, Pullman included, if you will tell me some things I want to know."

She agreed eagerly. Outside the window Hotchkiss was bending over, examining footprints in the drive.

"Now," I began, "there has been a Miss West staying here?"

"Yes."

"Mr. Sullivan was attentive to her?"

"Yes. She was the granddaughter of a wealthy man in Pittsburgh. My aunt has been in his family for twenty years. Mrs. Curtis wanted her brother to marry Miss West."

"Do you think he did marry her?" I could not keep the excitement out of my voice.

"No. There were reasons—" She stopped abruptly.

"Do you know anything of the family? Are they—were they New Yorkers?"

"They came from somewhere in the south. I have heard Mrs. Curtis say her mother was a Cuban. I don't know much about them, but Mr. Sullivan had a wicked temper, though he didn't look it. Folks say big, light-haired people are easy going, but I don't believe it, sir."

"How long was Miss West here?"

"Two weeks."

I hesitated about further questioning. Critical as my position was, I could not pry deeper into Alison West's affairs. If she had got into the hands of adventurers, as Sullivan and his sister appeared to have been, she was safely away from them again. But something of the situation in the car Ontario was forming itself in my mind: the incident at the farm-house lacked only motive to be complete. Was Sullivan, after all, a rascal or a criminal? Was the murderer Sullivan or Mrs. Conway? The lady or the tiger again.

Jennie was speaking.

"I hope Miss West was not hurt?" she asked. "We liked her, all of us. She was not like Mrs. Curtis."

I wanted to say that she was not like anybody in the world. Instead, "She escaped with some bruises," I said.

She glanced at my arm. "You were on the train?"

"Yes."

She waited for more questions, but none coming, she went to the door. Then she closed it softly and came back.

"Mrs. Curtis is dead? You are sure of it?" she asked.

"She was killed instantly, I believe. The body was not recovered. But I have reasons for believing that Mr. Sullivan is living."

"I knew it," she said. "I—I think he was here the night before last. That is why I went to the tower room. I believe he would kill me if he could." As nearly as her round and comely face could express it, Jennie's expression was tragic at that moment. I made a quick resolution, and acted on it at once.

"You are not entirely frank with me, Jennie," I protested. "And I am going to tell you more than I have. We are talking at cross purposes.

"I was on the wrecked train, in the same car with Mrs. Curtis, Miss West and Mr. Sullivan. During the night there was a crime committed in that car and Mr. Sullivan disappeared. But he left behind him a chain of circumstantial evidence that involved me completely, so that I may, at any time, be arrested."

Apparently she did not comprehend for a moment. Then, as if the meaning of my words had just dawned on her, she looked up and gasped.

"You mean—Mr. Sullivan committed the crime himself?"

"I think he did."

"What was it?"

"It was murder," I said deliberately.

Her hands clenched involuntarily, and she shrank back. "A woman?" She could scarcely form her words.

"No, a man; a Mr. Simon Harrington, of Pittsburgh."

Her effort to retain her self-control was pitiful. Then she broke down and cried, her head on the back of a tall chair.

"It was my fault," she said wretchedly, "my fault, I should not have sent them the word."

After a few minutes she grew quiet. She seemed to hesitate over something, and finally determined to say it.

"You will understand better, sir, when I say that I was raised in the Harrington family. Mr. Harrington was Mr. Sullivan's wife's father!"

Chapter XXV

At the Station

∞

So it had been the tiger, not the lady! Well, I had held to that theory all through. Jennie suddenly became a valuable person; if necessary, she could prove the connection between Sullivan and the murdered man, and show a motive for the crime. I was triumphant when Hotchkiss came in. When the girl had produced a photograph of Mrs. Sullivan, and I had recognized the bronze-haired girl of the train, we were both well satisfied—which goes to prove the ephemeral nature of most human contentments.

Jennie either had nothing more to say, or feared she had said too much. She was evidently uneasy before Hotchkiss. I told her that Mrs. Sullivan was recovering in a Baltimore hospital, but she already knew it, from some source, and merely nodded. She made a few preparations for leaving, while Hotchkiss and I compared notes, and then, with the cat in her arms, she climbed into the trap from the town. I sat with her, and on the way down she told me a little, not much.

"If you see Mrs. Sullivan," she advised, "and she is conscious, she probably thinks that both her husband and her father were killed in the wreck. She will be in a bad way, sir."

"You mean that she—still cares about her husband?"

The cat crawled over on to my knee, and rubbed its head against my hand invitingly. Jennie stared at the undulating line of the mountain crests, a colossal sun against a blue ocean of sky. "Yes, she cares," she said softly. "Women are made like that. They say they are cats, but Peter there in your lap wouldn't come back and lick your hand if you kicked him. If—if you have to tell her the truth, be as gentle as you can, sir. She has been good to me—that's why I have played the spy here all summer. It's a thankless thing, spying on people."

"It is that," I agreed soberly.

Hotchkiss and I arrived in Washington late that evening, and, rather than arouse the household, I went to the club. I was at the office early the next morning and admitted myself. McKnight rarely appeared before half after ten, and our modest office force some time after nine. I looked over my previous day's mail and waited, with such patience as I possessed, for McKnight. In the interval I called up Mrs. Klopton and announced that I would dine at home that night. What my household subsists on during my numerous absences I have never discovered. Tea, probably, and crackers. Diligent search when I have made a midnight arrival never reveals anything more substantial. Possibly I imagine it, but the announcement that I am about to make a journey always seems to create a general atmosphere of depression throughout the house, as though Euphemia and Eliza, and Thomas, the stableman, were already subsisting, in imagination, on Mrs. Klopton's meager fare.

So I called her up and announced my arrival. There was something unusual in her tone, as though her throat was tense with indignation. Always shrill, her elderly voice rasped my ear painfully through the receiver.

"I have changed the butcher, Mr. Lawrence," she announced portentously. "The last roast was a pound short, and his mutton chops—any self-respecting sheep would refuse to acknowledge them."

As I said before, I can always tell from the voice in which Mrs. Klopton conveys the most indifferent matters if something of real significance has occurred. Also, through long habit, I have learned how quickest to bring her to the point.

"You are pessimistic this morning," I returned. "What's the matter, Mrs. Klopton? You haven't used that tone since Euphemia baked a pie for the iceman. What is it now? Somebody poison the dog?"

She cleared her throat.

"The house has been broken into, Mr. Lawrence," she said. "I have lived in the best families, and never have I stood by and seen what I saw yesterday—every bureau drawer opened, and my—my most sacred belongings—" she choked.

"Did you notify the police?" I asked sharply.

"Police!" she sniffed. "Police! It was the police that did it—two detectives with a search warrant. I—I wouldn't dare tell you over the telephone what one of them said when he found the whisky and rock candy for my cough."

"Did they take anything?" I demanded, every nerve on edge.

"They took the cough medicine," she returned indignantly, "and they said—"

"Confound the cough medicine!" I was frantic. "Did they take anything else? Were they in my dressing room?"

"Yes. I threatened to sue them, and I told them what you would do when you came back. But they wouldn't listen. They took away that black sealskin bag you brought home from Pittsburgh with you!"

I knew then that my hours of freedom were numbered. To have found Sullivan and then, in support of my case against him, to have produced the bag, minus the bit of chain, had been my intention. But the police had the bag, and, beyond knowing something of Sullivan's history, I was practically no nearer his discovery than before. Hotchkiss hoped he had his man in the house off Washington Circle, but on the very night he had seen him Jennie claimed that Sullivan had tried to enter the Laurels. Then—suppose we found Sullivan and proved the satchel and its contents his? Since the police had the bit of chain it might mean involving Alison in the story. I sat down and buried my face in my hands. There was no escape. I figured it out despondingly.

Against me was the evidence of the survivors of the Ontario that I had been accused of the murder at the time. There had been bloodstains on my pillow and a hidden dagger. Into the bargain, in my possession had been found a traveling bag containing the dead man's pocketbook.

In my favor was McKnight's theory against Mrs. Conway. She had a motive for wishing to secure the notes, she believed I was in lower ten, and she had collapsed at the discovery of the crime in the morning.

Against both of these theories, I accuse a purely chimerical person named Sullivan, who was not seen by any of the survivors—save one, Alison, whom I could not bring into the case. I could find a motive for his murdering his father-in-law, whom he hated, but again—I would have to drag in the girl.

And not one of the theories explained the telegram and the broken necklace.

Outside the office force was arriving. They were comfortably ignorant of my presence, and over the transom floated scraps of dialogue and the stenographer's gurgling laugh. McKnight had a relative, who was reading law with him, in the intervals between calling up the young women of his acquaintance. He came in singing, and the office boy joined in with the uncertainty of voice of fifteen. I smiled grimly. I was too busy with my own troubles to find any joy in opening the door and startling them into silence. I even heard, without resentment, Blobs of the uncertain voice inquire when "Blake" would be back.

I hoped McKnight would arrive before the arrest occurred. There were many things to arrange. But when at last, impatient of his delay, I telephoned, I found he had been gone for more than an hour. Clearly he was not coming directly to the office, and with such resignation as I could muster I paced the floor and waited.

I felt more alone than I have ever felt in my life. "Born an orphan," as Richey said, I had made my own way, carved out myself such success as had been mine. I had built up my house of life on the props of law and order, and now some unknown hand had withdrawn the supports, and I stood among ruins.

I suppose it is the maternal in a woman that makes a man turn to her when everything else fails. The eternal boy in him goes to have his wounded pride bandaged, his tattered self-respect repaired. If he loves the woman, he wants her to kiss the hurt.

The longing to see Alison, always with me, was stronger than I was that morning. It might be that I would not see her again. I had nothing to say to her save one thing, and that, under the cloud that hung over me, I did not dare to say. But I wanted to see her, to touch her hand— as only a lonely man can crave it, I wanted the comfort of her, the peace that lay in her presence. And so, with every step outside the door a threat, I telephoned her.

She was gone! The disappointment was great, for my need was great. In a fury of revolt against the scheme of things, I heard that she had started home to Richmond—but that she might still be caught at the station.

To see her had by that time become an obsession. I picked up my hat, threw open the door, and, oblivious of the shock to the office force of my presence, followed so immediately by my exit, I dashed out to the elevator. As I went down in one cage I caught a glimpse of Johnson and two other men going up in the next. I hardly gave them a thought. There was no hansom in sight, and I jumped on a passing car. Let come what might, arrest, prison, disgrace, I was going to see Alison.

I saw her. I flung into the station, saw that it was empty—empty, for she was not there. Then I hurried back to the gates. She was there, a familiar figure in blue, the very gown in which I always thought of her, the one she had worn when, Heaven help me—I had kissed her, at the Carter farm. And she was not alone. Bending over her, talking earnestly, with all his boyish heart in his face, was Richey.

They did not see me, and I was glad of it. After all, it had been McKnight's game first. I turned on my heel and made my way blindly out of the station. Before I lost them I turned once and looked toward them, standing apart from the crowd, absorbed in each other. They were the only two people on earth that I cared about, and I left them there together. Then I went back miserably to the office and awaited arrest.

Chapter XXVI

On to Richmond

STRANGELY enough, I was not disturbed that day. McKnight did not appear at all. I sat at my desk and transacted routine business all afternoon, working with feverish energy. Like a man on the verge of a critical illness or a hazardous journey, I cleared up my correspondence, paid bills until I had writer's cramp from signing checks, read over my will, and paid up my life insurance, made to the benefit of an elderly sister of my mother's. I no longer dreaded arrest. After that morning in the station, I felt that anything would be a relief from the tension. I went home with perfect openness, courting the warrant that I knew was waiting, but I was not molested. The delay puzzled me. The early part of the evening was uneventful. I read until late, with occasional lapses, when my book lay at my elbow, and I smoked and thought. Mrs. Klopton closed the house with ostentatious caution, about eleven, and hung around waiting to enlarge on the outrageousness of the police search. I did not encourage her.

"One would think," she concluded pompously, one foot in the hall, "that you were something you oughtn't to be, Mr. Lawrence. They acted as though you had committed a crime."

"I'm not sure that I didn't, Mrs. Klopton," I said wearily. "Somebody did, the general verdict seems to point my way."

She stared at me in speechless indignation. Then she flounced out. She came back once to say that the paper predicted cooler weather, and that she had put a blanket on my bed, but, to her disappointment, I refused to reopen the subject.

At half past eleven McKnight and Hotchkiss came in. Richey has a habit of stopping his car in front of the house and honking until someone comes out. He has a code of signals with the horn, which I never remember. Two long and a short blast mean, I believe, "Send out a box of cigarettes," and six short blasts, which sound like a police call, mean "Can you lend me some money?" Tonight I knew something was up, for he got out and rang the doorbell like a Christian.

They came into the library, and Hotchkiss wiped his collar until it gleamed. McKnight was aggressively cheerful.

"Not pinched yet!" he exclaimed. "What do you think of that for luck! You always were a fortunate devil, Lawrence."

"Yes," I assented, with some bitterness, "I hardly know how to contain myself for joy sometimes. I suppose you know"—to Hotchkiss—"that the police were here while we were at Cresson, and that they found the bag that I brought from the wreck?"

"Things are coming to a head," he said thoughtfully, "unless a little plan that I have in mind—" He hesitated.

"I hope so; I am pretty nearly desperate," I said doggedly. "I've got a mental toothache, and the sooner it's pulled the better."

"Tut, tut," said McKnight, "think of the disgrace to the firm if its senior member goes up for life, or—" He twisted his handkerchief into a noose, and went through an elaborate pantomime.

"Although jail isn't so bad, anyhow," he finished, "there are fellows that get the habit and keep going back and going back." He looked at his watch, and I fancied his cheerfulness was strained. Hotchkiss was nervously fumbling my book.

"Did you ever read *The Purloined Letter*, Mr. Blakeley?" he inquired.

"Probably, years ago," I said. "Poe, isn't it?"

He was choked at my indifference. "It is a masterpiece," he said, with enthusiasm. "I reread it today."

"And what happened?"

"Then I inspected the rooms in the house off Washington Circle. I—I made some discoveries, Mr. Blakeley. For one thing, our man there is left-handed." He looked around for our approval. "There was a small cushion on the dresser, and the scarf pins in it had been stuck in with the left hand."

"Somebody may have twisted the cushion," I objected, but he looked hurt, and I desisted.

"There is only one discrepancy," he admitted, "but it troubles me. According to Mrs. Carter, at the farmhouse, our man wore gaudy pajamas, while I found here only the most severely plain nightshirts."

"Any buttons off?" McKnight inquired, looking again at his watch.

"The buttons were there," the amateur detective answered gravely, "but the buttonhole next the top one was torn through."

McKnight winked at me furtively.

"I am convinced of one thing," Hotchkiss went on, clearing his throat, "the papers are not in that room. Either he carries them with him, or he has sold them."

A sound on the street made both my visitors listen sharply. Whatever it was it passed on, however. I was growing curious and the restraint was telling on McKnight. He has no talent for secrecy. In the interval we discussed the strange occurrence at Cresson, which lost nothing by Hotchkiss' dry narration.

"And so," he concluded, "the woman in the Baltimore hospital is the wife of Henry Sullivan and the daughter of the man he murdered. No wonder he collapsed when he heard of the wreck."

"Joy, probably," McKnight put in. "Is that clock right, Lawrence? Never mind, it doesn't matter. By the way, Mrs. Conway dropped in the office yesterday, while you were away."

"What!" I sprang from my chair.

"Sure thing. Said she had heard great things of us, and wanted us to handle her case against the railroad."

"I would like to know what she is driving at," I reflected. "Is she trying to reach me through you?"

Richey's flippancy is often a cloak for deeper feeling. He dropped it now. "Yes," he said, "she's after the notes, of course. And I'll tell you I felt like a poltroon—whatever that may be—when I turned her down. She stood by the door with her face white, and told me contemptuously that I could save you from a murder charge and wouldn't do it. She made me feel like a cur. I was just as guilty as if I could have obliged her. She hinted that there were reasons and she laid my attitude to beastly motives."

"Nonsense," I said, as easily as I could. Hotchkiss had gone to the window. "She was excited. There are no 'reasons,' whatever she means."

Richey put his hand on my shoulder. "We've been together too long to let any 'reasons' or 'unreasons' come between us, old man," he said, not very steadily. Hotchkiss, who had been silent, here came forward in his most impressive manner. He put his hands under his coattails and coughed.

"Mr. Blakeley," he began, "by Mr. McKnight's advice we have arranged a little interview here tonight. If all has gone as I planned, Mr. Henry

Pinckney Sullivan is by this time under arrest. Within a very few minutes—he will be here."

"I wanted to talk to him before be was locked up," Richey explained. "He's clever enough to be worth knowing, and, besides, I'm not so cocksure of his guilt as our friend the Patch on the Seat of Government. No murderer worthy of the name needs six different motives for the same crime, beginning with robbery, and ending with an unpleasant father-in-law."

We were all silent for a while. McKnight stationed himself at a window, and Hotchkiss paced the floor expectantly. "It's a great day for modern detective methods," he chirruped. "While the police have been guarding houses and standing with their mouths open waiting for clues to fall in and choke them, we have pieced together, bit by bit, a fabric—"

The doorbell rang, followed immediately by sounds of footsteps in the hall. McKnight threw the door open, and Hotchkiss, raised on his toes, flung out his arm in a gesture of superb eloquence.

"Behold—your man!" he declaimed.

Through the open doorway came a tall, blond fellow, clad in light gray, wearing tan shoes, and followed closely by an officer.

"I brought him here as you suggested, Mr. McKnight," said the constable.

But McKnight was doubled over the library table in silent convulsions of mirth, and I was almost as bad. Little Hotchkiss stood up, his important attitude finally changing to one of chagrin, while the blond man ceased to look angry, and became sheepish.

It was Stuart, our confidential clerk for the last half dozen years!

McKnight sat up and wiped his eyes.

"Stuart," he said sternly, "there are two very serious things we have learned about you. First, you jab your scarf pins into your cushion with your left hand, which is most reprehensible; second, you wear—er—nightshirts, instead of pajamas. Worse than that, perhaps, we find that one of them has a buttonhole torn out at the neck."

Stuart was bewildered. He looked from McKnight to me, and then at the crestfallen Hotchkiss.

"I haven't any idea what it's all about," he said. "I was arrested as I reached my boardinghouse tonight, after the theater, and brought directly here. I told the officer it was a mistake."

Poor Hotchkiss tried bravely to justify the fiasco. "You cannot deny," he contended, "that Mr. Andrew Bronson followed you to your rooms last Monday evening."

Stuart looked at us and flushed.

"No, I don't deny it," he said, "but there was nothing criminal about it, on my part, at least. Mr. Bronson has been trying to induce me to secure the forged notes for him. But I did not even know where they were."

"And you were not on the wrecked *Washington Flier?*" persisted Hotchkiss. But McKnight interfered.

"There is no use trying to put the other man's identity on Stuart, Mr. Hotchkiss," he protested. "He has been our confidential clerk for six years, and has not been away from the office a day for a year. I am afraid that the beautiful fabric we have pieced out of all these scraps is going to be a crazy quilt." His tone was facetious, but I could detect the under-current of real disappointment.

I paid the constable for his trouble, and he departed. Stuart, still indignant, left to go back to Washington Circle. He shook hands with McKnight and myself magnanimously, but he hurled a look of utter hatred at Hotchkiss, sunk crestfallen in his chair.

"As far as I can see," said McKnight dryly, "we're exactly as far along as we were the day we met at the Carter place. We're not a step nearer to finding our man."

"We have one thing that may be of value," I suggested. "He is the husband of a bronze-haired woman at Van Kirk's hospital, and it is just possible we may trace him through her. I hope we are not going to lose your valuable cooperation, Mr. Hotchkiss?" I asked.

He roused at that to feeble interest. "I—oh, of course not, if you still care to have me, I—I was wondering about—the man who just went out, Stuart, you say? I—told his landlady tonight that he wouldn't need the room again. I hope she hasn't rented it to somebody else."

We cheered him as best we could, and I suggested that we go to Baltimore the next day and try to find the real Sullivan through his wife. He left sometime after midnight, and Richey and I were alone.

He drew a chair near the lamp and lighted a cigarette, and for a time we were silent. I was in the shadow, and I sat back and watched him. It was not surprising, I thought, that she cared for him: women had always loved him, perhaps because he always loved them. There was no disloyalty in the thought: it was the lad's nature to give and crave affection. Only—I was different. I had never really cared about a girl before, and my life had been singularly loveless. I had fought a lonely battle always. Once before, in college, we had both laid ourselves and our callow devotions at the feet of the same girl. Her name was Dorothy—I had forgotten the rest—but I remembered the sequel. In a spirit of quixotic youth I had relinquished my claim in favor of Richey and had gone cheerfully on my way, elevated by my heroic sacrifice to a somber, white-hot martyrdom. As is often the case, McKnight's first words showed our parallel lines of thought.

"I say, Lollie," he asked, "do you remember Dorothy Browne?" Browne, that was it!

"Dorothy Browne?" I repeated. "Oh—why yes, I recall her now. Why?"

"Nothing," he said. "I was thinking about her. That's all. You remember you were crazy about her, and dropped back because she preferred me."

"I got out," I said with dignity, "because you declared you would shoot yourself if she didn't go with you to something or other!"

"Oh, why yes, I recall now!" he mimicked. He tossed his cigarette in the general direction of the hearth and got up. We were both a little conscious, and he stood with his back to me, fingering a Japanese vase on the mantel.

"I was thinking," he began, turning the vase around, "that, if you feel pretty well again, and—and ready to take hold, that I should like to go away for a week or so. Things are fairly well cleaned up at the office."

"Do you mean—you are going to Richmond?" I asked, after a scarcely perceptible pause. He turned and faced me, with his hands thrust in his pockets.

"No. That's off, Lollie. The Sieberts are going for a week's cruise along the coast. I—the hot weather has played hob with me and the cruise means seven days' breeze and bridge."

I lighted a cigarette and offered him the box, but he refused. He was looking haggard and suddenly tired. I could not think of anything to say, and neither could he, evidently. The matter between us lay too deep for speech.

"How's Candida?" he asked.

"Martin says a month, and she will be all right," I returned, in the same tone. He picked up his hat, but he had something more to say. He blurted it out, finally, halfway to the door.

"The Sieberts are not going for a couple of days," he said, "and if you want a day or so off to go down to Richmond yourself—"

"Perhaps I shall," I returned, as indifferently as I could. "Not going yet, are you?"

"Yes. It is late." He drew in his breath as if he had something more to say, but the impulse passed. "Well, good night," he said from the doorway.

"Good night, old man."

The next moment the outer door slammed and I heard the engine of the Cannonball throbbing in the street. Then the quiet settled down around me again, and there in the lamplight I dreamed dreams. I was going to see her.

Suddenly the idea of being shut away, even temporarily, from so great and wonderful a world became intolerable. The possibility of arrest before I could get to Richmond was hideous, the night without end.

I made my escape the next morning through the stable back of the house, and then, by devious dark and winding ways, to the office. There, after a conference with Blobs, whose features fairly jerked with excitement, I double-locked the door of my private office and finished off some imperative work. By ten o'clock I was free, and for the twentieth time I consulted my train schedule. At five minutes after ten, with McKnight not yet in sight, Blobs knocked at the door, the double rap we had agreed upon, and on being admitted slipped in and quietly closed the door behind him. His eyes were glistening with excitement, and a purple dab of typewriter ink gave him a peculiarly villainous and stealthy expression.

"They're here," he said, "two of 'em, and that crazy Stuart wasn't on, and said you were somewhere in the building."

A door slammed outside, followed by steps on the uncarpeted outer office.

"This way," said Blobs, in a husky undertone, and, darting into a lavatory, threw open a door that I had always supposed locked. Thence into a back hall piled high with boxes and past the presses of a bookbindery to the freight elevator.

Greatly to Blobs' disappointment, there was no pursuit. I was exhilarated but out of breath when we emerged into an alleyway, and the sharp daylight shone on Blobs' excited face.

"Great sport, isn't it?" I panted, dropping a dollar into his palm, inked to correspond with his face. "Regular walk-away in the hundred-yard dash."

"Gimme two dollars more and I'll drop 'em down the elevator shaft," he suggested ferociously. I left him there with his bloodthirsty schemes, and started for the station. I had a tendency to look behind me now and then, but I reached the station unnoticed. The afternoon was hot, the train rolled slowly along, stopping to pant at sweltering stations, from whose roofs the heat rose in waves. But I noticed these things objectively, not subjectively, for at the end of the journey was a girl with blue eyes and dark brown hair, hair that could—had I not seen it?—hang loose in bewitching tangles or be twisted into little coils of delight.

Chapter XXVII
The Sea, the Sand, the Stars

⌘

I TELEPHONED as soon as I reached my hotel, and I had not known how much I had hoped from seeing her until I learned that she was out of town. I hung up the receiver, almost dizzy with disappointment, and it was fully five minutes before I thought of calling up again and asking if she was within telephone reach. It seemed she was down on the bay staying with the Samuel Forbeses.

Sammy Forbes! It was a name to conjure with just then. In the old days at college I had rather flouted him, but now I was ready to take him to my heart. I remembered that he had always meant well, anyhow, and that he was explosively generous. I called him up.

"By the fumes of gasoline!" he said, when I told him who I was. "Blakeley, the Fount of Wisdom against Woman! Blakeley, the Great Unkissed! Welcome to our city!"

Whereupon he proceeded to urge me to come down to the Shack, and to say that I was an agreeable surprise, because four times in two hours youths had called up to ask if Alison West was stopping with him, and to suggest that they had a vacant day or two. "Oh—Miss West!" I shouted politely. There was a buzzing on the line. "Is she there?" Sam had no suspicions. Was not I in his mind always the Great Unkissed?—which sounds like the Great Unwashed and is even more of a reproach. He asked me down promptly, as I had hoped, and thrust aside my objections.

"Nonsense," he said. "Bring yourself. The lady that keeps my boardinghouse is calling to me to insist. You remember Dorothy, don't you, Dorothy Browne? She says unless you have lost your figure you can wear my clothes all right. All you need here is a bathing suit for daytime and a dinner coat for evening."

"It sounds cool," I temporized. "If you are sure I won't put you out— very well, Sam, since you and your wife are good enough. I have a couple of days free. Give my love to Dorothy until I can do it myself."

Sam met me himself and drove me out to the Shack, which proved to be a substantial house overlooking the water. On the way he confided to me that lots of married men thought they were contented when they were merely resigned, but that it was the only life, and that Sam junior could swim like a duck. Incidentally, he said that Alison was his wife's cousin, their respective grandmothers having, at proper intervals, married the same man, and that Alison would lose her good looks if she was not careful.

"I say she's worried, and I stick to it," he said, as he threw the lines to a groom and prepared to get out. "You know her, and she's the kind of girl you think you can read like a book. But you can't; don't fool yourself. Take a good look at her at dinner, Blake; you won't lose your head like the other fellows—and then tell me what's wrong with her. We're mighty fond of Allie."

He went ponderously up the steps, for Sam had put on weight since I knew him. At the door he turned around. "Do you happen to know the MacLure's at Seal Harbor?" he asked irrelevantly, but Mrs. Sam came into the hall just then, both hands out to greet me, and, whatever Forbes had meant to say, he did not pick up the subject again.

"We are having tea in here," Dorothy said gaily, indicating the door behind her. "Tea by courtesy, because I think tea is the only beverage that isn't represented. And then we must dress, for this is hop night at the club."

"Which is as great a misnomer as the tea," Sam put in, ponderously struggling out of his linen driving coat. "It's bridge night, and the only hops are in the beer."

He was still gurgling over this as he took me upstairs. He showed me my room himself, and then began the fruitless search for evening raiment that kept me home that night from the club. For I couldn't wear Sam's clothes. That was clear, after a perspiring seance of a half hour.

"I won't do it, Sam," I said, when I had draped his dress-coat on me toga fashion. "Who am I to have clothing to spare, like this, when many a poor chap hasn't even a cellar door to cover him. I won't do it; I'm selfish, but not that selfish."

"Lord," he said, wiping his face, "how you've kept your figure! I can't wear a belt anymore; got to have suspenders."

He reflected over his grievance for some time, sitting on the side of the bed. "You could go as you are," he said finally. "We do it all the time, only tonight happens to be the annual something or other, and—" He trailed off into silence, trying to buckle my belt around him. "A good six inches," he sighed. "I never get into a hansom cab anymore that I don't expect to see the horse fly up into the air. Well, Allie isn't going either. She turned down Granger this afternoon, the Annapolis fellow you met on the stairs, pigeon-breasted chap—and she always gets a headache on those occasions."

He got up heavily and went to the door. "Granger is leaving," he said, "I may be able to get his dinner coat for you. How well do you know her?" he asked, with his hand on the knob.

"If you mean Dolly—?"

"Alison."

"Fairly well," I said cautiously. "Not as well as I would like to. I dined with her last week in Washington. And—I knew her before that."

Forbes touched the bell instead of going out, and told the servant who answered to see if Mr. Granger's suitcase had gone. If not, to bring it across the hall. Then he came back to his former position on the bed.

"You see, we feel responsible for Allie—near relation and all that," he began pompously. "And we can't talk to the people here at the house—all the men are in love with her, and all the women are jealous. Then—there's a lot of money, too, or will be."

"Confound the money!" I muttered. "That is—nothing. Razor slipped."

"I can tell you," he went on, "because you don't lose your head over every pretty face—although Allie is more than that, of course. But about a month ago she went away—to Seal Harbor, to visit Janet MacLure. Know her?

"She came home to Richmond yesterday, and then came down here—Allie, I mean. And yesterday afternoon Dolly had a letter from Janet—something about a second man—and saying she was disappointed not to have had Alison there, that she had promised them a two weeks' visit! What do you make of that? And that isn't the worst. Allie herself wasn't in the room, but there were eight other women, and because Dolly had put belladonna in her eyes the night before to see how she would look, and as a result couldn't see anything nearer than across the room, someone read the letter aloud to her, and the whole story is out. One of the cats told Granger and the boy proposed to Allie today, to show her he didn't care a tinker's dam where she had been."

"Good boy!" I said with enthusiasm. I liked the Granger fellow since he was out of the running. But Sam was looking at me with suspicion.

"Blake," he said, "if I didn't know you for what you are, I'd say you were interested there yourself."

Being so near her, under the same roof, with even the tie of a dubious secret between us, was making me heady. I pushed Forbes toward the door.

"I interested!" I retorted, holding him by the shoulders. "There isn't a word in your vocabulary to fit my condition. I am an island in a sunlit sea of emotion, Sam, a—an empty place surrounded by longing—a—"

"An empty place surrounded by longing!" he retorted. "You want your dinner, that's what's the matter with you—"

I shut the door on him then. He seemed suddenly sordid. Dinner, I thought! Although, as matter of fact, I made a very fair meal when, Granger's suitcase not having gone, in his coat and some other man's trousers, I was finally fit for the amenities. Alison did not come down to dinner, so it was clear she would not go over to the clubhouse dance. I pled my injured arm and a ficticious, vaguely located sprain from the wreck as an excuse for remaining at home. Sam regaled the table with accounts of my distrust of women, my one love affair—with Dorothy; to which I responded, as was expected, that only my failure there had kept me single all these years, and that if Sam should be mysteriously missing during the bathing hour tomorrow, and so on.

And when the endless meal was over, and yards of white veils had been tied over pounds of hair—or is it, too, bought by the yard?—and some eight ensembles with their abject complements had been packed into three automobiles and a trap, I drew a long breath and faced about. I had just then only one object in life—to find Alison, to assure her of my absolute faith and confidence in her, and to offer my help and my poor self, if she would let me, in her service.

She was not easy to find. I searched the lower floor, the verandas and the grounds, circumspectly. Then I ran into a little English girl who turned out to be her maid, and who also was searching. She was concerned because her mistress had had no dinner, and because the tray of food she carried would soon be cold. I took the tray from her, on the glimpse of something white on the shore, and that was how I met the girl again.

She was sitting on an over-turned boat, her chin in her hands, staring out to sea. The soft tide of the bay lapped almost at her feet, and the draperies of her white gown melted hazily into the sands. She looked like a wraith, a despondent phantom of the sea, although the adjective is redundant. Nobody ever thinks of a cheerful phantom. Strangely enough, considering her evident sadness, she was whistling softly to herself, over and over, some dreary little minor air that sounded like a Bohemian dirge. She glanced up quickly when I made a misstep and my dishes jingled. All considered, the tray was out of the picture: the sea, the misty starlight, the girl, with her beauty—even the sad little whistle that stopped now and then to go bravely on again, as though it fought against the odds of a trembling lip. And then I came, accompanied by a tray of little silver dishes that jingled and an unmistakable odor of broiled chicken!

"Oh!" she said quickly; and then, "Oh! I thought you were Jenkins."

"Timeo Danaos—what's the rest of it?" I asked, tendering my offering. "You didn't have any dinner, you know." I sat down beside her. "See, I'll be the table. What was the old fairy tale? 'Little goat bleat: little table appear!' I'm perfectly willing to be the goat, too."

She was laughing rather tremulously.

"We never do meet like other people, do we?" she asked. "We really ought to shake hands and say how are you."

"I don't want to meet you like other people, and I suppose you always think of me as wearing the other fellow's clothes," I returned meekly. "I'm doing it again: I don't seem to be able to help it. These are Granger's that I have on now."

She threw back her head and laughed again, joyously this time.

"Oh, it's so ridiculous," she said, "and you have never seen me when I was not eating! It's too prosaic!"

"Which reminds me that the chicken is getting cold, and the ice warm," I suggested. "At the time, I thought there could be no place better than the farmhouse kitchen—but this is. I ordered all this for something I want to say to you—the sea, the sand, the stars."

"How alliterative you are!" she said, trying to be flippant. "You are not to say anything until I have had my supper. Look how the things are spilled around!"

But she ate nothing, after all, and pretty soon I put the tray down in the sand. I said little; there was no hurry. We were together, and time meant nothing against that age-long wash of the sea. The air blew her hair in small damp curls against her face, and little by little the tide retreated, leaving our boat an oasis in a waste of gray sand.

"If seven maids with seven mops swept it for half a year/ Do you suppose, the walrus said, that they could get it clear?" she threw at me once when she must have known I was going to speak. I held her hand, and as long as I merely held it she let it lie warm in mine. But when I raised it to my lips, and kissed the soft, open palm, she drew it away without displeasure.

"Not that, please," she protested, and fell to whistling softly again, her chin in her hands. "I can't sing," she said, to break an awkward pause, "and so, when I'm fidgety, or have something on my mind, I whistle. I hope you don't dislike it?"

"I love it," I asserted warmly. I did; when she pursed her lips like that, I was mad to kiss them.

"I saw you—at the station," she said suddenly. "You—you were in a hurry to go." I did not say anything, and after a pause she drew a long breath. "Men are queer, aren't they?" she said, and fell to whistling again.

After a while she sat up as if she had made a resolution. "I am going to confess something," she announced suddenly. "You said, you know, that you had ordered all this for something you—you wanted to say to me. But the fact is, I fixed it all—came here, I mean, because—I knew you would come, and I had something to tell you. It was such a miserable thing I—needed the accessories to help me out."

"I don't want to hear anything that distresses you to tell," I assured her. "I didn't come here to force your confidence, Alison. I came because I couldn't help it." She did not object to my use of her name.

"Have you found—your papers?" she asked, looking directly at me for almost the first time.

"Not yet. We hope to."

"The—police have not interfered with you?"

"They haven't had any opportunity," I equivocated. "You needn't distress yourself about that, anyhow."

"But I do. I wonder why you still believe in me. Nobody else does."

"I wonder," I repeated, "why I do!"

"If you produce Harry Sullivan," she was saying, partly to herself, "and if you could connect him with Mr. Bronson, and get a full account of why he was on the train, and all that, it—it would help, wouldn't it?"

I acknowledged that it would. Now that the whole truth was almost in my possession, I was stricken with the old cowardice. I did not want to know what she might tell me. The yellow line on the horizon, where the moon was coming up, was a broken bit of golden chain; my heel in the sand was again pressed on a woman's yielding fingers. I pulled myself together with a jerk.

"In order that what you might tell me may help me, if it will," I said constrainedly, "it would be necessary, perhaps, that you tell it to the police. Since they have found the end of the necklace—"

"The end of the necklace!" she repeated slowly. "What about the end of the necklace?"

I stared at her. "Don't you remember"—I leaned forward—"the end of the cameo necklace, the part that was broken off, and was found in the black sealskin bag, stained with—with blood?"

"Blood," she said dully. "You mean that you found the broken end?

And then—you had my gold pocketbook, and you saw the necklace in it, and you—must have thought—"

"I didn't think anything," I hastened to assure her. "I tell you, Alison, I never thought of anything but that you were unhappy, and that I had no right to help you. God knows, I thought you didn't want me to help you."

She held out her hand to me and I took it between both of mine. No word of love had passed between us, but I felt that she knew and understood. It was one of the moments that come seldom in a lifetime, and then only in great crises, a moment of perfect understanding and trust.

Then she drew her hand away and sat, erect and determined, her fingers laced in her lap. As she talked the moon came up slowly and threw its bright pathway across the water. Back of us, in the trees beyond the sea wall, a sleepy bird chirruped drowsily, and a wave, larger and bolder than its brothers, sped up the sand, bringing the moon's silver to our very feet. I bent toward the girl.

"I am going to ask just one question."

"Anything you like." Her voice was almost dreary.

"Was it because of anything you are going to tell me that you refused Richey?"

She drew her breath in sharply.

"No," she said, without looking at me. "No. That was not the reason."

Chapter XXVIII

Alison's Story

SHE told her story evenly, with her eyes on the water, only now and then, when I, too, sat looking seaward, I thought she glanced at me furtively. And once, in the middle of it, she stopped altogether.

"You don't realize it, probably," she protested, "but you look like a— a war god. Your face is horrible."

"I will turn my back, if it will help any," I said stormily, "but if you expect me to look anything but murderous, why, you don't know what I am going through with. That's all."

The story of her meeting with the Curtis woman was brief enough.

They had met in Rome first, where Alison and her mother had taken a villa for a year. Mrs. Curtis had hovered on the ragged edges of society there, pleading the poverty of the south since the war as a reason for not going out more. There was talk of a brother, but Alison had not seen him, and after a scandal which implicated Mrs. Curtis and a young attache of the Austrian embassy, Alison had been forbidden to see the woman.

"The women had never liked her, anyhow," she said. "She did unconventional things, and they are very conventional there. And they said she did not always pay her—her gambling debts. I didn't like them. I thought they didn't like her because she was poor and popular. Then—we came home, and I almost forgot her, but last spring, when mother was not well—she had taken grandfather to the Riviera, and it always uses her up—we went to Virginia Hot Springs, and we met them there, the brother, too, this time. His name was Sullivan, Harry Pinckney Sullivan."

"I know. Go on."

"Mother had a nurse, and I was alone a great deal, and they were very kind to me. I—I saw a lot of them. The brother rather attracted me, partly—partly because he did not make love to me. He even seemed to avoid me, and I was piqued. I had been spoiled, I suppose. Most of the other men I knew had—had—"

"I know that, too," I said bitterly, and moved away from her a trifle. I was brutal, but the whole story was a long torture. I think she knew what I was suffering, for she showed no resentment.

"It was early and there were few people around—none that I cared about. And Mother and the nurse played cribbage eternally, until I felt as though the little pegs were driven into my brain. And when Mrs. Curtis arranged drives and picnics, I—I slipped away and went. I suppose you won't believe me, but I had never done that kind of thing before, and I—well, I have paid up, I think."

"What sort of looking chap was Sullivan?" I demanded. I had got up and was pacing back and forward on the sand. I remember kicking savagely at a bit of water-soaked board that lay in my way.

"Very handsome—as large as you are, but fair, and even more erect."

I drew my shoulders up sharply. I am straight enough, but I was fairly sagging with jealous rage.

"When mother began to get around, somebody told her that I had been going about with Mrs. Curtis and her brother, and we had a dreadful time. I was dragged home like a bad child. Did anybody ever do that to you?"

"Nobody ever cared. I was born an orphan," I said, with a cheerless attempt at levity. "Go on."

"If Mrs. Curtis knew, she never said anything. She wrote me charming letters, and in the summer, when they went to Cresson, she asked me to visit her there. I was too proud to let her know that I could not go where I wished, and so—I sent Polly, my maid, to her aunt's in the country, pretended to go to Seal Harbor, and really went to Cresson. You see, I warned you it would be an unpleasant story."

I went over and stood in front of her. All the accumulated jealousy of the last few weeks had been fired by what she told me. If Sullivan had come across the sands just then, I think I would have strangled him with my hands, out of pure hate.

"Did you marry him?" I demanded. My voice sounded hoarse and strange in my ears. "That's all I want to know. Did you marry him?"

"No."

I drew a long breath.

"You—cared about him?"

She hesitated.

"No," she said finally. "I did not care about him."

I sat down on the edge of the boat and mopped my hot face. I was heartily ashamed of myself, and mingled with my abasement was a great relief. If she had not married him, and had not cared for him, nothing else was of any importance.

"I was sorry, of course, the moment the train had started, but I had wired I was coming, and I could not go back, and then when I got there, the place was charming. There were no neighbors, but we fished and rode and motored, and—it was moonlight, like this."

I put my hand over both of hers, clasped in her lap. "I know," I acknowledged repentantly, "and—people do queer things when it is moonlight. The moon has got me tonight, Alison. If I am a boor, remember that, won't you?"

Her fingers lay quiet under mine. "And so," she went on with a little sigh, "I began to think perhaps I cared. But all the time felt that there was something not quite right. Now and then Mrs. Curtis would say or do something that gave me a queer start, as if she had dropped a mask for a moment. And there was trouble with the servants; they were almost insolent. I couldn't understand. I don't know when it dawned on me that the old Baron Cavalcanti had been right when he said they were not my kind of people. But I wanted to get away, wanted it desperately."

"Of course, they were not your kind," I cried. "The man was married! The girl Jennie, a housemaid, was a spy in Mrs. Sullivan's employ. If he had pretended to marry you, I would have killed him! Not only that, but the man he murdered, Harrington, was his wife's father. And I'll see him hang by the neck yet if it takes every energy and every penny I possess."

I could have told her so much more gently, have broken the shock for her; I have never been proud of that evening on the sand. I was alternately a boor and a ruffian—like a hurt youngster who passes the blow that has hurt him on to his playmate, that both may bawl together. And now Alison sat, white and cold, without speech.

"Married!" she said finally, in a small voice. "Why, I don't think it is possible, is it? I—I was on my way to Baltimore to marry him myself, when the wreck came."

"But you said you didn't care for him!" I protested, my heavy masculine mind unable to jump the gaps in her story. And then, without the slightest warning, I realized that she was crying. She shook off my hand and fumbled for her handkerchief, and failing to find it, she accepted the one I thrust into her wet fingers.

Then, little by little, she told me from the handkerchief, a sordid story of a motor trip in the mountains without Mrs. Curtis, of a lost road and a broken car, and a rainy night when they—she and Sullivan—tramped eternally and did not get home. And of Mrs. Curtis, when they got home at dawn, suddenly grown conventional and deeply shocked. Of her own proud, half-disdainful consent to make possible the hackneyed compromising situation by marrying the rascal, and then—of his disappearance from the train. It was so terrible to her, such a Heaven-sent relief to me, in spite of my rage against Sullivan, that I laughed aloud. At which she looked at me over the handkerchief.

"I know it's funny," she said, with a catch in her breath. "When I

think that I nearly married a murderer—and didn't—I cry for sheer joy."
Then she buried her face and cried again.

"Please don't," I protested unsteadily. "I won't be responsible if you keep on crying like that. I may forget that I have a capital charge hanging over my head, and that I may be arrested at any moment."

That brought her out of the handkerchief at once. "I meant to be so helpful," she said, "and I've thought of nothing but myself! There were some things I meant to tell you. If Jennie was—what you say, then I understand why she came to me just before I left. She had been packing my things and she must have seen what condition I was in, for she came over to me when I was getting my wraps on, to leave, and said, 'Don't do it, Miss West, I beg you won't do it; you'll be sorry ever after.' And just then Mrs. Curtis came in and Jennie slipped out."

"That was all?"

"No. As we went through the station the telegraph operator gave Har—Mr. Sullivan a message. He read it on the platform, and it excited him terribly. He took his sister aside and they talked together. He was white with either fear or anger—I don't know which. Then, when we boarded the train, a woman in black, with beautiful hair, who was standing on the car platform, touched him on the arm and then drew back. He looked at her and glanced away again, but she reeled as if he had struck her."

"Then what?" The situation was growing clearer.

"Mrs. Curtis and I had the drawing room. I had a dreadful night, just sleeping a little now and then. I dreaded to see dawn come. It was to be my wedding day. When we found Harry had disappeared in the night, Mrs. Curtis was in a frenzy. Then—I saw his cigarette case in your hand. I had given it to him. You wore his clothes. The murder was discovered and you were accused of it! What could I do? And then, afterward, when I saw him asleep at the farmhouse, I—I was panic-stricken. I locked him in and ran. I didn't know why he did it, but—he had killed a man."

Someone was calling Alison through a megaphone, from the veranda. It sounded like Sam. "All-ee," he called. "All-ee! I'm going to have some anchovies on toast! All-ee!" Neither of us heard.

"I wonder," I reflected, "if you would be willing to repeat a part of that story—just from the telegram on—to a couple of detectives, say on

Monday. If you would tell that, and—how the end of your necklace got into the sealskin bag—"

"My necklace!" she repeated. "But it isn't mine. I picked it up in the car."

"All-ee!" Sam again. "I see you down there. I'm making a julep!"

Alison turned and called through her hands. "Coming in a moment, Sam," she said, and rose. "It must be very late. Sam is home. We would better go back to the house."

"Don't," I begged her. "Anchovies and juleps and Sam will go on for-ever, and I have you such a little time. I suppose I am only one of a dozen or so, but—you are the only girl in the world. You know I love you, don't you, dear?"

Sam was whistling, an irritating bird call, over and over. She pursed her red lips and answered him in kind. It was more than I could endure.

"Sam or no Sam," I said firmly, "I am going to kiss you!"

But Sam's voice came strident through the megaphone. "Be good, you two," he bellowed, "I've got the binoculars!" And so, under fire, we walked sedately back to the house. My pulses were throbbing; the little swish of her dress beside me on the grass was pain and ecstasy. I had but to put out my hand to touch her, and I dared not.

Sam, armed with a megaphone and field glasses, bent over the rail and watched us with gleeful malignity.

"Home early, aren't you?" Alison called when we reached the steps.

"Led a club when my partner had doubled no-trumps, and she fainted. Damn the heart convention!" he said cheerfully. "The others are not here yet."

Three hours later I went up to bed. I had not seen Alison alone again. The noise was at its height below, and I glanced down into the garden, still bright in the moonlight. Leaning against a tree, and staring inter-estedly into the billiard room, was Johnson.

Chapter XXIX
In the Dining Room

THAT was Saturday night, two weeks after the wreck. The previous five days had been full of swift-following events—the woman in the house next door, the picture in the theater of a man about to leap from the doomed train, the dinner at the Dallases, and Richey's discovery that Alison was the girl in the case. In quick succession had come our visit to the Carter place, the finding of the rest of the telegram, my seeing Alison there, and the strange interview with Mrs. Conway. The Cresson trip stood out in my memory for its serio-comic horrors and its one real thrill. Then—the discovery by the police of the sealskin bag and the bit of chain; Hotchkiss producing triumphantly Stuart for Sullivan and his subsequent discomfiture; McKnight at the station with Alison, and later the confession that he was out of the running.

And yet, when I thought it all over, the entire week and its events were two sides of a triangle that was narrowing rapidly to an apex, a point. And the said apex was at that moment in the drive below my window, resting his long legs by sitting on a carriage block, and smoking a pipe that made the night hideous. The sense of the ridiculous is very close to the sense of tragedy. I opened my screen and whistled, and Johnson looked up and grinned. We said nothing. I held up a handful of cigars, he extended his hat, and when I finally went to sleep, it was to a soothing breeze that wafted in salt air and a faint aroma of good tobacco. I was thoroughly tired, but I slept restlessly, dreaming of two detectives with Pittsburgh warrants being held up by Hotchkiss at the point of a splint, while Alison fastened their hands with a chain that was broken and much too short. I was roused about dawn by a light rap at the door, and, opening it, I found Forbes, in a pair of trousers and a pajama coat. He was as pleasant as most fleshy people are when they have to get up at night, and he said the telephone had been ringing for an hour, and he didn't know why somebody else in the blankety-blank house couldn't have heard it. He wouldn't get to sleep until noon.

As he was palpably asleep on his feet, I left him grumbling and went to the telephone. It proved to be Richey, who had found me by the simple expedient of tracing Alison, and he was jubilant.

"You'll have to come back," he said. "Got a railroad schedule there?"

"I don't sleep with one in my pocket," I retorted, "but if you'll hold the line, I'll call out the window to Johnson. He's probably got one."

"Johnson!" I could hear the laugh with which McKnight comprehended the situation. He was still chuckling when I came back.

"Train to Richmond at six-thirty a.m.," I said. "What time is it now?"

"Four. Listen, Lollie. We've got him. Do you hear? Through the woman at Baltimore. Then the other woman, the lady of the restaurant"—he was obviously avoiding names—"she is playing our cards for us. No—I don't know why, and I don't care. But you be at the Incubator tonight at eight o'clock. If you can't shake Johnson, bring him, bless him."

To this day I believe the Sam Forbeses have not recovered from the surprise of my unexpected arrival, my one appearance at dinner in Granger's clothes, and the note on my dresser which informed them the next morning that I had folded my tents like the Arabs and silently stole away. For at half after five Johnson and I, the former as uninquisitive as ever, were on our way through the dust to the station, three miles away, and by four that afternoon we were in Washington. The journey had been uneventful. Johnson relaxed under the influence of my tobacco, and spoke at some length on the latest improvements in gallows, dilating on the absurdity of cutting out the former free passes to see the affair in operation. I remember, too, that he mentioned the curious anomaly that permits a man about to be hanged to eat a hearty meal. I did not enjoy my dinner that night.

Before we got into Washington I had made an arrangement with Johnson to surrender myself at two the following afternoon. Also, I had wired to Alison, asking her if she would carry out the contract she had made. The detective saw me home, and left me there. Mrs. Klopton received me with dignified reserve. The very tone in which she asked me when I would dine told me that something was wrong.

"Now—what is it, Mrs. Klopton?" I demanded finally, when she had informed me, in a patient and long-suffering tone, that she felt worn out and thought she needed a rest.

"When I lived with Mr. Justice Springer," she began acidly, her mending basket in her hands, "it was an orderly, well-conducted household. You can ask any of the neighbors. Meals were cooked and, what's more, they were eaten; there was none of this 'here one day and gone the next' business."

"Nonsense," I observed. "You're tired, that's all, Mrs. Klopton. And I wish you would go out; I want to bathe."

"That's not all," she said with dignity, from the doorway. "Women coming and going here, women whose shoes I am not fit—I mean, women who are not fit to touch my shoes—coming here as insolent as you please, and asking for you."

"Good Heavens!" I exclaimed. "What did you tell them—her—whichever it was?"

"Told her you were sick in a hospital and wouldn't be out for a year!" she said triumphantly. "And when she said she thought she'd come in and wait for you, I slammed the door on her."

"What time was she here?"

"Late last night. And she had a light-haired man across the street. If she thought I didn't see him, she don't know me." Then she closed the door and left me to my bath and my reflections.

At five minutes before eight I was at the Incubator, where I found Hotchkiss and McKnight. They were bending over a table, on which lay McKnight's total armament—a pair of pistols, an elephant gun and an old cavalry saber.

"Draw up a chair and help yourself to pie," he said, pointing to the arsenal. "This is for the benefit of our friend Hotchkiss here, who says he is a small man and fond of life."

Hotchkiss, who had been trying to get the wrong end of a cartridge into the barrel of one of the revolvers, straightened himself and mopped his face.

"We have desperate people to handle," he said pompously, "and we may need desperate means."

"Hotchkiss is like the small boy whose one ambition was to have people grow ashen and tremble at the mention of his name," McKnight jibed. But they were serious enough, both of them, under it all, and when they had told me what they planned, I was serious, too.

"You're compounding a felony," I remonstrated, when they had explained. "I'm not eager to be locked away, but, by Jove, to offer her the stolen notes in exchange for Sullivan!"

"We haven't got either of them, you know," McKnight remonstrated, "and we won't have, if we don't start. Come along, Fido," to Hotchkiss.

The plan was simplicity itself. According to Hotchkiss, Sullivan was to meet Bronson at Mrs. Conway's apartment, at eight-thirty that night, with the notes. He was to be paid there and the papers destroyed. "But just before that interesting finale," McKnight ended, "we will walk in, take the notes, grab Sullivan, and give the police a jolt that will put them out of the count."

I suppose not one of us, slewing around corners in the machine that night, had the faintest doubt that we were on the right track, or that Fate, scurvy enough before, was playing into our hands at last. Little Hotchkiss was in a state of fever; he alternately twitched and examined the revolver, and a fear that the two movements might be synchronous kept me uneasy. He produced and dilated on the scrap of pillow slip from the wreck, and showed me the stiletto, with its point in cotton batting for safekeeping. And in the intervals he implored Richey not to make such fine calculations at the corners.

We were all grave enough and very quiet, however, when we reached the large building where Mrs. Conway had her apartment. McKnight left the power on, in case we might want to make a quick getaway, and Hotchkiss gave a final look at the revolver. I had no weapon. Somehow it all seemed melodramatic to the verge of farce. In the doorway Hotchkiss was a half dozen feet ahead; Richey fell back beside me. He dropped his affectation of gaiety, and I thought he looked tired. "Same old Sam, I suppose?" he asked.

"Same, only more of him."

"I suppose Alison was there? How is she?" he inquired irrelevantly.

"Very well. I did not see her this morning."

Hotchkiss was waiting near the elevator. McKnight put his hand on my arm. "Now, look here, old man," he said, "I've got two arms and a revolver, and you've got one arm and a splint. If Hotchkiss is right, and there is a row, you crawl under a table."

"The deuce I will!" I declared scornfully.

We crowded out of the elevator at the fourth floor, and found ourselves in a rather theatrical hallway of draperies and armor. It was very quiet; we stood uncertainly after the car had gone, and looked at the two or three doors in sight. They were heavy, covered with metal, and soundproof. From somewhere above came the metallic accuracy of a player piano, and through the open window we could hear—or feel—the throb of the Cannonball's engine.

"Well, Sherlock," McKnight said, "what's the next move in the game? Is it our jump, or theirs? You brought us here."

None of us knew just what to do next. No sound of conversation penetrated the heavy doors. We waited uneasily for some minutes, and Hotchkiss looked at his watch. Then he put it to his ear.

"Good gracious!" he exclaimed, his head cocked on one side. "I believe it has stopped. I'm afraid we are late."

We were late. My watch and Hotchkiss' agreed at nine o'clock, and, with the discovery that our man might have come and gone, our zest in the adventure began to flag. McKnight motioned us away from the door and rang the bell. There was no response, no sound within. He rang it twice, the last time long and vigorously, without result. Then he turned and looked at us.

"I don't half like this," he said. "That woman is in; you heard me ask the elevator boy. For two cents I'd—"

I had seen it when he did. The door was ajar about an inch, and a narrow wedge of rose-colored light showed beyond. I pushed the door a little and listened. Then, with both men at my heels, I stepped into the private corridor of the apartment and looked around. It was a square reception hall, with rugs on the floor, a tall mahogany rack for hats, and a couple of chairs. A lantern of rose-colored glass and a desk light over a writing table across made the room bright and cheerful. It was empty.

None of us was comfortable. The place was full of feminine trifles that made us feel the weakness of our position. Some such instinct made McKnight suggest division.

"We look like an invading army," he said. "If she's here alone, we will startle her into a spasm. One of us could take a look around and—"

"What was that? Didn't you hear something?"

The sound, whatever it had been, was not repeated. We went awkwardly out into the hall, very uncomfortable, all of us, and flipped a coin. The choice fell to me, which was right enough, for the affair was mine, primarily.

"Wait just inside the door," I directed, "and if Sullivan comes, or anybody that answers his description, grab him without ceremony and ask him questions afterwards."

The apartment, save in the hallway, was unlighted. By one of those freaks of arrangement possible only in the modern flat, I found the kitchen first, and was struck a smart and unexpected blow by a swinging door. I carried a handful of matches, and by the time I had passed through a butler's pantry and a refrigerator room I was completely lost in the darkness. Until then the situation had been merely uncomfortable; suddenly it became grisly. From somewhere near came a long-sustained groan, followed almost instantly by the crash of something—glass or china—on the floor.

I struck a fresh match, and found myself in a narrow rear hallway. Behind me was the door by which I must have come; with a keen desire to get back to the place I had started from, I opened the door and attempted to cross the room. I thought I had kept my sense of direction, but I crashed without warning into what, from the resulting jangle, was the dining table, probably laid for dinner. I cursed my stupidity in getting into such a situation, and I cursed my nerves for making my hand shake when I tried to strike a match. The groan had not been repeated.

I braced myself against the table and struck the match sharply against the sole of my shoe. It flickered faintly and went out. And then, without the slightest warning, another dish went off the table. It fell with a thousand splinterings; the very air seemed broken into crashing waves of sound. I stood still, braced against the table, holding the red end of the dying match, and listened. I had not long to wait; the groan came again, and I recognized it, the cry of a dog in straits. I breathed again.

"Come, old fellow," I said. "Come on, old man. Let's have a look at you."

I could hear the thud of his tail on the floor, but he did not move. He only whimpered. There is something companionable in the presence of a dog, and I fancied this dog in trouble. Slowly I began to work my way around the table toward him.

"Good boy," I said as he whimpered. "We'll find the light, which ought to be somewhere or other around here, and then—"

I stumbled over something, and I drew back my foot almost instantly. "Did I step on you, old man?" I exclaimed, and bent to pat him. I remember straightening suddenly and hearing the dog pad softly toward me around the table. I recall even that I had put the matches down and could not find them. Then, with a bursting horror of the room and its contents, of the gibbering dark around me, I turned and made for the door by which I had entered.

I could not find it. I felt along the endless wainscoting, past miles of wall. The dog was beside me, I think, but he was part and parcel now, to my excited mind, with the thing under the table. And when, after eons of search, I found a knob and stumbled into the reception hall, I was as nearly in a panic as any man could be.

I was myself again in a second, and by the light from the hall I led the way back to the tragedy I had stumbled on. Bronson still sat at the table, his elbows propped on it, his cigarette still lighted, burning a hole in the cloth. Partly under the table lay Mrs. Conway facedown. The dog stood over her and wagged his tail.

McKnight pointed silently to a large copper ashtray, filled with ashes and charred bits of paper.

"The notes, probably," he said ruefully. "He got them after all, and burned them before her. It was more than she could stand. Stabbed him first and then herself."

Hotchkiss got up and took off his hat. "They are dead," he announced solemnly, and took his notebook out of his hatband.

McKnight and I did the only thing we could think of—drove Hotchkiss and the dog out of the room, and closed and locked the door. "It's a matter for the police," McKnight asserted. "I suppose you've got an officer tied to you somewhere, Lawrence? You usually have."

We left Hotchkiss in charge and went downstairs. It was McKnight who first saw Johnson, leaning against a park railing across the street, and called him over. We told him in a few words what we had found, and he grinned at me cheerfully.

"After a while, in a few weeks or months, Mr. Blakeley," he said, "when you get tired of monkeying around with the bloodstain and fingerprint specialist upstairs, you come to me. I've had that fellow you want under surveillance for ten days!"

Chapter XXX
Finer Details

⌐∞

AT TEN minutes before two the following day, Monday, I arrived at my office. I had spent the morning putting my affairs in shape, and in a trip to the stable. The afternoon would see me either a free man or a prisoner for an indefinite length of time, and, in spite of Johnson's promise to produce Sullivan, I was more prepared for the latter than the former.

Blobs was watching for me outside the door, and it was clear that he was in a state of excitement bordering on delirium. He did nothing, however, save to tip me a wink that meant "As man to man, I'm for you." I was too much engrossed either to reprove him or return the courtesy, but I heard him follow me down the hall to the small room where we keep outgrown lawbooks, typewriter supplies and, incidentally, our wraps. I was wondering vaguely if I would ever hang my hat on its nail again, when the door closed behind me. It shut firmly, without any particular amount of sound, and I was left in the dark. I groped my way to it, irritably, to find it locked on the outside. I shook it frantically, and was rewarded by a sibilant whisper through the keyhole.

"Keep quiet," Blobs was saying huskily. "You're in deadly peril. The police are waiting in your office, three of 'em. I'm goin' to lock the whole bunch in and throw the key out of the window."

"Come back here, you imp of Satan!" I called furiously, but I could hear him speeding down the corridor, and the slam of the outer office door by which he always announced his presence. And so I stood there in that ridiculous cupboard, hot with the heat of a steaming September day, musty with the smell of old leather bindings, littered with broken overshoes and handleless umbrellas. I was apoplectic with rage one minute, and choked with laughter the next. It seemed an hour before Blobs came back.

He came without haste, strutting with new dignity, and paused outside my prison door.

"Well, I guess that will hold them for a while," he remarked comfortably, and proceeded to turn the key. "I've got 'em fastened up like sardines in a can!" he explained, working with the lock. "Gee whiz! You'd ought to hear 'em!" When he got his breath after the shaking I gave him, he began to splutter. "How'd I know?" he demanded sulkily. "You nearly broke your neck gettin' away the other time. And I haven't got the old key. It's lost."

"Where's it lost?" I demanded, with another gesture toward his coat collar.

"Down the elevator shaft." There was a gleam of indignant satisfaction through his tears of rage and humiliation.

And so, while he hunted the key in the debris at the bottom of the shaft, I quieted his prisoners with the assurance that the lock had slipped, and that they would be free as lords as soon as we could find the janitor with a passkey. Stuart went down finally and discovered Blobs, with the key in his pocket, telling the engineer how he had tried to save me from arrest and failed. When Stuart came up he was almost cheerful, but Blobs did not appear again that day.

Simultaneous with the finding of the key came Hotchkiss, and we went in together. I shook hands with two men who, with Hotchkiss, made a not very animated group. The taller one, an oldish man, lean and hard, announced his errand at once.

"A Pittsburgh warrant?" I inquired, unlocking my cigar drawer.

"Yes. Allegheny County has assumed jurisdiction, the exact locality where the crime was committed being in doubt." He seemed to be the spokesman. The other, shorter and rotund, kept an amiable silence. "We hope you will see the wisdom of waiving extradition," he went on. "It will save time."

"I'll come, of course," I agreed. "The sooner the better. But I want you to give me an hour here, gentlemen. I think we can interest you. Have a cigar?"

The lean man took a cigar; the rotund man took three, putting two in his pocket.

"How about the catch of that door?" he inquired jovially. "Any danger of it going off again?" Really, considering the circumstances, they were remarkably cheerful. Hotchkiss, however, was not. He paced the floor uneasily, his hands under his coattails. The arrival of McKnight created a diversion; he carried a long package and a corkscrew, and shook hands with the police and opened the bottle with a single gesture.

"I always want something to cheer on these occasions," he said. "Where's the water, Blakeley? Everybody ready?" Then in French he toasted the two detectives.

"To your eternal discomfiture," he said, bowing ceremoniously. "May you go home and never come back! If you take Monsieur Blakeley with you, I hope you choke."

The lean man nodded gravely. "Prosit," he said. But the fat one leaned back and laughed consumedly.

Hotchkiss finished a mental synopsis of his position, and put down his glass. "Gentlemen," he said pompously, "within five minutes the man you want will be here, a murderer caught in a net of evidence so fine that a mosquito could not get through."

The detectives glanced at each other solemnly. Had they not in their possession a sealskin bag containing a wallet and a bit of gold chain, which, by putting the crime on me, would leave a gap big enough for Sullivan himself to crawl through?

"Why don't you say your little speech before Johnson brings the other man, Lawrence?" McKnight inquired. "They won't believe you, but it will help them to understand what is coming."

"You understand, of course," the lean man put in gravely, "that what you say may be used against you."

"I'll take the risk," I answered impatiently.

It took some time to tell the story of my worse than useless trip to Pittsburgh, and its sequel. They listened gravely, without interruption.

"Mr. Hotchkiss here," I finished, "believes that the man Sullivan, whom we are momentarily expecting, committed the crime. Mr. McKnight is inclined to implicate Mrs. Conway, who stabbed Bronson and then herself last night. As for myself, I am open to conviction."

"I hope not," said the stout detective quizzically. And then Alison was announced. My impulse to go out and meet her was forestalled by the detectives, who rose when I did. McKnight, therefore, brought her in, and I met her at the door.

"I have put you to a great deal of trouble," I said contritely when I saw her glance around the room. "I wish I had not—"

"It is only right that I should come," she replied, looking up at me.

"I am the unconscious cause of most of it, I am afraid. Mrs. Dallas is going to wait in the outer office."

I presented Hotchkiss and the two detectives, who eyed her with interest. In her poise, her beauty, even in her gown, I fancy she represented a new type to them. They remained standing until she sat down.

"I have brought the necklace," she began, holding out a white-wrapped box, "as you asked me to."

I passed it, unopened, to the detectives. "The necklace from which was broken the fragment you found in the sealskin bag," I explained. "Miss West found it on the floor of the car, near lower ten."

"When did you find it?" asked the lean detective, bending forward.

"In the morning, not long before the wreck."

"Did you ever see it before?"

"I am not certain," she replied. "I have seen one very much like it." Her tone was troubled. She glanced at me as if for help, but I was powerless.

"Where?" The detective was watching her closely. At that moment there came an interruption. The door opened without ceremony, and Johnson ushered in a tall, blond man, a stranger to all of us. I glanced at Alison; she was pale, but composed and scornful. She met the newcomer's eyes full, and, caught unawares, he took a hasty backward step.

"Sit down, Mr. Sullivan," McKnight beamed cordially. "Have a cigar? I beg your pardon, Alison, do you mind this smoke?"

"Not at all," she said composedly. Sullivan had had a second to sound his bearings.

"No—no, thanks," he mumbled. "If you will be good enough to explain—"

"But that's what you're to do," McKnight said cheerfully, pulling up a chair. "You've got the most attentive audience you could ask. These two gentlemen are detectives from Pittsburgh, and we are all curious to know the finer details of what happened on the car Ontario two weeks ago, the night your father-in-law was murdered." Sullivan gripped the arms of his chair. "We are not prejudiced, either. The gentlemen from Pittsburgh are betting on Mr. Blakeley, over there. Mr. Hotchkiss, the gentleman by the radiator, is ready to place ten to one odds on you. And some of us have still other theories."

"Gentlemen," Sullivan said slowly, "I give you my word of honor that I did not kill Simon Harrington, and that I do not know who did."

"Fiddlededee!" cried Hotchkiss, bustling forward. "Why, I can tell you—" But McKnight pushed him firmly into a chair and held him there.

"I am ready to plead guilty to the larceny," Sullivan went on. "I took Mr. Blakeley's clothes, I admit. If I can reimburse him in any way for the inconvenience—"

The stout detective was listening with his mouth open. "Do you mean to say," he demanded, "that you got into Mr. Blakeley's berth, as he contends, took his clothes and forged notes, and left the train before the wreck?"

"Yes."

"The notes, then?"

"I gave them to Bronson yesterday. Much good they did him!" Bitterly. We were all silent for a moment. The two detectives were adjusting themselves with difficulty to a new point of view; Sullivan was looking dejectedly at the floor, his hands hanging loose between his knees. I was watching Alison; from where I stood, behind her, I could almost touch the soft hair behind her ear.

"I have no intention of pressing any charge against you," I said with forced civility, for my hands were itching to get at him, "if you will give us a clear account of what happened on the Ontario that night."

Sullivan raised his handsome, haggard head and looked around at me. "I've seen you before, haven't I?" he asked. "Weren't you an uninvited guest at the Laurels a few days—or nights—ago? The cat, you remember, and the rug that slipped?"

"I remember," I said shortly. He glanced from me to Alison and quickly away.

"The truth can't hurt me," he said, "but it's devilish unpleasant. Alison, you know all this. You would better go out."

His use of her name crazed me. I stepped in front of her and stood over him. "You will not bring Miss West into the conversation," I threatened, "and she will stay if she wishes."

"Oh, very well," he said with assumed indifference. Hotchkiss just then escaped from Richey's grasp and crossed the room.

"Did you ever wear glasses?" he asked eagerly.

"Never." Sullivan glanced with some contempt at mine. "I'd better begin by going back a little," he went on sullenly. "I suppose you know I was married to Ida Harrington about five years ago. She was a good girl, and I thought a lot of her. But her father opposed the marriage—he'd never liked me, and he refused to make any sort of settlement.

"I had thought, of course, that there would be money, and it was a bad day when I found out I'd made a mistake. My sister was wild with disappointment. We were pretty hard up, my sister and I."

I was watching Alison. Her hands were tightly clasped in her lap, and she was staring out of the window at the cheerless roof below. She had set her lips a little, but that was all.

"You understand, of course, that I'm not defending myself," went on the sullen voice. "The day came when old Harrington put us both out of the house at the point of a revolver, and I threatened—I suppose you know that, too—I threatened to kill him.

"My sister and I had hard times after that. We lived on the continent for a while. I was at Monte Carlo and she was in Italy. She met a young lady there, the granddaughter of a steel manufacturer and an heiress, and she sent for me. When I got to Rome, the girl was gone. Last winter I was all in—social secretary to an Englishman, a whole-sale grocer with a new title, but we had a row, and I came home. I went out to the Heaton boys' ranch in Wyoming, and met Bronson there. He lent me money, and I've been doing his dirty work ever since."

Sullivan got up then and walked slowly forward and back as he talked, his eyes on the faded pattern of the office rug.

"If you want to live in hell," he said savagely, "put yourself in another man's power. Bronson got into trouble, forging John Gilmore's name to those notes, and in some way he learned that a man was bringing the papers back to Washington on the *Flier*. He even learned the number of his berth, and the night before the wreck, just as I was boarding the train, I got a telegram."

Hotchkiss stepped forward once more importantly. "Which read, I think: 'Man with papers in lower ten, car seven. Get them.' "

Sullivan looked at the little man with sulky blue eyes.

"It was something like that, anyhow. But it was a nasty business, and it made matters worse that he didn't care that a telegram which must pass through a half dozen hands was more or less incriminating to me.

"Then, to add to the unpleasantness of my position, just after we boarded the train—I was accompanying my sister and this young lady, Miss West—a woman touched me on the sleeve, and I turned to face my wife!

"That took away my last bit of nerve. I told my sister, and you can understand she was in a bad way, too. We knew what it meant. Ida had heard that I was going—"

He stopped and glanced uneasily at Alison.

"Go on," she said coldly. "It is too late to shield me. The time to have done that was when I was your guest."

"Well," he went on, his eyes turned carefully away from my face, which must have presented certainly anything but a pleasant sight, "Miss West was going to do me the honor to marry me, and—"

"You scoundrel!" I burst forth, thrusting past Alison West's chair. "You—you infernal cur!"

One of the detectives got up and stood between us. "You must remember, Mr. Blakeley, that you are forcing this story from this man. These details are unpleasant, but important. You were going to marry this young lady," he said, turning to Sullivan, "although you already had a wife living?"

"It was my sister's plan, and I was in a bad way for money. If I could marry, secretly, a wealthy girl and go to Europe, it was unlikely that Ida—that is, Mrs. Sullivan—would hear of it.

"So it was more than a shock to see my wife on the train, and to realize from her face that she knew what was going on. I don't know yet, unless some of the servants—well, never mind that.

"It meant that the whole thing had gone up. Old Harrington had carried a gun for me for years, and the same train wouldn't hold both of us. Of course, I thought that he was in the coach just behind ours."

Hotchkiss was leaning forward now, his eyes narrowed, his thin lips drawn to a line.

"Are you left-handed, Mr. Sullivan?" he asked.

Sullivan stopped in surprise.

"No," he said gruffly. "Can't do anything with my left hand." Hotchkiss subsided, crestfallen but alert. "I tore up that cursed telegram, but I was afraid to throw the scraps away. Then I looked around for lower ten. It was almost exactly across—my berth was lower seven, and it was, of course, a bit of exceptional luck for me that the car was number seven."

"Did you tell your sister of the telegram from Bronson?" I asked.

"No. It would do no good, and she was in a bad way without that to make her worse."

"Your sister was killed, I think." The shorter detective took a small package from his pocket and held it in his hand, snapping the rubber band which held it.

"Yes, she was killed," Sullivan said soberly. "What I say now can do her no harm."

He stopped to push back the heavy hair which dropped over his forehead, and went on more connectedly.

"It was late, after midnight, and we went at once to our berths. I undressed, and then I lay there for an hour, wondering how I was going to get the notes. Someone in lower nine was restless and wide-awake, but finally became quiet.

"The man in ten was sleeping heavily. I could hear his breathing, and it seemed to be only a question of getting across and behind the curtains of his berth without being seen. After that, it was a mere matter of quiet searching.

"The car became very still. I was about to try for the other berth, when someone brushed softly past, and I lay back again.

"Finally, however, when things had been quiet for a time, I got up, and after looking along the aisle, I slipped behind the curtains of lower ten. You understand, Mr. Blakeley, that I thought you were in lower ten, with the notes."

I nodded curtly.

"I'm not trying to defend myself," he went on. "I was ready to steal the notes—I had to. But murder!"

He wiped his forehead with his handkerchief.

"Well, I slipped across and behind the curtains. It was very still. The man in ten didn't move, although my heart was thumping until I thought he would hear it.

"I felt around cautiously. It was perfectly dark, and I came across a bit of chain, about as long as my finger. It seemed a queer thing to find there, and it was sticky, too."

He shuddered, and I could see Alison's hands clenching and unclenching with the strain.

"All at once it struck me that the man was strangely silent, and I think I lost my nerve. Anyhow, I drew the curtains open a little, and let the light fall on my hands. They were red, blood-red."

He leaned one hand on the back of the chair, and was silent for a moment, as though he lived over again the awful events of that more than awful night.

The stout detective had let his cigar go out; he was still drawing at it nervously. Richey had picked up a paperweight and was tossing it from hand to hand; when it slipped and fell to the floor, a startled shudder passed through the room.

"There was something glittering in there," Sullivan resumed, "and on impulse I picked it up. Then I dropped the curtains and stumbled back to my own berth."

"Where you wiped your hands on the bed-clothing and stuck the dirk into the pillow." Hotchkiss was seeing his carefully built structure crumbling to pieces, and he looked chagrined.

"I suppose I did—I'm not very clear about what happened then. But when I rallied a little, I saw a Russia leather wallet lying in the aisle almost at my feet, and, like a fool, I stuck it, with the bit of chain, into my bag.

"I sat there, shivering, for what seemed hours. It was still perfectly quiet, except for someone snoring. I thought that would drive me crazy.

"The more I thought of it the worse things looked. The telegram was the first thing against me—it would put the police on my track at once, when it was discovered that the man in lower ten had been killed.

"Then I remembered the notes, and I took out the wallet and opened it."

He stopped for a minute, as if the recalling of the next occurrence was almost beyond him.

"I took out the wallet," he said simply, "and opening it, held it to the light. In gilt letters was the name, Simon Harrington."

The detectives were leaning forward now, their eyes on his face.

"Things seemed to whirl around for a while. I sat there almost paralyzed, wondering what this new development meant for me.

"My wife, I knew, would swear I had killed her father; nobody would be likely to believe the truth.

"Do you believe me now?" He looked around at us defiantly. "I am telling the absolute truth, and not one of you believes me!

"After a bit the man in lower nine got up and walked along the aisle toward the smoking compartment. I heard him go, and, leaning from my berth, watched him out of sight.

"It was then I got the idea of changing berths with him, getting into his clothes, and leaving the train. I give you my word I had no idea of throwing suspicion on him."

Alison looked scornfully incredulous, but I felt that the man was telling the truth.

"I changed the numbers of the berths, and it worked well. I got into the other man's berth, and he came back to mine. The rest was easy. I dressed in his clothes—luckily, they fitted—and jumped the train not far from Baltimore, just before the wreck."

"There is something else you must clear up," I said. "Why did you try to telephone me from M-, and why did you change your mind about the message?"

He looked astounded.

"You knew I was at M-?" he stammered.

"Yes, we traced you. What about the message?"

"Well, it was this way. Of course, I did not know your name, Mr. Blakeley. The telegram said, 'Man with papers in lower ten, car seven,' and after I had made what I considered my escape, I began to think I had left the man in my berth in a bad way.

"He would probably be accused of the crime. So, although when the wreck occurred I supposed everyone connected with the affair had been killed, there was a chance that you had survived. I've not been of much account, but I didn't want a man to swing because I'd left him in my place. Besides, I began to have a theory of my own.

"As we entered the car a tall, dark woman passed us, with a glass of water in her hand, and I vaguely remembered her. She was amazingly like Blanche Conway.

"If she, too, thought the man with the notes was in lower ten, it explained a lot, including that piece of a woman's necklace. She was a fury, Blanche Conway, capable of anything."

"Then why did you countermand that message?" I asked curiously.

"When I got to the Carter house, and got to bed—I had sprained my ankle in the jump—I went through the alligator bag I had taken from lower nine. When I found your name, I sent the first message. Then, soon after, I came across the notes. It seemed too good to be true, and I was crazy for fear the message had gone.

"At first I was going to send them to Bronson; then I began to see what the possession of the notes meant to me. It meant power over Bronson, money, influence, everything. He was a devil, that man."

"Well, he's at home now," said McKnight, and we were glad to laugh and relieve the tension.

Alison put her hand over her eyes, as if to shut out the sight of the man she had so nearly married, and I furtively touched one of the soft little curls that nestled at the back of her neck.

"When I was able to walk," went on the sullen voice, "I came at once to Washington. I tried to sell the notes to Bronson, but he was almost at the end of his rope. Not even my threat to send them back to you, Mr. Blakeley, could make him meet my figure. He didn't have the money."

McKnight was triumphant.

"I think you gentlemen will see reason in my theory now," he said. "Mrs. Conway wanted the notes to force a legal marriage, I suppose?"

"Yes."

The detective with the small package carefully rolled off the rubber band, and unwrapped it. I held my breath as he took out, first, the Russia leather wallet.

"These things, Mr. Blakeley, we found in the sealskin bag Mr. Sullivan says he left you. This wallet, Mr. Sullivan—is this the one you found on the floor of the car?"

Sullivan opened it, and, glancing at the name inside, "Simon Harrington," nodded affirmatively.

"And this," went on the detective, "this is a piece of gold chain?"

"It seems to be," said Sullivan, recoiling at the bloodstained end.

"This, I believe, is the dagger." He held it up, and Alison gave a faint cry of astonishment and dismay. Sullivan's face grew ghastly, and he sat down weakly on the nearest chair.

The detective looked at him shrewdly, then at Alison's agitated face.

"Where have you seen this dagger before, young lady?" he asked, kindly enough.

"Oh, don't ask me!" she gasped breathlessly, her eyes turned on Sullivan. "It's—it's too terrible!"

"Tell him," I advised, leaning over to her. "It will be found out later, anyhow."

"Ask him," she said, nodding toward Sullivan. The detective unwrapped the small box Alison had brought, disclosing the trampled necklace and broken chain. With clumsy fingers he spread it on the table and fitted into place the bit of chain. There could be no doubt that it belonged there.

"Where did you find that chain?" Sullivan asked hoarsely, looking for the first time at Alison.

"On the floor, near the murdered man's berth."

"Now, Mr. Sullivan," said the detective civilly, "I believe you can tell us, in the light of these two exhibits, who really did murder Simon Harrington."

Sullivan looked again at the dagger, a sharp little bit of steel with a Florentine handle. Then he picked up the locket and pressed a hidden spring under one of the cameos. Inside, very neatly engraved, was the name and a date.

"Gentlemen," he said, his face ghastly, "it is of no use for me to attempt a denial. The dagger and necklace belonged to my sister, Alice Curtis!"

Chapter XXXI

And Only One Arm

∞

HOTCHKISS was the first to break the tension.

"Mr. Sullivan," he asked suddenly, "was your sister left-handed?"

"Yes."

Hotchkiss put away his notebook and looked around with an air of triumphant vindication. It gave us a chance to smile and look relieved. After all, Mrs. Curtis was dead. It was the happiest solution of the unhappy affair. McKnight brought Sullivan some whisky, and he braced up a little.

"I learned through the papers that my wife was in a Baltimore hospital, and yesterday I ventured there to see her. I felt if she would help me to keep straight, that now, with her father and my sister both dead, we might be happy together.

"I understand now what puzzled me then. It seemed that my sister went into the next car and tried to make my wife promise not to interfere. But Ida—Mrs. Sullivan—was firm, of course. She said her father had papers, certificates and so on, that would stop the marriage at once.

"She said, also, that her father was in our car, and that there would be the mischief to pay in the morning. It was probably when my sister tried to get the papers that he awakened, and she had to do—what she did."

It was over. Save for a technicality or two, I was a free man. Alison rose quietly and prepared to go; the men stood to let her pass, save Sullivan who sat crouched in his chair, his face buried in his hands. Hotchkiss, who had been tapping the desk with his pencil, looked up abruptly and pointed the pencil at me.

"If all this is true, and I believe it is—then who was in the house next door, Blakeley, the night you and Mr. Johnson searched? You remember, you said it was a woman's hand at the trapdoor."

I glanced hastily at Johnson, whose face was impassive. He had his hand on the knob of the door and he opened it before he spoke.

"There were a number of scratches on Mrs. Conway's right hand," he observed to the room in general. "Her wrist was bandaged and badly bruised."

He went out then, but he turned as he closed the door and threw at me a glance of half-amused, half-contemptuous tolerance.

McKnight saw Alison, with Mrs. Dallas, to their carriage, and came back again. The gathering in the office was breaking up. Sullivan, looking worn and old, was standing by the window, staring at the broken necklace in his hand. When he saw me watching him, he put it on the desk and picked up his hat.

"If I cannot do anything more—" He hesitated.

"I think you have done about enough," I replied grimly, and he went out.

I believe that Richey and Hotchkiss led me somewhere to dinner, and that, for fear I would be lonely without him, they sent for Johnson. And I recall a spirited discussion in which Hotchkiss told the detective that he could manage certain cases, but that he lacked induction. Richey and I were mainly silent. My thoughts would slip ahead to that hour, later in the evening, when I should see Alison again.

I dressed in savage haste finally, and was so particular about my tie that Mrs. Klopton gave up in despair.

"I wish, until your arm is better, that you would buy the kind that hooks on," she protested, almost tearfully. "I'm sure they look very nice, Mr. Lawrence. My late husband always—"

"That's a lover's knot you've tied this time," I snarled, and, jerking open the bow knot she had so painfully executed, looked out the window for Johnson—until I recalled that he no longer belonged in my perspective. I ended by driving frantically to the club and getting George to do it.

I was late, of course. The drawing room and library at the Dallas home were empty. I could hear billiard balls rolling somewhere, and I turned the other way. I found Alison at last on the balcony, sitting much as she had that night on the beach—her chin in her hands, her eyes fixed unseeingly on the trees and lights of the square across. She was even whistling a little, softly. But this time the plaintiveness was gone. It was a tender little tune. She did not move, as I stood beside her, looking down. And now, when the moment had come, all the thousand and one things I had been waiting to say forsook me, precipitately beat a retreat, and left me unsupported. The arc-moon sent little fugitive lights over her hair, her eyes, her gown.

"Don't—do that," I said unsteadily. "You—you know what I want to do when you whistle!"

She glanced up at me, and she did not stop. She did not stop! She went on whistling softly, a bit tremulously. And straightway I forgot the street, the chance of passersby, the voices in the house behind us. "The world doesn't hold anyone but you," I said reverently. "It is our world, sweetheart. I love you."

And I kissed her.

A boy was whistling on the pavement below. I let her go reluctantly and sat back where I could see her.

"I haven't done this the way I intended to at all," I confessed. "In books they get things all settled, and then kiss the lady."

"Settled?" she inquired.

"Oh, about getting married and that sort of thing," I explained with elaborate carelessness. "We—we could go down to Bermuda—or Jamaica, say in December."

She drew her hand away and faced me squarely.

"I believe you are afraid!" she declared. "I refuse to marry you unless you propose properly. Everybody does it. And it is a woman's privilege: she wants to have that to look back to."

"Very well," I consented with an exaggerated sigh. "If you will promise not to think I look like an idiot, I shall do it, knee and all."

I had to pass her to close the door behind us, but when I kissed her again she protested that we were not really engaged.

I turned to look down at her. "It is a terrible thing," I said exultantly, "to love a girl the way I love you, and to have only one arm!" Then I closed the door.

From across the street there came a sharp crescendo whistle, and a vaguely familiar figure separated itself from the perk railing.

"Say," he called, in a hoarse whisper, "shall I throw the key down the elevator shaft?"

The Window
at the
White Cat

Chapter I

Sentiment and Clues

⌐∞⌐

IN MY criminal work anything that wears skirts is a lady, until the law proves her otherwise. From the frayed and slovenly petticoats of the woman who owns a poultry stand in the market and who has grown wealthy by selling chickens at twelve ounces to the pound, or the silk sweep of Mamie Tracy, whose diamonds have been stolen down on the avenue, or the staidly respectable black and middle-aged skirt of the client whose husband has found an affinity partial to laces and fripperies, and has run off with her—all the wearers are ladies, and as such announced by Hawes. In fact, he carries it to excess. He speaks of his wash lady, with a husband who is an ash merchant, and he announced one day in some excitement that the lady who had just gone out had appropriated all the loose change out of the pocket of his overcoat.

So when Hawes announced a lady, I took my feet off my desk, put down the brief I had been reading, and rose perfunctorily. With my first glance at my visitor, however, I threw away my cigar, and I have heard since, settled my tie. That this client was different was borne in on me at once by the way she entered the room. She had poise in spite of embarrassment, and her face when she raised her veil was white, refined, and young.

"I did not send in my name," she said when she saw me glancing down for the card Hawes usually puts on my table. "It was advice I wanted, and I—I did not think the name would matter."

She was more composed, I think, when she found me considerably older than herself. I saw her looking furtively at the graying places over my ears. I am only thirty-five, as far as that goes, but my family, although it keeps its hair, turns gray early—a business asset but a social handicap.

"Won't you sit down?" I asked, pushing out a chair so that she would face the light, while I remained in shadow. Every doctor and every lawyer knows that trick. "As far as the name goes, perhaps you had better tell me the trouble first. Then, if I think it indispensable, you can tell me."

She acquiesced to this and sat for a moment silent, her gaze absently on the windows of the building across. In the morning light my first impression was verified. Only too often the raising of a woman's veil in my office reveals the ravages of tears, or rouge, or dissipation. My new client turned fearlessly to the window an unlined face, with a clear skin, healthily pale. From where I sat, her profile was beautiful, in spite of its drooping suggestion of trouble; her first embarrassment gone, she had forgotten herself and was intent on her errand.

"I hardly know how to begin," she said, "but suppose"—slowly— "suppose that a man, a well-known man, should leave home without warning, not taking any clothes except those he wore, and saying he was coming home to dinner and he—he—"

She stopped as if her voice had failed her.

"And he does not come?" I prompted.

She nodded, fumbling for her handkerchief in her bag.

"How long has he been gone?" I asked. I had heard exactly the same thing before, but to leave a woman like that, hardly more than a girl, and lovely!

"Ten days."

"I should think it ought to be looked into," I said decisively, and got up. Somehow I couldn't sit quietly. A lawyer who is worth anything is always a partisan, I suppose, and I never hear of a man deserting his wife that I am not indignant, the virtuous scorn of the unmarried man, perhaps. "But you will have to tell me more than that. Did this gentleman have any bad habits? That is, did he—er—drink?"

"Not to excess. He had been forbidden anything of that sort by his physician. He played bridge for money; but I believe he was rather lucky." She colored uncomfortably.

"Married, I suppose?" I asked casually.

"He had been. His wife died when I—" She stopped and bit her lips. Then it was not her husband, after all! Oddly enough, the sun came out just at that moment, spilling a pool of sunlight at her feet, on the dusty rug with its tobacco-bitten scars.

"It is my father," she said simply. I was absurdly relieved.

But with the realization that I had not a case of desertion on my hands, I had to view the situation from a new angle.

"You are absolutely at a loss to account for his disappearance?"

"Absolutely."

"You have had no word from him?"

"None."

"He never went away before for any length of time without telling you?"

"No. Never. He was away a great deal, but I always knew where to find him." Her voice broke again and her chin quivered. I thought it wise to reassure her.

"Don't let us worry about this until we are sure it is serious," I said. "Sometimes the things that seem most mysterious have the simplest explanations. He may have written and the letter have miscarried or— even a slight accident would account—" I saw I was blundering; she grew white and wide-eyed. "But, of course, that's unlikely too. He would have papers to identify him."

"His pockets were always full of envelopes and things like that," she assented eagerly.

"Don't you think I ought to know his name?" I asked. "It need not be known outside of the office, and this is a sort of confessional any-how, or worse. People tell things to their lawyer that they wouldn't think of telling the priest."

Her color was slowly coming back, and she smiled.

"My name is Fleming, Margery Fleming," she said after a second's hesitation, "and my father, Mr. Allan Fleming, is the man. Oh, Mr. Knox, what are we going to do? He has been gone for more than a week!"

No wonder she had wished to conceal the identity of the missing man. So Allan Fleming was lost! A good many highly respectable citizens would hope that he might never be found. Fleming, state treasurer, delightful companion, polished gentleman and successful politician of the criminal type. Outside in the corridor the office boy was singing under his breath. "Oh once there was a miller," he sang, "who lived in a mill." It brought back to my mind instantly the reform meeting at the city hall a year before, where for a few hours we had blown the feeble spark of protest against machine domination to a flame. We had sung a song to that very tune, and with this white-faced girl across from me, its words came back with revolting truth. It had been printed and circulated through the hall.

> "Oh, once there was a capitol
> That sat on a hill,
> As it's too big to steal away
> It's probably there still.
> The ring's hand in the treasury
> And Fleming with a sack.
> They take it out in wagon loads
> And never bring it back."

I put the song out of my mind with a shudder.

"I am more than sorry," I said. I was, too; whatever he may have been, he was *her* father. "And of course there are a number of reasons why this ought not to be known, for a time at least. After all, as I say, there may be a dozen simple explanations, and— There are exigencies in politics—"

"I hate politics!" she broke in suddenly. "The very name makes me ill. When I read of women wanting to—to vote and all that, I wonder if they know what it means to have to be polite to dreadful people, people who have even been convicts, and all that. Why, our last butler had been a prizefighter!" She sat upright with her hands on the arms of the chair. "That's another thing, too, Mr. Knox. The day after father went away, Carter left. And he has not come back."

"Carter was the butler?"

"Yes."

"A white man?"

"Oh, yes."

"And he left without giving you any warning?"

"Yes. He served luncheon the day after father went away, and the maids say he went away immediately after. He was not there that evening to serve dinner, but he came back late that night, and got into the house using his key to the servants' entrance. He slept there, the maids said, but he was gone before the servants were up and we have not seen him since."

I made a mental note of the butler.

"We'll go back to Carter again," I said. "Your father has not been ill, has he? I mean recently."

She considered.

"I cannot think of anything except that he had a tooth pulled." She was quick to resent my smile. "Oh, I know I'm not helping you," she exclaimed, "but I have thought over everything until I cannot think any more. I always end where I begin."

"You have not noticed any mental symptoms—any lack of memory?"

Her eyes filled.

"He forgot my birthday, two weeks ago," she said. "It was the first one he had ever forgotten, in nineteen of them."

Nineteen! Nineteen from thirty-five leaves sixteen!

"What I meant was this," I explained. "People sometimes have sudden and unaccountable lapses of memory and at those times they are apt to stray away from home. Has your father been worried lately?"

"He has not been himself at all. He has been irritable, even to me, and terrible to the servants. Only to Carter—he was never ugly to Carter. But I do not think it was a lapse of memory. When I remember how he looked that morning, I believe that he meant then to go away. It shows how he had changed, when he could think of going away without a word, and leaving me there alone."

"Then you have no brothers or sisters?"

"None. I came to you—" There she stopped.

"Please tell me how you happened to come to me," I urged. "I think you know that I am both honored and pleased."

"I didn't know where to go," she confessed, "so I took the telephone directory, the classified part under 'Attorneys,' and after I shut my eyes, I put my finger haphazardly on the page. It pointed to your name."

I am afraid I flushed at this, but it was a wholesome douche. In a moment I laughed.

"We will take it as an omen," I said, "and I will do all that I can. But I am not a detective, Miss Fleming. Don't you think we ought to have one?"

"Not the police!" she shuddered. "I thought you could do something without calling a detective."

"Suppose you tell me what happened the day your father left, and how he went away. Tell me the little things too. They may be straws that will point in a certain direction."

"In the first place," she began, "we live on Monmouth Avenue. There are just the two of us, and the servants: a cook, two housemaids, a laundress, a butler and a chauffeur. My father spends much of his time at the capital, and in the last two years, since my old governess went back to Germany, at those times I usually go to mother's sisters' at Bellwood—Miss Letitia and Miss Jane Maitland."

I nodded. I knew the Maitland ladies well. I had drawn four different wills for Miss Letitia in the last year.

"My father went way on the tenth of May. You say to tell you all about his going, but there is nothing to tell. We have a machine, but it was being repaired. Father got up from breakfast, picked up his hat and walked out of the house. He was irritated at a letter he had read at the table—"

"Could you find that letter?" I asked quickly.

"He took it with him. I knew he was disturbed, for he did not even say he was going. He took a car, and I thought he was on his way to his office. He did not come home that night and I went to the office the next morning. The stenographer said he had not been there. He is not at Plattsburg, because they have been trying to call him from there on the long-distance telephone every day."

In spite of her candid face, I was sure she was holding something back.

"Why don't you tell me everything?" I asked. "You may be keeping back the one essential point."

She flushed. Then she opened her pocketbook and gave me a slip of rough paper. On it, in careless figures, was the number "eleven twenty-two." That was all.

"I was afraid you would think it silly," she said. "It was such a meaningless thing. You see, the second night after father left, I was nervous and could not sleep. I expected him home at any time and I kept listening for his step downstairs. About three o'clock I was sure I heard someone in the room below mine—there was a creaking as if the person were walking carefully. I felt relieved, for I thought he had come back. But I did not hear the door into his bedroom close, and I got more and more wakeful. Finally I got up and slipped along the hall to his room. The door was open a few inches and I reached in and switched on the electric lights. I had a queer feeling before I turned on the light that there was someone standing close to me, but the room was empty, and the hall, too."

"And the paper?"

"When I saw the room was empty, I went in. The paper had been pinned to a pillow on the bed. At first I thought it had been dropped or had blown there. When I saw the pin, I was startled. I went back to my room and rang for Annie, the second housemaid, who is also a sort of personal maid of mine. It was half-past three o'clock when Annie came down. I took her into father's room and showed her the paper. She was sure it was not there when she folded back the bedclothes for the night at nine o'clock."

"Eleven twenty-two," I repeated. "Twice eleven is twenty-two. But that isn't very enlightening."

"No," she admitted. "I thought it might be a telephone number, and I called up all the eleven twenty-twos in the city."

In spite of myself, I laughed, and after a moment she smiled in sympathy.

"We are not brilliant, certainly," I said at last. "In the first place, Miss Fleming, if I thought the thing was very serious, I would not laugh—but no doubt a day or two will see everything straight. But, to go back to this eleven twenty-two—did you rouse the servants and have the house searched?"

"Yes. Annie said Carter had come back and she went to waken him, but although his door was locked inside, he did not answer. Annie and I switched on all the lights on the lower floor from the top of the stairs. Then we went down together and looked around. Every window and door was locked, but in father's study, on the first floor, two drawers of his desk were standing open. And in the library, the little compartment in my writing table, where I keep my house money, had been broken open and the money taken."

"Nothing else was gone?"

"Nothing. The silver on the sideboard in the dining room, plenty of valuable things in the cabinet in the drawing room—nothing was disturbed."

"It might have been Carter," I reflected. "Did he know where you kept your house money?"

"It is possible, but I hardly think so. Besides, if he was going to steal, there were so many more valuable things in the house. My mother's jewels as well as my own were in my dressing room, and the door was not locked."

"They were not disturbed?"

She hesitated.

"They had been disturbed," she admitted. "My grandmother left each of her children some unstrung pearls. They were a hobby with her. Aunt Jane and Aunt Letitia never had theirs strung, but my mother's were made into different things, all old-fashioned. I left them locked in a drawer in my sitting room, where I have always kept them. The following morning the drawer was unlocked and partly open, but nothing was missing."

"All your jewelry was there?"

"All but one ring, which I rarely remove from my finger." I followed her eyes. Under her glove was the outline of a ring, a solitaire stone.

"Nineteen from—" I shook myself together and got up.

"It does not sound like an ordinary burglary," I reflected. "But I am afraid I have no imagination. No doubt what you have told me would be meat and drink to a person with an analytical turn of mind. I can't deduct. Nineteen from thirty-five leaves sixteen, according to my mental process, although I know men who could make the difference nothing."

I believe she thought I was a little mad, for her face took on again its despairing look.

"We *must* find him, Mr. Knox," she insisted as she got up. "If you know of a detective that you can trust, please get him. But you can understand that the unexplained absence of the state treasurer must be kept secret. One thing I am sure of: He is being kept away. You don't know what enemies he has! Men like Mr. Schwartz, who have no scruples, no principle."

"Schwartz!" I repeated in surprise. Henry Schwartz was the boss of his party in the state; the man of whom one of his adversaries had said, with the distinct approval of the voting public, that he was so low on the scale of humanity that it would require a special dispensation of Heaven to raise him to the level of total degradation. But he and Fleming were generally supposed to be captain and first mate of the pirate craft that passed with us for the ship of state.

"Mr. Schwartz and my father are allies politically," the girl explained with heightened color, "but they are not friends. My father is a gentleman."

The inference I allowed to pass unnoticed, and as if she feared she had said too much, the girl rose. When she left, a few minutes later, it was with the promise that she would close the Monmouth Avenue house and go to her aunts' at Bellwood, at once. For myself, I pledged a thorough search for her father, and began it by watching the scarlet wing on her hat through the top of the elevator cage until it had descended out of sight.

I am afraid it was a queer hodgepodge of clues and sentiment that I poured out to Hunter, the detective, when he came up late that afternoon.

Hunter was quiet when I finished my story.

"They're rotten clear through," he reflected. "This administration is worse than the last, and *it* was a peach. There have been more suicides than I could count on my two hands, in the last ten years. I warn you—you'd be better out of this mess."

"What do you think about the eleven twenty-two?" I asked as he got up and buttoned his coat.

"Well, it might mean almost anything. It might be that many dollars, or the time a train starts, or it might be the eleventh and the twenty-second letters of the alphabet—k—v."

"K—v!" I repeated. "Why that would be the Latin *cave*—beware."

Hunter smiled cheerfully.

"You'd better stick to the law, Mr. Knox," he said from the door. "We don't use Latin in the detective business."

Chapter II
Uneasy Apprehensions

⌘⌘

PLATTSBURG was not the name of the capital, but it will do for this story. The state doesn't matter either. You may take your choice, like the story Mark Twain wrote, with all kinds of weather at the beginning, so the reader could take his pick.

We will say that my home city is Manchester. I live with my married brother, his wife and two boys. Fred is older than I am, and he is an exceptional brother. On the day he came home from his wedding trip, I went down with my traps on a hansom, in accordance with a pre-arranged schedule. Fred and Edith met me inside the door.

"Here's your latchkey, Jack," Fred said as he shook hands. "Only one stipulation—remember we are strangers in the vicinity and try to get home before the neighbors are up. We have our reputations to think of."

"There is no hour for breakfast," Edith said as she kissed me. "You have a bath of your own, and don't smoke in the drawing room."

Fred was always a lucky devil.

I had been there now for six years. I had helped to raise two young Knoxes—bully youngsters, too: the oldest one could use boxing gloves when he was four—and the finest collie pup in our end of the state. I wanted to raise other things—the boys liked pets—but Edith was like all women: she didn't care for animals.

I had a rabbit-hutch built and stocked in the laundry, and a dove-cote on the roof. I used the general bath and gave up my tub to a younger alligator I got in Florida, and every Sunday the youngsters and I had a great time trying to teach it to do tricks. I have always taken it a little hard that Edith took advantage of my getting the measles from Billy, to clear out every animal in the house. She broke the news to me gently, the day the rash began to fade, maintaining that, having lost one cook through the alligator escaping from his tub and being mistaken, in the gloom of the back stairs, for a rubber boot, and picked up under the same misapprehension, she could not risk another cook.

On the day that Margery Fleming came to me about her father, I went home in a state of mixed emotion. Dinner was not a quiet meal: Fred and I talked politics, generally, and as Fred was on one side and I on the other, there was always an argument on.

"What about Fleming?" I asked at last, when Fred had declared that in these days of corruption, no matter what the government was, he was "forninst" it. "Hasn't he been frightened into reform?"

"Bad egg," he said, jabbing his potato as if it had been a politician, "and there's no way to improve a bad egg except to hold your nose. That's what the public is doing; holding its nose."

"Hasn't he a daughter?" I asked casually.

"Yes—a lovely girl, too," Edith assented. "It is his only redeeming quality."

"Fleming is a rascal, daughter or no daughter," Fred persisted. "Ever since he and his gang got poor Butler into trouble and then left him to kill himself as the only way out, I have felt that there was something coming to all of them—Hansen, Schwartz and the rest. I saw Fleming on the street today."

"What!" I exclaimed, almost jumping out of my chair.

Fred surveyed me quizzically over his coffee cup.

" 'Hasn't he a daughter!' " he quoted. "Yes, I saw him, Jack, this very day, in an unromantic four-wheeler, and he was swearing at a policeman."

"Where was it?"

"Chestnut and Union. His cab had been struck by a car, and badly damaged, but the gentleman refused to get out. No doubt you could get the details from the cornerman."

"Look here, Fred," I said earnestly. "Keep that to yourself, will you? And you too, Edith? It's a queer story, and I'll tell you sometime."

As we left the dining room, Edith put her hand on my shoulder.

"Don't get mixed up with those people, Jack," she advised. "Margery's a dear girl, but her father practically killed Henry Butler, and Henry Butler married my cousin."

"You needn't make it a family affair," I protested. "I have only seen the girl once."

But Edith smiled. "I know what I know," she said. "How extravagant of you to send Bobby that enormous hobbyhorse!"

"The boy has to learn to ride sometime. In four years he can have a pony, and I'm going to see that he has it. He'll be eight by that time."

Edith laughed.

"In four years!" she said. "Why, in four years you'll—" Then she stopped.

"I'll what?" I demanded, blocking the door to the library.

"You'll be forty, Jack, and it's a mighty unattractive man who gets past forty without being sought and won by some woman. You'll be buying—"

"I will be thirty-nine," I said with dignity, "and as far as being sought and won goes, I am so overwhelmed by Fred's misery that I don't intend to marry at all. If I do—*if I do*—it will be to some girl who turns and runs the other way every time she sees me."

"The oldest trick in the box," Edith scoffed. "What's that thing Fred's always quoting: 'A woman is like a shadow; follow her, she flies; fly from her, she follows.' "

"Upon my word!" I said indignantly. "And you are a woman!"

"I'm different," she retorted. "I'm only a wife and mother."

In the library Fred got up from his desk and gathered up his papers. "I can't think with you two whispering there," he said. "I'm going to the den."

As he slammed the door into his workroom, Edith picked up her skirts and scuttled after him.

"How dare you run away like that?" she called. "You promised me—" The door closed behind her.

I went over and spoke through the panels.

" 'Follow her, she flies; fly from her, she follows'—oh, wife and mother!" I called.

"For Heaven's sake, Edith," Fred's voice rose irritably. "If you and Jack are going to talk all evening, go and sit on *his* knee and let me alone. The way you two flirt under my nose is a scandal. Do you hear that, Jack?"

"Good night, Edith," I called. "I have left you a kiss on the upper left-hand panel of the door. And I want to ask you one more question: what if I fly from the woman and she doesn't follow?"

"Thank your lucky stars," Fred called in a muffled voice, and I left them to themselves.

I had some work to do at the office, work that the interview with Hunter had interrupted, and half past eight that night found me at my desk. But my mind strayed from the papers before me. After a useless effort to concentrate, I gave it up as useless, and by ten o'clock I was on the street again, my evening wasted, the papers in the libel case of the *Star* against the *Eagle* untouched on my desk, and I the victim of an uneasy apprehension that took me, almost without volition, to the neighborhood of the Fleming house on Monmouth Avenue. For it had occurred to me that Miss Fleming might not have left the house that day as she had promised, might still be there, liable to another intrusion by the mysterious individual who had a key to the house.

It was a relief, consequently, when I reached its corner, to find no lights in the building. The girl had kept her word. Assured of that, I looked at the house curiously. It was one of the largest in the city, not wide, but running far back along the side street; a small yard with a low iron fence and a garage completed the property. The streetlights left the back of the house in shadow, and as I stopped in the shelter of the garage, I was positive that I heard someone working with a rear window of the empty house. A moment later the sounds ceased and muffled footsteps came down the cement walk. The intruder made no attempt to open the iron gate; against the light I saw him put a leg over the low fence, follow it up with the other, and start up the street, still with peculiar noiselessness of stride. He was a short, heavy-shouldered fellow in a cap, and his silhouette showed a prodigious length of arm.

I followed, I don't mind saying in some excitement. I had a vision of grabbing him from behind and leading him—or pushing him, under the circumstances—in triumph to the police station, and another mental picture, not so pleasant, of being found on the pavement by some passerby, with a small punctuation mark ending my sentence of life. But I was not apprehensive. I even remember wondering humorously if I should overtake him and press the cold end of my silver-mounted fountain pen into the nape of his neck, if he would throw up his hands and surrender. I had read somewhere of a burglar held up in a similar way with a shoehorn.

Our pace was easy. Once, the man just ahead stopped and lighted a cigarette, and the odor of a very fair Turkish tobacco came back to me. He glanced back over his shoulder at me and went on without quickening his pace. We met no policemen, and after perhaps five minutes walking, when the strain was growing tense, my gentleman of the rubber-soled shoes swung abruptly to the left and—entered the police station!

I had occasion to see Davidson many times after that, during the strange development of the Fleming case; I had the peculiar experience later of having him follow me as I had trailed him that night, and I had occasion once to test the strength of his long arms when he helped to thrust me through the transom at the White Cat, but I never met him without a recurrence of the sheepish feeling with which I watched him swagger up to the night sergeant and fall into easy conversation with the man behind the desk. Standing in the glare from the open window, I had much the lost pride and self-contempt of a wet cat sitting in the sun.

Two or three roundsmen were sitting against the wall, lazily, helmets off and coats open against the warmth of the early spring night. In a back room others were playing checkers and disputing noisily. Davidson's voice came distinctly through the open windows.

"The house is closed," he reported. "But one of the basement windows isn't shuttered and the lock is bad. I couldn't find Shields. He'd better keep an eye on it." He stopped and fished in his pockets with a grin. "This was tied to the knob of the kitchen door," he said, raising his voice for the benefit of the room, and holding aloft a piece of paper. "For Shields!" he explained, "and signed 'Delia.' "

The men gathered around him. Even the sergeant got up and leaned forward, his elbows on his desk.

"Read it," he said lazily. "Shields has got a wife, and her name ain't Delia."

"Dear Tom," Davidson read in a mincing falsetto. "We are closing up unexpected, so I won't be here tonight. I am going to Mamie Brennan's and if you want to talk to me you can get me by calling up Anderson's drugstore. The clerk is a gentleman friend of mine. Mr. Carter, the butler, told me before he left he would get me a place as parlor maid, so I'll have another situation soon. Delia."

The sergeant scowled. "I'm goin' to talk to Tom," he said, reaching out for the note. "He's got a nice family, and things like that're bad for the force."

I lighted the cigar, which had been my excuse for loitering on the pavement, and went on. It sounded involved for a novice, but if I could find Anderson's drugstore, I could find Mamie Brennan; through Mamie Brennan I would get Delia; and through Delia I might find Carter. I was vague from that point, but what Miss Fleming had said of Carter had made me suspicious of him. Under an arc light I made the first note in my new business of manhunter and it was something like this:

> Anderson's drugstore.
> Ask for Mamie Brennan.
> Find Delia.
> Advise Delia that a policeman with a family is a bad bet.
> Locate Carter.

It was late when I reached the corner of Chestnut and Union Streets, where Fred had said Allan Fleming had come to grief in a cab. But the cornerman had gone, and the night man on the beat knew nothing, of course, of any particular collision.

"There's plinty of 'em every day at this corner," he said cheerfully. "The department sends a wagon here every night to gather up the pieces, automobiles mainly. That trolley pole over there has been sliced off clean three times in the last month. They say a fellow ain't a gradu-ate of the automobile school till he can go around it on the sidewalk without hittin' it!"

I left him looking reminiscently at the pole, and went home to bed. I had made no headway, I had lost conceit with myself and a day and evening at the office, and I had gained the certainty that Margery Flem-ing was safe in Bellwood and the uncertain address of a servant who *might* know something about Mr. Fleming.

I was still awake at one o'clock and I got up impatiently and con-sulted the telephone directory. There were twelve Andersons in the city who conducted drugstores.

When I finally went to sleep, I dreamed that I was driving Margery Fleming along a street in a broken taxicab, and that all the buildings were pharmacies and numbered eleven twenty-two.

Chapter III
Ninety-eight Pearls

AFTER such a night I slept late. Edith still kept her honeymoon promise of no breakfast hour and she had gone out with Fred when I came downstairs.

I have a great admiration for Edith, for her tolerance with my uncertain hours, for her cheery breakfast room, and the smiling good nature of the servants she engages. I have a theory that, show me a sullen servant and I will show you a sullen mistress, although Edith herself disclaims all responsibility and lays credit for the smile with which Katie brings in my eggs and coffee to largess on my part. Be that as it may, Katie is a smiling and personable young woman, and I am convinced that had she picked up the alligator on the back stairs and lost part of the end of her thumb, she would have told Edith that she cut it off with the bread knife, and thus have saved to us Bessie the Beloved and her fascinating trick of taking the end of her tail in her mouth and spinning.

On that particular morning, Katie also brought me a letter, and I recognized the cramped and rather uncertain writing of Miss Jane Maitland.

> DEAR MR. KNOX:
>
> Sister Letitia wishes me to ask you if you can dine with us tonight, informally. She has changed her mind in regard to the Colored Orphans' Home, and would like to consult you about it.
>
> Very truly yours,
> Susan Jane Maitland

It was a very commonplace note: I had had one like it after every board meeting of the orphans' home, Miss Maitland being on principle an aggressive minority. Also, having considerable mind, changing it became almost as ponderous an operation as moving a barn, although not nearly so stable.

(Fred accuses me here of a very bad pun, and reminds me, quite undeservedly, that the pun is the lowest form of humor.)

I came across Miss Jane's letter the other day, when I was gathering the material for this narrative, and I sat for a time with it in my hand, thinking over again the chain of events in which it had been the first link, a series of strange happenings that began with my acceptance of the invitation, and that led through ways as dark and tricks as vain as Bret Harte's Heathen Chinese ever dreamed of, to the final scene at the White Cat. With the letter I had filed away a half dozen articles and I arranged them all on the desk in front of me: the letter, the bit of paper with eleven twenty-two on it, that Margery gave me the first time I saw her; a notebook filled with jerky characters that looked like Arabic and were newspaper shorthand; a railroad schedule; a bullet, the latter slightly flattened; a cube-shaped piece of chalk which I put back in its box, labeled poison, with a shudder, and a small gold buckle from a slipper, which I—at which I did not shudder.

I did not need to make the climaxes of my story. They lay before me.

I walked to the office that morning, and on the way I found and interviewed the cornerman at Chestnut and Union. But he was of small assistance. He remembered the incident, but the gentleman in the taxi-cab had not been hurt and refused to give his name, saying he was merely passing through the city from one railroad station to another, and did not wish any notoriety.

At eleven o'clock Hunter called; he said he was going after the affair himself, but that it was hard to stick a dip net into the political puddle without pulling out a lot more than you went after, or than it was healthy to get. He was inclined to be facetious, and wanted to know if I had come across any more k. v's. Whereupon I put away the notes I had made about Delia and Mamie Brennan and I heard him chuckle as I rang off.

I went to Bellwood that evening. It was a suburban town a dozen miles from the city, with a picturesque station, surrounded by lawns and cement walks. Streetcars had so far failed to spoil its tree-bordered streets, and it was exclusive to the point of stagnation. The Maitland place was at the head of the main street, which had at one time been its drive. Miss Letitia, who was seventy, had had sufficient commercial instinct, some years before, to cut her ancestral acres—*their* ancestral acres, although Miss Jane hardly counted—into building lots, except perhaps an acre which surrounded the house. Thus, the Maitland ladies were reputed to be extremely wealthy. And as they never spent any money, no doubt they were.

The homestead as I knew it was one of impeccable housekeeping and unmitigated gloom. There was a chill that rushed from the old-fashioned center hall to greet the newcomer on the porch, and that seemed to freeze up whatever in him was spontaneous and cheerful.

I had taken dinner at Bellwood before, and the memory was not hilarious. Miss Letitia was deaf, but chose to ignore the fact. With superb indifference she would break into the conversation with some wholly alien remark that necessitated a reassembling of one's ideas, making the meal a series of mental gymnastics. Miss Jane, through long practice, and because she only skimmed the surface of conversation, took her cerebral flights easily, but I am more unwieldy of mind.

Nor was Miss Letitia's dominance wholly conversational. Her sister Jane was her creature, alternately snubbed and bullied. To Miss Letitia, Jane, in spite of her sixty-five years, was still a child, and sometimes a bad one. Indeed many a child of ten is more sophisticated. Miss Letitia gave her expurgated books to read, and forbade her to read divorce court proceedings in the newspapers. Once a recreant housemaid presenting the establishment with a healthy male infant, Jane was sent to the country for a month and was only brought back when the house had been fumigated throughout.

Poor Miss Jane! She met me with fluttering cordiality in the hall that night, safe in being herself for once, with the knowledge that Miss Letitia always received me from a thronelike horsehair sofa in the back parlor. She wore a new lace cap, and was twitteringly excited.

"Our niece is here," she explained as I took off my coat—everything was "ours" with Jane; "mine" with Letitia—"and we are having an ice at dinner. Please say that ices are not injurious, Mr. Knox. My sister is so opposed to them and I had to beg for this."

"On the contrary, the doctors have ordered ices for my young nephews," I said gravely, "and I dote on them myself."

Miss Jane beamed. Indeed, there was something almost unnaturally gay about the little old lady all that evening. Perhaps it was the new lace cap. Later, I tried to analyze her manner, to recall exactly what she had said, to remember anything that could possibly help. But I could find no clue to what followed.

Miss Letitia received me as usual, in the back parlor. Miss Fleming was there also, sewing by a window, and in her straight white dress with her hair drawn back and braided around her head, she looked even younger than before. There was no time for conversation. Miss Letitia launched at once into the extravagance of both molasses and butter on the colored orphans' bread and after a glance at me, and a quick comprehension from my face that I had no news for her, the girl at the window bent over her sewing again.

"Molasses breeds worms," Miss Letitia said decisively. "So does pork. And yet those children think Heaven means ham and molasses three times a day."

"You have had no news at all?" Miss Fleming said cautiously, her head bent over her work.

"None," I returned, under cover of the table linen to which Miss Letitia's mind had veered. "I have a good man working on it." As she glanced at me questioningly, "It needed a detective, Miss Fleming." Evidently another day without news had lessened her distrust of the police, for she nodded acquiescence and went on with her sewing. Miss Letitia's monotonous monologue went on, and I gave it such attention as I might. For the lamps had been lighted, and with every movement of the girl across, I could see the gleaming of a diamond on her engagement finger.

"If I didn't watch her, Jane would ruin them," said Miss Letitia. "She gives 'em apples when they keep their faces clean, and the bills for soap have gone up double. Soap once a day's enough for a colored child. Do you smell anything burning, Knox?"

I sniffed and lied, whereupon Miss Letitia swept her black silk, her colored orphans and her majestic presence out of the room. As the door closed, Miss Fleming put down her sewing and rose. For the first time I saw how weary she looked.

"I do not dare to tell them, Mr. Knox," she said. "They are old, and they hate him anyhow. I couldn't sleep last night. Suppose he should have gone back, and found the house closed!"

"He would telephone here at once, wouldn't he?" I suggested.

"I suppose so, yes." She took up her sewing from the chair with a sigh. "But I'm afraid he won't come—not soon. I have hemmed tea towels for Aunt Letitia today until I am frantic, and all day I have been wondering over something you said yesterday. You said, you remember, that you were not a detective, that some men could take nineteen from thirty-five and leave nothing. What did you mean?"

I was speechless for a moment.

"The fact is—I—you see," I blundered, "it was a—merely a figure of speech, a—speech of figures is more accurate—" And then dinner was announced and I was saved. But although she said little or nothing during the meal, I caught her looking across at me once or twice in a bewildered, puzzled fashion. I could fairly see her revolving my detestable figures in her mind.

Miss Letitia presided over the table in garrulous majesty. The two old ladies picked at their food, and Miss Jane had a spot of pink in each withered cheek. Margery Fleming made a brave pretense, but left her plate almost untouched. As for me, I ate a substantial masculine meal and half apologized for my appetite, but Letitia did not hear. She tore the board of managers to shreds with the roast, and denounced them with the salad. But Jane was all anxious hospitality.

"Please *do* eat your dinner," she whispered. "I made the salad myself. And I know what it takes to keep a big man going. Harry eats more than Letitia and I together. Doesn't he, Margery?"

"Harry?" I asked.

"Mrs. Stevens is an unmitigated fool. I said if they elected her president, I'd not leave a penny to the home. That's why I sent for you, Knox." And to the maid, "Tell Heppie to wash those cups in lukewarm water. They're the best ones. And not to drink her coffee out of them. She let her teeth slip and bit a piece out of one the last time."

Miss Jane leaned forward to me after a smiling glance at her niece across.

"Harry Wardrop, a cousin's son, and—" she patted Margery's hand with its ring—"soon to be something closer."

The girl's face colored, but she returned Miss Jane's gentle pressure.

"They put up an iron fence," Miss Letitia reverted somberly to her grievance, "when a wooden one would have done. It was extravagance, ruinous extravagance."

"Harry stays with us when he is in Manchester," Miss Jane went on, nodding brightly across at Letitia as if she, too, were damning the executive board. "Lately, he has been almost all the time in Plattsburg. He is secretary to Margery's father. It is a position of considerable responsibility, and we are very proud of him."

I had expected something of the sort, but the remainder of the meal had somehow lost its savor. There was a lull in the conversation while dessert was being brought in. Miss Jane sat quivering, watching her sister's face for signs of trouble; the latter had subsided into muttered grumbling, and Miss Fleming sat, one hand on the table, staring absently at her engagement ring.

"You look like a fool in that cap, Jane," volunteered Letitia, while the plates were being brought in. "What's for dessert?"

"Ice cream," called Miss Jane, over the table.

"Well, you needn't," snapped Letitia. "I can hear you well enough. You told me it was junket."

"I said ice cream, and you said it would be all right," poor Jane shrieked. "If you drink a cup of hot water after it, it won't hurt you."

"Fiddle," Letitia snapped unpleasantly. "I'm not going to freeze my stomach and then thaw it out like a drain pipe. Tell Heppie to put my ice cream on the stove."

So we waited until Miss Letitia's had been heated, and was brought in, sicklied over with pale hues, not of thought, but of confectioners' dyes. Miss Letitia ate it resignedly. "Like as not I'll break out, I did the last time," she said gloomily. "I only hope I don't break out in colors."

The meal was over finally, but if I had hoped for another word alone with Margery Fleming that evening, I was foredoomed to disappointment. Letitia sent the girl, not ungently, to bed, and ordered Jane out of the room with a single curt gesture toward the door.

"You'd better wash those cups yourself, Jane," she said. "I don't see any sense anyhow in getting out the best china unless there's real company. Besides, I'm going to talk business."

Poor, meek, spiritless Miss Jane! The situation was absurd in spite of its pathos. She confided to me once that never in her sixty-five years of life had she bought herself a gown, or chosen the dinner. She was snubbed with painstaking perseverance, and sent out of the room when subjects requiring frank handling were under discussion. She was as unsophisticated as a child of ten, as unworldly as a baby, as—well, poor Miss Jane, again.

When the door had closed behind her, Miss Letitia listened for a moment, got up suddenly, and, crossing the room with amazing swiftness for her years, pounced on the knob and threw it open again. But the passage was empty; Miss Jane's slim little figure was disappearing into the kitchen. The older sister watched her out of sight, and then returned to her sofa without deigning explanation.

"I didn't want to see you about the will, Mr. Knox," she began without prelude. "The will can wait. I ain't going to die just yet—not if I know anything. But although I think you'd look a heap better and more responsible if you wore some hair on your face, still in most things I think you're a man of sense. And you're not too young. That's why I didn't send for Harry Wardrop; he's too young."

I winced at that. Miss Letitia leaned forward and put her bony hand on my knee.

"I've been robbed," she announced in a half whisper, and straightened to watch the effect of her words.

"Indeed!" I said, properly thunderstruck. I *was* surprised. I had always believed that only the use of the fourth dimension in space would enable anyone, not desired, to gain access to the Maitland house. "Of money?"

"Not money, although I had a good bit in the house." This also I knew. It was said of Miss Letitia that when money came into her possession, it went out of circulation.

"Not—the pearls?" I asked.

She answered my question with another.

"When you had those pearls appraised for me at the jewelers last year, how many were there?"

"Not quite one hundred. I think—yes, ninety-eight."

"Exactly," she corroborated in triumph. "They belonged to my mother. Margery's mother got some of them. That's a good many years ago, young man. They are worth more than they were then—a great deal more."

"Twenty-two thousand dollars," I repeated. "You remember, Miss Letitia, that I protested vigorously at the time against your keeping them in the house."

Miss Letitia ignored this, but before she went on, she repeated again her catlike pouncing at the door, only to find the hall empty as before. This time when she sat down it was knee to knee with me.

"Yesterday morning," she said gravely, "I got down the box; they have always been kept in the small safe at the top of my closet. When Jane found a picture of my niece, Margery Fleming, in Harry's room, I thought it likely there was some truth in the gossip Jane heard about the two, and—if there was going to be a wedding—why, the pearls were to go to Margery anyhow. But I found the door of the safe unlocked and a little bit open—and ten of the pearls were gone!"

"Gone!" I echoed. "Ten of them! Why, it's ridiculous! If ten, why not the whole ninety-eight?"

"How do I know?" she replied with asperity. "That's what I keep a lawyer for. That's why I sent for you."

For the second time in two days I protested the same thing.

"But you need a detective," I cried. "If you can find the thief, I will be glad to send him where he ought to be, but I couldn't find him."

"I will not have the police," she persisted inflexibly. "They will come around asking impertinent questions, and telling the newspapers that a foolish old woman had got what she deserved."

"Then you are going to send them to a bank?"

"You have less sense than I thought," she snapped. "I am going to leave them where they are, and watch. Whoever took the ten will be back for more, mark my words."

"I don't advise it," I said decidedly. "You have most of them now, and you might easily lose them all; not only that, but it is not safe for you or your sister."

"Stuff and nonsense!" the old lady said, with spirit. "As for Jane, she doesn't even know they are gone. I know who did it. It was the new housemaid, Bella MacKenzie. Nobody else could get in. I lock up the house myself at night, and I'm in the habit of doing a pretty thorough job of it. They went in the last three weeks, for I counted them Saturday three weeks ago myself. The only persons in the house in that time, except ourselves, were Harry, Bella and Hepsibah, who's been here for forty years and wouldn't know a pearl from a pickled onion."

"Then—what do you want me to do?" I asked. "Have Bella arrested and her trunk searched?"

I felt myself shrinking in the old lady's esteem every minute.

"Her trunk!" she said scornfully. "I turned it inside out this morning, pretending I thought she was stealing the laundry soap. Like as not she has them buried in the vegetable garden. What I want you to do is stay here for three or four nights, to be on hand. When I catch the thief, I want my lawyer right by."

It ended by my consenting, of course. Miss Letitia was seldom refused. I telephoned to Fred that I would not be home, listened for voices and decided Margery Fleming had gone to bed. Miss Jane lighted me to the door of the guest room, and saw that everything was comfortable. Her thin gray curls bobbed as she examined the water pitcher, saw to the towels, and felt the bed linen for dampness. At the door she stopped and turned around timidly.

"Has—has anything happened to disturb my sister?" she asked. "She has been almost irritable all day."

Almost!

"She is worried about her colored orphans," I evaded. "She does not approve of fireworks for them on the fourth of July."

Miss Jane was satisfied. I watched her little, old, black-robed figure go lightly down the hall. Then I bolted the door, opened all the windows, and proceeded to a surreptitious smoke.

Chapter IV

A Thief in the Night

⋯

THE windows being wide open, it was not long before a great moth came whirring in. He hurled himself at the light and then, dazzled and singed, began to beat with noisy thumps against the barrier of the ceiling. Finding no egress there, he was back at the lamp again, whirling in dizzy circles until at last, worn out, he dropped to the table, where he lay on his back, kicking impotently.

The room began to fill with tiny winged creatures that flung themselves headlong to destruction, so I put out the light and sat down near the window, with my cigar and my thoughts.

Miss Letitia's troubles I dismissed shortly. While it was odd that only ten pearls should have been taken, still—in every other way it bore the marks of an ordinary theft. The thief might have thought that by leaving the majority of the gems he could postpone discovery indefinitely. But the Fleming case was of a different order. Taken by itself, Fleming's disappearance could have been easily accounted for. There must be times in the lives of all unscrupulous individuals when they feel the need of retiring temporarily from the public eye. But the intrusion into the Fleming home, the ransacked desk and the broken money drawer—most of all, the bit of paper with eleven twenty-two on it— here was a hurdle my legal mind refused to take.

I had finished my second cigar, and was growing more and more wakeful, when I heard a footstep on the path around the house. It was black outside; when I looked out, as I did cautiously, I could not see even the gray-white of the cement walk. The steps had ceased, but there was a sound of fumbling at one of the shutters below. The catch clicked twice, as if some thin instrument was being slipped underneath to raise it, and once I caught a muttered exclamation.

I drew in my head and, puffing my cigar until it was glowing, managed by its light to see that it was a quarter to two. When I listened again, the housebreaker had moved to another window, and was shaking it cautiously.

With Miss Letitia's story of the pearls fresh in my mind, I felt at once that the thief, finding his ten a prize, had come back for more. My first impulse was to go to the head of my bed, where I am accustomed to keep a revolver. With the touch of the tall corner post, however, I remembered that I was not at home, and that it was not likely there was a weapon in the house.

Finally, after knocking over an ornament that shattered on the hearth and sounded like the crash of doom, I found on the mantel a heavy brass candlestick, and with it in my hand I stepped into the gloom of the hallway and felt my way to the stairs.

There were no night lights; the darkness was total. I found the stairs before I expected to, and came within an ace of pitching down, headlong. I had kicked off my shoes—a fact which I regretted later. Once down the stairs I was on more familiar territory. I went at once into the library, which was beneath my room, but the sounds at the window had ceased. I thought I heard steps on the walk, going toward the front of the house. I wheeled quickly and started for the door, when something struck me a terrific blow on the nose. I reeled back and sat down, dizzy and shocked. It was only when no second blow followed the first that I realized what had occurred.

With my two hands out before me in the blackness, I had groped, one hand on either side of the open door, which of course I had struck violently with my nose. Afterward I found it had bled considerably, and my collar and tie must have added to my ghastly appearance.

My candlestick had rolled under the table, and after crawling around on my hands and knees, I found it. I had lost, I suppose, three or four minutes, and I was raging at my awkwardness and stupidity. No one, however, seemed to have heard the noise. For all her boasted watchfulness, Miss Letitia must have been asleep. I got back into the hall and from there to the dining room. Someone was fumbling at the shutters there, and as I looked, they swung open. It was so dark outside, with the trees and the distance from the street, that only the creaking of the shutter told it had opened. I stood in the middle of the room, with one hand firmly clutching my candlestick.

But the window refused to move. The burglar seemed to have no proper tools; he got something under the sash, but it snapped, and through the heavy plate glass I could hear him swearing. Then he abruptly left the window and made for the front of the house.

I blundered in the same direction, my unshod feet striking on projecting furniture and causing me agonies, even through my excitement. When I reached the front door, however, I was amazed to find it unlocked, and standing open perhaps an inch. I stopped uncertainly. I was in a peculiar position; not even the most ardent admirers of antique brass candlesticks endorse them as weapons of offense or defense. But, there seeming to be nothing else to do, I opened the door quietly and stepped out into the darkness.

The next instant I was flung heavily to the porch floor. I am not a small man by any means, but under the fury of that onslaught I was a child. It was a porch chair, I think, that knocked me senseless; I know I folded up like a jackknife, and that was all I did know for a few minutes.

When I came to, I was lying where I had fallen, and a candle was burning beside me on the porch floor. It took me a minute to remember, and another minute to realize that I was looking into the barrel of a revolver. It occurred to me that I had never seen a more villainous face than that of the man who held it—which shows my state of mind—and that my position was the reverse of comfortable. Then the man behind the gun spoke.

"What did you do with that bag?" he demanded, and I felt his knee on my chest.

"What bag?" I inquired feebly. My head was jumping, and the candle was a volcanic eruption of sparks and smoke.

"Don't be a fool," the gentleman with the revolver persisted. "If I don't get that bag within five minutes, I'll fill you as full of holes as a cheese."

"I haven't seen any bag," I said stupidly. "What sort of bag?" I heard my own voice, drunk from the shock. "Paper bag, laundry bag—"

"You've hidden it in the house," he said, bringing the revolver a little closer with every word. My senses came back with a jerk and I struggled to free myself.

"Go in and look," I responded. "Let me up from here, and I'll take you in myself."

The man's face was a study in amazement and anger. "You'll take me in! You!" He got up without changing the menacing position of the gun. "You walk in there—here, carry the candle—and take me to that bag. Quick, do you hear?"

I was too bewildered to struggle. I got up dizzily, but when I tried to stoop for the candle, I almost fell on it. My head cleared after a moment, and when I had picked up the candle, I had a good chance to look at my assailant. He was staring at me, too. He was a young fellow, well dressed, and haggard beyond belief.

"I don't know anything about a bag," I persisted, "but if you will give me your word there was nothing in it belonging to this house, I will take you in and let you look for it."

The next moment he had lowered the revolver and clutched my arm.

"Who in the devil's name *are* you?" he asked wildly. I think the thing dawned on us both at the same moment.

"My name is Knox," I said coolly, feeling for my handkerchief—my head was bleeding from a cut over the ear—"John Knox."

"Knox!" Instead of showing relief, his manner showed greater consternation than ever. He snatched the candle from me and, holding it up, searched my face. "Then—good God—where is my traveling bag?"

"I have something in my head where you hit me," I said. "Perhaps that is it."

But my sarcasm was lost on him.

"I am Harry Wardrop," he said, "and I have been robbed, Mr. Knox. I was trying to get in the house without waking the family, and when I came back here to the front door, where I had left my valise, it was gone. I thought you were the thief when you came out, and—we've lost all this time. Somebody has followed me and robbed me!"

"What was in the bag?" I asked, stepping to the edge of the porch and looking around, with the help of the candle.

"Valuable papers," he said shortly. He seemed to be dazed and at a loss what to do next. We had both instinctively kept our voices low.

"You are certain you left it here?" I asked. The thing seemed incredible in the quiet and peace of that neighborhood.

"Where you are standing."

Once more I began a desultory search, going down the steps and looking among the cannas that bordered the porch. Something glistened beside the step, and stooping down I discovered a small brown leather traveling bag, apparently quite new.

"Here it is," I said, not so gracious as I might have been; I had suffered considerably for that traveling bag. The sight of it restored Wardrop's poise at once. His twitching features relaxed.

"By Jove, I'm glad to see it," he said. "I can't explain, but—tremendous things were depending on that bag, Mr. Knox. I don't know how to apologize to you; I must have nearly brained you."

"You did," I said grimly, and gave him the bag. The moment he took it I knew there was something wrong; he hurried into the house and lighted the library lamp. Then he opened the traveling bag with shaking fingers. It was empty!

He stood for a moment, staring incredulously into it. Then he hurled it down on the table and turned on me, as I stood beside him.

"It's a trick!" he said furiously. "You've hidden it somewhere. This is not my bag. You've substituted one just like it."

"Don't be a fool," I retorted. "How could I substitute an empty satchel for yours when up to fifteen minutes ago I had never seen you or your grip either? Use a little common sense. Someplace tonight you have put down that bag, and some clever thief has substituted a similar one. It's an old trick."

He dropped into a chair and buried his face in his hands.

"It's impossible," he said after a pause, while he seemed to be going over, minute by minute, the events of the night. "I was followed, as far as that goes, in Plattsburg. Two men watched me from the minute I got there, on Tuesday; I changed my hotel, and for all of yesterday— Wednesday, that is—I felt secure enough. But on my way to the train I felt that I was under surveillance again, and by turning quickly, I came face to face with one of the men."

"Would you know him?" I asked.

"Yes. I thought he was a detective; you know I've had a lot of that sort of thing lately, with election coming on. He didn't get on the train, however."

"But the other one may have done so."

"Yes, the other one may. The thing I don't understand is this, Mr. Knox. When we drew in at Bellwood Station, I distinctly remember opening the bag and putting my newspaper and railroad schedule inside. It was the right bag then; my clothing was in it, and my brushes."

I had been examining the empty bag as he talked.

"Where did you put your railroad schedule?" I asked.

"In the leather pocket at the side."

"It is here," I said, drawing out the yellow folder. For a moment my companion looked almost haunted. He pressed his hands to his head and began to pace the room like a crazy man.

"The whole thing is impossible. I tell you, that valise was heavy when I walked up from the station. I changed it from one hand to the other because of the weight. When I got here, I set it down on the edge of the porch and tried the door. When I found it locked—"

"But it wasn't locked," I broke in. "When I came downstairs to look for a burglar, I found it open at least an inch."

He stopped in his pacing up and down, and looked at me curiously.

"We're both crazy then," he asserted gravely. "I tell you, I tried every way I knew to unlock that door, and could hear the chain rattling.

Unlocked! You don't know the way this house is fastened up at night."

"Nevertheless, it was unlocked when I came down."

We were so engrossed that neither of us had heard steps on the stairs. The sound of a smothered exclamation from the doorway caused us both to turn suddenly. Standing there, in a loose gown of some sort, very much surprised and startled, was Margery Fleming. Wardrop pulled himself together at once. As for me, I knew what sort of figure I cut, my collar stained with blood, a lump on my forehead that felt as big as a doorknob, and no shoes.

"What is the matter?" she asked uncertainly. "I heard such queer noises, and I thought someone had broken into the house."

"Mr. Wardrop was trying to break in," I explained, "and I heard him and came down. On the way I had a bloody encounter with an open door, in which I came out the loser."

I don't think she quite believed me. She looked from my swollen head to the open bag, and then to Wardrop's pale face. Then I think, womanlike, she remembered the two great braids that hung over her shoulders and the dressing gown she wore, for she backed precipitately into the hall.

"I'm glad that's all it is," she called back cautiously, and we could hear her running up the stairs.

"You'd better go to bed," Wardrop said, picking up his hat. "I'm going down to the station. There's no train out of here between midnight and a flag train at four thirty a.m. It's not likely to be of any use, but I want to see who goes on that train."

"It is only half past two," I said, glancing at my watch. "We might look around outside first."

The necessity for action made him welcome any suggestion. Reticent as he was, his feverish excitement made me think that something vital hung on the recovery of the contents of that Russia leather bag. We found a lantern somewhere in the back of the house, and together we went over the grounds. It did not take long, and we found nothing.

As I look back on that night, the key to what had passed and to much that was coming was so simple, so direct—and yet we missed it entirely. Nor, when bigger things developed, and Hunter's trained senses were brought into play, did he do much better. It was some time before we learned the true inwardness of the events of that night.

At five o'clock in the morning Wardrop came back exhausted and nerveless. No one had taken the four thirty; the contents of the bag were gone, probably beyond recall. I put my dented candlestick back on the mantel, and prepared for a little sleep, blessing the deafness of old age which had enabled the Maitland ladies to sleep through it all. I tried to forget the queer events of the night, but the throbbing of my head kept me awake, and through it all one question obtruded itself— who had unlocked the front door and left it open?

Chapter V

Little Miss Jane

∞

I WAS almost unrecognizable when I looked at myself in the mirror the next morning, preparatory to dressing for breakfast. My nose boasted a new arch, like the back of an angry cat, making my profile Roman and ferocious, and the lump on my forehead from the chair was swollen, glassy and purple. I turned my back to the mirror and dressed in wrathful irritation and my yesterday's linen.

Miss Fleming was in the breakfast room when I got down, standing at a window, her back to me. I have carried with me, during all the months since that time, a mental picture of her as she stood there, in a pink morning frock of some sort. But only the other day, having mentioned this to her, she assured me that the frock was blue, that she didn't have a pink garment at the time this story opens and that if she did, she positively didn't have it on. And having thus flouted my eye for color, she maintains that she did *not* have her back to me, for she distinctly saw my newly raised bridge as I came down the stairs. So I amend this. Miss Fleming in a blue frock was facing the door when I went into the breakfast room. Of one thing I am certain. She came forward and held out her hand.

"Good morning," she said. "What a terrible face!"

"It isn't mine," I replied meekly. "My own face is beneath these excrescences. I tried to cover the bump on my forehead with French chalk, but it only accentuated the thing, like snow on a mountaintop."

" 'The purple peaks of Darien,' " she quoted, pouring me my coffee. "Do you know, I feel so much better since you have taken hold of things. Aunt Letitia thinks you are wonderful."

I thought ruefully of the failure of my first attempt to play the sleuth, and I disclaimed any right to Miss Letitia's high opinion of me. From my dogging the watchman to the police station, to Delia and her note, was a short mental step.

"Before anyone comes down, Miss Fleming," I said, "I want to ask a question or two. What was the name of the maid who helped you search the house that night?"

"Annie."

"What other maids did you say there were?"

"Delia and Rose."

"Do you know anything about them? Where they came from, or where they went?"

She smiled a little.

"What does one know about new servants?" she responded. "They bring you references, but references are the price most women pay to get rid of their servants without a fuss. Rose was fat and old, but Delia was pretty. I thought she rather liked Carter."

Carter as well as Shields, the policeman. I put Miss Delia down as a flirt.

"And you have no idea where Carter went?"

"None."

Wardrop came in then, and we spoke of other things. The two elderly ladies it seemed had tea and toast in their rooms when they wakened, and the three of us breakfasted together. But conversation languished with Wardrop's appearance; he looked haggard and worn, avoided Miss Fleming's eyes, and after ordering eggs instead of his chop, looked at his watch and left without touching anything.

"I want to get the nine thirty, Margie," he said, coming back with his hat in his hand. "I may not be out to dinner. Tell Miss Letitia, will you?" He turned to go, but on second thought came back to me and held out his hand.

"I may not see you again," he began.

"Not if I see you first," I interrupted. He glanced at my mutilated features and smiled.

"I have made you a Maitland," he said. "I didn't think that anything but a prodigal Nature could duplicate Miss Letitia's nose! I'm honestly sorry, Mr. Knox, and if you do not want Miss Jane at that bump with a cold silver knife and some butter, you'd better duck before she comes down. Good-bye, Margie."

I think the girl was as much baffled as I was by the change in his manner when he spoke to her. His smile faded and he hardly met her eyes: I thought that his aloofness puzzled rather than hurt her. When the house door had closed behind him, she dropped her chin in her hand and looked across the table.

"You did not tell me the truth last night, Mr. Knox," she said. "I have never seen Harry look like that. Something has happened to him."

"He was robbed of his traveling bag," I explained, on Fred's theory that half a truth is better than a poor lie. "It's a humiliating experience, I believe. A man will throw away thousands, or gamble them away, with more equanimity than he'll see someone making off with his hair brushes or his clean collars."

"His traveling bag!" she repeated scornfully. "Mr. Knox, something has happened to my father, and you and Harry are hiding it from me."

"On my honor, it is nothing of the sort," I hastened to assure her. "I saw him for only a few minutes, just long enough for him to wreck my appearance."

"He did not speak of Father?"

"No."

She got up and, crossing the wooden mantel, put her arms upon it and leaned her head against them. "I wanted to ask him," she said drearily, "but I am afraid to. Suppose he doesn't know and I should tell him! He would go to Mr. Schwartz at once, and Mr. Schwartz is treacherous. The papers would get it, too."

Her eyes filled with tears, and I felt as awkward as a man always does when a woman begins to cry. If he knows her well enough, he can go over and pat her on the shoulder and assure her it is going to be all right. If he does not know her, and there are two maiden aunts likely to come in at any minute, he sits still, as I did, and waits until the storm clears.

Miss Margery was not long in emerging from her handkerchief.

"I didn't sleep much," she explained, dabbing at her eyes, "and I am nervous, anyhow. Mr. Knox, are you sure it was only Harry trying to get into the house last night?"

"Only Harry," I repeated. "If Mr. Wardrop's attempt to get into the house leaves me in this condition, what would a real burglar have done to me!"

She was too intent to be sympathetic over my disfigured face.

"There was someone moving about upstairs not long before I came down," she said slowly.

"You heard me; I almost fell down the stairs."

"Did you brush past my door, and strike the knob?" she demanded.

"No, I was not near any door."

"Very well." Triumphantly. "Someone did. Not only that, but they were in the storeroom on the floor above. I could hear one person and perhaps two, going from one side of the room to the other and back again."

"You heard a goblin quadrille. First couple forward and back," I said facetiously.

"I heard real footsteps—unmistakable ones. The maids sleep back on the second floor, and— Don't tell me it was rats. There are no rats in my aunt Letitia's house."

I was more impressed than I cared to show. I found I had a half hour before train time, and as we were neither of us eating anything, I suggested that we explore the upper floor of the house. I did it, I explained, not because I expected to find anything, but because I was sure we would not.

We crept past the two closed doors behind which the ladies Maitland were presumably taking out their crimps and taking in their tea. Then up a narrow, obtrusively clean stairway to the upper floor.

It was an old-fashioned, sloping-roofed attic, with narrow windows and a bare floor. At one end a door opened into a large room, and in there were the family trunks of four generations of Maitlands. One on another they were all piled there—little hair trunks, squab-topped trunks, huge Saratogas—of the period when the two maiden ladies were in their late teens—and there were handsome, modem trunks, too. For Miss Fleming's satisfaction I made an examination of the room, but it showed nothing. There was little or no dust to have been disturbed; the windows were closed and locked.

In the main attic were two stepladders, some curtains drying on frames and an old chest of drawers with glass knobs and the veneering broken in places. One of the drawers stood open, and inside could be seen a red and white patchwork quilt, and a grayish thing that looked like flannel and smelled to heaven of camphor. We gave up finally, and started down.

Partway down the attic stairs Margery stopped, her eyes fixed on the white-scrubbed rail. Following her gaze, I stopped, too, and I felt a sort of chill go over me. No spot or blemish, no dirty fingerprint marked the whiteness of that stair rail, except in one place. On it, clear and distinct, every line of the palm showing, was the reddish imprint of a hand!

Margery did not speak; she had turned very white and closed her eyes, but she was not faint. When the first revulsion had passed, I reached over and touched the stain. It was quite dry, of course, but it was still reddish brown; another hour or two would see it black. It was evidently fresh—Hunter said afterward it must have been about six hours old, and as things transpired, he was right. The stain showed a hand somewhat short and broad, with widened fingertips; marked in ink, it would not have struck me so forcibly, perhaps, but there, its ugly red against the white wood, it seemed to me to be the imprint of a brutal, murderous hand.

Margery was essentially feminine.

"What did I tell you?" she asked. "Someone was in this house last night; I heard them distinctly. There must have been two, and they quarreled—" She shuddered.

We went on downstairs into the quiet and peace of the dining room again. I got some hot coffee for Margery, for she looked shaken, and found I had missed my train.

"I am beginning to think I am being pursued by a malicious spirit," she said, trying to smile. "I came away from home because people got into the house at night and left queer signs of their visits, and now, here at Bellwood, where nothing *ever* happens, the moment I arrive things begin to occur. And—just as it was at home—the house was so well locked last night."

I did not tell her of the open hall door, just as I had kept from her the fact that only the contents of Harry Wardrop's bag had been taken.

That it had all been the work of one person, and that that person, having in some way access to the house, had also stolen the pearls, was now my confident belief.

I looked at Bella—the maid—as she moved around the dining room; her stolid face was not even intelligent, certainly not cunning. Heppie, the cook and the only other servant, was partly blind and her horizon was the diameter of her largest kettle. No—it had not been a servant, this mysterious intruder who passed the Maitland silver on the sideboard without an attempt to take it, and who floundered around an attic at night, in search of nothing more valuable than patchwork quilts and winter flannels. It is strange to look back and think how quietly we sat there; that we could see nothing but burglary—or an attempt at it—in what we had found.

It must have been after nine o'clock when Bella came running into the room. Ordinarily a slow and clumsy creature, she almost flew. She had a tray in her hand, and the dishes were rattling and threatening overthrow at every step. She brought up against a chair, and a cup went flying. The breaking of a cup must have been a serious offense in Miss Letitia Maitland's house, but Bella took no notice whatever of it.

"Miss Jane," she gasped, "Miss Jane, she's—she's—"

"Hurt!" Margery exclaimed, rising and clutching at the table for support.

"No. Gone—she's gone! She's been run off with!"

"Nonsense!" I said, seeing Margery's horrified face. "Don't come in here with such a story. If Miss Jane is not in her room, she is somewhere else, that's all."

Bella stooped and gathered up the broken cup, her lips moving. Margery had recovered herself. She made Bella straighten and explain.

"Do you mean—she is not in her room?" she asked incredulously. "Isn't she somewhere around the house?"

"Go up and look at the room," the girl replied, and, with Margery leading, we ran up the stairs.

Miss Jane's room was empty. From somewhere near Miss Letitia could be heard lecturing Hepsibah about putting too much butter on the toast. Her high voice, pitched for Heppie's old ears, rasped me. Margery closed the door, and we surveyed the room together.

The bed had been occupied; its coverings had been thrown back, as if its occupant had risen hurriedly. The room itself was in a state of confusion; a rocker lay on its side, and Miss Jane's clothing, folded as she had taken it off, had slid off on to the floor. Her shoes stood neatly at the foot of the bed, and a bottle of toilet vinegar had been upset, pouring a stream over the marble top of the dresser and down on to the floor. Over the high wooden mantel the Maitland who had been governor of the state years ago hung at a waggish angle, and a clock had been pushed aside and stopped at half-past one.

Margery stared around her in bewilderment. Of course, it was not until later in the day that I saw all the details. My first impression was of confusion and disorder: the room seemed to have been the scene of a struggle. The overturned furniture, the clothes on the floor, the picture, coupled with the print of the hand on the staircase and Miss Jane's disappearance, all seemed to point to one thing.

And as if to prove it conclusively, Margery picked up Miss Jane's new lace cap from the floor. It was crumpled and spotted with blood.

"She has been killed," Margery said in a choking voice. "Killed, and she had not an enemy in the world!"

"But where is she?" I asked stupidly.

Margery had more presence of mind than I had; I suppose it is because woman's courage is mental and man's physical, that in times of great strain women always make the better showing. While I was standing in the middle of the room, staring at the confusion around me, Margery was already on her knees, looking under the high, four-post bed. Finding nothing there she went to the closet. It was undisturbed. Pathetic rows of limp black dresses and on the shelves two black crepe bonnets were mute reminders of the little old lady. But there was nothing else in the room.

"Call Robert, the gardener," Margery said quickly, "and have him help you search the grounds and cellars. I will take Bella and go through the house. Above everything, keep it from Aunt Letitia as long as possible."

I locked the door into the disordered room, and with my head whirling, I went to look for Robert.

It takes a short time to search an acre of lawn and shrubbery. There was no trace of the missing woman anywhere outside the house, and from Bella, as she sat at the foot of the front stairs with her apron over her head, I learned in a monosyllable that nothing had been found in the house. Margery was with Miss Letitia, and from the excited conversation I knew she was telling her—not harrowing details, but that Miss Jane had disappeared during the night.

The old lady was inclined to scoff at first.

"Look in the fruit closet in the storeroom" I heard her say. "She's let the spring lock shut on her twice; she was black in the face the last time we found her."

"I did look; she's not there," Margery screamed at her.

"Then she's out looking for stump water to take that wart off her neck. She said yesterday she was going for some."

"But her clothes are all here," Margery persisted. "We think someone must have got in the house."

"If all her clothes are there, she's been sleepwalking," Miss Letitia said calmly. "We used to have to tie her by a cord around her ankle and fasten it to the bedpost. When she tried to get up, the cord would pull and wake her."

I think after a time, however, some of Margery's uneasiness communicated itself to the older woman. She finished dressing, and fumed when we told her we had locked Miss Jane's door and mislaid the key. Finally, Margery got her settled in the back parlor with some peppermints and her knitting; she had a feeling, she said, that Jane had gone after the stump water and lost her way, and I told Margery to keep her in that state of mind as long as she could.

I sent for Hunter that morning and he came at three o'clock. I took him through the back entrance to avoid Miss Letitia. I think he had been skeptical until I threw open the door and showed him the upset chair, the old lady's clothing, and the bloodstained lace cap. His examination was quick and thorough. He took a crumpled sheet of notepaper out of the wastebasket and looked at it; then he stuffed it in his pocket. He sniffed the toilet water, called Margery, and asked her if any clothing was missing, and on receiving a negative answer asked if any shawls or wraps were gone from the halls or other rooms. Margery reported nothing missing.

Before he left the room, Hunter went back and moved the picture which had been disturbed over the mantel. What he saw made him get a chair and, standing on it, take the picture from its nail. Thus exposed, the wall showed an opening about a foot square, and perhaps eighteen inches deep. A metal door, opening in, was unfastened and ajar, and just inside was a copy of a recent sentimental novel and a bottle of some sort of complexion cream. In spite of myself, I smiled; it was so typical of the dear old lady, with the heart of a girl and a skin that was losing its roses. But there was something else in the receptacle, something that made Margery Fleming draw in her breath sharply, and made Hunter raise his eyebrows a little and glance at me. The something was a scrap of unruled white paper, and on it the figures eleven twenty-two!

Chapter VI

A Fountain Pen

∽∾

HARRY Wardrop came back from the city at four o'clock, while Hunter was in the midst of his investigation. I met him in the hall and told him what had happened, and with this new apprehension added to the shock of the night before, he looked as though his nerves were ready to snap.

Wardrop was a man of perhaps twenty-seven, as tall as I, although not so heavy, with direct blue eyes and fair hair; altogether a manly and prepossessing sort of fellow. I was not surprised that Margery Fleming had found him attractive—he had the blond hair and offhand manner that women seem to like. I am dark, myself.

He seemed surprised to find Hunter there, and not particularly pleased, but he followed us to the upper floor and watched silently while Hunter went over the two rooms. Beside the large chest of drawers in the main attic, Hunter found perhaps half a dozen drops of blood, and on the edge of the open drawer there were traces of more. In the inner room two trunks had been moved out nearly a foot, as he found by the faint dust that had been under them. With the stain on the stair rail, that was all he discovered, and it was little enough. Then he took out his notebook and there among the trunks we had a little seance of our own, in which Hunter asked questions, and whoever could do so answered them.

"Have you a pencil or pen, Mr. Knox?" he asked me, but I had none. Wardrop felt his pockets, with no better success.

"I have lost my fountain pen somewhere around the house today," he said irritably. "Here's a pencil—not much of one."

Hunter began his interrogations.

"How old was Miss Maitland—Miss Jane, I mean?"

"Sixty-five," from Margery.

"She had always seemed rational? Not eccentric, or childish?"

"Not at all; the sanest woman I ever knew." This from Wardrop.

"Has she ever, to your knowledge, received any threatening letters?"

"Never in all her life," from both of them promptly.

"You heard sounds, you say, Miss Fleming. At what time?"

"About half-past one or perhaps a few minutes later. The clock struck two while I was still awake and nervous."

"This person who was walking through the attics here—would you say it was a heavy person? A man, I mean?"

Margery stopped to think.

"Yes," she said finally. "It was very stealthy, but I think it was a man's step."

"You heard no sound of a struggle? No voices? No screams?"

"None at all," she said positively. And I added my quota.

"There could have been no such sounds," I said. "I sat in my room and smoked until a quarter to two. I heard nothing until then, when I heard Mr. Wardrop trying to get into the house. I went down to admit him, and—I found the front door open about an inch."

Hunter wheeled on Wardrop.

"A quarter to two?" he asked. "You were coming home from—the city?"

"Yes, from the station."

Hunter watched him closely.

"The last train gets in here at twelve thirty," he said slowly. "Does it always take you an hour and a quarter to walk the three squares to the house?"

Wardrop flushed uneasily, and I could see Margery's eyes dilate with amazement. As for me, I could only stare.

"I did not come directly home," he said, almost defiantly.

Hunter's voice was as smooth as silk.

"Then—will you be good enough to tell me where you did go?" he asked. "I have reasons for wanting to know."

"Damn your reasons—I beg your pardon, Margery. Look here, Mr. Hunter, do you think I would hurt a hair of that old lady's head? Do you think I came here last night and killed her, or whatever it is that has happened to her? And then went out and tried to get in again through the window?"

"Not necessarily," Hunter said, unruffled. "It merely occurred to me that we have at least an hour of your time last night, while this thing was going on, to account for. However, we can speak of that later. I am practically certain of one thing: Miss Maitland is not dead, or was not dead when she was taken away from this house."

"Taken away!" Margery repeated. "Then you think she was kidnapped?"

"Well, it is possible. It's a puzzling affair all through. You are certain there are no closets or unused rooms where, if there had been a murder, the body could be concealed."

"I never heard of any," Margery said, but I saw Wardrop's face change on the instant. He said nothing, however, but stood frowning at the floor, with his hands deep in his coat pockets.

Margery was beginning to show the effect of the long day's strain; she began to cry a little, and with an air of proprietorship that I resented, somehow Wardrop went over to her.

"You are going to lie down, Margery," he said, holding out his hand to help her up. "Mrs. Mellon will come over to Aunt Letitia, and you must get some sleep."

"Sleep!" she said with scorn, as he helped her to her feet. "Sleep, when things like this are occurring! Father first, and now dear old Aunt Jane! Harry, do you know where my father is?"

He faced her, as if he had known the question must come and was prepared for it.

"I know that he is all right, Margery. He has been—out of town. If it had not been for something unforeseen that—happened within the last few hours, he would have been home today."

She drew a long breath of relief.

"And Aunt Jane?" she asked Hunter, from the head of the attic stairs, "you do not think she is dead?"

"Not until we have found something more," he answered tactlessly. "It's like where there's smoke there's fire; where there's murder there's a body."

When they had both gone, Hunter sat down on a trunk and drew out a cigar that looked like a bomb.

"What do you think of it?" I asked, when he showed no disposition to talk.

"I'll be damned if I know," he responded, looking around for some place to expectorate and finding none.

"The window," I suggested, and he went over to it. When he came back, he had a rather peculiar expression. He sat down and puffed for a moment.

"In the first place," he began, "we can take it for granted that, unless she was crazy or sleepwalking, she didn't go out in her night-clothes, and there's nothing of hers missing. She wasn't taken in a carriage, providing she was taken at all. There's not a mark of wheels on that drive newer than a week, and besides, you say you heard nothing."

"Nothing," I said positively.

"Then, unless she went away in a balloon, where it wouldn't matter what she had on, she is still around the premises. It depends on how badly she was hurt."

"Are you sure it was she who was hurt?" I asked. "That print of a hand—that is not Miss Jane's."

In reply Hunter led the way down the stairs to the place where the stain on the stair rail stood out, ugly and distinct. He put his own heavy hand on the rail just below it.

"Suppose," he said, "suppose you grip something very hard. What happens to your hand?"

"It spreads," I acknowledged, seeing what he meant.

"Now, look at that stain. Look at the short fingers—why, it's a child's hand beside mine. The breadth is from pressure. It might be figured out this way. The fingers, you notice, point down the stairs. In some way, let us say, the burglar, for want of a better name, gets into the house. He used a ladder resting against that window by the chest of drawers.

"Ladder!" I exclaimed.

"Yes, there is a pruning ladder there. Now then—he comes down these stairs, and he has a definite object. He knows of something valuable in that cubbyhole over the mantel in Miss Jane's room. How does he get in? The door into the upper hall is closed and bolted, but the door into the bathroom is open. From there another door leads into the bedroom, and it has no bolt—only a key. That kind of a lock is only a three-minutes delay, or less. Now then, Miss Maitland was a light sleeper. When she wakened, she was too alarmed to scream; she tried to get to the door and was intercepted. Finally she got out the way the intruder got in, and ran along the hall. Every door was locked. In a frenzy she ran up the attic stairs and was captured up there. Which bears out Miss Margery's story of the footsteps back and forward."

"Good heavens, what an awful thing!" I gasped. "And I was sitting smoking just across the hall."

"He brings her down the stairs again, probably half dragging her. Once, she catches hold of the stair rail, and holds desperately to it, leaving the stain here."

"But why did he bring her down?" I asked, bewildered. "Why wouldn't he take what he was after and get away?"

Hunter smoked and meditated.

"She probably had to get the key of the iron door," he suggested. "It was hidden, and time was valuable. If there was a scapegrace member of the family, for instance, who knew where the old lady kept money, and who needed it badly, who knew all about the house, and who—"

"Fleming!" I exclaimed, aghast.

"Or even our young friend, Wardrop," Hunter said quietly. "He has an hour to account for. The trying to get in may have been a blind, and how do you know that what he says was stolen out of his satchel was not what he had just got from the iron box over the mantel in Miss Maitland's room?"

I was dizzy with trying to follow Hunter's facile imagination. The thing we were trying to do was to find the old lady, and, after all, here we were brought up against the same *impasse*.

"Then where is she now?" I asked. He meditated. He had sat down on the narrow stairs, and was rubbing his chin with a thoughtful forefinger. "One thirty, Miss Margery says, when she heard the noise. One forty-five when you heard Wardrop at the shutters. I tell you, Knox, it is one of two things: either that woman is dead somewhere in this house, or she ran out of the hall door just before you went downstairs, and in that case the Lord only knows where she is. If there is a room anywhere that we have not explored—"

"I am inclined to think there is," I broke in, thinking of Wardrop's face a few minutes before. And just then Wardrop himself joined us. He closed the door at the foot of the boxed-in staircase, and came quietly up.

"You spoke about an unused room or a secret closet, Mr. Hunter," he said, without any resentment in his tone. "We have nothing so sensational as that, but the old house is full of queer nooks and crannies, and perhaps, in one of them, we might find—" he stopped and gulped. Whatever Hunter might think, whatever I might have against Harry Wardrop, I determined then that he had had absolutely nothing to do with little Miss Maitland's strange disappearance.

The first place we explored was a closed and walled-in wine cellar, long unused, and to which access was gained by a small window in the stone foundation of the house. The cobwebs over the window made it practically an impossible place, but we put Robert, the gardener, through it, in spite of his protests.

"There's nothin' there, I tell you," he protested, with one leg over the coping. "God only knows what's down there, after all these years. I've been livin' here with the Miss Maitlands for twenty year, and I ain't never been put to goin' down into cellars on the end of a rope."

He went, because we were three to his one, but he was up again in sixty seconds, with the announcement that the place was as bare as the top of his head.

We moved every trunk in the storeroom, although it would have been a moral impossibility for anyone to have done it the night before without rousing the entire family, and were thus able to get to and open a large closet, which proved to contain neatly tied and labeled packages of religious weeklies, beginning in the sixties.

The grounds had been gone over inch by inch, without affording any clue, and now the three of us faced one another. The day was almost gone, and we were exactly where we started. Hunter had sent men through the town and the adjacent countryside, but no word had come from them. Miss Letitia had at last succumbed to the suspense and had gone to bed, where she lay quietly enough, as is the way with the old, but so mild that she was alarming.

At five o'clock Hawes called me from the office and almost tearfully implored me to come back and attend to my business. When I said it was impossible, I could hear him groan as he hung up the receiver. Hawes is of the opinion that by keeping fresh magazines in my waiting room and by persuading me to the extravagance of Turkish rugs, that he has built my practice to its present flourishing state. When I left the telephone, Hunter was preparing to go back to town and Wardrop was walking up and down the hall. Suddenly Wardrop stopped his uneasy promenade and hailed the detective on his way to the door.

"By George," he exclaimed, "I forgot to show you the closet under the attic stairs!"

We hurried up and Wardrop showed us the panel in the hall, which slid to one side when he pushed a bolt under the carpet. The blackness of the closet was horrible in its suggestion to me. I stepped back while Hunter struck a match and looked in.

The closet was empty.

"Better not go in," Wardrop said. "It hasn't been used for years and it's black with dust. I found it myself and showed it to Miss Jane. I don't believe Miss Letitia knows it is here."

"It hasn't been used for years!" reflected Hunter, looking around him curiously. "I suppose it has been some time since you were in here, Mr. Wardrop?"

"Several years," Wardrop replied carelessly. "I used to keep contraband here in my college days, cigarettes and that sort of thing. I haven't been in it since then."

Hunter took his foot off a small object that lay on the floor, and picking it up, held it out to Wardrop, with a grim smile.

"Here is the fountain pen you lost this morning, Mr. Wardrop," he said quietly.

Chapter VII
Concerning Margery

WHEN Hunter had finally gone at six o'clock, summoned to town on urgent business, we were very nearly where we had been before he came. He could only give us theories, and after all, what we wanted was fact—and Miss Jane. Many things, however, that he had unearthed puzzled me.

Why had Wardrop lied about so small a matter as his fountain pen? The closet was empty: what object could he have had in saying he had not been in it for years? I found that my belief in his sincerity of the night before was going. If he had been lying then, I owed him something for a lump on my head that made it difficult for me to wear my hat.

It would have been easy enough for him to rob himself, and, if he had an eye for the theatrical, to work out just some such plot. It was even possible that he had hidden for a few hours in the secret closet the contents of the Russia leather bag. But, whatever Wardrop might or might not be, he gave me little chance to find out, for he left the house before Hunter did that afternoon, and it was later, and under strange circumstances, that I met him again.

Hunter had not told me what was on the paper he had picked out of the basket in Miss Jane's room, and I knew he was as much puzzled as I at the scrap in the little cupboard, with eleven twenty-two on it. It occurred to me that it might mean the twenty-second day of the eleventh month, perhaps something that had happened on some momentous, long-buried twenty-second of November. But this was May, and the finding of two slips bearing the same number was too unusual.

After Hunter left I went back to the closet under the upper stairs, and with some difficulty got the panel open again. The space inside, perhaps eight feet high at one end and four at the other, was empty. There was a row of hooks, as if at some time clothing had been hung there, and a flat shelf at one end, gray with dust.

I struck another match and examined the shelf. On its surface were numerous scratchings in the dust layer, but at one end, marked out as if drawn on a blackboard, was a rectangular outline, apparently that of a smallish box, and fresh.

My match burned my fingers and I dropped it to the floor, where it expired in a sickly blue flame. At the last, however, it died heroically— like an old man to whom his last hours bring back some of the glory of his prime, burning brightly for a second and then fading into darkness. The last flash showed me, on the floor of the closet and wedged between two boards, a small white globule. I did not need another match to tell me it was a pearl.

I dug it out carefully and took it to my room. In the daylight there I recognized it as an unstrung pearl of fair size and considerable value. There could hardly be a doubt that I had stumbled on one of the stolen gems; but a pearl was only a pearl to me, after all. I didn't feel any of the inspirations which fiction detectives experience when they happen on an important clue.

I lit a cigar and put the pearl on the table in front of me. But no explanation formed itself in the tobacco smoke. If Wardrop took the pearls, I kept repeating over and over, if Wardrop took the pearls, who took Miss Jane?

I tried to forget the pearls, and to fathom the connection between Miss Maitland's disappearance and the absence of her brother-in-law. The scrap of paper, eleven twenty-two, must connect them, but how? A family scandal? Dismissed on the instant. There could be nothing that would touch the virginal remoteness of that little old lady. Insanity? Well, Miss Jane might have had a sudden aberration and wandered away, but that would leave Fleming out, and the paper dragged him in. A common enemy?

I smoked and considered for some time over this. An especially malignant foe might rob, or even murder, but it was almost ludicrous to think of his carrying away by force Miss Jane's ninety pounds of austere flesh. The solution, had it not been for the bloodstains, might have been a peaceful one, leaving out the pearls altogether, but later developments showed that the pearls refused to be omitted. To my mind, however, at that time, the issue seemed a double one. I believed that someone, perhaps Harry Wardrop, had stolen the pearls, hidden them in the secret closet, and disposed of them later. I made a note to try to follow up the missing pearls.

Then—I clung to the theory that Miss Maitland had been abducted and was being held for ransom. If I could have found traces of a vehicle of any sort near the house, I would almost have considered my contention proved. That anyone could have entered the house, intimidated and even slightly injured the old lady, and taken her quietly out the front door, while I sat smoking in my room with the window open, and Wardrop trying the shutters at the side of the house, seemed impossible. Yet there were the stains, the confusion, the open front door to prove it.

But—and I stuck here—the abductor who would steal an old woman, and take her out into the May night without any covering—not even shoes—clad only in her nightclothes, would run an almost certain risk of losing his prize by pneumonia. For a second search had shown not an article of wearing apparel missing from the house. Even the cedar chests were undisturbed; not a blanket was gone.

Just before dinner I made a second round of the grounds, this time looking for traces of wheels. I found none nearby, and it occurred to me that the boldest highwayman would hardly drive up to the door for his booty. When I had extended my search to cover the unpaved lane that separated the back of the Maitland place from its nearest neighbor, I was more fortunate.

The morning delivery wagons had made fresh trails, and at first I despaired. I sauntered up the lane to the right, however, and about a hundred feet beyond the boundary hedge I found circular tracks, broad and deep, where an automobile had backed and turned. The lane was separated by high hedges of osage orange from the properties on either side, and each house in that neighborhood had a drive of its own, which entered from the main street, circled the house and went out as it came.

There was no reason, or, so far as I could see, no legitimate reason, why a car should have stopped there, yet it had stopped and for some time. Deeper tracks in the sand at the side of the lane showed that.

I felt that I had made some progress: I had found where the pearls had been hidden after the theft, and this put Bella out of the question. And I had found—or thought I had—the way in which Miss Jane had been taken away from Bellwood.

I came back past the long rear wing of the house which contained, I presumed, the kitchen and the other mysterious regions which only women and architects comprehend. A long porch ran the length of the wing, and as I passed I heard my name called.

"In here in the old laundry," Margery's voice repeated, and I retraced my steps and went up on the porch. At the very end of the wing, dismantled, piled at the sides with firewood and broken furniture, was an old laundry. Its tubs were rusty, its walls mildewed and streaked, and it exhaled the musty odor of empty houses. On the floor in the middle of the room, undeniably dirty and disheveled, sat Margery Fleming.

"I thought you were never coming," she said petulantly. "I have been here alone for an hour."

"I'm sure I never guessed it," I apologized. "I should have been only too glad to come and sit with you."

She was fumbling with her hair, which threatened to come down any minute, and which hung, loosely knotted, over one small ear.

"I hate to look ridiculous," she said sharply, "and I detest being laughed at. I've been crying, and I haven't any handkerchief."

I proffered mine gravely, and she took it. She wiped the dusty streaks off her cheeks and pinned her hair in a funny knob on top of her head that would have made any other woman look like a caricature. But still she sat on the floor.

"Now," she said, when she had jabbed the last hairpin into place and tucked my handkerchief into her belt, "if you have been sufficiently amused, perhaps you will help me out of here."

"Out of where?"

"Do you suppose I'm sitting here because I like it?"

"You have sprained your ankle," I said, with sudden alarm.

In reply she brushed aside her gown, and for the first time I saw what had occurred. She was sitting half over a trapdoor in the floor, which had closed on her skirts and held her fast.

"The wretched thing!" she wailed. "And I have called until I am hoarse. I could shake Heppie! Then I tried to call you mentally. I fixed my mind on you and said over and over, 'Come, please come.' Didn't you feel anything at all?"

"Good old trapdoor!" I said. "I know I was thinking about you, but I never suspected the reason. And then to have walked past here twenty minutes ago! Why didn't you call me then?" I was tugging at the door, but it was fast, with the skirts to hold it tight.

"I looked such a fright," she explained. "Can't you pry it up with something?"

I tried several things without success, while Margery explained her plight.

"I was sure Robert had not looked carefully in the old wine cellar," she said, "and then I remembered this trapdoor opened into it. It was the only place we hadn't explored thoroughly. I put a ladder down and looked around. Ugh!"

"What did you find?" I asked, as my third broomstick lever snapped.

"Nothing—only I know now where Aunt Letitia's Edwin Booth went to. He was a cat," she explained, "and Aunt Letitia made the railroad pay for killing him."

I gave up finally and stood back.

"Couldn't you—er—get out of your garments, and—I could go out and close the door," I suggested delicately. "You see you are sitting on the trapdoor, and—"

But Margery scouted the suggestion with the proper scorn, and demanded a pair of scissors. She cut herself loose with vicious snips, while I paraphrased the old nursery rhyme, "She cut her petticoats all around about." Then she gathered up her outraged garments and fled precipitately.

She was unusually dignified at dinner. Neither of us cared to eat, and the empty places—Wardrop's and Miss Letitia's—Miss Jane's had not been set—were like skeletons at the board.

It was Margery who, after our pretense of a meal, voiced the suspicion I think we both felt.

"It is a strange time for Harry to go away," she said quietly, from the library window.

"He probably has a reason."

"Why don't you say it?" she said suddenly, turning on me. "I know what you think. You believe he only pretended he was robbed!"

"I should be sorry to think anything of the kind," I began. But she did not allow me to finish.

"I saw what you thought," she burst out bitterly. "The detective almost laughed in his face. Oh, you needn't think I don't know: I saw him last night, and the woman too. He brought her right to the gate. You treat me like a child, all of you!"

In sheer amazement I was silent. So a new character had been introduced into the play—a woman, too!

"You were not the only person, Mr. Knox, who could not sleep last night," she went on. "Oh, I know a great many things. I know about the pearls, and what you think about them, and I know more than that, I—"

She stopped then. She had said more than she intended to, and all at once her bravado left her, and she looked like a frightened child. I went over to her and took one trembling hand.

"I wish you didn't know all those things," I said. "But since you do, won't you let me share the burden? The only reason I am still here is on your account."

I had a sort of crazy desire to take her in my arms and comfort her, Wardrop or no Wardrop. But at that moment, luckily for me, perhaps, Miss Letitia's shrill old voice came from the stairway.

"Get out of my way, Heppie," she was saying tartly. "I'm not on my deathbed yet, not if I know it. Where's Knox?"

Whereupon I obediently went out and helped Miss Letitia into the room.

"I think I know where Jane is," she said, putting down her cane with a jerk. "I don't know why I didn't think about it before. She's gone to get her new teeth; she's been talkin' of it for a month. Not but what her old teeth would have done well enough."

"She would hardly go in the middle of the night," I returned. "She was a very timid woman, wasn't she?"

"She wasn't raised right," Miss Letitia said with a shake of her head. "She's the baby, and the youngest's always spoiled."

"Have you thought that this might be more than it appears to be?" I was feeling my way: she was a very old woman. "It—for instance, it might be abduction, kidnapping—for a ransom.

"Ransom!" Miss Letitia snapped. "Mr. Knox, my father made his money by working hard for it: I haven't wasted it—not that I know of. And if Jane Maitland was fool enough to be abducted, she'll stay a while before I pay anything for her. It looks to me as if this detective business is going to be expensive, anyhow."

My excuse for dwelling with such attention to detail on the preliminary story, the disappearance of Miss Jane Maitland and the peculiar circumstances surrounding it, will have to find its justification in the events that followed it. Miss Jane herself, and the solution of that mystery, solved the even more tragic one in which we were about to be involved. I say *we,* because it was borne in on me at about that time, that the things that concerned Margery Fleming must concern me henceforth, whether I willed it so or otherwise. For the first time in my life a woman's step on the stair was like no other sound in the world.

Chapter VIII

Too Late

∽

AT NINE o'clock that night things remained about the same. The man Hunter had sent to investigate the neighborhood and the country just outside of the town came to the house about eight, and reported "nothing discovered." Miss Letitia went to bed early, and Margery took her upstairs.

Hunter called me by telephone from town.

"Can you take the nine-thirty up?" he asked. I looked at my watch.

"Yes, I think so. Is there anything new?"

"Not yet; there may be. Take a cab at the station and come to the corner of Mulberry Street and Park Lane. You'd better dismiss your cab there and wait for me."

I sent word upstairs by Bella, who was sitting in the kitchen, her heavy face sodden with grief, and taking my hat and raincoat—it was raining a light spring drizzle—I hurried to the station. In twenty-four minutes I was in the city, and perhaps twelve minutes more saw me at the designated corner, with my cab driving away and the rain dropping off the rim of my hat and splashing on my shoulders.

I found a sort of refuge by standing under the wooden arch of a gate, and it occurred to me that, for all my years in the city, this particular neighborhood was altogether strange to me. Two blocks away, in any direction, I would have been in familiar territory again.

Back of me a warehouse lifted six or seven gloomy stories to the sky. The gate I stood in was evidently the entrance to its yard, and in fact, some uncomfortable movement of mine just then struck the latch, and almost precipitated me backward by its sudden opening. Beyond was a yard full of shadowy wheels and packing cases; the streetlights did not penetrate there, and with an uneasy feeling that almost anything, in this none too savory neighborhood, might be waiting there, I struck a match and looked at my watch. It was twenty minutes after ten. Once a man turned the corner and came toward me, his head down, his long ulster flapping around his legs. Confident that it was Hunter, I stepped out and touched him on the arm. He wheeled instantly, and in the light which shone on his face, I saw my error.

"Excuse me," I mumbled, "I mistook my man."

He went on again without speaking, only pulling his soft hat down lower on his face. I looked after him until he turned the next corner, and I knew I had not been mistaken; it was Wardrop.

The next minute Hunter appeared, from the same direction, and we walked quickly together. I told him who the man just ahead had been, and he nodded without surprise. But before we turned the next corner, he stopped.

"Did you ever hear of the White Cat?" he asked. "Little political club?"

"Never."

"I'm a member of it," he went on rapidly. "It's run by the city ring, or rather it runs itself. Be a good fellow while you're there, and keep your eyes open. It's a queer joint."

The corner we turned found us on a narrow, badly paved street. The broken windows of the warehouse still looked down on us, and across the street was an ice factory, with two deserted wagons standing along the curb. As well as I could see for the darkness, a lumberyard stretched beyond the warehouse, its piles of boards giving off in the rain the aromatic odor of fresh pine.

At a gate in the fence beyond the warehouse Hunter stopped. It was an ordinary wooden gate and it opened with a thumb latch. Beyond stretched a long, narrow, brick-paved alleyway, perhaps three feet wide, and lighted by the merest glimmer of a light ahead. Hunter went on regardless of puddles in the brick paving, and I stumbled after him. As we advanced, I could see that the light was a single electric bulb, hung over a second gate. While Hunter fumbled for a key in his pocket, I had time to see that this gate had a Yale lock, was provided, at the side, with an electric bell button, and had a letter slot cut in it.

Hunter opened the gate and preceded me through it. The gate swung to and clicked behind me. After the gloom of the passageway, the small brick-paved yard seemed brilliant with lights. Two wires were strung its length, dotted with many electric lamps. In a corner a striped tent stood out in grotesque relief; it seemed to be empty, and the weather was an easy explanation. From the two-story house beyond there came suddenly a burst of piano music and a none too steady masculine voice. Hunter turned to me, with his foot on the wooden steps.

"Above everything else," he warned, "keep your temper. Nobody gives a hang in here whether you're the mayor of the town, the champion pool player of the first ward, or the roundsman on the beat."

The door at the top of the steps was also Yale-locked. We stepped at once into the kitchen, from which I imagined that the house faced on another street, and that for obvious reasons only its rear entrance was used. The kitchen was bright and clean; it was littered, however, with half-cut loaves of bread, glasses and empty bottles. Over the range a man in his shirtsleeves was giving his whole attention to a slice of ham, sizzling on a skillet, and at a table nearby a young fellow, with his hair cut in a barber's oval over the back of his neck, was spreading slices of bread and cheese with mustard.

"How are you, Mr. Mayor?" Hunter said, as he shed his raincoat. "This is Mr. Knox, the man who's engineering the *Star-Eagle* fight."

The man over the range wiped one greasy hand and held it out to me.

"The Cat is purring a welcome," he said, indicating the frying ham. "If my cooking turns out right, I'll ask you to have some ham with me. I don't know why in thunder it gets black in the middle and won't cook around the edges."

I recognized the mayor. He was a big fellow, handsome in a heavy way, and "Tommy" to everyone who knew him. It seemed I was about to see my city government at play.

Hunter was thoroughly at home. He took my coat and his own and hung them somewhere to dry. Then he went into a sort of pantry opening off the kitchen and came out with four bottles of beer.

"We take care of ourselves here," he explained, as the newly barbered youth washed some glasses. "If you want a sandwich, there is cooked ham in the refrigerator and cheese—if our friend at the sink has left any."

The boy looked up from his glasses. "It's rat-trap cheese, that stuff," he growled.

"The other man out an hour ago and didn't come back," put in the mayor, grinning. "You can kill that with mustard, if it's too lively."

"Get some cigars, will you?" Hunter asked me. "They're on a shelf in the pantry. I have my hands full."

I went for the cigars, remembering to keep my eyes open. The pantry was a small room: it contained an icebox, stocked with drinkables, ham, eggs and butter. On shelves above were cards, cigars and liquors, and there, too, I saw a box with an endorsement which showed the "honor system" of the Cat Club.

"Sign checks and drop here," it read, and I thought about the old adage of honor among thieves and politicians.

When I came out with the cigars, Hunter was standing with a group of new arrivals; they included one of the city physicians, the director of public charities and a judge of a local court. The latter, McFeely, a little, thin Irishman, knew me and accosted me at once. The mayor was busy over the range, and was almost purple with heat and unwonted anxiety.

When the three newcomers went upstairs, instead of going into the grillroom, I looked at Hunter.

"Is this where the political game is played?" I asked.

"Yes, if the political game is poker," he replied, and led the way into the room which adjoined the kitchen.

No one paid any attention to us. Bare tables, a wooden floor, and almost as many cuspidors as chairs, comprised the furniture of the long room. In one corner was a battered upright piano, and there were two fireplaces with old-fashioned mantels. Perhaps a dozen men were sitting around, talking loudly, with much scraping of chairs on the bare floor. At one table they were throwing poker dice, but the rest were drinking beer and talking in a desultory way. At the piano a man with a red mustache was mimicking the sextette from *Lucia* and a roar of applause met us as we entered the room. Hunter led the way to a corner and put down his bottles.

"It's fairly quiet tonight," he said. "Tomorrow's the big night— Saturday."

"What time do they close up?" I asked. In answer Hunter pointed to a sign over the door. It was a card, neatly printed, and it said, "The White Cat never sleeps."

"There are only two rules here," he explained. "That is one, and the other is, 'If you get too noisy, and the patrol wagon comes, make the driver take you home.'"

The crowd was good-humored; it paid little or no attention to us, and when someone at the piano began to thump a waltz, Hunter, under cover of the noise, leaned over to me.

"We traced Fleming here, through your cornerman and the cabby," he said carefully. "I haven't seen him, but it is a moral certainty he is skulking in one of the upstairs rooms. His precious private secretary is here, too."

I glanced around the room, but no one was paying any attention to us.

"I don't know Fleming by sight," the detective went on, "and the pictures we have of him were taken a good while ago, when he wore a mustache. When he was in local politics, before he went to the legislature, he practically owned this place, paying for favors with membership tickets. A man could hide here for a year safely. The police never come here, and a man's business is his own."

"He is upstairs now?"

"Yes. There are four rooms up there for cards, and a bathroom. It's an old dwelling house. Would Fleming know you?"

"No, but of course Wardrop would."

As if in answer to my objection, Wardrop appeared at that moment. He ran down the painted wooden stairs and hurried through the room without looking to right or left. The piano kept on, and the men at the tables were still engrossed with their glasses and one another. Wardrop was very pale; he bolted into a man at the door, and pushed him aside without ceremony.

"You might go up now," Hunter said, rising. "I will see where the young gentleman is making for. Just open the door of the different rooms upstairs, look around for Fleming, and if anyone notices you, ask if Al Hunter is there. That will let you out."

He left me then, and after waiting perhaps a minute, I went upstairs alone. The second floor was the ordinary upper story of a small dwelling house. The doors were closed, but loud talking, smoke, and the rattle of chips floated out through open transoms. From below, the noise of the piano came up the staircase, unmelodious but rhythmical, and from the street on which the house faced, an automobile was starting its engine, with a series of shot-like explosions.

The noise was confusing, disconcerting. I opened two doors, to find only the usual poker table, with the winners sitting quietly, their cards bunched in the palms of their hands, and the losers, growing more voluble as the night went on, buying chips recklessly, drinking more than they should. The atmosphere was reeking with smoke.

The third door I opened was that of a dingy bathroom, with a zinc tub and a slovenly washstand. The next, however, was different. The light streamed out through the transom as in the other rooms, but there was no noise from within. With my hand on the door, I hesitated— then, with Hunter's injunction ringing in my ears, I opened it and looked in.

A breath of cool night air from an open window met me. There was no noise, no smoke, no sour odor of stale beer. A table had been drawn to the center of the small room, and was littered with papers, pen and ink. At one corner was a tray, containing the remnants of a meal; a pillow and a pair of blankets on a couch at one side showed the room had been serving as a bedchamber.

But none of these things caught my eye at first. At the table, leaning forward, his head on his arms, was a man. I coughed and, receiving no answer, stepped into the room.

"I beg your pardon," I said, "but I am looking for—"

Then the truth burst on me, overwhelmed me. A thin stream was spreading over the papers on the table, moving slowly, sluggishly, as is the way with blood when the heart pump is stopped. I hurried over and raised the heavy, wobbling, gray head. It was Allan Fleming and he had been shot through the forehead.

Chapter IX

Only One Eye Closed

MY FIRST impulse was to rouse the house; my second, to wait for Hunter. To turn loose that mob of half-drunken men in such a place seemed profanation. There was nothing of the majesty or panoply of death here, but the very sordidness of the surroundings made me resolve to guard the new dignity of that figure. I was shocked, of course; it would be absurd to say that I was emotionally unstrung. On the contrary, I was conscious of a distinct feeling of disappointment. Fleming had been our key to the Bellwood affair, and he had put himself beyond helping to solve any mystery. I locked the door and stood wondering what to do next. I should have called a doctor, no doubt, but I had seen enough of death to know that the man was beyond aid of any kind.

It was not until I had bolted the door that I discovered the absence of any weapon. Everything that had gone before had pointed to a position so untenable that suicide seemed its natural and inevitable result. With the discovery that there was no revolver on the table or floor, the thing was more ominous. I decided at once to call the young city physician in the room across the hall, and with something approximating panic, I threw open the door—to face Harry Wardrop, and behind him, Hunter.

I do not remember that anyone spoke. Hunter jumped past me into the room and took in in a single glance what I had labored to acquire in three minutes. As Wardrop came in, Hunter locked the door behind him, and we three stood staring at the prostrate figure over the table.

I watched Wardrop: I have never seen so suddenly abject a picture. He dropped into a chair, and feeling for his handkerchief, wiped his shaking lips; every particle of color left his face, and he was limp, unnerved.

"Did you hear the shot?" Hunter asked me. "It has been a matter of minutes since it happened."

"I don't know," I said, bewildered. "I heard a lot of explosions, but I thought it was an automobile, out in the street."

Hunter was listening while he examined the room, peering under the table, lifting the blankets that had trailed off the couch onto the floor. Someone outside tried the doorknob and, finding the door locked, shook it slightly.

"Fleming!" he called under his breath. "Fleming!"

We were silent, in response to a signal from Hunter, and the steps retreated heavily down the hall. The detective spread the blankets decently over the couch, and the three of us moved the body there. Wardrop was almost collapsing.

"Now," Hunter said quietly, "before I call in Dr. Gray from the room across, what do you know about this thing, Mr. Wardrop?" Wardrop looked dazed.

"He was in a bad way when I left this morning," he said huskily. "There isn't much use now trying to hide anything; God knows I've done all I could. But he has been using cocaine for years, and today he ran out of the stuff. When I got here, about half an hour ago, he was on the verge of killing himself. I got the revolver from him—he was like a crazy man, and as soon as I dared to leave him, I went out to try and find a doctor—"

"To get some cocaine?"

"Yes."

"Not—because he was already wounded, and you were afraid it was fatal?"

Wardrop shuddered; then he pulled himself together, and his tone was more natural.

"What's the use of lying about it?" he said wearily. "You won't believe me if I tell the truth, either, but—he was dead when I got here. I heard something like the bang of a door as I went upstairs, but the noise was terrific down below, and I couldn't tell. When I went in, he was just dropping forward, and—" he hesitated.

"The revolver?" Hunter queried, lynx-eyed.

"Was in his hand. He was dead then."

"Where is the revolver?"

"I will turn it over to the coroner."

"You will give it to me," Hunter replied sharply. And after a little fumbling, Wardrop produced it from his hip pocket. It was an ordinary thirty-eight. The detective opened it and glanced at it. Two chambers were empty.

"And you waited—say ten minutes—before you called for help, and even then you went outside hunting a doctor! What were you doing in those ten minutes?"

Wardrop shut his lips and refused to reply.

"If Mr. Fleming shot himself," the detective pursued relentlessly, "there would be powder marks around the wound. Then, too, he was in the act of writing a letter. It was a strange impulse, this—you see, he had only written a dozen words."

I glanced at the paper on the table. The letter had no superscription; it began abruptly:

"I shall have to leave here. The numbers have followed me. Tonight—"

That was all.

"This is not suicide," Hunter said gravely. "It is murder, and I warn you, Mr. Wardrop, to be careful what you say. Will you ask Dr. Gray to come in, Mr. Knox?"

I went across the hall to the room where the noise was loudest. Fortunately, Dr. Gray was out of the game. He was opening a can of caviar at a table in the corner and came out in response to a gesture. He did not ask any questions, and I let him go into the death chamber unprepared. The presence of death apparently had no effect on him, but the identity of the dead man almost stupefied him.

"Fleming!" he said, awed, as he looked down at the body. "Fleming, by all that's sacred! And a suicide!"

Hunter watched him grimly.

"How long has he been dead?" he asked.

The doctor glanced at the bullet wound in the forehead, and from there significantly to the group around the couch.

"Not an hour—probably less than half," he said. "It's strange we heard nothing, across the hall there."

Hunter took a clean folded handkerchief from his pocket and, opening it, laid it gently over the dead face. I think it was a relief to all of us. The doctor got up from his kneeling posture beside the couch and looked at Hunter inquiringly.

"What about getting him away from here?" he said. "There is sure to be a lot of noise about it, and—you remember what happened when Butler killed himself here."

"He was reported as being found dead in the lumberyard," Hunter said dryly. "Well, Doctor, this body stays where it is, and I don't give a whoop if the whole city government wants it moved. It won't be. This is murder, not suicide."

The doctor's expression was curious.

"Murder!" he repeated. "Why—who—"

But Hunter had many things to attend to; he broke in ruthlessly on the doctor's amazement.

"See if you can get the house empty, Doctor; just tell them he is dead—the story will get out soon enough."

As the doctor left the room, Hunter went to the open window, through which a fresh burst of rain was coming, and closed it. The window gave me an idea, and I went over and tried to see through the streaming pane. There was no shed or low building outside, but not five yards away the warehouse showed its ugly walls and broken windows.

"Look here, Hunter," I said. "Why could he not have been shot from the warehouse?"

"He could have been—but he wasn't," Hunter affirmed, glancing at Wardrop's drooping figure. "Mr. Wardrop, I am going to send for the coroner, and then I shall ask you to go with me to the office and tell the chief what you know about this. Knox, will you telephone the coroner?"

In an incredibly short time the clubhouse was emptied, and before midnight the coroner himself arrived and went up to the room. As for me, I had breakfasted, lunched and dined on horrors, and I sat in the deserted room downstairs and tried to think how I was to take the news to Margery.

At twelve thirty Wardrop, Hunter and the coroner came downstairs, leaving a detective in charge of the body until morning, when it could be taken home. The coroner had a cab waiting, and he took us at once to Hunter's chief. He had not gone to bed, and we filed into his library sepulchrally.

Wardrop told his story, but it was hardly convincing. The chief, a large man who said very little and leaned back with his eyes partly shut, listened in silence, only occasionally asking a question. The coroner, who was yawning steadily, left in the middle of Wardrop's story, as if in his mind, at least, the guilty man was as good as hanged.

"I am—I was—Mr. Allan Fleming's private secretary," Wardrop

began. "I secured the position through a relationship on his wife's side. I have held the position for three years. Before that I read law. For some time I have known that Mr. Fleming used a drug of some kind. Until a week ago I did not know what it was. On the ninth of May, Mr. Fleming sent for me. I was in Plattsburg at the time, and he was at home. He was in a terrible condition—not sleeping at all, and he said he was being followed by some person who meant to kill him. Finally he asked me to get him some cocaine, and when he had taken it, he was more like himself. I thought the pursuit was only in his own head. He had a man named Carter on guard in his house, and acting as butler.

"There was trouble of some sort in the organization; I do not know just what. Mr. Schwartz came here to meet Mr. Fleming, and it seemed there was money needed. Mr. Fleming had to have it at once. He gave me some securities to take to Plattsburg and turn into money. I went on the tenth—"

"Was that the day Mr. Fleming disappeared?" the chief interrupted.

"Yes. He went to the White Cat, and stayed there. No one but the caretaker and one other man knew he was there. On the night of the twenty-first, I came back, having turned my securities into money. I carried it in a package in a small Russia leather bag that never left my hand for a moment. Mr. Knox here suggested that I had put it down, and it had been exchanged for one just like it, but I did not let it out of my hand on that journey until I put it down on the porch at the Bellwood house, while I tried to get in. I live at Bellwood, with the Misses Maitland, sisters of Mr. Fleming's deceased wife. I don't pretend to know how it happened, but while I was trying to get into the house it was rifled. Mr. Knox will bear me out in that. I found my grip empty."

I affirmed it in a word. The chief was growing interested.

"What was in the bag?" he asked.

Wardrop tried to remember.

"A pair of pajamas," he said, "two military brushes and a clothes brush, two or three soft-bosomed shirts, perhaps a half-dozen collars, and a suit of underwear."

"And all this was taken, as well as the money?"

"The bag was left empty, except for my railroad schedule."

The chief and Hunter exchanged significant glances. Then—

"Go on, if you please," the detective said cheerfully.

I think Wardrop realized the absurdity of trying to make anyone believe that part of the story. He shut his lips and threw up his head as if he intended to say nothing further.

"Go on," I urged. If he could clear himself he must. I could not go back to Margery Fleming and tell her that her father had been murdered and her lover was accused of the crime.

"The bag was empty," he repeated. "I had not been five minutes trying to open the shutters, and yet the bag had been rifled. Mr. Knox here found it among the flowers below the veranda, empty."

The chief eyed me with awakened interest.

"You also live at Bellwood, Mr. Knox?"

"No. I am attorney to Miss Letitia Maitland, and was there one night as her guest. I found the bag as Mr. Wardrop described, empty."

The chief turned back to Wardrop.

"How much money was there in it when you—left it?"

"A hundred thousand dollars. I was afraid to tell Mr. Fleming, but I had to do it. We had a stormy scene, this morning. I think he thought the natural thing—that I had taken it."

"He struck you, I believe, and knocked you down?" asked Hunter smoothly.

Wardrop flushed.

"He was not himself; and, well, it meant a great deal to him. And he was out of cocaine; I left him raging, and when I went home I learned that Miss Jane Maitland had disappeared, been abducted, at the time my satchel had been emptied! It's no wonder I question my sanity."

"And then—tonight?" the chief persisted.

"Tonight, I felt that someone would have to look after Mr. Fleming; I was afraid he would kill himself. It was a bad time to leave while Miss Jane was missing. But—when I got to the White Cat I found him dead. He was sitting with his back to the door, and his head on the table."

"Was the revolver in his hand?"

"Yes."

"You are sure?" from Hunter. "Isn't it a fact, Mr. Wardrop, that you took Mr. Fleming's revolver from him this morning when he threatened you with it?"

Wardrop's face twitched nervously.

"You have been misinformed," he replied, but no one was impressed by his tone. It was wavering, uncertain. From Hunter's face I judged it had been a random shot, and had landed unexpectedly well.

"How many people knew that Mr. Fleming had been hiding at the White Cat?" from the chief.

"Very few—besides myself, only a man who looks after the club-house in the mornings, and Clarkson, the cashier of the Borough Bank, who met him there once by appointment."

The chief made no comment.

"Now, Mr. Knox, what about you?"

"I opened the door into Mr. Fleming's room, perhaps a couple of minutes after Mr. Wardrop went out," I said. "He was dead then, lean-ing on his outspread arms over the table; he had been shot in the fore-head."

"You heard no shot while you were in the hall?"

"There was considerable noise; I heard two or three sharp reports like the explosions of an automobile engine."

"Did they seem close at hand?"

"Not particularly; I thought, if I thought at all, that they were on the street."

"You are right about the automobile," Hunter said dryly. "The mayor sent his car away as I left to follow Mr. Wardrop. The sounds you heard were not shots."

"It is a strange thing," the chief reflected, "that a revolver could be fired in the upper room of an ordinary dwelling house, while that house was filled with people—and nobody hear it. Were there any powder marks on the body?"

"None," Hunter said.

The chief got up stiffly.

"Thank you very much, gentlemen," he spoke quietly. "I think that is all. Hunter, I would like to see you for a few minutes."

I think Wardrop was dazed at finding himself free; he had expected nothing less than an immediate charge of murder. As we walked to the corner for a car or cab, whichever materialized first, he looked back.

"I thought so," he said bitterly. A man was loitering after us along the street. The police were not asleep; they had only closed one eye.

The last train had gone. We took a night electric car to Wynton, and walked the three miles to Bellwood. Neither of us was talkative, and I imagine we were both thinking of Margery, and the news she would have to hear.

It had been raining, and the roads were vile. Once, Wardrop turned around to where we could hear the detective splashing along, well behind.

"I hope he's enjoying it," he said. "I brought you by this road so he'd have to wade in mud up to his neck."

"The devil you did!" I exclaimed. "I'll have to be scraped with a knife before I can get my clothes off."

We both felt better for the laugh; it was a sort of nervous reaction. The detective was well behind, but after a while Wardrop stood still, while I plowed along. They came up together presently, and the three of us trudged on, talking of immaterial things.

At the door Wardrop turned to the detective with a faint smile. "It's raining again," he said, "you'd better come in. You needn't worry about me; I'm not going to run away, and there's a couch in the library."

The detective grinned, and in the light from the hall I recognized the man I had followed to the police station two nights before.

"I guess I will," he said, looking apologetically at his muddy clothes. "This thing is only a matter of form, anyhow."

But he didn't lie down on the couch. He took a chair in the hall near the foot of the stairs, and we left him there, with the evening paper and a lamp. It was a queer situation, to say the least.

Chapter X

Breaking the News

⤙∞⤚

WARDROP looked so wretched that I asked him into my room, and mixed him some whisky and water. When I had given him a cigar, he began to look a little less hopeless.

"You've been a darned sight better to me than I would have been to you, under the circumstances," he said gratefully.

"I thought we had better arrange about Miss Margery before we try to settle down," I replied. "What she has gone through in the last twenty-four hours is nothing to what is coming tomorrow. Will you tell her about her father?"

He took a turn about the room.

"I believe it would come better from you," he said finally. "I am in the peculiar position of having been suspected by her father of robbing him, by you of carrying away her aunt, and now by the police and everybody else of murdering her father."

"I do not suspect you of anything," I justified myself. "I don't think you are entirely open, that is all, Wardrop. I think you are damaging yourself to shield someone else."

His expressive face was on its guard in a moment. He ceased his restless pacing, pausing impressively before me.

"I give you my word as a gentleman—I do not know who killed Mr. Fleming, and that when I first saw him dead, my only thought was that he had killed himself. He had threatened to, that day. Why, if you think I killed him, you would have to think I robbed him, too, in order to find a motive."

I did not tell him that that was precisely what Hunter *did* think. I evaded the issue.

"Mr. Wardrop, did you ever hear of the figures eleven twenty-two?" I inquired.

"Eleven twenty-two?" he repeated. "No, never in any unusual connection."

"You never heard Mr. Fleming use them?" I persisted.

He looked puzzled.

"Probably," he said. "In the very nature of Mr. Fleming's position, we used figures all the time. Eleven twenty-two. That's the time the theater train leaves the city for Bellwood. Not what you want, eh?"

"Not quite," I answered noncommittally, and began to wind my watch. He took the hint and prepared to leave.

"I'll not keep you up any longer," he said, picking up his raincoat. He opened the door and stared ruefully down at the detective in the hall below. "The old place is queer without Miss Jane," he said irrelevantly. "Well, good night, and thanks."

He went heavily along the hall and I closed my door. I heard him pass Margery's room and then go back and rap lightly. She was evidently awake.

"It's Harry," he called. "I thought you wouldn't worry if you knew I was in the house tonight."

She asked him something, for—

"Yes, he is here," he said. He stood there for a moment, hesitating over something, but whatever it was, he decided against it.

"Good night, dear," he said gently and went away. The little familiarity made me wince. Every unattached man has the same pang now and then. I have it sometimes when Edith sits on the arm of Fred's chair, or one of the youngsters leaves me to run to "daddy." And one of the sanest men I ever met went to his office and proposed to his stenographer in sheer craving for domesticity, after watching the wife of one of his friends run her hand over her husband's chin and give him a reproving slap for not having shaved!

I pulled myself up sharply, and after taking off my dripping coat, I went to the window and looked out into the May night. It seemed incredible that almost the same hour the previous night little Miss Jane had disappeared, had been taken away bodily through the peace of the warm spring darkness, and that I, as wide-awake as I was at that moment, acute enough of hearing to detect Wardrop's careful steps on the gravel walk below, had heard no struggle, had permitted this thing to happen without raising a finger in the old lady's defense. And she was gone as completely as if she had stepped over some psychic barrier into the fourth dimension!

I found myself avoiding the more recent occurrence at the White Cat. I was still too close to it to have gained any perspective. On that subject I was able to think clearly of only one thing: that I would have to tell Margery in the morning, and that I would have given anything I possessed for a little of Edith's diplomacy with which to break the bad news. It was Edith who broke the news to me that the moths had gotten into my evening clothes while I was hunting in the Rockies, by telling me that my dress coat made me look narrow across the shoulders and persuading me to buy a new one and give the old one to Fred. Then she broke the news of the moths to Fred!

I was ready for bed when Wardrop came back and rapped at my door. He was still dressed, and he had the leather bag in his hand.

"Look here," he said excitedly, when I had closed the door, "this is not my bag at all. Fool that I was, I never examined it carefully."

He held it out to me, and I carried it to the light. It was an ordinary eighteen-inch Russia leather traveling bag, tan in color, and with gold-plated mountings. It was empty, save for the railroad schedule that still rested in one side pocket. Wardrop pointed to the empty pocket on the other side.

"In my bag," he explained rapidly, "my name was written inside that pocket, in ink. I did it myself—my name and address."

I looked inside the pockets on both sides: nothing had been written in.

"Don't you see?" he asked excitedly. "Whoever stole my bag had this one to substitute for it. If we can succeed in tracing the bag here to the shop it came from, and from there to the purchaser, we have the thief."

"There's no maker's name in it," I said after a casual examination. Wardrop's face fell, and he took the bag from me despondently.

"No matter which way I turn," he said, "I run into a blind alley. If I were worth a damn, I suppose I could find a way out. But I'm not. Well, I'll let you sleep this time."

At the door, however, he turned around and put the bag on the floor, just inside.

"If you don't mind, I'll leave it here," he said.

"They'll be searching my room, I suppose, and I'd like to have the bag for future reference."

He went for good that time, and I put out the light. As an afterthought I opened my door perhaps six inches, and secured it with one of the pink conch shells which flanked either end of the stone hearth. I had failed the night before: I meant to be on hand that night.

I went to sleep immediately, I believe. I have no idea how much later it was that I roused. I wakened suddenly and sat up in bed. There had been a crash of some kind, for the shock was still vibrating along my nerves. Dawn was close; the window showed gray against the darkness inside, and I could make out dimly the larger objects in the room. I listened intently, but the house seemed quiet. Still I was not satisfied. I got up and, lighting the candle, got into my raincoat in lieu of a dressing gown, and prepared to investigate.

With the fatality that seemed to pursue my feet in that house, with my first step I trod squarely on top of the conch shell, and I fell back on to the edge of the bed swearing softly and holding the injured member. Only when the pain began to subside did I realize that I had left the shell on the doorsill, and that it had moved at least eight feet while I slept!

When I could walk, I put it on the mantel, its mate from the other end of the hearth beside it. Then I took my candle and went out into the hall. My door, which I had left open, I found closed; nothing else was disturbed. The leather bag sat just inside, as Wardrop had left it. Through Miss Maitland's transom were coming certain strangled and irregular sounds, now falsetto, now deep bass, that showed that worthy lady to be asleep. A glance down the staircase revealed Davidson, stretching in his chair and looking up at me.

"I'm frozen," he called up cautiously. "Throw me down a blanket or two, will you?"

I got a couple of blankets from my bed and took them down. He was examining his chair ruefully.

"There isn't any grip to this horsehair stuff," he complained. "Every time I doze off I dream I'm coasting down the old hill back on the farm, and when I wake up I'm sitting on the floor, with the end of my backbone bent like a hook."

He wrapped himself in the blankets and sat down again, taking the precaution this time to put his legs on another chair and thus anchor himself. Then he produced a couple of apples and a penknife and proceeded to pare and offer me one.

"Found 'em in the pantry," he said, biting into one. "I belong to the apple society. Eat one apple every day and keep healthy!" He stopped and stared intently at the apple. "I reckon I got a worm that time," he said, with less ardor.

"I'll get something to wash him down," I offered, rising, but he waved me back to my stair.

"Not on your life," he said with dignity. "Let him walk. How are things going upstairs?"

"You didn't happen to be up there a little while ago, did you?" I questioned in turn.

"No. I've been kept busy trying to sit tight where I am. Why?"

"Someone came into my room and wakened me," I explained. "I heard a racket, and when I got up, I found a shell that I had put on the doorsill to keep the door open, in the middle of the room. I stepped on it."

He examined a piece of apple before putting it in his mouth. Then he turned a pair of shrewd eyes on me.

"That's funny," he said. "Anything in the room disturbed?"

"Nothing."

"Where's the shell now?"

"On the mantel. I didn't want to step on it again." He thought for a minute, but his next remark was wholly facetious.

"No. I guess you won't step on it up there. Like the old woman: she says, 'Motorman, if I put my foot on the rail will I be electrocuted?' And he says, 'No, madam, not unless you put your other foot on the trolley wire.' "

I got up impatiently. There was no humor in the situation that night for me.

"Someone had been in the room," I reiterated. "The door was closed, although I had left it open."

He finished his apple and proceeded with great gravity to drop the parings down the immaculate register in the floor beside his chair. Then—

"I've only got one business here, Mr. Knox," he said in an undertone, "and you know what that is. But if it will relieve your mind of the thought that there was anything supernatural about your visitor, I'll tell you that it was Mr. Wardrop, and that to the best of my belief he was in your room, not once, but twice, in the last hour and a half. As far as that shell goes, it was I that kicked it, having gone up without my shoes."

I stared at him blankly.

"What could he have wanted?" I exclaimed. But with his revelation, Davidson's interest ceased; he drew the blanket up around his shoulders and shivered.

"Search me," he said and yawned.

I went back to bed, but not to sleep. I deliberately left the door wide open, but no intrusion occurred. Once, I got up and glanced down the stairs. For all his apparent drowsiness, Davidson heard my cautious movements, and saluted me in a husky whisper.

"Have you got any quinine?" he said. "I'm sneezing my head off."

But I had none. I gave him a box of cigarettes, and after partially dressing, I threw myself across the bed to wait for daylight. I was roused by the sun beating on my face, to hear Miss Letitia's tones from her room across.

"Nonsense," she was saying querulously. "Don't you suppose I can smell? Do you think because I'm a little hard of hearing that I've lost my other senses? Somebody's been smoking."

"It's me," Heppie shouted. "I—"

"You?" Miss Letitia snarled. "What are you smoking for? That ain't my shirt; it's my—"

"I ain't smokin'," yelled Heppie. "You won't let me tell you. I spilled vinegar on the stove; that's what you smell."

Miss Letitia's sardonic chuckle came through the door.

"Vinegar," she said with scorn. "Next thing you'll be telling me it's vinegar that Harry and Mr. Knox carry around in little boxes in their pockets. You've pinned my cap to my scalp."

I hurried downstairs to find Davidson gone. My blankets lay neatly folded, on the lower step, and the horsehair chairs were arranged along the wall as before. I looked around anxiously for telltale ashes, but there were none, save, at the edge of the spotless register, a trace. Evidently they had followed the apple parings. It grew cold a day or so later, and Miss Letitia had the furnace fired, and although it does not belong to my story, she and Heppie searched the house over to account for the odor of baking apples—a mystery that was never explained.

Wardrop did not appear at breakfast. Margery came downstairs as Bella was bringing me my coffee, and dropped languidly into her chair. She looked tired and white.

"Another day!" she said wearily. "Did you ever live through such an eternity as the last thirty-six hours?"

I responded absently; the duty I had assumed hung heavy over me. I had a frantic impulse to shirk the whole thing: to go to Wardrop and tell him it was his responsibility, not mine, to make this sad-eyed girl sadder still. That as I had not his privilege of comforting her, neither should I shoulder his responsibility of telling her. But the issue was forced on me sooner than I had expected, for at that moment I saw the glaring headlines of the morning paper, laid open at Wardrop's plate.

She must have followed my eyes, for we reached for it simultaneously. She was nearer than I, and her quick eye caught the name. Then I put my hand over the heading and she flushed with indignation.

"You are not to read it now," I said, meeting her astonished gaze as best I could. "Please let me have it. I promise you I will give it to you—almost immediately."

"You are very rude," she said without relinquishing the paper. "I saw a part of that; it is about my father!"

"Drink your coffee, please," I pleaded. "I will let you read it then. On my honor."

She looked at me; then she withdrew her hand and sat erect.

"How can you be so childish!" she exclaimed. "If there is anything in that paper that it—will hurt me to learn, is a cup of coffee going to make it any easier?"

I gave up then. I had always thought that people heard bad news better when they had been fortified with something to eat, and I had a very distinct recollection that Fred had made Edith drink something—tea probably—before he told her that Billy had fallen off the back fence and would have to have a stitch taken in his lip. Perhaps I should have offered Margery tea instead of coffee. But as it was, she sat, stonily erect, staring at the paper, and feeling that evasion would be useless, I told her what had happened, breaking the news as gently as I could.

I stood by her helplessly through the tearless agony that followed, and cursed myself for a blundering ass. I had said that he had been accidentally shot, and I said it with the paper behind me, but she put the evasion aside bitterly.

"Accidentally!" she repeated. The first storm of grief over, she lifted her head from where it had rested on her arms and looked at me, scorning my subterfuge. "He was murdered. That's the word I didn't have time to read! Murdered! And you sat back and let it happen. I went to you in time and you didn't do anything. No one did anything!"

I did not try to defend myself. How could I? And afterward when she sat up and pushed back the damp strands of hair from her eyes, she was more reasonable.

"I did not mean what I said about your not having done anything," she said, almost childishly. "No one could have done more. It was to happen, that's all."

But even then I knew she had trouble in store that she did not suspect. What would she do when she heard that Wardrop was under grave suspicion? Between her dead father and her lover, what? It was to be days before I knew, and in all that time I, who would have died, not cheerfully but at least stoically, for her, had to stand back and watch the struggle, not daring to hold out my hand to help, lest by the very gesture she divine my wild longing to hold her for myself.

She recovered bravely that morning from the shock, and refusing to go to her room and lie down—a suggestion, like the coffee, culled from my vicarious domestic life—she went out to the veranda and sat there in the morning sun, gazing across the lawn. I left her there finally, and broke the news of her brother-in-law's death to Miss Letitia. After the first surprise, the old lady took the news with what was nearer complacency than resignation.

"Shot!" she said, sitting up in bed, while Heppie shook her pillows. "It's a queer death for Allan Fleming; I always said he would be hanged."

After that, she apparently dismissed him from her mind, and we talked of her sister. Her mood had changed and it was depressing to find that she spoke of Jane always in the past tense. She could speak of her quite calmly—I suppose the sharpness of our emotions is in inverse ratio to our length of years, and she regretted that, under the circumstances, Jane would not rest in the family lot.

"We are all there," she said, "eleven of us, counting my sister Mary's husband, although he don't properly belong, and I always said we would take him out if we were crowded. It is the best lot in the Hopedale Cemetery; you can see the shaft for two miles in any direction."

We held a family council that morning around Miss Letitia's bed: Wardrop, who took little part in the proceedings and who stood at a window looking out most of the time; Margery on the bed, her arm around Miss Letitia's shriveled neck; and Heppie, who acted as interpreter and shouted into the old lady's ear such parts of the conversation as she considered essential.

"I have talked with Miss Fleming," I said, as clearly as I could, "and she seems to shrink from seeing people. The only friends she cares about are in Europe, and she tells me there are no other relatives."

Heppie condensed this into a vocal capsule, and thrust it into Miss Letitia's ear. The old lady nodded.

"No other relatives," she corroborated. "God be praised for that, anyhow."

"And yet," I went on, "there are things to look after, certain neces- sary duties that no one else can attend to. I don't want to insist, but she ought, if she is able, to go to the city house, for a few hours, at least."

"City house!" Heppie yelled in her ear.

"It ought to be cleaned," Miss Letitia acquiesced, "and fresh curtains put up. Jane would have been in her element; she was always handy at a funeral. And don't let them get one of those let-down-at-the-side coffins. They're leaky."

Luckily Margery did not notice this.

"I was going to suggest," I put in hurriedly, "that my brother's wife would be only too glad to help, and if Miss Fleming will go into town with me, I am sure Edith would know just what to do. She isn't curi- ous and she's very capable."

Margery threw me a grateful glance—grateful, I think, that I could understand how, under the circumstances, a stranger was more accept- able than curious friends could be.

"Mr. Knox's sister-in-law!" interpreted Heppie.

"When you have to say the letter S, turn your head away," Miss Leti- tia rebuked her. "Well, I don't object, if Knox's sister-in-law don't." She had an uncanny way of expanding Heppie's tabloid speeches. "You can take my white silk shawl to lay over the body, but be sure to bring it back. We may need it for Jane."

If the old lady's chin quivered a bit, while Margery threw her arms around her, she was mightily ashamed of it. But Heppie was made of weaker stuff. She broke into a sudden storm of sobs and left the room, to stick her head in the door a moment after.

"Kidneys or chops?" she shouted almost belligerently.

"Kidneys," Miss Letitia replied in kind.

Wardrop went with us to the station at noon, but he left us there, with a brief remark that he would be up that night. After I had put Margery in a seat, I went back to have a word with him alone. He was standing beside the train, trying to light a cigarette, but his hands shook almost beyond control, and after the fourth match he gave it up. My minute for speech was gone. As the train moved out, I saw him walking back along the platform, paying no attention to anything around him. Also, I had a fleeting glimpse of a man loafing on a bag- gage truck, his hat over his eyes. He was paring an apple with a penknife, and dropping the peelings with careful accuracy through a crack in the floor of the platform.

I had arranged over the telephone that Edith should meet the train, and it was a relief to see that she and Margery took to each other at once. We drove to the house immediately, and after a few tears when she saw the familiar things around her, Margery rose to the situation bravely. Miss Letitia had sent Bella to put the house in order, and it was evident that the idea of clean curtains for the funeral had been drilled into her until it had become an obsession. Not until Edith had concealed the stepladder were the hangings safe, and late in the afternoon we heard a crash from the library and found Bella twisted on the floor, the result of putting a teakwood tabouret on a table and from thence attacking the lace curtains of the library windows.

Edith gave her a good scolding and sent her off to soak her sprained ankle. Then she righted the tabouret, sat down on it and began on me.

"Do you know that you have not been to the office for two days?" she said severely. "And do you know that Hawes had hysterics in our front hall last night? You had a case in court yesterday, didn't you?"

"Nothing very much," I said, looking over her head. "Anyhow, I'm tired. I don't know when I'm going back. I need a vacation."

She reached behind her and, pulling the cord, sent the window shade to the top of the window. At the sight of my face thus revealed, she drew a long sigh.

"The biggest case you ever had, Jack! The biggest retainer you ever had—"

"I've spent that," I protested feebly

"A vacation, and you only back from Pinehurst!"

"The girl was in trouble—*is* in trouble, Edith," I burst out. "Anyone would have done the same thing. Even Fred would hardly have deserted that household. It's stricken, positively stricken."

My remark about Fred did not draw her from cover.

"Of course it's your own affair," she said, not looking at me, "and goodness knows I'm disinterested about it; you ruin the boys, both stomachs and dispositions, and I could use your room *splendidly* as a sewing room—"

"Edith! You abominable little liar!"

She dabbed at her eyes furiously with her handkerchief, and walked with great dignity to the door. Then she came back and put her hand on my arm.

"Oh, Jack, if we could only have saved you this!" she said, and a minute later, when I did not speak: "Who is the man, dear?"

"A distant relative, Harry Wardrop," I replied, with what I think was very nearly my natural tone. "Don't worry, Edith. It's all right. I've known it right along."

"Pooh!" Edith returned sagely. "So do I know I've got to die and be buried someday. Its being inevitable doesn't make it any more cheerful." She went out, but she came back in a moment and stuck her head through the door.

"*That's* the only inevitable thing there is," she said, taking up the conversation—an old habit of hers—where she had left off.

"I don't know what you are talking about," I retorted, turning my back on her. "And anyhow, I regard your suggestion as immoral." But when I turned again, she had gone.

That Saturday afternoon at four o'clock the body of Allan Fleming was brought home, and placed in state, in the music room of the house.

Miss Jane had been missing since Thursday night. I called Hunter by telephone, and he had nothing to report.

Chapter XI

A Night in the Fleming Home

I HAD a tearful message from Hawes late that afternoon, and a little after five I went to the office. I found him offering late editions of the evening paper to a couple of clients, who were edging toward the door. His expression when he saw me was pure relief, the clients', relief strongly mixed with irritation.

I put the best face on the matter that I could, saw my visitors, and left alone, prepared to explain to Hawes what I could hardly explain to myself.

"I've been unavoidably detained, Hawes," I said. "Miss Jane Maitland has disappeared from her home."

"So I understood you over the telephone." He had brought my mail and stood by impassively.

"Also, her brother-in-law is dead."

"The papers are full of it."

"There was no one to do anything, Hawes. I was obliged to stay," I apologized. I was ostentatiously examining my letters and Hawes said nothing. I looked up at him sideways, and he looked down at me. Not a muscle of his face quivered, save one eye, which has a peculiar twitching of the lid when he is excited. It gave him a sardonic appearance of winking. He winked at me then.

"Don't wait, Hawes," I said guiltily, and he took his hat and went out. Every line of his back was accusation. The sag of his shoulders told me I had let my biggest case go by default that day; the forward tilt of his head, that I was probably insane; the very grip with which he seized the doorknob, his "good night" from around the door, that he knew there was a woman at the bottom of it all. As he closed the door behind him, I put down my letters and dropped my face in my hands. Hawes was right. No amount of professional zeal could account for the interest I had taken. Partly through force of circumstances, partly of my own volition, I had placed myself in the position of first friend to a family with which I had had only professional relations; I had even enlisted Edith, when my acquaintance with Margery Fleming was only three days old! And at the thought of the girl, of Wardrop's inefficiency and my own hopelessness, I groaned aloud.

I had not heard the door open.

"I forgot to tell you that a gentleman was here half a dozen times today to see you. He didn't give any name."

I dropped my hands. From around the door Hawes' nervous eye was winking wildly.

"You're not sick, Mr. Knox?"

"Never felt better."

"I thought I heard—"

"I was singing," I lied, looking him straight in the eye.

He backed nervously to the door.

"I have a little sherry in my office, Mr. Knox—twenty-six years in the wood. If you—"

"For God's sake, Hawes, there's nothing the matter with me!" I exclaimed, and he went. But I heard him stand a perceptible time out-side the door before he tiptoed away.

Almost immediately after, someone entered the waiting room, and the next moment I was facing, in the doorway, a man I had never seen before.

He was a tall man, with a thin, colorless beard trimmed to a Vandyke point, and pale eyes blinking behind glasses. He had a soft hat crushed in his hand, and his whole manner was one of subdued excitement.

"Mr. Knox?" he asked, from the doorway.

"Yes. Come in."

"I have been here six times since noon," he said, dropping rather than sitting in a chair. "My name is Lightfoot. I am—was—Mr. Fleming's cashier."

"Yes?"

"I was terribly shocked at the news of his death," he stumbled on, getting no help from me. "I was in town and if I had known in time I could have kept some of the details out of the papers. Poor Fleming—to think he would end it that way."

"End it?"

"Shoot himself." He watched me closely.

"But he didn't," I protested. "It was not suicide, Mr. Lightfoot. According to the police, it was murder."

His cold eyes narrowed like a cat's. "Murder is an ugly word, Mr. Knox. Don't let us be sensational. Mr. Fleming had threatened to kill himself more than once; ask young Wardrop. He was sick and despon-dent; he left his home without a word, which points strongly to emo-tional insanity. He could have gone to any one of a half-dozen large clubs here, or at the capital. Instead, he goes to a little third-rate polit-ical club, where, presumably, he does his own cooking and hides in a dingy room. Is that sane? Murder! It was suicide, and that puppy Wardrop knows it well enough. I—I wish I had him by the throat!"

He had worked himself into quite a respectable rage, but now he calmed himself.

"I have seen the police," he went on. "They agree with me that it was suicide, and the party newspapers will straighten it out tomorrow. It is only unfortunate that the murder theory was given so much publicity. The *Times-Post*, which is Democratic, of course, I cannot handle."

I sat stupefied.

"Suicide!" I said finally. "With no weapon, no powder marks, and with a half-finished letter at his elbow."

He brushed my interruption aside.

"Mr. Fleming had been—careless," he said. "I can tell you in confidence, that some of the state funds had been deposited in the Borough Bank of Manchester, and—the Borough Bank closed its doors at ten o'clock today."

I was hardly surprised at that, but the whole trend of events was amazing.

"I arrived here last night," he said, "and I searched the city for Mr. Fleming. This morning I heard the news. I have just come from the house: his daughter referred me to you. After all, what I want is a small matter. Some papers—state documents—are missing, and no doubt are among Mr. Fleming's private effects. I would like to go through his papers, and leave tonight for the capital."

"I hardly have the authority," I replied doubtfully. "Miss Fleming, I suppose, would have no objection. His private secretary, Wardrop, would be the one to superintend such a search."

"Can you find Wardrop—at once?"

Something in his eagerness put me on my guard.

"I will make an attempt," I said. "Let me have the name of your hotel, and I will telephone you if it can be arranged for tonight."

He had to be satisfied with that, but his eagerness seemed to me to be almost desperation. Oddly enough, I could not locate Wardrop after all. I got the Maitland house by telephone, to learn that he had left there about three o'clock and had not come back.

I went to the Fleming house for dinner. Edith was still there, and we both tried to cheer Margery, a sad little figure in her black clothes. After the meal, I called Lightfoot at his hotel, and told him that I could not find Wardrop, that there were no papers at the house, and that the office safe would have to wait until Wardrop was found to open it. He was disappointed and furious; like a good many men who are physical cowards, he said a great deal over the telephone that he would not have dared to say to my face, and I cut him off by hanging up the receiver. From that minute, in the struggle that was coming, like Fred, I was "forninst" the government.

It was arranged that Edith should take Margery home with her for the night. I thought it a good idea; the very sight of Edith tucking in her babies and sitting down beside the library lamp to embroider me a scarfpin holder for Christmas would bring Margery back to normal again. Except in the matter of Christmas gifts, Edith is the sanest woman I know; I recognized it at the dinner table, where she had the little girl across from her planning her mourning hats before the dinner was half finished.

When we rose at last, Margery looked toward the music room, where the dead man lay in state. But Edith took her by the arm and pushed her toward the stairs.

"Get your hat on right away, while Jack calls a cab," she directed. "I must get home, or Fred will keep the boys up until nine o'clock. He is absolutely without principle."

When Margery came down, there was a little red spot burning in each pale cheek, and she ran down the stairs like a scared child. At the bottom she clutched the newel post and looked behind fearfully.

"What's the matter?" Edith demanded, glancing uneasily over her shoulder.

"Someone has been upstairs," Margery panted. "Somebody has been staying in the house while we were away."

"Nonsense," I said, seeing that her fright was infecting Edith. "What makes you think that?"

"Come and look," she said, gaining courage, I suppose, from a masculine presence. And so we went up the long stairs, the two girls clutching hands, and I leading the way and inclined to scoff.

At the door of a small room next to what had been Allan Fleming's bedroom, we paused and I turned on the light.

"Before we left," Margery said more quietly, "I closed this room myself. It had just been done over, and the pale blue soils so easily I came in the last thing, and saw covers put over everything. Now look at it!"

It was a sort of boudoir, filled with feminine knickknacks and mahogany lounging chairs. Wherever possible, a pale brocade had been used, on the empire couch, in panels in the wall, covering cushions on the window seat. It was evidently Margery's private sitting room.

The linen cover that had been thrown over the divan was folded back, and a pillow from the window seat bore the imprint of a head. The table was still covered, knobby protuberances indicating the pictures and books beneath. On one corner of the table, where the cover had been pushed aside, was a cup, empty and clean-washed, and as if to prove her contention, Margery picked up from the floor a newspaper, dated Friday morning, the twenty-second.

A used towel in the bathroom nearby completed the inventory. Margery had been right; someone had used the room while the house was closed.

"Might it not have been your—father?" Edith asked, when we stood again at the foot of the stairs. "He could have come here to look for something, and lain down to rest."

"I don't think so," Margery said wanly. "I left the door so he could get in with his key, but—he always used his study coach. I don't think he ever spent five minutes in my sitting room in his life."

We had to let it go at that finally. I put them in a cab, and saw them start away; then I went back into the house. I had arranged to sleep there and generally to look after things—as I said before. Whatever scruples I had had about taking charge of Margery Fleming and her affairs had faded with Wardrop's defection and the new mystery of the blue boudoir.

The lower floor of the house was full of people that night, local and state politicians, newspaper men and the usual crowd of the morbidly curious. The undertaker took everything in hand, and late that evening I could hear them carrying in tropical plants and stands for the flowers that were already arriving. Whatever panoply the death scene had lacked, Allan Fleming was lying in state now.

At midnight things grew quiet. I sat in the library, reading, until then, when an undertaker's assistant in a pink shirt and polka-dot cravat came to tell me that everything was done.

"Is it customary for somebody to stay up, on occasions like this?" I asked. "Isn't there an impression that wandering cats may get into the room, or something of that sort?"

"I don't think it will be necessary, sir," he said, trying to conceal a smile. "It's all a matter of taste. Some people like to take their troubles hard. Since they don't put money on their eyes anymore, nobody wants to rob the dead."

He left with that cheerful remark, and I closed and locked the house after him. I found Bella in the basement kitchen with all the lights burning full, and I stood at the foot of the stairs while she scooted to bed like a scared rabbit. She was a strange creature, Bella—not so stupid as she looked, but sullen, morose—"smoldering" about expresses it.

I closed the doors into the dining room and, leaving one light in the hall, went up to bed. A guest room in the third story had been assigned me, and I was tired enough to have slept on the floor. The telephone bell rang just after I got into bed, and grumbling at my luck, I went down to the lower floor.

It was the *Times-Post,* and the man at the telephone was in a hurry.

"This is the *Times-Post.* Is Mr. Wardrop there?"

"No."

"Who is this?"

"This is John Knox."

"The attorney?"

"Yes."

"Mr. Knox, are you willing to put yourself on record that Mr. Fleming committed suicide?"

"I am not going to put myself on record at all."

"Tonight's *Star* says you call it suicide, and that you found him with the revolver in his hand."

"The *Star* lies!" I retorted, and the man at the other end chuckled.

"Many thanks," he said, and rang off.

I went back to bed, irritated that I had betrayed myself. Loss of sleep for two nights, however, had told on me: in a short time I was sound asleep.

I wakened with difficulty. My head felt stupid and heavy, and I was burning with thirst. I sat up and wondered vaguely if I were going to be ill, and I remember that I felt too weary to get a drink. As I roused, however, I found that part of my discomfort came from bad ventilation, and I opened a window and looked out.

The window was a side one, opening on to a space perhaps eight feet wide, which separated it from its neighbor. Across from me was only a blank red wall, but the night air greeted me refreshingly. The wind was blowing hard, and a shutter was banging somewhere below. I leaned out and looked down into the well-like space beneath me. It was one of those apparently chance movements that have vital consequences, and that have always made me believe in the old Calvinistic creed of foreordination.

Below me, on the wall across, was a rectangle of yellow light, reflected from the library window of the Fleming home. There was someone in the house.

As I still stared, the light was slowly blotted out—not as if the light had been switched off, but by a gradual decreasing in size of the lighted area. The library shade had been drawn.

My first thought was burglars: my second—Lightfoot. No matter who it was, there was no one who had business there. Luckily, I had brought my revolver with me from Fred's that day, and it was under my pillow; to get it, put out the light and open the door quietly, took only a minute. I was in pajamas, barefoot, as on another almost similar occasion, but I was better armed than before.

I got to the second floor without hearing or seeing anything suspicious, but from there I could see that the light in the hall had been extinguished. The unfamiliarity of the house, the knowledge of the silent figure in the drawing room at the foot of the stairs, and of whatever might be waiting in the library beyond, made my position uncomfortable, to say the least.

I don't believe in the man who is never afraid: he doesn't deserve the credit he gets. It's the fellow who is scared to death, whose knees knock together, and who totters rather than walks into danger, who is the real hero. Not that I was as bad as that, but I would have liked to know where the electric switch was, and to have seen the trap before I put my head in.

The stairs were solidly built, and did not creak. I felt my way down by the baluster, which required my right hand, and threw my revolver to my left. I got safely to the bottom, and around the newel post; there was still a light in the library, and the door was not entirely closed. Then, with my usual bad luck, I ran into a heap of folding chairs that had been left by the undertaker, and if the crash paralyzed me, I don't know what it did to the intruder in the library.

The light was out in an instant, and with concealment at an end, I broke for the door and threw it open, standing there with my revolver leveled. We—the man in the room and I—were both in absolute darkness. He had the advantage of me. He knew my location, and I could not guess his.

"Who is here?" I demanded.

Only silence, except that I seemed to hear rapid breathing.

"Speak up, or I'll shoot!" I said, not without an ugly feeling that he might be—even probably was—taking careful aim by my voice. The darkness was intolerable: I reached cautiously to the left and found, just beyond the door frame, the electric switch. As I turned it, the light flashed up. The room was empty, but a portière in a doorway at my right was still shaking.

I leaped for the curtain and dragged it aside, to have a door just close in my face. When I had jerked it open, I found myself in a short hall, and there were footsteps to my left. I blundered along in the semi-darkness, into a black void which must have been the dining room, for my outstretched hand skirted the table. The footsteps seemed only beyond my reach, and at the other side of the room the swinging door into the pantry was still swaying when I caught it.

I made a misstep in the pantry, and brought up against a blank wall. It seemed to me I heard the sound of feet running up steps, and when I found a door at last, I threw it open and dashed in.

The next moment the solid earth slipped from under my feet, I threw out my hand, and it met a cold wall, smooth as glass. Then I fell—fell an incalculable distance, and the blackness of the night came over me and smothered me.

Chapter XII

My Commission

⤜⤛

WHEN I came to, I was lying in darkness, and the stillness was absolute. When I tried to move, I found I was practically a prisoner: I had fallen into an air shaft, or something of the kind. I could not move my arms, where they were pinioned to my sides, and I was half-lying, half-crouching, in a semi-vertical position. I worked one arm loose and managed to make out that my prison was probably the dumbwaiter shaft to the basement kitchen.

I had landed on top of the slide, and I seemed to be tied in a knot. The revolver was under me, and if it had exploded during the fall it had done no damage. I can hardly imagine a more unpleasant position. If the man I had been following had so chosen, he could have made away with me in any one of a dozen unpleasant ways—he could have filled me as full of holes as a sieve, or scalded me, or done anything, pretty much, that he chose. But nothing happened. The house was impressively quiet.

I had fallen feet first, evidently, and then crumpled up unconscious, for one of my ankles was throbbing. It was some time before I could stand erect, and even by reaching, I could not touch the doorway above me. It must have taken five minutes for my confused senses to remember the wire cable, and to tug at it. I was a heavy load for the slide, accustomed to nothing weightier than political dinners, but with much creaking I got myself at last to the floor above, and stepped out, still into darkness, but free.

I still held the revolver, and I lighted the whole lower floor. But I found nothing in the dining room or the pantry. Everything was locked and in good order. A small alcove off the library came next; it was undisturbed, but a tabouret lay on its side, and a half-dozen books had been taken from a low bookcase, and lay heaped on a chair. In the library, however, everything was confusion. Desk drawers stood open— one of the linen shades had been pulled partly off its roller, a chair had been drawn up to the long mahogany table in the center of the room, with the electric dome overhead, and everywhere, on chairs, over the floor, heaped in stacks on the table, were papers.

After searching the lower floor, and finding everything securely locked, I went upstairs, convinced the intruder was still in the house. I made a systematic search of every room, looking into closets and under beds. Several times I had an impression, as I turned a corner, that someone was just ahead of me, but I was always disappointed. I gave up at last and, going down to the library, made myself as comfortable as I could, and waited for morning.

I heard Bella coming down the stairs, after seven sometime; she came slowly, with flagging footsteps, as if the slightest sound would send her scurrying to the upper regions again. A little later I heard her rattling the range in the basement kitchen, and I went upstairs and dressed.

I was too tired to have a theory about the night visitor; in fact, from that time on, I tried to have no theories of any kind. I was impressed with only one thing—that the enemy or enemies of the late Allan Fleming evidently carried their antagonism beyond the grave. As I put on my collar I wondered how long I could stay in this game, as I now meant to, and avoid lying in state in Edith's little drawing room, with flowers around and a gentleman in black gloves at the door.

I had my ankle strapped with adhesive that morning by my doctor and it gave me no more trouble. But I caught him looking curiously at the blue bruise on my forehead where Wardrop had struck me with the chair, and at my nose, no longer swollen, but mustard-yellow at the bridge.

"Been doing any boxing lately?" he asked, as I laced up my shoe.

"Not for two or three years."

"New machine?"

"No."

He smiled at me quizzically from his desk.

"How does the other fellow look?" he inquired, and to my haltingly invented explanation of my battered appearance, he returned the same enigmatical smile.

That day was uneventful. Margery and Edith came to the house for about an hour and went back to Fred's again.

A cousin of the dead man, an elderly bachelor named Parker, appeared that morning and signified his willingness to take charge of the house during that day. The very hush of his voice and his black tie prompted Edith to remove Margery from him as soon as she could, and as the girl dreaded the curious eyes of the crowd that filled the house, she was glad to go.

It was Sunday, and I went to the office only long enough to look over my mail. I dined in the middle of the day at Fred's, and felt heavy and stupid all afternoon as a result of thus reversing the habits of the week. In the afternoon I had my first conversation with Fred and Edith, while Margery and the boys talked quietly in the nursery. They had taken a great fancy to her, and she was almost cheerful when she was with them.

Fred had the morning papers around him on the floor, and was in his usual Sunday argumentative mood.

"Well," he said, when the nursery door upstairs had closed, "what was it, Jack? Suicide?"

"I don't know," I replied bluntly.

"What do you think?" he insisted.

"How can I tell?" Irritably. "The police say it was suicide, and they ought to know."

"The *Times-Post* says it was murder, and that they will prove it. And they claim the police have been called off."

I said nothing of Mr. Lightfoot, and his visit to the office, but I made a mental note to see the *Times-Post* people and learn, if I could, what they knew.

"I cannot help thinking that he deserved very nearly what he got," Edith broke in, looking much less vindictive than her words. "When one thinks of the ruin he brought to poor Henry Butler, and that Ellen has been practically an invalid ever since, I can't be sorry for him."

"What was the Butler story?" I asked. But Fred did not know, and Edith was as vague as women usually are in politics.

"Henry Butler was treasurer of the state, and Mr. Fleming was his cashier. I don't know just what the trouble was. But you remember that Henry Butler killed himself after he got out of the penitentiary, and Ellen has been in one hospital after another. I would like to have her come here for a few weeks, Fred," she said appealingly. "She is in some sanatorium or other now, and we might cheer her a little."

Fred moaned.

"Have her if you like, petty," he said resignedly, "but I refuse to be cheerful unless I feel like it. What about this young Wardrop, Jack? It looks to me as if the *Times-Post* reporter had a line on him."

"Hush," Edith said softly. "He is Margery's fiancé, and she might hear you."

"How do you know?" Fred demanded. "Did she tell you?"

"Look at her engagement ring," Edith threw back triumphantly. "And it's a perfectly beautiful solitaire, too."

I caught Fred's eye on me, and the very speed with which he shifted his gaze made me uncomfortable. I made my escape as soon as I could, on the plea of going out to Bellwood, and in the hall upstairs I met Margery.

"I saw Bella today," she said. "Mr. Knox, will you tell me why you stayed up last night? What happened in the house?"

"I—thought I heard someone in the library," I stammered, "but I found no one."

"Is that all the truth or only part of it?" she asked. "Why do men always evade issues with a woman?" Luckily, womanlike, she did not wait for a reply. She closed the nursery door and stood with her hand on the knob, looking down.

"I wonder what you believe about all this," she said. "Do you think my father—killed himself? You were there; you know. If someone would only tell me everything!"

It seemed to me it was her right to know. The boys were romping noisily in the nursery. Downstairs Fred and Edith were having their Sunday afternoon discussion of what in the world had become of the money from Fred's latest book. Margery and I sat down on the stairs, and, as well as I could remember the details, I told her what had happened at the White Cat. She heard me through quietly.

"And so the police have given up the case!" she said despairingly. "And if they had not, Harry would have been arrested. Is there nothing I can do? Do I have to sit back with my hands folded?"

"The police have not exactly given up the case," I told her, "but there is such a thing, of course, as stirring up a lot of dust and then running to cover like blazes before it settles. By the time the public has wiped it out of its eyes and sneezed it out of its nose and coughed it out of its larynx, the dust has settled in a heavy layer, clues are obliterated, and the public lifts its skirts and chooses another direction. The NO THOROUGHFARE sign is up."

She sat there for fifteen minutes, interrupted by occasional noisy excursions from the nursery, which resulted in her acquiring by degrees a lapful of broken wheels, three-legged horses and a live water beetle which the boys had found under the kitchen sink and imprisoned in a glass-topped box, where, to its bewilderment, they were assiduously offering it dead and mangled flies. But our last five minutes were undisturbed, and the girl brought out with an effort the request she had tried to make all day.

"Whoever killed my father—and it was murder, Mr. Knox—whoever did it is going free to save a scandal. All my friends"—she smiled bitterly—"are afraid of the same thing. But I cannot sit quiet and think nothing can be done. I *must* know, and you are the only one who seems willing to try to find out."

So it was, that when I left the house a half hour later, I was committed. I had been commissioned by the girl I loved—for it had come to that—to clear her lover of her father's murder, and so give him back to her—not in so many words, but I was to follow up the crime, and the rest followed. And I was morally certain of two things—first, that her lover was not worthy of her, and second, and more to the point, that innocent or guilty, he was indirectly implicated in the crime.

I had promised her also to see Miss Letitia that day if I could, and I turned over the events of the preceding night as I walked toward the station, but I made nothing of them. One thing occurred to me, however. Bella had told Margery that I had been up all night. Could Bella—? But I dismissed the thought as absurd—Bella, who had scuttled to bed in a panic of fright, would never have dared the lower floor alone, and Bella, given all the courage in the world, could never have moved with the swiftness and light certainty of my midnight prowler. It had not been Bella.

But after all, I did not go to Bellwood. I met Hunter on my way to the station, and he turned around and walked with me.

"So you've lain down on the case!" I said, when we had gone a few steps without speaking.

He grumbled something unintelligible and probably unrepeatable.

"Of course," I persisted, "being a simple and uncomplicated case of suicide, there was nothing in it anyhow. If it had been a murder, under peculiar circumstances—"

He stopped and gripped my arm.

"For ten cents," he said gravely, "I would tell the chief and a few others what I think of them. And then I'd go out and get full."

"Not on ten cents!"

"I'm going out of the business," he stormed. "I'm going to drive a garbage wagon: it's cleaner than this job. Suicide! I never saw a cleaner case of—" He stopped suddenly. "Do you know Burton—of the *Times-Post?*"

"No, I've heard of him."

"Well, he's your man. They're dead against the ring, and Burton's been given the case. He's as sharp as a steel trap. You two get together."

He paused at a corner. "Good-bye," he said dejectedly. "I'm off to hunt some boys that have been stealing milk bottles. That's about my size, these days." He turned around, however, before he had gone many steps and came back.

"Wardrop has been missing since yesterday afternoon," he said. "That is, he thinks he's missing. We've got him all right."

I gave up my Bellwood visit for the time, and taking a car downtown, I went to the *Times-Post* office. The Monday morning edition was already under way, as far as the staff was concerned, and from the waiting room I could see three or four men, with their hats on, most of them rattling typewriters. Burton came in in a moment, a red-haired young fellow, with a short thick nose and a muggy skin. He was rather stocky in build, and the pugnacity of his features did not hide the shrewdness of his eyes.

I introduced myself, and at my name his perfunctory manner changed.

"Knox!" he said. "I called you last night over the phone."

"Can't we talk in a more private place?" I asked, trying to raise my voice above the confusion of the next room. In reply he took me into a tiny office, containing a desk and two chairs, and separated by an eight-foot partition from the other room.

"This is the best we have," he explained cheerfully. "Newspapers are agents of publicity, not privacy—if you don't care what you say."

I liked Burton. There was something genuine about him; after Wardrop's kid-glove finish, he was a relief.

"Hunter, of the detective bureau, sent me here," I proceeded, "about the Fleming case."

He took out his notebook. "You are the fourth today," he said. "Hunter himself, Lightfoot from Plattsburg, and McFeely here in town.

Well, Mr. Knox, are you willing now to put yourself on record that Fleming committed suicide?"

"No," I said firmly. "It is my belief that he was murdered."

"And that the secretary fellow, what's his name?—Wardrop?—that he killed him?"

"Possibly."

In reply Burton fumbled in his pocket and brought up a pasteboard box, filled with jeweler's cotton. Underneath was a small object, which he passed to me with care.

"I got it from the coroner's physician, who performed the autopsy," he said casually. "You will notice that it is a thirty-two, and that the revolver they took from Wardrop was a thirty-eight. Question, where's the other gun?"

I gave him back the bullet, and he rolled it around on the palm of his hand.

"Little thing, isn't it?" he said. "We think we're lords of creation, until we see a quarter-inch bichloride tablet, or a bit of lead like this. Look here." He dived into his pocket again and drew out a roll of ordinary brown paper. When he opened it, a bit of white chalk fell on the desk.

"Look at that," he said dramatically. "Kill an army with it, and they'd never know what struck them. Cyanide of potassium—and the druggist that sold it ought to be choked."

"Where did it come from?" I asked curiously. Burton smiled his cheerful smile.

"It's a beautiful case, all around," he said, as he got his hat. "I haven't had any Sunday dinner yet, and it's five o'clock. Oh—the cyanide? Clarkson, the cashier of the bank Fleming ruined, took a bite off that corner right there, this morning."

"Clarkson!" I exclaimed. "How is he?"

"God only knows," said Burton gravely, from which I took it Clarkson was dead.

Chapter XIII

Sizzling Metal

❦

BURTON listened while he ate, and his cheerful comments were welcome enough after the depression of the last few days. I told him, after some hesitation, the whole thing, beginning with the Maitland pearls and ending with my drop down the dumbwaiter. I knew I was absolutely safe in doing so: there is no person to whom I would rather tell a secret than a newspaperman. He will go out of his way to keep it: he will lock it in the depth of his bosom, and keep it until seventy times seven. Also, you may threaten the rack or offer a larger salary; the seal does not come off his lips until the word is given. If then he makes a scarehead of it, and gets in three columns of space and as many photographs, it is his just reward.

So—I told Burton everything, and he ate enough beefsteak for two men, and missed not a word I said.

"The money Wardrop had in the grip—that's easy enough explained," he said. "Fleming used the Borough Bank to deposit state funds in. He must have known it was rotten: he and Clarkson were as thick as thieves. According to a time-honored custom in our land of the brave and home of the free, a state treasurer who is crooked can, in such a case, draw on such a bank without security, on his personal note, which is usually worth its value by the pound as old paper."

"And Fleming did that?"

"He did. Then things got bad at the Borough Bank. Fleming had had to divide with Schwartz and the Lord only knows who all, but it was Fleming who had to put in the money to avert a crash—the word crash being synonymous with scandal in this case. He scrapes together a paltry hundred thousand, which Wardrop gets at the capital, and brings on. Wardrop is robbed, or says he is; the bank collapses and Clarkson, driven to the wall, kills himself, just after Fleming is murdered. What does that sound like?"

"Like Clarkson!" I exclaimed. "And Clarkson knew Fleming was hiding at the White Cat!"

"Now, then, take the other theory," he said, pushing aside his cup. "Wardrop goes in to Fleming with a story that he has been robbed: Fleming gets crazy and attacks him. All that is in the morning—Friday. Now, then—Wardrop goes back there that night. Within twenty minutes after he enters the club he rushes out, and when Hunter follows him, he says he is looking for a doctor, to get cocaine for a gentleman upstairs. He is white and trembling. They go back together, and find you there, and Fleming dead. Wardrop tells two stories: first he says Fleming committed suicide just before he left. Then he changes it and says he was dead when he arrived there. He produces the weapon with which Fleming is supposed to have killed himself, and which, by the way, Miss Fleming identified yesterday as her father's. But there are two discrepancies. Wardrop practically admitted that he had taken that revolver from Fleming—not that night, but the morning before— during the quarrel."

"And the other discrepancy?"

"The bullet. Nobody ever fired a thirty-two bullet out of a thirty-eight caliber revolver—unless he was trying to shoot a double-compound curve. Now, then, who does it look like?"

"Like Wardrop," I confessed. "By Jove, they didn't both do it."

"And he didn't do it himself for two good reasons: he had no revolver that night, and there were no powder marks."

"And the eleven twenty-two, and Miss Maitland's disappearance?"

He looked at me with his quizzical smile.

"I'll have to have another steak, if I'm to settle that," he said. "I can only solve one murder on one steak. But disappearances are my specialty; perhaps, if I have a piece of pie and some cheese—"

But I got him away at last, and we walked together down the street.

"I can't quite see the old lady in it," he confessed. "She hadn't any grudge against Fleming, had she? Wouldn't be likely to forget herself temporarily and kill him?"

"Good Lord!" I said. "Why, she's sixty-five, and as timid and gentle a little old lady as ever lived."

"Curls?" he asked, turning his bright blue eyes on me.

"Yes," I admitted.

"Wouldn't be likely to have eloped with the minister or advertised for a husband, or anything like that?"

"You would have to know her to understand," I said resignedly. "But she didn't do any of those things, and she didn't run off to join a theatrical troupe. Burton, who do you think was in the Fleming house last night?"

"Lightfoot," he said succinctly.

He stopped under a streetlamp and looked at his watch.

"I believe I'll run over to the capital tonight," he said. "While I'm gone—I'll be back tomorrow night or the next morning—I wish you would do two things. Find Rosie O'Grady, or whatever her name is, and locate Carter. That's probably not his name, but it will answer for a while. Then get your friend Hunter to keep him in sight for a while, until I come back anyhow. I'm beginning to enjoy this; it's more fun than a picture puzzle. We're going to make the police department look like a kindergarten playing jackstraws."

"And the second thing I am to do?"

"Go to Bellwood and find out a few things. It's all well enough to say the old lady was a meek and timid person, but if you want to know her peculiarities, go to her neighbors. When people leave the beaten path, the neighbors always know it before the families."

He stopped before a drugstore.

"I'll have to pack for my little jaunt," he said, and purchased a toothbrush, which proved to be the extent of his preparations. We separated at the station, Burton to take his red hair and his toothbrush to Plattsburg, I to take a taxicab, and armed with a page torn from the classified directory to inquire at as many of the twelve Anderson's drugstores as might be necessary to locate Delia's gentleman friend, "the clerk," through him Delia, and through Delia, the mysterious Carter, "who was not really a butler."

It occurred to me somewhat tardily, that I knew nothing of Delia but her given name. A telephone talk with Margery was of little assistance: Delia had been a new maid, and if she had heard her other name, she had forgotten it.

I had checked off eight of the Andersons on my list, without result, and the taximeter showed something over nineteen dollars, when the driver drew up at the curb.

"Gentleman in the other cab is hailing you, sir," he said over his shoulder.

"The other cab?"

"The one that has been following us."

I opened the door and glanced behind. A duplicate of my cab stood perhaps fifty feet behind, and from it a familiar figure was slowly emerging, carrying on a high-pitched argument with the chauffeur. The figure stopped to read the taximeter, shook his fist at the chauffeur, and approached me, muttering audibly. It was Davidson.

"That liar and thief back there has got me rung up for nineteen dollars," he said, ignoring my amazement. "Nineteen dollars and forty cents! He must have the thing counting the revolutions of all four wheels!"

He walked around and surveyed my expense account, at the driver's elbow. Then he hit the meter a smart slap, but the figures did not change.

"Nineteen dollars!" he repeated, dazed. "Nineteen dollars and—look here," he called to his driver, who had brought the cab close, "it's only thirty cents here. Your clock's ten cents fast."

"But how—" I began.

"You back up to nineteen dollars and thirty cents," he persisted, ignoring me. "If you'll back up to twelve dollars, I'll pay it. That's all I've got." Then he turned on me irritably. "Good heavens, man," he exclaimed, "do you mean to tell me you've been to eight drugstores this Sunday evening and spent nineteen dollars and thirty cents, and haven't got a drink yet?"

"Do you think I'm after a drink?" I asked him. "Now look here, Davidson, I rather think you know what I am after. If you don't, it doesn't matter. But since you are coming along anyhow, pay your man off and come with me. I don't like to be followed."

He agreed without hesitation, borrowed eight dollars from me to augment his twelve and crawled in with me.

"The next address on the list is the right one," he said, as the man waited for directions. "I did the same round yesterday, but not being a plutocrat, I used the streetcars and my legs. And because you're a decent fellow and don't have to be chloroformed to have an idea injected, I'm going to tell you something. There were eleven roundsmen as well as the sergeant who heard me read the note I found at the Fleming house that night. You may have counted them through the window. A dozen plainclothesmen read it before morning. When the news of Mr. Fleming's mur— death came out, I thought this fellow Carter might know something, and I trailed Delia through this Mamie Brennan. When I got there I found Tom Brannigan and four other detectives sitting in the parlor, and Miss Delia, in a blue silk waist, making eyes at every mother's son of them."

I laughed in spite of my disappointment. Davidson leaned forward and closed the window at the driver's back. Then he squared around and faced me.

"Understand me, Mr. Knox," he said. "Mr. Fleming killed himself. You and I are agreed on that. Even if you aren't just convinced of it, I'm telling you, and—better let it drop, sir." Under his quiet manner I felt a threat: it served to rouse me.

"I'll let it drop when I'm through with it," I asserted, and got out my list of addresses.

"You'll let it drop because it's too hot to hold," he retorted, with the suspicion of a smile. "If you are determined to know about Carter, I can tell you everything that is necessary."

The chauffeur stopped his engine with an exasperated jerk and settled down in his seat, every line of his back bristling with irritation.

"I prefer learning from Carter himself."

He leaned back in his seat and produced an apple from the pocket of his coat.

"You'll have to travel some to do it, son," he said. "Carter left for parts unknown last night, taking with him enough money to keep him in comfort for some little time."

"Until all this blows over," I said bitterly.

"The trip was for the benefit of his health. He has been suffering— and is still suffering—from a curious lapse of memory." Davidson smiled at me engagingly. "He has entirely forgotten everything that occurred from the time he entered Mr. Fleming's employment, until that gentleman left home. I doubt if he will ever recover."

With Carter gone, his retreat covered by the police, supplied with funds from some problematical source, further search for him was worse than useless. In fact, Davidson strongly intimated that it might be dangerous and would certainly be unpleasant. I yielded ungraciously and ordered the cab to take me home. But on the way, I cursed my folly for not having followed this obvious clue earlier, and I wondered what this thing could be that Carter knew, that was at least surmised by various headquarters men, and yet was so carefully hidden from the world at large.

The party newspapers had come out that day with a signed statement from Mr. Fleming's physician in Plattsburg that he had been in ill health and inclined to melancholia for some time. The air was thick with rumors of differences with his party: the dust cloud covered everything; pretty soon it would settle and hide the tracks of those who had hurried to cover under its protection.

Davidson left me at a corner downtown. He turned to give me a parting admonition.

"There's an old axiom in the mills around here, 'Never sit down on a piece of metal until you spit on it.' If it sizzles, don't sit." He grinned. "Your best position just now, young man, is standing, with your hands over your head. Confidentially, there ain't anything within expectorating distance just now that ain't pretty well het up."

He left me with that, and I did not see him again until the night at the White Cat, when he helped put me through the transom. Recently, however, I have met him several times. He invariably mentions the eight dollars and his intention of repaying it. Unfortunately, the desire and the ability have not yet happened to coincide.

I took the evening train to Bellwood, and got there shortly after eight, in the midst of the Sunday evening calm, and the calm of a place like Bellwood is the peace of death without the hope of resurrection.

I walked slowly up the main street, which was lined with residences; the town relegated its few shops to less desirable neighborhoods. My first intention had been to see the Episcopal minister, but the rectory was dark, and a burst of organ music from the church near reminded me again of the Sunday evening services.

Promiscuous inquiry was not advisable. So far, Miss Jane's disappearance was known to very few, and Hunter had advised caution. I wandered up the street and turned at random to the right; a few doors ahead a newish red brick building proclaimed itself the post office, and gave the only sign of life in the neighborhood. It occurred to me that here inside was the one individual who, theoretically at least, in a small place always knows the idiosyncrasies of its people.

The door was partly open, for the spring night was sultry. The postmaster proved to be a one-armed veteran of the Civil War, and he was sorting rapidly the contents of a mailbag, emptied on the counter.

"No delivery tonight," he said shortly. "Sunday delivery, two to three."

"I suppose, then, I couldn't get a dollar's worth of stamps," I regretted. He looked up over his glasses.

"We don't sell stamps on Sunday nights," he explained, more politely. "But if you're in a hurry for them—"

"I am," I lied. And after he had gotten them out, counting them with a wrinkled finger, and tearing them off the sheet with the deliberation of age, I opened a general conversation.

"I suppose you do a good bit of business here?" I asked. "It seems like a thriving place."

"Not so bad; big mail here sometimes. First of the quarter, when bills are coming round, we have a rush, and holidays and Easter we've got to hire an express wagon."

It was when I asked him about his empty sleeve, however, and he had told me that he lost his arm at Chancellorsville, that we became really friendly. When he said he had been a corporal in General Maitland's command, my path was one of ease.

"The Maitland ladies! I should say I do," he said warmly. "I've been fighting with Letitia Maitland as long as I can remember. That woman will scrap with the angel Gabriel at the resurrection, if he wakes her up before she's had her sleep out."

"Miss Jane is not that sort, is she?"

"Miss Jane? She's an angel—she is that. She could have been married a dozen times when she was a girl, but Letitia wouldn't have it. I was after her myself, forty-five years ago. This was the Maitland farm in those days, and my father kept a country store down where the railroad station is now."

"I suppose from that the Maitland ladies are wealthy."

"Wealthy! They don't know what they're worth—not that it matters a mite to Jane Maitland. She hasn't called her soul her own for so long that I guess the good Lord won't hold her responsible for it."

All of which was entertaining, but it was much like an old-fashioned seesaw; it kept going, but it didn't make much progress. But now at last we took a step ahead.

"It's a shameful thing," the old man pursued, "that a woman as old as Jane should have to get her letters surreptitiously. For more than a year now she's been coming here twice a week for her mail, and I've been keeping it for her. Rain or shine, Mondays and Thursdays, she's been coming, and a sight of letters she's been getting, too."

"Did she come last Thursday?" I asked overeagerly. The postmaster, all at once, regarded me with suspicion.

"I don't know whether she did or not," he said coldly, and my further attempts to beguile him into conversation failed. I pocketed my stamps, and by that time his resentment at my curiosity was fading. He followed me to the door, and lowered his voice cautiously.

"Any news of the old lady?" he asked. "It ain't generally known around here that she's missing, but Heppie, the cook there, is a relation of my wife's."

"We have no news," I replied, "and don't let it get around, will you?"

He promised gravely.

"I was tellin' the missus the other day," he said, "that there is an old walled-up cellar under the Maitland place. Have you looked there?" He was disappointed when I said we had, and I was about to go when he called me back.

"Miss Jane didn't get her mail on Thursday, but on Friday that niece of hers came for it—two letters, one from the city and one from New York."

"Thanks," I returned, and went out into the quiet street.

I walked past the Maitland place, but the windows were dark and the house closed. Haphazard inquiry being out of the question, I took the ten-o'clock train back to the city. I had learned little enough, and that little I was at a loss to know how to use. For why had Margery gone for Miss Jane's mail *after* the little lady was missing? And why did Miss Jane carry on a clandestine correspondence?

The family had retired when I got home except Fred, who called from his study to ask for a rhyme for mosque. I could not think of one and suggested that he change the word to "temple." At two o'clock he banged on my door in a temper, said he had changed the rhythm to fit, and now he couldn't find a rhyme for "temple!" I suggested "dimple" drowsily, whereat he kicked the panel of the door and went to bed.

Chapter XIV

A Walk in the Park

∽⊗∽

THE funeral occurred on Monday. It was an ostentatious affair, with a long list of honorary pallbearers, a picked corps of city firemen in uniform ranged around the casket, and enough money wasted in floral pillows and sheaves of wheat tied with purple ribbon, to have given all the hungry children in town a square meal.

Amid all this state Margery moved, stricken and isolated. She went to the cemetery with Edith, Miss Letitia having sent a message that, having never broken her neck to see the man living, she wasn't going to do it to see him dead. The music was very fine, and the eulogy spoke of this patriot who had served his country so long and so well. "Following the flag," Fred commented under his breath, "as long as there was an appropriation attached to it."

And when it was all over, we went back to Fred's until the Fleming house could be put into order again. It was the best place in the world for Margery, for, with the children demanding her attention and applause every minute, she had no time to be blue.

Mrs. Butler arrived that day, which made Fred suspicious that Edith's plan to bring her far antedated his consent. But she was there when we got home from the funeral, and after one glimpse at her thin face and hollow eyes, I begged Edith to keep her away from Margery, for that day at least.

Fortunately, Mrs. Butler was exhausted by her journey, and retired to her room almost immediately. I watched her slender figure go up the stairs, and, with her black trailing gown and colorless face, she was an embodiment of all that is lonely and helpless. Fred closed the door behind her and stood looking at Edith and me.

"I tell you, honey," he declared, *"that* brought into a cheerful home is sufficient cause for divorce. Isn't it, Jack?"

"She is ill," Edith maintained valiantly. "She is my cousin, too, which gives her some claim on me, and my guest, which gives her more."

"Lady-love," Fred said solemnly, "if you do not give me the key to the cellarette, I shall have a chill. And let me beg this of you: if I ever get tired of this life, and shuffle off my mortality in a lumberyard, or a political club, and you go around like that, I shall haunt you. I swear it."

"Shuffle off," I dared him. "I will see that Edith is cheerful and happy."

From somewhere above, there came a sudden crash, followed by the announcement, made by a scared housemaid, that Mrs. Butler had fainted. Fred sniffed as Edith scurried upstairs.

"Hipped," he said shortly. "For two cents I'd go up and give her a good whiff of ammonia—not this aromatic stuff, but the genuine article. That would make her sit up and take notice. Upon my word, I can't think what possessed Edith; these spineless, soft-spoken, timid women are leeches on one's sympathies."

But Mrs. Butler was really ill, and Margery insisted on looking after her. It was an odd coincidence, the widow of one state treasurer and the orphaned daughter of his successor; both men had died violent deaths, in each case when a boiling under the political lid had threatened to blow it off.

The boys were allowed to have their dinner with the family that evening, in honor of Mrs. Butler's arrival, and it was a riotous meal. Margery got back a little of her color. As I sat across from her, and watched her expressions change, from sadness to resignation, and even gradually to amusement at the boys' antics, I wondered just how much she knew, or suspected, that she refused to tell me.

I remembered a woman—a client of mine—who said that whenever she sat near a railroad track and watched an engine thundering toward her, she tortured herself by picturing a child on the track, and wondering whether, under such circumstances, she would risk her life to save the child.

I felt a good bit that way; I was firmly embarked on the case now, and I tortured myself with one idea. Suppose I should find Wardrop guilty, and I should find extenuating circumstances—what would I do? Publish the truth, see him hanged or imprisoned, and break Margery's heart? Or keep back the truth, let her marry him, and try to forget that I had had a hand in the whole wretched business?

After all, I decided to try to stop my imaginary train. Prove Wardrop innocent, I reasoned with myself, get to the bottom of this thing, and then—it would be man and man. A fair field and no favor. I suppose my proper attitude, romantically taken, was to consider Margery's engagement ring an indissoluble barrier. But this was not romance; I was fighting for my life happiness, and as to the ring—well, I am of the opinion that if a man really loves a woman, and thinks he can make her happy, he will tell her so if she is strung with engagement rings to the ends of her fingers. Dangerous doctrine? Well, this is not propaganda.

Tuesday found us all more normal. Mrs. Butler had slept some, and very commendably allowed herself to be tea'd and toasted in bed. The boys were started to kindergarten, after ten minutes of frenzied caphunting. Margery went with me along the hall when I started for the office.

"You have not learned anything?" she asked cautiously, glancing back to Edith, at the telephone calling the grocer frantically for the Monday morning supply of soap and starch.

"Not much," I evaded. "Nothing definite, anyhow. Margery, you are not going back to the Monmouth Avenue house again, are you?"

"Not just yet; I don't think I could. I suppose, later, it will have to be sold, but not at once. I shall go to Aunt Letitia's first."

"Very well," I said. "Then you are going to take a walk with me this afternoon in the park. I won't take no; you need the exercise, and I need—to talk to you," I finished lamely.

When she had agreed, I went to the office. It was not much after nine, but, to my surprise, Burton was already there. He had struck up an acquaintance with Miss Grant, the stenographer, and that usually frigid person had melted under the warmth of his red hair and his smile. She was telling him about her sister's baby having the whooping cough, when I went in.

"I wish I had studied law," he threw at me. " 'What shall it profit a man to become a lawyer and lose his own soul?' as the psalmist says. I like this ten-to-four business."

When we had gone into the inner office, and shut out Miss Grant and the whooping cough, he was serious instantly.

"Well," he said, sitting on the radiator and dangling his foot, "I guess we've got Wardrop for theft, anyhow."

"Theft?" I inquired.

"Well, larceny, if you prefer legal terms. I found where he sold the pearls—in Plattsburg, to a wholesale jeweler named, suggestively, Cashdollar."

"Then," I said conclusively, "if he took the pearls and sold them, as sure as I sit here, he took the money out of that Russia leather bag."

Burton swung his foot rhythmically against the pipes.

"I'm not so darned sure of it," he said calmly.

If he had any reason, he refused to give it. I told him, in my turn, of Carter's escape, aided by the police, and he smiled. "For a suicide it's causing a lot of excitement," he remarked. When I told him the little incident of the post office, he was much interested.

"The old lady's in it, somehow," he maintained. "She may have been lending Fleming money, for one thing. How do you know it wasn't her hundred thousand that was stolen?"

"I don't think she ever had the uncontrolled disposal of a dollar in her life."

"There's only one thing to do," Burton said finally, "and that is, find Miss Jane. If she's alive, she can tell something. I'll stake my fountain pen on that—and it's my dearest possession on earth, next to my mother. If Miss Jane is dead—well, somebody killed her, and it's time it was being found out."

"It's easy enough to say find her."

"It's easy enough to find her," he exploded. "Make a noise about it; send up rockets. Put a half-column ad in every paper in town, or—better still—give the story to the reporters and let them find her for you. I'd do it, if I wasn't tied up with this Fleming case. Describe her, how she walked, what she liked to eat, what she wore—in this case what she didn't wear. Lord, I wish I had that assignment! In forty-eight hours she will have been seen in a hundred different places, and one of them will be right. It will be a question of selection—that is, if she is alive."

In spite of his airy tone, I knew he was serious, and I felt he was right. The publicity part of it I left to him, and I sent a special delivery that morning to Bellwood, asking Miss Letitia to say nothing and to refer reporters to me. I had already been besieged with them, since my connection with the Fleming case, and a few more made no difference.

Burton attended to the matter thoroughly. The one-o'clock edition of an afternoon paper contained a short and vivid scarlet account of Miss Jane's disappearance. The evening editions were full, and while vague as to the manner of her leaving, were minute as regarded her personal appearance and characteristics.

To escape the threatened inundation of the morning paper men, I left the office early, and at four o'clock Margery and I stepped from a hill car into the park. She had been wearing a short, crepe-edged veil, but once away from the gaze of the curious, she took it off. I was glad to see she had lost the air of detachment she had worn for the last three days.

"Hold your shoulders well back," I directed, when we had found an isolated path, "and take long breaths. Try breathing in while I count ten."

She was very tractable—unusually so, I imagined, for her. We swung along together for almost a half hour, hardly talking. I was content merely to be with her, and the sheer joy of the exercise after her enforced confinement kept her silent. When she began to flag a little, I found a bench, and we sat down together. The bench had been lately painted, and although it seemed dry enough, I spread my handkerchief for her to sit on. Whereupon she called me "Sir Walter," and at the familiar jest we laughed like a pair of children.

I had made the stipulation that, for this one time, her father's death and her other troubles should be taboo, and we adhered to it religiously. A robin in the path was industriously digging out a worm; he had tackled a long one, and it was all he could manage. He took the available end in his beak and hopped back with the expression of one who sets his jaws and determines that this which should be, is to be. The worm stretched into a pinkish and attenuated line, but it neither broke nor gave.

"Horrid thing!" Margery said. "That is a disgraceful, heartless exhibition.

"The robin is a parent," I reminded her. "It is precisely the same as Fred, who twists, jerks, distorts and attenuates the English language in his magazine work, in order to have bread and ice cream and jelly cake for his two blooming youngsters."

She had taken off her gloves, and sat with her hands loosely clasped in her lap.

"I wish someone depended on me," she said pensively. "It's a terrible thing to feel that it doesn't matter to anyone—not vitally, anyhow—whether one is around or not. To have all my responsibilities taken away at once, and just to drift around, like this—oh, it's dreadful."

"You were going to be good," I reminded her.

"I didn't promise to be cheerful," she returned. "Besides my father, there was only one person in the world who cared about me, and I don't know where she is. Dear Aunt Jane!"

The sunlight caught the ring on her engagement finger, and she flushed suddenly as she saw me looking at it. We sat there for a while saying nothing; the long May afternoon was coming to a close. The paths began to fill with long lines of hurrying homeseekers, their day in office or factory at an end.

Margery got up at last and buttoned her coat. Then impulsively she held out her hand to me.

"You have been more than kind to me," she said hurriedly. "You have taken me into your home—and helped me through these dreadful days—and I will never forget it; never."

"I am not virtuous," I replied, looking down at her. "I couldn't help it. You walked into my life when you came to my office—was it only last week? The evil days are coming, I suppose, but just now nothing matters at all, save that you are you, and I am me."

She dropped her veil quickly, and we went back to the car. The prosaic world wrapped around us again; there was a heavy odor of restaurant coffee in the air; people bumped and jolted past us. To me they were only shadows; the real world was a girl in black and myself and the girl wore a betrothal ring which was not mine.

Chapter XV
Find the Woman

⤜✦⤛

MRS. Butler came down to dinner that night. She was more cheerful than I had yet seen her, and she had changed her mournful garments to something a trifle less depressing. With her masses of fair hair dressed high, and her face slightly animated, I realized what I had not done before—that she was the wreck of a very beautiful woman. Frail as she was, almost shrinkingly timid in her manner, there were times when she drew up her tall figure in something like its former stateliness. She had beautiful eyebrows, nearly black and perfectly penciled; they were almost incongruous in her colorless face.

She was very weak; she used a cane when she walked, and after dinner, in the library, she was content to sit impassive, detached, propped with cushions, while Margery read to the boys in their night nursery and Edith embroidered.

Fred had been fussing over a play for some time, and he had gone to read it to some manager or other. Edith was already spending the royalties.

"We could go a little ways out of town," she was saying, "and we could have an automobile; Margery says theirs will be sold, and it will certainly be a bargain. Jack, are you laughing at me?"

"Certainly *not*," I replied gravely. "Dream on, Edith. Shall we train the boys as chauffeurs, or shall we buy in the Fleming man, also cheap."

"I am sure," Edith said aggrieved, "that it costs more for horse feed this minute for your gray, Jack, than it would for gasoline."

"But Lady Gray won't eat gasoline," I protested. "She doesn't like it."

Edith turned her back on me and sewed. Near me, Mrs. Butler had languidly taken up the paper; suddenly she dropped it, and when I stooped and picked it up I noticed she was trembling.

"Is it true?" she demanded. "Is Robert Clarkson dead?"

"Yes," I assented. "He has been dead since Sunday morning—a suicide."

Edith had risen and come over to her. But Mrs. Butler was not fainting.

"I'm glad, glad," she said. Then she grew weak and semi-hysterical, laughing and crying in the same breath. When she had been helped upstairs, for in her weakened state it had been more of a shock than we realized, Margery came down and we tried to forget the scene we had just gone through.

"I am glad Fred was not here," Edith confided to me. "Ellen is a lovely woman, and as kind as she is mild; but in one of her—attacks, she is a little bit trying."

It was strange to contrast the way in which the two women took their similar bereavements. Margery represented the best type of normal American womanhood; Ellen Butler the neurasthenic; she demanded everything by her very helplessness and timidity. She was a constant drain on Edith's ready sympathy. That night, while I closed the house— Fred had not come in—I advised her to let Mrs. Butler go back to her sanatorium.

At twelve thirty I was still downstairs; Fred was out, and I waited for him, being curious to know the verdict on the play. The bell rang a few minutes before one, and I went to the door; someone in the vestibule was tapping the floor impatiently with his foot. When I opened the door, I was surprised to find that the late visitor was Wardrop.

He came in quietly, and I had a chance to see him well, under the hall light; the change three days had made was shocking. His eyes were sunk deep in his head, his reddened lids and twitching mouth told of little sleep, of nerves ready to snap. He was untidy, too, and a three days' beard hardly improved him.

"I'm glad it's you," he said, by way of greeting. "I was afraid you'd have gone to bed."

"It's the top of the evening yet," I replied perfunctorily, as I led the way into the library. Once inside, Wardrop closed the door and looked around him like an animal at bay.

"I came here," he said nervously, looking at the windows, "because I had an idea you'd keep your head. Mine's gone; I'm either crazy, or I'm on my way there."

"Sit down, man." I pushed a chair to him. "You don't look as if you have been in bed for a couple of nights."

He went to each of the windows and examined the closed shutters before he answered me.

"I haven't. You wouldn't go to bed either, if you thought you would never wake up."

"Nonsense."

"Well, it's true enough. Knox, there are people following me wherever I go; they eat where I eat; if I doze in my chair they come into my dreams!" He stopped there; then he laughed a little wildly. "That last isn't sane, but it's true. There's a man across the street now, eating an apple under a lamppost."

"Suppose you *are* under surveillance," I said. "It's annoying to have a detective following you around, but it's hardly serious. The police say now that Mr. Fleming killed himself; that was your own contention."

He leaned forward in his chair and, resting his hands on his knees, gazed at me somberly.

"Suppose I say he didn't kill himself?" Slowly. "Suppose I say he was murdered? Suppose—good God—suppose I killed him myself?"

I drew back in stupefaction, but he hurried on.

"For the last two days I've been wondering—if I did it! He hadn't any weapon; I had one, his. I hated him that day; I had tried to save him, and couldn't. My God, Knox, I might have gone off my head and done it—and not remember it. There have been cases like that."

His condition was pitiable. I looked around for some whisky, but the best I could do was a little port on the sideboard. When I came back he was sitting with bent head, his forehead on his palms.

"I've thought it all out," he said painfully. "My mother had spells of emotional insanity. Perhaps I went there, without knowing it, and killed him. I can see him, in the night, when I daren't sleep, toppling over onto that table, with a bullet wound in his head, and I am in the room, and I have his revolver in my pocket!"

"You give me your word you have no conscious recollection of hearing a shot fired."

"My word before Heaven," he said fervently. "But I tell you, Knox, he had no weapon. No one came out of that room as I went in and yet he was only swaying forward, as if I had shot him one moment, and caught him as he fell, the next. I was dazed; I don't remember yet what I told the police."

The expression of fear in his eyes was terrible to see. A gust of wind shook the shutters, and he jumped almost out of his chair.

"You will have to be careful," I said. "There have been cases where men confessed murders they never committed, driven by Heaven knows what method of undermining their mental resistance. You expose your imagination to 'third degree' torture of your own invention, and in two days more you will be able to add full details of the crime."

"I knew you would think me crazy," he put in, a little less somberly, "but just try it once: sit in a room by yourself all day and all night, with detectives watching you; sit there and puzzle over a murder of a man you are suspected of killing; you know you felt like killing him, and you have a revolver, and he is shot. Wouldn't you begin to think as I do?"

"Wardrop," I asked, trying to fix his wavering eyes with mine, "do you own a thirty-two-caliber revolver?"

"Yes."

I was startled beyond any necessity, under the circumstances. Many people have thirty-twos.

"That is, I had," he corrected himself. "It was in the leather bag that was stolen at Bellwood."

"I can relieve your mind of one thing," I said. "If your revolver was stolen with the leather bag, you had nothing to do with the murder. Fleming was shot with a thirty-two." He looked first incredulous, then relieved.

"Now, then," I pursued, "suppose Mr. Fleming had an enemy, a relentless one who would stoop to anything to compass his ruin. In his position he would be likely to have enemies. This person, let us say, knows what you carry in your grip, and steals it, taking away the funds that would have helped to keep the lid on Fleming's mismanagement for a time. In the grip is your revolver; would you know it again?"

He nodded affirmatively.

"This person—this enemy—finds the revolver, pockets it and at the first opportunity, having ruined Fleming, proceeds humanely to put him out of his suffering. Is it far-fetched?"

"There were a dozen—a hundred—people who would have been glad to ruin him." His gaze wavered again suddenly. It was evident that I had renewed an old train of thought.

"For instance?" I suggested, but he was on guard again.

"You forget one thing, Knox," he said, after a moment. "There was nobody else who could have shot him: the room was empty."

"Nonsense," I replied. "Don't forget the warehouse."

"The warehouse!"

"There is no doubt in my mind that he was shot from there. He was facing the open window, sitting directly under the light, writing. A shot fired through a broken pane of one of the warehouse windows would meet every requirement of the case: the empty room, the absence of powder marks—even the fact that no shot was heard. There was a report, of course, but the noise in the clubhouse and the thunderstorm outside covered it."

"By George!" he exclaimed. "The warehouse, of course. I never thought of it." He was relieved, for some reason.

"It's a question now of how many people knew he was at the club, and which of them hated him enough to kill him."

"Clarkson knew it," Wardrop said, "but he didn't do it."

"Why?"

"Because it was he who came to the door of the room while the detectives and you and I were inside, and called Fleming."

I pulled out my pocketbook and took out the scrap of paper which Margery had found pinned to the pillow in her father's bedroom. "Do you know what that means?" I asked, watching Wardrop's face. "That was found in Mr. Fleming's room two days after he left home. A similar scrap was found in Miss Jane Maitland's room when she disappeared. When Fleming was murdered, he was writing a letter; he said: 'The figures have followed me here.' When we know what those figures mean, Wardrop, we know why he was killed and who did it."

He shook his head hopelessly.

"I do not know," he said, and I believed him. He had gotten up and taken his hat, but I stopped him inside the door.

"You can help this thing in two ways," I told him. "I am going to give you something to do: you will have less time to be morbid. Find out, if you can, all about Fleming's private life in the last dozen years, especially the last three. See if there are any women mixed up in it, and try to find out something about this eleven twenty-two."

"Eleven twenty-two," he repeated, but I had not missed his change of expression when I said women.

"Also," I went on, "I want you to tell me who was with you the night you tried to break into the house at Bellwood."

He was taken completely by surprise: when he had gathered himself together his perplexity was overdone.

"With me!" he repeated. "I was alone, of course."

"I mean—the woman at the gate."

He lost his composure altogether then. I put my back against the door and waited for him to get himself in hand.

"There was a woman," I persisted, "and what is more, Wardrop, at this minute you believe she took your Russia leather bag and left a substitute."

He fell into the trap.

"But she couldn't," he quavered. "I've thought until my brain is going, and I don't see how she could have done it."

He became sullen when he saw what he had done, refused any more information, and left almost immediately.

Fred came soon after, and in the meantime I had made some notes like this:

1. Examine warehouse and yard.
2. Attempt to trace Carter.
3. See station agent at Bellwood.
4. Inquire Wardrop's immediate past.
5. Take Wardrop to Dr. Anderson, the specialist.
6. Send Margery violets.

Chapter XVI
Eleven Twenty-two Again

⟨∞⟩

BURTON'S idea of exploiting Miss Jane's disappearance began to bear fruit the next morning. I went to the office early, anxious to get my more pressing business out of the way, to have the afternoon with Burton to inspect the warehouse. At nine o'clock came a call from the morgue.

"Small woman, well dressed, gray hair?" I repeated. "I think I'll go up and see. Where was the body found?"

"In the river at Monica Station," was the reply. "There is a scar diagonally across the cheek to the corner of the mouth."

"A fresh injury?"

"No, an old scar."

With a breath of relief I said it was not the person we were seeking and tried to get down to work again. But Burton's prophecy had been right. Miss Jane had been seen in a hundred different places: one perhaps was right; which one?

A reporter for the *Eagle* had been working on the case all night: he came in for a more detailed description of the missing woman, and he had a theory, to fit which he was quite ready to cut and trim the facts.

"It's Rowe," he said confidently. "You can see his hand in it right through. I was put on the Benson kidnapping case. You remember, the boy who was kept for three months in a deserted lumber camp in the mountains? Well, sir, every person in the Benson house swore that youngster was in bed at midnight, when the house was closed for the night. Every door and window bolted in the morning, and the boy gone. When we found Rowe—after the mother had put on mourning—and found the kid, ten pounds heavier than he had been before he was abducted, and strutting around like a turkey cock, Rowe told us that he and the boy took in the theater that night, and were there for the first act. How did he do it? He offered to take the boy to the show if he would pretend to go to bed, and then slide down a porch pillar and meet him. The boy didn't want to go home when we found him."

"There can't be any mistake about the time in this case," I commented. "I saw her myself after eleven, and said good night."

The *Eagle* man consulted his notebook. "Oh, yes," he asked, "did she have a diagonal cut across her cheek?"

"No," I said for the second time.

My next visitor was a cabman. On the night in question he had taken a small and a very nervous old woman to the Omega ferry. She appeared excited and almost forgot to pay him. She carried a small satchel, and wore a black veil. What did she look like? She had gray hair, and she seemed to have a scar on her face that drew the corner of her mouth.

At ten o'clock I telephoned Burton: "For Heaven's sake," I said, "if anybody has lost a little old lady in a black dress, wearing a black veil, carrying a satchel, and with a scar diagonally across her cheek from her eye to her mouth, I can tell them all about her, and where she is now."

"That's funny," he said. "We're stirring up the pool and bringing up things we didn't expect. The police have been looking for that woman quietly for a week: she's the widow of a coal baron, and her son-in-law's under suspicion of making away with her."

"Well, he didn't," I affirmed. "She committed suicide from an Omega ferry boat and she's at the morgue this morning."

"Bully," he returned. "Keep on; you'll get lots of clues, and remember one will be right."

It was not until noon, however, that anything concrete developed. In the two hours between, I had interviewed seven more people. I had followed the depressing last hours of the coal baron's widow, and jumped with her, mentally, into the black river that night. I had learned of a small fairish-haired girl who had tried to buy cyanide of potassium at three drugstores on the same street, and of a tall, light woman who had taken a room for three days at a hotel and was apparently demented.

At twelve, however, my reward came. Two men walked in, almost at the same time: one was a motorman, in his official clothes, brass buttons and patches around the pockets. The other was a taxicab driver. Both had the uncertain gait of men who by occupation are unused to anything stationary under them, and each eyed the other suspiciously.

The motorman claimed priority by a nose, so I took him first into my private office. His story, shorn of his own opinions at the time and later, was as follows:

On the night in question, Thursday of the week before, he took his car out of the barn for the eleven-o'clock run. Barney was his conductor. They went from the barn, at Hays Street, downtown, and then started out for Wynton. The controller blew out, and two or three things went wrong: all told they lost forty minutes. They got to Wynton at five minutes after two; their time there was one twenty-five.

The car went to the bad again at Wynton, and he and Barney tinkered with it until two forty. They got it in shape to go back to the barn, but that was all. Just as they were ready to start, a passenger got on, a woman, alone—a small woman with a brown veil. She wore a black dress or a suit—he was vague about everything but the color, and he noticed her especially because she was fidgety and excited. Half a block farther a man boarded the car, and sat across from the woman. Barney said afterward that the man tried twice to speak to the woman, but she looked away each time. No, he hadn't heard what he said.

The man got out when the car went into the barn, but the woman stayed on. He and Barney got another car and took it out, and the woman went with them. She made a complete round-trip this time, going out to Wynton and back to the end of the line downtown. It was just daylight when she got off at last, at First and Day Streets.

Asked if he had thought at the time that the veiled woman was young or old, he said he had thought she was probably middle-aged. Very young or very old women would not put in the night riding in a streetcar. Yes, he had had men who rode around a couple of times at night, mostly to sober up before they went home. But he never saw a woman do it before.

I took his name and address and thanked him. The chauffeur came next, and his story was equally pertinent.

On the night of the previous Thursday he had been engaged to take a sick woman from a downtown hotel to a house at Bellwood. The woman's husband was with her, and they went slowly to avoid jolting. It was after twelve when he drove away from the house and started home. At a corner—he did not know the names of the streets—a woman hailed the cab and asked him if he belonged in Bellwood or was going to the city. She had missed the last train. When he told her he was going into town, she promptly engaged him, and showed him where to wait for her, a narrow road off the main street.

"I waited an hour," he finished, "before she came; I dropped to sleep or I would have gone without her. About half-past one she came along, and a gentleman with her. He put her in the cab, and I took her to the city. When I saw in the paper that a lady had disappeared from Bellwood that night, I knew right off that it was my party."

"Would you know the man again?"

"I would know his voice, I expect, sir; I could not see much: he wore a slouch hat and had a traveling bag of some kind."

"What did he say to the woman?" I asked.

"He didn't say much. Before he closed the door, he said, 'You have put me in a terrible position,' or something like that. From the traveling bag and all, I thought perhaps it was an elopement, and the lady had decided to throw him down."

"Was it a young woman or an old one?" I asked again. This time the cabby's tone was assured.

"Young," he asserted, "slim and quick: dressed in black, with a black veil. Soft voice. She got out at Market Square, and I have an idea she took a crosstown car there."

"I hardly think it was Miss Maitland," I said. "She was past sixty, and besides—I don't think she went that way. Still it is worth following up. Is that all?"

He fumbled in his pocket, and after a minute brought up a small black pocketbook and held it out to me. It was the small coin purse out of a leather handbag.

"She dropped this in the cab, sir," he said. "I took it home to the missus—not knowing what else to do with it. It had no money in it— only that bit of paper."

I opened the purse and took out a small white card, without engraving. On it was written in a pencil the figures:

C 1122

Chapter XVII

His Second Wife

⌒∾⌒

WHEN the cabman had gone, I sat down and tried to think things out. As I have said many times in the course of this narrative, I lack imagination: moreover, a long experience of witnesses in court had taught me the unreliability of average observation. The very fact that two men swore to having taken solitary women away from Bellwood that night, made me doubt if either one had really seen the missing woman.

Of the two stories, the taxicab driver's was the more probable, as far as Miss Jane was concerned. Knowing her childlike nature, her timidity, her shrinking and shamefaced fear of the dark, it was almost incredible that she would walk the three miles to Wynton, voluntarily, and from there lose herself in the city. Besides, such an explanation would not fit the bloodstains, or the fact that she had gone, as far as we could find out, in her nightclothes.

Still—she had left the village that night, either by cab or on foot. If the driver had been correct in his time, however, the taxicab was almost eliminated; he said the woman got into the cab at one thirty. It was between one thirty and one forty-five when Margery heard the footsteps in the attic.

I think for the first time it came to me, that day, that there was at least a possibility that Miss Jane had not been attacked, robbed or injured: that she had left home voluntarily, under stress of great excitement. But if she had, why? The mystery was hardly less for being stripped of its gruesome details. Nothing in my knowledge of the missing woman gave me a clue. I had a vague hope that, if she had gone voluntarily, she would see the newspapers and let us know where she was.

To my list of exhibits I added the purse with its enclosure. The secret drawer of my desk now contained, besides the purse, the slip marked eleven twenty-two that had been pinned to Fleming's pillow; the similar scrap found over Miss Jane's mantel; the pearl I had found on the floor of the closet; and the cyanide, which, as well as the bullet, Burton had given me. Add to these the still tender place on my head where Wardrop had almost brained me with a chair, and a blue ankle, now becoming spotted with yellow, where I had fallen down the dumb-waiter, and my list of visible reminders of the double mystery grew to eight.

I was not proud of the part I had played. So far, I had blundered, it seemed to me, at every point where a blunder was possible. I had fallen over folding chairs and down a shaft; I had been a half-hour too late to save Allan Fleming; I had been up and awake, and Miss Jane had got out of the house under my very nose. Last, and by no means least, I had waited thirty-five years to find the right woman, and when I found her, someone else had won her. I was in the depths that day when Burton came in.

He walked into the office jauntily and presented Miss Grant with a club sandwich neatly done up in waxed paper. Then he came into my private room and closed the door behind him.

"Avaunt, dull care!" he exclaimed, taking in my dejected attitude and exhibits on the desk at a glance. "Look up and grin, my friend." He had his hands behind him.

"Don't be a fool," I snapped. "I'll not grin unless I feel like it."

"Grin, darn you," he said, and put something on the desk in front of me. It was a Russia leather bag.

"*The* leather bag!" he pointed proudly.

"Where did you get it?" I exclaimed, incredulous. Burton fumbled with the lock while he explained.

"It was found in Boston," he said. "How do you open the thing, anyhow?"

It was not locked, and I got it open in a minute. As I had expected, it was empty.

"Then—perhaps Wardrop was telling the truth," I exclaimed. "By Jove, Burton, he was robbed by the woman in the cab, and he can't tell about her on account of Miss Fleming! She made a haul, for certain."

I told him then of the two women who had left Bellwood on the night of Miss Jane's disappearance, and showed him the purse and its enclosure. The C puzzled him as it had me. "It might be anything," he said as he gave it back, "from a book, chapter and verse in the Bible to a prescription for rheumatism at a drugstore. As to the lady in the cab, I think perhaps you are right," he said, examining the interior of the bag, where Wardrop's name in ink told its story. "Of course, we have only Wardrop's word that he brought the bag to Bellwood; if we grant that we can grant the rest—that he was robbed, that the thief emptied the bag, and either took it or shipped it to Boston."

"How on earth did you get it?"

"It was a coincidence. There have been a shrewd lot of baggage thieves in two or three eastern cities lately, mostly Boston. The method, the police say, was something like this—one of them, the chief of the gang, would get a wagon, dress like an expressman and go around the depots looking at baggage. He would make a mental note of the numbers, go away and forge a check to match, and secure the pieces he had taken a fancy to. Then he merely drove around to headquarters, and the trunk was rifled. The police got on, raided the place, and found, among others, our Russia leather bag. It was shipped back, empty, to the address inside, at Bellwood."

"At Bellwood? Then how—"

"It came while I was lunching with Miss Letitia," he said easily. "We're very chummy—thick as thieves. What I want to know is"— disregarding my astonishment—"where is the hundred thousand?"

"Find the woman."

"Did you ever hear of Anderson, the nerve specialist?" he asked, without apparent relevancy.

"I have been thinking of him," I answered. "If we could get Wardrop there, on some plausible excuse, it would take Anderson about ten minutes with his instruments and experimental psychology, to know everything Wardrop ever forgot."

"I'll go on one condition," Burton said, preparing to leave. "I'll promise to get Wardrop and have him on the spot at two o'clock tomorrow, if you'll promise me one thing: if Anderson fixes me with his eye, and I begin to look dotty and tell about my past life, I want you to take me by the flap of my ear and lead me gently home."

"I promise," I said, and Burton left.

The recovery of the bag was only one of the many astonishing things that happened that day and the following night. Hawes, who knew little of what it all meant, and disapproved a great deal, ended that afternoon by locking himself, blinking furiously, in his private office. To Hawes any practice that was not lucrative was bad practice. About four o'clock, when I had shut myself away from the crowd in the outer office, and was letting Miss Grant take their depositions as to when and where they had seen a little old lady, probably demented, wandering around the streets, a woman came who refused to be turned away.

"Young woman," I heard her say, speaking to Miss Grant, "he may have important business, but I guess mine's just a little more so."

I interfered then, and let her come in. She was a woman of medium height, quietly dressed, and fairly handsome. My first impression was favorable; she moved with a certain dignity, and she was not laced, crimped or made up. I am more sophisticated now; The Lady Who Tells Me Things says that the respectable women nowadays, out-rouge, out-crimp and out-lace the unrespectable.

However, the illusion was gone the moment she began to speak. Her voice was heavy, throaty, expressionless. She threw it like a weapon: I am perfectly honest in saying that for a moment the surprise of her voice outweighed the remarkable thing she was saying.

"I am Mrs. Allan Fleming," she said, with a certain husky defiance.

"I beg your pardon," I said, after a minute. "You mean—the Allan Fleming who just died?"

She nodded. I could see she was unable, just then, to speak. She had nerved herself to the interview, but it was evident that there was a real grief. She fumbled for a black-bordered handkerchief, and her throat worked convulsively. I saw now that she was in mourning.

"Do you mean," I asked incredulously, "that Mr. Fleming married a second time?"

"He married me three years ago, in Plattsburg. I came from there last night. I—couldn't leave before."

"Does Miss Fleming know about this second marriage?"

"No. Nobody knew about it. I have had to put up with a great deal, Mr. Knox. It's a hard thing for a woman to know that people are talking about her, and all the time she's married as tight as ring and book can do it."

"I suppose," I hazarded, "if that is the case, you have come about the estate."

"Estate!" Her tone was scornful. "I guess I'll take what's coming to me, as far as that goes—and it won't be much. No, I came to ask what they mean by saying Allan Fleming killed himself."

"Don't you think he did?"

"I know he did not," she said tensely. "Not only that: I know who did it. It was Schwartz—Henry Schwartz."

"Schwartz! But what on earth—"

"You don't know Schwartz," she said grimly. "I was married to him for fifteen years. I took him when he had a saloon in the Fifth Ward, at Plattsburg. The next year he was alderman: I didn't expect in those days to see him riding around in an automobile—not but what he was malting money—Henry Schwartz is a moneymaker. That's why he's boss of the state now."

"And you divorced him?"

"He was a brute," she said vindictively. "He wanted me to go back to him, and I told him I would rather die. I took a big house, and kept bachelor suites for gentlemen. Mr. Fleming lived there, and—he married me three years ago. He and Schwartz had to stand together, but they hated each other."

"Schwartz?" I meditated. "Do you happen to know if Senator Schwartz was in Plattsburg at the time of the mur—of Mr. Fleming's death?"

"He was here in Manchester."

"He had threatened Mr. Fleming's life?"

"He had already tried to kill him, the day we were married. He stabbed him twice, but not deep enough."

I looked at her in wonder. For this woman, not extraordinarily handsome, two men had fought and one had died—according to her story.

"I can prove everything I say," she went on rapidly. "I have letters from Mr. Fleming telling me what to do in case he was shot down; I have papers—canceled notes—that would put Schwartz in the penitentiary— that is," she said cunningly, "I did have them. Mr. Fleming took them away."

"Aren't you afraid for yourself?" I asked.

"Yes, I'm afraid—afraid he'll get me back yet. It would please him to see me crawl back on my knees."

"But—he cannot force you to go back to him."

"Yes, he can," she shivered. From which I knew she had told me only a part of her story.

After all she had nothing more to tell. Fleming had been shot; Schwartz had been in the city about the Borough Bank; he had threatened Fleming before, but a political peace had been patched; Schwartz knew the White Cat. That was all.

Before she left she told me something I had not known.

"I know a lot about inside politics," she said, as she got up. "I have seen the state divided up with the roast at my table, and served around with the dessert, and I can tell you something you don't know about your White Cat. A back staircase leads to one of the upstairs rooms, and shuts off with a locked door. It opens below, out a side entrance, not supposed to be used. Only a few know of it. Henry Butler was found dead at the foot of that staircase."

"He shot himself, didn't he?"

"The police said so," she replied, with her grim smile. "There is such a thing as murdering a man by driving him to suicide."

She wrote an address on a card and gave it to me.

"Just a minute," I said, as she was about to go. "Have you ever heard Mr. Fleming speak of the Misses Maitland?"

"They were—his first wife's sisters. No, he never talked of them, but I believe, just before he left Plattsburg, he tried to borrow some money from them."

"And failed?"

"The oldest one telegraphed the refusal, collect," she said, smiling faintly.

"There is something else," I said. "Did you ever hear of the number eleven twenty-two?"

"No—or—why, yes—" she said. "It is the number of my house."

It seemed rather ridiculous, when she had gone, and I sat down to think it over. It was anticlimax, to say the least. If the mysterious number meant only the address of this very ordinary woman, then— it was probable her story of Schwartz was true enough. But I could not reconcile myself to it, nor could I imagine Schwartz, with his great bulk, skulking around pinning scraps of paper to pillows.

It would have been more like the fearlessness and passion of the man to have shot Fleming down in the statehouse corridor, or on the street, and to have trusted to his influence to set him free. For the first time it occurred to me that there was something essentially feminine in the revenge of the figures that had haunted the dead man.

I wondered if Mrs. Fleming had told me all, or only half the truth.

That night, at the most peaceful spot I had ever known, Fred's home, occurred another inexplicable affair, one that left us all with racked nerves and listening, fearful ears.

Chapter XVIII

Edith's Cousin

⌒∞⌒

THAT was to be Margery's last evening at Fred's. Edith had kept her as long as she could, but the girl felt that her place was with Miss Letitia. Edith was desolate.

"I don't know what I am going to do without you, she said that night when we were all together in the library, with a wood fire, for light and coziness more than heat. Margery was sitting before the fire, and while the others talked she sat mostly silent, looking into the blaze.

The May night was cold and rainy, and Fred had been reading us a poem he had just finished, receiving with indifference my comment on it, and basking in Edith's rapture.

"Do you know yourself what it is about?" I inquired caustically.

"If it's about anything, it isn't poetry," he replied. "Poetry appeals to the ear. It is primarily sensuous. If it is more than that it ceases to be poetry and becomes verse."

Edith yawned.

"I'm afraid I'm getting old," she said. "I'm getting the nap habit after dinner. Fred, run up, will you, and see if Katie put blankets over the boys?"

Fred stuffed his poem in his pocket and went resignedly upstairs. Edith yawned again, and prepared to retire to the den for forty winks.

"If Ellen decides to come downstairs," she called back over her shoulder, "please come and wake me. She said she felt better and might come down."

At the door she turned, behind Margery's back, and made me a sweeping and comprehensive signal. She finished it off with a double wink, Edith having never been able to wink one eye alone, and crossing the hall, closed the door of the den with an obtrusive bang.

Margery and I were alone. The girl looked at me, smiled a little, and drew a long breath.

"It's queer about Edith," I said. "I never before knew her to get drowsy after dinner. If she were not beyond suspicion, I would think it a deep-laid scheme, and she and Fred sitting and holding hands in a corner somewhere."

"But why—a scheme?" She had folded her hands in her lap, and the eternal ring sparkled malignantly.

"They might think I wanted to talk to you," I suggested.

"To me?"

"To you. The fact is, I do."

Perhaps I was morbid about the ring: it seemed to me she lifted her hand and looked at it.

"It's drafty in here. Don't you think so?" she asked suddenly, looking back of her. Probably she had not meant it, but I got up and closed the door into the hall. When I came back I took the chair next to her, and for a moment we said nothing. The log threw out tiny red devil sparks, and the clock chimed eight, very slowly.

"Harry Wardrop was here last night," I said, poking down the log with my heel.

"Here?"

"Yes. I suppose I was wrong, but I did not say you were here."

She turned and looked at me closely, out of the most beautiful eyes I ever saw.

"I'm not afraid to see him," she said proudly, "and he ought not to be afraid to see me."

"I want to tell you something before you see him. Last night, before he came, I thought that—well, that at least he knew something of—the things we want to know."

"Yes?"

"In justice to him, and because I want to fight fair, I tell you tonight that I don't believe he knows anything about your father's death, and that I believe he was robbed that night at Bellwood."

"What about the pearls he sold at Plattsburg?" she asked suddenly.

"I think when the proper time comes, he will tell about that too, Margery." I did not notice my use of her name until too late. If she heard, she failed to resent it. "After all, if you love him, hardly anything else matters, does it? How do we know but that he was in trouble, and that Aunt Jane herself gave them to him?"

She looked at me with a little perplexity.

"You plead his case very well," she said. "Did he ask you to speak to me?"

"I won't run a race with a man who is lame," I said quietly. "Ethically, I ought to go away and leave you to your dreams, but I am not going to do it. If you love Wardrop as a woman ought to love the man she marries, then marry him and I hope you will be happy. If you don't— no, let me finish. I have made up my mind to clear him if I can; to bring him to you with a clear slate. Then, I know it is audacious, but I am going to come, too, and—I'm going to plead for myself then, unless you send me away."

She sat with her head bent, her color coming and going nervously. Now she looked up at me with what was the ghost of a smile.

"It sounds like a threat," she said in a low voice. "And you—I wonder if you always get what you want?"

Then, of course, Fred came in, and fell over a hassock looking for matches. Edith opened the door of the den and called him to her irritably, but Fred declined to leave the wood fire, and settled down in his easy chair. After a while Edith came over and joined us, but she snubbed Fred the entire evening, to his bewilderment. And when conversation lagged, during the evening that followed, I tried to remember what I had said, and knew I had done very badly. Only one thing cheered me: she had not been angry, and she had understood. Blessed be the woman that understands!

We broke up for the night about eleven. Mrs. Butler had come down for a while, and had even played a little, something of Tschaikovsky's, a singing, plaintive theme that brought sadness back into Margery's face, and made me think, for no reason, of a wet country road and a plodding, back-burdened peasant.

Fred and I sat in the library for a while after the rest had gone, and I told him a little of what I had learned that afternoon.

"A second wife!" he said, "and a primitive type, eh? Well, did she shoot him, or did Schwartz? The Lady or the Democratic Tiger?"

"The Tiger," I said firmly.

"The Lady," said Fred, with equal assurance.

Fred closed the house with his usual care. It required the combined efforts of the maids followed up by Fred, to lock the windows, it being his confident assertion that in seven years of keeping house, he had never failed to find at least one unlocked window.

On that night, I remember, he went around with his usual scrupulous care. Then we went up to bed, leaving a small light at the telephone in the lower hall—nothing else.

The house was a double one, built around a square hall below, which served the purpose of a general sitting room. From the front door a short, narrow hall led back to this, with a room on either side, and from it doors led into the rest of the lower floor. At one side the stairs took the ascent easily, with two stops for landings, and upstairs the bedrooms opened from a similar, slightly smaller square hall. The staircase to the third floor went up from somewhere back in the nursery wing.

My bedroom was over the library, and Mrs. Butler and Margery Fleming had connecting rooms, across the hall. Fred and Edith slept in the nursery wing, so they would be near the children. In the square upper hall there was a big reading table, a lamp, and some comfortable chairs. Here, when they were alone, Fred read aloud the evening paper, or his latest short story, and Edith's sewing basket showed how she put in what women miscall their leisure.

I did not go to sleep at once. Naturally the rather vital step I had taken in the library insisted on being considered and almost regretted. I tried reading myself to sleep, and when that failed, I tried the soothing combination of a cigarette and a book. That worked like a charm; the last thing I remember is of holding the cigarette in a death grip as I lay with my pillows propped back of me, my head to the light, and a delightful languor creeping over me.

I was wakened by the pungent acrid smell of smoke, and I sat up and blinked my eyes open. The side of the bed was sending up a steady column of gray smoke, and there was a smart crackle of fire under me somewhere. I jumped out of bed and saw the trouble instantly. My cigarette had dropped from my hand, still lighted, and as is the way with cigarettes, determined to burn to the end. In so doing it had fired my bed, the rug under the bed and pretty nearly the man on the bed.

It took some sharp work to get it all out without rousing the house. Then I stood amid the wreckage and looked ruefully at Edith's pretty room. I could see, mentally, the spot of water on the library ceiling the next morning, and I could hear Fred's strictures on the heedlessness and indifference to property of bachelors in general and me in particular.

Three pitchers of water on the bed had made it an impossible couch. I put on a dressing gown, and, with a blanket over my arm, I went out to hunt some sort of place to sleep. I decided on the davenport in the hall just outside, and as quietly as I could, I put a screen around it and settled down for the night.

I was wakened by the touch of a hand on my face. I started, I think, and the hand was jerked away—I am not sure: I was still drowsy. I lay very quiet, listening for footsteps, but none came. With the feeling that there was someone behind the screen, I jumped up. The hall was dark and quiet. When I found no one, I concluded it had been only a vivid dream, and I sat down on the edge of the davenport and yawned.

I heard Edith moving back in the nursery: she has an uncomfortable habit of wandering around in the night, covering the children, closing windows, and sniffing for fire. I was afraid some of the smoke from my conflagration had reached her suspicious nose, but she did not come into the front hall. I was wide-awake by that time, and it was then, I think, that I noticed a heavy, sweetish odor in the air. At first I thought one of the children might be ill, and that Edith was dosing him with one of the choice concoctions that she kept in the bathroom medicine closet. When she closed her door, however, and went back to bed, I knew I had been mistaken.

The sweetish smell was almost nauseating. For some reason or other—association of certain odors with certain events—I found myself recalling the time I had a wisdom tooth taken out, and that when I came around I was being sat on by the dentist and his assistant, and the latter had a black eye. Then, suddenly, I knew. The sickly odor was chloroform!

I had the light on in a moment, and was rapping at Margery's door. It was locked, and I got no answer. A pale light shone over the transom, but everything was ominously quiet, beyond the door. I went to Mrs. Butler's door, next; it was unlocked and partly open. One glance at the empty bed and the confusion of the place, and I rushed without ceremony through the connecting door into Margery's room.

The atmosphere was reeking with chloroform. The girl was in bed, apparently sleeping quietly. One arm was thrown up over her head, and the other lay relaxed on the white cover. A folded towel had been laid across her face, and when I jerked it away I saw she was breathing very slowly, stertorously, with her eyes partly open and fixed.

I threw up all the windows, before I roused the family, and as soon as Edith was in the room I telephoned for the doctor. I hardly remember what I did until he came: I know we tried to rouse Margery and failed, and I know that Fred went downstairs and said the silver was intact and the back kitchen door open. And then the doctor came, and I was put out in the hall, and for an eternity, I walked up and down, eight steps one way, eight steps back, unable to think, unable even to hope.

Not until the doctor came out to me, and said she was better, and would I call a maid to make some strong black coffee, did I come out of my stupor. The chance of doing something, anything, made me determined to make the coffee myself. They still speak of that coffee at Fred's.

It was Edith who brought Mrs. Butler to my mind. Fred had maintained that she had fled before the intruders, and was probably in some closet or corner of the upper floor. I was afraid our solicitude was long in coming. It was almost an hour before we organized a searching party to look for her. Fred went upstairs, and I took the lower floor.

It was I who found her, after all, lying full length on the grass in the little square yard back of the house. She was in a dead faint, and she was a much more difficult patient than Margery.

We could get no story from either of them that night. The two rooms had been ransacked, but apparently nothing had been stolen. Fred vowed he had locked and bolted the kitchen door, and that it had been opened from within.

It was a strange experience, that night intrusion into the house, without robbery as a motive. If Margery knew or suspected the reason for the outrage, she refused to say. As for Mrs. Butler, to mention the occurrence put her into hysteria. It was Fred who put forth the most startling theory of the lot.

"By George," he said the next morning when we had failed to find tracks in the yard, and Edith had reported every silver spoon in its place. "By George, it wouldn't surprise me if the lady in the grave clothes did it herself. There isn't anything an hysterical woman won't do to rouse your interest in her, if it begins to flag. How did anyone get in through that kitchen door, when it was locked inside and bolted? I tell you, she opened it herself."

I did not like to force Margery's confidence, but I believe that the outrage was directly for the purpose of searching her room, perhaps for papers that had been her father's. Mrs. Butler came around enough by morning to tell a semi-connected story in which she claimed that two men had come in from a veranda roof, and tried to chloroform her. That she had pretended to be asleep and had taken the first opportunity, while they were in the other room, to run downstairs and into the yard. Edith thought it likely enough, being a credulous person.

As it turned out, Edith's intuition was more reliable than my skepticism—or Fred's.

Chapter XIX

Back to Bellwood

THE inability of Margery Fleming to tell who had chloroformed her, and Mrs. Butler's white face and brooding eyes made a very respectable mystery out of the affair. Only Fred, Edith and I came down to breakfast that morning. Fred's expression was half amused, half puzzled. Edith fluttered uneasily over the coffee machine, her cheeks as red as the bow of ribbon at her throat. I was preoccupied, and, like Fred, I propped the morning paper in front of me and proceeded to think in its shelter.

"Did you find anything, Fred?" Edith asked. Fred did not reply, so she repeated the question with some emphasis.

"Eh—what?" Fred inquired, peering around the corner of the paper.

"Did—you—find—any—clue?"

"Yes, dear—that is, no. Nothing to amount to anything. Upon my soul, Jack, if I wrote the editorials of this paper, I'd *say* something." He subsided into inarticulate growls behind the paper, and everything was quiet. Then I heard a sniffle, distinctly. I looked up. Edith was crying—pouring cream into a coffee cup, and feeling blindly for the sugar, with her pretty face twisted and her pretty eyes obscured. In a second I was up, had crumpled the newspapers, including Fred's, into a ball, and had lifted him bodily out of his chair.

"When I am married," I said fiercely, jerking him around to Edith and pushing him into a chair beside her, "if I ever read the paper at breakfast when my wife is bursting for conversation, may I have some good and faithful friend who will bring me back to a sense of my duty." I drew a chair to Edith's other side. "Now, let's talk," I said.

She wiped her eyes shamelessly with her table napkin. "There isn't a soul in this house I can talk to," she wailed. "All kinds of awful things happening—and we had to send for coffee this morning, Jack. You must have used four pounds last night—and nobody will tell me a thing. There's no use asking Margery— she's sick at her stomach from the chloroform—and Ellen never talks except about herself, and she's horribly—uninteresting. And Fred and you make a ba-barricade out of newspapers, and fire 'yes' at me when you mean 'no'."

"I put the coffee back where I got it, Edith," I protested stoutly. "I know we're barbarians, but I'll swear to that." And then I stopped, for I had a sudden recollection of going upstairs with something fat and tinny in my arms, of finding it in my way, and of hastily thrusting it into the boys' boot closet under the nursery stair.

Fred had said nothing. He had taken her hand and was patting it gently, the while his eyes sought the headlines on the wad of morning paper.

"You burned that blue rug," she said to me disconsolately, with a threat of fresh tears. "It took me ages to find the right shade of blue."

"I will buy you that Shirvan you wanted," I hastened to assure her.

"Yes, to take away when you get married." There is a hint of the shrew in all good women.

"I will buy the Shirvan and *not* get married."

Here, I regret to say, Edith suddenly laughed. She threw her head back and jeered at me.

"You!" she chortled, and pointed one slim finger at me mockingly. "You, who are so mad about one girl that you love all women for her sake! You, who go white instead of red when she comes into the room! You, who have let your practice go to the dogs to be near her, and then never speak to her when she's around, but sit with your mouth open like a puppy begging for candy, ready to snap up every word she throws you and wiggle with joy!"

I was terrified.

"Honestly, Edith, do I do that?" I gasped. But she did not answer; she only leaned over and kissed Fred.

"Women like men to be awful fools about them," she said. "That's why I'm so crazy about Freddie." He writhed.

"If I tell you something nice, Jack, will you make it a room-size rug?"

"Room size it is.

"Then, Margery's engagement ring was stolen last night and when I commiserated her she said, 'Dear me, the lamp's out and the coffee is cold!' "

"Remarkable speech, under the circumstances," said Fred.

Edith rang the bell and seemed to be thinking. "Perhaps we'd better make it four small rugs instead of one large one," she said.

"Not a rug until you have told me what Margery said." Firmly.

"Oh, that! Why, she said it didn't really matter about the ring. She had never cared much about it anyway."

"But that's only a matter of taste," I protested, somewhat disappointed. But Edith got up and patted me on the top of my head.

"Silly," she said. "If the right man came along and gave her a rubber teething ring, she'd be crazy about it for his sake."

"Edith!" Fred said, shocked. But Edith had gone.

She took me upstairs before I left for the office to measure for the Shirvan, Edith being a person who believes in obtaining a thing while the desire for it is in its first bloom. Across the hall Fred was talking to Margery through the transom.

"Mustard leaves are mighty helpful," he was saying. "I always take 'em on shipboard. And cheer up: land's in sight."

I would have given much for Fred's ease of manner when, a few minutes later, Edith having decided on four Shirvans and a hall runner, she took me to the door of Margery's room.

She was lying very still and pale in the center of the white bed, and she tried bravely to smile at us.

"I hope you are better," I said. "Don't let Edith convince you that my coffee has poisoned you."

She said she was a little better, and that she didn't know she had had any coffee. That was the extent of the conversation. I, who have a local reputation of a sort before a jury, could not think of another word to say. I stood there for a minute uneasily, with Edith poking me with her finger to go inside the door and speak and act like an intelligent human being. But I only muttered something about a busy day before me and fled. It was a singular thing, but as I stood in the doorway, I had a vivid mental picture of Edith's description of me, sitting up puppylike to beg for a kind word, and wiggling with delight when I got it. If I slunk into my office that morning like a dog scourged to his kennel, Edith was responsible.

At the office I found a note from Miss Letitia, and after a glance at it I looked in my railroad schedule for the first train. The note was brief; unlike the similar epistle I had received from Miss Jane the day she disappeared, this one was very formal.

MR. JOHN KNOX:

Dear Sir—Kindly oblige me by coming to see me as soon as you get this. Some things have happened, not that I think they are worth a row of pins, but Hepsibah is an old fool, and she says she did not put the note in the milk bottle.

Yours very respectfully,
LETITIA ANN MAITLAND

I had an appointment with Burton for the afternoon, to take Wardrop; if we could get him on some pretext, to Dr. Anderson. That day, also, I had two cases on the trial list. I got Humphreys, across the hall, to take them over, and evading Hawes' resentful blink, I went on my way to Bellwood. It was nine days since Miss Jane had disappeared. On my way out in the train I jotted down the things that had happened in that time: Allan Fleming had died and been buried; the Borough Bank had failed; someone had gotten into the Fleming house and gone through the papers there; Clarkson had killed himself; we had found that Wardrop had sold the pearls; the leather bag had been returned;

Fleming's second wife had appeared, and someone had broken into my own house and, intentionally or not, had almost sent Margery Fleming over the borderland.

It seemed to me everything pointed in one direction, to a malignity against Fleming that extended itself to the daughter. I thought of what the woman who claimed to be the dead man's second wife had said the day before. If the staircase she had spoken of opened into the room where Fleming was shot, and if Schwartz was in town at the time, then, in view of her story that he had already tried once to kill him, the likelihood was that Schwartz was at least implicated.

If Wardrop knew that, why had he not denounced him? Was I to believe that, after all the mystery, the number eleven twenty-two was to resolve itself into the number of a house? Would it be typical of the Schwartz I knew to pin bits of paper to a man's pillow? On the other hand, if he had reason to think that Fleming had papers that would incriminate him, it would be like Schwartz to hire someone to search for them, and he would be equal to having Wardrop robbed of the money he was taking to Fleming.

Granting that Schwartz had killed Fleming—then who was the woman with Wardrop the night he was robbed? Why did he take the pearls and sell them? How did the number eleven twenty-two come into Aunt Jane's possession? How did the leather bag get to Boston? Who had chloroformed Margery? Who had been using the Fleming house while it was closed? Most important of all now—where was Aunt Jane?

The house at Bellwood looked almost cheerful in the May sunshine, as I went up the walk. Nothing ever changed the straight folds of the old-fashioned lace curtains; no dog ever tracked the porch, or buried sacrilegious and odorous bones on the level lawn; the birds were nesting in the trees, well above the reach of Robert's ladder, but they were decorous, well-behaved birds, whose prim courting never partook of the exuberance of their neighbors', bursting their little throats in an elm above the baby perambulator in the next yard.

When Bella had let me in, and I stood once more in the straight hall, with the green rep chairs and the Japanese umbrella stand, involuntarily I listened for the tap of Miss Jane's small feet on the stairs. Instead came Bella's heavy tread, and a request from Miss Letitia that I go upstairs.

The old lady was sitting by a window of her bedroom, in a chintz upholstered chair. She did not appear to be feeble; the only change I noticed was a relaxation in the severe tidiness of her dress. I guessed that Miss Jane's exquisite neatness had been responsible for the white ruchings, the soft caps, and the spotless shoulder shawls which had made lovely their latter years.

"You've taken your own time about coming, haven't you?" Miss Letitia asked sourly. "If it hadn't been for that cousin of yours you sent here, Burton, I'd have been driven to sending for Amelia Miles, and when I send for Amelia Miles for company, I'm in a bad way."

"I have had a great deal to attend to," I said as loud as I could. "I came some days ago to tell you Mr. Fleming was dead; after that we had to bury him, and close the house. It's been a very sad—"

"Did he leave anything?" she interrupted. "It isn't sad at all unless he didn't leave anything."

"He left very little. The house, perhaps, and I regret to have to tell you that a woman came to me yesterday who claims to be a second wife."

She took off her glasses, wiped them and put them on again.

"Then," she said with a snap, "there's one other woman in the world as big a fool as my sister Martha was. I didn't know there were two of 'em. What do you hear about Jane?"

"The last time I was here," I shouted, "you thought she was dead; have you changed your mind?"

"The last time you were here," she said with dignity, "I thought a good many things that were wrong. I thought I had lost some of the pearls, but I hadn't."

"What!" I exclaimed incredulously. She put her hands on the arms of her chair, and leaning forward, shot the words at me viciously.

"I—said—I—had—lost—some—of—the—pearls—well—I—haven't."

She didn't expect me to believe her, any more than she believed it herself. But why on earth she had changed her attitude about the pearls was beyond me. I merely nodded comprehensively.

"Very well," I said, "I'm glad to know it was a mistake. Now, the next thing is to find Miss Jane."

"We have found her," she said tartly. "That's what I sent for you about."

"Found her!" This time I did get out of my chair. "What on earth do you mean, Miss Letitia? Why, we've been scouring the country for her."

She opened a religious monthly on the table beside her, and took out a folded paper. I had to control my impatience while she changed her glasses and read it slowly.

"Heppie found it on the back porch, under a milk bottle," she prefaced. Then she read it to me. I do not remember the wording, and Miss Letitia refused, both then and later, to let it out of her hands. As a result, unlike the other manuscripts in the case, I have not even a copy. The substance, shorn of its bad spelling and grammar, was this:

The writer knew where Miss Jane was; the inference being that he was responsible. She was well and happy, but she had happened to read a newspaper with an account of her disappearance, and it had worried her. The payment of the small sum of five thousand dollars would send her back as well as the day she left. The amount, left in a tin can on the base of the Maitland shaft in the cemetery, would bring the missing lady back within twenty-four hours. On the contrary, if the recipient of the letter notified the police, it would go hard with Miss Jane.

"What do you think of it?" she asked, looking at me over her glasses. "If she was fool enough to be carried away by a man that spells cemetery with one m, she deserves what she's got. And I won't pay five thousand, anyhow, it's entirely too much."

"It doesn't sound quite genuine to me," I said, reading it over. "I should certainly not leave any money until we had tried to find who left this."

"I'm not so sure but what she'd better stay a while anyhow," Miss Letitia pursued. "Now that we know she's living, I ain't so particular when she gets back. She's been notionate lately anyhow."

I had been reading the note again. "There's one thing here that makes me doubt the whole story," I said. "What's this about her reading the papers? I thought her reading glasses were found in the library."

Miss Letitia snatched the paper from me and read it again.

"Reading the paper!" she sniffed. "You've got more sense than I've been giving you credit for, Knox. Her glasses are here this minute; without them she can't see to scratch her nose."

It was a disappointment to me, although the explanation was simple enough. It was surprising that we had not had more attempts to play on our fears. But the really important thing bearing on Miss Jane's departure was when Heppie came into the room, with her apron turned up like a pocket and her dust cap pushed down over her eyes like the slouch hat of a bowery tough.

When she got to the middle of the room she stopped and abruptly dropped the corners of her apron. There rolled out a heterogenous collection of things: a white muslin garment which proved to be a nightgown, with long sleeves and high collar; a half-dozen hair curlers—I knew those—Edith had been seen, in midnight emergencies, with her hair twisted around just such instruments of torture; a shoe buttoner; a railroad map; and one new and unworn black kid glove.

Miss Letitia changed her glasses deliberately, and took a comprehensive survey of the things on the floor.

"Where did you get 'em?" she said, fixing Heppie with an awful eye.

"I found 'em stuffed under the blankets in the chest of drawers in the attic," Heppie shouted at her. "If we'd washed the blankets last week, as I wanted to—"

"Shut up!" Miss Letitia said shortly, and Heppie's thin lips closed with a snap. "Now then, Knox, what do you make of that?"

"If that's the nightgown she was wearing the night she disappeared, I think it shows one thing very clearly, Miss Maitland. She was not abducted, and she knew perfectly well what she was about. None of her clothes were missing, and that threw us off the track; but look at this new glove! She may have had new things to put on and left the old. The map—well, she was going somewhere, with a definite purpose. When we find out what took her away, we will find her."

"Humph!"

"She didn't go unexpectedly—that is, she was prepared for whatever it was."

"I don't believe a word of it," the old lady burst out. "She didn't have a secret; she was the kind that couldn't keep a secret. She wasn't responsible, I tell you; she was extravagant. Look at that glove! And she had three pairs half worn in her bureau."

"Miss Maitland," I asked suddenly, "did you ever hear of eleven twenty-two?"

"Eleven twenty-two what?"

"*Just* the number, eleven twenty-two," I repeated. "Does it mean anything to you? Has it any significance?"

"I should say it has," she retorted. "In the last ten years the Colored Orphans' Home has cared for, fed, clothed, and pampered exactly eleven hundred and twenty-two colored children, of every condition of shape and misshape, brains and no brains."

"It has no other connection?"

"Eleven twenty-two? Twice eleven is twenty-two, if that's any help. No, I can't think of anything. I loaned Allan Fleming a thousand dollars once; I guess my mind was failing. It would be about eleven twenty-two by this time."

Neither of these explanations sufficed for the little scrap found in Miss Jane's room. What connection, if any, had it with her flight? Where was she now? What was eleven twenty-two? And why did Miss Letitia deny that she had lost the pearls, when I already knew that nine of the ten had been sold, who had bought them, and approximately how much he had paid?

Chapter XX

Association of Ideas

I ATE a light lunch at Bellwood, alone, with Bella to look after me in the dining room. She was very solicitous, and when she had brought my tea, I thought she wanted to say something. She stood awkwardly near the door, and watched me.

"You needn't wait, Bella," I said.

"I beg your pardon, sir, but—I wanted to ask you—is Miss Fleming well?"

"She was not very well this morning, but I don't think it is serious, Bella," I replied. She turned to go, but I fancied she hesitated.

"Oh, Bella," I called, as she was going out. "I want to ask you something. The night at the Fleming home, when you and I watched the house, didn't you hear some person running along the hall outside your door? About two o'clock, I think?"

She looked at me stolidly.

"No, sir, I slept all night."

"That's strange. And you didn't hear me when I fell down the dumb-waiter shaft?"

"Holy saints!" she ejaculated. "Was *that* where you fell?"

She stopped herself abruptly.

"You heard that," I asked gently, "and yet you slept all night? Bella, there's a hitch somewhere. You didn't sleep that night, at all; you told Miss Fleming I had been up all night. How did you know that? If I didn't know that you couldn't possibly get around as fast as the—person in the house that night, I would say you had been in Mr. Fleming's desk, looking for—let us say, postage stamps. May I have another cup of coffee?"

She turned a sickly yellow white, and gathered up my cup and saucer with trembling hands. When the coffee finally came back it was brought grumblingly by old Heppie. "She says she's turned her ankle," she sniffed. "Turned it on a lathe, like a table leg, I should say, from the shape of it." Before I left the dining room I put another line in my notebook:

What does Bella know?

I got back to the city somewhat late for my appointment with Burton. I found Wardrop waiting for me at the office, and if I had been astonished at the change in him two nights before, I was shocked now. He seemed to have shrunk in his clothes; his eyeballs were bloodshot from drinking, and his fair hair had dropped, neglected, over his fore-head. He was sitting in his familiar attitude, his elbows on his knees, his chin on his palms.

He looked at me with dull eyes when I went in. I did not see Burton at first. He was sitting on my desk, holding a flat can in his hand, and digging out with a wooden toothpick one sardine after another and bolting them whole.

"Your good health," he said, poising one in the air where it threat-ened oily tears over the carpet. "As an appetite-quencher and thirst-producer, give me the festive sardine. How lovely it would be if we could eat 'em without smelling 'em!"

"Don't you do anything but eat?" Wardrop asked, without enthusiasm.

Burton eyed him reproachfully. "Is that what I get for doing without lunch, in order to prove to you that you are not crazy?" He appealed to me. "He says he's crazy—lost his think works. Now, I ask you, Knox,

when I go to the trouble to find out for him that he's got as many con-
volutions as anybody, and that they've only got a little convolved, is it
fair, I ask you, for him to reproach me about my food?"

"I didn't know you knew each other," I put in, while Burton took
another sardine.

"He says we do," Wardrop said wearily. "Says he used to knock me
around at college."

Burton winked at me solemnly.

"He doesn't remember me, but he will," he said. "It's his nerves that
are gone, and we'll have him restrung with new wires, like an old
piano, in a week."

Wardrop had that after-debauch suspicion of all men, but I think he
grasped at me as a dependability.

"He wants me to go to a doctor," he said. "I'm not sick; it's only—"
He was trying to light a cigarette, but the match dropped from his
shaking fingers.

"Better see one, Wardrop," I urged—and I felt mean enough about
doing it. "You need something to brace you up."

Burton gave him a very small drink, for he could scarcely stand, and
we went down in the elevator. My contempt for the victim between
us was as great as my contempt for myself. That Wardrop was in a
bad position there could be no doubt; there might be more men
than Fleming who had known about the money in the leather bag,
and who thought he had taken it and probably killed Fleming to hide
the theft.

It seemed incredible that an innocent man would collapse as he had
done, and yet—at this minute I can name a dozen men who, under the
club of public disapproval, have fallen into paresis, insanity and the
grave. We are all indifferent to our fellowmen until they are against us.

Burton knew the specialist very well—in fact, there seemed to be few
people he did not know. And considering the way he had got hold of
Miss Letitia and Wardrop, it was not surprising. He had evidently
arranged with the doctor, for the waiting room was empty and we were
after hours.

The doctor was a large man, his size emphasized by the clothes he
wore, very light in color, and unprofessional in cut. He was sandy-
haired, inclined to be bald, and with shrewd, light blue eyes behind his

glasses. Not particularly impressive, except as to size, on first acquaintance; a good fellow, with a brisk voice, and an amazingly light tread.

He began by sending Wardrop into a sort of examining room in the rear of the suite somewhere, to take off his coat and collar. When he had gone the doctor looked at a slip of paper in his hand.

"I think I've got it all from Mr. Burton," he said. "Of course, Mr. Knox, this is a little out of my line; a nerve specialist has as much business with psychotherapy as a piano tuner has with musical technique. But the idea is Munsterburg's, and I've had some good results. I'll give him a short physical examination, and when I ring the bell one of you may come in. Are you a newspaperman, Mr. Knox?"

"An attorney," I said briefly.

"Press man, lawyer, or doctor," Burton broke in, "we all fatten on the other fellow's troubles, don't we?"

"We don't fatten very much," I corrected. "We live."

The doctor blinked behind his glasses.

"I never saw a lawyer yet who would admit he was making money," he said. "Look at the way a doctor grinds for a pittance! He's just as capable as the lawyer; he works a damn sight harder, and he makes a tenth the income. A man will pay his lawyer ten thousand dollars for keeping him out of jail for six months, and he'll kick like a steer if his doctor charges him a hundred to keep him out of hell for life! Which of you will come in? I'm afraid two would distract him."

"I guess it is Knox's butt-in," Burton conceded, "but I get it later, Doctor; you promised."

The physical examination was very brief; when I was called in, Wardrop was standing at the window looking down into the street below, and the doctor was writing at his desk. Behind Wardrop's back he gave me the slip he had written.

> Test is for association of ideas. Watch length of time between word I give and his reply. I often get hold of facts forgotten by the patient. A wait before the answering word is given shows an attempt at concealment.

"Now, Mr. Wardrop," he said, "will you sit here, please?"

He drew a chair to the center table for Wardrop, and another, just across, for himself. I sat back and to one side of the patient, where I could see Wardrop's haggard profile and every movement of the specialist.

On the table was an electric instrument like a small clock, and the doctor's first action was to attach it to two wires with small, black rubber mouthpieces.

"Now, Mr. Wardrop," he said, "we will go on with the test. Your other condition is fair, as I told you; I think you can dismiss the idea of insanity without a second thought, but there is something more than brain and body to be considered; in other words, you have been through a storm, and some of your nervous wires are down. Put the mouthpiece between your lips, please; you see, I do the same with mine. And when I give you a word, speak as quickly as possible the association it brings to your mind. For instance, I say 'noise.' Your first association might be 'street,' 'band,' 'drum,' almost anything associated with the word. As quickly as possible, please."

The first few words went simply enough. Wardrop's replies came almost instantly. To "light" he replied "lamp"; "touch" brought the response "hand"; "eat" brought "Burton," and both the doctor and I smiled. Wardrop was intensely serious. Then—

"Taxicab," said the doctor, and, after an almost imperceptible pause, "road" came for the association. All at once I began to see the possibilities.

"Desk." "Pen."

"Pipe." "Smoke."

"Head." After a perceptible pause the answer came uncertainly. "Hair." But the association of ideas would not be denied, for in answer to the next word, which was "ice," he gave "blood," evidently following up the previous word "head."

I found myself gripping the arms of my chair. The dial on the doctor's clocklike instrument was measuring the interval; I could see that now. The doctor took a record of every word and its response. Wardrop's eyes were shifting nervously.

"Hot." "Cold."

"White." "Black."

"Whisky." "Glass," all in less than a second.

"Pearls." A little hesitation, then "box."

"Taxicab" again. "Night."

"Silly." "Wise."

"Shot." After a pause, "revolver."

"Night." "Dark."

"Blood." "Head."

"Water." "Drink."

"Traveling bag." He brought out the word "train" after an evident struggle, but in answer to the next word "lost," instead of the obvious "found," he said "woman." He had not had sufficient mental agility to get away from the association with "bag." The "woman" belonged there.

"Murder" brought "dead," but "shot," following immediately after, brought "staircase."

I think Wardrop was on his guard by that time, but the conscious effort to hide truths that might be damaging made the intervals longer, from that time on. Already I felt sure that Allan Fleming's widow had been right; he had been shot from the locked back staircase. But by whom?

"Blow" brought "chair."

"Gone." "Bag" came like a flash.

In quick succession, without pause, came the words—

"Bank." "Note."

"Door." "Bolt."

"Money." "Letters," without any apparent connection.

Wardrop was going to the bad. When, to the next word, "staircase," again, he said "scar," his demoralization was almost complete. As for me, the scene in Wardrop's mind was already in mine—Schwartz, with the scar across his ugly forehead, and the bolted door to the staircase open!

On again with the test.

"Flour," after perhaps two seconds, from the preceding shock, brought "bread."

"Trees." "Leaves."

"Night." "Dark."

"Gate." He stopped here so long, I thought he was not going to answer at all. Presently, with an effort, he said "wood," but as before, the association idea came out in the next word; for "electric light" he gave "letters."

"Attic" brought "trunks" at once.

"Closet." After perhaps a second and a half came "dust," showing what closet was in his mind, and immediately after, to "match" he gave "pen."

A long list of words followed which told nothing, to my mind, although the doctor's eyes were snapping with excitement. Then "traveling bag" again, and instead of his previous association, "woman," this time he gave "yellow." But, to the next word, "house," he gave "guest." It came to me that in his mental processes I was the guest, the substitute bag was in his mind, as being in my possession. Quick as a flash the doctor followed up—

"Guest." And Wardrop fell. "Letters," he said.

To a great many words, as I said before, I could attach no significance. Here and there I got a ray.

"Elderly" brought "black."

"Warehouse." "Yard," for no apparent reason.

"Eleven twenty-two." "C" was the answer, given without a second's hesitation.

Eleven twenty-two C! He gave no evidence of having noticed any peculiarity in what he said; I doubt if he realized his answer. To me, he gave the impression of repeating something he had apparently forgotten. As if a number and its association had been subconscious, and brought to the surface by the psychologist; as if, for instance, someone prompted a—b, and the corollary "c" came without summoning.

The psychologist took the small mouthpiece from his lips, and motioned Wardrop to do the same. The test was over.

"I don't call that bad condition, Mr.—Wardrop," the doctor said. "You are nervous, and you need a little more care in your habits. You want to exercise, regularly, and you will have to cut out everything in the way of stimulants for a while. Oh, yes, a couple of drinks a day at first, then one a day, and then none. And you are to stop worrying—when trouble comes round, and stares at you, don't ask it to have a drink. Take it out in the air and kill it; oxygen is as fatal to anxiety as it is to tuberculosis."

"How would Bellwood do?" I asked. "Or should it be the country?"

"Bellwood, of course," the doctor responded heartily. "Ten miles a day, four cigarettes, and three meals—which is more than you have been taking, Mr. Wardrop, by two."

I put him on the train for Bellwood myself, and late that afternoon the three of us—the doctor, Burton and myself—met in my office and went over the doctor's record.

"When the answer comes in four-fifths of a second," he said, before we began, "it is hardly worth comment. There is no time in such an interval for any mental reservation. Only those words that showed noticeable hesitation need be considered."

We worked until almost seven. At the end of that time the doctor leaned back in his chair, and thrust his hands deep in his trousers pockets.

"I got the story from Burton," he said, after a deep breath. "I had no conclusion formed, and of course I am not a detective. Things looked black for Mr. Wardrop, in view of the money lost, the quarrel with Fleming that morning at the White Cat, and the circumstance of his leaving the club and hunting a doctor outside, instead of raising the alarm. Still, no two men ever act alike in an emergency. Psychology is as exact a science as mathematics; it gets information from the source, and a man cannot lie in four-fifths of a second. 'Head,' you noticed, brought 'hair' in a second and three quarters, and the next word, 'ice,' brought the 'blood' that he had held back before. That doesn't show anything. He tried to avoid what was horrible to him.

"But I gave him 'traveling bag'; after a pause, he responded with 'train.' The next word, 'lost,' showed what was in his mind; instead of 'found,' he said 'woman.' Now then, I believe he was either robbed by a woman, or he thinks he was. After all, we can only get what he believes himself."

" 'Money—letters'—another slip."

" 'Shot—staircase'—where are the stairs at the White Cat?"

"I learned yesterday of a back staircase that leads into one of the upper rooms," I said. "It opens on a side entrance, and is used in emergency."

The doctor smiled confidently.

"We look there for our criminal," he said. "Nothing hides from the chronoscope. Now then, 'staircase—scar.' Isn't that significant? The association is clear: a scar that is vivid enough, disfiguring enough, to be the first thing that enters his mind."

"Schwartz!" Burton said with awe. "Doctor, what on earth does 'eleven twenty-two C' mean?"

"I think that is up to you, gentlemen. The C belongs there, without doubt. Briefly, looking over these slips, I make it something like this: Wardrop thinks a woman took his traveling bag. Three times he gave the word 'letters,' in response to 'gate,' 'guest' and 'money.' Did he have a guest at the time all this happened at Bellwood?"

"I was a guest in the house at the time."

"Did you offer him money for letters?"

"No."

"Did he give you any letters to keep for him?"

"He gave me the bag that was substituted for his."

"Locked?"

"Yes. By Jove, I wonder if there is anything in it? I have reason to know that he came into my room that night at least once after I went asleep."

"I think it very likely," he said dryly. "One thing we have not touched on, and I believe Mr. Wardrop knows nothing of it. That is, the disappearance of the old lady. There is a psychological study for you! My conclusion? Well, I should say that Mr. Wardrop is not guilty of the murder. He knows, or thinks he knows, who is. He has a theory of his own, about someone with a scar: it may be only a theory. He does not necessarily know, but he hopes. He is in a state of abject fear. Also, he is hiding something concerning letters, and from the word 'money' in that connection, I believe he either sold or bought some damaging papers. He is not a criminal, but he is what is almost worse."

The doctor rose and picked up his hat. "He is a weakling," he said, from the doorway.

Burton looked at his watch. "By George!" he said. "Seven twenty, and I've had nothing since lunch but a box of sardines. I'm off to chase the festive mutton chop. Oh, by the way, Knox, where is that locked bag?"

"In my office safe."

"I'll drop around in the morning and assist you to compound a felony," he said easily. But as it happened, he did not.

Chapter XXI

A Proscenium Box

I WAS very late for dinner. Fred and Edith were getting ready for a concert, and the two semi-invalids were playing pinochle in Fred's den. Neither one looked much the worse for her previous night's experience; Mrs. Butler was always pale, and Margery had been so since her father's death.

The game was over when I went into the den. As usual, Mrs. Butler left the room almost immediately, and went to the piano across the hall. I had grown to accept her avoidance of me without question. Fred said it was because my overwhelming vitality oppressed her. Personally, I think it was because the neurasthenic type of woman is repulsive to me. No doubt Mrs. Butler deserved sympathy, but her open demand for it found me cold and unresponsive.

I told Margery briefly of my visit to Bellwood that morning. She was as puzzled as I was about the things Heppie had found in the chest. She was relieved, too.

"I am just as sure, now, that she is living, as I was a week ago that she was dead," she said, leaning back in her big chair. "But what terrible thing took her away? Unless—"

"Unless what?"

"She had loaned my father a great deal of money," Margery said, with heightened color. "She had not dared to tell Aunt Letitia, and the money was to be returned before she found it out. Then—things went wrong with the Borough Bank, and—the money did not come back. If you know Aunt Jane, and how afraid she is of Aunt Letitia, you will understand how terrible it was for her. I have wondered if she would go—to Plattsburg, and try to find Father there."

"The *Eagle* man is working on that theory now," I replied. "Margery, if there was a letter 'C' added to eleven twenty-two, would you know what it meant?"

She shook her head in the negative.

"Will you answer two more questions?" I asked.

"Yes, if I can."

"Do you know why you were chloroformed last night, and who did it?"

"I think I know who did it, but I don't understand. I have been trying all day to think it out. I'm afraid to go to sleep tonight."

"You need not be," I assured her. "If necessary, we will have the city police in a ring around the house. If you know and don't tell, Margery, you are running a risk, and more than that, you are protecting a person who ought to be in jail."

"I'm not sure," she persisted. "Don't ask me about it, please."

"What does Mrs. Butler say?"

"Just what she said this morning. And she says valuable papers were taken from under her pillow. She was very ill—hysterical, all afternoon."

The gloom and smouldering fire of the *Sonata Apassionata* came to us from across the hall. I leaned over and took Margery's small hand between my two big ones.

"Why don't you tell me?" I urged. "Or—you needn't tell me, I know what you think. But there isn't any motive that I can see, and why would she chloroform you?"

"I don't know," Margery shuddered. "Sometimes—I wonder—do you think she is altogether sane?"

The music ended with the crash of a minor chord. Fred and Edith came down the stairs, and the next moment we were all together, and the chance for a quiet conversation was gone. At the door Fred turned and came back.

"Watch the house," he said. "And by the way, I guess"—he lowered his voice—"the lady's story was probably straight. I looked around again this afternoon, and there are fresh scratches on the porch roof under her window. It looks queer, doesn't it?"

It was a relief to know that, after all, Mrs. Butler was an enemy and a dangerous person to nobody but herself. She retired to her room almost as soon as Fred and Edith had gone. I was wondering whether or not to tell Margery about the experiment that afternoon; debating how to ask her what letters she had got from the postmaster at Bell-wood addressed to Miss Jane, and what she knew of Bella. At the same time—bear with me, oh masculine reader, the gentle reader will, for she cares a great deal more for the love story than for all the crime and mystery put together—bear with me, I say, if I hold back the account of the terrible events that came that night, to tell how beautiful Margery looked as the lamplight fell on her brown hair and pure profile, and how the impulse came over me to kiss her as she sat there; and how I didn't, after all—poor gentle reader!—and only stooped over and kissed the pink palm of her hand.

She didn't mind it; speaking as nearly as possible from an impersonal standpoint, I doubt if she was even surprised. You see, the ring was gone and—it had only been an engagement ring anyhow, and everybody knows how binding they are!

And then an angel with a burning sword came and scourged me out of my Eden. And the angel was Burton, and the sword was a dripping umbrella.

"I hate to take you out," he said. "The bottom's dropped out of the sky; but I want you to make a little experiment with me." He caught sight of Margery through the portéires, and the imp of mischief in him prompted his next speech. "She said she must see you," he said, very distinctly, and leered at me.

"Don't be an ass," I said angrily. "I don't know that I care to go out tonight."

He changed his manner then.

"Let's go and take a look at the staircase you fellows have been talking about," he said. "I don't believe there is a staircase there, except the main one. I have hounded every politician in the city into or out of that joint, and I have never heard of it."

I felt some hesitation about leaving the house—and Margery—after the events of the previous night. But Margery had caught enough of the conversation to be anxious to have me to go, and when I went in to consult her she laughed at my fears.

"Lightning never strikes twice in the same place," she said bravely. "I will ask Katie to come down with me if I am nervous, and I shall wait up for the family."

I went without enthusiasm. Margery's departure had been delayed for a day only, and I had counted on the evening with her. In fact, I had sent the concert tickets to Edith with an eye single to that idea. But

Burton's plan was right. It was, in view of what we knew, to go over the ground at the White Cat again, and Saturday night, with the place full of men, would be a good time to look around, unnoticed.

"I don't hang so much to this staircase idea," Burton said, "and I have a good reason for it. I think we will find it is the warehouse, yet."

"You can depend on it, Burton," I maintained, "that the staircase is the place to look. If you had seen Wardrop's face today, and his agony of mind when he knew he had associated 'staircase' with 'shot,' you would think just as I do. A man like Schwartz, who knew the ropes, could go quietly up the stairs, unbolt the door into the room, shoot Fleming and get out. Wardrop suspects Schwartz, and he's afraid of him. If he opened the door just in time to see Schwartz, we will say, backing out the door and going down the stairs, or to see the door closing and suspect who had just gone, we would have the whole situation, as I see it, including the two motives of deadly hate and jealousy."

"Suppose the stairs open into the back of the room? He was sitting facing the window. Do you think Schwartz would go in, walk around the table and shoot him from in front? Pooh! Fudge!"

"He had a neck," I retorted. "I suppose he might have turned his head to look around."

We had been walking through the rain. The White Cat, as far off as the poles socially, was only a half-dozen blocks actually from the best residence portion of the city. At the corner of the warehouse, Burton stopped and looked up at it.

"I always get mad when I look at this building," he said. "My great-grandfather had a truck garden on this exact spot seventy years ago, and the old idiot sold out for three hundred dollars and a pair of mules! How do you get in?"

"What are you going in for?" I asked.

"I was wondering if I had a grudge—I have, for that matter—against the mayor, and I wanted to shoot him, how I would go about it. I think I should find a point of vantage, like an overlooking window in an empty building like this, and I would wait for a muggy night, also like this, when the windows were up and the lights going. I could pot him with a thirty-eight at a dozen yards, with my eyes crossed."

We had stopped near the arched gate where I had stood and waited for Hunter, a week before. Suddenly Burton darted away from me and tried the gate. It opened easily, and I heard him splashing through a puddle in the gloomy yard.

"Come in," he called softly. "The water's fine."

The gate swung to behind me, and I could not see six inches from my nose. Burton caught my elbow and steered me, by touching the fence, toward the building.

"If it isn't locked too tight," he was saying, "we can get in, perhaps through a window, and get upstairs. From there we ought to be able to see down into the club. What the devil's that?"

It was a rat, I think, and it scrambled away among the loose boards in a frenzy of excitement. Burton struck a match; it burned faintly in the dampness, and in a moment went out, having shown us only the approximate location of the heavy, arched double doors. A second match showed us a bar and a rusty padlock; there was no entrance to be gained in that way.

The windows were of the eight-paned variety, and in better repair than the ones on the upper floors. By good luck, we found one unlocked and not entirely closed; it shrieked hideously as we pried it up, but an opportune clap of thunder covered the sound.

By this time I was ready for anything that came; I was wet to my knees, muddy, disreputable. While Burton held the window, I crawled into the warehouse, and turned to perform the same service for him. At first I could not see him, outside. Then I heard his voice, a whisper, from beyond the sill.

"Duck," he said. "Cop!"

I dropped below the window, and above the rain I could hear the squash of the watchman's boots in the mud. He flashed a night lamp in at the window next to ours, but he was not very near, and the open window escaped his notice. I felt all the nervous dread of a real malefactor, and when I heard the gate close behind him, and saw Burton put a leg over the sill, I was almost as relieved as I would have been had somebody's family plate, tied up in a tablecloth, been reposing at my feet.

Burton had an instinct for getting around in the dark. I lighted another match as soon as he had closed the window, and we made out our general direction toward where the stairs ought to be. When the match went out, we felt our way in the dark; I had only one box of wax matches, and Burton had dropped his in a puddle.

We got to the second floor, finally, and without any worse mishap than Burton banging his arm against a wheel of some sort. Unlike the first floor, the second was subdivided into rooms; it took a dozen precious matches to find our way to the side of the building overlooking the club, and another dozen to find the window we wanted. When we were there at last, Burton leaned his elbows on the sill, and looked down and across.

"Could anything be better!" he said. "There's our theater, and we've got a proscenium box. That room over there stands out like a spotlight."

He was right. Not more than fifteen feet away, and perhaps a foot lower than our window, was the window of the room where Fleming had been killed. It was empty, as far as we could see; the table, neat enough now, was where it had been before, directly under the light. Anyone who sat there would be an illuminated target from our window. Not only that, but an arm could be steadied on the sill, allowing for an almost perfect aim.

"Now, where's your staircase?" Burton jeered.

The club was evidently full of men, as he had prophesied. Above the rattle of the rain came the thump-thump of the piano, and a half-dozen male voices. The shutters below were closed; we could see nothing.

I think it was then that Burton had his inspiration.

"I'll bet you a five-dollar bill," he said, "that if I fire off my revolver here, now, not one of those fellows down there would pay the slightest attention."

"I'll take that bet," I returned. "I'll wager that every time anybody drops a poker, since Fleming was shot, the entire club turns out to investigate."

In reply Burton got out his revolver, and examined it by holding it against the light from across the way.

"I'll tell you what I'll do," he said. "Everybody down there knows me; I'll drop in for a bottle of beer, and you fire a shot into the floor here, or into somebody across, if you happen to see anyone you don't care for. I suggest that you stay and fire the shot, because if you went, my friend, and nobody heard it, you would accuse me of shooting from the back of the building somewhere."

He gave me the revolver and left me with a final injunction.

"Wait for ten minutes," he said. "It will take five for me to get out of here, and five more to get into the clubhouse. Perhaps you'd better make it fifteen?"

Chapter XXII

In the Room over the Way

HE WENT away into the darkness, and I sat down on an empty box by the window and waited. Had anyone asked me, at that minute, how near we were to the solution of our double mystery, I would have said we had made no progress—save by eliminating Wardrop. Not for one instant did I dream that I was within less than half an hour of a revelation that changed my whole conception of the crime.

I timed the interval by using one of my precious matches to see my watch when he left. I sat there for what seemed ten minutes, listening to the rush of the rain and the creaking of a door behind me in the darkness somewhere, that swung back and forth rustily in the draft from the broken windows. The gloom was infinitely depressing; away from Burton's enthusiasm, his scheme lacked point; his argument, that the night duplicated the weather conditions of that other night, a week ago, seemed less worthy of consideration.

Besides, I have a horror of making myself ridiculous, and I had an idea that it would be hard to explain my position, alone in the warehouse, firing a revolver into the floor, if my own argument was right, and the club should rouse to a search. I looked again at my watch: only six minutes.

Eight minutes.

Nine minutes.

Everyone who has counted the passing of seconds knows how they drag. With my eyes on the room across, and my finger on the trigger, I waited as best I could. At ten minutes I was conscious there was someone in the room over the way. And then he came into view from the side somewhere, and went to the table. He had his back to me, and I could only see that he was a large man, with massive shoulders and dark hair.

It was difficult to make out what he was doing. After a half-minute, however, he stepped to one side, and I saw that he had lighted a candle, and was systematically reading and then burning certain papers, throwing the charred fragments on the table. With the same glance that told me that, I knew the man. It was Schwartz.

I was so engrossed in watching him that when he turned and came directly to the window, I stood perfectly still, staring at him. With the light at his back, I felt certain I had been discovered, but I was wrong. He shook the newspaper which had held the fragments, out of the window, lighted a cigarette and flung the match out also, and turned back into the room. As a second thought, he went back and jerked at the cord of the window shade, but it refused to move.

He was not alone, for from the window he turned and addressed someone in the room behind.

"You are sure you got them all?" he said.

The other occupant of the room came within range of vision. It was Davidson.

"All there were, Mr. Schwartz," he replied. "We were nearly finished before the woman made a bolt." He was fumbling in his pockets. I think I expected him to produce an apple and a penknife, but he held out a small object on the palm of his hand.

"I would rather have done it alone, Mr. Schwartz," he said. "I found this ring in Brigg's pocket this morning. It belongs to the girl."

Schwartz swore and, picking up the ring, held it to the light. Then he made an angry motion to throw it out of the window, but his German cupidity got the better of him. He slid it into his vest pocket instead.

"You're damned poor stuff, Davidson," he said, with a snarl. "If she hasn't got them, then Wardrop has. You'll bungle this job and there'll be hell to pay. Tell McFeely I want to see him."

Davidson left, for I heard the door close. Schwartz took the ring out and held it to the light. I looked at my watch. The time was almost up.

A fresh burst of noise came from below. I leaned out cautiously and

looked down at the lower windows; they were still closed and shuttered. When I raised my eyes again to the level of the room across, I
was amazed to see a second figure in the room—a woman, at that.

Schwartz had not seen her. He stood with his back to her, looking
at the ring in his hand. The woman had thrown her veil back, but I
could see nothing of her face as she stood. She looked small beside
Schwartz's towering height, and she wore black.

She must have said something just then, very quietly, for Schwartz
suddenly lifted his head and wheeled on her. I had a clear view of him,
and if ever guilt, rage, and white-lipped fear showed on a man's face,
it showed on his. He replied—a half-dozen words, in a low tone, and
made a motion to offer her a chair. But she paid no attention.

I have no idea how long a time they talked. The fresh outburst of
noise below made it impossible to hear what they said, and there was
always the maddening fact that I could not see her face. I thought of
Mrs. Fleming, but this woman seemed younger and more slender.
Schwartz was arguing, I imagined, but she stood immobile, scornful,
watching him. She seemed to have made a request, and the man's eva-
sions moved her no whit.

It may have been only two or three minutes, but it seemed longer.
Schwartz had given up the argument, whatever it was, and by pointing out the window, I supposed he was telling her he had thrown what
she wanted out there. Even then she did not turn toward me; I could
not see even her profile.

What happened next was so unexpected that it remains little more
than a picture in my mind. The man threw out his hands as if to show
he could not or would not accede to her request; he was flushed with
rage, and even at that distance the ugly scar on his forehead stood out
like a welt. The next moment I saw the woman raise her right hand,
with something in it.

I yelled to Schwartz to warn him, but he had already seen the
revolver. As he struck her hand aside, the explosion came; I saw her
stagger, clutch at a chair, and fall backward beyond my range of
vision.

Then the light went out, and I was staring at a black, brick wall.

I turned and ran frantically toward the stairs. Luckily, I found them
easily. I fell rather than ran down to the floor below. Then I made a

wrong turning and lost some time. My last match set me right and I got into the yard somehow, and to the street.

It was raining harder than ever, and the thunder was incessant. I ran around the corner of the street, and found the gate to the White Cat without trouble. The inner gate was unlocked, as Burton had said he would leave it, and from the steps of the club I could hear laughter and the refrain of a popular song. The door opened just as I reached the top step, and I half tumbled inside.

Burton was there in the kitchen, with two other men whom I did not recognize, each one holding a stein of beer. Burton had two, and he held one out to me as I stood trying to get my breath.

"You win," he said. "Although I'm a hardworking journalist and need the money, I won't lie. This is Osborne of the *Star* and McTighe of the *Eagle,* Mr. Knox. They heard the shot in there, and if I hadn't told the story, there would have been a panic. What's the matter with you?"

I shut the door into the grillroom and faced the three men.

"For God's sake, Burton," I panted, "let's get upstairs quietly. I didn't fire any shot. There's a woman dead up there."

With characteristic poise, the three reporters took the situation quietly. We filed through the grillroom as casually as we could; with the door closed, however, we threw caution aside. I led the way up the stairs to the room where I had found Fleming's body, and where I expected to find another.

On the landing at the top of the stairs I came face to face with Davidson, the detective, and behind him Judge McFeely. Davidson was trying to open the door of the room where Fleming had been shot, with a skeleton key. But it was bolted inside. There was only one thing to do: I climbed on the shoulders of one of the men, a tall fellow, whose face to this day I don't remember, and by careful maneuvering and the assistance of Davidson's long arms, I got through the transom and dropped into the room.

I hardly know what I expected. I was in total darkness. I know that when I got the door open at last, when the cheerful light from the hall streamed in, and I had not felt Schwartz's heavy hand at my throat, I drew a long breath of relief. Burton found the electric light switch and turned it on. And then—I could hardly believe my senses. The room was empty.

One of the men laughed a little.

"Stung!" he said lightly. "What sort of a story have you and your friend framed up, Burton?"

But I stopped at that minute and picked up a small nickel-plated revolver from the floor. I held it out, on my palm, and the others eyed it respectfully.

Burton, after all, was the quickest-witted of the lot. He threw open one of the two doors in the room, revealing a shallow closet, with papered walls and a row of hooks. The other door stuck tight. One of the men pointed to the floor; a bit of black cloth had wedged it, from the other side. Our combined efforts got it open at last, and we crowded in the doorway, looking down a flight of stairs.

Huddled just below us, her head at our feet, was the body of the missing woman.

"My God," Burton said hoarsely, "who is it?"

Chapter XXIII

A Box of Crown Derby

WE GOT her into the room and on the couch before I knew her. Her fair hair had fallen loose over her face, and one long, thin hand clutched still at the bosom of her gown. It was Ellen Butler!

She was living, but not much more. We gathered around and stood looking down at her in helpless pity. A current of cold night air came up the staircase from an open door below, and set the hanging light to swaying, throwing our shadows in a sort of ghastly dance over her quiet face.

I was too much shocked to be surprised. Burton had picked up her hat, and put it beside her.

"She's got about an hour, I should say," said one of the newspapermen. "See if Gray is around, will you, Jim? He's mostly here Saturday night."

"Is it—Miss Maitland?" Burton asked, in a strangely subdued voice.

"No; it is Henry Butler's widow," I returned, and the three men were reporters again, at once.

Gray was there and came immediately. Whatever surprise he may have felt at seeing a woman there, and dying, he made no comment. He said she might live six hours, but the end was certain. We got a hospital ambulance, and with the clang of its bell as it turned the corner and hurried away, the White Cat drops out of this story, so far as action is concerned.

Three detectives and as many reporters hunted Schwartz all of that night and the next day, to get his story. But he remained in hiding. He had a start of over an hour, from the time he switched off the light and escaped down the built-in staircase. Even in her agony, Ellen Butler's hate had carried her through the doorway after him, to collapse on the stairs.

I got home just as the cab, with Fred and Edith, stopped at the door. I did not let them get out; a half-dozen words, without comment or explanation, and they were driving madly to the hospital.

Katie let me in, and I gave her some money to stay up and watch the place while we were away. Then, not finding a cab, I took a car and rode to the hospital.

The building was appallingly quiet. The elevator cage, without a light, crept spectrally up and down; my footsteps on the tiled floor echoed and reechoed above my head. A night watchman, in felt shoes, admitted me, and took me upstairs.

There was another long wait while the surgeon finished his examination, and a nurse with a basin of water and some towels came out of the room, and another one with dressings went in. And then the surgeon came out, in a white coat with the sleeves rolled above his elbows, and said I might go in.

The cover was drawn up to the injured woman's chin, where it was folded neatly back. Her face was bloodless, and her fair hair had been gathered up in a shaggy knot. She was breathing slowly, but regularly, and her expression was relaxed—more restful than I had ever seen it. As I stood at the foot of the bed and looked down at her, I knew that as surely as death was coming, it would be welcome.

Edith had been calm, before, but when she saw me she lost her self-control. She put her head on my shoulder, and sobbed out the shock and the horror of the thing. As for Fred, his imaginative temperament made him particularly sensitive to suffering in others. As he sat there beside the bed I knew by his face that he was repeating and repenting every unkind word he had said about Ellen Butler.

She was conscious; we realized that after a time. Once she asked for water, without opening her eyes, and Fred slipped a bit of ice between her white lips. Later in the night she looked up for an instant, at me.

"He—struck my—hand," she said with difficulty, and closed her eyes again.

During the long night hours I told the story, as I knew it, in an undertone, and there was a new kindliness in Fred's face as he looked at her.

She was still living by morning, and was rallying a little from the shock. I got Fred to take Edith home, and I took her place by the bed. Someone brought me coffee about eight, and at nine o'clock I was asked to leave the room, while four surgeons held a consultation there. The decision to operate was made shortly after.

"There is only a chance," a gray-haired surgeon told me in brisk short-dipped words. "The bullet went down, and has penetrated the abdomen. Sometimes, taken early enough, we can repair the damage, to a certain extent, and nature does the rest. The family is willing, I suppose?"

I knew of no family but Edith, and over the telephone she said, with something of her natural tone, to do what the surgeons considered best.

I hoped to get some sort of statement before the injured woman was taken to the operating room, but she lay in a stupor, and I had to give up the idea. It was two days before I got her deposition, and in that time I had learned many things.

On Monday I took Margery to Bellwood. She had received the news about Mrs. Butler more calmly than I had expected.

"I do not think she was quite sane, poor woman," she said with a shudder. "She had had a great deal of trouble. But how strange—a murder and an attempt at murder—at that little club in a week!"

She did not connect the two, and I let the thing rest at that. Once, on the train, she turned to me suddenly, after she had been plunged in thought for several minutes.

"Don't you think," she asked, "that she had a sort of homicidal mania, and that she tried to kill me with chloroform?"

"I hardly think so," I returned evasively. "I am inclined to think someone actually got in over the porch roof."

"I am afraid," she said, pressing her gloved hands tight together. "Wherever I go, something happens that I cannot understand. I never willfully hurt anyone, and yet—these terrible things follow me. I am afraid—to go back to Bellwood, with Aunt Jane still gone, and you— in the city."

"A lot of help I have been to you," I retorted bitterly. "Can you think of a single instance where I have been able to save you trouble or anxiety? Why, I allowed you to be chloroformed within an inch of eternity, before I found you."

"But you did find me," she cheered me. "And just to know that you are doing all you can—"

"My poor best," I supplemented.

"It is very comforting to have a friend one can rely on," she finished, and the little bit of kindness went to my head. If she had not got a cinder in her eye at that psychological moment, I'm afraid I would figuratively have trampled Wardrop underfoot, right there. As it was, I got the cinder, after a great deal of looking into one beautiful eye—which is not as satisfactory by half as looking into two—and then we were at Bellwood.

We found Miss Letitia in the lower hall, and Heppie on her knees with a hatchet. Between them sat a packing box, and they were having a spirited discussion as to how it should be opened.

"Here, give it to me," Miss Letitia demanded, as we stopped in the doorway. "You've got stove lengths there for two days if you don't chop 'em up into splinters."

With the hatchet poised in midair she saw us, but she let it descend with considerable accuracy nevertheless, and our greeting was made between thumps.

"Come in"—thump—"like as not it's a mistake"—bang—"but the expressage was prepaid. If it's mineral water—" crash. Something broke inside.

"If it's mineral water," I said, "you'd better let me open it. Mineral water is meant for internal use, and not for hall carpets." I got the hatchet from her gradually. "I knew a case once where a bottle of hair tonic was spilled on a rag carpet, and in a year they had it dyed with spots over it and called it a tiger skin."

She watched me suspiciously while I straightened the nails she had bent, and lifted the boards. In the matter of curiosity, Miss Letitia was truly feminine; great handfuls of excelsior she dragged out herself, and heaped on Heppie's blue apron, stretched out on the floor.

The article that had smashed under the vigor of Miss Letitia's seventy years lay on the top. It had been a teapot, of some very beautiful ware. I have called just now from my study, to ask what sort of ware it was, and the lady who sets me right says it was Crown Derby. Then there were rows of cups and saucers, and heterogeneous articles in the same material that the women folk seemed to understand. At the last, when the excitement seemed over, they found a toast rack in a lower corner of the box and the "Ohs" and "Ahs" had to be done all over again.

Not until Miss Letitia had arranged it all on the dining-room table, and Margery had taken off her wraps and admired from all four corners, did Miss Letitia begin to ask where they had come from. And by that time Heppie had the crate in the woodbox, and the excelsior was a black and smoking mass at the kitchen end of the grounds.

There was not the slightest clue to the sender, but while Miss Letitia rated Heppie loudly in the kitchen, and Bella swept up the hall, Margery voiced the same idea that had occurred to me.

"If—if Aunt Jane were—all right," she said tremulously, "it would be just the sort of thing she loves to do."

I had intended to go back to the city at once, but Miss Letitia's box had put her in an almost cheerful humor, and she insisted that I go with her to Miss Jane's room, and see how it was prepared for its owner's return.

"I'm not pretending to know what took Jane Maitland away from this house in the middle of the night," she said. "She was a good bit of a fool, Jane was; she never grew up. But if I know Jane Maitland, she will come back and be buried with her people, if it's only to put Mary's husband out of the end of the lot.

"And another thing, Knox," she went on, and I saw her old hands were shaking. "I told you the last time you were here that I hadn't been robbed of any of the pearls, after all. Half of those pearls were Jane's and—she had a perfect right to take forty-nine of them if she wanted. She—she told me she was going to take some, and it—slipped my mind."

I believe it was the first lie she had ever told in her hard, conscientious old life. Was she right? I wondered. Had Miss Jane taken the pearls, and if she had, why?

Wardrop had been taking a long walk; he got back about five, and as Miss Letitia was in the middle of a diatribe against white undergarments for colored children, Margery and he had a half-hour alone together. I had known, of course, that it must come, but under the circumstances, with my whole future existence at stake, I was vague as to whether it was colored undergarments on white orphans or the other way round.

When I got away at last, I found Bella waiting for me in the hall. Her eyes were red with crying, and she had a crumpled newspaper in her hand. She broke down when she tried to speak, but I got the newspaper from her, and she pointed with one work-hardened finger to a column on the first page. It was the announcement of Mrs. Butler's tragic accident, and the mystery that surrounded it. There was no mention of Schwartz.

"Is she—dead?" Bella choked out at last.

"Not yet, but there is very little hope."

Amid fresh tears and shakings of her heavy shoulders, as she sat in her favorite place, on the stairs, Bella told me, briefly, that she had lived with Mrs. Butler since she was sixteen, and had only left when the husband's suicide had broken up the home. I could get nothing else out of her, but gradually Bella's share in the mystery was coming to light.

Slowly, too—it was a new business for me—I was forming a theory of my own. It was a strange one, but it seemed to fit the facts as I knew them. With the story Wardrop told that afternoon came my first glimmer of light.

He was looking better than he had when I saw him before, but the news of Mrs. Butler's approaching death and the manner of her injury affected him strangely. He had seen the paper, like Bella, and he turned on me almost fiercely when I entered the library. Margery was in her old position at the window, looking out, and I knew the despondent droop of her shoulders.

"Is she conscious?" Wardrop asked eagerly, indicating the article in the paper.

"No, not now—at least, it is not likely."

He looked relieved at that, but only for a moment. Then he began to pace the room nervously, evidently debating some move. His next action showed the development of a resolution, for he pushed forward two chairs for Margery and myself.

"Sit down, both of you," he directed. "I've got a lot to say, and I want you both to listen. When Margery has heard the whole story, she will probably despise me for the rest of her life. I can't help it. I've got to tell all I know, and it isn't so much after all. You didn't fool me yesterday, Knox; I knew what that doctor was after. But he couldn't make me tell who killed Mr. Fleming, because, before God, I didn't know."

Chapter XXIV
Wardrop's Story

∽

"I HAVE to go back to the night Miss Jane disappeared—and that's another thing that has driven me desperate. Will you tell me why I should be suspected of having a hand in that, when she had been a mother to me? If she is dead, she can't exonerate me; if she is living, and we find her, she will tell you what I tell you—that I know nothing of the whole terrible business."

"I am quite certain of that, Wardrop," I interposed. "Besides, I think I have gotten to the bottom of that mystery."

Margery looked at me quickly, but I shook my head. It was too early to tell my suspicions.

"The things that looked black against me were bad enough, but they had nothing to do with Miss Jane. I will have to go back to before the night she—went away, back to the time Mr. Butler was the state treasurer, and your father, Margery, was his cashier.

"Butler was not a businessman. He let too much responsibility lie with his subordinates—and then, according to the story, he couldn't do much anyhow, against Schwartz. The cashier was entirely under machine control, and Butler was neglectful. You remember, Knox, the crash, when three banks, rotten to the core, went under, and it was found a large amount of state money had gone too. It was Fleming who did it—I am sorry, Margery, but this is no time to mince words. It was

Fleming who deposited the money in the wrecked banks, knowing what would happen. When the crash came, Butler's sureties, to save themselves, confiscated every dollar he had in the world. Butler went to the penitentiary for six months, on some minor count, and when he got out, after writing to Fleming and Schwartz, protesting his innocence, and asking for enough out of the fortune they had robbed him of to support his wife, he killed himself, at the White Cat."

Margery was very pale, but quiet. She sat with her fingers locked in her lap, and her eyes on Wardrop.

"It was a bad business," Wardrop went on wearily. "Fleming moved into Butler's place as treasurer, and took Lightfoot as his cashier. That kept the lid on. Once or twice, when there was an unexpected call for funds, the treasury was almost empty, and Schwartz carried things over himself. I went to Plattsburg as Mr. Fleming's private secretary when he became treasurer, and from the first I knew things were even worse than the average state government.

"Schwartz and Fleming had to hold together; they hated each other, and the feeling was trebled when Fleming married Schwartz's divorced wife."

Margery looked at me with startled, incredulous eyes. What she must have seen confirmed Wardrop's words, and she leaned back in her chair, limp and unnerved. But she heard and comprehended every word Wardrop was saying.

"The woman was a very ordinary person, but it seems Schwartz cared for her, and he tried to stab Mr. Fleming shortly after her marriage. About a year ago Mr. Fleming said another attempt had been made on his life, with poison; he was very much alarmed, and I noticed a change in him from that time on. Things were not going well at the treasury; Schwartz and his crowd were making demands that were hard to supply, and behind all that, Fleming was afraid to go out alone at night.

"He employed a man to protect him, a man named Carter, who had been a bartender in Plattsburg. When things began to happen here in Manchester, he took Carter to the home as a butler.

"Then the Borough Bank got shaky. If it went down there would be an ugly scandal, and Fleming would go too. His notes for half a million were there, without security, and he dared not show the canceled notes he had, with Schwartz's endorsement.

"I'm not proud of the rest of the story, Margery." He stopped his nervous pacing and stood looking down at her. "I was engaged to marry a girl who was everything on earth to me, and—I was private secretary to the state treasurer, with the princely salary of such a position!

"Mr. Fleming came back here when the Borough Bank threatened failure, and tried to get money enough to tide over the trouble. A half million would have done it, but he couldn't get it. He was in Butler's position exactly, only he was guilty and Butler was innocent. He raised a little money here, and I went to Plattsburg with securities and letters. It isn't necessary to go over the things I suffered there; I brought back one hundred and ten thousand dollars, in a package in my Russia leather bag. And—I had something else."

He wavered for the first time in his recital. He went on more rapidly, and without looking at either of us.

"I carried, not in the valise, a bundle of letters, five in all, which had been written by Henry Butler to Mr. Fleming, letters that showed what a dupe Butler had been, that he had been negligent, but not criminal; accusing Fleming of having ruined him, and demanding certain notes that would have proved it. If Butler could have produced the letters at the time of his trial, things would have been different."

"Were you going to sell the letters?" Margery demanded, with quick scorn.

"I intended to, but—I didn't. It was a little bit too dirty, after all. I met Mrs. Butler for the second time in my life, at the gate down there, as I came up from the train the night I got here from Plattsburg. She had offered to buy the letters, and I had brought them to sell to her. And then, at the last minute, I lied. I said I couldn't get them—that they were locked in the Monmouth Avenue house. I put her in a taxicab that she had waiting, and she went back to town. I felt like a cad; she wanted to clear her husband's memory, and I—well, Mr. Fleming was your father, Margery. I couldn't hurt you like that."

"Do you think Mrs. Butler took your leather bag?" I asked.

"I do not think so. It seems to be the only explanation, but I did not let it out of my hand one moment while we were talking. My hand was cramped from holding it, when she gave up in despair at last, and went back to the city."

"What did you do with the letters she wanted?"

"I kept them with me that night, and the next morning hid them in the secret closet. That was when I dropped my fountain pen!"

"And the pearls?" Margery asked suddenly. "When did you get them, Harry?"

To my surprise his face did not change. He appeared to be thinking.

"Two days before I left," he said. "We were using every method to get money, and your father said to sacrifice them, if necessary."

"My father!"

He wheeled on us both.

"Did you think I stole them?" he demanded. And I confess that I was ashamed to say I had thought precisely that.

"Your father gave me nine unmounted pearls to sell," he reiterated. "I got about a thousand dollars for them—eleven hundred and something, I believe."

Margery looked at me. I think she was fairly stunned. To learn that her father had married again, that he had been the keystone in an arch of villainy that, with him gone, was now about to fall, and to associate him with so small and mean a thing as the theft of a handful of pearls—she was fairly stunned.

"Then," I said, to bring Wardrop back to his story, "you found you had been robbed of the money, and you went in to tell Mr. Fleming. You had some words, didn't you?"

"He thought what you all thought," Wardrop said bitterly. "He accused me of stealing the money. I felt worse than a thief. He was desperate, and I took his revolver from him."

Margery had put her hands over her eyes. It was a terrible strain for her, but when I suggested that she wait for the rest of the story, she refused vehemently.

"I came back here to Bellwood, and the first thing I learned was about Miss Jane. When I saw the bloody print on the stair rail, I thought she was murdered, and I had more than I could stand. I took the letters out of the secret closet, before I could show it to you and Hunter, and later I put them in the leather bag I gave you, and locked it. You have it, haven't you, Knox?"

I nodded.

"As for that night at the club, I told the truth then, but not all the truth. I suppose I am a coward, but I was afraid to. If you knew Schwartz, you would understand."

With the memory of his huge figure and the heavy undershot face that I had seen the night before, I could understand very well, knowing Wardrop.

"I went to that room at the White Cat that night, because I was afraid not to go. Fleming might kill himself or someone else. I went up the stairs, slowly, and I heard no shot. At the door I hesitated, then opened it quietly. The door into the built-in staircase was just closing. It must have taken me only an instant to realize what had happened. Fleming was swaying forward as I caught him. I jumped to the staircase and looked down, but I was too late. The door below had closed. I knew in another minute who had been there, and escaped. It was raining, you remember, and Schwartz had forgotten to take his umbrella with his name on the handle!"

"Schwartz!"

"Now do you understand why I was being followed?" he demanded. "I have been under surveillance every minute since that night. There's probably someone hanging around the gate now. Anyhow, I was frantic. I saw how it looked for me, and if I had brought Schwartz into it, I would have been knifed in forty-eight hours. I hardly remember what I did. I know I ran for a doctor, and I took the umbrella with me and left it in the vestibule of the first house I saw with a doctor's sign. I rang the bell like a crazy man, and then Hunter came along and said to go back; Dr. Gray was at the club.

"That is all I know. I'm not proud of it, Margery, but it might have been worse, and it's the truth. It clears up something, but not all. It doesn't tell where Aunt Jane is, or who has the hundred thousand. But it does show who killed your father. And if you know what is good for you, Knox, you will let it go at that. You can't fight the police and the courts single-handedly. Look how the whole thing was dropped, and the most cold-blooded kind of murder turned into suicide. Suicide without a weapon! Bah!"

"I am not so sure about Schwartz," I said thoughtfully. "We haven't yet learned about eleven twenty-two C."

Chapter XXV
Measure for Measure

⟨∞⟩

MISS Jane Maitland had been missing for ten days. In that time not one word had come from her. The reporter from the *Eagle* had located her in a dozen places, and was growing thin and haggard following little old ladies along the street—and being sent about his business tartly when he tried to make inquiries.

Some things puzzled me more than ever in the light of Wardrop's story. For the third time I asked myself why Miss Letitia denied the loss of the pearls. There was nothing in what he had learned either, to tell why Miss Jane had gone away—to ascribe a motive.

How she had gone, in view of Wardrop's story of the cab, was clear. She had gone by streetcar, walking the three miles to Wynton alone at two o'clock in the morning, although she had never stirred around the house at night without a candle, and was privately known to sleep with a light when Miss Letitia went to bed first, and could not see it through the transom.

The theory I had formed seemed absurd at first, but as I thought it over, its probabilities grew on me. I took dinner at Bellwood and started for town almost immediately after.

Margery had gone to Miss Letitia's room, and Wardrop was pacing up and down the veranda, smoking. He looked dejected and anxious, and he welcomed my suggestion that he walk down to the station with me. As we went, a man emerged from the trees across and came slowly after us.

"You see, I am only nominally a free agent," he said morosely. "They'll poison me yet; I know too much."

We said little on the way to the train. Just before it came thundering along, however, he spoke again.

"I am going away, Knox. There isn't anything in this political game for me, and the law is too long. I have a chum in Mexico, and he wants me to go down there."

"Permanently?"

"Yes. There's nothing to hold me here now," he said.

I turned and faced him in the glare of the station lights.

"What do you mean?" I demanded.

"I mean that there isn't any longer a reason why one part of the earth is better than another. Mexico or Alaska, it's all the same to me."

He turned on his heel and left me. I watched him swing up the path, with his head down; I saw the shadowy figure of the other man fall into line behind him. Then I caught the platform of the last car as it passed, and that short ride into town was a triumphal procession with the wheels beating time and singing: "It's all the same—the same—to me—to me."

I called Burton by telephone, and was lucky enough to find him at the office. He said he had just got in, and as usual, he wanted something to eat. We arranged to meet at a little Chinese restaurant, where at that hour, nine o'clock, we would be almost alone. Later on, after the theater, I knew that the place would be full of people, and conversation impossible.

Burton knew the place well, as he did every restaurant in the city.

"Hello, Mike," he said to the unctuous Chinaman who admitted us. And "Mike" smiled a slant-eyed welcome. The room was empty; it was an unpretentious affair, with lace curtains at the windows and small, very clean tables. At one corner a cable and slide communicated through a hole in the ceiling with the floor above, and through the aperture, Burton's order for chicken and rice, and the inevitable tea, was barked.

Burton listened attentively to Wardrop's story, as I repeated it.

"So Schwartz did it, after all!" he said regretfully, when I finished. "It's a tame ending. It had all the elements of the unusual, and it resolves itself into an ordinary, everyday, man-to-man feud. I'm disappointed; we can't touch Schwartz."

"I thought the *Times-Post* was hot after him."

"Schwartz bought the *Times-Post* at three o'clock this afternoon," Burton said, with repressed rage. "I'm called off. Tomorrow we run a photograph of Schwartzwold, his place at Plattsburg, and the next day we eulogize the administration. I'm going down the river on an excursion boat, and write up the pig-killing contest at the union butchers' picnic."

"How is Mrs. Butler?" I asked, as his rage subsided to mere rumbling in his throat

"Delirious"—shortly. "She's going to croak, Wardrop's going to Mexico, Schwartz will be next governor, and Miss Maitland's body will be found in a cistern. The whole thing has petered out. What's the use of finding the murderer if he's coated with asbestos and lined with money? Mike, I want some more tea to drown my troubles."

We called up the hospital about ten thirty, and learned that Mrs. Butler was sinking. Fred was there, and without much hope of getting anything, we went over. I took Burton in as a nephew of the dying woman, and I was glad I had done it. She was quite conscious, but very weak. She told the story to Fred and myself, and in a corner Burton took it down in shorthand. We got her to sign it about daylight sometime, and she died very quietly shortly after Edith arrived at eight.

To give her story as she gave it would be impossible; the ramblings of a sick mind, the terrible pathos of it all, is impossible to repeat. She lay there, her long, thin body practically dead, fighting the death rattle in her throat. There were pauses when for five minutes she would lie in a stupor, only to rouse and go forward from the very word where she had stopped.

She began with her married life, and to understand the beauty of it is to understand the things that came after. She was perfectly, ideally, illogically happy. Then one day Henry Butler accepted the nomination for state treasurer, and with that things changed. During his term in office he altered greatly; his wife could only guess that things were wrong, for he refused to talk.

The crash came, after all, with terrible suddenness. There had been an all-night conference at the Butler home, and Mr. Butler, in a frenzy at finding himself a dupe, had called the butler from bed and forcibly ejected Fleming and Schwartz from the house. Ellen Butler had been horrified, sickened by what she regarded as the vulgarity of the occurrence. But her loyalty to her husband never wavered.

Butler was one honest man against a complete organization of unscrupulous ones. His disgrace, imprisonment and suicide at the White Cat had followed in rapid succession. With his death, all that was worthwhile in his wife died. Her health was destroyed; she became one of the wretched army of neurasthenics, with only one idea: to retaliate, to pay back in measure full and running over, her wrecked life, her dead husband, her grief and her shame.

She laid her plans with the caution and absolute recklessness of a diseased mentality. Normally a shrinking, nervous woman, she became cold, passionless, deliberate in her revenge. To disgrace Schwartz and Fleming was her original intention. But she could not get the papers.

She resorted to hounding Fleming, meaning to drive him to suicide. And she chose a method that had more nearly driven him to madness. Wherever he turned he found the figures eleven twenty-two C. Sometimes just the number, without the letter. It had been Henry Butler's cell number during his imprisonment, and if they were graven on his wife's soul, they burned themselves in lines of fire on Fleming's brain. For over a year she pursued this course—sometimes through the mail, at other times in the most unexpected places, wherever she could bribe a messenger to carry the paper. Sane? No, hardly sane, but inevitable as fate.

The time came when other things went badly with Fleming, as I had already heard from Wardrop. He fled to the White Cat, and for a week Ellen Butler hunted him vainly. She had decided to kill him, and on the night Margery Fleming had found the paper on the pillow, she had been in the house. She was not the only intruder in the house that night. Someone—presumably Fleming himself—had been there before her. She found a ladies desk broken open and a small drawer empty. Evidently Fleming, unable to draw a check while in hiding, had needed ready money. As to the jewels that had been disturbed in Margery's boudoir, I could only surmise the impulse that, after prompting him to take them, had failed at the sight of his dead wife's jewels. Surprised by the girl's appearance, Mrs. Butler had crept to the upper floor and concealed herself in an empty bedroom. It had been almost dawn before she got out. No doubt this was the room belonging to the butler, Carter, which Margery had reported as locked that night.

She took a key from the door of a side entrance, and locked the door behind her when she left. Within a couple of nights she had learned that Wardrop was coming home from Plattsburg, and she met him at Bellwood. We already knew the nature of that meeting. She drove back to town, half maddened by her failure to secure the letters that would have cleared her husband's memory, but the wiser by one thing; Wardrop had inadvertently told her where Fleming was hiding.

The next night she went to the White Cat and tried to get in. She knew from her husband of the secret staircase, for many a political meeting of the deepest significance had been possible by its use. But the door was locked, and she had no key.

Above her the warehouse raised its empty height, and it was not long before she decided to see what she could learn from its upper windows. She went in at the gate and felt her way, through the rain, to the windows. At that moment the gate opened suddenly, and a man muttered something in the darkness. The shock was terrible.

I had no idea, that night, of what my innocent stumbling into the warehouse yard had meant to a half-crazed woman just beyond my range of vision. After a little she got her courage again, and she pried up an unlocked window.

The rest of her progress must have been much as ours had been, a few nights later. She found a window that commanded the club, and with three possibilities that she would lose, and would see the wrong room, she won the fourth. The room lay directly before her, distinct in every outline, with Fleming seated at the table, facing her and sorting some papers.

She rested her revolver on the sill and took absolutely deliberate aim. Her hands were cold, and she even rubbed them together, to make them steady. Then she fired, and a crash of thunder at the very instant covered the sound.

Fleming sat for a moment before he swayed forward. On that instant she realized that there was someone else in the room—a man who took an uncertain step or two forward into view, threw up his hands and disappeared as silently as he had come. It was Schwartz. Then she saw the door into the hall open, saw Wardrop come slowly in and close it, watched his sickening realization of what had occurred; then a sudden panic seized her. Arms seemed to stretch out from the darkness behind her, to draw her into it. She tried to get away, to run, even to scream— then she fainted. It was gray dawn when she recovered her senses and got back to the hotel room she had taken under an assumed name.

By night she was quieter. She read the news of Fleming's death in the papers, and she gloated over it. But there was more to be done; she was only beginning. She meant to ruin Schwartz, to kill his credit, to fell him with the club of public disfavor. Wardrop had told her that her husband's letters were with other papers at the Monmouth Avenue house, where he could not get them.

Fleming's body was taken home that day, Saturday, but she had gone too far to stop. She wanted the papers before Lightfoot could get at them and destroy the incriminating ones. That night she got into the Fleming house, using the key she had taken. She ransacked the library, finding not the letters that Wardrop had said were there, but others, equally or more incriminating, canceled notes, private accounts that would have ruined Schwartz forever.

It was then that I saw the light and went downstairs. My unlucky stumble gave her warning enough to turn out the light. For the rest, the chase through the back hall, the dining room and the pantry, had culminated in her escape up the back stairs, while I had fallen down the dumbwaiter shaft. She had run into Bella on the upper floor— Bella, who had almost fainted, and who knew her and kept her until morning, petting her and soothing her, and finally getting her into a troubled sleep.

That day she realized that she was being followed. When Edith's invitation came she accepted it at once, for the sake of losing herself and her papers, until she was ready to use them. It had disconcerted her to find Margery there, but she managed to get along. For several days everything had gone well: she was getting stronger again, ready for the second act of the play, prepared to blackmail Schwartz, and then expose him. She would have killed him later, probably; she wanted her measure full and running over, and so she would disgrace him first.

Then—Schwartz must have learned of the loss of the papers from the Fleming house, and guessed the rest. She felt sure he had known from the first who had killed Fleming. However that might be, he had had her room entered, Margery chloroformed in the connecting room, and her papers were taken from under her pillow while she was pretending anesthesia. She had followed the two men through the house and out the kitchen door, where she had fainted on the grass.

The next night, when she had retired early, leaving Margery and me downstairs, it had been an excuse to slip out of the house. How she found that Schwartz was at the White Cat, how she got through the side entrance, we never knew. He had burned the papers before she got there, and when she tried to kill him, he had struck her hand aside.

When we were out in the cheerful light of day again, Burton turned his shrewd, blue eyes on me.

"Awful story, isn't it?" he said. "Those are primitive emotions, if you like. Do you know, Knox, there is only one explanation we haven't worked on for the rest of this mystery—I believe in my soul you carried off the old lady and the Russia leather bag yourself."

Chapter XXVI

Lovers and a Letter

AT NOON that day I telephoned to Margery.

"Come up," I said, "and bring the keys to the Monmouth Avenue house. I have some things to tell you, and—some things to ask you."

I met her at the station with Lady Gray and the trap. My plans for that afternoon were comprehensive; they included what I hoped to be the solution of the Aunt Jane mystery; also, they included a little drive through the park, and a—well, I shall tell about that, all I am going to tell, at the proper time.

To play propriety, Edith met us at the house. It was still closed, and even in the short time that had elapsed it smelled close and musty.

At the door into the drawing room I stopped them. "Now, this is going to be a sort of game," I explained. "It's a sort of button, button, who's got the button, without the button. We are looking for a drawer, receptacle or closet, which shall contain, bunched together, and without regard to whether they should be there or not, a small revolver, two military brushes and a clothes brush, two or three soft bosomed shirts, perhaps a half-dozen collars, and a suit of underwear. Also a small flat package about eight inches long and three wide."

"What in the world are you talking about?" Edith asked.

"I am not talking, I am theorizing," I explained. "I have a theory, and according to it the things should be here. If they are not, it is my misfortune, not my fault."

I think Margery caught my idea at once, and as Edith was ready for anything, we commenced the search. Edith took the top floor, being accustomed, she said, to finding unexpected things in the servants' quarters; Margery took the lower floor, and for certain reasons I took the second.

For ten minutes there was no result. At the end of that time I had finished two rooms, and commenced on the blue boudoir. And here, on the top shelf of a three-corner Empire cupboard, with glass doors and spindle legs, I found what I was looking for. Every article was there. I stuffed a small package into my pocket, and called the two girls.

"The lost is found," I stated calmly, when we were all together in the library.

"When did you lose anything?" Edith demanded. "Do you mean to say, Jack Knox, that you brought us here to help you find a suit of gaudy pajamas and a pair of military brushes?"

"I brought you here to find Aunt Jane," I said soberly, taking a letter and the flat package out of my pocket. "You see, my theory worked out. *Here* is Aunt Jane, and *there* is the money from the Russia leather bag."

I laid the packet in Margery's lap, and without ceremony opened the letter. It began:

My Dearest Niece:

I am writing to you, because I cannot think what to say to Sister Letitia. I am running away! I—am—running—away! My dear, it scares me even to write it, all alone in this empty house. I have had a cup of tea out of one of your lovely cups, and a nap on your pretty couch, and just as soon as it is dark I am going to take the train for Boston. When you get this, I will be on the ocean, the ocean, my dear, that I have read about, and dreamed about, and never seen.

I am going to realize a dream of forty years—more than twice as long as you have lived. Your dear mother saw the continent before she died, but the things I have wanted have always been denied me. I have been of those that have eyes to see and see not. So—I have run away. I am going to London and Paris, and even to Italy, if the money your father gave me for the pearls will hold out. For a year

now I have been getting steamship circulars, and I have taken a little French through a correspondence school. That was why I always
made you sing French songs, dearie: I wanted to learn the accent. I
think I should do very well if I could only sing my French instead
of speaking it.

I am afraid that Sister Letitia discovered that I had taken some of
the pearls. But—half of them were mine, from our mother, and
although I had wanted a pearl ring all my life, I have never had one.
I am going to buy me a hat, instead of a bonnet, and clothes, and
pretty things underneath, and a switch; Margery, I have wanted a
switch for thirty years.

I suppose Letitia will never want me back. Perhaps I shall not
want to come. I tried to write to her when I was leaving, but I had
cut my hand in the attic, where I had hidden away my clothes, and
it bled on the paper. I have been worried since for fear your Aunt
Letitia would find the paper in the basket, and be alarmed at the
stains. I wanted to leave things in order—please tell Letitia—but I
was so nervous, and in such a hurry. I walked three miles to Wynton and took a streetcar. I just made up my mind I was going to do
it. I am sixty-five, and it is time I have a chance to do the things I
like.

I came in on the car, and came directly here. I got in with the second key on your keyring. Did you miss it? And I did the strangest
thing at Bellwood. I got down the stairs very quietly and out onto
the porch. I set down my empty traveling bag—I was going to buy
everything new in the city—to close the door behind me. Then I
was sure I heard someone at the side of the house, and I picked it
up and ran down the path in the dark.

You can imagine my surprise when I opened the bag this morning to find I had picked up Harry's. I am emptying it and taking it
with me, for he has mine.

If you find this right away, please don't tell Sister Letitia for a day
or two. You know how firm your Aunt Letitia is. I shall send her a
present from Boston to pacify her, and perhaps when I come back
in three or four months, she will be over the worst.

I am not quite comfortable about your father, Margery. He is not
like himself. The last time I saw him he gave me a little piece of
paper with a number on it and he said they followed him every-

where, and were driving him crazy. Try to have him see a doctor. And I left a bottle of complexion cream in the little closet over my mantel, where I had hidden my hat and shoes that I wore. Please destroy it before your Aunt Letitia sees it.

Good-bye, my dear niece. I suppose I am growing frivolous in my old age, but I am going to have silk linings in my clothes before I die.

Your Loving Aunt Jane

When Margery stopped reading, there was an amazed silence. Then we all three burst into relieved, uncontrolled mirth. The dear, little, old lady with her new independence and her sixty-five-year-old, romantic, starved heart!

Then we opened the packet, which was a sadder business, for it had represented Allan Fleming's last clutch at his waning public credit.

Edith ran to the telephone with the news for Fred, and for the first time that day Margery and I were alone. She was standing with one hand on the library table; in the other she held Aunt Jane's letter, half tremulous, wholly tender. I put my hand over hers, on the table.

"Margery!" I said. She did not stir.

"Margery, I want my answer, dear. I love you—love you; it isn't possible to tell you how much. There isn't enough time in all existence to tell you. You are mine, Margery—mine. You can't get away from that."

She turned, very slowly, and looked at me with her level eyes. "Yours!" she replied softly, and I took her in my arms.

Edith was still at the telephone.

"I don't know," she was saying. "Just wait until I see."

As she came toward the door, Margery squirmed, but I held her tight. In the doorway Edith stopped and stared; then she went swiftly back to the telephone.

"Yes, dear," she said sweetly. "They are, this minute."

The Buckled Bag

Chapter I

I HAVE broken down in health lately—nothing serious; but a nurse lasts only so long, and during the last five years I have been under a double strain. Caring for the sick has been only a part of it. The other?

Well, put it like this: The world's pretty crowded after all. We are always touching elbows, and there is never a deviation from the usual, the normal, that is not felt all the way down the line. Stand a row of dominoes on edge and knock down the end one. Do you see? And generally somebody goes down for fair. We do not know much about it among the poor; they have to manage the best way they can, and maybe they are blunted—some of them. They have not the time for mental agony. And the thing works both ways. Their lapses are generally obvious—cause and result; motive and crime.

In the lower walks of life people are more elemental. But get up higher. Crime exists there; but, instead of a passion, it is a craft. In its detection it is brain against brain, not intellect against brute force or instinct. If anything gives, it is the body.

Illness follows crime—it does not always follow the criminal; but somebody goes down for fair. There is a breach in the wall. The doctor and the clergyman come in then. One way and another they get the story. There is nothing hidden from them. They get it, but they do not want it. They cannot use it. The clergyman's vows and the medical man's legal status forbid their using their knowledge; but, where a few years ago there were only two, now each crisis, mental or physical, finds three—the trained nurse.

Do you see what I mean? The thing is thrust at her. She does not want the story either. Her business is bodies, doctors' orders, nourishments; but unless she's a fool, she ends by holding the family secret in the hollow of her hand. It worries her. She needs her hands. She gets rid of it as soon as she can and forgets it. She is safe; the secret is safe. Without the clergyman's vows or the doctor's legal status, she is as silent as either.

That is the ethical side. That is what the nurse does. There is another side, which is mine. The criminal uses every means against society. Why not society against the criminal? And this is my defense. Every trained nurse plays a game, a sort of sporting proposition—her wits against wretchedness. I play a double game—the fight against misery and the fight against crime—like a man running two chessboards at once.

I hated it in the beginning. It has me by the throat now. It is the criminal I find absorbing. And I have learned some things—not new, of course: that to be honest because one is untempted is to be strong with the strength of a child; that the great virtues often link arms with the great vices; that the big criminal thinks big thoughts.

I have had my chance to learn and I know. A nurse gets under the very skin of the soul. She finds a mind surrendered, all the crooked little motives that have fired the guns of life revealed in their pitifulness. Even now, sometimes, it hurts me to look back.

IT IS five years since George L. Patton was shot in the leg during a raid on the Hengst Place, in Cherry Run. He is at the head of one of the big private agencies now, but he was a county detective then; and Hengst shot him from a cupboard. Well, that does not matter particularly, except that Mr. Patton was brought to the hospital that night and I was given the case.

He took it very calmly—said he guessed he would rest awhile, now he had the chance, and slept eighteen hours without moving. I made caps, I remember, and tried to plan what I would do when I left the house. My time was about up and I dreaded private duty. I had been accustomed to the excitement of a hospital, and there was something horrible to me in the idea of spending the rest of my life in darkened rooms, with the doctor's daily visit for excitement and a walk round the block for recreation.

I gave Mr. Patton his dinner that night and we had our first clash. He looked at the soup and toast, and demanded steak and onions.

"I'm sorry," I said. "You're to have light diet for a day or two. We don't want any fever from that leg."

"Leg! What has my leg to do with my stomach? I want a medium steak. I'll do without the onions if I have to."

"Doctor's orders," I said firmly. "You may have an egg custard if you want it, or some cornstarch."

We had a downright argument and he took the soup. When he had finished, he looked up at me and smiled.

"I don't like you," he said, "but darned if I don't respect you, young woman. Absolute obedience to orders is about the hardest thing in the world to get. And now send for that fool intern and we'll have a steak for breakfast."

Well, he did; and pretty soon he was getting about everything the hospital could give him. He was a politician, of course, and we depended on our state appropriation for support; but he got nothing from me without an order. He always said he did not like me, but I think he did after a while. I could beat him at chess, for one thing.

"You have a good head, Miss Adams," he said to me one day when he was almost well. "Are you going to spend the rest of your life changing pillow slips and shaking down a thermometer?"

"I've thought of institutional work; I daresay I'd be changing nurses and shaking down interns," I said with some bitterness.

"How old are you? Not, of course, for publication."

"Twenty-nine."

"Any family?"

"The nearest relatives I have are two old aunts, in the country."

He was silent for a minute or two. Then, "I've been thinking of something; I may take it up with you later. There's only one objection—you're rather too good-looking."

"I'm not really good-looking at all," I admitted frankly. "I have too high a forehead. It's the cap."

"Like 'em high!" said Mr. Patton.

I made an eggnog and brought it in to him. He was sitting propped in a chair, and when I gave him the glass, he smiled up at me. He had never attempted any sentimentalities with me, which is more than can be said of the usual convalescent male over forty.

"It isn't all the cap," he said.

That afternoon he tried to learn from me something about the other patients on the floor, but of course I would tell him nothing. He seemed rather irritated and tried to bully me, but I was firm.

"Don't be childish, Mr. Patton!" I said at last. "We don't tell about other patients. If you want to find out, get one of your men in here." To my surprise he laughed.

"Good girl!" he said. "You've stood a cracking test and come through A one. You've got silence and obedience to orders, and you have a brain. I've mentioned the forehead. Now I'm going to make my proposition. Has it ever occurred to you that every crisis, practically, among the better classes, finds a trained nurse on hand?"

"Cause or result?"

"Result, of course. Upset the ordinary routine of a family, have a robbery, an elopement or a murder, and somebody goes to bed, with a trained nurse in attendance. Fact, isn't it?" I admitted it. "It's a fault of the tension people live under," he went on. "Any extra strain and something snaps. And who is it who is in the very bosom of the family? You know and I know. The nurse gets it all—the intimate details that the police miss; the family disputes, the inner motives; the— You go to your room and think it over. And when you decide, I have a case for you."

I tried to object, but he cut me short; so I put the thermometer in his mouth and managed to tell him how I felt.

"It just doesn't seem honest," I finished. "I'm in a position of confidence and I violate it. That's the truth. A nurse is supposed to work for good; if she has any place, it's an uplift—if you can see what I mean. And to go into a house and pry out its secrets—"

He jerked the thermometer out wrathfully.

"Uplift!" he said. "Isn't it uplifting to place a criminal where he won't injure society? If you can't see it that way, we don't want you. Now go away and think about it."

I went up to my room and stood in front of the mirror, which is where I do most of my thinking. I talk things over with myself, I suppose. And I saw the lines beside my ears that said, "Twenty-nine, almost thirty!" And I thought of institutional work, with its daily round of small worries, its monotonous years, with my soul gradually shrinking and shaping itself to fit a set of rules. And over against it all I put Mr. Patton's offer.

I recall it all—the color that came to my face at the chance to use my head instead of only a trained obedience to orders; the prospect of adventure; the chance to pit my wits against other wits and perhaps win out. I put on one of the new caps and went down to Mr. Patton's room.

"I'll do it!" I said calmly.

MY TIME was up two days later. Mr. Patton was practically well and gave me my instructions while I helped him pack his bag.

"Do the things the other nurses do," he advised. "Go to the Nurses' Home, but don't register for cases right away. Make an excuse that you're tired and need a few days' rest. When I telephone you, I shall call myself Dr. Patton—not that I pretend to do any medical work, but for extra caution."

"You said you had a case for me."

"I had, but it isn't big enough. I want you for something worthwhile, and it will be along soon. It's about due."

"And—just one thing, Mr. Patton: I will take my first case on trial. If I find that I am doing harm and not good by revealing the secrets of a family, I shall give it up. A doctor would be answerable to the law for doing the things I am about to do."

"You have no legal status."

"I have a moral status," I replied grimly, and he found no answer to that.

Before he left, however, he said something that rather cheered me.

"You will never be required to tell anything you learn, except what is directly pertinent to the matter in hand," he said. "I would not give such latitude to any other woman I know, but you have brains and you will know what we want."

"I cannot work in the dark. I must know what you are after."

"We will lay all our cards on your table faceup. I wouldn't insult you by asking you to play blindfolded. And remember this, Miss Adams—

it's as high a duty to explore and heal the moral sores of a community as it is to probe and dress, for instance, the wound of a man who has been shot in the leg."

Two days later I left the hospital and took a room at the Nurses' Home he had recommended. He would arrange with the secretary, he said, that I should be called for any case on which he wished me placed.

I put in a bad week. One of the staff of the hospital located me and called me to a case. I got out of it by saying I needed a few days' rest, and he rang off irritably. Then, on the third day, I had my handbag cut off my arm in a department store, and went home depressed and ill-humored.

"You're a fine detective!" I said to myself in the mirror. "You're not so clever as Mr. Patton thinks, and if you're honest, you'll go and tell him so."

I think I should have done so—I was so abashed; but our arrangement was that I should not try to see him under any circumstances. There was to be no suspicion of me in any way. He would see me when necessary. I still had the strap of my bag, which had been left hanging to my arm; and, as a constant reminder, I fastened it to the frame of my mirror. Even now, when the department gives me its best cases, and when I have been successful enough to justify a little pride, I look at that bit of leather and become meek and normal again.

Chapter II

IN SPITE of Mr. Patton's promise, I went on my first case for him without any preparation. Miss Shinn, the secretary, asked me if I would take a case that evening.

"For whom?"

She was turning over the pages of her ledger in the parlor office of the Home and she did not look up.

"A Dr. Patton telephoned," she said. "I believe he had spoken to you of the case."

My throat tightened, but, after all, this was what I had been waiting for. "Do you know what sort of case it is?" I asked. "I'm not doing obstetrics, you know."

"It is not an obstetric case. You are to take a taxicab at eight o'clock tonight."

Miss Shinn was a heavy, rather bilious brunette, who rarely smiled, but I caught an amused twinkle as she glanced up. Quite suddenly I liked her. Clearly she knew what I was about to do and she did not disapprove; and yet she was a very ethical person. I gathered that she would be very hard on a nurse who wore frivolous uniforms, or gossiped about her patients, or went to the theater with a doctor, or cut rates. And yet she was indulgent to me—she was more than indulgent. I was certain, somehow, from the very quiver of her wide back as she marked me ENGAGED on her register, that she was wildly interested and curious. It gave me confidence.

At eight o'clock that evening I went downstairs with my suitcase and ordered a taxicab. No word had come from Mr. Patton and I had nothing but a name and address to go by. The name—we will call it G. W. March. It was not, of course. You would know the name at once if I told it. The address was a street fronting one of the parks—a good neighborhood, I knew—old families, substantial properties, traditions, all that sort of thing. Certainly not a place to look for crime.

As I waited for the cab, I searched the newspapers for something to throw light on my new enterprise. There was nothing at all except a notice that Mr. and Mrs. George W. March had returned from their summer home on the Maine coast a few days before and had opened their city home.

It looked like a robbery. I was vaguely disappointed. I had it all worked out in five minutes—Mrs. March in bed, collapsed; missing pictures or jewels; house full of trusted servants; and myself trying to solve the mystery between an alcohol rub and a dose of bromide. I hated to go on with it, but I was ashamed not to. I said to myself savagely that I was not a quitter, and got into the taxicab.

The March case was not a robbery, however. It was, strictly speaking, not a criminal case at all. It concerned the disappearance of a girl, and in some ways it was a remarkable mystery—particularly baffling because for so long it seemed to be a result without a cause. How we found the cause at last; how we located the family in Brickyard Road and solved the puzzle of the buckled bag; how we learned the identity of the little old woman with the jet bonnet, and her connection with the garden door—all this makes up the record of my first case.

The buckled bag is lying on my desk now. It is a shabby, quaint old bag, about eight inches long, round-bellied, brown with wear. It still contains what was in it when Mr. Patton found it: a cotton handkerchief, marked with a J; two keys—one a house-door key, the other a flat one; a scrawled note in a soiled lavender envelope; a newspaper clipping of a sale of blankets.

It is one of my most painful memories that for a month I examined that newspaper cutting frequently and that I failed entirely to grasp the significance of the reverse side. We all have a mental blind spot. That was mine.

Clare March was missing. That was my case: to find her, or to help to find her, was my task at first. Later it grew more complicated. I had not thought Mr. Patton would violate our agreement about working in the dark, and my confidence was justified. At the first corner he hailed the machine and got in.

"Fine work!" he said. "You're a dependable person, Miss Adams."

"I'm rather a scared person."

"Nonsense! And don't take yourself or this affair too seriously. Do your durnedest—'Angels could do no more.' "

"Is it something stolen?"

"A small matter of a daughter. It's a queer thing, Miss Adams. I'll tell you about it." He asked the driver to go slowly. "Time us to get there at eight thirty," he said. "Now, Miss Adams, here are the facts: You are going to the home of George March, the banker—you probably know the name—Mrs. March is your patient. She's not ill; she's hysterical and frightened—that's all. It's not a hard case."

"It's the hardest sort of a case."

"Well, you like work," he replied cheerfully. "The family has been away for four months. Until a month ago, Clare, the daughter, was with them. One month ago, on the third of September, Clare, who is an only child, twenty years old, left the country place in Maine for home. She traveled alone, leaving her maid in the country. The city house had not been closed; a housekeeper and two maids were there through the summer. She was expected at the house for breakfast on the morning of the fourth. She did not arrive—or, rather, she did not go home. She reached the city safely. We have traced her into the railroad station and out again—and that has been about all. She's not been seen since."

"Perhaps she has eloped."

"Possibly; but the man she is engaged to is in the city, almost frantic. Besides, there is more than I have told you. We know that she took a taxicab at the station; that before she got in, she met and accepted a small parcel from a blond young man, rather shabbily dressed; and that they seemed to be having an argument, though a quiet one. We have found the taxicab she took, and a shop where she bought a couple of books—a Browning and a recent novel. From the bookshop she went to a department store. There she dismissed the taxicab. We have traced her in the store to a department where she bought a pair of blankets. They made a large parcel, but she took it with her. From that time we have lost her absolutely."

"The third of September, and this is the fifth of October—almost five weeks!"

"Exactly," he said dryly. "That's why I've sent for you. We have tried all the usual things; we've combed the city fine—and we are just where we started. If we could make a noise about it, we should have some chance. Set the general public looking—that's the way to get information. You get a million clues worth nothing, and out of the lot one that helps. But you know these people. They won't listen to any publicity. They have only one argument—if she is dead, publicity won't help her, and if she is alive, it will hurt her."

I was conscious of a vague disappointment. In the last half hour I had keyed myself to the highest pitch. I was seeing red, really—nothing but the bloodiest sort of crime would have come up to my expectation. Certainly nothing less than a murder had been in my thoughts.

"I don't see how I can help," I said, a bit resentfully. "You've had five weeks and got nowhere," I continued, "and if you are going to ask me to put myself in her place, and try to imagine what could have happened, and to follow her mental processes, I can't do it. I can't imagine myself idle and rich and twenty. I can't imagine taking a taxicab when a streetcar would do, or having a lady's maid—"

Mr. Patton laid a hand on my arm.

"Did you ever hear Lincoln's story of the little Mississippi steamboat with a whistle so large that every time they blew it the boat stopped? . . . No? Well, no matter. I don't want you to put yourself in her place; I want a little inside help—that's all. There's a curious story behind this case, Miss Adams. We've only scratched the top. Get in there and get their confidence. They won't talk to me—too much family pride. Get the mother to talk. That's part of her trouble—family pride and bottling up her emotions. I can't get close to any of them. After five weeks Mrs. March still calls me Mr. Peyton." He smiled ruefully.

"She bought blankets! That's curious, isn't it?"

"It's almost ridiculous under the circumstances. You may not be able to imagine yourself twenty, and so on, but you can certainly get your wits to work on those blankets. If she had bought a revolver now—but blankets!"

"She was engaged, you say? Were there any other men who—who liked her?"

"Half a dozen, I believe—all accounted for."

"Any neurasthenic tendency?"

"In the half dozen? I daresay yes, when she announced her engagement; in the girl—I think not. She was temperamental rather. The picture I get of her is of an attractive and indulged young woman, engaged to a man she seems to have cared about. And yet, with all the gods smiling, she disappears."

I sat thoughtful. The cab was moving along beside the park now. We were almost there.

"She may be dead," I said at last.

"She may, indeed."

He asked the driver to stop and got out, with a quick handshake.

"Now go to it!" he said. "Go out for a breath of air between seven and eight each evening, and keep your eyes open. I have a hunch that you'll get this thing—beginner's luck."

The March house was an old-fashioned, rather stately residence. Instead of a drawing room upstairs, there was a reception room opening into the lower hall. Behind that was a music room and, still farther back, a library.

At the very rear of the lower floor was a dining room, quite the largest room in the house, extending as it did the entire width of the building.

In it was a large bay window looking onto a city garden, and in the bay, shut off by tall plants, was a small table, where the family breakfasted and even, when alone, sometimes dined.

A long flight of stairs, uncarpeted, led to the second floor. On that first evening I got merely the vaguest outlines of the house, of course. It was silent, immaculate, rather heavy. I had a glimpse of two men in the library talking—one middle-aged, rather stout; the other much younger. Over everything hung the hush of suspense—that hush which accompanies birth and death and great trouble.

A parlor maid admitted me and led me upstairs to my room.

"Mr. March would like to see you in the library when you have taken off your things," she said.

I changed quickly into my uniform—all white, of course, with rubber-soled white shoes. With the familiar garb I was myself again; I could face anything, do anything. Clothes are queer things.

Mr. March turned when he heard me at the door and rose.

"I am Miss Adams, the nurse," I said. "Do you wish to see me?"

"Will you come in, Miss Adams? This is Mr. Plummer. Have you seen Mrs. March?"

"No. I thought it best to see you first."

"I am glad of that. Perhaps I ought to tell you—we are in great trouble, Miss Adams. Our—our only daughter has gone away, disappeared. It is over a month since—" He stopped.

"That is very terrible," I said. I liked his face.

"We wish absolute secrecy—of course I need hardly say that; but you understand Mrs. March is highly nervous. I—I hope you can quiet her. What we want you to do is to be as cheerful and optimistic as possible. You know what I mean. She will talk to you about Clare—about Miss March. Reassure her if you can. Be certain that Miss March will be found soon.

"I will do what I can. Has the doctor left any orders?"

"Very few. She is to be soothed. There's a bromide, I believe. Her maid has the instructions."

There was nothing for me in that glimpse of the two men most nearly concerned—two gentlemen unaffectedly distressed and under great strain in a quiet, well-ordered house. It looked like poor material, from Mr. Patton's point of view. Mr. March followed me into the hall.

"If you need anything, let me know, Miss Adams. Or will you speak to the servants?"

"I can tell better later on. If I am going to be up tonight—and I think I'd better be, this first night anyhow—I should like a lunch; something cold on a tray."

"Do you wish it upstairs?"

I hesitated. There was a picture in a silver frame on the library table—I thought it probably one of the missing girl. I wanted to see it. "It will be a change to come down."

"Very well," he said. "There will be a supper left in the dining room. There is a small table there in the bay window. It will be more comfortable—not quite so lonely."

"Thank you," I replied and started upstairs. Opposite the library door I glanced in. I had been right about the picture. Mr. Plummer had picked it up and was looking at it. I felt certain that he was the fiancé—a manly looking fellow; not very tall, but solid and dependable-looking, with a good head and earnest eyes.

My patient was in bed—a pretty little woman in a frilly bed jacket, with a pink light beside her. She held out a nervous hand.

"How big and strong and competent you look!" she said, and quite unexpectedly fell to crying. I had a difficult evening. She was entirely unstrung—must have me sit down by the bed at once and listen to the trouble, as she called it—and as it was, indeed.

"She wouldn't go away and leave me like this!" she said more than once. "If you only knew her, Miss Adams—so full of character, so determined, so gifted! And beautiful—haven't you seen her picture in the newspapers?"

I evaded that. I never read society news.

"And happy, too?" I said. "She must have been very happy."

I saw a change in Mrs. March's rather childish face.

"We thought she was, of course; but lately— I've remembered so many things while I've been lying here. She was very strange all summer—moody sometimes, and again so gay that she frightened me."

"Perhaps she was gay when Mr. Plummer was there and moody when he was away."

"But he wasn't there at all. That's another thing, Miss Adams. She would not let me ask Walter up. She—she really kept him away all summer. I don't believe Mr. March told the detective that. He forgot so many things."

She wanted me to telephone this piece of information to the police at once, but I persuaded her to wait. I gave her an alcohol rub and a cup of hot milk; and finding them without effect, I took a massage vibrator I found on her dressing table and ran it up and down her spine. She finally relaxed with the treatment and even asked me to use it on her face.

"I'm an old woman with all the worry," she said apologetically. "It will tone up the facial muscles, won't it? And would you mind putting some cold cream on first?"

I did not mind; and after a time she fell asleep. I was glad of a respite. In my two hours over the bed I had accumulated many ill-assorted bits of information. I wanted time to catalogue them in my mind. I have the notes I made that night on one of my records:

"C. has been missing since September third; today is October fifth—a total of thirty-two days.

"Was moody all summer—would not see Mr. Plummer, but wrote him daily.

"She had been engaged once before, to a Wilson Page, but broke engagement. Cause of trouble not known. C. suffered much at the time. Note—Have Mr. P. look up Wilson Page.

"C. usually undemonstrative, but rather affected when she said good-bye to her mother. Was she planning something, unknown to them?

"But if she was planning an elopement, why did she make careful appointments with her dressmakers and milliners? Is she more crafty than they think, or was her decision made unexpectedly?

"She forgot her jewel case, which she always carried with her. An inventory reveals only a part of her jewelry. She wore, when she left, only the sapphire ring Mr. Plummer gave her. She had less than a hundred dollars in cash.

"Wilson Page is dark. The man who met her in the station was thin and fair.

"Her picture is on her mother's dressing table—an attractive face: dark-eyed, full of character, but rather wistful. A thoughtful face. Is she living or dead? Did she go voluntarily or was she lured away? If she went voluntarily—why?"

I looked round the handsome room where my patient slept calmly, her petulant features relaxed and peaceful. I glanced across the hall to Miss Clare's room, where a light burned every evening; where an ivory dressing set, with carved monogram, was spread on the toilet table; where every luxury a young woman could demand had been gathered together for her use. And I recalled the look in the face of the man downstairs as he gazed at her picture—the tragedy in the eyes of her father. How had she gone, and why? How and why?

Chapter III

My FIRST night at the March house was marked by a disagreeable and rather mystifying occurrence. I had got my patient quiet and asleep and had had a telephone talk with the doctor by eleven.

"There is very little to do," the doctor said. "I'll come in in the morning. Just keep her comfortable and cheerful. She needs someone to talk to. Let her talk all she wants."

I darkened the room where she lay and placed a screen in the hall outside the door, with a comfortable chair beside it and a shaded lamp. I had made up my mind to sit up for that one night at least. I had had nervous cases before; and I knew that sometime between then and morning she would waken, and that the sight of someone alert and watchful would be a comfort.

At midnight I took off my cap, eased my hair and loosened my uniform collar. With the neck of my dress turned in, I was fairly comfortable. It was too early to eat. I got a book from the library and read.

At two o'clock Mrs. March was still sleeping quietly and I decided to get my night supper. I slipped down the stairs as noiselessly as possible. An English hall lamp was turned on in the lower hall near the music-room door, and far back in the dining room a candle light in a wall bracket showed me where to go.

My progress in my rubber-soled shoes was practically noiseless. I made my way along the hall back to the dining room. The room was very large, as I have said before, paneled in oak, with a heavy fireplace and a tapestry in an overmantel above. At one corner, beside the deep bay window, were French doors, hung with casement cloths, evidently leading out into the garden.

I was deliberate in all my movements, I remember. I went to the fireplace and stood looking up at the overmantel; I found the switch that would throw the light over my small table and thus give me a more cheerful place to eat. The bay, walled off by palms and flowering oleanders in tubs, was dark and rather uninviting at that hour. I made no particular attempt to be silent, but I daresay it is a result of my training that I make no unnecessary noise.

One of the older nurses once said to me, "When you go out on private duty, you'll have to fuss about your night supper generally. An orange and a glass of milk is about what most cooks set out. Keep them up to the mark. Insist on cold meat or sandwiches; and if there's an alcohol coffeepot, have them leave it ready. Coffee is your best friend at three in the morning, and your next best is a shawl to lay over your knees."

I was thinking of that and rather smiling when I entered the recess and sat down at the small table. I was absolutely calm and beginning to be mightily interested in my case. The tray was ready; and there was a small alcohol coffeepot ready, with a box of matches beside it.

I lit the lamp and inspected the tray. The cook seemed to have been trained by some predecessor. There was chicken, a bit of salad, brown bread and fruit. I ate slowly while my coffee cooked—ate with an ear toward the staircase for a sound from my patient above, and with an occasional eye toward the garden below. A late moon showed a brick terrace under the windows, and three steps lower was a formal design of flower bed and path, with a small cement circle, evidently a pool in summer. Somehow the garden looked uncanny—bushes became figures, moving about, waving arms in the breeze. I was a distinct object from outside as I sat in my nook; and having eaten and waiting only for the coffee, I stood up and extinguished the light over my head.

It was then, still standing, that I saw the hand. It was coming down the staircase rail, moving slowly and grasping tight. It was near the music room when I saw it first and therefore going away from me, but descending. There was something terribly stealthy about it. It must have been that quality in it which made me shrink back behind an oleander.

Surely there was nothing unusual in people being about in a house where there was both illness and trouble, and yet . . .

At the foot of the stairs the hand, still on the rail, hesitated, disappeared. A moment later there rounded the newel post a little old woman dressed in black. She limped slightly, but for all that she came swiftly. Every detail is stamped on my mind. I can see her now, bent forward, something that was probably jet on her old-fashioned bonnet catching the faint light as she came. She had on a quaint loose black wrap—a dolman, I think they used to call them—and hanging to her arm a shabby leather handbag.

Stealthy as her movements were, they were extremely natural. Just inside the door she stopped, took off her spectacles and put them in a case, which she put in her bag, and then extracted from it another pair, which she put on. The bag was a quaint one, fastened with two straps and steel buckles. The buckles were troublesome and she was in a hurry. More than once she turned and looked back.

I waited for her to see me. It was an old servant, of course, come to tell me I was wanted upstairs. I was so sure of it that I bent down and put out my alcohol lamp. When I straightened up, she had passed the bay and was at the French door leading to the garden. She opened the door, went out, closed it noiselessly behind her, and was gone. I tried to see her in the garden, but if she went that way, she was lost in the shadows.

Even then I was rather amused than puzzled. I went over to the door and tried it. There was a lock on it. Unless she had a key, she had locked herself out.

I drank my coffee and went upstairs. My patient was still asleep. From Mr. March's room came heavy, deep breathing, telling that he was forgetting his anxieties, for a time at least. But my book—the book I had left on my chair in the hall—was gone!

It seemed rather absurd. I thought I might have taken it with me; and I searched the dining room, without result. It was not to be found. I thought of the little old housekeeper, or whatever she was—but that was ridiculous. Besides, she had carried no book. She had a black leather handbag over her arm. She might, of course, have put the book— What idiocy was I thinking! The book must be somewhere about. Everyone has laid things down and had them disappear. Sometimes they turn up and sometimes they do not—the fourth dimension, perhaps.

I MET MR. PATTON THE NEXT EVENING as he had arranged. He fell into step beside me.

"How's it going?" he asked.

"I'm learning to be a first-rate lady's maid," I said rather peevishly I am afraid. "I massage, manicure and give scalp treatments, and I've got a smirk from trying to look cheerful. The experiment is a failure, Mr. Patton. I'm not nursing, for there's no real illness; and I'm not helping you any. And the dreadful decorum of the house gets me. If I were twenty, I'd run away, too. Nothing ever gets dusty or out of place. No door ever slams. When I raise a window for air, I put in a gauze-filled frame to keep the dirt out!"

"Has the mother talked at all?"

"All the time—about herself. I've learned a little, of course. The girl has been moody, would not let Mr. Plummer, her fiancé, visit her this summer. Seemed to be in trouble, but confided in no one. The family relationships seem to have been all right. They adore her."

"Have you seen many of the people who come and go about the house? Anyone who could answer the description of the man she met at the station—the light-haired chap?"

I considered.

"None, I am sure."

"She and her mother got along well?"

"I think so. They were always together."

"Is there any trace of another love affair?"

"Yes, she was engaged once before. To a Mr. Wilson Page. She broke the engagement herself."

That interested him. He said he would look up Mr. Page.

"And don't be impatient," he advised me. We had made our circuit of the block and were in sight of the house again. "These are long cases sometimes—but the longer the time, the more sure I am that the girl is alive. Murder will out; it's self-limiting, like a case of measles. But take a girl who wants to stay hidden, and if she's intelligent, there's hardly any way to locate her. How many servants in the house?"

"Seven, I believe."

"Keep an eye on them. If one of them is garrulous, let her talk. They know more of the family than any member of it."

This brought to my mind the curious episode of the old woman, and I told him about it. He listened without interruption.

"When you say old, how old?"

"Seventy, I should say. She was stooped—and rather lame, but very active."

"You are sure you saw her? You could not possibly have been dozing?"

"I was making coffee; I don't customarily do that in my sleep. I think it must have been the cook. She is the only servant I have not seen. And, as to dozing, does anybody dream a handbag with straps and buckles?"

He put a hand on my arm impressively.

"It may interest you to know," he said, "that the cook is a young woman; I interviewed her myself. There is no person such as you describe in the house!"

"But why—at three in the morning—"

"Exactly," he said dryly. "Why? That's for us to find out."

He got a careful description of the old woman from me, and an account of her exit by the French door from the dining room into the garden. He was excited, for him, and rather triumphant.

"Now was it a mistake to put you there?" he demanded. "Of course not! And the next thing is to find the old lady. You can help there. Tell your story to the family. Set them to wondering and guessing. They may place her for us at once. In this business, try direct methods whenever you can. They save time."

He left me at the corner and I went on alone. Just before I reached the house, a man ran down the steps and went away rapidly. The parlor maid was just closing the door.

"Did that gentleman inquire for me, Mimi?" I asked. "I am expecting my brother." I was learning!

"No, miss. He asked for Miss March." Her eyes were wide and excited. "When I said she was not here, he ran down the steps in a hurry."

"My brother," I persisted, "is short and dark. Perhaps you—"

"He asked for Miss March," she repeated. "And, anyhow, he was thin and lightish." She turned to see whether any of the family might overhear. "He's been here before, miss," she confided, lowering her voice. "Twice, in the last week. He—he isn't one of Miss March's friends—I know that. And tonight he left this."

She showed me her tray on the hall table. There was a note on it addressed: "Miss Clare March. Important."

"I'll take this up to Mrs. March, Mimi," I said. "And if he comes again, ask him in and call me."

"Call you, miss?"

"Call me," I said quietly. "When he asks for Miss March, merely ask him to come in. Then call me. Mrs. March has requested me to see him."

I took the letter and went upstairs, but I did not give it to Mrs. March at once. That night, while I made my coffee, I steamed open the envelope and read the contents. It was on pale lavender paper and was as follows:

"I implore you to see me as soon as posible. Come to the old place. I am up against it for sure. Don't let this go any longer! It's life or death with me!"

I made a careful copy of the note, even to the misspelled word, and sealed it again. Mr. March was out that night—a girl had been found in a hospital. He was always following some such forlorn hope, returning each time a little sadder, a little grayer.

Mrs. March was unusually exacting the next morning. She wakened at dawn with a cry and I went to her. I was sleeping on the couch at the foot of the bed. She was sitting up, terrified, in the gray dawn. She wailed that Clare needed her, was calling for her. She had heard her distinctly.

"Surely you do not believe in dreams!" I said sternly.

"Not in dreams, perhaps," she replied. She was still pallid. "But don't you think, Miss Adams, that people hear things in sleep that waking ears do not catch? You know what I mean. It's subconscious, or something."

"It's subnormal," I commented, and brought her back to earth with a cup of hot tea.

That morning I gave Mr. March the note. We were at breakfast and Mr. Plummer had dropped in, as he usually did, on his way to his downtown office. Mr. March read it without comment and passed it to the other man. He was younger, less poised. I saw him change color.

"Who brought this?" he demanded.

"Mimi got it. It was left by a thin, fair-haired young man."

They called Mimi, but she knew no more than I had told them, except for one fact: She said the man had tried to push by her into the house and that he had insisted that Miss March was at home. They sent the girl out. They seemed to have no scruple about talking before me.

"It is mystifying enough," Mr. Plummer said. "Patton ought to see it. But it doesn't help much. Whoever wrote that did not know that Clare was not at home."

"Thin and fair-haired!" repeated Mr. March. "That's what Patton said, Walter—about the man at the railroad station, isn't it?"

"Patton is a fool!"

I gathered that the idea of the fair-haired man was extremely distasteful to him. He was almost surly.

We were sitting at the small breakfast table in the bay. I thought it a good time to speak about the little old woman. Any lingering doubt I may have had as to her right to be where I had seen her was dispelled by their manner. They were abstracted at first, then interested, then astounded.

"But, my dear young woman," Mr. March exclaimed, "why did you not rouse the house? And why did you wait for thirty hours before telling us?"

"It would be necessary for you to have seen her in order to understand. It never occurred to me that she was not a member of the household—she was so respectable. Only now, when I have seen all the servants, I begin to realize . . . She went out through that door."

"Is anything missing?" Mr. Plummer asked. "Mrs. March's jewels?"

"Still in the safe-deposit vault. We have had no heart to think of them."

Nevertheless a search of the house was made that day. Nothing was missing. Under Mrs. March's flushed directions, as she sat up in bed, I went round with great bunches of keys, verifying lists, looking up laces, locating furs. Such jewelry as she had about was safe.

As for the old lady with the jet on her bonnet, with the dolman and the buckled handbag—none of the family had ever known such a person. She answered no description, fitted into no place. Family and servants alike disclaimed her.

Life has a curious way of picking up threads and dropping them. The romantic young man with the blond hair, the little old lady with the limp, had come and gone; and for two weeks there was nothing more. Clare March remained missing. Mrs. March spoke of her in the past tense. Mr. Plummer grew thinner and took to coming into Mrs. March's room and sitting for long stretches without speech, his hands hanging listlessly between his knees.

I had my first real talk with Mr. Plummer late one afternoon while the invalid dozed in her chair. He was a good-looking man, something over thirty and already growing gray. He had sat for some time, apparently busy with his own thoughts—in reality watching me as I put away Mrs. March's various pretty trifles. She was always littered—ribbon bows, a nail file, a magazine, letters.

"Do you never make an unnecessary movement?" he asked at last.

"Frequently, I'm afraid."

"Must you put all those things away? Or will you sit down and talk for five minutes?"

I sat down near him. Mrs. March was now sound asleep.

"Do you want me to sit down and talk, or to sit down and listen?"

"To listen, and to answer some questions. Just a minute." He went quietly to the dressing table, returning with the photograph of Clare that stood there.

"You nurses know a lot about people," he said. "That's your business. You're a psychologist even if you don't realize it. I've watched you with Mrs. March. Now what do you read in that picture?"

"It is a lovely face," I replied, doing my best but feeling utterly inadequate. Womanlike, I daresay I was anxious to say the thing he wanted to hear. "A—a pleasant face, I should say, but with character and temperament."

"What about the eyes?"

"They are well apart—that's a good sign, though cows are that way, aren't they! They are very direct and honest, too. Really, Mr. Plummer—"

"Here is a later picture, taken this summer. Now, what do you see?"

I was puzzled and uncomfortable.

"She looks older, more serious."

"Look at the eyes."

Well, there was a difference. I could not say where it lay. The effect was curious. In the early picture she was looking at the camera, and the eyes were limpid and clear. In the picture he had taken from his pocketbook she gazed into the camera also; but there was a sort of elusiveness about the eyes. It gave me a strange feeling of indirectness, evasion—I hardly know what. They might have been the eyes of a woman who had lived hard and suffered. And yet this girl of twenty had hardly lived as yet. It was almost a tragic face. I have seen the same drooping lines in eye cases, where vision is faulty and seeing an effort. What was this, then—astigmatism or evasion?

"You see it, don't you? Miss Adams, she has had some real trouble to make a change of that sort. I—I thought she was happy in our engagement; but as I look back, there are things—"

Mrs. March stirred and opened her eyes.

"I hate to waken," she said querulously. "It is only when I am asleep that I can forget, and even then I dream. Co out now, please, Walter; Miss Adams is going to use the vibrator."

That afternoon at five o'clock Mr. Patton called me on the telephone for the first time.

"I think we have something," he said. "When you go out for your walk tonight, dress for the street. There will be a taxicab at the corner and I shall be inside."

"At what time?"

"Seven thirty."

"Will an hour be enough?"

"Ask for two hours."

Mrs. March was rather peevish about my going out.

"I daresay you need air," she said, "but you could get it by opening a window. And what about my hot milk?"

"I'll ask Hortense to sit with you and she will heat the milk. I do not need air, of course. But I do need some exercise."

She let me go grudgingly. Mr. Patton would not tell me where we were going, but insisted on talking of indifferent things. As it turned out, we were headed for a police station; and at last he voiced his errand.

"We are going to show you a lot of handbags," he said. "A woman pickpocket was brought in here yesterday with four in a pocket under a skirt. I was looking over them today and it occurred to me that you might recognize one of them."

"Mine! I hope you send her up for a year!"

"Not yours. And do not jump to conclusions; it is fatal in this business."

I knew the bag at once when I saw it. Surely no other bag of that size in the city had two straps fastened with steel buckles. The handles of two of the other bags had been cut off, but the heavy leather handle of this one was entire.

"This is the one you mean, of course. Yes, it looks like the one the old lady carried, but there may be others. It is foreign, isn't it?"

"What was she doing that night when you noticed the bag?"

"She opened it and put in a pair of spectacles in a case."

He unfastened the bag and emptied onto a table a tin spectacle case, as quaint as the bag; two keys, one for a patent lock, the other an ordinary house key. Last of all he drew from a pocket inside the bag a soiled and creased lavender envelope, stamped and ready for mailing. It was addressed in pencil to Mrs. March and had been opened. Mr. Patton drew out the communication inside and watched me as I read it. It was hardly decipherable and was written on a piece of wrapping paper:

"Am all right. Clare."

I stared at it.

"Interesting, isn't it?" commented Mr. Patton. "Did she write it or didn't she? If she's all right, why isn't she home? Why do all our little communications arrive in lavender envelopes? Who's the old lady? What was she doing in the house that night? What's the answer?"

"That could be the key to the garden door," I said dully.

Chapter IV

⋙

THE doctor made a late call that night and dismissed Mrs. March as a patient.

"I'll drop in now and then to learn what the news is," he said as he prepared to leave. "You don't need me professionally. Just keep cheerful. It will all come out right."

I followed him into the hall. It seemed to me that if anyone knew the inside history I had failed to secure, it was he. And up to that time I had failed with him.

"I hope you will stay on, Miss Adams. I am leaving her in your hands—remember, no drugs so long as she is normal; at any symptoms of nervousness again, start them early."

"It's a trying case," I said slowly. "It takes it out of me, Doctor. She asks me for theories, and—of course I didn't know the girl or her life— I cannot give her what she wants."

He hesitated. We were in the lower hall by that time.

"Just what does she want?"

"Encouragement."

"That Clare is living, of course. Well, tell her this the next time she is down. It is true enough. Tell her Clare was unhappy in her engagement and that I believe there is another man; that she has eloped with him and that her message to the family has miscarried."

"Wilson Page?"

He eyed me. For the first time it occurred to me that he suspected my business in the house and that he was giving me information that ethically he would have refused.

"No. A blond fellow, rather thin. I have seen her meeting him in the park, and once I believe she met him in my reception room."

He seemed to regret this information the moment I had it and left immediately.

That night, after I had rubbed Mrs. March with coconut oil, used the vibrator, given her hot milk and finally read her to sleep, I slipped into my room and sat down by the window. The autumn garden lay beneath, with no moon to bring out its geometrical desolation. And there, elbows on the sill, the chill air blowing about me, I tried to piece together the scraps I held: the little old lady, the blond man and his frantic note, the letter in the buckled bag. And again I recalled the conversation Mr. Patton and I had had in the taxicab that evening.

"She's alive," he had said, "and she is in the city—if that note is hers, and I think it is. I'll show it to the father and the other chap in the morning. Then she is in hiding. Why?"

I LAY down on a couch at the foot of Mrs. March's bed, but did not get to sleep, for some reason. The slightest movement of my patient found me wide-eyed and alert. Small sounds were exaggerated. A regular foot-step that seemed to ascend the stairs for hours turned out to be a drip from a bathroom tap. The slow chiming of the hall clock set me crazy.

At two o'clock I got up and went downstairs. In the waitress's pantry, off the dining room, there were beef cubes. It seemed to me that if I drank a cup of bouillon I might sleep. As usual the light was burning in the lower hall. The dining room was dark—I no longer required a night supper—and the little table in the bay window was bare. A street light beyond the garden showed the window and the longer rectangle of the garden door. I was not nervous.

I made my way through the unlighted dining room to the pantry, a small room, painted white, with a butler's slide to the basement kitchen, and a small white glass-and-silver refrigerator built into the wall, where the waitress kept the dining-room butter and cream. The electric light was out of order there; I pressed the switch, but there was no answering flood of light. I had matches with me for the alcohol lamp, however, and found my bouillon cubes easily. Thus I was still in darkness when I opened the swinging door into the dining room.

Someone was trying the lock of the garden door! I do not mind say-ing I was terrified. The door was glass. To cross the room to the lighted hall would throw my whole figure into relief. I shrank back, breathing with difficulty, into my corner. Beyond the thin casement cloth of the door I could see a moving shadow.

The lock did not give. It seemed to me, all at once, that I knew the silhouette—that here again was the little old lady, but now without her key. My heart ceased pounding. I was able to think, to calculate. I won-dered whether she would break the glass. I planned to let her get in if she could and then to cut off her retreat by advancing on her from behind. I was very calm by that time—rather exalted, I daresay, at my own bravery. I put the packet of beef cubes into my pocket in order to have both hands free.

I do not know just when I realized that it was not the little old lady—I believe it was after one of the panes had been broken and had fallen with a soft crash onto the rug inside. The figure straight-ened; it was much taller than I had expected. I recall that my heart almost stopped and then raced on at a mad pace; I saw what I knew was a hand put through the opening; I heard the lock turn and the cautious opening of the door. The intruder was in the room with me.

Panic possessed me then. I turned wildly and threw myself headlong against the swinging pantry door. It was madness, of course. There was no exit from the little room, no way to fasten the door. I was in a cul-de-sac and in the black dark. I believe I opened a drawer and got a cake knife; at least, eons after, I found myself clutching one. I do not remember how I got it.

The swinging door remained undisturbed. When I could hear—above the pounding in my ears—there was no sound anywhere except the hall clock's slow chiming.

Many things I have never recalled clearly about that hideous night. I do not know, for instance, how long I stood at bay in the pantry; or how my courage rose from my knees, which ceased trembling, to my spinal cord, to my pulse, which went down from about a hundred and eighty, thin and stringy, to what I judged was almost normal, still irregular, but stronger. When my courage reached my brain, which was in perhaps fifteen minutes, though I would have sworn it was daylight by that time and I had stood there most of the night, I put my ear against the door and listened. There was no sound.

The instinct of my training asserted itself. Whatever was happening, my patient must not be alone. I must get up to the sickroom. In a few moments it was an obsession. I must get back. My sense of duty was stronger than my terror.

I made the break at last, opening the door an inch or so. The room was quiet. With infinite caution I pushed the door farther open. I could see the room, solidly handsome, rather heavy, empty! I made my first few steps of progress with deliberate slowness. I knew that if I ran, panic would follow at my heels. I dared not look over my shoulder. Even the lighted hall brought small comfort, with the dark rooms opening off it, sheltering I knew not what; but I reached the foot of the stairs in safety. There I stopped.

A woman, dressed in rags, lay huddled on the bottom steps in a faint. She lay facedown. Even when I had turned her over and had recognized the features of the photographs in the house, I was still incredulous. Nevertheless it was true. Bruised and torn, clad in rags, gaunt to the point of emaciation, Clare March had come home again.

It was the end of one mystery—the beginning of another.

Chapter V

MY FIRST feeling was one of horror. Her condition was frankly terrible. I even feared at first that she was dead. I found a pulse, however. I am big and strong; I got her down off the staircase and laid her flat on the floor. All the time, I was praying that none of the family or the servants had been roused. I did not want anyone to see her yet.

I brought down some aromatic ammonia and gave it to her in water. Mrs. March was sleeping calmly; across the hall Mr. March also slept, audibly. I had a little time; I wanted an hour—maybe two.

She came to very gradually, throwing an arm over her head, moving a little, and finally opening her eyes. I talked soothingly to her.

"Now don't be alarmed," I said over and over. "You are at home and everything is all right. I am a nurse. Everything is all right."

"I want—Julie," she said at last, feebly.

I had never heard the name.

"Julie is coming. Can you sit up if I hold you?"

She made an effort, and by degrees I got her into the music room, where she collapsed again; and, there being no couch, I put her down on the floor with a cushion under her head. Terrible thoughts had been running through my head. The papers had been full of abduction stories, and I confess I thought nothing else could explain her condition, her rags.

"I am hungry," she said when I got her settled. "I am—I am starving! I don't know when I have had anything to eat."

She looked it, too. I had the beef cubes in my pocket and I left her there while I made some broth. I brought it back, with crackers. She was sitting in a chair by that time, and she drank the stuff greedily, blistering hot as it was.

I had my first chance to take an inventory of her appearance. It was startling. Her hands were abraded and blistered. She held one out to me pathetically, but without comment. Over one eye was a deep bluish bruise. Her face was almost colorless, and her forearm, where one sleeve had been torn away, was thin to emaciation. Every trace of beauty was eclipsed for the time. She was shocking—that is all.

Her clothing was thin and inadequate: a torn white waist, much soiled; a short, ragged black skirt; and satin bedroom slippers, frayed and cut. She had nothing on her head and no wrap, though the night was cold. She looked up at me when she held out the empty cup.

"How is Mother?"

"She has not been well."

"Was it worry?"

"Yes. Do you think you can get up the stairs?"

"Is that all I am to have to eat?"

"I'll get more soon. You mustn't take too much at once."

She rose and I put my arm around her. She had taken me for granted, childishly, but at the foot of the stairs she halted our further progress to ask me, "Who are you? You are not a servant."

"I am a trained nurse. I've been caring for your mother during her illness."

We went up the stairs and into her room.

Mrs. March wakened about the time I had got the girl to her own room. "Don't tell Mother yet," she begged. "Give me a little time. I—I'd frighten her now."

I promised.

When I went back, half an hour later, Clare had undressed herself and put on a negligee from the closet. She was sitting in front of the fire I had lighted, brushing out her hair. For the first time she was reminiscent of the girl of the photographs. She was not like them yet—she was too gaunt.

I tried to coax her to bed, but she would not go. I was puzzled. Her nervous excitement was extreme; more than once she stopped, with brush poised, as if she were on the point of asking me some question; but she never asked it—her courage evidently failed her. It was a horrible night. I sat inside the door of my patient's room, in darkness, and watched the door opposite. I could hear the girl pacing back and forth; I was almost crazy.

I offered her a bromide, which she refused to take; but about half past three I heard her lie down on the bed, and some of the tension relaxed. I had a chance to think, to work out a course of action. Mr. Patton should be notified at once; and as soon as the girl was really composed, I would rouse Mr. March. I knew I would be criticized in the family for not rousing them all at once, but I am always willing to take the responsibility for what I do. The doctor's orders first and my own judgment next is my motto. And there have been times when the doctor's orders— But never mind about that.

I looked at my watch. It was almost four o'clock and still black dark. I went down to the library, where the telephone stood on a stand behind a teakwood screen, and called up Mr. Patton's apartment; but I could not get him.

I hung up the receiver and sat there in the darkness, meaning to try again in a moment or so. It was while I was still there that I heard Clare on the stairs.

She came slowly and painfully—a step, a pause for rest, another step. Once down in the lower hall, she made better progress. She came directly into the library, through the music room, and turned on the lights.

I was curious. It was easy to watch her through the carved margin of the screen. It was only curiosity. I had no idea there would be further mystery to solve. In the morning she would tell her story, the law would take hold, and that would be all. But I recall distinctly every movement she made.

First she went to the long table littered with magazines, with the bronze reading lamp in the center. She glanced over the magazines as they lay, picked up the framed picture of herself and looked at it for a long moment, her hands visibly trembling. Then she took a survey of the room.

There was an English fender about the fireplace, with a tufted leather top. Mr. Plummer habitually sat there, with his back to the fire. And just inside, thrown carelessly, lay a newspaper. It was the newspaper she wanted. It was not easy for her to reach it in her weakened condition. She stooped, staggered, bent again, and got it.

The wood fire had burned itself out, but the warm bricks and ashes still threw out a comforting heat. She curled up on the floor by the fender and proceeded to go over the pages, running a shaking finger through paragraph after paragraph. I was most uncomfortable, half ashamed, and cramped from my position.

When I felt that I could stand no more, she found what she was looking for. I heard her gasp and then saw her throw herself forward, her face in her arms, crying silently but fiercely, her shoulders shaking. She paid no attention when I bent over her, except to draw herself away from my hand. When I tried to take the newspaper, however, she snatched it from my hand and sat up.

"Go away!" she said hysterically. "Stop following me and watching me. Can't I even cry alone?"

I was rather offended. I drew back, like a fool, and lost a clue that we did not find until weeks later.

"I'm sorry you feel that way," I said coldly, and went out and up the stairs.

She burned the paper before she made a laborious and faltering ascent of the staircase half an hour later—at least, when I went down, there was no sign of it or of any of the newspapers that had littered the room. And, though Mr. Patton secured copies of them all later and we went over them patiently, we could find nothing that seemed to have the remotest bearing on what we were trying to learn.

SHE was much better by morning—had slept a little; was calmer; had a bit of color in her ears, which had been wax-white; but the bruise on her forehead was blacker.

I broke the news of her return very gently to Mr. March at dawn and left it to him to tell his wife. I went to her afterward and found her hysterically impatient to see her daughter. I induced her to wait, however, until she had had an egg and a piece of toast. I do not believe in excitement on an entirely empty stomach. We covered the bruise with a loop of Clare's heavy hair; and then her father and mother went in and I closed the door.

Somebody had telephoned for Mr. Plummer; but she sent her father out to say she would not see him just yet. It was like a blow in the face. He almost reeled.

"That's the message, boy," Mr. March said. "I don't understand it any more than you do. She's in frightful condition; we've sent for the doctor. Tomorrow I am sure—"

"But what does she say?" Mr. Plummer broke in. "Where has she been? I'll wait until she wants to see me, of course, but for God's sake tell me where she has been!"

"She has told us very little," Mr. March had to confess. "She is hardly coherent yet. She says she will talk to the police sometime today. She has been imprisoned—that is all we know."

Mrs. March's sitting room was open and Mr. Plummer went in and sat down heavily. Sometime later, as I passed the door, he called me in.

"You saw her first, didn't you?" he asked. "Will you sit down and tell me all you know about it?"

I was glad to talk—I had been bottled up for so long. I told him everything—except my reason for being down in the library behind the screen.

"Did she ask for me at all?" he asked when I had finished.

"I—I think so. Naturally she would."

He smiled at me wryly.

"You know she did not ask for me," he said, and got up.

I was very sorry for him. He was so earnest, so bewildered. He waited round all morning, hoping for a message, and about noon she said she would see him. Her own maid dressed her and together we put a little rouge on her face and touched up her colorless lips. Except for the hollows in her cheeks, she looked lovely. I gave her message to him.

"Tell him I want to see him," she said to me. "But he is not to ask a lot of questions, and he is to stay only a minute or two—I am so very tired."

He was uncertain of his welcome, I think. I took him to the door. She was on a couch, propped up with pillows, and the bruise was covered. And when I saw the look in his eyes and the assuring flame in hers, I knew that, whatever else was wrong, it was nothing that lay between them. The vision of the blond man as Clare's lover died at that moment and never came to life again.

The story of the almost two months of Clare March's disappearance she told to Mr. Patton that afternoon. She would not allow her father and mother to be present, and only Mr. Patton's insistence that the nurse should be there to see that she did not overtax her strength secured my admission. The story was short and was told haltingly. It gave me the impression of truth, but of being only a part of the truth. Her descriptions of the people and of the surroundings, for instance, were undoubtedly drawn from painful memory. They were photographic—raw with truth. The same was true of her story of the escape.

"It was on the third of September that you started home," Mr. Patton said. "We know that, and that you arrived on the morning of the fourth. We lost you from the time you got into a taxicab at the station. Did you order the man to drive you home?"

"Not directly. I went to—" She named the department store to which she had been traced. "I had made my purchase when a young man came up to me and introduced himself. He said I did not know him, but that he was living in the same house with an old German teacher of mine, Fräulein Julie Schlenker. She had taught me at boarding school and I was very fond of her. He said she was—dying."

Tears came into her eyes. Mr. Patton caught my eye for the fraction of a second.

"Was this before you bought the blankets or after?"

She looked startled, but he was smiling pleasantly. If she had to reassemble her story, she did it well and quickly.

"Before. I was terribly worried about Julie," she said. "I agreed to go there at once, and I asked him what I could take her to make her comfortable. He said she couldn't eat, but perhaps blankets—or something like that. I bought blankets and had them put in the taxicab."

"What address did this blond young man give you?"

"I did not say he was a blond young man," she objected. "I do not remember what he looked like. I should not know him again."

Mr. Patton nodded gravely.

"My mistake," he said. "Was this the same taxicab?"

"No. I had dismissed the other. I got into the taxicab and the man gave an address to the driver. I paid no attention to it. I was upset about Julie. I hardly looked out. We went very fast. All the time I was seeing Julie lying dead, with her poor old face—" She shuddered. Clearly that part of the story was true enough and painful. "We drove for a long time. I was worried about the bill. When the register said four dollars, I was anxious. I had checks, but very little money."

She stopped herself suddenly and gave Mr. Patton a startled glance, but he was blandness itself.

"Four dollars!" he said. "Did you know the neighborhood?"

"Not at all. I was angry and accused the driver of taking a roundabout way. He said he had gone directly and offered to ask a policeman."

"You were still in the city then?"

"Yes, but it was far out. When the driver drew up, I had just enough money to pay him. It was almost five dollars."

"Can you remember exactly?"

"Four dollars and eighty cents. I gave that man five dollars. I had only a dollar left."

"The young man was still with you?"

"No, indeed. I was quite alone. I wish you would not interrupt me."

Mr. Patton sat back good-humoredly and folded his hands. I knew why he had continually broken in on the story. I thought he had caught something, by his look.

"I got out. I had the blankets and they were bulky. The man carried them to the doorstep and drove away. I thought it was a queer neighborhood. It was a mean little house, off by itself, with only an unoccupied house near.

"I felt very strange, but Julie was always queer.

"I asked for Julie. A hideous old woman answered the door. The whole place was filthy. I felt terribly for Julie—she was always so neat. I went in and up the stairs. The stairs were narrow and steep, and shut off below with a door. All I could think of was Julie in that horrible place. There were cobwebs along the stairs. We turned toward the back of the house and stopped before a door. The old woman did not rap. She opened it and said, 'In here, miss.' I went in. The room was empty. I said, 'Why, where is Julie?' But the old woman had gone. I heard her outside locking the door."

That was a strange story we listened to that afternoon—a story of futile calls for help; of bread and water passed through a broken panel in the door; of a drugged sleep, from which she wakened to find her clothing gone and rags substituted; of drunken revels below; and of the constant, maddening surveillance through the panel by a man with a squint. She described the room with absolute accuracy and even drew it roughly for Mr. Patton: a low attic room with two small windows, a sloping roof, discolored plaster from a leak above, a washstand without bowl or pitcher; for light a glass lamp with a smoked chimney; and for furniture a cot under the lowest part of the ceiling, and a chair.

Once a day, she said, the old woman brought her a tin basin for washing, and a towel, rough-dried. The basin had a red string to hang it up by, she said. The towels were checked—pink and white.

"Like glass towels," she said. "There was a grate for coal and a wooden shelf above it, with an old steel engraving tacked up on the wall. One corner was loose, and if I left the window open, it flapped all the time. I had a fire only once; but I did not suffer from cold—the kitchen was beneath, and the flue was always warm."

"This steel engraving—do you remember what it was?"

"The Landing of the Pilgrims," she said promptly. "Someone had colored a part of it with crayons—a child probably."

Mr. Patton looked puzzled. She might have invented the panel in the door or the man with the squint; but parts of her story bore the absolute imprint of truth: the chimney flue being warm, the flapping picture, the rough-dried towels, the basin with a red string through its rim.

"In a moment I want you to tell us how you got away," Mr. Patton said, "but first, I want a reason for all this. Was it— Did they try to force you to anything?"

"Nothing at all."

"They were not white slavers then?"

She colored. "No."

"They never threatened you?"

She hesitated, considered.

"Only when I cried out—and that did no good. There was only an empty house near."

"Miss March, this is an almost incredible story. A crime must have a motive. You are saying that you were imprisoned in an isolated house for nearly two months, were unharmed and unthreatened, but under constant surveillance, and finally made your escape. And you can imagine no reason for it!"

"I haven't said that at all—I imagined plenty of reasons. Couldn't they have wanted a ransom?"

"They made no attempt to secure one."

She told of her escape rather briefly. If I can give in so many words my impression of her story, it was that here and there she was on sure ground, and that the escape was drawn absolutely from memory and was accurate in every detail.

"Every now and then they all got drunk," she said. "I—I always thought they would set the house on fire. The two younger women would sing—and it was horrible."

"You did not say there were younger women."

She was confused.

"There were two. One was married to the man. They called the old woman Ma. And there was a man with a wooden leg who visited the house. He came over the field; I saw him often. For two days they'd been drinking, and the old woman fell down and hurt herself. I could hear her groaning. And I was hungry—I was terribly hungry." She looked at me. "You know how hungry I was. I had not even water."

"She was starving," I said.

"Nobody came. I was frightened. I kept thinking that something had happened." She checked herself, started again. "All evening I lay in darkness. I could hear them yelling and singing, and now and then the old woman groaning. And I was so thirsty I hoped it would rain and the roof would leak. That's how thirsty I was. I slept a little—not very much. Mostly I walked about and worried. The house was so quiet that it drove me crazy."

"Quiet! Were they asleep?"

She looked at him quickly.

"They went away—all of them. There was only the old woman, and she was hurt. When I called, nobody answered."

"How was your door fastened?"

"On the outside."

"Couldn't you have put your arm through the broken panel and unlocked it?"

"The key was not in the lock. It never was. It was always on a nail at the top of the staircase. I could see it."

No one could have doubted her. The key was kept at the top of the stairs on a nail. It takes a perceptible second to invent such a detail. She had not invented it.

"All the next day no one came near me. One of the windowpanes was broken. I called through it for help. Sometimes there were people in the fields beyond the house. There was nobody that day except some little boys. They paid no attention; perhaps they did not hear me. I was getting weaker all the time. I thought that pretty soon I would be too weak to try to escape. The fire was out below and my room was cold. My hands were so stiff I could hardly move them. I worked a long time at the window. They had driven nails in all round it. I worked them loose."

She held out her hands. They were cut and blistered.

"I got them out at last, but I broke a pane of glass. I hardly cared whether it was heard or not. I had never been able before to see what lay below the window. There was a sort of shed there.

"I had to wait until night. The room was freezing, with the window out. They were still away, except the old woman. She lay and groaned down below. I lay on the mattress the rest of the day and shivered. As soon as it was dark, I crawled up on the windowsill. I was frightened—it looked so far down. I lowered myself by my hands and then dropped; but I slipped. I thought I had broken my ankle. The loose boards on the shed made a frightful noise."

"How did you find your way home?"

"I walked for hours. I do not know anything about the streets. I just walked toward the glow of the city lights against the sky. When I got into the city proper, I knew where I was."

"Where were you when you first recognized your surroundings?"

"I saw the North Market."

"Do you remember from which direction you approached it?"

"The west side, I believe." Her tone was reluctant.

Mr. Patton drew a soiled lavender envelope from his pocket and took out its enclosure.

" 'Am all right. Clare,' " he read. "Now, Miss March, just when and where did you write this little note?"

Her only answer was to break into hysterical crying. "Julie! Julie!" she cried. She absolutely refused to explain the note. It was an *impasse*. She could neither explain it nor ignore it. She took refuge in tears and silence.

That was the end of Clare March's story. It sounded like madness; but there was proof of a sort—her general condition; her hands; her brief but photographic descriptions. It was true—at least in part. It was not the whole truth. She had not spoken of the blond man or of the little old lady in black; and yet I was convinced she knew about them both. Mr. Patton thought as I did; for when she was quieter, he asked for a description of the old woman of her story.

"She was very stout," she said slowly, "and very dirty. She always wore the same things—a blue calico dress and an apron. She seemed to be washing all the time; the apron was always wet and soapy. And she had thin gray hair drawn into a hard knot."

"Could you tell her nationality by her voice—her accent?"

"I'm afraid not."

"Did you ever see her dressed for the street?"

"Never."

"Then you never saw her in a black bonnet trimmed with jet, and an old-fashioned dolman, and carrying a pocketbook fastened with two buckles?"

She leaned over suddenly and caught Mr. Patton by the wrist.

"I can't stand it any longer!" she cried. "What do you know? Was the paper wrong?"

When she saw by his face that he did not understand and could not help her, she sank back among her pillows. She would not answer any more questions and lapsed into a watchful silence.

Chapter VI

NATURALLY I have never taken any credit for the solution of the Clare March mystery. Even now, when I am writing under an assumed name, I am uneasy. To be suspected would be my professional ruin. So far I have been able to keep my double calling a profound secret. I may have been in your house. Think it over, those of you who have something to conceal. Are you certain that the soft-walking, starched young woman to whom in your weakness you talked so freely—are you sure it was not myself? Under the skin, I said in the beginning—aye, and under the flesh and its weaknesses. Do you recall that day when you and a visitor talked at the bedside and I wrote letters in a corner by a window? How do you know but that your entire conversation, word by word, was at the Central Office in two hours? Did it ever occur to you before?

I wrote many letters that week. Mrs. March was up and about, bustling and busy; Clare was my patient. I no longer met Mr. Patton in the evenings. He was combing the outskirts of the city, I believe, and interviewing taxicab drivers. I sent a daily report to him by mail:

MONDAY—I notice one curious thing: She will not let me do much for her. Hortense, her maid, does some things—not much. She gets rid of us both whenever she can. I feel worse than useless. I have offered to give her massage, but she refuses. Mr. Plummer only comes to the door—she does not wish him to come in.

TUESDAY—Still weak and inert. A box of flowers every day from Mr. Plummer. I had once thought possibly she did not care for him; but today I saw her eyes again when she looked at the roses—I believe she is crazy about him. She would like to get rid of me, but her parents insist she needs me. Her hands are healing. There is one curious thing— her wrists are abraded. Did she say her hands were tied?

WEDNESDAY—The blond man has been here. I saw him from the stairs and went down. He is not what we thought at all. He is untidy and shabby. He was waiting inside the door, turning his hat round in his hands. I told him Miss March was ill, but he refused to leave. He said, "Tell her it is Samuels, and this is the last call. She'll know what I mean." I said, "I think she has had a letter from you." He turned livid. "Then she got it!" he stormed. "And she paid no attention to it! You tell her, for me, that she'll fix things with me now—today—or I'll tell the whole story!" He felt in his watch pocket and seemed to remember that his watch was gone. That added to his rage. "You tell her that. Tell her she'll have it at the old place by three this afternoon or I'll go to her precious sweetheart and tell him some things he ought to know." I tried to follow him when he left, but by the time I'd got my hat and ulster, he was out of sight. If Samuels is his real name, you can probably find him. He is blond and smooth-shaved, and has a gold tooth—right side, upper jaw; wears a tan overcoat and a soft green felt hat.

WEDNESDAY, FOUR P.M.—I have just come back from an errand for Clare. I have been to the "old place" with a parcel for Samuels. It was money. He was so greedy that he tore it open while I waited. It seemed to be considerable—well over a hundred dollars. When he had counted it, he put it in his pocket. He looked better than in the morning and was calmer. He looked at me after he had counted it. "Don't look so damned virtuous!" he said. "This isn't blackmail. It's for value received."

The "old place" is at the corner of Tenth Street and the Embankment. We stood in the doorway of a vacant building and talked. Samuels looks decayed—as if he has seen better days. I tried to get you by telephone to follow me. You were out.

THURSDAY—A very curious thing happened today: Clare asked for some chicken cooked in cream. The cook had never done it and I volunteered. It took some time; I was in the basement more than an hour. When I came up with the chicken, she had disappeared. We were all terribly frightened. I called the office twice, but you were out as usual—you will have to arrange some way for me to get you in emergencies. She had taken her wraps and gone out by the garden door. The parlor maid had not seen her. It was two hours later when she came back, exhausted. She locked herself in her room and it was almost the dinner hour before she would admit me.

Her father had a talk with her tonight. He said, "You must not do such unwise things. You will drive your mother frantic."

"Poor Mother!" she replied. "I'll tell you before long where I was. Don't ask me."

I thought she had been crying. I believe she has pawned or sold her sapphire ring; I do not see it.

THAT last letter, sent special delivery, and unsigned as all of them were, brought a telephone message from the detective and an appointment for that evening.

"Ask for an evening off," he said. "I think I've got it. And I want to talk to you."

He had a taxi at the corner that night. It was when it was well under way that he began to talk.

"We've got the house," he said. "The man with the squint did it—but that's a long story. In Miss March's anxiety to tell as much as she dared of the truth, she went a little too far. Given a four-dollar-and-eighty-cent taxicab radius, an isolated house with two young women, an old hag and a man with a squint—put a shed on the back of the house and a bad reputation all over it—and you have perhaps two dozen possibilities. Add such graphic touches as a built-in stairway and a tin basin hung up by a red string as identification marks, and an empty house and a man with a wooden leg for neighbors, and out of the two dozen there will be one house that fits. We've found it."

"Is that where we are going?"

"To that neighborhood. I really wanted a chance to go over the whole thing with you. Now, then, what do you think? You've been close to the case—closer than I have. How much of that story of hers is true?"

"About half of it."

"Which half?"

"Well, I think she was not a prisoner. I believe she was a voluntary guest in the house she described and that she was hiding from something."

"I see. And not expecting us to find the house, she gave a circumstantial description. But what was she hiding from? So far as we can learn, her past has been an open book—she was away at school for four years, and spent a year abroad with a party of girls and a chaperone. She came out two years ago—I remember reading about the coming-out ball, something very elaborate. That first winter she went about with young Page, became engaged and broke it off. Page has been away ever since. It can't have anything to do with Page. Last spring she took on this Plummer—has been with her family all summer—has never, except during the year abroad, been away from her mother for any length of time. That doesn't look like anything to hide from. What do you think of the Julie story?"

"I don't believe it. But there is a Julie."

"Does the family know the name?"

"No. The girl is paying blackmail, Mr. Patton."

"The blond chap?"

"Yes."

"That was rotten luck, my being out of touch that day. If we had him—or if we had your friend, the little old lady!"

He stopped the taxicab shortly after and we got out. We were well out of the center of town, in a scattering suburb. I had never seen it. And before us stretched one of those empty spaces that are left here and there, without apparent cause, during the growth of the city. House builders are gregarious—they build in clusters. Perhaps it's a matter of sewers or of gas and water. To right and left of us stretched a sort of field, almost bare of grass, with straggling paths across it. Long before, a street had been cut through; its edges were still intact— a pitfall for the unwary.

I did not see all this that night. It was late October and very dark. Mr. Patton had a pocket flash, and with that and his hand I managed fairly. Our destination was before us—a little house, faintly lighted.

"I'm afraid this isn't very pleasant, Miss Adams," he apologized. "And I haven't a good reason for bringing you. But I'm up against it in a way. I want you to see this place and perhaps your instinct will tell you what I fail to make out. I've been here once today and it stumps me. They swear they've never had a girl there; that the man with the wooden leg sleeps in the garret sometimes. He's a watchman at the railroad over there. By the way, did she speak of a railroad?"

"I think not."

"It's a bad place. The police protection doesn't amount to much, but over there in the town they say it's a speakeasy. The cellar's full of beer. They say other things, too—that the old woman is a white slaver, for one thing. That bears out the story partly. And another thing does also—the hag hurt herself lately. She's going about with a cane. On the other hand—well, if they were lying today, they did a good piece of work."

There was a wagon near the house as we approached. At first we thought they were moving out. Then Mr. Patton laughed.

"Getting rid of the beer and the empties," he said. "Got them scared! Now don't be nervous. You needn't speak to them. I want you to keep your eyes open—that's all."

I was nervous. There was something sinister about the very location. I have even now rather a hazy recollection of Mr. Patton's rap at the door, the imperious summons of the law, and of a hideous old woman who peered out into the darkness.

"Well, Mother," Mr. Patton said cheerfully, "here I am again. I want to look round a little."

The hag made as if to close the door, but a woman spoke from behind.

"Let him in, Ma," she said. "We ain't got nothing to hide. Come in, mister."

A man came up from a cellarway with a box of bottles. I can still see his face over the bottles—his sickening pallor, his squint. He thought it was a raid, clearly. Then he saw me and his color came back.

"I guess a man's 'ouse is 'is own," he snarled. "We drink a little beer ourselves. That ain't agin' the law, I reckon."

"Not at all," Mr. Patton said good-humoredly. "I'll have a lamp, please."

It appeared to be a four-roomed house. We stood in the front room, an untidy place with a bed in a corner, and heavy with stale odors. Behind, there was a kitchen containing a table littered with the remains of the evening meal. Between the two rooms was a narrow, steep staircase shut off with a door below and ending above in a small landing. From this landing two doorways opened—one into a front room, the other into a half room, or attic, over the kitchen. It was into this room that Mr. Patton, carrying a smoky lamp, led the way.

"This is the room," he said. "That is the window with the shed below. Here is where the flue comes up from the kitchen."

I looked round. It was a sordid, filthy place. The plaster had broken away here and there. Where it was intact it was discolored from a leaking roof. For furniture there was a mattress on the floor, with soiled bedding, a chair with a broken seat and a washstand. Clare had said the washstand was unfurnished, but had mentioned a tin basin. Here was a tin basin with a red string. Mr. Patton was watching me grimly.

"Well, what do you make of it?" he said.

"It looks queer," I admitted. "Only there are some things—the panel in the door, for instance. There is no door."

"I asked about that. They say it came off the hinges a month or so ago and they chopped it up for firewood."

I was still looking about. He had stooped and was examining the door hinges.

"She said she broke the glass. One window is broken, but this one over the shed is not."

He came over and ran his hand over the window frame.

"Sash is nailed in, which I believe was also mentioned!" he said. Our eyes met in the dim light—a friendly clash; he was so sure of the place and I was so doubtful.

As I stood there peering into the squalid corners of the attic, I remembered the daintiness of the girl's room at home—its bright chintz and shining silver, its soft lamps, its cushions, its white bath beyond. I remembered the exquisite service of the March household and tried to picture the hag below climbing that ladder of a staircase with a platter of greasy food. I tried to forget Clare in her lovely negligee, and to recall the haggard creature who had dropped in her rags at the foot of the staircase. And I tried to place the wretched girl of that night in this wretched place. I could not do it. There was something wrong.

Mr. Patton turned to me, gravely smiling.

"Now, then, your instinct against my training," he said. "Is this the place?"

"I do not believe she was ever here," I said. "Don't ask me why—I just don't believe it." But a moment later I felt that my instinct had received a justification. "Do you remember," I said, "a graphic description of a steel engraving that flapped in the wind?"

"By George!"

"There is not only no engraving—there are no nail holes in the plaster. There has never been such an engraving here," I said in triumph.

Chapter VII

I HAVE often wondered what would have happened had we taken Clare March the next day to that untidy house in Brickyard Road. Brickyard Road was the local name of the street that had been cut through and forgotten.

Would she have told the real story or not? If not, how would she have explained the discrepancy, for instance, of the missing engraving? Would she have taken refuge in silence? Had she hoped by the very detail of her description to throw us off the track? Did she wonder, those dreadful days, how the bag with the buckles had come into the hands of the police and yet had not led us further? Did she suspect me at any time?

Sometimes I thought she did. She would not let me do much for her. I gave her the medicines that were ordered, saw to her nourishment, read to her occasionally. Her own maid looked after her personally. It rather irritated me. More than once I found her watching me. I would glance up from my book and find her eyes on me with a question in them; but she never asked it.

Mr. Patton was waiting eagerly to take her out to Brickyard Road, but she was still very weak and she showed a distaste for the excursion that was understandable enough under the circumstances. Other things puzzled me, however—her unwillingness to see Mr. Plummer was one. Yet she sat for hours looking at his picture. I suspected, too, that her maid was closely in her confidence. More than once I caught a glance of understanding between them. Sometimes I wondered if Clare was quite normal—not insane, of course, but with some queer mental bias.

Outwardly everything was calm. She lay or sat in her fairylike room, with flowers all about her. Her color was coming back. In her soft negligees she looked flowerlike herself. The picture was quite complete: a lovely convalescent, a starched and capped nurse, a maid in black and white, flowers, order, decorum, with a lover hovering in the background. But the nurse was making notes on her record that were not of symptoms; the maid was not clever enough to mask her air of mystery; and the lover paced back and forth downstairs waiting for a word that never came.

On the day following my excursion with Mr. Patton, going into my own room unexpectedly, I found Hortense, the maid, in my clothes closet. She made profuse apologies and backed out. She had been looking, she said, for a frock that had been mislaid. I did not believe her.

After she had gone, I made a careful examination of the closet. A row of my white linen dresses hung there, my street clothes, my mackintosh. In a far end, where I had placed them the night she arrived, were the ragged garments in which Clare had come home. I locked my door and, taking them out, went over them carefully.

There was a worn black skirt, rather short; a ragged and filthy waist of poor material and carelessly made, put together by hand with large stitches and coarse thread. The undergarments were similarly sewed. They might have come from just such a place as the house in Brickyard

Road. The skirt was different. Though ragged, it was well made, and it had been shortened.

I found something just then. On the inside of the belt was woven the name of one of the leading tailors in the city. I thought that over awhile. The skirt could hardly belong to Brickyard Road. It seemed to me that this was a valuable clue. It seemed to me that Hortense knew this also, and that there was no time to be lost.

The situation was put up to me that day in an unexpected fashion. Mr. Patton slipped on the first ice of the season and injured the leg that had been hurt before. He was almost wild with vexation.

"Just keep wide-awake," he wrote me by special delivery, "and send me the usual daily bulletins. If anything very important happens, come round and see me. The people we saw are being watched. If you meet the blond chap, follow him until you get a chance to telephone. I'll send someone to relieve you. We haven't got it all yet by any means."

It rather knocked my plans, especially as I could tell by the shaky writing that he was suffering when he wrote the letter. It seemed to me that for a day or so I should have to get along alone.

But I could do something—I could perhaps trace the skirt.

I had been in the March house now for eight weeks and had had practically no time off. When I asked for two hours, Mrs. March offered me the remainder of the day.

I took it; I was glad to get it.

I took the skirt along, carrying it out quite calmly under Hortense's not too friendly eyes. I wanted to identify the skirt. If it had been made for Clare, her story of having had all her clothing taken away from her would fall to shreds. If it had not, I meant to trace it. And trace it I did that autumn afternoon, while the dead leaves in the park made crackling eddies under the trees, while the wind held me back at every corner, while fashionable women donned the first furs of the season and sallied forth to the tailors for their winter garments. I, too, went to a tailor.

I daresay I was not fashionable enough to be worthwhile. It was a long time before I received attention and my few hours were flying. When at last the manager turned to me, I indicated my bundle.

"I want to trace a skirt that was made here," I began. "Your name is on the belt. It is very important."

"But, madam," he said, "we cannot give any information that concerns our customers."

"This is vitally important."

"It would be impossible. We turn out a great many costumes. We keep no record of the styles."

"There is a number on the belt."

I believe he suspected me of divorce proclivities. He held out both hands, palms up.

"Madam surely understands—it is impossible!"

I turned over the lapel of my coat and he saw a badge that Mr. Patton had given me. He had said, "Don't use it unless you need to; but when the time comes, flash it!"

I flashed it. I got my information within ten minutes, but it did not help at first. He gave me the name of the woman for whom it had been made. I had never heard of her—a Mrs. Kershaw.

"You are quite positive?"

"Positive, madam. The number is distinct. Also one of the skirtmakers recalls—it was part of a trousseau a year or so ago."

A sort of lust of investigation seized me. I had started the thing and I would see it out. With a new deference the tailor handed me my rewrapped bundle and saw me to the door.

"No trouble with the Kershaws, I hope?" he said.

"None whatever," I answered at random. "She gave a skirt away and I am tracing it."

That was it, of course. I said it first and believed it afterward. She had given the skirt away.

It took an hour and a half of my shortening afternoon to locate and interview Mrs. Kershaw. She was quite affable. I did not show my badge—it was not necessary. I made up a story about some stolen goods, with this skirt among them. She was anxious to help, she said, but . . .

"I hardly remember," she said. "I gave away a lot of my wedding clothes—the styles changed so quickly. Why, I remember exactly what I did with that! I gave it to the Fräulein—Fräulein Schlenker. But stolen goods! She's the honestest old soul in the world."

"She is old then?"

"Oh, yes—quite. Such a quaint little figure. She taught me at boarding school; she seemed old even then. Poor Fräulein Julie!"

My lips were dry. Julie!

"Would you mind describing the Fräulein, Mrs. Kershaw?"

"You do not suspect her of anything?"

"No, indeed; but I should like to find her."

"Well, she is a little thing, stooped and lame. She hurt her ankle after I knew her first. She is very saving—we all thought she was rich; but I believe not. There's a brother, or someone, that she helps. She wears a rusty black bonnet with jet on it, and a queer old wrap; and—oh, yes— she always carries the same bag—a foreign one, with buckles. I really think the bag was the reason we thought she was wealthy. It seemed such a secure affair."

Julie, then, was my little old lady of the dining room and the garden door! And there was more than that—the school was the school from which Clare had graduated.

"Have you seen the Fräulein lately?"

"We have been away all summer. She may have called. I'll ask."

The little old lady had not called, however. I got her address. It seemed to me that things were closing up.

It was quite dark when I left the Kershaw house. It was very cold and I was hungry; but excitement would not let me eat. I was getting my first zest for this new game I was playing, and I was losing my shrinking horror of spying into affairs that were not my own. It seemed to me that my cause was just; for if Clare March had not been incarcerated in the Brickyard Road house, she might still, out of terror of the truth, insist that she had been. Hysterical young women had done such things before. I held no brief for the family in Brickyard Road; but if they were innocent, they were not to suffer. I was after the truth, and I felt that I should get it. I had no course of action mapped out. I wanted to confront the little old lady—I got no further.

It was seven o'clock when I reached the house. I had crossed the city again. I was hungry and shivering with cold, and I still carried the parcel under my arm. For the first time that day I was nervous. The fear of failure assailed me. I used to have the same feeling when I had charge of the operating room and a strange surgeon was about to operate. Would he want silk or catgut? What solutions did he use? Would the assistant get there in time to lay out the instruments? So now with the Fräulein—would she deny the skirt? If she did, should I accuse her of the night visit to the March house? Or of the letter in the buckled bag?

The house was a small one on a by-street, a comfortable two-story brick, with a wooden stoop and a cheerful glow through the curtains of a vestibule door. The woman who answered my ring was clearly the mistress. She wore a white apron and there was an agreeable odor of cooking food in the air.

"Fräulein Schlenker?" she said. "Yes. She made her home here. She is not here now."

"Can't you tell me where I may find her?"

She hesitated.

"I don't know exactly. We've been anxious about her lately. She went away for a vacation about two months ago. Did you want to see her about renting the house in Brickyard Road?"

For just a minute I distinctly saw two white aprons and two vestibule doors!

"Yes," I said as coolly as I could. "When—when will it be empty?"

"It is empty," she replied. "I hardly know what to do. She's been anxious to rent it; but now that she's away and no word from her . . . Would you like the key?"

The empty house in Brickyard Road!

"If I might have it."

"You'll return it soon, won't you?" She went into the hall and got a key from the drawer of a table. "She'll do anything that's reasonable— paper the lower floor and fix the roof. It's a nice little house." I took the key, still rather dazed. "It's a growing neighborhood out that way," she went on, evidently eager to do her roomer a good turn. "Some of these days that street will be paved." She had an air of doubt; she was clearly divided between eagerness and trepidation. "You'll be sure to return the key?"

"I'll have it back here tomorrow."

She watched me down the street, still vaguely uneasy. I tried to make my back honest, to step as one who walks the straight and narrow path. I had a feeling that she might suddenly change her mind and pursue me, commanding the return of the key. I hardly breathed until I had turned the corner.

I got something to eat at the first restaurant I saw. I needed food and time to think. I meant at first to telephone Mr. Patton. As I grew warmer and less fatigued, I decided to go on alone. It was my first case; I wanted to make good—frankly I desired Mr. Patton's approval, and something he had once said to me came back.

"In this business," he said, "there are times when two's a crowd." I remembered that.

I ate deliberately. I never hurry with my food—I've seen too many stomachs treated like coal cellars on the first cold day of fall. And as I ate, the key lay before me on the cloth. It had a yellow tag tied to it, endorsed in a small, neat script, very German.

"Key to the house in Brickyard Road," it said. "Kitchen door."

I had, at the best, about two hours and a half when I left the restaurant. That meant a taxicab. I counted my money. I had thirteen dollars. It would surely be enough.

Brickyard Road lay a square or two away from where I alighted. I retained the cab—out there in that potter's field of dead-and-gone real-estate hopes it was a tie with the living world. Its lamps made a comfortable glow. The driver was broad-shouldered. I borrowed a box of matches from him. I have often wondered since what he thought.

The house Mr. Patton and I had examined was dimly lighted, as before. I passed it at a safe distance. The empty house, that was the only other building in Brickyard Road, was my destination. The two houses were alike—clearly built by the same builder. Only the courage of an idea took me on. In the lighted house the crone was singing—a maudlin voice. Someone was walking along the rickety boardwalk round the place—a step and a tap, a step and a tap—the one-legged man, of course.

There is something horrible about an empty house at night. A house is an intimate place; its every emanation is human. Life has begun and ended in it. Thoughts are things, I have always believed—things that leave their mark.

I had such a feeling about the little house in Brickyard Road. I was very nervous. The other house was near enough to be dangerous—too far away to be company. I felt terribly alone. There was not even starlight. I stumbled and fumbled along, feeling my way by the side of the house to the rear. There was a dispute going on next door. The crone had ceased singing. Someone broke a bottle with a crash.

I found the kitchen door at last. To reach it I had to go through a wooden shed. In the safety of the shed I struck a match and found the keyhole. The key turned easily. As I opened the door, a breath of musty air greeted me and blew out my match. The thick darkness closed down on me like a veil; I was frightened.

It was a moment or two before I could light a fresh match, and it took more than that for me to survey the kitchen. It had been in use not very long before. There was a kettle on the stove and a few odds and ends of dishes in orderly stacks on an upturned box. And there was a loaf of bread, covered with gray-green mold. There was no table, no chair—but in a corner, there was a cot bed, neatly made up. I remember distinctly the comfort of discovering that orderly bed, with a log-cabin quilt spread over it.

My match went out, but the box was almost full. I was not uneasy now. The peace of the log-cabin quilt was on my soul. I found a smoky lamp with very little oil in it, and lighted it. My nerves are pretty good. I've laid out more than one body in the mortuary at night and alone. I was not going to be daunted by an empty house. Nevertheless the glow of the lamp was comforting. I put down my bundle and went into the front room.

I had a real fright there. Something shadowy stood in the center of the room, moving very slightly. I almost dropped the lamp. I had a patient once who used to say her heart "dropped a stitch." Mine did. Then I saw that it was a woman's black dress hanging on a gas fixture and moving in the air from the open kitchen door.

I began to feel uneasy. What if the house were inhabited? Certainly it had been occupied recently. I daresay I move softly by habit, but I doubled my ordinary caution. I wanted to get away, but I wanted more than that. I wanted desperately to see whether there was a steel engraving of the Landing of the Pilgrims in the attic room over the kitchen. If I was right—if in this house Clare March had been imprisoned—if her detail of the house next door was merely what she had gained from a window—what was the meaning of it all? Where was Julie? If I knew anything, this old black silk swaying in the air belonged to her.

Not, of course, that I reasoned all this out. I felt it partly; for the next moment I heard a door open at the top of the stairs. I blew out the lamp instantly, but a sort of paralysis of fright kept me from flight. I could have made it. The stairs, as in the house next door, were closed off with a door—a dash past this door and I should have been in the kitchen; but I hesitated, and it was too late. The steps were at the lower door.

Now and then since that evening I have a nightmare, and it is always the same. I am standing in a dark room and there are stealthy steps drawing nearer and nearer. At last the thing comes toward me. I can hear it; but there is nothing to see. And then it touches me with ice-cold hands—and I waken with a scream. I frightened a nervous patient almost into convulsions once because of that dream of mine.

The darkness was terrible. Behind me the dress swayed, touched me. I almost fainted. The staircase door did not open immediately. I wondered frantically what was standing and waiting there. It showed my abnormal mental condition when it occurred to me that perhaps the old woman, Julie—perhaps she was dead, and that this on the staircase was she again, come back. I almost dropped the lamp.

I braced myself against I knew not what when I heard the door opening. Whoever it was, was listening, I felt sure. Through the open kitchen door came the sound of singing from next door and of someone hammering on a table in time. It covered my gasping breaths, I daresay. The stair door opened wider and someone stepped down into the tiny passage. We were perhaps eight feet apart.

I lived a century, waiting to hear which way the footsteps turned. They went toward the kitchen, still stealthily, with a caution that was more terrible than curses. I had a moment's respite then, and I felt my way toward the front door. If the key was there, I might yet escape. I found the door. The key was gone. Even in that moment of frenzy I knew where the key was—in the buckled bag at the police station. I was trapped!

There were various sounds now from the kitchen: a match struck, and a wavering search, probably for the lamp I held; then a dim but steady light, as though from a candle, followed by the cautious lifting of stovelids and much rustling of paper. The paper reminded me of something—my bundle lay on the cot!

I knew the exact moment when it was discovered. I heard it torn open and I shivered in the silence that followed. Then the candle went out and there was complete silence again; but this time it was the quiet of strained ears and quickened senses. I dream of that, too, sometimes—of a silence that is a horror.

I dared not move a muscle. I felt that if I relaxed, I should stagger. I breathed with only the upper part of my lungs. Then, very slowly, there was movement in the next room—a step and then another. It was coming. While the light was burning, I had been terrified by something desperate, but at least quick with life. Now, in the darkness, it became disembodied horror again! It came slowly but inevitably, and directly toward me. I tried to move, but I could not. The black dress moved in the air; a chill breath blew on me. Then, out of the black void all round, a cold hand touched my cheek. I must have collapsed without a sound.

Chapter VIII

WHEN I came to, I was lying on the floor of the empty room, with the black dress swaying above me. There was a faint light in the room. By turning my head, I saw that it came from the kitchen. Someone was moving quickly there; there was a rattle of china. A moment later a figure appeared in the doorway and peered in.

"Are you awake, Miss Adams?"

It was Clare! I struggled to a sitting position and stared at her.

"Was it—you—before?" I asked.

"Yes. Don't talk about it just now. I have a fire going and soon we can have some tea. I think you are almost frozen—and I know I am."

It was curious to see how our positions had been reversed. And there was a change in Clare—she was almost cheerful. She helped me out into the kitchen and onto the cot, and then busied herself about the room.

"I am sure there is tea somewhere," she said. "Julie was always making tea."

She was dressed for the street—suit and hat and furs. She tried to make talk as she moved about the room, but the really vital things of the evening she avoided. She fussed with the fire, filled the kettle afresh from a hydrant outside, rinsed out two cups, found tea, searched for sugar. And still her eyes had not met mine.

She found me staring at an engraving that lay on the floor, however, and she dropped her artificial manner.

"The Landing of the Pilgrims!" she said gravely. "I was going to burn it."

The sounds in the next house died away. The kettle on the stove began to boil cheerfully. The little room grew bright with firelight. Clare drew the box before the cot and poured two steaming cups of tea.

"We will drink our tea," she said, "and then I shall tell you, Miss Adams. I am very happy tonight—I have only one grief."

What that was she did not say. She had found a box of biscuits and opened it. She took very little herself. She was plainly intent on making up to me for my fright. She seemed to bear me no malice for being there. It was not until I had drained my cup that she put hers down.

"Now we'll begin," she said, and took off her jacket. Next she drew up the sleeve of the soft blouse she wore beneath and held out her arm for me to see. I gave a shocked exclamation.

"Cocaine!" she said briefly. "The other arm is also scarred. I got it first at school for toothache." I could not say anything; I only stared. "But that's all over now," she went on briskly. "Today I have—but I'll tell you about that later. I knew there was only one way out, Miss Adams—to do it myself. Father and Mother would have helped me, of course; but it would have been their will, not mine. I had to educate my own will to be strong enough. Oh, I'd thought it all out. And then—I did not want them to know. Even now, when I know it's over, I'm afraid to have them know. I've lied to keep it from them; but the detective knew it wasn't true."

She told me the whole story eagerly, frankly. It was clearly a relief. She had made her plans that summer and made them thoroughly. She had tried before and failed. This time there was the great incentive—she wished to marry.

"I wanted to bring children into the world, Miss Adams," she said. "I should not have dared—the way things were. All summer I tried and broke over. I was almost crazy. Then I got a letter from Julie—she had been my German teacher at school and I was fond of her. She had been taking care of an insane brother, who had died. She wanted to work again. Poor Julie!

"I thought she could help me. I knew it would be hard, though I didn't know—well, I wrote her the whole story and told her my plan. I had been here to see the brother with her; I knew the house. I asked her to send out after dark for just enough to keep us going for a time. I did not want the house opened. I thought there would be a hue and cry and they might trace me to Julie."

"Your father and mother said they knew of no one named Julie."

"They would have known of her as Fräulein Schlenker. They had never seen her. I came to the city, bought some blankets and a book or two, and came out here. She was here and partly settled. She was against the plan even then; but I showed her my arms and she knew I was desperate. I had a supply of cocaine—I had got it in town. I was to have it—I should have died without—but she was to reduce the quantity. I locked myself in and gave her the key."

"You had been getting the cocaine from the man with the blond hair?"

"Yes. He was in a pharmacy at first—where I got the prescription filled. He suspected me after a time. After he lost his position, he still got it for me. I met him wherever I could—on the street, in the park, anywhere; but generally we met by the Embankment. He robbed me, I think. I owed him a great deal finally. He took to bothering me about it. I used up all my allowance and more.

"I gave Julie the cocaine; and she was to reduce it—a little at a time. I suffered the tortures of the lost, Miss Adams—but perhaps you know. There were many days when I wanted to kill myself; and once Julie tied my hands behind my back. She was wonderful—wonderful! I owe it all to her. I was lost, Miss Adams—I would lie, steal, almost murder, to get the cocaine. I lived for it."

"All this was here in this house?"

"Upstairs—in the back room one window looked out over a field and could be kept unshuttered. I chose it. Besides, the fire from below heated it. We had only a little coal left in the cellar, and we could get none. Julie went out after dark and did our buying. It—it all took longer than I had thought. I planned for a month. It was more than that. We were running out of money. At the end of five weeks we were desperate—and I sent Julie to the house."

I remembered that well enough! But I did not interrupt.

"Father always gave me the fees from directors' meetings; and, as they were in gold, I dropped them under the cushion of a silver box on my dressing table. Sometimes there would be several; most of them went eventually to—to the man I spoke of. Before we went away in the summer, I had put some there; I could not remember how many—my mind was hazy—but I was sure there was perhaps fifty dollars. I had my own house keys with me and I gave Julie the key to the garden door. She was terribly frightened, but we were desperate. She got in without any trouble and got it. There was forty dollars."

I remembered something. "Forty dollars and a book," I said, smiling.

"Forty dollars and a book— Was it yours? The day came when she told me I had had no cocaine for a week. I was faint and dizzy, but I wrote a line to Father and Mother. I shouldn't have written it. It could never be reconciled with anything but the truth, and I was morbid about that. They were never to know. I did not want Mr. Plummer to know—I thought he would never trust me again. But I wrote it and Julie took it out. She never came back—and I was locked in, upstairs!"

"She never came back!"

"She was killed—struck by an automobile. I thought— Didn't the detective know that? He had her bag."

So my little old lady was dead after all! I was sorry. What a spirit she had!

"I was locked in," Clare was saying. "I waited—and she did not come. I had not eaten for a day or so before, and there were two days and a night without even water. I was so desperate that I tried to call the other house; but the old woman had hurt herself, and there was no one about outside. I tried to break down the door. There was a panel in it—for the brother who was crazy. I could almost reach the key on the nail outside. The last day I think I was delirious. The key made faces at me through the panel. I told you, didn't I, about getting out of the window?"

"Yes. When did you learn about Julie?"

"The night I went home. As you know, I went down to the library and searched the newspapers. I felt that she had been hurt. As soon as I was strong enough, I slipped away from the house, and—they were going to give her a pauper's burial—I pawned a ring, and at least she did not have that."

She broke down, after keeping up bravely for so long. I gathered from broken sentences her terrible fear of having the facts known; her despair over the tissue of falsehood and truth that she had told Mr. Patton; her fear of seeing her lover again until she was sure of herself; her grief for Julie's death and her self-accusation of it; her terror that day when Hortense had told her that I had taken her skirt from my closet. But after a time she looked up, smiling through her tears.

"I am really only crying over Julie," she said. "The rest is—all gone, Miss Adams. I am cured—really cured! Today I sat for an hour with a bottle of cocaine beside me, and—I did not touch it!"

THAT was my first case for Mr. Patton; and though I really discovered nothing that Clare would not have told eventually herself, he was kind enough to say some very pleasant things.

"Though," he said, wincing as he tried to move his leg, "courage carried to the nth power is often foolishness! What possessed you to go to that house alone?"

"I wanted to locate the Landing of the Pilgrims."

He leaned back and looked up at me, smiling.

"Curiosity!" he said. "That was the only quality I was afraid you lacked." He took an envelope from the stand at his elbow and held it out.

"Your check, as per agreement."

"I don't want money, Mr. Patton. I— Don't think I am silly; but I had my reward—if I deserve one, which, of course, I don't—when I saw Mr. Plummer's eyes last night. She went straight into his arms."

"You won't take the check?"

"No, thank you."

"Then I'll bank it for you. We are going to have some interesting cases together, Miss Adams, but I wish you were back here to look after me. There's a spineless creature here who lets me bully her. Do you know— you're a queer woman! Taking as remuneration the sight of a young girl going into her lover's arms!"

"I've taken most of my pleasures and all of my sentiment vicariously for a number of years," I retorted. "And, even if it's the other person's, sentiment one has to have!"

"Yes," said Mr. Patton, looking at me curiously. "Sentiment one has to have!"

THE bag is before me as I write. There are two keys—one to the house in Brickyard Road; the other to the garden door at the March home. The lavender envelope is there and its scrawled note from Clare—simply explained, as are all confusing things when one has a key. The envelope had contained the vial of cocaine that Clare took with her on her flight, and had come, of course, from the pharmacy clerk. I never examined the clipping carefully until today. It is curious to locate one's mental blind spot. I had read it many times.

The reverse is an advertisement for the cure of the drug habit.

The Principal Works of Mary Roberts Rinehart

⟡

NOVELS AND SHORT STORY COLLECTIONS

1936 *The Doctor*
1937 *Tish Marches On*
1938 *The Wall*
1940 *The Great Mistake*
1942 *The Haunted Lady*
1944 *Alibi for Isabel*

1945 *The Yellow Room*
1950 *Episode of the Wandering Knife*
1952 *The Swimming Pool*
1953 *The Frightened Wife and Other Murder Stories*

NONFICTION

1915 *Kings, Queens, and Pawns: An American Woman at the Front*
1916 *Through Glacier Park: Seeing America First with Howard Eaton*
1917 *The Altar of Freedom*
1918 *Tenting To-night: A Chronicle of Sport and Adventure in Glacier Park and the Cascade Mountains*
1920 *Isn't That Just Like a Man!*
1922 *The Out Trail*
1926 *Nomad's Land*
1939 *Writing Is Work* (published by The Writer, Inc.)

PLAYS
(DATE OF FIRST PRODUCTION)

1906 *A Double Life*
1909 *Seven Days* (based on *When a Man Marries*)
1912 *Cheer Up*
1919 *Tumble In* (musical version of *When a Man Marries*)
1920 *Spanish Love*
1920 *The Bat*
1920 *Tish*
1920 *Bab*
1923 *The Breaking Point*

FILMS

1915 *The Circular Staircase* (silent)
1926 *The Bat* (silent)
1930 *The Bat Whispers* (starring Chester Morris and Una Merkel)
1932 *Miss Pinkerton* (starring Joan Blondell and George Brent)
1935 *The Case of Elinor Norton* (British)
1941 *The Nurse's Secret*
1956 *The Circular Staircase* (Climax TV production with Judith Anderson)
1957 *Telephone Time* (TV adaptation of *The After House*)
1959 *The Bat* (starring Vincent Price and Agnes Moorehead)

AUTOBIOGRAPHY

My Story, Farrar and Rinehart, 1931.
My Story: A New Edition and Seventeen New Years, Rinehart, 1948.